THE DEATH OF CHE GUEVARA

THE DEATH OF
CHE
GUEVARA
A NOVEL BY
JAY CANTOR

VINTAGE BOOKS
A DIVISION OF RANDOM HOUSE
NEW YORK

First Vintage Books Edition, August 1984

Portions of this book have appeared previously, in slightly different form, in the following publications: *Canto, Raritan,* and *Triquarterly.*

In addition, there are fragments from the translation of Che Guevara's Bolivian diaries from both *Ramparts Magazine* (July 27, 1968) and Daniel James's *The Complete Bolivian Diaries of Che Guevara* (Stein and Day), and fragments from the translations of Inca documents in John Hemmings's *The Conquest of the Incas* (Harcourt Brace Jovanovich, Inc., 1973). "Life is not a walk across an open field" is from Boris Pasternak's poem "Hamlet."

Grateful acknowledgment is made to The Johns Hopkins University Press for permission to reprint excerpts from *The Critical Difference* by Barbara Johnson. Copyright © 1980 by The Johns Hopkins University Press. Reprinted by permission.

Library of Congress Cataloging in Publication Data

Cantor, Jay.
The death of Che Guevara.

1. Guevara, Ernesto, 1982–1967—Fiction.
2. Cuba—History—Revolution, 1959—Fiction.
I. Title. [PS3535.A5475D4 1984]   813'.54   84-40028
ISBN 0-394-72592-1 (pbk.)

*My part in this story
is for my father,
Alfred Joseph Cantor.
One of the thirty-six.*

Contents

II
THE DIARIES OF THE
BOLIVIAN CAMPAIGN

THE DEATH OF
CHE GUEVARA

Dates

<u>1927</u> The Communist Party of China leads an uprising in Shanghai, a general strike, an assault on the police station to gain arms for the rebels. The uprising —badly coordinated, poorly armed—misfires, is put down, is . . . (but what word for political error, historical misfortune might make vivid so many deaths?) . . . by Kuomintang troops. Thirty-five years later, Regis Debray, a French theoretician, gathers up the dead from the streets of Shanghai, orders them into the cunning of history, draws a lesson, a moral: "But the blood shed in Shanghai must not be inscribed in the deficit column of the Revolution, as though it were the result of an error of judgment . . . the theoretical proof that an isolated urban insurrection cannot achieve victory in a semi-colonial country had to be made in practice." (The country surrounds the city.) <u>1928</u> Profitable outlets cannot be found for the reinvestment of profits made by the industrial monopolies. Money is drained from the economy or wagered pointlessly. Inventories build. These manufactured things, things that too few can buy, stand against their makers, menace them. <u>1929</u> Panic on Wall Street, and in the City of London. Argentina, whose wealth is beef sold to the industrialized countries, discovers again that it does not make history, but, like a terrified dreamer, merely suffers events. <u>1930</u> Irigoyen, the blind, now unpopular President of Argentina, sits alone in an unlit room. He is overthrown by the Army under General Uriburu. In China, Chiang's troops move against the Communist bases in Kiangsi, Fukien, Hopeh. Gandhi gaily walks two hundred miles across India to the Arabian Sea. In defiance of British law, he picks up some salt from the shore. His gesture enters the imagination of the Indian masses, is completed by them, becomes an action. Thousands join Gandhi in defiance, illegally dry seawater on the rooftops for salt, hawk it openly in the streets. Nonviolent marchers move towards the Dharasana Salt Works, the British monopoly. (Their chests are naked, their ribs exposed.) Native policemen, goaded on by their British officers, shatter the marchers' heads with steel lathes. The marchers do not even raise their arms against the blows. Enraged by this passivity, this restraint, the police fracture men's skulls,

kick and stab marchers in the testicles.   **1931** The Roca-Runciman Agreement is signed: the British to buy Argentine beef; the Argentines to purchase British manufactured goods. Few national industries are developed in Argentina. Through this, and other measures, the large landowners secure their power over the country.   **1934** The Long March of the Chinese Red Army begins, away from Kiangsi and into northern Shensi, away from the cities and deep into the countryside. (The country surrounds the city.) Tens of thousands of soldiers die on the march, from lack of food, from lack of warm clothing, from lack of boots. (This is not the sort of world where a fellow can take his boots off.) In Cuba, Sergeant Fulgencio Batista leads the overthrow of the government of Grau San Martin. Those who protest are tortured and then shot. (Batista himself sets the style for his administration: He announces his coup to a meeting of his fellow officers. A colleague objects. Batista puts his arm around the man's shoulders, and shoots his fellow officer's head off with his own service revolver.) The United States extends recognition to the new government.   **1935** Hitler defies the Versailles Treaty, and establishes military training for all Germans. The Comintern, in the Soviet Union, calls for formation of Popular Front governments. The Soviet Union announces that when the capitalist jackals fight, it will side with the capitalist democracies against the Fascists.   **1936** General Franco leads a rising of dissident troops against the Spanish Republican government. Irregular forces of Anarchist miners and P.O.U.M. (Partido Oberero de Unificacion Marxista) resist the advance of the Fascists. A Revolutionary Committee comes to power in Barcelona. The Germans send ten thousand troops to the aid of Franco. The Fascists begin a massive aerial bombardment of soldiers and civilians, of the men, women, and children of Madrid. In Argentina, the Radical Party wins the congressional elections. An Argentine Popular Front is organized. It is a hopeful time (for even bad marriages seem full of possibility at the start). Victory in the next presidential election seems certain. In the Soviet Union the show trials of Zinoviev and Kamenev begin. (They will be executed by firing squad as "agents of Trotsky and spies of the Nazis.")   **1937** Fraudulent elections are held in Argentina. The army candidates defeat the Popular Front. General Ortiz, a diabetic, takes power. His fellow officers find him too weak towards the opposition. He will resign in favor of General Castillo. The Soviet Union sends advisers and guns to the Republicans in Spain. The Communist Party reads the Agenda of History for the Spanish people. The time for a Communist revolution is . . . not yet. There can be only one leadership, one direction, one vanguard party. Negrin takes over as head of the Republican government. He declares, "The War must be won before the Revolution can be carried further." By command of the party, the P.O.U.M. is suppressed, its leaders jailed or killed. The miners' militias are not sent arms or supplies, are left to die before the Fascist advance. Other socialist, but non-party, units are dissolved, and their men are reintegrated into brigades of the regular Army. Their officers are jailed. Throughout the Left there is a pervasive confusion about what is happening in Spain, an icy wind that leaves each person isolated, afraid to move for fear of touching something unintentionally, while his limbs are tender. Had the Communists betrayed the miners so as not to disturb the digestion of their new allies, the Paris bourgeoisie? Or were the miners treach-erously undisciplined cowards, the class enemy in one of the many disguises that only the Party can penetrate? The confusion—the lack of clarity—is worse for the Left (the Argentine left) than even the worst knowledge might have been. It invades all their certainties, makes them unsure of all they thought they knew, ironic towards themselves, paralyzed. **1938** The Communist Party of Cuba begins cooperation with the Batista government. The Munich Pact is signed. Germany occupies Austria. The Soviet show trials of Bukharin, Rykov, and Yagoda end with their sham confessions. **1939** The Soviets sign a ten-year nonaggression pact with Germany. (No longer able to locate the hero in this movie, one twists uncomfortably in one's seat.) Franco takes Barcelona, executing tens of thousands of Loyalists. During the Spanish Civil War seven hundred thousand men are killed in battle. Fifteen thousand people die (that solemn word!) in aerial bombardment. Three hundred thousand are executed or assassinated. (You and he are of the same family. He must be annihilated utterly.) **1940** Batista makes himself President of Cuba. (A day's work for the dictator: he chooses his clothes, ties his tie, puts commas in letters, reties his tie.) **1941** Argentina, its army officers sympathetic to fascism and op-posed to Britain and the United States, refuses to join with the other American republics in breaking with the Axis. Yugoslavia surrenders to Germany, but partisan guerrilla units continue to fight in the mountains. Chinese Commu-nist guerrillas and regular units lead the resistance to the Japanese invaders. **1943** In Argentina a group of German-trained army officers overthrow the government of General Castillo. General Ramirez becomes head of state. The Ministry of Education is turned over to a fascist and anti-Semite, Gustavo Zuirria. He purges all democratic teachers from the schools. Catholic educa-tion is restored. Students protest (even in the mountain province of Cordoba, a place good for one's asthma but far from the metropole). The German Sixth Army surrenders at Stalingrad. Six hundred thousand soldiers and civilians die in the battle, or are destroyed by cold and famine. **1944** The United States, its attention elsewhere, relaxes its hold on Latin America, for a time; a national-ist revolution, led by the army, begins in Guatemala. In Argentina, Colonel Peron becomes Minister of Labor. He raises wages and gains the support of the grandsons of Italian and Spanish immigrants, his "shirtless ones." **1945** Colonel Peron is forced to resign by Argentina's generals, who fear his growing power. They imprison Peron on Martin Garcia Island. His wife, Evita, an actress, rallies his supporters, leads a demonstration in Buenos Aires of millions of workers. They take over the streets and squares of the city. The unions call for a general strike. Peron is freed. Ho Chi Minh, who led the guerrilla forces against the Japanese in Indochina, proclaims the independence of Vietnam from France. He begins a "regular" war against the French, to free Vietnam, and make all of Indochina one state. France has the "Republic of Cochin China" declared at Saigon. **1946** Fidel Castro, an ambitious man, is elected President of the Association of Cuban Law Students. Peron is overwhelmingly elected President of Argentina. The French bombard the port and people of Haiphong. **1947** Castro, an adventurous man, joins an expedition to liberate the Dominican Republic from the tyrant Trujillo. The expedition fails, most of the band is killed, but Castro, a fortunate man, escapes. Civil war spreads throughout China, the Communist forces against those of the Kuomintang. Peron, in conflict with Great Britain and the United States, purges the courts of all but the most loyal Peronistas. After years of mass unrest, nonviolent demonstrations, and sporadic rioting, the British find that it is no longer in their interest to remain in India as its colonial rulers. The colony is freed. **1948** Fidel Castro, a convincing man, attends the Conference of Latin American Students in Bogota, Colombia. During the conference Eliecer Gaitan, a popular Colombian leader, is assassinated by rightists. There is a vast rising in the city. It is said later (by the United States ambassador to Cuba) that Castro's voice was heard over the radio, announcing, inciting, instructing, cajoling the rising. The demonstrations are put down. **1949** The Argentine Constitution is changed, so that Peron can succeed himself. The Communists are victorious in China. (The country surrounds the city.) Mao Tse-tung heads the new government. **1950** War begins between the Korean Communists and the Koreans who have the support of the United States. **1951** Paz Estenssoro, a leader of the nationalist and anti-feudal forces, is elected President of Bolivia. But the election is annulled by the army. (Pieces of a new interpretation: In Latin America power belongs to the army. And to whoever can purchase the army. This thesis will be inscribed, and reinscribed, on the body of the Latin American masses.) The Vietnamese Communists return to guerrilla tactics against the French. (The country surrounds the city.) **1952** In Cuba, the Ortodoxos party wins the general election. Batista (now General Batista) annuls the elections and takes power again. (He has telephone conversations taped all over the island and sent to him. What do people say about him? How do they live?) Fidel Castro, a courageous man, brings charges against Batista in the Cuban courts, accusing him of violating the Constitution. (Castro's gesture, his tactic, will become theory: a people's war cannot be begun until every hope of legal redress has been exhausted.) General Perez Jimenez takes over Venezuela by coup. In Bolivia a force made up of Indians, peasants, miners, and cadre of the Movement for a National Revolution smash the regular army and bring Paz Estenssoro to power. (Pieces of a new interpretaion: if power belongs to the army, or those who can purchase the army, then only another armed force can defeat the regular army, gain power for the people. In Latin America the peasant will be the base of the Revolution.) In Argentina, Peron's policies, the corruption of his government, and the opposition of the industrialized countries have crippled the Argentine economy. Land reform begins in China. In Guatemala, Colonel Jacobo Arbenz Guzman signs a land-reform bill expropriating 225,000 acres of United Fruit Company land, for distribution to the peasantry. The United Fruit Company, and the State Department of the United States, express their displeasure. The United States takes over the financing of French forces in Vietnam. (Greece, Macedonia, Rome, Spain, Portugal, France, Great Britain, as all schoolchildren know, had empires.) In Argentina, Eva Peron, Protector of the Forsaken, Defender of the Workers, Guiding Light of the Children, dies. Peron, perhaps not sensitive enough to the country's feelings, takes up with a series of attractive women. **1953** Fidel Castro, a reckless man, leads a hundred twenty people in an attack against the Moncada barracks in Santiago. They plan to seize arms, and by their actions spark a general uprising. The attack occurs during the confusion of carnival time. The rebels, disguised in carnival costumes, had planned to emerge from the crowd, and move on the barracks. Badly coordinated, poorly armed, the insurgents lose their way in the streets of Santiago. Those who make it to the barracks are defeated by the soldiers. The rebel reinforcements, wandering in the unfamiliar streets, never arrive. Most of the insurgents are captured, tortured, and then killed by the police. Fidel Castro, a fortunate man, escapes to the mountains, and is not discovered until after the Bishop of Santiago has interceded to stop the executions. Fidel Castro, isolated, is tried in secret for the rebellion. A rhetorical man when menaced, Castro delivers a speech to the court, concluding that "History will absolve me." He is sentenced to fifteen years in prison on the Isle of Pines. The United States, no longer diverted, has recovered economically from the war. The State Department, and the CIA, begin operations to overthrow the government of Guatemala. They train mercenaries in Honduras for the invasion. Bolivia nationalizes its tin mines and passes land-reform laws that are acceptable to the United States. The Vietnamese Communists have an army now of 125,000. The French have 230,000 soldiers in Vietnam. The main center of

French strength is the huge entrenched (and doomed) camp at Dien Bien Phu. **1954** Batista again declares himself President of Cuba. (He takes the commas out of letters, reties his tie. He plays canasta for hours, sitting on the edge of his bed. He has the television stations show more horror movies, his favorites.) Peron begins an attack against the Catholic Church and its power. There is an insurrection in the city of Algiers against the French. The insurrection is quelled. (Certain theoretical proofs must be made in practice.) The war against the French will continue in the countryside for seven more years. In Vietnam Dien Bien Phu falls, overrun by the Communist forces. (The country surrounds the city: a children's nursery rhyme.) Peron makes all labor decrees of his government binding on the now powerless unions. General Castillo Armas, leading his army of CIA-trained mercenaries (their symbol: the cross and the sword), overthrows the nationalist government of Guatemala. **1955** Batista, hoping to increase his popularity, establish some legitimacy, declares a general amnesty for political prisoners. Fidel Castro, a free man, goes to Mexico, Costa Rica, and the United States, to organize Cuban exiles and prepare an armed landing. In a suburban house near Mexico City, he meets an asthmatic Argentine doctor, Ernesto Guevara. They talk through the night. Peron bars Catholic education in the schools. He is excommunicated by the Pope. Peron signs an agreement with Standard Oil. Eva gone, and his economic programs in shambles, enthusiasm for Peron wanes in working-class quarters. They wish him well, but they do not wish to die for him. He is overthrown by the air force and the navy. Demonstrators for Peron in the public squares of Buenos Aires are bombed by air force planes. The Geneva Accords are signed, ending the fighting in Vietnam. The United States does not sign. Elections called for by the accords are never held. The United States establishes a puppet regime in Saigon. **1956** Fidel Castro, a bold man, announces in Mexico, "This year we will be free or else martyrs." His boat, the *Granma,* leaves Mexico for Cuba, with eighty-two rebels aboard. To coincide with their landing, an armed rising is to be led by Frank Pais in Santiago. But the *Granma* is delayed by choppy seas. The rising in Santiago is put down. ("Put down"? And if one could find the words that would make so much death palpable? And to what end?) The rebels land, but they are betrayed by a guide and are surprised by the army in a sugar-cane field near Alegria de Pio. They are strafed from the air and the ground. Twelve men (or was it twenty? Mythology—or is it propaganda?—here has needs that long ago overwhelmed history) survive. The men, isolated, in small groups, lost, are helped by peasants, and make their way to the Sierra Maestra Mountains. There they are reunited with Castro. A few men, most of their weapons lost, wander in land barely known to them. "The days of the dictatorship," Castro says, "are numbered." An uprising in the city of Budapest is crushed by the Soviet Army. 1957 Duvalier, a juju man, seizes power in Haiti. The Cuban guerrillas make successful attacks on the army barracks at La Plata, and at El Uvero. The army, the police, the militia arrest any suspected rebels throughout the island. The police shoot down Frank Pais on the streets of Santiago. A spontaneous strike is sparked by Pais's death, paralyzing the western provinces of the island. Demonstrators and mourners at Pais's funeral are machine-gunned by the army. Radicals leave the cities and make their way to join Castro in the mountains. Castro forms a second rebel column in the Sierras, under the command of Ernesto Guevara. The guerrillas declare El Hombrito, in the Sierras, a "free territory." They decree a land reform for the region, set up a shoe "factory" to make boots for the peasants and soldiers, and they establish a radio station, a rebel newspaper, and a hospital. The urban resistance organizes a series of attacks on power plants and government buildings in Havana and Santiago. These urban rebels suffer heavy losses to the army and the police. More than twenty thousand will die during the Revolution. (In the Cuban Revolution death is in the cities.) 1958 The urban movement blows up the electric plant and the water works in Havana. Airport runways are cratered by rebel bombs. Raul Castro, with sixty-seven men, opens a second front in the northern provinces. Fidel Castro, an inspired leader, calls for a general strike in Havana. But the plans for the strike fall into government hands, and it is crushed, its leaders arrested and shot. Street battles break out in several towns throughout the island. The army begins a major offensive against the Sierra strongholds. (In a guerrilla war, one does not engage in battle unless certain of victory.) The army occupies rebel positions at Las Mercedes, and continues to advance, terrorizing the peasants who have been sympathetic to the rebels, and who are now without protection. The army occupies Las Vegas, four hours' march from the rebel "capital." The rebels begin a counteroffensive at the San Domingo River. Two army battalions are routed, fleeing in disorder. At El Jigue the rebels take two hundred fifty army prisoners and hand them over to the Red Cross, as part of "Operation Trojan Horse." (That is: the Cuban Army vindictively tortures and then kills rebel prisoners. Thus there is no point in surrendering to the government, you may as well fight until you are killed. But the rebels free prisoners unharmed. In any engagement government soldiers can save their lives simply by giving up.) The columns of Che Guevara and Camillo Cienfuegos recapture Las Vegas. The army, its spirit broken, turns and withdraws from the Sierras. The Guevara and Cienfuegos columns begin a march down from the mountains, into the plains, towards the cities. Fidel Castro's column descends into Oriente Province. Raul Castro organizes a Congress of Peasants in the liberated areas. Guevara's column moves across the length of the island, to Santa Clara. Batista's air force bombards the outskirts of Santa Clara. The columns of Guevara and Cienfuegos, raggedy, tired, hungry, and footsore from the march, meet outside the city, and begin the battle. The army garrison capitulates. Batista flees to the Dominican Republic. In Algeria, the French Army revolts. De Gaulle becomes President of France. In Venezuela, Perez Jimenez is overthrown by nationalist army officers under Fabricio Ojeda. In Peru, Hugo Blanco begins organizing peasant unions. 1959 Che and Camillo's columns advance on Havana. Fidel Castro's column crosses the island, and the three enter the capital in triumph. Guerrillas appear in the countryside in Paraguay. There are rebellions in Panama, Nicaragua, and the Dominican Republic. (All are defeated by the army.) Haiti is invaded by rebels (the rebellion fails). Peronist guerrillas appear in Argentina. The Peasant Leagues are organized by Juliao in Brazil. The Vietnamese Communists organize guerrilla resistance to the United States. Before his eyes, the world of the second half of the century appears to take shape. Death from hunger, death from parasites, death from cold, these have been the most ordinary facts for most of the people of the world. Suddenly, with the success of the Chinese Revolution, the Vietnamese Revolution, the Algerian Revolution, the Cuban Revolution, these facts seem extraordinary. The people of the industrialized countries will learn that there is not, has never been silence. What was called a time of peace was only the moment before the victim cried out. The Chinese Revolution, the Vietnamese Revolution, the Algerian Revolution, the Cuban Revolution: a nursery refrain: the country surrounds the city: the revolution is in the countryside, among the peasants. Colonialism is a city being strangled, and as it dies it releases its final savagery. It becomes a fire on the skin of the colonized countries. *But colonialism is dying.* 1960 (Year of the Agrarian Reform) Cuba and the Soviet Union sign a commercial treaty. Eisenhower orders the CIA to train Cuban exiles for an invasion of the island. (The CIA are in this text, but as a subtext, in secret. One will not know of them until, like a pun, a mistake, a slip of the tongue—that joke just kills me!—they break the surface, break cover.) A French ship, carrying arms for the Cuban government, explodes in Havana Harbor, killing seventy; Castro, a suspicious man, accuses the CIA of sabotage. The United States refuses to buy the remainder of that year's Cuban sugar quota, some seven hundred thousand pounds of sweet stuff; the Soviet Union agrees to purchase this residue. At a mass meeting outside the Presidential Palace in Havana, Ernesto Guevara thanks the Soviet Union: "Cuba is a glorious island in the center of the Caribbean, defended by the rockets of the greatest power in history." The Cuban government nationalizes the telephone company, the sugar mills, the oil refineries—belonging, as so much of the island does, to U.S. corporations. The United States declares a partial embargo on trade with Cuba. (The steps seem now as ordained, as formal, as some terrible dance . . . but you are unwilling . . . your partner comes towards you.) The Chinese government denounces its "Elder Brother" the Soviet Union for its unfamilial dictatorial ways. The Soviet Union recalls all its technicians from China and begins its own economic blockade. In Guatemala, Yon Sosa, a dissident army officer, establishes a guerrilla center. It is a lyric time in Latin America. Rebels hope that the bourgeoisie of their country will "side with the nation" against the imperialists. Once power is gained a social revolution can be carried out under the protection of Soviet missiles (Cuba's example is a difficult poem to interpret). Paz Estenssoro, leader of the Bolivian MNR, grown rich, his party rotten with U.S. money, becomes, once again, President of Bolivia. The Belgian Congo declares its independence. Moise Tshombe, financed by Belgian mining interests, leads a secessionist movement in Katanga Province. Prime Minister Lumumba appeals to the United Nations. Lumumba, betrayed, ignored by the UN forces, his death desired, plotted by the CIA (those jokers!), will be delivered to his enemies and assassinated. Tshombe becomes head of the Congo.   1961 (Year of Education) One hundred thousand young people leave Havana to begin a great literacy campaign in the countryside; peasants of all ages will be taught to read. The United States breaks off all diplomatic relations with Cuba. Ernesto Guevara—an advocate of strong central planning, and of socialist development based not on "profit accounting" but on the social needs of the people, becomes Minister of Industries. He begins an ambitious program of factory development. (The epic of industrialization, read as the epic of national independence: plans for the construction of a sulpho-metallic plant, "Patrice Lumumba," producing three hundred metric tons of sulphuric acid daily; a brush factory; a screw factory; an iron and steel foundry; a factory for picks and shovels; factories for welding electrodes; barbed-wire factories; a cement plant; the island has iron ores, hemalites, magnetites, laterites, nickel, cobalt, chromite, manganese, silicon, dolomites, limestone, copper; plans for a shipping industry; sucrochemistry, fermentation of sugar, paper pulp from bagazo, synthetic fibers from sugar, plywood from sugar pulp; machinery for cutting cane; technical training for workers; radio and television courses. "We must perfect the plan's control mechanisms, eliminate unemployment, establish work standards, avoid supply shortages, subsidize laid-off workers, establish complete salary justice." Cuba will read the poem of industrialization not in two hundred years, but in ten years! To arrive, within the shortest possible time, at socialism.) The Central Intelligence Agency, and the anti-Castro forces trained by them, bomb the Havana and Santiago airports, to prepare for the landing of their expeditionary force. At the funeral for the victims of this bombing,

Castro, an angry man, declares the socialist character of the Cuban Revolution. The anti-Castro forces land from U.S. ships at the Bay of Pigs. Their plan: to set up a small beachhead, declare themselves the free government of Cuba, and, as that "government," request that the U.S. military invade. But the Cuban Army and militia surround the invaders, and within two days take twelve hundred prisoners. The U.S. declares a total embargo on all trade with Cuba. (An embargo: All Cuban machinery before the Revolution was made in the United States; all spare parts and supplies have come from there. Now each machine feeds on the others, till there are no parts left.) John Kennedy begins the Alliance for Progress in Latin America, to "promote the continent's development" (or at least that development which does not infringe on the prerogatives of the United States). The U.S., a generous donor, will provide the bullets for the army, the penicillin for the hospitals, the textbooks for the schools, the ideas for the government, the most modern techniques for the police . . . the bullets for the army. Fidel Castro establishes the United Party of Socialist Revolution: "I am a Marxist-Leninist, and I shall remain one until the end of my life." The United States has formed its own interpretation of the Cuban poem. And it will enforce it. Kennedy intensifies the anti-guerrilla campaigns in Latin America, in Vietnam and Laos, increasing the number of elite forces and advisers. The Venezuelan ruling party splits over the extent (and the evil) of United States control of their industries, their country. Fabricio Ojeda, now a prominent parliamentary delegate, resigns and joins the guerrillas. The nationalist party in Peru, APRA, divides over the necessity of armed struggle for the independence of Peru. (Second Havana Declaration: "We cannot stand in our doorway and watch the corpse of imperialism carried by, with the national bourgeoisie and the Soviet Union as pallbearers. It is the duty of revolutionaries to make the revolution. One cannot make the revolution without willing it.") Luis de la Puente sets up the "Rebel APRA."

1962 (Year of Planning) The Organization of American States expels Cuba. Cuba institutes the Integrated Revolutionary Organizations, the block-level organs of party rule, party participation, party surveillance, party control. Rationing is introduced for food and clothing, with severe penalties for speculators, hoarders, and (that useful but vague category) counterrevolutionaries. (Many will be arrested, imprisoned; at the end of each of these declarations, these sentences, many will find themselves sentenced. Many more, when allowed, and with very few of their possessions unconfiscated, will flee Cuba for the wealthier United States.) The United States warns the Soviet Union that it must remove its missiles from Cuba. The U.S. Navy is sent to blockade the island and turn back all Soviet ships. The U.S. Marines prepare for invasion; the people of North America, speechless audience to their kings, think on last things, and sweat. Cuba, too, prepares for invasion and (but how does one do this, except by resigning oneself, conforming oneself, to one's own rhetoric) prepares for nuclear attack. Guevara says: "What we affirm is that we must proceed along the path of liberation even if this costs millions of atomic victims. The Cuban people are advancing fearlessly towards the hecatomb which specifies final redemption." But Cuba finds itself another spectator at the court of kings, almost a jester, excessive in its rhetoric, clownish. It may comment, it may howl, but it only observes. Soviet ships on their way towards Cuba are told by their government to turn about from "final redemption"; the missiles are dismantled and withdrawn. Castro is not consulted but only, eventually, informed. Hearing the news, he swears, kicks the walls, throws a glass to the floor in impotent fury: "They betrayed us as they did in Spain." (Pieces of his new, his always changing, interpretation: The Soviet Union will not protect an independent government in Latin America; Latin America must protect itself. Only a united Third World, struggling together, can defeat the savagery of imperialism.) President Frondizi of Argentina is deposed by the military. Guerrilla groups, mostly of students, appear briefly, flicker, and are put out in Ecuador, forty-eight hours after taking to the mountains. Leftist elements of the military in Venezuela rebel against the government and are put down; survivors join the guerrillas under Douglas Bravo. Guerrillas in Guatemala, under Turcios Lima and Yon Sosa, inflict casualties on the army. Haya de la Torre, the much-compromised nationalist leader in Peru, wins the presidential election but is prevented from taking office by the military. The Rebel APRA under de la Puente and Javier Heraud begins guerrilla operations. China condemns the Soviet Union as revisionists, betrayers of Communism, and social imperialists; it is inevitable, they declare, that One Splits into Two. (This quarrel will divide the Communist world; and sharp fragments—of propaganda that keeps people from moving, of supplies not delivered, of betrayal—will enter the hearts of many Latin American guerrilla movements, splintering them, rendering them, often, immobile, dead.) Algeria, its long war finally over, becomes independent of France. **1963** (Year of Organization) Fidel Castro visits the Soviet Union; he negotiates large sugar purchases by the Russians. Ernesto Guevara visits Algeria to establish economic cooperation among the socialist countries of the Third World. (Do they have something more to share than their poverty?) The Second Agrarian Reform Law in Cuba restricts all privately held estates to no more than a hundred acres. Jorge Masetti, an Argentine journalist who had first come to Cuba to interview his famous countryman Che Guevara, is encouraged by Guevara to establish a guerrilla center in Argentina. Masetti's men gather at a Bolivian farm near the Argentine jungle. (Piece of his new interpretation: guerrilla war is the method for class struggle on our continent.) In Bolivia the tin miners of Catavi go on strike against the government. President Ydigoras Fuentes of Guatemala is overthrown by the military. Hugo Blanco, the peasant organizer, alone and sick with fever, is captured in Peru. Javier Heraud, the Peruvian guerrilla leader, is killed, and his men decimated by the army at Puerto Maldonado. **1964** (Year of the Economy) The voice reading the epic of industrialization reads too quickly, stumbles over its words, makes disastrous mistakes. Blockade (the lack of spare parts, of raw materials), sabotage (defective ball bearings insinuated into shipments from Europe to destroy machinery), absenteeism (working for oneself under socialism—and with few things to buy—one gives oneself a vacation), poor planning (peasants leaving the land to move to the factories, wounding agricultural production; factories built far from transport, without roads, without access to materials; factories producing quantities of sulphuric acid before there is a place in the industrial process for sulphuric acid), all these things damage, nearly cripple, the Cuban economy. The Soviets advise their Cuban comrades, their Cuban clients, to concentrate on agriculture, to see themselves as interdependent with the Soviet bloc; agriculture will provide foreign exchange for future development. (Perhaps, they suggest, Guevara's idea that workers do not require material incentives, that they will produce for "moral" reasons—to build socialism, to destroy imperialism—is idealistic, unrealistic.) The bourgeoisie of Brazil make it clear that even the mildest nationalism offends them; with the aid of the United States, Marshal Castelo Branco leads a military overthrow of President Goulart. (Further piece of his new interpretation: the national bourgeoisie, such as it is, is a weak parasite, in the pay of the imperialists.) In Bolivia, Paz Estenssoro is elected President again, only to be overthrown by Generals Ovando and Barrientos. In Peru, Hugo Blanco is sentenced to twenty-five years in jail. **1965** (Year of Agriculture) Guevara tours Congo-Brazzaville, Ghana, Guinea, Algeria, establishing new links between Africa and Cuba. (Do they have more to offer each other than their poverty? The Third World, he says, must draw together, like soldiers at the front line, to make themselves independent of the first world.) Fidel Castro, Premier of Cuba, makes himself Minister of Agriculture. A trade agreement is signed with the Soviet Union, granting Cuba a credit of 167 million dollars. Che Guevara, at the second Afro-Asian Solidarity Conference—and as if in dissidence to the Soviet loans—criticizes those "so-called socialist methods of aid which are no different from capitalism, that still leave one partner subservient to the other." Upon his return to Cuba, Guevara drops from sight. Castro declares: "Major Ernesto Guevara will be found where he is most useful to the revolution." Ben Bella, in Algeria, is overthrown by the rightist Colonel Boumedienne. A U.S.-financed military coup in Indonesia, led by Suharto, overthrows President Sukarno. Coordinated with CIA help, a massacre of Indonesia's Communists follows; in a few months half a million people will be killed. The United States sends twenty-two thousand Marines to the Dominican Republic, to prevent the election of Juan Bosch. At Catavi, the Bolivian miners do not become a mobile force, a guerrilla force; they remain with their homes and families. The Bolivian military blockades the area: the miners have no milk to give their children, no cough syrup for their silicosis. General Barrientos declares: "We will keep faith with the nation." (A joke, repeated over and over, becomes threatening.) The Bolivian military occupies the mining area of Catavi and massacres the leaders of the strike. Luis de la Puente, the new leader of the Peruvian guerrillas, is killed. The Communist guerrilla base in Colombia, the "independent Republic of La Pato," is eliminated by government troops. Camillo Torres, a Jesuit priest of prominent family, condemns the government for collaborating in the poverty of the people, and leaves the priesthood to join the guerrillas; in a few months his body is brought back to the capital by the army. Splits between the pro-Chinese and pro-Soviet Communist parties mar the activities of the Peruvian guerrillas; the parties guard their ideological purity; neither aids the guerrillas. The Venezuelan Communist Party, like the Bolivian Communist Party, rejects the Cuban thesis, embraces the Soviet line of "peaceful coexistence." One must support and strengthen the national bourgeoisie; competition between the national bourgeoisie and the United States will weaken the imperialists. Then, revolution will be on the agenda. Now one must distribute leaflets, build the consciousness of the masses. The party—not the guerrillas—is, and will remain, the vanguard of the Revolution, that Revolution whose time is not yet. (Piece of a new interpretation: the orthodox Communist parties are so much debris to be swept up by the guerrilla movement and the revolution they will lead.) Jorge Masetti's guerrillas, containing both Argentines and Cubans, are infiltrated by the army and betrayed before ever attacking. Some of the men retreat into the jungle; there they are decimated by starvation, by internal disputes, by disease. Masetti, alone, goes deeper into the jungle to hide, to die. (A Cuban guerrilla, Joaquin, escapes to tell the story.) U.S. military action, delayed briefly by a presidential election, "escalates" in Vietnam. Half a million troops are sent to aid the regime in Saigon. The daily bombing of North Vietnam—Operation Rolling Thunder—begins. Areas of the South are "carpet bombed." A new vocabulary for the world: forced urbanization (if the country surrounds the city, destroy the countryside so that none can live there), pacification (stillness, death, peace, all made the same); new words: they mean a fire in the home, in the bed, on the skin. (Pieces of his new interpretation: Only an armed people, prepared for a long march, for a struggle like that of the Vietnamese, can oppose the imperialists. The revolution must be made by and for the peasants; it must offer them socialism from the start. Only the New Man created by the struggle, by the fires and crucible of revolution, by violence, will build and defend socialism. "Now is the time of the furnaces, and only light should be seen.") Fidel Castro reads the farewell letter of Ernesto Guevara to the Cuban people.   **1966**

I

CRITICISM, SELF-CRITICISM

Isle of Pines, June 1965

Again this morning I walked across the open field outside our house, down to the ocean. Once, when I was eleven, I looked into one of my mother's black notebooks and read from her angular hand, "Life is not a walk across an open field." But in this field, for now, the only ambushes are specters.

I stood for a minute or two on the beach, staring abstractedly at the water breaking in high white waves. My head was still fuzzy from sleep. Small clear lines, transparent hairs, floated annoyingly in front of me, and yet inside my eyes where I couldn't get at them, like mistakes in theory or flaws in character. The brightness made my head hurt. The ocean meant nothing to me this morning, empty of correspondences. I turned and started back through the tall scratchy grass that grows along the edge of the field, by the fence.

Today I stopped halfway up to watch the prisoners, leaning forward with my hands against the thick strands of wire mesh, testing one of the sharp barbs with my fingertip. I drew a drop of blood. Sometimes a small sharp pain breaks through the fuzz in my head, focuses my attention. The fuzz remained; my finger stung. I placed my hands carefully between the barbs, my head down so I wouldn't be recognized. I was dressed in fatigues, as the guards would be —probably I'd be taken for one of them.

The prisoners worked among young trees with long thin waxy leaves, orange trees I think. They were shoveling fertilizer into the dry earth around the roots, mixing it under. The revolution is in growing things, you said; each tree a soldier of revolution. Heat wavered up from the mounds of black earth in the wheelbarrows, a warm sharp smell that I like. The day was just beginning, but circles of sweat were already spreading under the men's arms, and across the backs of their gray shirts. I thought of a phrase: there's no way to put an end to prison, except to make the whole island a prison, each man in the care of every other, as guerrillas are, each man his brother's keeper, teacher, guard. (—Hard to imagine the country where one could use that in a speech!)

I put my fingertip to my mouth and sucked a drop of blood from it: it was less salty than I expected.

One of the prisoners turned from his comrades and picked up a long green leafy weed with two pale-red flowers on its stem. His eyes closed, he pressed the flower against his lips for a moment, as if feeling its pleasant soft texture. With a few quick bites he ate both flowers, and an inch or two of stem. He dropped the stalk to the ground and returned to his shoveling. They must not have enough to eat in the prisons. The pollen from the grass began to make my nose stuffy, so I headed back to the house.

Walter—comrade, bodyguard, keeper—was sitting on the porch. He said hello in his painful raspy voice. Nodes had grown on his vocal cords during the war and had had to wait for the victory of the revolution to be cut away. His voice now is a harsh whisper he hates the sound of; he doesn't talk as much as he did in the Sierras. I said hello, and he returned to his reading.

He had on a newly laundered olive-green uniform, and sat tilted back in the shade of the veranda, keeping himself fresh. My friend has become a fastidious man, almost prissy. He takes care of himself in such a way that he hardly sweats. He has become a smart dresser too. Seven years ago, when he joined my column in the Sierras, he was a raggedy grimy boy in a floppy straw hat and torn pants. He appeared one day, barefoot, his feet so small that there was nothing in our stores that fit him but a pair of Celia's shoes, hand-tooled Mexican boots, women's shoes, an occasion for mockery. Walter enjoyed the jokes and the boots, made the shoes his trademark and his charm against danger. (Floppy straw hats already identified—and protected—Camilo.) The magical boots were the beginning of his interest in clothing. He wears such small fancy things still, and always slightly alters his clothes to show his taste. A dandy with limited resources. Today he has folded back the sleeves of his shirt in huge cuffs, to give them a little style. (It did look good, I thought.)

I stopped near the steps, and thinking of our talks stared at Walter, focusing my meditation on him. He was eating sunflower seeds and reading *The Charterhouse of Parma.* He had come to the Revolution illiterate, perhaps seventeen years old (he lied about his age, about everything), a boy who told stories about himself, arduous adventures, narrow escapes from the police on his way to us, true romances, fabulous crimes he'd committed, very odd jobs he'd done. If you said you were a baker, he would start a story saying, "I was a baker for a while, too," or "I played cards with a baker once. He was a sharp. But cleverly I . . . ," or "I went out with a vicious baker's daughter. But she could do things with her tongue that . . ." He told his tales in a goodhearted way, not expecting to be believed, not offended if you didn't believe him. He wanted to interest you; he wanted you to like him. If you accused him of lying he would smile, as if pleased by your cleverness in seeing through him; and for some reason (I never asked) he would spit in his hand and wipe it on his pants. (In those days he was quite slovenly. He has rewoven himself as if he were one of his own stories.) In a few minutes he began telling you another myth, in a high-pitched, excited voice, an unbroken thread of words. He hardly took breaths, afraid of losing your attention; he never paused for invention (quite common among liars, I've noticed—the products of the imagination suggest their own continuations in a way life does not). If you again pointed out some preposterous contradiction (he had just said he was a baker in Santiago, when now, at the same time, he was having an affair with a gangster's wife in Manzanillo), he drew breath for a second, and then explained the problem away in a rush, restitching the fabric boldly, implausibly, a grotesque yellow zigzag across a red mass, trying to turn the figure of a woman into the outline of a city. ("Did I say I knew a woman like that? I mean one who came from there.") He got on the nerves of some comrades in those days: perhaps they felt his incredible lies showed a contempt for their intelligence. Perhaps his constant interruptions annoyed them. Maybe he talked too much. No longer. The Revolution had demanded the sacrifice of his voice, and in return it had taught him how to read. Now he spent his spare time following other people's fictions.

Walter is a small strong black man; compact-looking, self-possessed. I turned him into a picture, an unshaded drawing. I rubbed away at his skin, the way you might erase a sketch, smudging him, making a dirty whiteness, destroying his outline so that a human form was barely recognizable. But this was amusement, rhetoric, not a real imagination of his dying. I made a bloodstain appear on his clean shirt, but it looked too much like wax. I made the stain melt, spread like sweat across his shirt, from the center of his stomach (but I couldn't, in my mind, see the expression on his face, the shock, the pain). I had him rise and stumble forward, take the positions of some of those I have seen die, one pose after another, like bits of film cut together, a little jump between each image. Walter's long thin fingers grabbed at air; his slender body lay on the ground with his legs open; his body lurched forward and upward, as if struck from behind; then, spliced in by accident, there was an image of a dead child, his head shaven for lice, lying in a grassy field like the one behind me, his skinny arms bent akimbo underneath him; then Walter again, his small body about to fall into the dirt, his head with its high smooth forehead lolling to one side. His chair gave a little wobble. He stuck his hands out for balance, and caught my eye, surprised to find me still standing there, staring at him. I stopped my experiments (do I want him, my friend, to die?). It was a pointless game.

"What's the story?" Walter said, raising his eyebrows, and cocking his head to the side. He put his hand into a small brown bag by his chair and popped a few seeds into his mouth.

The sound of his voice made my throat feel dry and scratchy. "I was thinking about the prisoners," I lied, gesturing to the fence, "the ones putting in the fruit trees over there. I saw one of them eat a flower"—as if that would make my lie more credible. I felt ashamed of what I had been doing to his image: killing it over and over, and magically making his chair wobble.

"Not prisoners," Walter said, omitting as he often now did the noncrucial parts of his sentences. "Volunteers. Young Communists. Didn't you see the women?" He was undoubtedly telling the truth. Only the ornate fiction, the wordy picaresque, had ever interested him. And he didn't tell stories anymore.

"Well, appearances are deceiving," I said, sententiously, wondering what that made of my aphorism about prisons.

I went in to my work, my writing, my self-criticism. On the way I reached into Walter's bag for a few salty seeds.

For a moment, when I came into the shadows, spots of light with blue centers bloomed on the bedroom furniture, the gray metal cot, the straight-backed chair. It reminded me of something you had said about my rhetoric (as opposed, say, to yours): that too much light can blind a person. I held up my hand. The gray-and-white seeds were visible in the center of my palm, but parts of my fingers were gone, eaten by spots of light. A metaphorical point for you. Another game. ("Make shadows," you might have said, "so they can see what they wish." "But you know they're deceiving themselves," I would say. "And later we'll have to deal with them anyway." You turn away, "Let them think what they wish. Later we'll be strong enough to deal with them as *we* wish.")

I write in my bedroom, on the desk that was here waiting for me, a long white board standing on two sawhorses. It faces the window that looks out on the field and the ocean. The prerevolutionary owner of the house, a Yanqui, has left a memento on the wall by the bed: a copy of Coleridge's "Kubla Khan," mounted in a plain wooden frame.

Preface:
Self-criticism, to overcome that rhetoric that makes the world go away in a flare. To overcome my pride, my egotism, to see things plainly, to break these stones, to bring this old man to an end.
"To bring this old man to an end"—it's already too rhetorical. Cross it out.

Self-criticism: crossing parts of myself out, rewriting myself. Instead of killing myself or my comrades, a metaphorical way to sacrifice myself.

"Sacrifice myself"—more rhetoric! Cross it out.

Endless redefinition instead of the activity itself.

The boy with his head shaved lying in the field. My mother once shaved my head that way. He could have me killed. My plane could disappear, out to sea.

Impossible! We're married for life. (My mother once brought a pistol to the breakfast table, laid it down by her plate. I was fourteen. It was an absurd charade, to show my father how serious she was about her position in some political argument. But what if, while I watched, she raised that pistol and pointed it at his forehead?)

Impossible. It's waiting like this. It makes me crazy.

My finger throbs a little where I pricked it.

The stuffiness in my nose is liquid on my upper lip. My lungs strain and hurt. When I was a child

I have to get my inhalator.

JUNE 14

I am thirty-seven years old today. The time has come when I must think about my future as a guerrilla.

Walter baked a cake for us, for me.

JUNE 15

At breakfast Walter told me that he had heard over Voice of America that I am dead. (Walter is insomniac. When he is too tired to read, he lies in the dark and listens to the voices on the shortwave radio.) Last night informed sources murmured of a serious split in the ruling circles of Cuba. Castro has purged me, executed me, as I have executed so many. So end tyrants. Perhaps, reliable sources whisper (and Walter rasps), it was for my criticism of the Soviet trade agreements; perhaps for the failures of my policy of industrialization— it is known that Castro is critical of my "idealistic stand" on moral incentives; or perhaps he and Raul are jealous of my following. Informed sources are uncertain; they had their ears to the door, but the voices were indistinct. The actors emerged and one of the players was gone. A dumb show. They conjectured a plot.

The only certainty is that I am dead.

Fidel Castro, Premier of Cuba, is silent, neither confirming or denying.

Fidel is silent. The afternoon of our talk, after the ride from the airport in which we each shouted and punched the air, ended in silence, that to some uncanny silence of his, when he joins the world of mineral things, when the most talkative of men, whose life is a stream, river, torrent vapor cloud stream, etc., of words, shuts up; when his gestures, too, his hand reaching out and upward to punctuate a point, to squeeze a shoulder, come to an end. His hands lie open by his sides.

We sat facing each other, neither of us speaking, on the crow's-nest platform he had built in the middle of his room. (To reach it we walked up a circular metal stairway that winds about a thick metal pole. The pole supports the wooden platform.) Fidel sat in a rounded wooden desk chair on rollers (a triumph for someone to have gotten up that ladder), and I made myself comfortable in a small straight-backed wooden chair. We were eight feet off the ground, talking, smoking; not talking. I looked down at his room. His single bed was neatly made, the blue and red blanket tucked tight. (He rarely sleeps here. Uneasy in Havana, he travels all over the island, wandering, in a caravan of jeeps. And in Havana he prefers others' beds.) Iron weights were scattered on the floor, dumbbells, a rowing machine, baseball bats, baseball and boxing gloves, the wide white cross-weave of a trampoline. Fidel does not want to get fat; or old; or die. The trampoline was useless for exercise, though; books were piled all over it. Books were everywhere, books on farming, on soil science, on cattle raising, books on crop hybridization, books half read, books stacked on the seat of the rowing machine, with red ribbon place-markers sticking out from their pages. Books on the red reclining chair and on the wobbly leopard-skin footrest, books opened and spread face down on the floor, their spines cracking. Scattered about among the wilderness of books were the musical instruments he has tried to play from time to time—a guitar, a bright new brass trumpet, an accordion. (A one-man mariachi band!) For a bad moment I looked about, at the scattered books on agriculture, and the musical instruments he had abandoned (each time he gave up on the project before he had learned to play even a simple tune. Not enough time, not enough patience. There is only one instrument for him: the crowded plaza, his orchestra); and I thought of the factories—my ministry's responsibility—many of them idle or half used, hobbled for lack of raw materials or trained workers, or spare parts. The Revolution was an old engraving I saw once, as a child: a pensive bearded man, a broken god, with a ruined city in the background, a collection of useless instruments around him, a magic square whose impotent charm means nothing beyond itself, a pile of books under his elbow on the spectral unproductive science of alchemy, that promises so much and accomplishes nothing; only one tool: a reaper, instrument of some dubious harvest.

I looked back at Fidel. His eyes were distant, tired. He'd been up the night before, perhaps discussing my arrival, perhaps with a woman. His hands lay on his lap (he'd moved them when I looked away. It made me smile; he didn't respond). He was still now. Immobile. Mineral.

I was exhausted by my plane trip, and would usually have been fretful. I had a clammy smell. But I knew my thoughts. I stretched my legs out and looked at my boots. I put my hands in my lap. I sat.

This silence of his was tactical. (All of Fidel's actions, all his gestures are —or by his genius could later be gathered up into—a tactic.) It was a rare tactic, but not unfamiliar. Occasionally, in committee meetings, in planning sessions (earlier ones, when consent was still often at issue) he would do this immobility business, as if his motor ("the little motor that sets the big motor —the masses—in motion") had run down, finally, for good and all. His hands, which had been busy curling and uncurling the thick hair of his sideburns, fell, as if he'd died, to his sides. His mouth fell open a bit, almost doltishly, if it hadn't been for the intelligence of his eyes, which looked as if they were seeing something puzzling, distasteful. The others chattered on for a bit, until they saw him; then, one by one, they too grew quiet; waited.

His silence was another manner of argument (silence is argument carried on by other means). When he had said all he could think to say (and that meant hours), when he had run out of rhetoric, examples, dialectical twists, and you —a broad, bearded comrade from the mountains, a too-open man—were still obstinate, obdurate, unconvinced, then he would sit like this. You thought the Revolution had promised land to the peasants, land they would own, land they would work themselves. Now Fidel was talking of reserving land for state farms, cooperative enterprises. You glared at those around the table. You were in uniform; some of them wore suit jackets. They weren't comrades; they were shit. No one looked back at you. Fidel's silence meant, "examine your motives"; it meant, "I do not know why you are so obstinate, it's something dark in you that you won't admit to us, perhaps because you haven't admitted it to yourself; some desire for personal power, some petit-bourgeois prejudice; some mulish pride that keeps you attached to your mistake. But I am more obdurate than you. We'll sit here until you discover your error. Or, if you fail, I will end this meeting in silence."

And perhaps you would discover your blindness; or perhaps his silence was (in so many ways) too terrifying to be abided—as if you thought he (or someone) was dying. He, the principle of Revolution, was being absorbed into the nonhuman world. You would do what you must to bring him back, to save him (or someone). You would indeed (and why not call your motive concern, loyalty, love for him whether he was right or wrong?). For perhaps there was, you felt, a glacial change going on within that silence, a change that would be irreversible; a mountain was being gouged from the land by the slow progress of a huge silent mass of ice. You were falling away from him, you were falling down that mountain, out of his confidence. He might smile suddenly and end the meeting. We would get up and leave the high-ceilinged room; and it would be far too late. You would find yourself at a distance from him, in a province, in exile, in jail, dead. His silence prefigured an abandonment, an absence, a death. Maybe yours.

But to revive him now, to bring him back up the chain of being from rock to man, required a lot of talk from you. You could not anymore simply acquiesce in his plan. You must indicate thoroughly your hidden motive, now discovered, for disagreement. You must show that you had apprehended the flaw in your character, and so seen your theoretical mistake. You must display your understanding of his idea: economies of scale, creation of a new man, destruction of the petit-bourgeois element. You must elaborate for a while on why you now agreed—hard to do, for he had exhausted most of the means of elaboration himself. Perhaps you could use anecdotes from the war: when we had redistributed expropriated cattle to the peasants they had immediately slaughtered and eaten them, afraid the cows would be taken away again. Only state cooperatives could prevent this. I had seen you, a courageous man, drag a wounded comrade from a field strafed by gunfire, but sweat covered your body now as you showed yourself before your comrades. I could smell it: an acrid unpleasant odor. You clasped your fingers together with strain, in prayer, as I had seen you do when you first tried to learn to read. Again, words were failing to come to you. Comrades stared at the light from the high windows, or the discolored rectangles on the wall where the portraits of Cuba's betrayers had hung. (I, however, watched you perform. You caught my eye and I smiled and nodded. You hated me ever after.) You went on till he spoke, for his silence was a waste of snow you might have to wander in till your heart froze in confusion and terror.

And often, as the holdout heard himself talk, he found that he now agreed with Fidel, not simply for show, but deeply. (Or was this pride's ruse to save one's dignity?) Even as you nervously spoke (I have been told) you found that something recalcitrant in you had melted. Fidel *was* right. Of course he was right. Who better could interpret that exacting god, the Revolution? You turned about before our eyes; he had turned you; you wanted even to thank him; you saw things freshly. You didn't feel you had abandoned your position exactly (something you would never have done in a battle, when the enemy was clearly uniformed, when you thought you had known what you were fighting for); rather you simply couldn't find your old position from your new perspective.

But such silence was an extreme tactic for Fidel. He preferred interpretation and reinterpretation, a reworking of everyone's arguments that found opposition to be not opposition at all, but an unsuspected fundamental agreement with him (for the moment), that made you feel that your point was subsumed in his, and that the later working-out of things would join you both (till death do you part).

Or, alas, later some other solution would be found.

Fidel's silence is so powerful because all vitality is in his voice. Once there was. No, this should have a fairy-tale beginning. Once upon a time there was a CIA plot to damage the Revolution by putting lysergic acid in one of Fidel's cigars. (What appears to them to be a broom is a creature with ears; they have their informed sources, we have ours.) He would smoke the funny cigar before making an important speech to the nation, and become psychotic during the speech, talk all crazy out of his head. This would demoralize the masses.

And there was a dreamlike truth to their idea. Fidel's voice is the Cuban Revolution. Not his presence, but his voice. It is as if the island were a narrative of his, a continual improvisation by a master storyteller. He is making them up as we go along; creating characters (was there a proletariat in the way that the revolution required it before he named it, made it know its responsibilities, its power?); and yet one feels at each turn that the story could not be other than it is. He has done this by listening: to hear Fidel speak is to hear a man responding, always; he hears a murmur in the crowd; it becomes a voice inside him; he speaks it; he gives the mass the words it wished but did not know, did not even know that it wished except as an uncertainty, a painful anxiety. The Revolution is the long delirium of Fidel's speeches. Every citizen is a sentence in that story, as he covers the country with words, makes it out of words, crossing and revising and crisscrossing the island as if it were a giant piece of paper. Fidel gone mad would be the Revolution become farce. They would build big factories to make cookies in the shape of obscene body parts; they would declare war on the Eskimos and load their guns with potatoes and soap; they would dig up sugar cane and plant transistors, waiting patiently for their harvest of radios. And they would become strange to each other, having lost the common term, the common hero, the common language that he is for them. There is no life in Cuba outside the Revolution, outside of his voice.

Thus the anxiety when he shuts up. In the first year of the Revolution, when we still had to make gestures to the national bourgeoisie, and to the North Americans, we made Judge Urrutia the President. He was an old courageous man, a judge under Batista who had voted freedom for the captured men of the *Granma*. But he would not go along with the First Agrarian Reform Law, mild though it was. He accused Communists—myself among them—of subverting the government, misleading Fidel. (For Fidel had made shadows, allowed the national bourgeoisie to believe what it liked about him.) Fidel resigned. The Cabinet tried to meet in his absence; but nothing could be done without him. Urrutia telephoned Castro and his call was refused. Castro was silent. The Cabinet met again to deal with this crisis; but again they could not agree, they could not calculate his silence, they could not improvise an action. The ministers left the Presidential Palace. Rumors spread. Fidel was silent, neither confirming nor denying. The sugar workers, a union we controlled, called for Urrutia's resignation, that Fidel might be returned to them. The people waited. Was the Revolution at an end? Would Fidel, indefatigable rebel, take arms against the government? That night Fidel spoke on television. He enumerated Urrutia's faults, his mistaken appointments, his too-large house, his too-large salary. "Personally," Fidel said, "I neither have nor want anything. Disinterest is a garment I wear everywhere." What did he need money for if he trusted the people to provide for him? Urrutia was making up the idea of a Communist plot to provoke aggression from the United States. Urrutia planned to flee Cuba, return after the invasion, and run the country for the North Americans. Urrutia made it impossible for him to work, made him impotent, defenseless, exhausted by Urrutia's hysterical anti-Communist declarations that caused international embarrassment and conflict with the good people in the United States. *Urrutia made him silent.* That was what was intolerable. Cuba had found its hero, its epic, this man who spoke in rhythmic cadenced sentences of audacious plans, of future gaiety, of sublime and necessary cruelty, and this gray-haired old man had shut him up, denied them Fidel's voice. Crowds gathered around the Presidential Palace demanding the judge's life. Urrutia fled out the back door. We placed him under house arrest, then let him flee ignominiously to Venezuela. From that time on we ruled Cuba.

I have seen him use his silence as a military tactic too. He would have us wait in ambush, in terrain that we controlled, and watch, watch as the soldiers entered our territory, strung out in a line across a field of tall grass, watch as their bold steps became more hesitant. They had known they were entering our zone, they had steeled themselves for the battle, they had taken the step, the leap, to face the danger, the firing, their death; *why hadn't the firing begun?* they couldn't believe they were safe; how much longer before it began; how much longer would they have to wait? it is terrible to feel in yourself a longing for an attack to begin, a longing for the sight of friends falling around you, perhaps for your own death; so divided, it is difficult to hold your resolve, to hold yourself ready; the line bunched near the front (we always shot the man on point first, so that soon no man would be willing to enter our zone first); you could see the sweat on their faces, under their arms, the terror in their eyes. The silence demoralized them. Then we killed them.

JUNE 16

Notes for statement on Vietnam

We cannot remain silent towards Vietnam. We cannot treat the struggles of the Vietnamese people as if they were theater, a show we are audience at, a spectacle, a tragedy to provoke our pity, our tears. We have cried and applauded, but we have done nothing.

We must not abandon Vietnam.

Vietnam, like Cuba, should have been made, irrevocably, and no matter what the cost, a part of the Socialist world, to be defended by the missiles of the Socialist world, even—if the imperialists forced it—to the point of nuclear holocaust. This was not done. She was abandoned to fight alone.

Vietnam is the vanguard of the struggle against imperialism. We must aid her with our hands.

> Sketch of world situation since WWII.
> Use figure of hands/of fire
>
> A map on fire
> fire/light   destruction/illumination
> A fire in a field on a shirt
> a body on fire
> The hands of a young woman in
> Vietnam (I see dirt under her nails)/
> our hands—the nails bitten down
> with anxiety; source of the
> anxiety? too psychological
> The people of Vietnam must be as
> real to us as our own hands.

This morning I sat at the table in the main room with Walter, keeping him company during breakfast. My asthma has been very bad the last few days, and I can't make myself eat much. There is a dank smell for me everywhere that takes away my appetite and my strength. I sipped a cup of mate, mostly for the warmth on my hands.

Walter said, chewing some bread and jam, "Why are we here?"

"A metaphysical question?" I said. I knew what he meant; it was odd, I thought, that he hadn't asked before. But often he waits patiently for situations to unfold themselves, to reveal their meanings; he is a watchful man. "I'm here," I said, "waiting to find out what Fidel will do. He can help my plans; he could damage them greatly. I'm here to write my self-criticism, to make myself sure of my next step. I am writing a message about Vietnam, a call to arms." Walter looked at me, and said nothing. "But I'm not writing." My last words came in a wheeze; but I couldn't use the epinephrine, again, yet.

"What happened?"

"You're a poem, Walter. I don't understand what you mean."

"Between you and our leader." He *was* a poem—it was difficult ever to know if he were ironic.

"We talked. We fought. We sat silently."

"What did he say?"

"A great deal. At the end he said that perhaps I wanted to sacrifice myself and my closest comrades to appease my guilt. He said that I had sent many people to prove my theories, and they had died; and now I felt troubled. I couldn't stand to live when they were dead on my account. I had to prove that my theories were good—they were *my* theories during this conversation—that they had died from mistakes of their own. Or I had to die myself, and appease my guilt. Maybe, he said, I wanted to die." Talking like this made an anxious flutter in my chest; my lungs ached. "I think it's nonsense, a way for him to avoid the question facing us. But I must wait for his help."

Walter stared at me, as I had at him a few days ago. Do I want him to die? I returned his look. He has large brown watchful eyes. His small face tilts backward from his chin to the brow. The last week he has grown a wispy black mustache. I wheezed more deeply. The outline of his face wavered in the bad air.

"Very metaphysical," he said. "Very psychological. Not like him. Not like you. Things must have gone very far between you."

"We had been looking at each other a long time, up on that platform he has. Neither of us had spoken. We'd exhausted our arguments. He had known

of my plans. He had to decide what he would do. We sat. Then he spoke that
. . . nonsense—very slowly, his voice was hoarse, far away, a low murmur—there
were pauses between his sentences, not his style at all. He knew he was avoiding
the question. But I must wait. I said I would come here and think about what
he had said."

"What happened before?"

"The rise and decline of the Roman, Spanish, and British Empires. The
whole history of imperialism. The Cuban Revolution." I wheezed out a laugh.
I laughed alone; Walter said nothing; Walter watched, his eyes melancholy,
quiet. My laugh exhausted me. I gasped for breath. "Don't stare at me," I said,
and sipped some tea. "I repeated to him what I'd said in Africa about the trade
agreements, what I had said to him, to you, before: We'd be dependent on
the Soviets for oil. We'd produce sugar, they'd trade us manufactured goods.
Industrialization would come to an end. Everything would be the same as
before."

"And?" The harshness of his voice made his words peremptory, almost a
command.

"And he said, Fine. Cuba was an agricultural country, should be an agricultural country. The cities were corrupt. Havana was the most corrupt, a whore
to tourists, a white vampire that had sucked the wealth of the rest of the island.
It had to wander in the wilderness forty years, return to wilderness until it was
fit for freedom. Havana should be allowed to die; its sewers to break; its streets
to decay; grass would grow between the paving stones. The peasants, he said,
are the only trustworthy ones in the country. Farming was a beautiful thing,
to work the land was a beautiful thing, the land itself was a beautiful thing.
His hand reached out then and patted the air, as if he were stroking the island.
The world, he said, was hungry, and growing hungrier. There would always be
many hungry nations to buy our crops. The Soviets were right about some
things, even if their reasons were crude. We had no internal market for
industrial products. But we had a gift for breeding things. He talked about
cows, about the different kinds of cows, about cross-breeding of cows, about
raising new kinds of cattle on the state farms, about kudzu."

"You don't like cows?" Walter smiled, as he would have in the mountains
many years ago, about to begin a story; somewhere in the past I heard his old
voice say, there had been an important cow, an interesting cow. But he said
no more. The smile was all that was left of the story, the smile and his ghostly
voice.

"I don't know much about cows. He knows a great deal. He's really in love
with it, his pastoral. He's going to make himself Minister of Agriculture. He
repeated that only the peasants understand the Revolution, understand it in

their being. The Revolution is in growing things, in crops, in grain, in cane, in cattle. The seasons are the rhythm of the Cuban Revolution. The people working the state farms are the base of the Revolution, the new proletariat."

Walter laughed. "I remember when the rhythm of the revolution was the pachanga. Socialism with the pachanga." His body shook in slow motion; each stage of his laugh was superimposed on another, a blur of forms. "And?" he said. His voice was very dry; he could hardly get the word out. His mouth had spittle around it, a lot of white foam. I lifted my arm from the table (a great effort it was, a great weight), and pointed. Walter narrowed his eyes at me, quizzically. "What?"

The foam disappeared. "Nothing."

"And?" That ghostly sound; I always expected something else; I could not accommodate to it.

I drank some smoky tea, bringing my face close to the table. "And I said the Soviets wouldn't protect us from the United States. They'd rubbed our faces in that in '62. They'd made clowns of us. They'd abandoned us then and they had abandoned Vietnam to the most savage attack. They would abandon us again."

"Abandon," Walter rasped. "Forlorn word. Word from a love story. He said?"

"He didn't say anything to that. He knew what I said was true. I had used his own phrases. He looked disappointed. I said that whatever we produced, still Cuba must have markets here, in Latin America. And it must have allies. It must break the encirclement, the blockade. And now was the right time. The Vietnamese had made an opportunity for us. Once begun, guerrilla warfare will spread throughout the continent. The United States cannot struggle here and in Asia. Our blow, now, will be decisive."

Walter brought his hands from the table, and clapped them together twice, slowly. Delighted, or ironic. "And?" He put something to his mouth that looked like a handkerchief; he brought it away covered with blood. "What is that?" I said, horrified, pointing at his bloody hand. "Is your throat bleeding?" A sudden spasm of anxiety: his cancer had recurred.

Walter looked at me, as if I were crazy. "A piece of bread. With jam. Are you all right?"

"Oh." I tried to pull myself back from that world. "Yes. It's the asthma. I'm seeing things." When I had gestured at his bread I had spilled tea all over my hand, my arm, my leg. I liked the sharp pain. But it turned lukewarm; the damp splotches here and there on my body annoyed me; they made me feel in fragments. I strained to remember what Walter and I had been talking about. I saw Fidel sitting stonily in a wooden desk chair. "He didn't speak for a while. We had thought these things, we had spoken these things to each other many times. My way was clear. In that silence I became even more certain. I wasn't intimidated by his stillness; it didn't cause me a moment's doubt. I thought it pointless. He wanted to sidestep the issue; he wanted me to take back the truth I had spoken. But there's no way to go back. Then he said, Argentina is impossible. The masses there still dream of Peron, there is no way to discredit a dream, the dream of a just king. Nothing could be done there until the matter of Peron was settled. I agreed. He said that Latin America was too nationalist for me to operate anywhere else but in Argentina. And the other parties wouldn't support a guerrilla movement I led. They'd be terrified of me. I'd be condemned as an adventurer. They'd follow the Russian line. We could say what we would about their cowardice, we could rub their faces in their own shit. But they wouldn't change. They were craven opportunists, and the Russians fed them. The Russians owned their balls, etc."

"You said?" Walter sounded like a child who wanted more story—making allowances for a voice so very old it was not human but a tree's.

"I said what he's heard me say, what you have heard me say, a thousand times. Once we begin, the parties will have to support us or be swept away in the war. The Revolution must be continental, a struggle on many fronts. The imperialists will bleed from a hundred places. But he wasn't listening. He was distracted inwardly, twirling the edges of his sideburns between his fingers. We stopped then, and smoked. He said, musingly, You must move slowly with bureaucrats, bring them along, neutralize them, until they don't know what they've gotten into. He was coming round to my way of thinking. He was silent again. And we sat. Then he talked about guilt, and sacrifice, those things I've told you about already."

Walter picked up a knife from beside his plate. He spread his other hand on the table, and poked the knife rapidly back and forth between his long thin fingers, into the wood of the table. He was like a shuttle. Was this a riddle about sacrifice? He was in a trance. I didn't want to startle him, afraid he would jab himself. I asked softly, "Why are you poking yourself?"

"I'm not. You look awful."

"An attack. It will pass."

"Couldn't you lie?"

"To whom?"

Walter looked astonished. "I said you should lie down."

"No. I'll be all right. I want to tell you the rest. I want to know what you think."

"What else did you say?"

"I said I'd consider his points. He said he'd think about what he could do for me. There's a great deal he could do, must do—financing, arrangements with other parties, propaganda. But it would anger many people. I should go away for a while, and think things through. I needed a rest after my trip. And I infuriate the Russians. It would be easier to operate if I were out of the way for a while. He grew angry. Fuck them, he said, they can go fuck themselves. But I wondered if he would prefer me . . . more obscure."

Walter smiled. "No. He's thinking of what to do with you. He knows there's a use for everything. Especially a piece as valuable as you. He's figuring what that use is. He'll support you. It's only your name that can unite the guerrillas on the continent. Yours or his. If you leave Cuba you will be the great rebel, the adventurer. He'll be the stay-at-home, the housewife. That's hard for him." This was a very long speech for Ponco. There were flecks of blood around his mouth. Of jam, I mean. "But in the end he'll back you. Once, in the mountains, when I first joined, Fidel said to me, 'I am all the names of rebellion in history.'"

I laughed gleefully.

Ponco stared at me. "Are horns growing from my head? Is milk pouring from my ears?"

"No. He said that to me, too. The first time we met, in a kitchen in Mexico. I thought he was crazy. I told him so."

"*I* thought it was beautiful. I was sixteen. I'm that type. You see? He doesn't *waste* anything. He had held on to the remark for three years. It didn't work for you. Okay. A middle-class doctor. Wrong sort. He had to find the right sort of character. He waits till he finds the right use for things. He knows how to wait." His voice became raspier as he spoke, but he continued. "The Russians will be angry. One Vietnam is enough, they think. No one becomes too upset. The United States loses a little territory, but it gets rid of its crap. Two Vietnams! Unthinkable! But he will support you. Your arguments are good. And what kind of rebel is he if he is afraid? He'll come round. You should work on your writing. It would be interesting to read."

"I've lost the taste for reflection. I taught myself to think only of what must be done. I know now what must be done. Where do I begin?" We were two men speaking in whispers, in gasps, at a table, on an island in the ocean. It seemed funny to me, our weak voices, rasping, two breaths barely exhaled, in pain.

"At the beginning. Here. Once upon a time there was a prince on an enchanted island where prisoners changed into young Communists." Ponco looked thin and nervous. His body bent over the table. It was my mother.

"You sound like my mother," I said.

"You're seeing things again." He drew back from the table. "You know,

I'm jealous of your childhood. Stupid." As he stood up he mimed crying, a silent waah. "No one to read me stories. No one knew how to read. No stories. I like stories. You should write me a story. Many people would like to know the story of your life." He picked up his book from the chair by the door. "No more talking now. My voice hurts."

I went in to lie down on my cot. Images floated before me, fully colored, and were replaced by other images, as in the moment before sleep. My mother reading to me at dinner. The smoky light of my childhood dining room that makes Ponco jealous. The dank and bad-smelling air that began when I began and that follows me everywhere. An attack. Careening down the hall of my parents' house. The foot of my parents' bed, where I have fallen.

Argentina, 1928

My Asthma

When I was a child I choked on the air; I coughed; I tried to spit my pain out into my hands in hard knots of dark slippery sputum. My asthma began before my memory begins, and so I can never know its root. When my father and mother were arguing—and they often were, for they were both proud, spirited people—my father said that my asthma came from her, that it had come to me because my mother was a selfish woman, she cared for her pleasure more than she loved her own son. She had been careless with me. (She had to do whatever she wanted, had to go swimming when no one else would, when a storm was about to begin, when it was criminal to expose a child to the wind.) One overcast chilly day, when I was an infant, my mother had taken me to the yacht club (she despised the other members, but liked to have a private beach), so that she could play in the ocean.

Often when I was a child, hearing my father's voice as they argued at the dinner table, I felt as if I were remembering that day. I saw my mother standing by the edge of the ocean, wearing a blue bathing suit that showed her long pale legs. Her red hair was entirely tucked up under a white rubber cap that made her features severe, strange to me—it wasn't a woman's face. Her muscles were taut. The water will be cold at first, a little painful, but it will open into her pleasure: she loves to swim. Her mouth was slightly open, but not slack. Her face was intent, expectant, she was thinking of her pleasure. Her face was empty of thoughts of me! She turned from me and walked forward slowly, down the deserted shoreline, away from me, towards a sea that became dark cloud at the horizon. And then suddenly she vanished, diving into, swallowed up by, a wavering hand of green and white water, a huge angry wave.

She had left me covered on the sand, but I crawled from under my woolen blanket into a sharp wind. When she came out of the ocean I was blue and shaking, my arms and legs moving in grasping spasms, clutching air.

I had had my first attack.

Because she had been careless with me. Or so my father said when they argued (and they argued always before me: I was the point). And carried along for a moment by his strength, the self-righteous rage in his precise, his furious voice, I too became angry at her. There was a sickening haze around the electric lights. The night's meat soured in my stomach. *She had abandoned me!*

But this anger quickly became a bewilderment of tears in my throat, a clog in my chest, for I knew that my pain had no beginning; the thick impossible air had always been there; there had been no betrayal.

And in times of peace between them my father affirmed this, exonerated her: my asthma was not her, or anyone's fault; no particular incident had anything to do with bringing it about; it would have begun sometime in any case; it was outside history; it was heredity; my body; fate. But she didn't believe him then. She was a strong smart woman, but she bent without defense to that blow, never answering back; for she was as hard on herself as she was on others (and egotistical too: taking responsibility where she had none). She thought that truth was in anger always, and so in her husband's accusation only, that any other explanation was a way of comforting her, letting her off, a lie. To her death she believed my pain had come from her, from her having indulged her love of the ocean that cold fall day. And often, watching her as she argued with him at the dinner table, I thought I saw that sad thought enter her; it was a hesitation when she was making one of her sharp witty caricatures; she glanced at me; a fear clouded the bright brown intelligence of her eyes, suddenly stilled the lovely O almost wicked vivacity of her face. She looked for a moment—my mother, Celia de la Serna Guevara!—as if she were cringing slightly. Her malicious remark would trail off into ". . . but still, I suppose he's doing the best he can"—a kind inanity that was not her style at all.

So the terrain of my childhood was a place where I was menaced. My enemy, the air, might come at me at any time, turn suddenly heavy, bad.

I might be lying in bed, watching the shadows pass back and forth over the cracks in the cream-colored ceiling—a map, a land rich with wide rivers that I might dreamwalk. Waiting for sleep, I passed my two friends, Left and Right, the red tassels of the blanket edges, back and forth between my fingers, telling myself a story about them: they were being trained by my fingers, their captain, to do fantastic feats, ones that would make them much-admired performers. My eyes closed to a trapeze, a crowd in wooden stands. Men in white coats passed back and forth selling candy and small whips that whistled sharply when cracked in the air. Then it was that the air might thicken on my skin, a cream curdling around me. *I had not been careful enough, vigilant enough!* My upper lip was wet with snot; I coughed; and soon, as the attack grew worse, a bad smell, and the worst pain came. My parents, in the kitchen discussing the evening newspapers with each other, heard me, and ran to my bed—for whenever they spoke together they were listening also for that third voice, their son's anguished breathing.

Or an attack might come late at night, when my parents were asleep (the nights, with their chill, were the worst time for me, especially if there were any dampness in the air, any sign of storm). I woke to my own clangorous breathing; dazed; uncertain for a moment whose sound it was; woke to a constriction in my chest that was a big hand inside me, holding my lungs in its palm while it balled into a fist. I thought: *No one will hear me, no one will come to me.* Bumping against the walls, I made my way down the long hall to my parents' room.

The heavy air at the foot of their bed made me sway from side to side. My mother was repeating odd sounds to herself, over and over, in a hoarse voice. A different spirit was inside her at night. The bedroom smelled strange, musty. Fascinated by my parents' bodies, turning jerkily under the sheets, dimly illuminated by the pale light from the windows, I forgot, almost forgot, my pain. I thought: *I must be sure I'm having an attack, I mustn't wake them unless I'm having an attack.* I stood in my pajamas in the darkness at the foot of their bed, listening to my own breathing, listing my symptoms to myself, concentrating inwardly, and biting my fingers to keep from crying out and waking them before I was certain I was having an attack.

And often I waited too long, no longer had the strength to tug at my father's beard, or pull his shoulder and wake him. I pushed the air to beat it back from me, I took small steps forward towards them, trying to break the air's encirclement; I stood still, in a last attempt to hide from it. But then I could do no more; it took all my strength to get the thick stuff, the air, inside me. I gasped, my thin body shook with a continuous tremor from the effort, the terrible effort, of breathing. I was brought to my knees. My mind, tormented animal, was panicked towards one sharp thought, *I must breathe, I have to breathe!* My arms, my legs, every muscle was strained, trying to breathe. The air pushed back, formed itself into a hand that brought me down, till I rolled from side to side on the floor by the foot of my parents' bed.

My wheezing—how loud it was for such a small boy!—entered their dreams, woke them. *It wasn't my fault though, it was my pain that disturbed them.* And unless my consciousness was flickering out, reduced to the animal movement of my throat and lungs, I was filled with joy at my father bending over me in his loose white nightshirt. The feeling of rescue flooded me, a buoyant light.

But really there was no rescue, very little anyone, even he, could do. My father picked me up from the floor. My head lolled against the man's sleep-warmed shoulder. He carried me back to my bed.

But by then the bad air was in the bedroom too, and it was impossible to rest. I lay in bed clutching the blanket edges, squeezing them rhythmically in my palms. The cracks in the ceiling moved about, the ceiling wavered, breathed in and out as I did. It grew intolerably light in the room, though there was only one lamp (made from a blue toy train engine), and its single bulb was softened by a square yellow shade. Still, the rays of light were thick, they had a nauseating substance. The light overwhelmed the furniture, washed at the wooden bureau, the large mirror, the light was a sickening acid fog that took away all contours.

I wiped my nose on the sheets. The cotton was cool against my lips, gave me a momentary sense of comfort, a reassurance that the world would not be washed away. But then I grew sweaty again, and again a hand was pressing down on me, crushing me into the bed. I gasped for air, my lungs fluttered painfully. The room shook with my effort to breathe; the painted nursery-rhyme figures on the wall, the bureau, vibrated, went fuzzy. The sheet I held against my cheek for reassurance thickened, till I felt all the fibers crawling like hard tiny worms against my skin. Convulsively I threw the bedclothes down around my waist. They bunched there like the folds of a statue's drapery, pressing into my waist with dull heavy edges.

My father stayed by me throughout the night, to tend me as best he could. A muscular short man of great energy and strength, he sat quietly in a child's wooden chair by the head of the bed, unable to act, to use his strength. My father's eyes were set deep in his face, under bushy brows; he had a large straight nose, a large face, and a brown beard; he was, if he wished, a fierce-looking man. Now, his empty hands resting on his thighs, he watched me tenderly, until, I think, his consciousness was only an adumbration of his son's shaking body, his son's difficult breathing, until his own lungs strained within him. My pain took away my father's moralism, his deepest habit (where was the fault here? where was the lesson?). He was a doctor, but he could do nothing for his son; there was no action to take, no use for his fortitude, his fierceness, his love. He could do nothing but make gestures: hold my arm, wipe my forehead with a washcloth. There were no injections yet for asthma, only a black powder that was burnt in a cup by my bedside. It made a thick foul smoke that did little to help. But it was burnt anyway, another gesture, a rite more than a medicine.

As the night went on the air began to stink to me, not only heavy but dank, bad smelling, like rotting meat. The attack clawed at my chest constantly, my body moved in spasms. My father held my body against his own (for once I'd told him that that made the pain less) and rocked me back and forth.

I was dazed. My father's large neatly manicured fingers, his thick veins that showed clearly beneath the skin on the back of his hand, looked monstrous to me then, they pulsed and changed in shape, as if I were seeing, grotesquely enlarged, the life of the cells in his hand. With my own hand I grabbed at the tight scratchy curls of his beard, squeezed them weakly to tell him—though it accomplished nothing—when the pain was worst. Then he spoke to me soothingly—if only he could take the pain into himself! He told me of all the things we would do when I was better. But I was gagging, without will or thought, my throat and lungs moving in insistent, agonizing, frantic spasms, trying to bring up, to spit out, the thick black and yellow knots of sputum that had suddenly flowered inside my chest, that were choking the life out of me. My body arched upwards from the bed; the strain ran through me like a current. I was behind walls of pain: I heard distorted fragments of sound, saw my father's lips move (they were too large now, rubbery, clownish) but I couldn't understand what the man was saying to me.

And then, a little later, when I was six, shots were discovered that were effective for asthma, an injection of epinephrine that, if administered at the beginning of an attack, would, after a time, become a hand smoothing out the inside of my chest. But I barely connected the injections with the relief that came later. I hated the shots, hated them more than I hated the attacks.

Perhaps I was attached to the concern, the love, that my pain made for me in my parents. During the hard days my mother sat on the end of my bed and drew pictures with me on a big pad. And in the late afternoon my father left his paying patients to come sit with us in the small wooden chair. He put a book across his lap, so I could see the pictures, and read to my mother and me.

And perhaps I confused the disease with myself, my will; to lose one was to lose the other. For I was terrified of the needle, hated and feared my father when I saw him preparing the long glass and silver syringe. To give up my sickness to my father's cure was, or so it felt to me, to fall, to lose power over myself.

He carefully raised the glass plunger to suck up the liquid. I promised him then that my attack would soon be over, it would be over in just a moment, it was only a little one this time. I promised that this was the last attack I'd have for a long time, if only they'd just talk to me they'd understand I was serious. I didn't need the injection. I'd really never have another attack, if they would just not give me the shot (I was screaming now, crying from fear and the strain of breathing), I wouldn't complain anymore, I wouldn't have any more trouble breathing, I wouldn't wake them up at night to help me.

My mother held me hard against her to keep me still. She was standing by the foot of my bed, holding me to her. I was overpowered, I was falling, losing myself, falling. "Stop wriggling now," he said; "we don't want the needle to break inside you." He took down my pajama bottoms and put the needle into my buttock.

Soon my father could no longer bear to give me the shots. He was afraid that his son would be formed by this fear of him, would grow up half hating him for these injections. So a nurse—whose wages I realize now they already could not afford—was hired to watch over me, to give me my shots, preserve my love for him.

My Asthma, Their Indulgence

Brought to the world frail, unable to tolerate its air, I bought with my infirmities all my parents' indulgent love. Anything I wanted I was given, they were so thankful that I continued to live from moment to moment, a constant rejoicing. There was no discipline for me, not even toilet training. A child, my mother said, was naturally good, curious, and capable of learning many things for himself (given an occasional timely hint from an adult). Especially such a bright child as her own was.

These ideas formed for her after an exhaustive study of the newest books on child rearing. She particularly enjoyed studying those new ideas that went against the common grain, that went, if possible, against common sense altogether. And she liked those ideas that required no disciplining of the child— not from laziness, for she had an uneven but fierce energy for certain kinds of work—but because she herself was in rebellion against any form of imposed discipline. (Once, when she was a child, she had been told that children learn best from pain: they learn not to touch hot things by being burned. She hated this vulgar and cruel idea, and to show that it wasn't true she immediately put her right hand on a flaming candle, and said, "It doesn't hurt." Someone pulled her hand away, but it was marked, her palm was scarred, puckered all over with fine lines.)

My mother had been born into a wealthy and aristocratic family—an ancestor of hers, of mine, was the last Spanish Viceroy of the River Plate— but she found she could not bear the tedious restraints of her class. A woman of great, if sometimes erratic, intelligence, she had come of age in the nineteen-twenties, and had set styles, been a leader of her generation. She was the first woman in Argentina to have her own bank account, the first woman to drive a car in downtown Buenos Aires (often on sidewalks according to my father, terrifying innocent people—like the Toad in an English children's story she delighted in telling me). My mother had been an activist, a militant, of the Radical Party. She'd led demonstrations for women's suffrage (failed: thirty years later that most hated woman, Eva Peron, would autocratically accomplish this pointless reform). She was a tall woman, often slightly stooped when she stood, as if embarrassed by her height. I think she was a beauty, with a fine face, long and thin, sharp, but lively and engaging features, a mouth that curved interestingly (if a little critically), downward. I think, from certain hints that my father gave in arguments (ones I didn't understand but were charged enough for me to remember), that she had done some drinking, and had several affairs (though after her marriage her friends were mostly women, and I never saw her drink anything but quantities of black bitter coffee).

My mother believed that people could, should, do what they wished. The world could be remade according to our desires. (It would be easy enough to mock her and add, if you have the money. But I mocked her often enough during my childhood—following my father's lead—and now I'd like to say something in her favor. For bound though she was to the ideas of her class— so thoroughly bound that she did not see how they betrayed her project, made it look stylish, a little eccentric—*yet she wished to be free.*)

So, a rebel herself, she never imposed any discipline on her son. I ate what I wanted, dressed as I pleased, rarely brushed my teeth (Oh, once every few weeks perhaps, when I was suddenly seized by a fear that they were rotting out of my mouth). Her pale son could ride his tricycle from the front door, through the long carpeted living room, past our guests, and out the back, if that was the quickest route.

And I was always en route, by preference the quickest, somewhere. I was a child possessed by an enormous amount of nervous energy. When I wasn't in bed with an attack—and especially just after I'd recovered—I couldn't sit still, had to move around. If I was excited, or frustrated—particularly if I didn't understand something my parents were saying to each other—I had to use my body, to fling myself about until I came to an understanding, until the tension, the knot, had been worked out through my motion. At dinner in the Guevara home it was perfectly allowable for me to skate round and round the marble floors of the dining room in my stockinged feet. And while still eating my food —kept chipmunk-like in pouches in my cheeks—I carried on a gay conversation with my amused parents. They leaned back laughing in their carved wooden armchairs.

But despite my mother's free and easy attitude, I was, at first, more my father's child. Ernesto was my given name, named after my father, by my father, according to an Argentine custom that my mother (who hated the customary) was then too weak to protest against. *(And how did he feel when I changed my name to that nonsense syllable, a cry in the streets?)* When she left her childbed she refused to use his name, calling me instead Tete— supposedly to avoid confusion between myself and my father.

A confusion I did everything I could to encourage. I imitated him constantly, even to the harsh jokes he made about his wife, blunt remarks about the way she ate (too loudly, she chewed the way cows do, mouth open, it got on his nerves, how could he enjoy eating with her?—and a small orbiting voice added: Go moo, Mother). Or the way she wore her hair (too severely, it was unfeminine); or the way she kept house (a mess, with books and magazines all over attracting dust. It was bad for the child). My father was an anxious, angry man, but Celia was his equal in force. Tactically astute, she feigned indifference to his criticism. She didn't care for his style of battle—crude complaint from an imagined vantage of moral superiority. So she waited till he was off guard—puffed up—and then struck. (For there were hard things to say about him. He was in the process of squandering her considerable inheritance in "cunning investments" in mate fields.) It was a fair fight—until her husband made an ally, one she loved and felt she had wronged. How could she reply to her son's childish insults? Not until after I'd left home did I allow myself to think of the many evenings at dinner when my mother turned her body away from me—Go moo, Mother—so that I could not see her face.

Yet he did love her, too (though the rebelliousness, wit, and energy that had once been so attractive to him became a more uneven joy, I suppose, when he was the authority she turned on.—But he loved being the authority). One day, I remember, when he was feeling close with her, my father wrote in chalk letters on the tall brown doors that led to the dining room: "This is what Ernesto Guevara said to his mother . . ." and then there followed some of my mean remarks, ones that even now I would rather not recall. It was unbearable to me that the children who came to see us that day should see my father's sign.

For those children were my mother's friends as much as mine. On her walks downtown she recruited playfellows for me. Newspaper boys, her friends' children, the maids' children at her friends' houses, caddies, shoeshine boys, they were all invited to come visit us. Perhaps this was a contemptuous gesture towards her parents, her upbringing, a way of shocking her friends—for she certainly wasn't beyond using people that way. But there was something more to it: she liked gossiping with people from all over town, finding things out from them, adding to her never completed education. (Isolated and without theory, anything might be a clue to her nameless project.)

So it was a special shame to me that these children should see how I had treated her when they weren't there. I cried in front of those chalk marks until I was overcome by a tightening in my chest. I vowed I'd never again be nasty to her (within a few days I'd broken my vow). But I cried most strongly because *he* had betrayed me. A hole had opened in the world, and I'd fallen through. For hadn't I simply been doing what he did? And was there no safety in that either?

My Vocation

I was to be a son worthy of my parents, a prodigy (no matter how meager my abilities were). I was to become, as my father was, a doctor. But I would be a surgeon also, a famous man certainly, one who discovers the cures for many diseases.

When I was six years old my father began to prepare me for my calling, teaching me, each evening, a few of the bones of the body. We sat together on the deep white sofa in the living room, our thighs touching, holding across our two unequal laps the large red anatomy book my father had used in medical school. My father's strong fingers, red and rough around the knuckles from so much scrubbing, outlined the pictures of the bones, and traced for me their gray spidery covering of musculature.

He pointed to places on his body, and asked me the names of the bones beneath. I rose from the cushions and paced about the room, swinging my arms back and forth as I recited the Latin words in a rapid singsong. It meant nothing to me. I didn't want to imagine a connection between the shadowy pictures and the life beneath my father's skin. (That would mean he could die!) But I learned the right responses, for my father, because it meant so much to him. Soon I could chant the names of thirty or so bones for my parents' guests.

My parents took me everywhere with them, to educate me, to show me off (and perhaps, too, they liked my company). I was entertained, when we still lived in Buenos Aires and they had money, by plays where I didn't understand a word. But the ritual of showgoing, the feel of the plush seats, the lukewarm fruit juice, the bitter taste of the program that I chewed on during the show, all this pleased me (even though I had to sit more or less still). I told myself I would be an actor too, a great doctor-actor. I practiced for it by being the entertainment at parties, where Mr. Bones did his Latin routine, and was rewarded by the hostess with bogus praise and delicious greasy hors d'oeuvres.

Newspapers

I was invited, too, despite my precarious health, to stay up with my parents most of the night, to listen as they discussed the newspapers with each other. This newspaper reading was a serious business for them, was ritual, was their way of having commerce with forces greater than they were, of connecting themselves with a more impassioned life, with their nation, with history. I felt the pleasure and gravity in them as each evening they cleared away the dinner dishes, laid out their hot drinks and papers on the glass kitchen table. They were serious, even courtly with each other in the white stone kitchen. It would be a good time. There would be nothing said about how my mother chewed her food, or my father's stupid investments.

My father, in a loose brown sweater with big wooden buttons, rocked back and forth in his wicker chair as he read from the paper to my mother and me. My mother, like me, couldn't sit still while being read to, she had to be moving about, even when engaged in some essentially still activity—though she managed to confine her motion (or over the years it had been confined) to her hands. They fluttered about her constantly as her husband read. (I wanted to reach out, to trap her scarred hand, but I couldn't; it might annoy him; I was only his assistant.) She bit her fingernails, ran her hand through her red hair, cut out something from one of the papers, tapped her leg with a pencil, dug the point into her thigh, reached for one of the dozens of black notebooks she had scattered across the tabletop, made a note to herself. She chain-smoked cigarettes, rarely using the ashtray, for she would forget in one of her argumentative gestures that there was something held between her long fingers, a cigarette burned down to a shaky gray worm. As she spoke her hands strewed ash on the glass table, on the stone floor, on her blouse—all her blouses had charcoal stains—or into her coffee. Not noticing, or not caring (it was the vitality she wanted, not the taste) she drank it anyway.

After the reading of an article my father strained a cup of mate for himself (he despised her "vile" coffee) and clipped the end of a cigar. Then one of my parents, usually my mother, analyzed the article for us, talked about the way it lied, the distortions it contained, the way the papers had been bought by Britain, the United States, part of the piecemeal dismemberment and auction of that fallen god, our country. My mother mocked whoever spoke in the article, Justo, Chamberlain, Blum, Roosevelt. She would turn him into, reveal him as, a raving fool. My father smiled, enjoying her performance. He puffed his cigar, filling the large stone kitchen with a foul earthy smell (an odor that permeated the history of my infancy, and still makes the events of '33–'35, when they occur in conversation, slightly distasteful to me. Small stoic, I never complained to him. And by the Spanish Civil War I was used to it, a veteran). Delighted by my mother I happily sipped up some mate through a silver straw that fit neatly into my own yellow and brown gourd.

The procedure was the same each night. The points made were usually the same points; the lies the government told, the same lies. And as a child I particularly liked the repetition, the energy summoned to frame the same wonderful remarks, turn the same figures into clowns with the same invective (fool, tool, puppet, traitor), the same mock accents (British, American, provincial Argentine), the same gestures of disgust: my mother pursing her lips, puffing out her cheeks till they were round and smooth, sticking out her tongue crookedly. History for me was my mother making faces. And yet, through it all, her thin face, her voice remained recognizably—but barely, barely—still my mother's. That was the special pleasure of it for me as I danced about the table staring at her: the there and not-there, peekaboo from around the edges, then disappearing back into her mockery. As a little boy I liked the ritual of the evening, and it was only very gradually that I began to understand what any of it meant, this constant hopeless procession of villains, this nightly morality play of history—though the parade was meant in large part for my benefit, my education.

I walked round and round the glass table, trying to comprehend by movement what my parents were saying, until, brought low by fatigue, and my father's cigars, I lay down on the cold whitewashed stone floor.

My father saw me down there, rubbing my eyes. "Ernesto," he said, "this can't be very interesting to you. I can see you're tired. Time for bed."

"But I *am* interested," I said crankily. "I don't want to go to bed. I *do* understand what you're saying. I want to stay up with you."

And when, as occasionally happened, I was sent to bed, I couldn't sleep. The murmur of their impassioned voices, overheard in my bed upstairs, the words hanging always on the edge of sense, was like a wall my whole body yearned to fling itself against, to break down, or batter myself into exhaustion and tears trying.

And really my parents wanted me to stay with them. So I made history my bedtime story, drifted off to sleep on the floor of the big white kitchen, listening to my parents' voices. Even when I was too groggy to understand their meaning I loved to lie there watching my mother's hands moving constantly, like two caged birds fluttering in the air before her face. My eyes closed and their words entered the texture of my dreams. I saw the Roca-Runciman Agreement (two fat men with oddly colored duck-billed caps), the vile General Justo (a fat black spider). I dreamt myself wasting away with Gandhi; the cold white stones my cheek lay against were my prison pillows. Or I wore the tall soft leather boots I'd seen on the soldiers in the city squares, ready to step out with the Eighth Route Army on the Long March.

When I awoke the next morning I was magically in my own bed, with three paper cigar rings on my fingers. I had survived another night's acrid smoke, mate, irony, and shameful political betrayals.

My Enemies, My Asthma

The start of my schooling was a disastrous change for me. I was used to being stage center, with my own spotlight and an audience that was certain to admire my routines. In school the teacher misjudged me: she found me no more precious than thirty others. And the other children weren't amused by me. I was weaker than they were, odd looking, with dark rings under my eyes and an invalid's concave chest and stooped figure. Yet I carried myself as if I were special. *They* were indifferent to my knowing the bones of the body. They would not abide an attitude of superiority from someone physically weaker than they were. So they bullied me.

They pushed me about when we stood in lines, and I lost my place. They pulled my hair. (My mother had allowed me to grow it as long as I liked; I liked it down to my shoulders—so I could run my hands through strands of it as if they were blanket edges. My long hair and my habit of playing with it were more signs of my queerness, my fitness for being tortured.)

They stole my things. They made fun of my—and my father's!—name.

"Here's your cap, Ernesto Banana, Banana Guevara," a freckled boy says with mock politeness, offering it to me. I reach for it, and the boy tosses it over my head to a friend.

"No, he doesn't have it anymore," the friend says, "I do."

My chest constricts with sobs like hard glass bubbles, blocking my breath. Crying, I hurl myself at my tormentors, flailing out with my fists, windmill-style, hitting air. My body begins to shake with hatred, frustration, bewilderment. I want to hit them in the face, rip their flesh, make blood run from his freckled nose. The children, the schoolyard, blur. I am terrified, the world is shaking apart, everything trembles with my rage, everything is disappearing!

The freckled boy grabs my wrist and bends my arm behind my back, spinning me around. I scream with pain and fury. The boy pushes me over to the water basin. Another boy (I can't see his face) pulls my head down hard by the hair. With the flat of his hand the freckled boy forces my face under the tap and runs cold water over me. I gasp desperately, spitting water and sputum, falling to the ground, no longer able to stand, clutching the dirt in my hands as if it would keep me from dying.

The other children stand around and stare, a blur of white smocks and imprisoning legs, the bad air incarnate. They watch an animal, howling in pain, rolling on the ground, trapped in the circle of their legs, with no control over himself.

The spectacle unnerved them. They ran away.

Soon asthma attacks kept me out of school one day out of three. I was far behind the other children, a complete rather than partial illiterate, classed, humiliatingly, with the other slow ones as barely worth the teacher's attention. Lines of print filled me with bafflement and anger (and in that anger was the remnant of my aristocratic heritage: this humiliation was unfair: I was special; I was entitled to understand). If only they would let me walk around during lessons, as I walked around the tables at home, then I could learn! But in school we were forbidden to move about. We could not leave our seats without permission. We even had to hold our hands still in front of ourselves, on our desks. My understanding was blocked—for as some people have to draw a figure with their hands in order to understand it (though it is not the figure but the act of drawing that resolves the tension, brings understanding), so I had to have movement, the thought making its way through my body. I hated staying still when I didn't understand something; I kicked my bare legs against the table legs, or twined them around the chair leg, I felt a fluttering start in my chest, I grew anxious, and flushed. Deprived of motion, I was deprived along with it of the ability to reason.

Scared I might be called on in class, I hid for hours in the school bathroom, locked in one of the slat-sided wooden stalls, breathing as quietly as I could, to elude discovery. (From that day in the schoolyard I had learned my first *lesson: how to hide.)* I wasn't discovered in the bathroom, wasn't even searched for, wasn't even missed. And yet, at the same time, I wanted to be missed, discovered, called on, touched, made much of.

I withdrew more and more into my solitude, playing the role of a sickly child, withdrawn, moody, anxious, whining whenever I could about my illness, my pain—for my sickness was now my only distinction, my secret knowledge, though I could not put it into words. My asthma attacks came more frequently, were more severe when they came. I fell further behind. I was scared of all the other children, beings who were so completely contemptuous of me, who, without warning or reason, might turn on me. Even the girls were bigger than I was! Mornings after breakfast, waiting for my mother to drive me to school, filled me with dread. As soon as the meal was over I ran to the small downstairs bathroom, and threw up bitter lumps of bread and jam.

I was too weak to play their games, even if they had let me. And they had not. If I wanted a friend to play with during recess I had to bribe him. The boy with the freckled face rented me his companionship in return for pieces of chocolate.

To get the candy I sneaked downstairs Sunday mornings when my parents were asleep, to pilfer from the scalloped silver trays that they had set out for their party. I sat for hours on the fluffy white sofa that still retained the odor of perfume from their guests (and my mother's perfume as well). I watched the dusty light of early morning enter through the tall doors to the patio. It was the only happy time of the week for me. No one was there to taunt me, to scare me, to make me feel ugly, clumsy, pathetic. Solitude soothed me, made me disappear in the play of the sun and dust. I was empty, light. *(I have never entirely left that solitude.)*

Monday I delivered over the stolen candy, misshapen and covered with white lint from my pocket. My poorer companion sold me so many minutes of catch per piece. It was fair trade. I wasn't much fun to play with. The ball was too big for me. I tried to catch the way a girl would, trapping it against my chest. But it usually got away, caroming off towards the fence.

"You throw it hard on purpose," I whined. "You *want* me to miss. You know I can't run after it." This game was an agony of self-consciousness for me. My whole body was hot. I could not stop thinking, *Am I doing all right? Did he tell the other children about the candy? Do they all laugh at me afterwards?*

The freckled boy was a natural athlete, everyone's favorite child, and I hoped to seem more competent—all right, at least acceptable—by being seen playing with him. But the boy kept his round freckled face as expressionless as a doll's. That way it would be clear to everyone on the playground that I wasn't his friend, that he wasn't contaminated by my cooties just because he was playing with me.

Aside from his bought companionship, though, I had no pals.

I hated myself, small, pale, wheezing, skinny, weak, unable even to throw a ball accurately. I thought myself as contemptible as the others thought me. And at the same time, equally strongly, I hated them all, despised them, thought them coarser and stupider than I was. I had special qualities the others knew nothing about. I was funny, brilliant, knew all the bones of the body, was a great violinist (like a boy in a storybook my mother had read me). I was Martin Fierro, leader of the gaucho army, clever, fierce with a knife. I was a Spanish prince, soon to be revealed as the rightful King of Argentina. I lived in those stories that my parents told me at meals. And unless someone read to me I refused to eat. Like most of my tastes, this one was catered to. I was so sickly that my parents were afraid I'd waste away if I missed a meal. So they gave in to my blackmail, took turns amusing me as they ate their own food. My mother read to me from storybooks, or from whatever book she was studying. My father read to me from *Heroes of Medicine*. (Each hero, as I remember it, lived a version of the same life: persisting, despite the contempt of other doctors, in some folly that history revealed to be an intuition of genius.) Or he made up a story for me, one episode at each meal. The story I liked best was about a pottery maker who was sad and lonely because he had no children. One day he made statues of the children he wanted from a magic clay in his back yard. And the potter's love and longing brought the figures to life.

My Education

Finally my father took me in hand and taught me how to read, one word at a time, and every word a test of my worthiness to be his son. Lists of words, like the lists of bones I'd learned in my prodigy days, neatly arranged in the double columns of a black wire-bound teachers' manual. We sat beside each other on the white sofa, and I climbed this ladder of words, both of us delighted at my accomplishments, at each step I took, each step of the world I mastered.

But this climb was a perilous one. I trembled inwardly at every word, every new challenge, for one mistake might send me hurtling into a void where I was next to nothing, contemptible to my father, small, worthless, insignificant. — Though the punishment never came from his hands. He never struck me. His punishment was a simple gesture of his disappointment, a thinning of his lips, a slight frown. Or worse: a way of smiling he had, turning his lips up without showing his teeth. A smile of infinite condescension: I felt myself a deeply offensive person, for even my presence required so much of my father's tolerance. "No," the doctor said, annoyed, "that's wrong, Ernesto, try it again." And my given name was a terror to me then, for my father used it only when I did badly; when I did well he called me son.

My father brought with him, wherever we went, his own grave air. I had spied on him at parties; there was a distance between him and those he stood talking with, a way he had of holding himself back from people, some final sense of a moral life that he had that would not be budged by smiles, compliments, jokes. This made people want to please him. They failed. But *I* could please him. My father was generous with his praise when I did well. He had a broad smile for me then that showed all his spotted uneven teeth (perhaps shame had been the first motive for his tight-lipped smile). His smile lit up my world. I was "Brilliant! A genius! Much smarter than I was at your age." And when he said it, I believed him. I was ecstatic.

But no praise was ever permanent. And that inner distance that had so impressed me when the man was my protector was now awful to me, for my father's judgment, which could not be conned, was on me. I banged my thigh with my fist. I stood up on the sofa, balancing precariously. I sat down with my legs under me. I marched about the room, filled with confusion and anxiety. For my essence was wagered on my performance, on the next word, no matter what praise I'd gathered in the past. My smiles, my kisses on my father's rough cheeks, these made no difference to him. Any error and I was once more out of favor, plunged into deeper anxiety, on the brink of nonexistence! And I wanted to please him, I loved him so.

Newspapers

So I began to take a more active part in their newspaper ritual, reading to them, but not commenting yet on what I read—for it was hard for me (I was nine) to get the line of their dialectic right (it was theoretically inconsistent in the extreme, vertiginously so). But it was fun showing off to them. And we were happy being together. (When my father read, he would make up lies, absurd ones, and insert them into the text, to see if we were awake, to make us laugh.) It was a hopeful time for us: the beginning of the war in Spain.

My parents, of course, were both on the side of the Republic and the anarchist miners. My father supported them, for their cause was just. But my mother loved them, for they, too, were a small beleaguered group on the side of justice, an aristocracy of the oppressed, kindred noble spirits. Those nights, as I orbited the table, they made me so ardent for the cause that I named my dog Negrina.

And chose for friends the children of Spanish refugees who were already flowing into Argentina, even to the mountain province, Cordoba, where we now lived. (We had moved for my health. The air would be crisp, dry, less painful for me than the humid weather of Buenos Aires.) My mother's sister, her closest friend, had married a Spanish Communist poet, and their son, Fernando Alvarados, a boy a few years older than I was, became my companion. We had much in common: we were outcasts. He lived, as I did, in an unfamiliar, menacing world, my native land. (And he didn't know yet that I was hateful, smelly, weak.)

It was from him (thin survivor, floating downstream, clinging to a log) that I heard of the heroic resistance of a city, a place where all men were comrades, and, as in stories, shared out their food with each other. There, in that enchanted place, boys only a few years older than we were had run over open fields to capture machine guns and turn the battle. I felt grand when I was with the refugee children, hearing their stories. Death was only a solemn word to me. So tragedy made me feel courageous, exalted.

My parents and their friends, too, were filled with a new exuberance by the war in Spain. Masses were in motion, large issues were being contested. (Death was only a solemn word to them.) My mother's pale face had more color. She slept more easily, the dark rings had disappeared from under her eyes. Despite our money problems—my father was having trouble finding patients in the town—they argued less.

I felt the energy in them when we went together to street demonstrations. (It was the time of Popular Fronts, and even bad marriages seem full of possibility at the start.) My mother joked with the people standing around her. (Mostly men. There weren't many women of her class there.) She smiled constantly, a little nervously perhaps, speaking always, it seemed, more rapidly than the others around her, gesturing more sharply. She was a sound film star trapped among silent movie clowns, traveling forever at the wrong speed. Yet people seemed to be happy to be near her (though, like my father, they must have felt themselves a little sluggish in her presence, a little slow). It was a pleasure to be in on her jokes, to laugh with her.

I too enjoyed the marches. I liked being part of a slowly forming crowd, hearing political talk. I held my father's hand and listened to my mother talk with our companions in a high, excited voice. I liked my mother's quick rhythms, the tumbling movement of her hurrying intellect. I liked her clever logic. She showed us (my father, of course, already knew, was beyond her—as I would be someday—into a realm of absolutes) how good and evil subtly changed form in the dialectic. Out of the strong came the sweet, the first became last, and the last (despite their *blunders*) first. There was magic for me in her voice as she negotiated the rapid turns of her argument, made categories shift shape, transform themselves, a stick turn into a snake into a dove. Oh, what seemed evil worked often to some good end, and pious sentiments were only a disguise for the most awful acts and many mean deaths. There was a hidden face to things in politics, a truth behind the show, and my mother let us in on the secret, unmasked it for us through her analysis, unwove the veil of lies. Her hands turned in the sunlight. I was lost in the austere beauty of this terrible system, this hard world. Bewitched, I saw how even evil was necessary, and worked against its will for the Cunning of Reason, of History.

My father, too, was happy. He stood more easily with the other men, chatting, almost expansive in the way he laughed or gestured with his cigar. He was wearing a blue suit, and he looked more sharply outlined than anyone else. He had, I felt, with his strong hands, his beard, the dignity of a prophet. Others felt this too, and leaned towards him (he did not lean; he stood straight). You enjoyed arguing with my mother, but wanted my father's agreement. I too loved my father's rightness, admired it, wanted it for my own, felt that I participated in it when I nodded assent to his grave shapely sentences.

I let his voice fill me, his seriousness make me still (my mother's voice made me want to laugh, to hop around). When my father spoke I was grown up, someone who mattered, an actor in the drama.

I let go of his hand, and went over to be with my new friends. We were on the outskirts of town, among the small uneven farm plots, the wire-meshed cages of dirty chickens. I took sharp breaths, whiffing the interesting hot odor of dung fertilizer. The late afternoon sunlight warmed me through my thin jacket as I chatted with the other children. Here I had friends, had escaped for the moment (I *knew* they would catch up with me) my tormentors in Buenos Aires.

We marched. I helped my parents hold aloft cloth banners that floated between two thin wooden poles. No one had thought to punch holes in the cloth, so the wind bellied the banners, bent the sticks. My hands ached from the strain and my arms hurt from holding my pole up even with my father's. We chanted as we walked, making the birds squawk with our nursery-rhyme slogans, our singsong refrains that kept time with our stamping feet, our swinging arms and legs.

When we came to the main square of Cordoba, towards evening (we took the long way around, through every street in town), we raised our voices, made our chants angrier, shouted our defiance at the indifferent soldiers who lined the square. Young men with Indian faces, made more dour-looking by their Nazi-style helmets, they stared at us, unimpressed. Our chants moved with wings through the darkening air, rose over the soldiers' heads, battered themselves against the massive stone cathedral. Our words returned to us transformed, their sound larger, more powerful in the echo, but also strange, wintery, vast, our own words now almost unrecognizable to us.

My mother's jokes soon became more bitter. You hesitated in joining her. Her rhythm was wrong. (Who was the joke on?) There was something dark and mean in her laughter.

Franco was moving triumphantly through the Spanish countryside. (Had the Communists betrayed the miners, so as not to disturb their new allies, the Paris bourgeoisie? Or were the miners treacherous undisciplined cowards, the class enemy in one of the disguises only the Party could penetrate?) My mother fought viciously with her sister, and her brother-in-law, as if over a family inheritance. My father's bearing stiffened. My mother's face became colorless again. She was restless at night. (I heard her get up again after we'd all gone to bed, the rustle of her bathrobe, the soft fall of her slippers moving past my bedroom. She would go to the kitchen, sit and read all night. Lying in bed I was invaded by these sounds, and turned, unable to sleep, near tears, staring at the shadowy ceiling. Why was she doing this to us?)

My father's practice was not making much money. The people here didn't like him. My mother's inheritance was completely gone, squandered on bad investments in mate fields. We would have to move to a smaller house in Cordoba. They fought now, worse than before.

In time we stopped going to rallies. The crowds had grown smaller. Working-class people no longer came. The Popular Front had been defeated. Fascism was coming to Argentina. The street demonstrations of Communist militants—my parents long since absent—were met in the church square by more army conscripts with lackluster eyes. They fired indifferently into the crowd.

Of course, my mother explained to us, our demonstrations never mattered. It had always been a farce. The Anglos ran the puppet show. We would have more colonels. We would always have more colonels. The country had an endless supply of colonels.

We were sitting in the kitchen of our new home, around the glass table. The table was too big for this room. The wicker chairs were almost against the wall. They would have cramped me if I still walked around the table. My mother scissored out an article for one of her black notebooks. "You were right,

Tete," she said, for they both liked to give me credit for their own insights. I nodded, happy, sipping up some mate. "We were fools to get involved in this election nonsense."

She was right. Every political convulsion that shook my country throughout my childhood (see? newspaper pictures of thousands filling the plazas of Buenos Aires) always gave issue in a monstrous birth, the rigged election of another colonel. There was neither reason nor cunning to history.

Soon strikes were forbidden. The schools were purged of leftist teachers. Union leaders were jailed and then disappeared. People's lives were an unpleasant series of pointless shocks. They became obscurely violent even to themselves, driven back to their burrows. My parents' friends talked of their sun signs, their predestined life, determined from birth, immutable, beyond history, the stars, fate.

We—my parents and I—at least gathered together in our blue kitchen, drinking our hot drinks, reading to each other, keeping enlightenment alive. My father, in his ragged but unpatched sweater, swayed back and forth in his chair, the newspaper his prayer and his bereavement. My mother sat surrounded by her growing clutter of coffee cups and notebooks, her scarred hand running nervously over and over her hair, smoothing it down, smoothing it down. I read to them. We were keeping reason alive in a dark age. How important our mission was! We were the intelligence of a dark time.

My Regimen, My Vocation

I could read, I was acquiring a political education. But I was still marked as queer at school, as an invalid, by my sunken chest and sloped shoulders. So, for my body, there was what my father called "the Regimen," making his improvised series of exercises sound military, magical, certain of success.

There were long walks to start, far too long for me. My father—though time would reveal him as a short man—took monster steps. I scurried like a crab to keep up, dancing along as best I could, and chattering to him, trying to amuse him. My father strode forward in his walking outfit, black pants, a red flannel shirt, wide suspenders, and a brave hat: a brown duck-billed hunting cap with red ear flaps that tied up on top with a thin red ribbon. He was splendidly indifferent to the looks from people we passed.

We walked all over the city, through the most desolate slums (for even if crowded in every inch they still looked empty, deserted, enormous spaces between things, like the bombed-out cities of Europe that I saw in the newspaper at night). My father listened to my talk as if I were an adult too, a performer, one who delighted him. He was lavish with his attention, took my silliest plans (to discover the cure for a dozen diseases) seriously. It was deeply satisfying to talk with him, it made me giddy with pleasure at my own seriousness, until I grew so full of my own power and interest that I wanted to throw my arms out and spin round and round in front of him. But I wouldn't, I was too serious, too profound, too adult, to do that.

My father spoke to me of history, of imperialism, told me over and over —until I understood it well—the story of Latin America, our unredeemed continent, and the cause of its misery: the terrible cowardice, the moral failure of its leaders, its people's degeneracy. My father grew angry as he spoke, balling his hands into fists. But how could a man do anything? How could anyone make the people see reason? How could he strike a blow at the United States?

My father, though, would never have struck anyone. Gandhi was one of the few leaders he admired, a man like himself, strongly moral and without violence. He told me often of the Salt March, the little man in a loincloth walking hundreds of miles to the sea and picking up on the shore a small fragment of salt. The British wouldn't allow this and went crazy with anger. But other Indians, when they saw what Gandhi had done, were deeply stirred, wanted to do it too, to show that they also knew what was right. I loved the story. My Gandhi looked like Charlie Chaplin, marching to the sea with a bow-legged walk. I was moved by his courage, his solitude, moved most of all by his obvious vulnerability. He was skinny. He had no shirt. His ribs showed. Like me.

My father, like Gandhi, despised violent people. His work was to save life, and that was to be my work too. He said I'd already begun it by doctoring myself, giving myself my epinephrine injections. (What I had hated to have him do to me I was proud to do to myself for love of him. And every time I put the needle into my arm I felt I was mastering something, gaining knowledge by using my own body. It was an intellectual pleasure. I had to test the new medicine on myself, take the risk of being turned into a gibbering moron, a monkey monster.)

It was worth the risk. To be a doctor, my father showed me on our walks, was the highest calling. Everything in the world, all its rich and powerful people, "the imperialists," worked against my father and me. Hard, unfeeling, immoral men, they starved the people of our country, kept them ignorant and superstitious, so they didn't even want the medicines my father offered them. The poor lived in disgusting unsanitary ratholes, like the ones down the street from our new house. Could I imagine what life was like in a place like that? We walked by quickly. It was a dirt lot with shacks scattered across it. Children played among the clotheslines. They had no real shoes, but here and there a mother had wrapped one of her children's feet in rags and newspapers and tied them up with string—a floppy clown's shoes. Dogs ran all over the place. There was a terrible smell from the unpainted wooden outhouses. The women bent over long black iron basins near the back edge of the lot. One of them shouted to a child to stay away from the line. Could I imagine the dirt, the squalor they lived in? (I was with the other children in the slum, someone was shouting at me, warning me of something. My clothes were dirty, torn, crawling against my skin. I was running along, shouting, shouting something, it didn't mean anything, just sound shouted up at the sky. I felt as if I were falling into this life, losing myself.) I took my father's hand. He was moving faster than I was, pulling me along. We passed by.

It was difficult, it was nearly impossible, my father said, to save even one life the way *we* did. People were like eggs. They could be cracked just like that. (I imagined: inside our eggshell heads we had white brains with runny yellow centers.) It was easy to kill people. You could do it with dust, a maggot, a closed door, a heavy weight. But that was something for weak people to do, ones without character, "imperialists."

Excited by his rightness he strode ahead. I walked faster to get back into hearing range. A little refrain began in my head. *Death from accident, death from drowning, death from hunger.* Each time my foot hit the ground I thought of another kind of death. *Dead from disease, dead drunk, dead tired.* My chest was tightening. I panted up air painfully, my legs grew awfully heavy. Of course, he continued, that wasn't the way the world felt. No, they admired killers, thought you were a hero if you killed enough, put up a statue to you. Most people were beneath our contempt. They were incapable of knowing right from wrong. You know what they admired most of all? If you used up a person's life so as to turn him into money! (I understood: capitalism: a top-hatted magician turning dead people into round gold coins.) But only real men, like my father and me (I was eleven), could save another man's life. When we arrived back at the door each day I was dizzy from the strain of keeping up with him, from the grandness of my mission.

On Contradiction

Before taking up my medical career, I had to finish primary school. My father and I studied my school lessons together, practiced my spelling on our walks. We went over my mathematics as we played chess. He had taught me the game with a crumbling set of black and red stone pieces that often broke when we accidentally tipped them over. I loved chess, though playing against my father was never very satisfying. I could not win. For even if I won, as I frequently did, I felt my father had let me win, had cunningly set up positions where I couldn't avoid capturing his pieces. My father denied this. "No, son, I'm glad when you win. But you have to take your victories the way you just did, by your own strength. I'll never give you anything in a contest." But my father smiled when he spoke to me and I couldn't believe him. *(Perhaps he wanted me to doubt my victories, still think him superior to me?)*

Nights after I'd won games were the ones most likely to find me in bed crying, confused, resentful.

On Practice

The walks, the tutoring, the games of chess, all had their effect. I was hungry for more certain victories.

Given importance by my father, I became a prima donna at school. I went not to learn (I did that with my father) but to perform before the others. I was far ahead of the other children now, pretended that I knew more than the teacher did—the dialectical reverse of my previous abasement.

One day the teacher warned us not to put ink or chalk in our mouths. They were poisonous. "Nonsense," I said, during recess. We were standing in the classroom, by our wooden desks, about to run into the yard. "I don't believe him. They're not poisonous." But I was talking through my hat. I didn't know. I just wanted to hold the others around me.

"What do you know about it?" one of the boys said. A dark squat child, he had the same stony quality as my old adversary, the freckled boy. We were enemies, with the bone-shaking hatred of childhood. I wanted to make his nose go crooked and bleed. I would have *annihilated* him if I could have.

"I think," I said, "that they're not poisonous. And I'm a scientist. I'm going to *test my hypothesis*. I'm going to find out if I'm right." My heart trembled at where this was leading. I'd no idea if they were poisonous. But I made a point of contradicting everything the teacher said—unless I knew from my lessons with my father that it was true. Now, if I wanted to know about the ink I had to taste it, use my own body.

The children clustered about my desk in a half-circle. I felt that by daring something the others wouldn't I could bind them to my will—by exercising my will in front of them on myself. I was like Gandhi, cleaning the latrines of the untouchables, or walking barefoot through India. I would move men by my example. And so secure a further hold over them, make a distance between us; a distance I would be safe in—safe from their irritation, their anger, their casual blows.

"How will you find out?" my enemy said. Usually no one taunted me. But my authority was personal: I had to renew it at every moment. This time my voice was shaky, so my hold on the others wavered.

"I'll show you how," I said, and I bit off a piece of the powdery chalk. "I think I'll wash it down with a drink of this," I added, gagging as I reached across my desk for my ink bottle. I felt as if I were watching my hand from above; I was conducting an experiment; I would know the truth.

"Don't, Guevara," my friend Alvarados said. "Don't kill yourself."

I thought, He's worried my father will hold him responsible. He'll have to carry my body home. Stand in the doorway holding me in his arms. Mrs. Guevara, he's dead. He ate chalk and drank ink. He'll hand me to my mother and run away.

The thought of Alvarados carrying me made me laugh giddily. I took a sip of the oily black ink. Made nervous by my cousin, I drank more than I meant. *This is it, I'm going to die.* I wanted to stick my finger down my throat to make myself throw up. I wanted to go screaming for a doctor before the dust and oil destroyed me.

But my fear of humiliation before the others was greater, apparently, than my will to live. I could not show weakness. So, with a sublimity of gesture available only to eleven-year-olds who believe they are about to die, I casually patted my mouth with a piece of blotting paper from my desk. "Mmm, good," I murmured. "Tasty. Would anyone else like some? Would you like some?" I asked the squat boy. My enemy said no and looked at his shoes, ashamed of himself, remorseful that he'd driven me to suicide.

To clinch the demonstration I added some phrases of my father's, in my father's precise phrasing. "Take nothing on faith, children. That's not the scientific way. Don't believe things you haven't tested for yourself. Most of what people believe is just nonsense that everyone believes." Everyone looked at me wonderingly—not for my wisdom, but because I had poison in my veins. I had stepped over to that farther shore.

The rest of the day the others sneaked glances at me from behind their books. They were waiting for the fearful spectacle of my going into convulsions, gripping my stomach, falling off my chair, writhing on the floor, my eyes rolling up white as I passed away. That would be marvelous.

I, too, waited. When the teacher's back was turned I took my arm from the table and held my hand in front of me. Had it started to shake? *It will when the ink reaches my brain.* I saw my brain, dyed black like a rotten nut. *I'll go crazy then.* I repeated my address to myself to show myself that I was still sane. *But when I've forgotten, will I remember that I've forgotten and know I'm mad?* I pushed a book off my desk, so that while bending over to pick it up I could stick out my tongue, and check for the color change that would precede death. *It was black!* I bit it. *It was going numb!* Would the teacher, please God, notice that my teeth were inky and send me to the doctor?

The teacher didn't notice. I was called on to recite. I stood by my desk and rolled my eyes around while I spelled out my word, to show I was in distress. I beat my hand against my thigh, sending out the S O S in Morse code. The teacher didn't pick it up.

In fact, nothing out of the ordinary happened the rest of the day. Only a slight dizziness; and that came from imagining angels, their wings beating rapidly, as they hovered in place overhead, waiting to gather me to their bosom.

The Regimen

As I grew stronger from our walks my father started me running, more and more distance each day. He held a gold watch in his palm, and clocked off my time per block as I ran through the streets near our house. I was twelve, filled with a fierce energy. (I liked experimenting with my body, feeling pain. Pain sheared me from my body: I watched myself, and so gained a power over my fate.) He charted my progress on a large piece of brown paper that we'd ruled off together and tacked to the wall by my bed. It was the first thing I saw when I woke up.

Each afternoon in my bedroom, embarrassed at being naked before my father, I quickly put on my running costume: white tennis shorts, a plaid scarf, a sweatshirt, and a heavy blue sweater (worn in all weathers, to protect my throat and chest).

He passed his hands back and forth over my head, in small circles. "Shazam," he said, the word that transformed small, asthmatic Ernesto Guevara into strong Captain Amazing, the man whose exploits transfixed us both every Sunday at the movies.

I was finishing primary school then, was nearly grown up; and despite my father's magical incantation, I could not become someone else, could not mime my father's, or an actor's, indifference to my audience. I felt a fool running down the unpaved streets in wide white shorts that were much too big for me. Groups of children from the slums nearby came to watch me. These children had once been guests at our house, and I was painfully conscious of their laughter, their mocking gestures.

Sometimes one of them ran alongside me for a few steps, imitating my loud puffing sound. His rags flapped in the wind, his face was as emaciated as mine was, his legs bowed out, thinner, ricketier than mine. A bad smell came from him. I said to myself, as my father would have, *Do these people never wash?*

But it was an attack starting. Soon the scratchy feeling in my lungs took away all self-consciousness, and I coughed and retched at once. My father would not relent on the day's running until this happened, and so I ran always until I could not go on running. (Nor would *I* relent. How far could I go? How much pain could I stand? It was an experiment; we would chart it; I would know the truth.) The doctor held his son's shaking body, and beyond self-consciousness, I threw up in the street.

My father tied a tin can to a tree branch in our back yard. I was to shoot at it with a .22 rifle. "It will teach you to concentrate," my father said, "and how to remain calm. It will train your eye and hand for surgery."—For that was the promised end of all our work for me. Someday I would join him in practice.

The man shouted encouragement. "Make that can dance, son! Make it hop!" And I enjoyed the shooting. There was something powerful in those rare times I hit the metal, something beyond my control, and yet—for I pulled the trigger—done by me (it was as if grace, or the gods, had entered into it). Usually I missed. The rifle was too heavy. It made my arms tremble.

"Hold your breath," my father instructed from behind me. "And count to eight." (He had read a book: *The Hindu Science of Breath Control.*) "Now gradually let it out as you squeeze." I took another breath before pulling the trigger. The rifle wavered again. I was becoming dizzy. I waited for the dizziness to pass and took another breath. By the end of a half-hour of this I was ready to pass out. My arms ached and I wanted to cry.

But my father did not relent. I grew stronger, calmer, better able to control my demonic energies. The doctor added a new aspect to our workout: swimming. I was terrified of water. And the vision of undressing with other people in a cold white tile room made my bowels hurt. *They'll see me naked, my chest exposed. They'll see how weak I am, naked, open, small.*

My mother encouraged me. She spoke of the pleasures of swimming, the water resisting you and yet holding you up. "You move without effort Tete. The water takes care of you, supports you. It's cold at first. But don't panic. Just let yourself go. You'll float. And you'll have a wonderful time." I was not convinced.

But my father insisted, and I was ashamed to show fear before him, to disobey him. He was so jolly, so matter of fact about it. We went to the country club swimming pool.

But at the edge of the pool I buckled. Panic possessed me. "I'll go tomorrow. Let's come back tomorrow. Okay? I'm just not ready yet. I promise I'll go tomorrow though. I just don't feel like it now. Please don't make me go. I can't. Please." I hated being nearly naked like this. I wanted to go away from there.

He was my father; I was his son.

The man threw me in.

I swallowed water. It burned my nose. My hands beat frantically. *He won't let me die. He couldn't. But what if he's angry at me because I cried?* I was too panicked even to scream for help, scared of dying, of failing my father. I had made some terrible mistake, like the time he had written my insults on the door. A hole had opened in the world. *He didn't care about me anymore!*

The people on the chairs alongside the pool laughed good-naturedly. My father appeared through a blur of water, a little apart from the others. The man in blue boxer shorts, his chest covered with curly hair, smiled at me, shouted encouragement. But I was nearly rigid in the water, sure that if I relaxed my vigilance even for a moment I would go under, fail him utterly, and die.

Encouraged by my parents to test my new skills I organized a soccer team. *(I was their captain, had to be, had to be their leader, have that distance between us, that distance that was my safety, my protection. It might happen as I was playing soccer with them; I might have an attack. They would see again what they could do to me. They would turn again into my tormentors. They had taken me by the hair, had pulled my face down into an iron trough. Their legs had gathered around me. They had gaped at me as I writhed on the ground. What more would they do? They'd done nothing more: to see me gasp was all they wanted, all they could imagine to want. But imprisoned by their bare legs I had known: I was helpless. I remembered this often, could not keep myself from remembering it: it was an image, a confusion, an anxiety that gnawed at my side, that I had to act constantly to resolve.)* The other players were the children from our little street, and from the slum near our house. I arranged matches against the country-club kids. I was their captain. *(Remembering, I felt as if I were naked, stretched out on a board where anyone could touch me. I had to have a distance.)* These games were a joy for me, for I loved to strain my body, loved the concentration on movement, delighted in the rasping pain in my chest as I gasped down air. I could stand it. I was great with it.

The boys I led were quicker to violence than our opponents were. I led them in this also. *(I had to make a distance between us, hold them off by the exercise of my will on myself, by the actions I might improvise that they were afraid to perform.)* Our violence inspired fear, created a hesitancy of movement in the other children that we could exploit. Usually we won.

And when we won we followed the losers home, to the best residential sections of Cordoba, the paved streets—where my parents could no longer afford to live.

"Time to go home and cry."

"Have your mama wash you and put you to bed."

I danced at the head of this raggedy army of mine, abusing their mothers in my mother's voice. We were crows, we had raucous voices, we pursued the birds of rare plumage through the gilded evening air.

"Have her get in bed with you."

"Send us your mamas next time."

Oh, I was gay, I was giddy with triumph and exhaustion (for both were sweet to me). The sweat chilled on my skin. I was so tired I could barely breathe. We had won. A phrase came into my head as we walked home. *I have done my utmost.* The big houses and lawns were sharply outlined still. Every blade of grass was itself, was clear to me. The world had a message for me, was on the edge of speaking. My legs were heavy, and I had to will them to take each step. *I have done my utmost.* I smiled at the other children, my comrades. It was evening. The world would slowly grow dark around us. Their dirt and sweat were beautiful. I loved them.

Adversaries

So, for a time, my strength, my leadership, had no limits. I was confident in myself, my power, my hold on the others. But gradually, in my late adolescence, I found that my magic was waning, for I was divided within myself, and so brought my own power to an end. I have three memories (a man with no legs; a boy in jail; a game of rugby) of what taught me of my limits.

For the first memory I must remind you that in the town where I grew up the different classes often lived close together. Society is still, in many of its forms, feudal: each class knew its proper, its fated role. No matter how near our bodies might be to each other, our spirits would remain untouched; my class's natural superiority would remain undiminished. The block where we now lived was a row of neat bourgeois houses. Not in the best section of town anymore, but each house had a garden, and there were servants and gardeners. Across the street—an unpaved one that had to be watered by the gardeners to keep down the dust—there was a waste land, an open tract of dirt. Scattered over it were dozens of shacks made from scraps of cardboard and tin.

My wealthier friends and I sat on the grass near our houses, to watch what went on across the street (for the poor did much of their living in public). Only one of the slum dwellers was more painful than interesting to see, even for young boys. He was called No Legs. Groups of kids used to follow him around when he was drunk and sing songs about him. Such as: "No Legs / Hard Luck / Has to Beg / Can't Fuck."

"Want me to bring Jesus's mother by, so you can fuck her, No Legs?"

And sometimes No Legs would say, "I can fuck her with my tongue," and leer amiably, and lick his lips. Sometimes he cursed at the children, with the inhuman coldness of someone who has too often repeated a prayer for vengeance. Sometimes he cried and went back to his shack.

To get around No Legs had made a flat wooden cart. He strapped himself to the floor, and his dogs were attached to the whole by a leather harness. It was hard for the dogs to drag him from his hut, for the ground had been worn away by years of their use and had turned his home into a hole, a burrow. They howled as he beat them to make them pull harder, lift him up over the ridge.

When he appeared above the ridge, outside, his face was constricted from rage and effort. His leather thong rose and fell powerfully on the dogs in time to his litany of insults. He had a terrible fury about him. A frightening man.

One cold fall morning when I was working outside our front door, adjusting the brakes on my bicycle, I heard the whine of the dogs from inside No Legs' hut, and the man's dark abuse. A gang of slum kids suddenly gathered at the sound, like blackbirds coming down for scattered grain. No Legs was on his way out to beg his living in front of the church in the main square. Many families in the slum lived from his earnings. This, perhaps, made the children hate him more. When he emerged at the rim of the hole they hurled stones at their benefactor, sang their songs about him, offered to go down to the store for spare parts.

The stones hit the little man on his chest as he struggled to get over the rim. The dogs whined, and tried to turn in the harness. The man bellowed with pain, trying to keep his balance on the cart. He wouldn't go back to his burrow. He couldn't raise an arm to protect himself for he would have had to let go of the reins, and the dogs would have turned and tipped him over on the ground. He had to whip them harder, for they were his chance of escape.

The man's animal bellowing shook me. I knew that feeling. Being driven back to that point where you are no longer human, but only a consciousness of pain and a will to continue. His vulnerability reminded me of myself, and so moved me. My chest and stomach filled with that sweet giddy feeling of self-righteous anger, of being just in someone else's cause.

I ran across the street, my white oil rag flapping from my hand as I went, shouting, "Goddamn it stop that!" The children ran away as I came across the dirt. Perhaps they fled because I was their captain, and they were ashamed before me. Or perhaps they were used to taking orders from people who shouted at them with authority, people like me. Something about the ease with which I could dismiss them unsettled me.

After the children fled, the man got his cart up over the rim of the hole. He pulled the leather reins and stopped the cart in front of me. He looked me up and down, his misshapen face filled with a hatred, something worse than winter in his eyes. I shivered under the examination. I had helped him. Why did he hate me so? He stared at me. The man had been handsome once, but now his face was eaten away, pocked, reddened by drinking, the veins broken. The shiny black sports jacket he wore looked comical on him—it reminded you that he had no lower half. He was a stump tied to a wooden cart by leather thongs. I could brush him into the dirt with a sweep of my hands. My hands balled into fists. My tender protectiveness, refused, soured into resentment and anger. The man looked at me a moment more and then spat into my face. Slowly he whipped his dogs and drove away.

The son of a bitch, I thought, he's counting on my honor, his weakness to protect him. Well, I have no honor, I told myself, stepping after him. But I couldn't. I was rooted. I wiped the spit from my face with my white oil rag, wanting to kill the runt, destroy him utterly, knock his little stumpy body into the dirt and kick it around like a soccer ball, a soccer ball with a mouth that would scream for mercy but get none from me. I contained my rage. It sank to my stomach, a painful heat.

I was shaking, my body shimmered with anger. I was indifferent to the dirt I crossed, the children watching me walk back to my house. My mother, when she heard my story, insisted on immediately scrubbing my face herself, to calm me.

"Well, what did you expect," she said, working away roughly with a white washcloth, as though the half-man's spit were dangerous, infectious, "that he'd be grateful? You fool! Of course not! They can't *think*, Ernesto, can't reason. None of them. It's like this Peron business. They think their friends are their enemies, and their enemies are their friends. They're deluded. You know that. When you want to be a friend, and offer your hand, they bite it. But if you treat them like dogs, the way Peron does, they lick your hand and fawn on you." She was rubbing at my face, so worked up—as she often was when angry—that I think she'd forgotten what she was doing. I remembered that on one of her rare cooking nights I'd seen her vengefully hack a chicken to bits while insulting the Fat Man and the Self-righteous Cripple, the Allied war leaders. "Scions of wealthy families," she said contemptuously (forgetting the origin of a certain Celia de la Serna), "who pretend to be the little fathers of the common man, so they can send common men off to die for them." They were stinking imperialists, who wanted to win the war so they could divide up the world! Chicken bits flew about the tiled counter till there was nothing to do with the bird but make a tasteless soup of it. I worried for my cheeks.

I was sitting in one of the wicker chairs in the kitchen. A piece of wicker had unraveled and its sharp edge was sticking into my back. I twisted my body a bit.

"Sit still, child," she said. "Oh, it was a perfectly natural thing for him to do." She drew out the word "natural." "Perfectly natural, once you understand that they're all crazy nowadays. We are the last sane people in this insane country, in my opinion. He was like those others exactly, can't think, can't reason." —"Those others" were some people at a rally for Peron in our town's central square. My mother and her sister—reunited by Peron—had gone to shout some sense into them. In return several Peronistas had tried to grab them and tear them to pieces. *If it hadn't been for the police they would have!* she said, when she returned home (pretending to be not merely hysterical, but a little amused, incredulous). *Can you imagine that! I was going to hit a policeman with my pocketbook when I realized he was protecting me! Your mother! Reduced to being protected by the police!*

"Ernesto," she concluded, giving my red cheeks a final dab, "this whole country has gone crazy. *Complètement fou!* Out of its mind!"

"I can see the newspapers now," I said, catching her manic mood. My mother and I rarely touched each other. Even this rough tenderness with a washcloth made us both a little uncomfortable. When we were alone together we usually put our energy into a kind of wit, a kind of caring, of playing with each other. "It's sure to make the newspapers. Banner headlines for the Peronist press: Heroic Resistance with Spit. Subhead: Crippled Beggar Shows Upper Class Busybody a Thing or Two. Or for *La Prensa* we can have something more genteel: Beggar Hurls Spitball Without Ball at Young Soccer Captain." I ran on for a bit in the same way, puerile stuff. It wasn't very witty, I knew, but it was in the right style. It worked to transform the heat that still rose in waves from my stomach into a feeling more controlled. It made me feel for a moment the master of events, able, like my mother, to make epigrams —of a sort—out of them.

And yet I felt, even then, that her wit, my imitation of it, was somehow missing the point. Outside on the field I had come close to learning something. But as my mother scrubbed me, spoke with me, that revelation was obscuring itself, going into hiding again. For a moment I was irritable, about to cry. I gripped the glass edge of the table hard in my hand. Then my mother said something more; and I replied; and she laughed; and I was pleased with and delighted in her laughter. Soon I forgot what had annoyed me. The stumpy man went back into his burrow. I was happy in our irony.

My Irony

We are the last sane people in this insane country. I believed that then and it delighted me. I was circumstance's superior, ironic, understanding others better than they understood themselves. In school, or as I walked about the town with friends, I often had a supercilious smile. I *knew.* I had the goods on others. A doctor in a madhouse. I was sane; I understood history; and by understanding it stood outside it, though it dragged others down. By irony I was saved. My sanity was more than sanity; it was a kind of genius.

Or so I thought. I remember that in 1943 my cousin Alvarados, lacking the inoculation of irony, had succumbed to madness. He had led a series of student demonstrations in Cordoba, against the restoration of Catholic education. The crazy people put him in jail.

Alvarados, though he was two years older than I was, had always been a good amiable friend to me, the sort who retold the plots of movies in detail —agreeable at first on the long motorcycle trips we took together as teen-agers, yet the way he told them made them turn boring, a mechanical series of occurrences that rendered even tragedy into slapstick. And, like the projectionists in Cordoba, Alvarados often put the parts in any order. At the end, right before the finale, seeing how blank I looked, how anxious to get into my sleeping bag, he'd say, "Did I tell you they were on board an ocean liner? I didn't! Well, they were on board an ocean liner. And they were leaning out a porthole. I mentioned that? I didn't! Well, it was a very rough sea. And one of the women was his first wife, right? I didn't say that? And Gable was on deck. . . ."

But now, since he had begun college, Alvarados had been transformed. He had lost his clownish air, become a leader of his class. Along with his physical grace there was a seriousness to Fernando that was more important than the irregular way he organized his discourse. That moral seriousness had in fact gathered up and transformed his oddity as well, as it sometimes will our clownish qualities, and made it a sign of his sincerity: you were constantly reminded that what he said was all that mattered to Fernando, not his own eloquence in saying it.

I got a note from Fernando in jail. He had a job for me. He wanted me to organize the high school students to demonstrate against the arrest of the university students. I went down to the jail to talk with him.

"You can do it Ernesto. I've seen how they listen to you. They all admire you. As I do. All these high school students in the street to support us! Did I say I wanted you to organize them in our support?"

I nodded. I was standing in the cement corridor of the jail, talking to Fernando through the bars of his cell. There were only a few lights in the corridor, and they too had little wire cages around them. There were no lights in the cell. A guard let you in and out of the corridor. I hated it. The air was pressing in on me. I couldn't breathe well. I wanted to get this over with and get out of there.

Alvarados had grown thin in jail. His tall frame was bony again, as when I'd first met him, my aunt's child, a refugee. His brown eyes looked feverish in his skull. They had bruised him badly on the cheeks. *You bastard this isn't your country,* they would say when they hit him, *this isn't your country,* holding him, working him over, not caring whether their work showed. This isn't your country. As if that explained it.

"They'll know then, the colonels will know, that we're serious. Repression won't work. Jails won't work. We won't stand for this Catholic crap. We just need to stand up to them." He was emphatic, convinced. But *he* couldn't stand up that well. He leaned forward, holding the bars to steady himself, staring at me, as if my image would keep him from falling.

I nodded again, but my mind was on his bruises. There were big purplish swellings under his eyes. As he spoke to me I heard the voices of our kitchen, my mother's voice, talking along with Fernando, taking his words just a few seconds after he said them, and twisting them slightly, mocking him. I spoke *(she spoke),* "Fernando, what will we do when they arrest us? Organize the primary grades? Toddlers against Fascism. No. That's crazy, Fernando. I love you." —That was true. I had never cared for him so much as I did at that moment when I refused him. I wanted to hug his thin body to me, to protect him. He *needed* protection, from the police, from his good heart, from his own insanity. "But this won't work, Fernando. If we go out into the street, the same thing will happen to us. They'll grab some of us and beat us to the ground with sticks. The rest will run away." I was speaking with my mother's hurried phrasing, quick, reasonable, ironic, even moving my hands in the air, suddenly, as she did. "Look at you," I said, "blood caked over your hair like pomade." But I didn't feel ironic. I was horrified, near hysteria, barely controlling myself with this impassioned analytic tone. I hardly saw Fernando, leaning forward into the light. My mind was filled with images of what the police might do to me if they had power over me. They would strip off my shirt, they would beat me across the chest. Every blow would violate me. "Didn't your blood teach you anything? We're not going to destroy them with our moral resistance, the good-natured way we offer them our heads. If we go out in the streets it should be serious. It should be a real fight." I *meant* it: a real fight: for as I spoke my fear changed, showed this other face: that they would *spare* me. They would be merciful towards me because I looked weak. I wanted the fight to be real. I wanted it to be serious. I wasn't sick, I wasn't ugly, I wasn't contemptible, I was not helpless, and I could not have stood to suffer their mercy. (Or so I thought: death was still only a solemn word to me.) Their mercy would make me small, insignificant. "If it's not a real fight, Fernando, people will have contempt for us. They'll say we're students play-acting. If you give me a gun I'll go out there. But if we're not serious we shouldn't show how damn helpless we are. Why demonstrate our powerlessness? Everybody already knows about that. If we're going to fight I want a gun. I want to fight back. I don't want to play games." But my voice had gone on now too long without response. It sounded hollow in my chest. I felt hot all over, flushed. What did I know about guns? I was a pretentious impostor, a fraud. A fool. (What would my father have thought of my violent words? I felt deeply ashamed. How contemptible he would have found me!)

Alvarados moved a little, supporting his shoulders against the bars of his cell. The weakness of his body, the curve, called to me. I wanted to embrace him fraternally, be his comrade, act with him. Against the pull of irony I admired him. But his action was stupid. Or was it? Was it the stupidity I hated, or the risk, the blows across my face, being put into a rotten hole? And in someone else's power. My penis shrank, as if something cold were touching it. But I was right! What he did *was* stupid! But if I'm right why do I feel ashamed before him? I hated looking at him. (And at the same time I wanted to stare at his face, his bruises. They transfixed me.)

Alvarados, though, simply believed my words, even if he didn't agree with them. We argued for a little while.

"Give my love to your family," he said, reaching out his hand through the bars. I hesitated, clasped it lightly; let it fall.

I turned and walked from his cell, calling to a guard to let me out of the corridor. I hated being enclosed in this damp stifling place.

Alvarados believed me, didn't think me a coward. Alvarados believed me, but I no longer believed myself. He even continued to admire me. We remained the closest of friends.

My Asthma, My Enemies

My third memory:
We are playing rugby. A bleak windy day. A cold rain starts that whips against our faces and will soon turn the field to mud. But we continue our game. My

father, hands thrust into his jacket pockets, wearing his red hunting cap, watches from the sidelines with a few other men. They run back and forth a few steps, carried along by the game. I am the captain of the team (I had to be captain), and play scrum half. I carry an asthma inhaler in the top pocket of a sweater that I wear under my blue cotton jersey. But in scrimmage I am knocked down, and the inhaler falls from the pocket. There isn't time to look for it in the muck.

Soon the air turns thick on my skin. *It's the storm,* I think, *the humidity, a change in air pressure.* I begin to sweat too much, and gasp, but do not leave the field. My father is watching me. I continue, to my own surprise, to run about, to shout out plays. I feel as if I'm watching myself from the air, watching my body move around. My head is floating far above my legs, far above the field itself. My body is enormously elongated; I look down from a great distance. During the scrimmage I am unable to fight back; to push anyone is impossible. I fall to the wet ground, gasping, and am too weak to lift my arms, to cover my head and protect myself. The other players swarm about my body, their legs darken the air. They kick me, and I think, ever a slow student, *They don't know I don't have the ball. No,* I realized suddenly, *it's because I'm down, because they can.* They repeat the lesson, their blows come hard, rapid, they pummel me, until I learn: *They do this because they hate me!* They pound me to make their hatred clear. *But it's only a game for God's sake.* No, they say with their blows. This is as you want it, this is not a game, not accident, or play, we want to hurt you badly now, do you damage, really smash you down. We do this because you keep yourself distant from us, think yourself our leader, our superior, better than us, because you're arrogant. This is your pride come home; you've practiced making us keep our distance, compelled our admiration, and this is how we show it to you. I can do nothing against their blows but huddle up to protect my head, my balls. They pile on me, jumping at my body, hitting at my chest and legs with their knees hands cleats. My body's twisted, my arm's buried under me, broken, pushed down slanting into the mud. My lips and nose are struck, they tear sharply and begin to bleed. *Why doesn't someone stop them?* Blood is running from my nose, down my throat. I taste salt blood mixed with balls of sputum and dirt, it clogs my throat, choking me. *Get them off me!* I can't cough, the press of bodies stops my chest from moving. I can't move my chest to breathe, I'm stifling, shaking with hatred and rage and pain and fear. I want to be, to go on being! There is a sharp ripping pain across the skin of my stomach, where my jersey has ridden up. My ribs will crack, my chest is caving in. *They'll smother me!* The beating goes on forever and ever. *Do they want me dead? Why doesn't someone help me?* The blood from my nostrils runs together with the rain and the sweat that streams from me. I'm in panic, shaking with spasms, physical sensation is gone, my whole consciousness is fear that they're going to kill me, no one will help me. My head's tilted back against the ground. My wounds release a film of blood that covers my eyes. *Stop them, Father, for God's sake stop them! My eyes are bleeding, my eyes are bleeding! Do you want me to die!*

They rise and pass, my tormentors. Long ago they beat me because I was helpless; helpless, I became arrogant so they would not dare to beat me; when I was arrogant, they waited for me to be helpless, so they might beat me for my arrogance. The game goes on. The world is running motion, cries and runs, and clots of reddish light. Someone notices me. The rugby game is stopped for a moment. My teammates carry me over to the sidelines. When I come to it will be in a hospital bed. As in my childhood my father will be sitting beside me. I'll think, brought back to ordinary life by my father's presence, *It couldn't have been as I thought, so much hatred in their blows. It was asthma, it was hallucination.* . . .

The last thing I remember from before I passed out is the sound of my own wheezing, too loud, too loud, and my father's face, leaning close to me, too close, his features distorted, enlarged, his huge hand pulsing as it clumsily, tenderly, brushes the water and blood from my face. And he is whispering, soothingly, "Good boy, son, good boy."

I have done my utmost.

Argentina, 1952

My Letter

University of Buenos Aires
May 1952

Dear Father: This work, this life

Dear Father:
I cannot do this work you've chosen. I write this letter

Dear Father: This work, this life you've chosen
    I have not chosen, I cannot yet find the will

Dear Father, I have written this letter to you over and over this last year, my last year of school, to tell you of my decision not to join you in practice. A letter —for we cannot speak to each other anymore. Yet I never stop speaking with you. So many nights here in this damp city, or while I walked in the mountains, or picked my way among the numinous stones of Peru, I spoke with you in my mind, trying to piece these things out. And your voice was always in my mind, answering me, your voice always speaking, always

Dear Father: I write this letter to you over and over in my mind, night after night. But I can't send it to you, I can't let you read it, and I can't stop writing it, explaining myself to you, accusing you, justifying my ways, justifying

Dear Father, This letter is meant for you, but it will always remain with me. That is our nature: to think more than we say, to hold back, but to let everyone know, by our distant manner, that we are holding back, observing, judging. We drop their hand a moment after shaking it. We withdraw at a party, sit in a corner, not speaking, while others bob up and down in a drunken dance. Their judge, understanding all, forgiving nothing, our verdict contained in our thin-lipped smile. (My lips do it too.) We'll forgive the drunken dancers eventually —the kind of forgiveness extended to children and countrypeople—if they're contrite and accept our judgment of them, our right to judge.

I do not like our character. I must change. I will find the will to change. The will to change that

I will not be like you. Not in the way that is most important to you. I will not join you in practice.

When I was a child we filled my head with visions of my future glory as a doctor. Those visions (garishly colored, like cheap pictures of the saints) now live inside me. I can't enact them, and I can't rid myself of them.

You and I said I would be not just a doctor, but a great doctor, a Prince of Medicine. You told me stories of our country's sickness, the diseases inflicted by poverty, by imperialism. But that misery was opportunity, was the field for my future exploits. I would cure the sickness. When I was twelve I imagined myself featured in a series of movie serials. I saw myself unobtrusively standing in line on the dirty mosaic sidewalk outside our movie theater, buying a ticket like everyone else, and sitting anonymously among the audience. A modest smile crossed my lips as I watched the very slightly exaggerated re-enactments of my achievements. Each episode was devoted to one of my discoveries. At the age of nineteen I would be the man who discovered the cure for (I kept dropping some diseases from the list and adding others) polio, cancer, leprosy, and—always—asthma. (It was given to me not as an affliction only, but as a sign.)

And I still believed, five years ago, when I came to medical school—already a little behind in my schedule of discoveries—that I would find out something about asthma. The pain would put me intuitively in touch with some piece of knowledge about that disease, knowledge that I would recognize, because it would speak to me a truth about my own character; it would be self-knowledge.

Now I know my asthma is my pain only; it means nothing.

from a journal 3/50   The faces in the street, "nothing, nothing you can do." Broken, even their anger gone. And what is it I wanted really by becoming a doctor? To exercise my compassion on a princely scale for these people. To discover a cure that would save thousands. And now?

I hear my father's voice. "You know what you remind me of, Ernesto? Those monks who keep a death's head before them, to remind themselves that the world's a wicked place. You hold up these poor like a memento. You say, I can't do enough for them. So I won't do anything at all."

—But imperialism is an inferno, it is the Fire of London that consumes millions. Still, he is right, of course—one must work tirelessly to do what one can.

Father, I worked hard at medicine, though it was very difficult for me. I felt as if I were breaking my will, memorizing, sitting quietly, sitting still and solitary with my books. It's hard for you, you told me once a week throughout my third year here, because you don't work steadily enough. Things came too easily for you in the past. You have no staying power when things are difficult. You give up.

That was unfair. And yet, like all your words, they cut me to the heart. Or wounded my pride. For if I accepted your lifelong judgment—that I was especially gifted, a genius—then I had to accept your reasons for my difficulty: I wasn't trying hard enough. For I could do *anything* I really wanted to.

The other students, my competitors, made me jumpy. Within a year my old comrades from the student union had fallen away from me. The times are cold, frightening. Peron has us at each other's throats. As Mother says, tell a group of Argentine leftists to form a firing squad and they'll make a circle. We were isolated, sullen; we could not find an action; we turned back on ourselves, made gestures—for a while. Soon we were terrified to do even that. We talked. Afraid to demonstrate, be beaten pointlessly, sent to jail, disappear, we hid our terror from one another, and talked. Near the university there are huge billboards, pictures of Eva and the General. No words. Just enormous pictures, lit up at night. The image of our world. Outside of them there is nothing.

from a journal 6/50   Often now I am overcome with that same madness that seized me throughout my childhood. When I am in class, or walking in the city, or at one of the political meetings, I will see someone who rubs me the wrong way: perhaps he is condescending to me, or to someone else, or I simply don't like the way he looks. I am seized by a sudden savage lightheadedness. I want to throw myself upon him, to wrench his head back, I want to humble him utterly, to tear at his skin, smash his nose till it bleeds. My head is pushed upward by anger. All I know of myself disappears suddenly into this harsh wind that makes my body tremble. I can feel my muscles strain, feel the man's flesh as if I were actually tearing it. The street, the room, the whole world, shakes for me, as it does during one of my attacks. I feel as if there is a terrible force inside me; if I were to turn it outward I couldn't control it; it would surely destroy someone. The wind would shake him, shake the world, to bits.

I became arrogant, rude, made others nervous by my anxiety, my knifing mean sentences, my fingers twisting my hair into knots and ripping the knots away, my foot tapping out the desperation samba. My old friendships had been grounded in their admiration for me. I was hard to admire now.

from a journal 9/50   Operating theater. They bring patients before us as if the whole thing were a show staged for our benefit, to gratify our already bloated egos.

And how cowed the sick are before us, the men in the white jackets. The men who will cure them. The men who will judge them. Judges like my father and I: doctors. Even if you don't intend it the moralism invades your manner. Disease is a sign against the patient, it is his fault. We know better. We explain and treat the disease physically. But it always has an unacknowledged phantom dimension, a moral, a spiritual dimension: his soul. For if there weren't this fault in the patient's soul, if there weren't his culpability, his complicity in his disease, then the world would be too senseless a place. The suffering would be too pointless, too out of control, for us to bear it.

So without even knowing what we are doing we affix responsibility for his sickness on the patient, we give coherence to the world. He has sinned, he has fallen. (My asthma had to be my mother's fault. Or it had to be a sign.)

Perhaps the patient wants the coherence too. It gives him the illusion he has power over his own life, that somehow he did this to himself, brought this suffering on himself by his own bad character.

In any case, the white coat, the distant, scientific manner terrify him into accepting our judgment. It's terrified everyone in my father's life. (Except Mother.)

So much that I had thought of as his character is really his role. The doctors who train us are like him at his worst, cranky, bad tempered if their judgment is questioned. And like him they often find things wanting. Why don't things stay under control, obedient? Why does she chew so loudly when she knows it annoys him? Why is his home so disordered?

It has a terrible price. He's in control of his own life, responsible. He is as exacting and severe with himself as with the patients. So many afternoons he simply withdrew from us, not speaking at meals. Or locked himself in his study, his withdrawal filling the house with lassitude, despair. He sat in judgment on himself: his failures were his own fault only.

How to be a doctor without becoming like him?

from a journal 5/52   This last summer is the only decent work I have done. I wasn't particularly useful there. Anyone could have done as well. But I was in a decent relation to things. And I was learning.

I felt there was some warmth, some comradeship there (as if only certain knowledge of one's death could release you from this fierceness). Their scabbed pustulant bodies filled others with disgust, had put them in exile. But they had absorbed their own disgust with themselves. They looked with dispassion on each other. All were under the same sentence. That is at least a kind of comradeship. And they didn't concentrate so much on themselves (perhaps they couldn't bear to, for that would mean concentrating on their own disfigurement, disease, death). They knew the shape of their death, were free of anxiety. They were released into the world.

Alvarados and I were popular with them. We were healthy, and would touch them. (So they weren't beyond caring about others' opinions.) The doctors wore face masks, ate wearing gloves, stayed over on their own side of the river, rarely crossing to the colony. Alvarados and I took them on monkey hunts, toured the Indian villages. And everything had a great clarity for me then, it was all sharply outlined.

The patients wanted our acceptance, and we could give it. A cheap trick. The other staff gave them their thermometers tied to long sticks. Alvarados and I, fearless children of the Enlightenment, put thermometers into their hands. As if that meant we did not despise them, did not judge them!

They poled themselves across the river on a raft to say goodbye to us. A farewell party. They pulled up on the shore where we lived with the other physicians. George played for us. He had been a night-club saxophone player in his other life, before his slow dying began. The music was frantic, sweet, tender, like George himself, with his quick motions, his kindness. (It was also a fire to burn his scabs, his skin, his disgrace away from his bones. He had lived a long time with self-loathing; he transformed it to this terrible heat.)

It was foggy and raining, but we came out on the shore to dance. The doctors and the nurses dancing on the green shore. The lepers bobbed unsteadily on their log raft. (But I couldn't dance, couldn't tell a mambo from a tango.) The rain made small circles in the blue-green river. The raft, held steady by long poles, rocked back and forth with a light swishing sound, accompaniment for George's tune. They were losing sensation in their hands and feet, dying from the skin to the heart, turning colors like leaves before their final paleness. My friend George, the gentle high-cheekboned Negro could no longer feel the silver keys he played.

The lepers on the raft floated back to their quarters in the rain, grew invisible in the mist. Only sounds remained, the plunk of their poles, the raft gliding forward, the wail of George's saxophone, still playing.

This whole year since has been spent in a fog. Now there has come this time, when nothing touches, nothing tastes. My chest hurts constantly. My hands holding a book, or a cup, shake slightly with an old man's palsy. I have a vague achy restlessness all the time that makes it impossible to study. I feel as if there were a wound down my side, something pressing slightly on my ribs.

Anxiety breaks the contours of my world, and any pleasure I might take in it, its food, its women, its colors. My consciousness is broken, divided a hundred ways, as if I were making love, but it wasn't reaching me, I am fitfully momentarily conscious of everything, of my lover's hands touching the small of my neck, of the crumbs in the bed, a slight pain in my stomach, a cramp in my leg, things left undone. My hands move over her legs, but I don't have a constant feeling, touch too is in fragments. That is the way I feel now, nearly all the time. And the world proves to be a very discreet lover, and does not care to seduce me.

My own body has begun to displease me. I am uncomfortable with my own

*stink. My asthma has become severe now. Perhaps it is the season. The shots
barely keep the attacks under control. Difficulty eating. Weight 120.*

Father, you were insistent this year that I finish up quickly, not go on any
more trips, come join you in practice. You were worried that I'd change my
mind, wasn't going to work with you, would go off on another of my desperate
trips. (But I cannot join you, cannot compete with you for her.)

We stood together in my room. We faced each other, you in a badly fitting
brown suit, I wearing baggy pants held up by a piece of rope. The apartment,
you said, was slovenly. Dishes crusted up with food. One day's meal making
the sauce for the next. My shirts, you said, reeked. Hadn't anyone mentioned
it? You picked up a piece of my underwear, and smiled, after our fashion. Was
I old enough, you wondered, to care for myself?

I understood, Father: Your work was being wrecked before your eyes. You
tried to prop things up, get them back under control with your moralism, bind
my will to yours and raise it. You went on at me about my returned invalid's
stoop, my poor work habits. "And you know what would be especially painful
to your mother? The way you look now." And it would: my face was broken
out, my hair was matted, oily. She'd grown neglectful of her own good looks,
but she still took pride in mine.

Silent, each of us enraged, we faced each other. We couldn't touch each
other, not in the casual ways of childhood, hugging each other, kissing for
greeting. And the absence of contact was palpable to both of us. The air itself
was thick and resisted our motion. You moved to touch my arm, and I flinched
as if you meant to cause me pain. As if nothing we could do with each other
would be understood! Our actions, thwarted, turned back on ourselves; we were
forced to watch our hands; the smooth motion of reaching out became self-
conscious, crooked, a gesture. Our love was impotent. And then the great anger
came that follows in each of us when our love is misunderstood, rejected. We
looked at each other in the middle of that small dirty room, by the foot of my
unmade bed, wanting to make contact, to be able to speak, wanting to touch,
to strike each other, to hit hard across the face.

I felt constricted in your presence, Father, as if you used up all the air in
the room. It was impossible to talk, to tell you my thoughts, for my words had
to cross an enormous distance. To speak even one sentence, some joke intended
to turn aside your worry, left me spent, empty of breath.

I am standing in front of a tall wooden door with words chalked on it. I am pacing about the living room, trying to remember the sound of a word, terrified that you might frown, that you might send me tumbling into that void where I am worthless. I cannot be that child. I need a world where the feelings between us are unambiguous, permanent, even hatred will do, so long as it's sharply defined, without those dizzying drops into nothingness you sent me on by your disapproval, a thinning of the lips. Yes, even hatred will do, unreconcilable opposition, if only it is *clear*. But I can never attain that clarity with you, only this bewildering fuzzy anger that is too much like love.

I have to leave Argentina, put some distance between us. I cannot stay here and be a doctor the way you are. I do not want to be like you, a sad stern isolated moralist. I cannot compete with you.

Father, you are poisoning my air.

from a journal 6/52   I stood in the dirty corridor outside Alvarados's cell, and I could not reach out to him, could not, honestly, and with my own voice, speak to him. My own voice! My mother's voice spoke in my head, took my cousin's words a little after he spoke them, as if they were words from a newspaper article, and mocked them. She made him, the voice made him, sound foolish, crazy, suicidal.

That voice closes me off from my world still, closes me off from my own possibilities. I cannot test myself, act, make myself known, for it makes all action seem silly, foolish, absurd. Everything goes into that sausage machine for epigrams.

So my boldness in front of Alvarados: Give me a gun! That boldness was merely speculative. What a terrible fierce fighter I'd be against fascism, when the Voice told me the right time had come. But would I, would It, ever think the right time had come? I must have known that we couldn't fight them on my terms, for life or death. We'd lose, all be indifferently killed by those young dour soldiers. Any reasonable person could see that (I expected them to see it and stop me). Alvarados was at least keeping alive the idea of resistance.

No, any reasonable person, Tete, could see that he was only keeping alive the idea of defeat.

Then I was right? I don't know. I can't act, and so can't ever know. But Alvarados has fought the colonels and I haven't. He at least knew there were some things he wouldn't stand for. And I? I am all talk? A coward?

I couldn't reach out to him. And when he took my hand I was filled with confusion and shame.

But the political talk at the university is stupid. *The voice comes and takes the words and shows me that.*

And the students here sound no different from my parents. I can hear my parents' tones in theirs: pride, isolation, moralism, the bitter edge of some solitary rightness carried on too long, the edge of madness.

I want to silence that voice, the voice of reason. I want to have one voice, one action. I want to make myself known, directly, and without irony.

There's glass between me and the streets of the city, thick as the veil of asthma. I can't reach out, can't connect. The only time I've felt free these last few years was when I was walking the continent, working as a ship loader, or a nurse tending the lepers. Do you remember our walks, Father, when I would scurry along beside you? Now that I have a man's step, as long as yours, I think I have the step of a giant—I can take a continent in my stride. I am going to walk America awhile, be a tourist, without class or country, gain knowledge, go to and fro, perhaps find a way that I can be a doctor, act decently.

I am a tourist here anyway, living outside Eva's mausoleum. Peronism is like a foreign language to all of us, one that I can't speak, should speak. It is like nights I spent in bed as a boy, overhearing your voices in the kitchen; it trembles always, frustratingly, on the edge of sense. The people in the Plaza for Peron, there is an energy there that I want, but cannot share. (And so it fills me with fear. The words are like stones. The words are guns pointed at my head—I dream I am in a crowd at the Plaza, a small boy, lost in between their legs. I can't move. I'm rooted with terror.) I can do nothing here but feel purposeless. And, like you and Mother, have opinions, make gestures.

Do you remember, Father, we would go out walking through the town, where the poor lived. You don't have to be a master diagnostician, you told your eleven-year-old, to diagnose poverty. You shook your fist at the yard, and through it at the imperialists. A gesture of opposition that speaks, by being a gesture—this is all a man can do, make gestures—of your innocence. Nothing, nothing you can do. You *are* innocent Father. But neither you nor Mother believed that. And that voluptuous sense of guilt, how you cling to it, poke at it like a delicious hurting bruise! Mother sits at the kitchen table, cutting off her fingers with a razor blade, pasting them into one of her notebooks. You pour a pitcher of hot water on your lap. Your guilt shows how much better you are than others of your class. You at least feel guilty.

I don't know what's to be done. I have nowhere to stand. I don't know what's to be done that will not be more terror in a world overfull of violence.

But I know that I want to feed what I am, feel it, nourish it with my own body. And I will never do that here.

For now I have no voice, or many different voices, none of them mine, parts of you and Mother, and the radio, and the books I read, political speeches, and movies, magazines, and each of them has an opinion. I want to have one voice, one single action. And if that's not possible I want to quiet those voices, learn silence, achieve silence.

I hardly have the words to say what I want; such words do not yet exist for me. Unhappy, this pampered doctor cannot explain the lack, the insufficiency, that makes him unhappy. I have to work constantly to make my unhappiness my own, to keep it before me, my possession. And nothing is more ridiculous than working at one's alienation. But if I don't, this feeling easily cuts loose of me, permeates my world, as a disgust that makes everything slightly distasteful. I become then like Mother and you, a kind of aristocrat. I give way to—no, I find everywhere—a despair, a disgust that is simply the existence of things.

So I speak of action, but that is not exactly what I want, that is the barest simulacrum of my need, for my need is not that at all. It is more like rest, stillness, pleasure. An action is not what I need, but what I will accept, for I am unable to get, even express what I need.

Father, I can hear your voice. Your voice says there's something more, that I want out not because of some rigmarole about wanting to make a new character for myself, find the work I can do for people. No, I'm leaving because I'm lazy and impatient, and spoiled. I can't sit still. I don't want to work at anything with an adult's patience. That's why I want to wander aimlessly.

And—though you won't say this, will never say this, only show that you are thinking it—you think I am leaving because I am pointlessly spiteful about your help, your concern, your love, because I hate you, I want to smash down all your hopes, all that keeps you alive. I want to destroy you. I want your death. Every child's dream. But I can do it simply by absenting myself. Because you allowed yourself to trust me. Of all people, you allowed yourself, as best you could, to love me.

You see, letters written late at night, like this, eventually engorge too much irony. Never sent, they go a little crazy.

So a hug, Father, from your son,

Ernesto

My Farewell

My father never made much money in Cordoba. The people of the region were peasants, or the children of peasants. They found my father too severe, unsympathetic. They were wary of him. And though there were few doctors, still many of those who could afford medical care went to folk doctors, astrologers, curers, magic men, rather than to my father.

My father had bought us the smaller house, in a decent section but, as I said, abutting a slum. It was to this small stucco house, its red paint flaking off, this constant symbol of their sacrifices for me—of me, I thought moodily as I walked in the door—that I came to offer my ingratitude, my betrayal.

It was evening. My parents were in the kitchen, reading their newspapers, sipping their hot drinks. Lapsed Catholics, the newspaper was their wafer. Not that they would have said this—for who would admit that his connection with the deepest life of his time was a newspaper? I remembered that in my childhood these newspaper sessions had been the best part of the day. My parents were calm, kind to each other, intent. Perhaps it was simply that these evenings were a time when they still felt comfortable with each other, as they no longer did in their bedroom, for they were engaged here in a common project, were free even to argue with each other without bitterness. But that moment was past. The bitterness now was everywhere.

My mother's drink, her potion, had grown more bitter too. A few years before, with the joy of Balboa, she had discovered instant coffee. She made it with hot water, directly from the tap, not bothering about boiling. I think over the years she must have tanned the inside of her mouth, for I had tasted this stuff once and it was, as my father said, "a truly vile drink."

So I refused her offer of coffee, poured myself some hot water from the gray pitcher, and made myself a cup of mate. I took a seat over in the corner, pushed back against the wall, as if I were joining them.

My father, though he sat with my mother, hadn't participated in these newspaper sessions for years. Not, that is, the way his wife still did, with vehemence and energy. He was present, now wearing a gray tweed jacket from England (it needed patching at the elbows), and he fashioned from his august bearded presence his method of participation, that of judge. His eyes were deeper in his sockets. His face was thinner, was stripping down to bone (a kind of declaration of his distaste for the world). He withdrew more and more into an abstract and—as my mother pointed out to him—"perfectly sententious moralism." With a doctor's conviction of rightness, he rendered judgments that were indisputable.

My mother nonetheless disputed. So he withdrew further, rarely spoke—perhaps out of strategy, for my mother would be intentionally provoking when he did speak. And she was hard to keep up with in an argument—she had so much passion for it. She had little else besides arguments, while he was worn from work, and waiting for work.

My mother, though, had grown more and more involved in these newspaper sessions, driven by Peronism into greater and more elaborate inventions of invective. Peron and his late wife, "those fascists," were "truly unbelievable" to her. And this absurdity was, at least, a comic opportunity for her.

That night—for my benefit I suppose (for he was a little above such joking)—she did a decent imitation of that other energetic implacable woman, Eva Peron. She lacked only the desolation of Evita's singsong voice, the near hysteria of a child whose main amusement had been to watch the trains pull through her town. (She stands on the tracks as long as she can until panic overcomes her and she leaps aside. The train passes by. It is her lover, of course, taking her almost to the point of destruction. It is her own power. The last car shakes her. It has passed by. She is desolate. The town looks shitty. It is shitty.) *That* my mother could not imagine, that aridity she could not mimic. My mother made her voice throaty, seductive, but, like Eva's, mechanical in its rise and fall. "Oh, I grew up in terrible poverty myself, so I know the people very well. I wear these feathers, this joowelery for them. Of course it's a terrible burden for me! Just think how much it weighs! But they're happy to see me in beautiful clothes and joowels. I can't deny them that pleasure. I can't deny them anything you know, I'm so fond of them. I was trained as a tragedienne you know"—here my mother, released from her usual modesty by the drama, did, before her son, a very moderate, very restrained, bump and grind. "And this I feel is part of my costume, part of the role the people delight in my playing for them. It's part of my sacrifice for them, so they have someone a little bit like them to tell stories about."

My mother continued in her own voice, speaking to me. "And do you know what's most nauseating? They love her! They swoon before her like teen-agers at a burlesque show. When their homes are washed away they say" —meek voice like a cartoon mouse— " 'Eva will take care of us.' Now that she's dead they tell each other her body wouldn't burn when the army tried to destroy it. I heard two idiot women saying that just this week! They pray to her for Christ's sake! Our stripper who art in heaven!" There was real disgust and anger in her voice, her look, the way she gestured, pointing her cigarette at me with a sharp stabbing motion. But there was delight too. I laughed, and carefully put my drink down on the table, and clapped, to show my appreciation. Polite guest. For really this show brought me to the edge of despair. She had done this little act for me, because once it had pleased me. But it did no longer. Once this mockery had been my bedtime story. But now I felt like a grown-up being fed a sticky treat his mother assures him was his childhood favorite. I was an adolescent being read a children's book. I wanted to shout out, like that rebellious adolescent, I'm too old for this! I'm no longer a child, Mother! But I couldn't—for why wasn't she too old for it?

And this *was* just like what had delighted me in my childhood, this performance, my mother and not my mother, peekaboo from around the edges. But she was always like that, performing or not, even in her *real* life, her family. For the roles she'd been given to play in that life were too small for her. She overflowed them, was them and not them at once. A great actress in a very provincial company, trapped in a minor role, too much intelligence and talent had gone into her small part; her qualities called attention to themselves, as if it were not a character you were watching, but someone who made you exclaim at each moment: Now there's a great actress! It gave a heightened quality to her least gesture—her hand moving through her hair, her conversation at parties—but it destroyed the verisimilitude of what she was doing. My mother, you see, seemed to be *playing herself.* And so she was always ironic —as if what was most important about her could not be expressed, could not manifest itself, but could only, ever, hint at its existence.

I leaned back in my chair, trying to get comfortable. Now there were dozens of frayed or unraveled pieces of wicker. My parents did not make repairs. My parents (and myself) had the necessity of economy but none of its habits. I think this got on my father's nerves (though he never found time to do anything about it). But my mother didn't seem to notice. (Any more than she saw her own mess. Half-filled notebooks, ashtrays, coffee cups, crumpled cigarette packs, magazines and books were scattered all over the table.) She was indifferent to her surroundings. She belabored my father for losing her money, but that was only for purposes of argument; she never seemed to want very much the things the money could have bought, never seemed unhappy about their worsening circumstances. A true intellectual, she didn't care about such things. Or perhaps she was simply too aristocratic to show her feelings.

Or perhaps she showed them constantly. I thought of her love for the Spanish Anarchists. She wanted to be not only on the side of justice, but part of a small beleaguered and necessarily doomed group on the side of justice. The smallness, isolation, and consequent doomedness of the group were, I think, very important to her. Against the aristocracy that she rebelled against, that she truly wanted no part of, she posed this other aristocracy, an elite that her family and friends would want no part of, because it was an aristocracy of the oppressed, it was against them. But it would be an aristocracy nonetheless, the purest of the left, kindred, chosen, noble spirits. And as the miners had lost more and more battles, more and more men, more and more territory, she had, I remembered, become that much more ardent for their cause, her fund raising for them that much more active. As if the Spanish miners, so far away, were an image of her own defeat in the world, her own coming down, because they too were part of an elite that was too good for this world. Beyond the political position of the defeated, it was the defeat that was important.

Peronism, I saw from my corner, sipping my smoky liquid, Peronism was perfect for my parents in an awful way, the final justification of their style: her irony, his judgments. With their hatred of the oligarchy they'd come from and with the workers on the side of "that madman," there was no one good enough for them to make common cause with. And once the Communists were cut off from the masses, from any possibility of success, once they had become a persecuted secret *debating* club, my parents became fellow travelers of the Communists, on the side of an imaginary, doomed, empty-handed proletariat, a proletariat of dreams.

The masses that did exist in our homeland were, alas, "irrational, driven insane by the smell of that woman's sex." Those masses had once, in fact, tried to tear my mother limb from limb. My mother, my parents, were, of course, rational, and it was clear to any rational person that there was nothing to do but to condemn this madness and wait for everyone to come to his senses. And they were right, I thought, their reasoning was faultless. (So it was reason itself I was running away from? Sanity that I wanted to be cured of? Doctor, make me mad!)

Why for God's sake didn't the masses follow decent leaders—for my mother was not for a mindless leaderless leveling, but for a natural aristocracy of leaders, one, I think, she was certain that, with her talent, ideas, education, she'd be a part of. (And she should be, I thought, listening to her analyze the Marshall Plan. She was brilliant.) If only the people had brought their sorrows to her instead of to that actress, she would have known how to teach them to lament. Then something might be done. But now—nothing.

Trapped forever with feelings they could neither act on, nor let go of, my parents had, for years, argued fiercely about politics with everyone—for there was nothing to do but argue. All their energy went into baiting their acquaintances, their friends, and then—the circle, like this glass table, closing in on itself—each other. They were constantly insulting each other. (My mother went so far once as to bring a small nickel-plated pistol to the table, to indicate just what might happen to my father if he pushed her sorely tried patience any further with his deliberate, his obstinate stupidity. The next night he too laid a pistol by his cup. They kept up this charade for a week.)

They took their ideas so seriously because they couldn't find a way to take them seriously at all—they were always and ever only ideas. For the less you do the more strictly you have to define the difference of opinion between you and the class enemy (the oligarchy, the imperialists), you have to draw the line ever more sharply, because under Peron the main difference between you and that enemy (they, too, were against Peron) were your opinions.

So my mother grew funnier, more bitter, more talkative. In her heart she would, I think, rather have done something against Peron, like her fund raising, her rallygoing, during the Spanish War—for she became more witty at her own expense as well, making self-deprecating jokes, jokes about her own absurdity, jokes tinged with self-hatred. (Could she have stood, after all these years, so much accumulated self-dislike, to be on the winning side?) But there was no way to win, nothing to do, nothing but this endless bickering with everyone, until she was tired of her own voice.

If only my mother could have found some way to act—but for that, though she couldn't see it, she would have had to turn herself inside out, become someone else, unrecognizable to herself. (I knew this because, as I lay in my damp bed in Buenos Aires, I had felt this truth for myself.) If only there had been some outlet for her energy! But there never had been, not her whole married life. My father had his work, my father had (or so it had seemed to all of us) me, and she had only her books, memories, a few admiring friends. So she made Peronism the stuff of an intellectual triumph; she could lampoon them, caricature them endlessly, destroy them with her wit. She threw herself into abusiveness as completely as she could (but how little of her this used!).

And as she abused the world it disappeared for her. History was only an excuse for her verbal structures; and at the end only a little bit of it remained in them, like a newspaper picture or some other found object that's glued into the corner of a collage. The political world, which existed for them not as a sphere of action but as a subject constantly judged, constantly parodied or condemned, fell away. And soon it was barely discernible what they were contemptuous of—for this crazy world, called up only in ridicule, had left of itself only the merest distorted fragments. And so my mother's abuse that had been at first her way of reaching out to the world, making it her own, mastering it, had by this time twisted the world out of anyone else's recognition, and sealed her isolation.

Alone now in this small blue kitchen (the wallpaper had milkmaids and oddly, sheep, on it; it had come with the place), alone, the rail splitter asleep, the miner asleep, the gaucho asleep (the gardeners, I suppose, out drinking), they were the only ones awake in the house, in the country, vigilant, sipping from clay mugs, reading the newspaper, talking. They seemed loony to me, as I waited now for them to run down, to finish this talking to no one—not even to each other—about nothing. I had long ago stopped listening. (Though I was still marked by these sessions, and knew myself marked.)

When they were nearly exhausted I told them of my determination to leave Argentina. My father's hand, holding the silver strainer for the glistening mate leaves, shook. The veins of his hand were thicker, more prominent than I remembered. He knew that I meant my departure, at least in part, as a blow at him, a way of separating us utterly. But his hand shaking like that, it was not, after all, a very gratifying sight. He was a lonely man. The peasants distrusted him, wouldn't accept his care; there was a bewildering distance between himself and his wife that was, he knew, as much his character as her refusal.

And I, who was the last person he could simply love, was deserting him.

"Your generation is weak," my father said, "not like mine. Very weak really, don't you think. Your mother spoiled you with her stupid ideas about raising children. We were more men than you are. We were able to carry on our fathers' work. We didn't go running off at a challenge the way you do. But you're all perpetual children now, you have no internal strength. I tell you this quite frankly, Ernesto, that's what you all lack. When it becomes difficult you give up, go running off. Not like us, not like us at all. Not like my people"— meaning, I suppose, the Guevaras, gold miners, ranchers. He was repeating his words like an old man, in a cranky voice, mechanically shaking his head at me. And the skin of his throat quivered; it had formed into loose folds and wrinkles; an old man's skin. Who was this old man? I barely recognized my father in him. "Weak," he went on, "weak. I should have expected it from you, of course. It's been too easy for you. Your mother always spoiled you. It's been so easy that the slightest difficulty, like this Peron business, makes you squeal. A little discomfort and you cave in, just as you did when you were a child. In a way you're effeminate, Ernesto. I'm being frank with you, that's my opinion. She would have spoiled you worse if she could have. You're weak, you have no courage. It's been too easy for you."

Why did he want to destroy my myth, the myth of my heroic struggle against asthma, the myth of the weak child who became a hero, the myth he'd been chief author of? I suppose it was his way of fighting back. And it stung, for he could still stir me if he wanted, his casual blows had power. And his accusations were too close to my own fears.

But I'd defeated him, this old man, that was clear, this old man with his crankiness about the younger generation. Not quite the feeling of triumph I'd expected when I arrived that evening. Did he read the strength of my will in my eyes and decide not to make a fight about my leaving—knowing that my will was as strong as his, was his, only younger?

I promised again that I'd return in a year. I whispered good-bye to the old man, but didn't try to kiss him. We did not touch each other much anymore, not the way we once had. I rose, and kissed my mother's cheek. She stood and hugged me—but lightly, hardly touching me, hugging me in the crook of her elbow, keeping the lit cigarette in her scarred hand away from her hair. When had this pretty woman, too, become old? Her own force, turned back on itself, had raked lines into her face. Her lovely eyes were darkly ringed again, permanently so. Her skin bagged beneath them now. "You will come back to us, Ernesto," she said in a soft voice.

Opening her pocketbook on the table, she gave me fifteen dollars in pesos. If I got as far as the United States, I was to buy her a lace dress and bring it back to her on my return. But I felt that she was playing this out for my father, and knew better herself; I felt, in fact, that she, who knew something of traps, for I myself had been hers—was giving me her blessing. "You will come back with my dress."

"Of course I will, Celia," I said.

And of course I never did.

Isle of Pines, June 1965

JUNE 23

Yesterday evening, after our beans and rice, I gave Ponco my account, a hundred handwritten pages. He took it back to his room immediately, and spent the rest of the night reading. I could see his light, a thin strip underneath the door.

That light kept me awake, fidgeting in my bed, twisting the sheets about my body to cover myself. I couldn't get comfortable; either the sheet stuck to my skin, or, kicking it away, I was too chilly, too exposed. It was not exactly, I think, a writer's vanity that made me turn in my bed, not "What does he think of my work, my talent?" not even "What does he think of me, how does he, knowing these secrets, judge me?" But I felt as if I weren't in my own hands anymore; I wondered, what does he *make* of me? Behind that door, in that light, he was reading me; I was entering his imagination; he was creating *a version* of me.

I was up before Ponco, sitting at the table, drinking mate when he came in, waiting for him. I wanted his version; I wanted to gaze at that funny reflection of myself. "What did you think of it?" I asked. "I've written history before but never in this way. Before I was writing from the outside, an observer, describing battles I was at. You know, you've read them. I acted in those battles, but I never spoke of how they formed me. But this is different, a history that cuts across and into me, that forms me. I feel as if I haven't given you an account, but my childhood itself." I was pompous from embarrassment. I was ashamed to say with real directness what I wanted: let's tell a story about me.

Ponco smiled, the peculiar way he has when nervous, quickly lifting his lips over his teeth, then letting them drop as if a switch had been thrown. "I enjoyed it very much."

I was disappointed. I wanted him to present myself to myself. "Say something more." My curiosity was a deep desire; it made me rude, imperious.

It only made Ponco more agitated. He bit the edge of a finger. "It's a good story," he said. "It made me wonder what happens next."

"It's all right. You can be critical." That wasn't what I meant either. I didn't want his artistic judgment on my plotting. I wanted to know his construction of me.

"Something critical," Ponco said, and paused. He then made a gesture that I had never before seen on this earth: he put one hand in his ear, palm out, and one on his head, like the comb of a rooster. He stuck his tongue out at me, and waggled his hands.

"What in God's name does that mean? Is it a Cuban thing?"

"No. It's critical. Called a Bronx cheer. Never seen one. Only read it."

"I don't think you have it right. I've seen one. Once, when I was in Miami, when I was twenty-one, I was mouthing off to old men in a cafeteria, and the FBI took me in for questioning. I told them what I thought of the United States, and one of the agents gave me a Bronx cheer." I did it for Walter. A fleck of spit landed on my mate gourd. Ponco laughed: dry husks scraping each other. "The agent had a fat face, and with his cheeks bulged out he looked obscene, as if he were shitting his thumb. But don't you have anything more to say about my story, my life?"

Walter fidgeted in his chair. (I saw my body turning in bed the night before and thought, that's what my account is good for, to make people fidget.) He scratched his face, pulled the smooth skin tight. He was nervous; he wanted to go read, to be somewhere else entirely. But I didn't care. Walter was silent for a while, scratching under his arm, up and down his chest, a breach of his fastidiousness. Then: "Nuh wdgmmugh."

Sometimes Ponco's voice is so low and so harsh it is hard to make out the words. I leaned more closely towards him. "What?"

"No women?"

"My mother."

"Yes. But no women. Didn't you have women? Or think about them? I heard Che was a ladies' man before the Revolution. A Don Juan."

"It's not a story about women."

"I suppose not." He drank some coffee. "Do you think often about your family?"

"What do you mean?"

He put his hands to his head, on each side, and pushed them together like a vise.

I understood. "You mean psychology. Psychoanalysis? Oedipus complex? Freud?"

He drew his lips up, clicked them shut, nodded.

A party game: charades. The loss of his voice had opened into new languages. "I thought you read only fiction."

"A fellow told me about it. Good story. Demons."

"I used to think a lot about it once, in that way. I was absorbed by Freud when I was in medical school, and after, until the beginning of the Revolution. Until I met Fidel. Hilda and I used to argue about psychoanalysis. She thought it was a bourgeois idea." Walter had met Hilda a few times, when she came to Havana with the baby, after the Revolution. I was not always comfortable seeing her after the divorce, and I sometimes sent Walter with gifts for the child, my child. "We used to argue in Guatemala about Freud and Sartre. It was during my existentialist period. Sartre, she said, was bourgeois, too. All that talk of *anxiety*, she'd say disgustedly, as if the word were dirty. Anxiety was a luxury item, more expensive than Paris perfume. It was only for Europeans. Latin Americans didn't have the spare change for it. For us the only choice was unremitting struggle, or having your face shoved in shit, not whether to commit suicide or not. With so many people trying to kill you, why give them the satisfaction? Of course, you know, she would never have said 'shit.' She doesn't talk like that. She doesn't speak ironically. She spoke of the struggle for social justice, the fight against exploitation, hunger, bad health, illiteracy, that's the way she talked, very clearly, very directly, not bitterly, not ironically. When we met in Guatemala she was in exile. Not self-chosen exile, like mine.

She had led the APRA group at the university in Lima, and after the coup she had had to flee. She had the right to talk the way she did. Is this interesting you?"

Ponco nodded happily, a real smile. "Very. I've never heard you talk like this."

"It's the writing. Once you begin explaining yourself there's no end to the process. In any case, Hilda believed in Pavlov, not Freud. He explained people's behavior in a way more acceptable to her. You know Pavlov? The dog trainer? Sartre and Freud paid too much attention to individuals, she said, not enough to the social struggle. And she found Freud disgusting. Nothing but sex drives and dirty thoughts! She said it wasn't a complete picture of a human being. I remember that phrase of hers. Political fighters were not sick men acting from frustrated sex drives. They were normal human beings, acting as we all should, freely accepting their responsibility to society. Very contradictory to Pavlov's poor doggies. She only liked Pavlov, really, because of her sympathy with the Soviets. I pointed that out to her. It was late at night, in her boardinghouse in Guatemala. Time for me to go she would say."

Out of my reverie, expelled from Hilda's house, I looked at Walter and saw (or imagined) the sidelong glance, the tightened lips of a leer. "No," I said emphatically. "Not a Don Juan. Not a conquest. Hilda was very serious, almost stern. There was nothing *light* about her. As I say, she was unironic, she didn't want to play, usually, only to get at the truth and act on it. She was not at all like my mother. I suppose that's a point against Freud. You know if she hadn't been pregnant she would have asked Fidel to let her join the expedition. Instead she went to my parents' house to wait for me. Each night she wore a flannel bathrobe I'd left behind. When she came after the victory of the revolution I told her immediately about Celia. I couldn't wait. I felt like dung. I said, 'It would be better if I'd died in battle.' I know: very self-dramatizing. Very self-pitying. She stopped crying immediately. 'No,' she said, 'the Revolution needs you.' You see what I mean?"

"Yes. You were made for each other." He was smiling at me; talking of my life, I had opened myself to this tender irony in others.

I paused, remembering her, going deeper into my trance. A boardinghouse in Guatemala. She was plump, with a round face, her mouth turned down, her eyes thin, Indian-looking. She wasn't pretty in the ways I was familiar with, but her looks fascinated me. I couldn't get them to come out right, and I felt there was something valuable there I didn't understand, as if, if I could learn to find her beauty, I would have deepened myself, changed for the better, solved a problem. Sometimes I knew she wasn't attractive, sometimes I thought everyone would think her beautiful, and sometimes I knew she was beautiful and knew also that no one else would see it. "I remember sitting in her living room, with our friends and her roommates. They were giddy things by comparison with Hilda. She always had fresh fruit for me, for my asthma, and hot water for my mate. In the days before the mercenaries invaded, I slept on a golf course, and I would come over in the morning to wash up. She took care of me. I think that was why she liked me, at first, because I needed her attention, because of my asthma. I wasn't like other Argentines, she said, stuck up, with overdeveloped European ways. I wasn't like other men. I think she meant I had a visible weakness, though I tried to hide it. After we were married she told me that at first she had thought I was haughty because of the way I stuck out my chest like a rooster. But when she found out from Soto that it was to ease the pain of my asthma, she found it touching, I was like a little boy bravely hiding his illness. That's a deep part of her nature: she's a very compassionate person. And very courageous. After the invasion of Guatemala she went to prison rather than tell the police where I hid. And in prison she went on a hunger strike because they denied her the rights of a political exile. It was an amazing performance."

"You gave up Freud for her?"

"What?" Walter meant well, but he was calling me back for no reason, for a silly joke. "No. Because of Hilda's arguments? No. Then we would have nothing to fight about. I only explained things to her in a Freudian way to tease her. It was a way of talking to her about sex—it was many, many months before we made love. She was right in a way. Freud may help us to see what parts of ourselves need changing. Then we must find the material conditions that must be changed to change ourselves. So Freud becomes Marxism. And then Gramsci's right: the revolutionary must be his own psychoanalyst. It is a matter of freeing the will to act."

Walter looked away. He didn't care for theory unless he could read it allegorically, make characters out of the abstractions, battles of Spirit, Will, Heart, Head.

"You must stop me talking," I said. "What do you think of my childhood?" He owed me something—not for my theory, but for my reminiscences.

And finally I goaded a response. "You were a violent child."

"I was? I thought your childhood more violent than mine."

"No. Mine had more hitting. All kinds of hitting. My mother and uncle raised me. Don't doubt. He was a fag, he didn't wear socks. You don't know?"

"About socks? No."

Ponco laughed. At me. "Yes. Much of Cuba is figures to you. The ones who wear sandals without socks are making a statement. He embarrassed me. Started my career as a liar. And he hit me. Often. When I was fourteen he knifed someone, and ran to the United States. I shot him at Playa Giron."

"Figuratively you mean." I thought his old ways were returning, brought back by my pressuring him to speak. (Or by my example.)

"No. Literally. Or someone did. He was in the group that landed from the *Travis*. My area. He died there. My mother hated him. Her brother. Now she calls a fag a 'Travis.' She calls her late brother Travis. See. He doesn't have a name anymore. He's dead for her. When she's angry at me, she says I'm like Travis. I'm a Travis." He stopped to drink some coffee, as if he could moisten that dryness. "See, in my family, if you were angry at someone, you hit. As hard as you could. Really angry, you killed. Bam! Pow! You people, you carried it around inside you. It becomes personal. Sharp." He paused, waiting for the right words. "Icy," he said in his hot, harsh voice.

"I suppose. At night, in high school, before sleep, I imagined shooting people from the windows of the house. Bad people. Fascist police. They had the house surrounded. I shot at them from the windows. Where could I stand where the bullets wouldn't hit me? My first strategic problem. I found it soothing."

Ponco laughed, a long time, the merest sound, warm breath coughed up from his chest, grating the roof of his mouth.

"This is strange talk," I said. "I've written more about my life than I ever wanted to. Or so I thought. And now we're talking, as you say, in a way we never have before."

"You mean I tell the truth."

I smiled. "Not just that. But talking about myself makes me talk more about myself. I can't stop! It's like a trance. You remember one thing, God knows from where, the edge of a blanket you had as a child, and it reminds you of something else you would have thought was gone forever if you ever thought about it, like the way the fruit bowl looked in the mornings in Hilda's living room, or the quality of dust in the light in my parents' house."

"You should go back to work." He got up from the table and went towards the porch and someone else's story. He was afraid, perhaps, of more questions; he didn't want to talk about me.

JUNE 24

And next? The goal is raising the production of zinc. The goal is increasing the participation in factory councils. The goal is taking that outpost. The goal is This business doesn't seem to work like that. Where am I going here? I don't know how to name it to myself. The goal is how I became the person that I am? That is: a certain will: the struggle must begin now. The beginning of revolutionary violence will unite the masses, throwing them in one direction, in one way. The Third World will rise to save Vietnam, to end colonialism forever.

But how can that catechism be the story of my adolescence?

Before I asked: is it possible, can it be done? Is that like asking now: is it true? And then I think, but what about its opposite? Isn't that part of the truth?

And next? Each sentence I write just stops. Dead. Like that. To know what comes next, after this sentence, I must imagine from the end backward. What is the end? (My plane lost over the sea? Some town in Bolivia? Or somewhere like Bolivia?) Make the life fit the death. To write one's life story is to be already dead.

Is that true?

JUNE 25

This morning, Ponco, up before me, had left a note on the table next to my mate gourd. (He had read my thoughts!) He provided direction.

Is it true
you killed a man in Bolivia?

After tea and bread I took this note back to my room, placed it before me on my board.

My day's work:

No.
I vomited on a man in Bolivia.
In Guatemala I killed a mercenary.

I left the page by Ponco's plate at dinner. He looked at it quizzically, folded it up into a very small square, and put it in his shirt pocket.

JUNE 26

This morning's note:

You always seem so certain.
Were you always so certain about everything?
Were you certain about Fidel?

I labored hard on that one.

No.

Yes.

Yes, I have always been certain. Imperialism is the enemy of mankind. But my tactics have changed. Once I was a follower of Gandhi, or so I thought. I believed in chastity, abstinence, humbling my body for my soul's sake. I believed in nonviolence and the life of the Indian villages. I was against industrialization. Gandhi, I thought, had shown the way to defeat the imperialists.

And then there was an in-between time. The space between the sentences. Have you ever seen a strip of motion-picture stock? In between the frames there is a thin white line. On the screen the motion looks continuous, a man turning round or walking out a door. But there is really that line. A discontinuous dialectic that looks smooth.

When I didn't know what should be done the world seemed hateful, nonsensical, rotten. It was like having a stomach ache.

But I was certain about Fidel. I had awaited him.

At dinner Walter smiled, pointing at me. "Gandhi?"

"In Bolivia," I said, returning his smile, remembering that young man's sermons.

"Chastity?"

"Yes." I nodded. There was something chaste in Walter's harshness. "The body is evil, unruly. Form yourself by cutting into the flesh."

Walter laughed, gasp gasp gasp, but said no more.

JUNE 27

You don't get the point.

Not an interview.

I meant a story. Tell a story about those things, about you.

Argentina-Bolivia, 1953

My Book

THE DISCOVERY OF LATIN AMERICA

Notes on Gandhi's Importance for the Latin American Revolution:

To the colonial intellectual—before Gandhi—revolution had meant aping Imperialist talk, Imperial culture, Imperial attitudes, even the Imperialists' contempt for oneself, his contempt for "natives." One wanted to be <u>modern</u>. Gandhi said No to this, Gandhi lived No. Western civilization, Western industry, Western Imperialism, Western science—that is the real savagery!

Gandhi showed us the way for Latin America, as for India. Gandhi drove the intellectuals into the villages. A spindly-legged little man in a white home-spun loincloth, he sat by a wooden hand loom, spinning out cotton, spinning the world "backward," away from the West, away from History. Let our ways replace imperialist machinery, imperialist wage slavery. Hand weaving: a symbol of the people's unity, a source of quiet meditation, sustenance, independence. Through that meditation we can learn stillness, learn to renounce our lust for violence, renounce the degrading lusts of our bodies.

—That was a piece of my notes on Gandhi and the Latin American Revolution (as I then imagined it!), a piece of the book I began on leaving Argentina, on the train to Bolivia. (Alvarados and I were on our way back to the leprosarium in San Pablo, Venezuela.) The "book" remained urgent homiletic notes—notes revised, notes added to with feverish exultation, notes re-written, but always only notes, the preparation for a project not quite ever begun, a sermon never quite preached (except to Fernando, my congregation of one). The book was to be, I imagined, a tour de force; a political tract, a travel journal that was also the discovery of a self—in the existential sense. Whatever that meant. (I thought it meant "an active emptiness," or "a continual venturing." And I thought that meant . . .) I didn't know what the book would be exactly. (I didn't know exactly what a self was "in the existential sense.") I thought that once it began it would all work itself out. (I thought the same about the self.) So I rewrote my notes, expecting from the writing a clue as to what to write next; and when it didn't come, I made more notes. My script shook as the train from Buenos Aires swayed from side to side on its worn tracks; the notebook bounced against my knees and splotched "lust." I crossed out the spotted paragraphs (I would recopy them soon in almost identical words) and looked about for the paper bag filled with oranges. It was next to Alvarados, on the outside of our wooden bench. Alvarados, tired, had given up reading an article on allergies and, like a bird folding its wings across its eyes for the night, had put the back of his left arm against his right ear. He shifted slightly in his sleep as my shirt sleeve brushed the bottom of his nose.

My mother had given me the notebook I wrote in, late my last night at home, when I had told her of my plans for a book. My father, in anger and disappointment (so cunningly mixed together that I could not reply to his fury with the force of my own), had gone off to bed. "I tire so easily lately," he said to my mother, who must surely have known. It was for me to overhear, for I could no longer be spoken to. He would not even look at me. I was a dead man for him; or I was his executioner; anyway someone had died. Watching him my body grew rigid.

He stooped over as he walked, his hands pressed into the pockets of his jacket, and he pushed out the white swinging door from the kitchen with his shoulder, as if he were too fatigued to lift his hands up before him. A shameless charade, I thought bitterly. I wanted to rise and hug him to me. I could not. My body was stiff, held in an arc of love and rebellion; if I were to reach out to him he would bend my gesture against me, misinterpret it, make me cry. I made myself hard. I was a knife, I thought grandly, as if it were all so basic to me, this problem, so deep in my soul, that it was beyond choice; not a family quarrel but a damnation.

"He'll get over it," I said. My voice sounded harsh, angry. The tone surprised me. I had meant it (I thought) as a gentle prayer.

"Are you sure you want him to?"

Her voice was calm, almost clinical. But it was a severe remark. Stupid amateur psychoanalysis, I wanted to say, but didn't. She had hurt me. I sat sunk in my chair, not speaking. After a while I told her of my idea for a book, my existential travelogue. "I'll make something of myself."

"A book? You mean you'll make a story out of yourself?" But she was smiling again.

"Yes. And I'll dedicate the book of myself to you and Father." She closed her eyes, putting her hands out on the glass table, palms downward. She was silent. I thought she found my offering—a dedication—a paltry thing compared with the pain I'd caused my father. But I was glad to have the chance to stare at her face, to look without being seen. Her face fascinated me, and I have never looked my fill. It was thin; and old; and lovely; and ruined; a relief map. I felt protective towards her, and tender, though there was nothing I could protect her against. Perhaps, if we had been a different sort of family, I would have touched her cheek then, run my finger in one of the hollows of her face. I wanted to, but I didn't.

"Yes," she intoned, from her long silence. Her voice was low, and, I thought, intentionally "mysterious." Her eyes remained closed. "I can see it. You will have many different adventures in many different climates. And you will be like me, cynical, and too trusting."

I laughed nervously at her theatrical self-description, her fortunetelling act, her peekaboo around the edges. The performance was unsettling, a low voice, hers and not hers, coming from that impassive old face with its large closed eyelids. And it was uncanny most of all, I think, because her hands were (as they never were) still, her long fingers not tapping on the table before her. (A song called "I'm More Alive Than This Place Will Bear!") "You need an earring," I said. "For one ear. Fortunes told."

She opened her eyes, reanimated her face and hands. "No, I'm sorry for joking, darling. I really mean it. I could feel it. It was like a strong wave buoying me up, buoying you up, because I felt *I was you.* Some rich fate awaits you, Tete. I'm more sure of it than ever." She rose from her chair suddenly and clapped her hands together. "It's a wonderful idea. You should write a book. You will do what I have all these years only made notes for, only dreamed of doing." For she too, she often said, when I saw her jotting something into one of her notebooks, was writing a book. It was to be called (self-mockingly, of course) *The Complete History of the World in Its Many Disguises.* (I think she did have some historical work planned, a scathing of all the criminals, pimps, whores, charlatans, and clowns of our country, our continent, our world. That is: everybody, everywhere.) An interesting reversal this evening, I thought placidly. (Her buoyancy made me calm, as if I, too, were contemplating my rich fate from afar.) I have disappointed my father, I thought, but I will complete my mother's destiny ("I felt *I was you*"), fulfill her desire. (The calm lasted only a few hours. Then, again, my adolescent mood returned; I felt myself as separate as a knife.)

From a pile of papers on the table she extracted one of her black notebooks, one that didn't have any newspaper clippings sticking out from between its pages. She leaned over as if looking in a mirror, and in spidery script inscribed a sentence on the title page: "Life is not a walk across an open field." A cigarette clasped between her lips, her eyes sparkling, she gave me the notebook with both hands. A presentation volume.

A little puzzle solved: what I had spied at age eleven was the motto that began all her notebooks. What dangers, I wondered, did my mother fear? What reassurance had she taken from this bitter reminder of . . . of what? unfortunate accidents? (not me, I hoped) cunning pitfalls? malevolent enemies? (my father? myself?) Of all beings, I thought, she is the most mysterious to me. But I didn't ask what the sentence meant to her. I wanted to, but I didn't.

I left the notebook with Hilda in Mexico, "by accident"; and she, by accident, left it behind when she went to my parents' house to wait for word from (or of) me. But someone in the boardinghouse (the police, perhaps) found it and sent it on to Argentina (it was my parents' address I had written underneath my mother's emblem on the flyleaf). Hilda brought it with her to Cuba, and handed it to me on the day I told her our marriage was over (a presentation volume). Bad penny, I've given up on losing it, have kept it with me since. I thought, I suppose, that I had left a necessary message in it for myself, that some quality that would make me whole would come back to me through its words. So every so often I would look into it. And shut it again quickly after reading a few pages, overcome by embarrassment. Until this morning. For then, as I looked over the entries, pages rippled from waterlogging, ink blurred, I felt myself hovering fondly, protectively, helplessly over the young man who wrote them, speeding over the continent towards his "rich fate." (There is nothing I can protect him from. I am the fate that awaits him.) Brave lad, he does need someone's advice. He seems to have brought a traveling pulpit with him everywhere! even on a train!

The book mine was to be modeled on, and took its title from, the book I found my task in, was Nehru's *The Discovery of India*. It was there, in the year that ended with the struggle with my father—that insecure and tasteless victory—that I discovered Gandhi.

In Gandhi, in those days, I found truly radical words, an intransigent nationalism that would shear down to the core, that would die (that solemn word! I felt *he* knew its meaning) rather than compromise. Gandhi's vision was far more radical than the old "nationalist" leaders and their jejune accommodations with imperialism—as if the point of revolution were not to change us deeply, but only to turn us more rapidly into North Americans, allow greater scope for our greed. And Gandhi's broken speech was poetry compared to the desiccated slogans of the left, the remnants of the Communist parties, whose messages, distributed clandestinely or in weak radio broadcasts, intoned always that no action was possible, not yet, not here, now, where you stood.

But most of all Gandhi was chasteness, simplicity, a relief from personality; he was the spiritual value of solitude (an isolation I must not allow myself to bridge; my feelings would betray me, would make me a child again, running for his approval until I could run no more, till nausea overtook me). Gandhi was *restraint.* Violence, my father had taught me, was for the weak ones, the ones without character. Outside of Fernando's cell, demanding a gun, I had forgotten that. But Gandhi's nonviolence was not the passivity I feared there; it was a constant task. I could define myself continually by all I would not do. And not doing, if the temptation were strong enough, would let me feel my will as well as doing would.

For *my* anger, I thought, was a terrifying power; fierce, punishing; I wanted to kill (at the very least). When I felt my fury my mind filled with images of indifferent young recruits firing into crowds, bodies bleeding onto stones, policemen feeding electric shocks into the mouths of prisoners, miners left to be slaughtered because of "ideological differences." The violence I had heard about or seen in my childhood issued always in defeat, in accommodation with imperialism, or in the nationalist charade of Peronism, empty spectacles of defiance to bewilder the masses. My father was right: anyone could make the human body suffer; it was work for stupid men. Though my fate would be, I thought, a rich one, on a public stage, it would not be to add to that pain. And Gandhi justified this self-dramatization. To be angry was evil; the angry man was no better than the imperialist; to conquer anger made one a noble individual. My continent required such individuals. My personal struggle against my inward violence was of *historical* importance. Anger sublimated, my catechism went, can conquer the world.

I poked Alvarados in the ribs to wake him. I wanted to read my paragraphs to him. Over the last months I had spoken to him ceaselessly of Gandhi; he had become my first convert. As I went deeper into the matter (or said the same thing in different words), I needed to try out my ideas on him, nourish myself from the quality of his attention. During our talks he held his body still, curved almost meditatively, as if his spirit were turned wholly towards my communication. Only his face moved, displaying (or miming) the passage of thought as I spoke, a continuous response—drawing his brows together, or pushing his cheek out with his tongue—a muscular process of understanding that marked its authenticity for me. (And perhaps that was his kind intention.)

Fernando inclined his head towards me.

"I want to read you my new opening paragraphs."

He smiled sweetly, if a little blankly, and I began.

He held up his hands to stop me.

"Bored already?"

"No. Wait. I can't hear you." He turned in his seat, so that he nearly faced me, his right ear very close to my mouth. I had forgotten: he was deaf on his left side from a beating the police had given him in jail. But there was, I thought, no bitterness in him about it. He had had no Gandhian philosophy that explained to him why he shouldn't be resentful. There was nothing cloyingly brave in his smile now as he waited for me to begin. He just wasn't bitter. Jail had made him more serious—he no longer told the plots of movies with parts misplaced; he no longer told them at all. And his face had grown thinner, almost fragile-looking since his time in jail. He had a long sharp nose, and the planes of his cheeks formed a broad triangle, the tip of it his chin. The bones stood out sharply, defining the sides of a theorem.

I read him my paragraphs.

"I don't really understand that, Ernesto." He looked puzzled, squinting his eyes, biting his lower lip. He made it a point of honor to find clear, easily readable gestures for his feelings. A complicated, decent person, he wanted to be *plain*. But his effort showed in the constant gestures, and so betrayed the difficulties in himself that he disliked, the complexities he wanted to overcome. (They leaked out anyway, in *wit*.)

Fernando twisted his lips into a quizzical half-smile. " 'The degrading lusts of our bodies?' "

"Yes," I said. "Yes. Until we can speak to each other clearly, with real respect, not using each other as instruments, until then we must abstain. And we can sharpen our will by practicing restraint of our bodies." My voice sounded too insistent. I could not truly explain to Fernando what I felt. When I thought of making love there was a ghostly urinous taste in my mouth. I felt covered in dirty sweat. Only denying myself, feeling my will, cleansed me, allowed me to feel myself as bright, pure, sharp. But I couldn't say that, not even to Alberto.

Fernando looked at me steadily, brought his brows together to indicate "considering." But he said nothing. I had to speak again. He had to assent to my willfulness, confirm me in it.

The task for Latin America (I read) *is the making of its soul. Each of us must learn to conquer his appetites. He must, by the continual exercise of his will, free himself from lust. The independent soul is made by cutting into the body, by making it a servant of the will. We have to turn the energy of our lust and anger against ourselves, against our own bodies. One must bring the body under control.* (I felt as if carried away by my speech, my prayer, my curse. A strong alien force lived in my words, a rough harsh wind that took the world away. Good; peace for myself could only come from this long strenuous denial.) *The body is evil. To be free individuals, self-governing nations, we must first govern our appetites. The body turns us into slaves of the Imperialists. We fear for it, or we want something for it. The body is worse than hell!*

I felt the exhilaration of the clenched fist.

When the train returned I saw that Fernando had turned his face from me. He looked at the seat in front. He had turned a deaf ear to me! I reached out, took his head between my hands, and turned him again until he faced me. His lips puckered sourly. "I couldn't bear it." He stopped, cast into himself. "You sounded like one of the nuns. I loathed the nuns."

He wasn't bitter at the police, who had broken his eardrum, but at the nuns! What could they have done to him, those equivocal enemies? He doubted me, but I had his good ear again.

Is Gandhi mad? I can hear my mother's voice: Hand looms! Spinning the world backward, indeed! And no penicillin, I suppose? No epinephrine for your asthma! But perhaps I must accept that, Mother, perhaps I need that pain to humble my body, to make it the servant of my will. Perhaps I need that suffering to make my soul strong. Perhaps that is the price of real revolution, real inner freedom. I must bear my suffering gladly. What nonsense this must sound to you! But perhaps it is from an overdose of your very modern cynicism that I seek a purge from this religious man.

The truth is in the villages. The villagers, once they have conquered their bodies, can live in voluntary simplicity. Latin American countrypeople don't need manufactured goods. They don't need North American barbarism, North American industry. Latin America can regain the socialism of the Incas. Each Andean village was an organ whose veins were the Inca roads. The villages formed a single human body, incarnated and imaged in the Inca. The Latin American Revolution does not require violence, only noncooperation with the Imperialists, with their panderings to our lusts. With noncooperation the Imperialists will evaporate like specters.

"Yes!" Fernando said, once again my ally, once again in enthusiastic agreement. He took a bite of an orange, avidly. "Not violence! Not *their* politics! Something else! These last few months, in our talks about Gandhi, I feel that I'm seeing things for the first time. A way for each individual to regain his dignity. Simple work done a little at a time. Helping people in the villages rediscover the value of their crafts, teaching them hygiene. Not politics, not speeches, not theories!" Fernando squeezed the orange in his excitement; juice squirted over his hand. Was that what I meant? Simple work done a little at a time? Fernando's agreement, my favorite drug, confused me. I found I wasn't sure. Still, I was happy with his approval; his delight was my food.

I went on reading. Fernando licked his hand clean.

Where is he, our Gandhi? (My voice gained confidence and volume from Fernando's vigorous nodding. Passengers turned to look at us. "Pianissimo," Fernando said, pressing the air down with his palms. "We're still in Argentina.") *Where are our leaders who might say no with the force of their souls? Where is our leader who does not grow gross on their bribes?*

"That crap!" Fernando said. He spat the words out, as if they had a foul taste. Naturally fastidious, Fernando rarely cursed.

Still my demons forced me to correct him. "Don't say 'crap.' " (If only I could enter these pages, restrain that dour young man!) "Shit—feces, I mean —isn't bad or good. It's part of life. It's false idealism that makes us think we're too sublime for shit. So if we feel disillusioned or angry, we say that life is shit. But shit, I mean feces, isn't bad. It's useful. For fertilizer." I was not, even then, so far gone that I didn't feel an ass as I finished. But I was so afraid of irony, its corrosive joy, its bitter exhilaration, that I embraced instead the secure fat berth of pomposity.

Fernando said nothing. He was surprised at my lecture (as was I. Who did I think I was? Gandhi?); he was miffed at my rebuke.

There's nothing sycophantic about Nehru's love for Gandhi. I could see Fernando was angry. (The better part of me even sympathized. After one of my little fits I often felt as disconnected from it as any observer might. I wondered why my friend didn't hit me.) Fernando clenched his jaws. The muscles bulged the tight skin of his cheeks. (I.e. "Restrained Fury.") But I went on. He must hear and respond to all of it. (Respond, I'm afraid, meant agree.) *Gandhi didn't subsume or subordinate Nehru. Gandhi made him, made India, more courageous, more itself. Nehru's love for Gandhi ennobles them both.*

Where is he, our Gandhi?

"I've never understood that part, either, Ernesto." Fernando scratched his head. (I.e. "Puzzlement.") Wanting to be plain meant that his gestures often tended towards cliche. "Why do we need a leader?" Fernando asked. "We know what needs to be done. We must make ourselves strong individuals."

Was that right? Over the weeks Fernando had joined my conversion to Gandhi (minus some austerities that horrified him). But now, reading my thoughts to him again, watching his enthusiasm, I felt for the first time no longer sure within myself. His excitement for work done a little at a time was distant from me. Whatever he had heard me say, I felt still that my rich fate was larger than that unassuming goodness so natural to Fernando. There was something in me that craved a larger stage, and Gandhi was a way for me to find that role. I thought that the violence I felt, my unsteadying rage at imperialism, at all that thwarted our lives, would, if properly used, turned inward, do more than form my soul. It would astound others. Nonviolence was a piece of magic meant to conjure up an audience. It would make me worthy of being chosen by one who knew what direction our further actions should take, one who could unite all who could be united against the North Americans. Gandhi's principles were a gaudy costume, all the more flamboyant in that they were a costume of homespun, of poverty. His way was a vivid speech I could give to make myself noticed, a speech to show my integrity to that unknown leader I longed for. There was that in me which wanted more from our travels than to help the lepers, more even than the formation of my soul. I wanted to know the name of the leader in whose cause I might find my work. The book that I wanted to write, the story I wanted to make of myself, was the story of that work, of my startling career.

A few moments ago I had been buoyed up by Fernando's eager approval, the vigorous nodding of his head. But now my divided and secret intentions made me uneasy before him, daunted not by disapproval, but by agreement.

"We don't need leaders," Fernando repeated emphatically. "We know what needs to be done. We're on our way to begin it."

I tried to rest myself in his certainty.

Bolivia, 1953

The Country of Exiles

Where are our leaders who might say no with the force of their souls?

I was not the only person of my generation troubled by such questions; and I would soon meet, in the country of exiles, many others willing to speak such grand big things aloud. A national movement had triumphed in Bolivia. The exiles, from Argentina, Peru, Venezuela, came to La Paz; perhaps in the improvisations of this revolution there would be a clue, a task, a map of return. Some, like myself, were exiles by choice; others, the aristocrats of the community, had been forbidden their homes by a dictator's edict. Democratically, we moved together through the pilgrims' makeshift way stations—from cafe tables where we asserted hypothetical militancies, to the houses of wealthy sympathizers, to discussions in crowded ministry offices, to sleep at last (tired from so much articulation) on the hard floors of rooms with no furniture (a nail in the plaster held up a stained leather bag filled with all one's caked underwear and sour shirts). We waited; waited for the plausible leader to declare himself; waited for the situation at home to decay; waited for a course of action we could believe in; waited and talked. *One must talk:* one's hope, one's politics, one's homeland, was alive now only in one's mouth, and not to talk of it, its melancholy past, its unhappy current state, its sublime future, was criminal, was to let it die and find oneself wandering in exile forever. (No, not even in exile, which is division, but without even the possibility of a place; not quite here, and without a *there* anymore.) Talk was the work of exile (talk was the thread through the maze; it could become the maze itself); no other career should be pursued; one's future was home; one must wait vigilantly—and vigilance was talk—for the hour of return. The Country of Exiles, that land whose science is remembrance, was wider than my parents' kitchen, but like it, for the world's epic, the inhabitants insisted, must be apprehended in political terms, and politics was, for the moment, for most of them, mostly talk. "They had fallen with a prince's fall; they might rise with a new prince's ascent; no wonder," my mother might say, "that court gossip was their life." (She would ignore in her attack how much her own home was *her* place of exile.)

But sometimes, Mother, it was better than gossip. A year before in Bolivia, on April 9, something had happened worth talking about. The tin miners of Oruro and the Indians who lived near the mines had joined together against the conscript army of the feudal order, the army paid for by the landowners, the mine companies, and the imperialists. The miners had the dynamite they used in blasting, the peasants had old-fashioned rifles that their fathers had seized in a failed insurrection thirty years before and hidden away for the time of rising. The feudal army had new North American weapons, had machine guns; it was certain of victory.

On the same day, in La Paz, a force of workers led by the Movement for a National Liberation and joined by rebellious police units attacked the army barracks and the Presidential Palace. Government troops stationed at the military academy fought back. The battle was joined in the center of the city, in the market square of La Paz. *But the nation had discovered its unity* (I wrote in my notebook, with a copy for the Guevara household).*The MNR had found symbols of national regeneration, an Indo-American ideology. It was this unity, not force of arms, that defeated the army. Each conscript, too, was part of the nation; that spark turned against him, shamed him. The market women of La Paz walked out into the square during the battle, and took the guns from the bewildered recruits' hands.* (Cc. Fernando Alvarados & the Guevaras.) The army retreated, leaving its dead in the streets. Cadets from the police academy dismantled the army's gun batteries on the rim of the plateau overlooking La Paz. *The workers had marched beneath guns meant to terrify them into submission, turn them to stone. The revolution became possible not when they were willing to kill, but when they were willing to die.* (Cc. Nehru, J. P. Sartre, S. de Beauvoir, and my father.) The miners and Indians from Oruro, victorious also, entered the city. Paz Estenssoro, head of the MNR, became President of Bolivia.

An Indian people (they bear all, the average wisdom had muttered; they are mute, the cry forever frozen in their bodies) had risen up; an ice age had ended in one Holy Week, drowning out the chatter of the average wisdom in a torrent of new excited voices. The Revolution, a voice released from trees and stones, was freedom to talk, possibility and occasion to speculate. How should the state be built? The new government nationalized the mines and began a land reform. Should the former mine owners be compensated? How large did a landlord's holdings have to be before his land became national property? Or should each family have only enough land to feed itself, as the Incas had decreed? (It was Gandhi's favorite question: How much land does a man need? With it, he would sound the depths of the universe. It was such a simple question! How could he be denied?) Should the landlords be paid for their seized plantations? Or was their property no more than theft from the nation? Should the peasant militias be disarmed? Should the military academy be reopened, and the army reorganized under the new middle-class officers? And I, too, had questions to ask in these interchanges: What is my role? What is my real name? Questions too impolite, too urgent, to ask directly. One spoke them by hints, enacted them in the imperious way one asked some other, more innocent, question.

Fernando and I walked the hot dry streets of La Paz (each breath at this altitude was hard work for low wages) reading the wall posters, surrounded by Indian families. (A man ran his fingertips over the print, forcing bits of stone through the thin newsprint, a hidden text.) I rejoiced; I hopped from foot to painful foot, wheezing with excitement. When I looked up at the mountains where the gun emplacements had looked down on the marchers, I felt as if I'd swallowed a strong warming drink. A test had taken place here that I longed for. When I imagined those battles I felt my hand could exalt itself to stroke the moon. I wanted (but how, in what words?) to declare myself to this man with his striped bundle across his shoulders, his eyes narrowed in thought. For it was in a movement like this that Gandhi had found his place, spoken his saving words. The MNR was bound to hear those words, for they were more than one man's thoughts; they were the common substratum that dissolved all class differences, the land itself showing through. In the unconscious that is Indian custom, there is a continual memory of the socialism of the Incas. Land then had been allotted according to need. The community worked the land of the old, the sick, of those drafted for the magnificent building projects of the Inca, aqueducts to bring water four hundred miles to desert regions, roads, across the Andes. Surplus crops from a fortunate village were distributed under the Inca's direction to those areas that had suffered drought, the gods' displeasure. Fleece from the llamas and alpacas went to the Inca's storehouses, to be distributed equally to the women's looms. From each according to his ability, to each according to his need. Paz Estenssoro would recognize—the Indians would force that recognition—that the peasants should not be made to work for wages and buy manufactured goods, that the farce of Western history, of money economies, of industrialization should be refused. The truth of the Andes was not in manufactured goods and the degraded life of the cities, but in agriculture, in the self-sufficient life of the peasantry, the villages, bound into one nation by land and custom, as once they had been each a word in the Inca's mouth.

"Pretty posters," Fernando said, smiling.

The MNR posters stated the positions of a generation of Latin American nationalists, of all those parties who searched for an Indo-American solution free of European or North American ideas. The MNR was the national movement of unity among classes against the feudal order. (It was *not* that Marxism which Gandhi called diabolic, which preached division, as if a nation's classes were not parts of the same family.)

This was the democratic Left, parties like Accion Democratica in Venezuela, the APRA of Peru; and I had thought (for my wisdom was average) that they were without a chance of success; and I was wrong. In the Bolivian Revolution, and in the democratic left, I was certain that I would find the leadership that would begin the struggle against imperialism, that would invent the next, the necessary step to make Latin America independent. I felt that I would find here the cause I could join myself to. For Bolivia was the first of a series of national revolutions bound to triumph; it was a small theater for a large audience (a place to find out what lines I might have it in me to speak). The debates of this revolution were in everyone's mouth; they were common bread, the food of nationhood; criticism let one chew the spirit of rebellion, assimilate it to one's own body. These were words I wanted to hear, conversations I wanted to enter. Bolivia, to me, was glorious talk.

Comrades

Mornings, Fernando and I walked near the Camacho market, listening to the town, buying fruit from the market women for our lunch. Early afternoons, we went to the cafes of the 16 de Julio Avenue, bought the newspapers that had bloomed in the heat of the Revolution (*Intransigencia*—from the Trotskyite Peasant Union; *El Ferroviario*—the railroad workers' paper; *La Nacion*, the right-wing *Ultimo Horo*, and *El Diario;* the psychotic smudged mimeographed sheets of the outlawed Falange). The papers and the cafes resonated almost to shattering with rumors of war. The Trotskyites threatened revolutionary violence against the enemies of the Revolution. The Falange cursed (and killed) those "agents of international conspiracies who betrayed the sacred soil of the Bolivian nation." There were rumors that opponents of Paz Estenssoro had been taken to empty fields and shot, that the CIA (perhaps in collaboration with Paz Estenssoro himself, perhaps with the Falange) had sent its murderers to La Paz. Prominent leftist leaders, and obscure militants, had been found dead in the back of La Paz's pathetic Model T taxis (one way of getting a taxi, the saying went). There was talk of cars without license plates paying calls at night, of men in long black jackets. The Archbishop of Bolivia advised parishioners to store food—for the crisis would surely deteriorate into armed struggle. Civil war was days away—the final convulsion, and triumph, of the revolution. This constant staccato talk of violence (all that I disapproved of, which fragmented the nation like the body of an anxious man) gave a solemnity and consequence to one's words. It was dangerous in La Paz if the wrong parties overheard you. It was fatal to speak the wrong opinions in certain places. Bolivian talk, like the words the priest spoke over the wafers, had mortal consequences, and just to speak (and I didn't yet know what else to do) was an *act*.

Throughout the day, wherever you were in the city, you heard the sound of automatic weapons. Probably an Indian emptying his clip into a wall somewhere. Probably no one was standing in front of the wall.

Fernando and I were joined at the cafe by our new friends, "Chaco" Francisco, the child, like Fernando, of Spanish refugees, a countryman of ours (and so twice exiled); and Ricardo Gadea, a heavyset Peruvian, an activist of APRA.

We spread the papers out on the round white cafe tables, discussed the announcements of the Ministry of Peasant Affairs (the most progressive wing of the MNR), the week's rate of inflation, the food shortages in the capital and their effect on the national will, the blank demand of Milton Eisenhower on behalf of the U.S. "aid" mission: the former mine owners must receive more money or U.S. aid, food, and technology would be "terminated."

The MNR, Ricardo said, would never allow this interference in its national sovereignty. He spoke solemnly, as if reading from stone tablets. Ricardo's words were heavy; you could walk around them and they would show the same from any side. "The people," Ricardo said, "would rather accept any sacrifice than be dictated to by North Americans."

Chaco laughed and pounded his feet up and down like an excited child. But who, or what, was he laughing at? The masses? Ricardo's faith? The United States? One never knew with Chaco. A second-year medical student, he would (he swore) never return to school. "Doctors," he told me, "are all Mr. Me's. Bloated 'I's in green leotards with big fat bellies. They'd be just as happy inflicting pain as curing it, if they could see the patient jump." Chaco had no positive idea of what he should do. So he spoke his search in irony and skewed whimsy. The world of our fathers, his words said, is a facade, a joke. He wanted to slander it, to push it down, to trample it. But, his tone said, wait, there'll be nothing behind it! Good! his gestures snickered, he longed for that emptiness. And feared it.

We were versions of each other, Chaco and I: a generation that had lost faith in its fathers' world. And I admired Chaco's intelligence. He had a deep feeling, an almost connoisseur's admiration, for the convoluted duplicities of this world. His every paragraph was an atonal concerto of conflicting voices. But he also got on my nerves. For the MNR had won. Impossible event! Another world had become possible, a world besides our fathers'. Chaco must make his voice single, surrender his self-lacerating irony, find other work than crafting complicated riddles with no answers.

Two Indian men carrying automatic rifles with long clips walked by on the avenue, in front of our table. They didn't speak, and moved with determination, as if under orders. The style of their rifles said that they had taken part in the battles near Oruro, had seized their weapons from dead soldiers. (The country surrounds the city. The Indians had come into their city.)

Chaco shuddered, a long uncontrollable tremor, like a fever.

We stared at him.

"I can't help it." He put his head down towards the table, and glanced up at us, looking for sympathy. "They terrify me, those Indians with their guns. I can't tell what they're thinking. They're like a bad dream. Someone holds up a potato in your face, and you know that if you say the word 'potato' you'll die, and you know you're going to say it. I feel like they might not like the way I hold my coffee cup, and just turn and shoot me."

There had been stories of such things. Men dragged out of bars by groups of Indian militiamen, their bodies found half burned. Why burned? Why them? No one could say why they had been taken, what law violated. Perhaps it was just the way they looked? What way? Who understands the darkness of the Indian's thoughts, corridors of shadows you might be lost in, to emerge transformed, unrecognizable to yourself. (Half burned.) It didn't bear too much thinking. (Is this what it meant for an Indian people to take possession of their city?)

But there were all kinds of stories.

The Battle of the Hotel Austria Bar

In the late afternoon we left our cafe for the bar of the Hotel Austria, a fancy place with a good view of the Plaza Murillo and the Presidential Palace. This week the government would give out certificates for land to any citizen who would devote his life to farming. Thousands of Indians walked around us as we made our way across the plaza. They lived in the streets, waiting for the processing of applicants to begin, built their charcoal fires on the conquistadors' stones, unrolled their blankets at night, and slept, village by village, in different areas of the hard wide place, a tribal quilt, a quilt of tribes. Each village even kept its separate feast days.

Around the high stone column in the center of the square, women sat in long wide skirts, piled one over another, red over blue, fold following fold. Heaped on blankets in front of them, like tiny ruins, were piles of cooking charcoal, coca leaves, little brown metal tins.

A woman with a round face grabbed my hand and pulled me backward. She wore a gray felt stovepipe sort of hat with an embroidered band around the crown.

"You have trouble breathing," she said. Her lower lip was mottled, partly eaten away. She rose from her blanket, still holding my hand. Her hand was dry.

How could she have known of my difficulty? It had begun just that moment, as I passed her blanket, the smoke from the cooking fires choking me.

She held her right hand towards me. In the lined palm there was a small round tin, stamped with the comical-looking profile of a wigged man. It held my attention as a hypnotist's object might (but my trance had begun the moment she had named me).

I opened my shirt, immediately, in the middle of the plaza. A few Indians smiled at me. The salve slid across my chest, a useless temporary warmth; I still couldn't breathe; I was still myself. My chest hairs stuck together in little clumps, like the beards of mussels. I looked up towards the sun.

"This doesn't work," I said. "It's just some manufactured garbage, mentholated vaseline."

She turned away from me when I spoke.

I touched her shoulder; I wanted to turn her towards my instruction.

The Indians near us, the other women by their blankets, grew suddenly still, a forest after a shot has been fired. My hand rested on the rough wool of her black poncho. I couldn't move, pinned there by their eyes. It seemed as if a thousand people hushed. An anger beyond noise.

"Damn you," Chaco said, "get your hand off her! They're going to kill us!" His body shook again.

She turned her face towards me. "You don't know who I am."

I stepped backward, stumbling over Alvarados.

We retreated into the doorway of the bar. "Why did she say that?" I asked Ricardo. Her words had undone me. I felt faint from that condemnation.

"Say what?" he said. "It was Quechua, wasn't it? I don't speak Quechua." He looked towards Fernando.

"Me neither." Fernando looked worried about me.

"But she spoke Spanish. She told me I have trouble breathing."

"No," Ricardo said. "She spoke Quechua."

There was no curse. There was no magic naming. It all never happened. I stood in the doorway, feeling my relief and my loss; my eyes adjusted to the darkness. This bar was a fancy place. Bow windows overlooked the square, but the topmost panes were frosted; the harsh light of the afternoon became something creamier, gentler. Red plush banquettes ran along the sides of the room. The bourgeois of the city, Austrian engineers (waiting for the mines to be returned to those who knew how to run them), Bolivian construction company owners, North American aid officials, UN personnel, talked quietly, drank.

We took a table by the window, ordered. A waiter brought us three cold bottles of beer on a round wooden tray, with a dish towel across it. "Nothing for you, sir?" the waiter asked me again.

"A glass of water."

"Water?" the waiter said, his face expressionless. He was a mestizo in a short red jacket.

"He wants to drink," Fernando said, "so he doesn't. He doesn't touch women, either. He wants to, so he doesn't. Get it?"

Chaco looked at me queerly, his thin lower lip pushed out. "He's one tough guy."

"Water," I said, smiling. I took pleasure in denying myself things, even mate; a small exaltation of willfulness. Fernando didn't yet understand the joy of austerities. My chastities repelled him also. He allowed himself ironies.

The waiter snapped the caps from the beer, and foam gushed from the bottles. He clasped the froth in his hand and wiped it on his towel.

We sipped our drinks and watched the plaza. An old man walked slowly about, trading furs from a deep pile on his shoulders; a forest creature prepared for an awful winter; a line drawing from a children's book, the young hero's half-human grandfather, teacher. I wanted to hug him to me. The city was filled with snares against him. His life could be turned to infertile garbage by paper money, by bright evenly woven textiles, by manufactured shoes that would, by an infamous irony, be the death of his gods. Every few steps the old man stumbled. Fernando saw others in the plaza jerk forward a bit too as they walked, like mechanical toys whose gears mesh unevenly. A small mystery. It didn't long engage my friends. They elaborated militant responses to Eisenhower's demands.

My friends ordered three more beers. Chaco took two mangoes from his pants pocket. Fernando had two limes in the breast pocket of his Eisenhower jacket. We sliced up the fruit for lunch, a sweet tart flavor that tasted to me of chastity and health. The waiter came back with the bottles. The price had gone up.

"Why?" Ricardo asked. He was a serious man; each indignity, no matter how often repeated, must be questioned.

The waiter shrugged his shoulders. "That is what prices do, gentlemen. They're like children. They grow up. You gentlemen can afford it?" He looked at me, my shirt still open, my chest hairs covered with a grease that had been totally lacking in magic. The waiter had a broad Indian face with dark brows. He stared openly, without embarrassment.

We didn't look as if we could afford it. Chaco's jacket and pants were all folds; he had slept in them for days. Fernando had peculiar shoes. Ricardo had dirty fingernails and gave off a rich acrid body odor. I wore wide brown pants, held up by a piece of rope, a stained nylon shirt, unmatched shoes, and a brown leather jacket, grime in its creases, strips of leather hanging from its sides. (An outfit emblematic of a vow.) The waiter's eyes narrowed. (Not the place to explain about my vow.)

"Of course we can afford it. And we can afford waiters to open it for us," Chaco said in a friendly way, as if his cruelty had been an accidental flick.

The waiter snapped the caps open. Chaco and Fernando both grabbed for the foam.

"Money will come to you," the waiter said amiably to Chaco.

"But probably, alas, in bolivianos." When Chaco talked he twisted his lips to one side, and squinched his eyes shut. One couldn't decipher the inflection this was meant to give his words. Perhaps that was the point. This constant face-making said: "This is a world of buffoons (I know, I am one); it is impossible to be serious. And yet it is too painful a world not to be serious. So make of my sentences what you like." Even at rest Chaco's puss was grotesque. His nose extended at least five centimeters into the air in front of him. His ears, too, were large, triangular. The frame of his face, supporting all this stuff, was narrow, with little chin. And his hair was very thin, wispy. (He was vain about it, though. Once, when he thought no one was looking, I saw him rub a tin of President's Cream into his hair, to make it seem thicker.) His forehead was wrinkled, like a nut. The whole ensemble was by turns funny, charming, and hideous; a gnome, an animal, a clown, a dwarf. What kind of creature was he? How should one take his words?

"Why does beer cost so much?" Ricardo asked, slowly. Was still asking. Repartee with waiters didn't interest him. Other thoughts didn't intervene when he held a question. He would worry the question slowly, slowly, until the bitter taste was gone.

"I will explain," Chaco said. " 'My first talk on the price of beer.' A drama for two players, called: 'Why Isn't There More Beer?' Or: 'The Boozer's Lament.'

"You ask" (he turned to Ricardo, and imitated him, talking slowly, in a deep voice)," 'Why isn't there more beer?'

"Chaco says"—and here he imitated himself, exaggerating his facial tics —" 'Because in a revolution everyone wants a drink, and because this is a national revolution, the government thinks everybody should have a drink. So they give everybody money so they can buy something to drink. There isn't more beer, only more money. So the price goes up.'

"So you say to Chaco"—and here he put his hands on the table, the way Ricardo would, and made his face motionless—" 'Chaco,' you say, 'why isn't there more beer?'

"And Chaco replies, 'Because there's more hard currency to be made smuggling it into Paraguay than selling it here. So the beer goes to Paraguay. It's the religious law of supply and demand. The law called, The devil eats where he can.'

"And you say—because you're a goodhearted serious man, the likes of which I've never seen before—you say, 'Chaco, you're confusing me. Why do they send the beer to Paraguay, if people want it here?'

"And I say, 'Ricardo, you goodhearted serious man, the likes of which I've never seen before, it's because Paraguay's currency is sounder.'

"And you say, 'Why isn't Bolivia's currency sound?'"

"And I say, 'Ricardo, you're making me dizzy. I told you, it's because prices keep going up.'"

"And of course you're not content with that, and you say, 'Why do prices keep going up?'"

"And Chaco says, wearily, 'I told you Ricardo, it's because the government loves the people and wants them to have a drink, so they can toast the health of the democratic revolution.'"

Ricardo, the real Ricardo, stared at him. Ricardo and the waiter looked alike; they both had broad faces. Ricardo's dark brows weren't drawn together in puzzlement. He sat, indifferent to Chaco's vaudeville. "Why does beer cost so much?" he asked. A placard for a slow march.

"I will explain," Chaco said. He stood up by our table, weaving. At this altitude two beers could make you tipsy. " 'MY SECOND TALK ON THE PRICE OF BEER.' "

"How did you know before that there would be a second talk?" Fernando asked.

Despite myself, I smiled; for the moment Chaco delighted me.

"What?"

"Before, you said that that was your first talk on the price of beer, as if you knew there'd be a second one."

"Oh. Well, this is an old story," he said. "And no one ever understands a talk on economics the first time. They let their minds wander. And then it's too late. This time be attentive. *You* especially." He leaned towards me admonishingly, bringing his tapir's nose close to my face. Prehensile thing; he should be able to pick up silverware with it.

"Now certain manufacturers," he said, "friends of the government, and their friends, and their friends' friends, are given a special right, called a 'cupo.' The cupo is magic. With it you can not only turn straw into gold, but shit into North American dollars. The holder of a cupo can exchange bolivianos for U.S. dollars at the rate of 190 bolivianos per dollar. The market rate, out in that square, is 13,000 per dollar. Get it? No? Well, follow me. I take a dollar out into that square, and I get 13,000 bolivianos. I take my bolivianos over to the national bank, and give them my name. They consult a ledger, and find I hold a cupo. Lucky me! They give me 68 U.S. dollars. I take my 68 dollars out into that square and get 884,000 bolivianos. I take my wheelbarrow of money over to the bank, they're not even surprised to see me—maybe I'll remember them come Christmastime—and they give me 4,652 dollars. Your eyes glaze, Guevara. But it's too late. It's already happened. The price of beer has gone up. You can check my figures. They're correct. I run through them at night on the floor to put myself to sleep. Now, why does the government give cupos? Are they crazy, like Chaco? No. It's to allow a subsidy from the government to promote national industry, so the manufacturers can buy the machinery they need inexpensively, from North America. National industry should develop. But it's more profitable just to manufacture inflation. And instead of machinery they buy luxury items, science-fiction cars, and television sets where there's no television station. If they do produce any beer or silk or bread they smuggle it into Paraguay, where they can get a good price in a sound currency. Your eyes glaze again, Mr. Guevara. I knew they would. But too late. The line for the few remaining food items forms at the right. It's already happened."

"That explains nothing," Ricardo said. He put his large fists on the table, like the character in Chaco's play, and spoke with consideration, judiciously, slowly.

"Yes," Fernando said. "That just explains *how* it happens. Not why. Not really."

"Why does beer cost so much?" Ricardo thought he would sound the depths of the universe if only he held to his simple question. How could he be denied?

"I don't know, Ricardo," Chaco said. He looked exhausted, and sat down. "Perhaps we speak the wrong language." He jerked his head at something behind him.

At a table nearer the center of the room four men in business suits were talking in English to each other. They were officers of the Department Bank, or the International Cooperation Administration. Or the Economic Commission for Latin America. Or the Export-Import Bank. Or the International Bank for Reconstruction. Or they were lawyers come to negotiate leases for the international oil companies. Or agents of the mines come to determine repayment schedules more acceptable to the former owners. Ricardo looked down. His silly question would be answered with per-capita production figures amortized over the life of, and renegotiation rates for, recapitalized loans. Or with indifferent silence. The bitter taste would just go on, no matter how long he chewed it. In Bolivia the price of beer goes up because the price of beer goes up.

I felt disgusted by Chaco's fooling, by North Americans, by the sophistical science of economics. I wanted to pull Ricardo's hair and force his head back up. Chaco was right: my eyes glazed. I hated this sort of thing. I hated Ricardo's cowed posture. I didn't want to understand Chaco's nonsense. Every way you walked imperialism tripped you up, hampered you. Chaco delighted in surreal twists: that if you wanted to develop the silk industry it caused lines to form outside the grocery each night, people waiting for the morning's opening, praying something might be left on the shelves. (A new national industry had developed: waiting in line at night for wealthier people.) Chaco liked that; it proved the mind's inadequacy to its tasks; he delighted in proving failure over and over. (What else could be done? his burlesque implied.) I despised it. The point of morality was not to revel in your own destruction, but to rise above the urinous snares of this world. I wanted to burn this world up with my indignation. "I'll tell you why beer is so expensive. It's not cupos. It's human greed. That's the root of the problem. That's what Chaco is really talking about. Greed. We have to change ourselves basically, radically, totally. We're greedy because our lives are empty, and we're afraid to die. We think if we get enough money we won't be empty, we won't die. Human greed is the problem. And people don't need beer. It's pois—"

Ricardo turned and stared at me. His frank gaze interrupted my thoughts. He put his fist down on the table. "I think you're right about greed. People are too greedy. They don't want to work. But I don't ever want to hear that shit again about beer. You don't like beer. Fine. Don't drink it. But I like it. So no more of that Gandhi shit." He put his glass to his mouth.

"Oh, no," Fernando cried, wincing theatrically, pursing his lips around a sour taste. "Oh, no. Please Ricardo, don't say 'shit.' Anything but that. I couldn't stand hearing about that again."

Ricardo and I laughed. Fernando had reconciled us, restored us to the world that the language of the men at the center table had garbled up.

"I think I would like another beer," Ricardo said; enormous spaces opened between each small word. He wiped his lips with the sleeve of his brown sports coat.

Fernando and I put some money on the table.

I turned towards the window and marched dizzily in the dry sun with the Indians. What did we care for cupos or lines in front of the city grocery stores? The world would be just again when we returned to our proper place, our villages. Our demand was simple: land to grow our food on. Hundreds of small processions walked back and forth, up and down the narrow colonial side streets, in military formations, scattered like colored ribbons on the hills about the center of town. Over their heads the balconies almost touched, the stone leaves of a feudal forest. Men waltzed gravely, in groups, machetes attached to their belts like ceremonial swords, tools home from a savage harvest. They held their hands together in front of their chests, and walked as if to measure. Women in bowler hats, and black ponchos striped with green and red bands, carried their babies trussed to their backs, and followed after the men, running thread as they walked, bobbins dangled and jumped at their feet, familiars kept in place by spells.

The Indians moved with profound, inexplicable deliberateness, like monkeys, children, growing trees. Ten or eleven sat in the square; suddenly they all rose and walked off together in a short parade, as if a single vein ran through them; they circled about the plaza once, then returned to their spot and, as if on signal, sat down. "I feel like there's a secret they all know," I said to Fernando. "It's a dance. Each one has a part. And I can't even hear the music."

"If it's a dance," Fernando said, smiling fondly, remembering my debacles in Buenos Aires night clubs, "you'll never get it. Even if you hear the music."

"Look at the way they move around," I said. It filled me with a deep excitement, as if there were a solemnity to it. "They're so curious. They've come into their mansion, some rich strange place they built but were always excluded from. They want to walk in all the rooms. They're serious about the furniture. They don't know what any of it is for. See? Look! That family, the little boy in a woolen hat walking between his parents, they go up and down the same street, stopping at every store window. Boxes that voices come from."

"Dead people's voices," Chaco said.

"Yellow coats on plaster figures?"

"Saints of *these* people," Chaco interpreted.

"They want to palpate the city, feel the stones against their bodies, taste it, see every inch of it." It gave me joy to imagine this. "They don't want to *live* in the house. They didn't think of building something like this in the first place. They don't want to buy that silly junk. They don't even know what money is. If they got some they'd only bury it under a rock. This is what ownership means to them. That they can look their fill."

"Idealist." Fernando laughed tenderly. "That's what *you* think. You don't know *them*. Those are *your* Indians. If I were one of them I'd like to have one of those yellow raincoats, to wear, for my own."

"No. Not them. They have it already, all they want of it, the sight of it. They bought that during Holy Week. The city is theirs now. They're marching through their domain, their inheritance, taking possession of it by walking in it, seeing it. Anyway, where would you wear a thing like a raincoat? Would you wear it to go planting?"

"I would if it were raining," Chaco said, nodding, his head turned to the side. "But I'll tell you what I'd really like if I were one of those Indians. I'd like a ballpoint pen! I really would."

"But you wouldn't know how to write," Fernando said.

"The MNR will teach them how to write." Ricardo made a covenant. APRA and the MNR shared the same promises. (I was sure then that he was right.)

Four men in loose-fitting white pants and colored belts walked by our window, carrying rifles. Their wives followed after, wearing leather bandilleras.

Chaco waved to the people near us, construction-company owners. (In a government office somewhere, a man drew red lines like welts all over a map, planning roads. Roads would cause the land to prosper.) The men looked out the window at Chaco's direction. The middle class of La Paz sat terrified of the Indian militias. They demanded the government disarm them, reorganize a regular army to protect them. (Who knows these Indians? They might suddenly, as if on signal—one that we couldn't hear, that we couldn't see— go berserk in the capital. A dummy in a store window might order them to kill us all.) Chaco smiled at the others, his fingers and thumb forming a gun pointed at their heads. One of the men frowned severely. Chaco scratched his thick earlobe with his gun barrel.

No, I thought, fear is not the way to produce national unity before imperialism, the common enemy. It is the readiness to die for what one believes that impresses others and would unite all classes of the nation. But Chaco's flapping earlobe made me smile.

Near our window two men in brown felt hats blew on long wooden Indian flutes, wide ones, tied round the top with blue thread. The song was a few high notes played over and over. A simple song, a children's song, even I could tap out its rhythm. A group of dancers stepped out to the center of the square in broad steps, six men in wide white pants and long red-and-yellow woolen caps that formed tasseled peaks. Around their waists and necks they wore woven squares of cloth thick with an intricate embroidery of smaller and smaller squares. The flaps of cloth overlapped one upon the other, like the tiles of a roof. These embroidered men formed a line. Three other men, taller ones, stood opposite. They wore black ponchos over white pants.

The man in the center of the embroidered men, the line of six, carried a light-red silk cloth. He walked to the tall men, and the other bright men followed, forming a "V." He stamped his feet before the taller men, as if in anger, hard, over and over, to the beat of the flutes. The tall men stared at him, and did nothing. The red man walked over to one of the other men and stamped his feet in anger. The man stared at him but did nothing. Over and over, he went back and forth between the three tall men, and stamped his feet. He looked behind him at the men in his group. One of these men went over to the tall ones, and stood with them, taking off his hat; and it seemed to me that he became taller too. Then another of his men went over. Finally there was a line of eight men, and the one man still wearing a round red cap stood alone, facing the man in the middle of the other line. He stamped his feet, first one, then the other, raising his knees high into the air, bringing his legs down, rocking back and forth, flinging the cloth up and whipping it down. When it came down, the flutes grew quiet, as if there were an ending. Or a separation. Then the flutes began again; played their short tune; and stopped as he brought his red cloth down. And began again. In the intervals of silence I lost myself, felt myself falling into the silence, like an unraveling, the letters that made up my name scattering all over the page. I didn't know who he was he means I am. There. In that place. The flutes began again, that breathy whistling, and reknit me note by note. One of the tall men turned his back to the single man. Then another. Then they all had their backs turned. The single man became more and more furious in his motions. There was nothing beautiful about it. It was far from beautiful. I thought he was in pain. He couldn't breathe. He flailed about in the thin air. The line of men formed a circle around him, with their backs to him. I could see him between their legs and bodies, he stamped his feet and leapt up, and his red hat looked like the tip of a flame. His body was wound round with the scarf, not artfully, but as if he'd become tangled in it. The circle dispersed, and there was no one in the middle. The music of the flutes went on. I loved the Bolivian Revolution. I wanted to dance my love. (I knew those steps! This ugly dance I'd done all my life!) I wanted to jump up and down and circle the table.

A North American scowled at me, his lips pursed in distaste. I stared back at him. I have come into my city! I have come to dance its possession!

Our eyes met. He must look away first. I would never harm him, but I would not look away; I would be recognized. And this man felt the same! A vivid current of hatred ran between us. I despised this man's face, middle-aged but still perfectly smooth, the face of congealed adolescence. He had been sent from Washington, to bring the Bolivian Revolution to heel! I loathed his thinning blond hair and small blue eyes, that he would not take from mine until I submitted to his look, to his possession of me. "You'll lose," I said quietly, in English. "It may take time, but we will win."

"Are you speaking to me, pal?" my enemy said, in Spanish. He even used the Argentine slang— "che." "It would be better for you, pal, if you didn't talk to me."

Anger must be sublimated! Nobility is self-rule! But I rose from the table without volition. A glass shattered. Fernando pulled hard on my sleeve, and I came back to myself, half out of my seat. My principles would not let me go forward. But I would not look away.

"Damn you Ernesto," Chaco said quietly. He tugged at my sleeve. "You're going to get us killed. These guys talk to the guys who do the bad things for these guys. Be still, child, please! I'm begging you!"

"I'm telling you, pal," my enemy said, "it would be better for you to sit back down. You don't know who I am. You don't know who you're talking to."

You don't know who I am. I laughed, puzzled and delighted by this repetition, as if, strolling in a foreign city, I'd found a favorite childhood toy of mine—discolored on the right paw by the glass of milk I'd spilled on it—displayed in a museum. My anger dissolved. I felt as if I were in someone's story. I felt chosen for instruction.

"What are you laughing at, you shithead?"

"You remind me of an old woman, a friend of mine."

He said something to his companions, without looking away. My jacket in tatters, my chest covered with grease—was I a madman?

Anger must be sublimated, I thought calmly. "Don't worry," I said. "I won't hurt you."

That enraged him. His face flushed. "Fucking goddamn right *you* won't hurt me, pal!"

An arm—I saw Chaco's long thin fingers—took me around the shoulder. "Ernesto dear," he said, "it was so good of you to come today." Chaco spoke English. "We're very glad to have your opinion. And we have so much to talk about with the minister. Let's walk over to the palace now." The North American, confused by this travesty, thought he'd misjudged me. Who knew in this crazy place, where a thousand Indians slept in the streets, what my role might be? He looked away. Chaco pulled me from the table, and Fernando took me under the arm. We walked out into the bright sun, the swirl of Indians, the pungent odor of cooking oil and spent rifle shells, the gaiety of inheritors.

"I know what you want to know," Chaco said. He patted me reassuringly on the back of my neck, to calm me, gentling the ponies. He was proud of himself. He thought he had saved our lives. Maybe he had.

My heart beat quickly, and my chest and throat hurt, heavy with blood, flushed with anger and some shame. I had risen from my chair to hurt that man; my anger had been a sun nearly blotting out my principles. I was still an undisciplined disciple. But mostly the whole thing seemed funny to me. Two big horned toads, sitting on the plush banquettes of the bar, puffing our chests with air and hissing.

"It's called Lucifer's Fall."

"What?" For a moment I thought that Chaco knew my fears about my discipleship.

"The dance. You're wondering what the dance meant."

But I wasn't. That movement had been, for me, sufficient in itself. I had moved in those bodies, I had stamped and leapt and suffered with that man's ugly shaking. I didn't wonder what it meant. *They were cutting off his air.*

"Lucifer and the band of former angels rise from hell to challenge the Trinity. And fail. And fall. Lucifer cast out. Get it?"

"Sure." I didn't want to hear more. "It's time for dinner."

"Yes. Oh, yes," Ricardo agreed. Hunger made him poetic.

"Yes," Fernando said.

I didn't want Chaco to talk. I wanted what I had seen. Or anyway, not his story.

An Open Field

Dinner was six miles away, at Isaias Nougues's house in Calacoto. There, two or three times a week, Nougues, an Argentine, served stew to the citizens of exile.

Isaias, leader and financier of a provincial Argentine party, a former member of our country's Parliament, had interests across several borders. I found his massive poem of woe, the contempt he suffered from Peron, a little hard to swallow (and a stanza had to be taken with dinner), for the cost of his opposition was paid down in gold from his sugar plantations, and there was still enough of that sweetness left to feed us all.

He was welcoming always to Fernando and myself, a friend of our families. (And this was the most nourishing food we had in La Paz.) "Your mother," he said to me, "has a sharp tongue, a great wit, and an immense heart. She tries to hide it, but she cannot. I think her cutting wit is meant to protect, to mask, her tender heart." Perhaps true—though Isaias spoke always only in compliment or complaint. Towards him, though, as phrases in her letters revealed—and we shamelessly used his house for mail—her heart was a lump of coal. She found him, as she did so much of her life, preposterous. "Isaias tells his beads, while his accountant keeps his books. Try please to eat him out of house and home."

The house was a light-pink stucco ranch, a long "L" with a pale red tile roof. Masses of shrubs with dark-red blooms surrounded it. We were rarely inside the house, except to use the bathroom; business was conducted in the fields. There were cultivated areas mixed with wildness, and artistry—according to Fernando—had gone into their counterpointing. (I didn't care about the setting. Landscapes were no clue—not yet.) I remember a large vegetable garden where burlap bags on tall sticks stood over the mounds of earth, and the green runners of potato plants. It made me uneasy to see the empty men flapping in the wind. (The bags, Isaias explained, had been coated with dried blood, to keep creatures away from the garden.) There was a small cornfield, with attendant ghouls, and long meadows, only partly mowed, with trees and large rocks in them. A river. I remember that. It ran between the house and the fields where we ate.

Fernando, Chaco, Ricardo, and I stepped carefully, single file, across the narrow footbridge, overlapping boards hammered together, with ropes for supports and railings. The bridge swayed. Chaco put one arm on my shoulder to steady himself. He closed his eyes, though we were only a few feet over the narrow river. Water terrified him.

Thirty others stood scattered in the field before us, waiting for dinner. Isaias had promised that Paz Estenssoro, leader of the MNR, would be in the field tonight. Helena, a nervous young exile from Peru, raised her arm in greeting to Ricardo, her fiance. Hunger, and the difficulty of breathing, made her form waver in front of me, as if she had several overlapping hands. The damp air from the river was thick on my skin. I pulled the matted wool collar of my jacket up around my neck, and eagerly pushed Ricardo forward into the land of shadows.

Paz Estenssoro's name had cut through my uneasiness and my deep dream of stew. I wanted to feel the force of his vision, the emanation of his leadership. I wanted to ask him my questions, and press his answers against Gandhi's words. I thought that Paz Estenssoro might be the leader in whose cause I might find my work.

"Damn," Chaco said, already afraid. "You be careful what you say Ernesto. Paz Estenssoro hates criticism. Do you understand me? Lots of hard guys do what he says."

The household staff came out from the side of the house, carrying saw-horses and boards across the bridge. They constructed a table by the river, near a new useless white washing machine.

The kitchen people came out from the side of the house, a processional of seven men, led by the cook carrying a bright tin ladle. Each of the staff held a black pot filled with stew.

"Blood for the ghosts," I said to Ricardo. "To make them talk."

"What?"

"Grub first," Chaco paraphrased. "Then talk."

"They're serving," Ricardo said, turning away with surprising speed before we finished speaking.

The food was dished up on tin plates. A good stew with thick pieces of beef, potatoes, and large chunks of corn on the cob, sweet, freshly picked. We ate with big wooden spoons, strolling about the grounds, absently, unconcerned with sad history, or each other, or their wandering intersection, at least until we'd had our dinner.

History, though, went on without us, and as the light waned (it didn't so much wane as become bit by bit opaque, as if we watched flakes of mica overlap) you could hear shooting from the city, and the roads around it, short high staccato bursts, echoing faintly from the mountains around us, like pebbles in a padded bucket. Each day this week had brought new violence. The smudged mimeographed sheets of the Falange had grown shrill with threats. "The Army and the Falange fight for the redemption of Bolivia's Martyrs. We will be avenged." Yesterday, they—or someone—attempted to assassinate Paz Estenssoro as he spoke from the steps of the Presidential Palace. A militiaman had been killed. The day before armed fascist groups attacked the government radio station and fire-bombed the office of *Intransigencia.* The gunshots we heard now were the Indians, the vigilant ones, guarding their revolution. My heart beat faster; I felt a solemn excitement. I remembered the militiamen I'd seen guarding the square in La Paz, I saw them lying in blood on the steps of the Presidential Palace. I imagined the cathedral in ruins, as if it had been bombed from the air. I felt that if I gave way to the angers I felt inside me at the enemies of this revolution, showed my fury to the North American in the bar whose words would rot this revolution like mold on fresh bread, my anger would drown the world in blood. But, I reminded myself, there had been enough suffering on my continent; streams of blood veined it. *Our* work was to save life. (I allowed myself to feed on the imagination of battle, and on the more intimate thoughts of ripping their tongues out, driving their noses back into their brains, crushing their eggshell heads—all, that is, that I would not do.) I looked over at Helena, who brought the large spoon to her mouth. She didn't place the whole spoonful in, but nibbled quickly at the contents. How dear she looked! I wanted to ask her to dance. "Odd dinner music," I said to Fernando, for no reason. I didn't want to think anymore about the source of my gaiety.

He looked at me blankly. "Good stew," he said, taking another mouthful.

Many of the other guests tonight, I noticed—when I'd put enough inside to look about—were Argentines, pilots whose plot against Peron had been broken. They wore long uniform jackets for dinner, though they worked during the day in their undershirts, building an asphalt road far away, between Cochabamba and Santa Cruz. (Wouldn't so many roads be bound to conjure vehicles richly laden to run down them?) The soldiers were landscape. The people I wanted to speak to were the leaders of the MNR, and the sun in that galaxy, Paz Estenssoro.

Isaias, a thin graying man with a white mustache, moved about the field in a long white Mexican wedding shirt, a genial ghost. After saying hello to each of us, he would disappear into the house for a fifteen-minute nap. (The meal, of course, continued without him.)

"Just the people I wanted to see," Isaias said, smiling warmly. "I wonder if one of you doctors could feel this bulge in my stomach. At least I think it's a bulge." He lifted up his white shirt and placed my hand, still holding one of his spoons, on his stomach. "Is it a bulge? Or nothing at all? I'm worried about my kidneys, you understand. Urination has been very painful."

This dinnertime consultation made me feel fondly towards Isaias. He knew how false our pride in our bodies is, and how unimportant courtesy was compared with pain. "It's just gas," I said in what I hoped was a reassuring manner. I returned to my stew.

"That can't be good for you," Isaias said, turning his paternal attention to me, "eating that fast."

I cast my eyes upward from my plate. "Good stew," I said. He raised his pale eyebrows in concern, or surprise, as I picked up speed, my wooden spoon striking the tin clickety-clack. I raced against a competitive crowd. It was a mournful moment for us all when those big black pots wended their empty way homeward.

"It's a reserve meal," Fernando explained. "Hasn't he told you his theory of reserve meals? His theory is, Eat when you can, eat as much as you can, and store up food like a camel."

"Or a cow," Isaias added, a little glumly.

"Good stew," I said.

"Well, you're the doctor," Isaias said, regaining his hostly equanimity. "You know what's best."

"Good stew is best," I said, spooning up more of it. The competition for thirds would be fierce.

After a few platefuls I'd lost my appetite, even the memory of my appetite. But I continued. I ate for the future. Tomorrow the only meal would be for my will, the cold ecstasy of not indulging my body.

We got our thirds. Eating more slowly, forcing myself to swallow (tomorrow I would force myself not to), I circulated about the field with Fernando, searching for interesting talk. Tonight, listening to two young Bolivians, I heard gloomy news. Paz Estenssoro had reopened the military and police academies. New officers would be recruited from the middle class and the peasants. The U.S. had sent experts on detection and interrogation. I knew what this meant: the attempt on his life had terrified Paz, broken his will. He thought a more efficient police force—trained by imperialism—would protect him. He was wrong. Only the will of the people could protect him. But he did not have the courage of Gandhi, the willingness to march beneath the guns, to die.

Fernando smiled wanly at me, shaking his head as I told him my thoughts. He found my talk of death too exalted, the misty sublime of the effete poet looking out at a contrived sea. His shaking head stopped me. Did I have any real imagination of death? Of dying, dead, death? Just a word? I imagined: a coldness spreading in my limbs. Or was it like being paralyzed piece by piece, then altogether stone? This field with myself absent, but all else present, round, colored, warm? Or the field gone, nothing, blankness, without even the imagining (by me) of blankness? Everything gone, even the imagining? Whatever it was, it was to be faced fearlessly. I would. (Would I? If only I had been here during Holy Week! Then I would know about myself!) I returned Fernando's smile.

There were good, vital signs tonight, too. A new board to oversee the mines had been elected, strongly nationalist and uncompromising. No more compensation would be paid the U.S. owners. If the United States threatened to cut off its purchases or withdraw its loans, then Bolivia would look elsewhere for buyers.

Behind us, as we listened to these men, Chaco hummed a song. It had no melody, and little rhyme. He would raise his voice here and there as if he'd suddenly been prodded, or remembered fitfully that there was something particular about what people called "a song."

> There are many people in his field tonight,
> —O how can Isaias feed them all?
> But far away in New York tonight
> The price of tin started to fall,
> To fall. Can you hear it?
> A dollar twenty a ton.

Why did Chaco demand defeat? He continued to follow us, whining his song:

> Many people ate in his field that night.
> How can Isaias feed them all?
> But a consortium met (what's a consortium?
> Is it a road? or is it a wall?),
> A consortium decided (if you don't know, too bad for you!).

He stopped. "Damn. Nothing rhymes with 'consortium.'"

> Well, rhyming or not, tin had to fall.
> Let me whisper it: ninety-five cents a ton.
> Ninety-five cents a ton? That's not very much for a hole
>   in the ground.
> And a deeper hole in your lung.
>
> A final voice, profundo:
> Ninety-five cents a ton!

"You're very clever," Fernando said, shaking Chaco's skinny hand.

"I'm not just clever," Chaco replied. "I'm also very profound." He looked at me, head to the side, eyes squinted. "But I can tell Ernesto doesn't like my singing."

"You long for loss," I said. "You hate yourself. You want defeat."

"You don't like my song?" He pretended a hurt whimpery tone, pushing out his lower lip like a child. "I know you, Ernesto. You want to scream at my music, don't you? NO! NO! NO!"

I nodded. Chaco was a perspicacious man.

"Don't you see, Ernesto? I'm not making this song up, such as it is. And your shouting NO doesn't put an end to it. It's just another note in the chorus."

I turned my back on him.

Noncooperation

Near an old tree a broad-shouldered man of about forty, in a light-brown sports coat, had drawn an attentive group of five or six people. A familiar face, thinner and more vulnerable than I remembered: I had seen it in the newspapers. Voting. Speaking from the steps of the palace. "We must build the nation," he declaimed, "in the framework of international cooperation." Was he saying that now, as the sun set, or was it a caption on a photograph I'd seen? Fernando and I drifted over to the tree, our clown following after, humming to himself.

The man held an empty plate, thinly filmed with gravy, turned on its side, with the wooden spoon pressed against it by his large thumb. He gestured broadly, with a cigarette held in his other hand, sweeping the arc of the circle. The man's hair formed a sharp "V" in front, with large areas of scalp on either side. His voice had authority but was a little toneless, as if he were reading a speech. "If Bolivia goes too far, too rapidly with its nationalization, without paying the *necessary* compensation, it will make for a nice gesture, but it will only endanger the Revolution."

"Yes," Isaias agreed gravely, back from his nap. His face looked fuddled from sleep. "Some young people don't understand the particular problems this nation faces."

The balding man nodded. Bolivia, he explained, could lose its only market for tin, its chief supplier of machinery and manufactured goods. "And that would only bankrupt the nation in futile gestures of defiance."

Heads nodded in the circle at the pathetic irreality of gestures. *For they did not understand the aura of symbols, how they could reach in and transform the sleeping soul!* "Bolivia," I said, displaying the shining words, "could continue as a nation without tin mines or machinery. Perhaps it would find itself for the first time."

Chaco's high voice from behind my shoulder interrupted me, thwarted the lifting of my chalice. "You sound like a Baptist preacher, Ernesto. 'Bo-li-vi-a' " —he made his voice a minister's singsong, from Voice of the Andes— " 'whores after manufactured goods.' You know, Ernesto, you confuse the sin of sex and the degradation of industry. You're a modern artist. You can't tell a woman from a machine."

"I'm sorry," the broad-shouldered man said, politely, eagerly, wanting a debate, "but I don't understand you." (Anyone could tell that Chaco was vaudeville, entertainment between the acts.)

I admired Paz Estenssoro, the leader of the MNR, President of the Bolivian Republic, for I was certain that he was the broad-shouldered man whose picture I'd seen. Drawn to him I wanted to test him. Perhaps my work, my place, would be here. I stepped forward into the circle and spoke of a people finding their nationhood in the collective sacrifices they made. Independence from the imperialists meant self-rule. And ruling the self meant voluntary sacrifice, feeling one's will. That's the place (I said) for gestures. The leadership can show by its own sacrifices how little material things, even life, matter, that dignity is the essential.

"Dignity," whined a tapir's voice behind me, "that means not having things. The naked man in the naked room."

"It means," I said, without turning round, "not being ruled by things." Chaco must offer up his whimsy. An Indian people had risen. New possibilities for work were upon us. Europe and irony were over. "It means not letting those who give you things or money be your masters. If the United States threatens Bolivia's independence it should be defied. We can do without it."

"Are you a Communist, Ernesto?" Isaias asked. He was more shocked by that possibility than by the rapid delivery of stew to my mouth.

I was astounded. In Gandhi's words I had found an alternative to the desiccated slogans of the Argentine Communists. But I wouldn't give the old man the satisfaction of a denial. "I don't see what difference it makes."

"Others can," Chaco said quietly. He put a hand on my arm to calm me.

Two or three of the Argentine pilots stirred uneasily, raised their shoulders. And two men with pistols jammed into their belts stood too still and looked from me to Paz Estenssoro, and then at each other. One of them nodded. One of them turned his back.

"Oh, damn you," Chaco muttered to the ground. "Oh, damn you, Ernesto."

"Can we do without the United States?" Isaias said. "Bolivia, you know, needs its neighbors' cooperation."

"Or perhaps you're unfamiliar with our geography?" Paz Estenssoro added condescendingly. "Bolivia has no port. And we also need U.S. loans. The tin ore is harder to get than it was at first. The mines need new machinery."

Chaco, the bard, sang tunelessly (fear had flattened his voice):

> Once Bolivia was as thick with tin
> as the varicose veins on a fat woman's legs.
> Now the tin is as far away
> as the money an Indian begs.
>
> The price, sir?
> Seventy-five cents a ton.

People laughed. Their laughter made the air shake before me. Paz Estenssoro was not the man I had thought. Pressed against Gandhi's vision, he crumbled. He had only words of accommodation, of slow surrender.

"You know," Paz Estenssoro mused rhetorically, "I wonder if you people have thought about the consequences of your gestures? It could cause, as Isaias says, a blockade of Bolivia. It could cause armed intervention, and unparalleled suffering for the Bolivian people. That's what I mean about the cost of gestures." He looked about. "The costs are difficult to compute, but they should be figured precisely."

This last bit delighted Isaias. He clapped his hands together and laughed. I could see the ropy veins on his ugly, skinny hands as if they made glowing lines in the dusk.

"If there is a struggle," I said, "we should follow the Gandhian tactic of noncooperation." It would be an opportunity to share suffering, I went on, a chance for the national will to triumph over greed and fear. People would go to prison gaily, as the masses in India had.

"Nobody cares what you think, Ernesto!" Chaco laughed too loudly, a mechanical sound, without resonance. He placed his head on my shoulder, digging down sharply with what little chin he had. "Please remember who you're talking to, Ernesto," he said quietly, insistently. "Don't talk too much. Don't say the wrong things to the wrong people. Don't say anything. Don't talk. Shut up, damn you!"

"He won't stop," Fernando said. "I mean he likes to tell people things they hate hearing. But Chaco's right, Ernesto. Let's go."

"This is all very abstract," Paz Estenssoro said, "like most theories. War wouldn't be so abstract." He looked about the group for approval. The dead, I thought, require reassurance, the lie that they are still carnal; ghosts feed upon reflections.

Ricardo grabbed my arm and pushed it up behind my back, forcing my plate from my hand. My muscles stretched painfully, then agonizingly. "How far do you think this nonviolent *shit* will take you, Ernesto? Do you like this? I think if I tell you to bend down now, you will." He pulled upward on my arm. It hurt terribly, a stinging pain all the way to the shoulder. But I would not bend. I wasn't angry with Ricardo, though. At least this wasn't more talk. This was serious. This hurt. I pressed the spoon in my other hand hard into my own thigh.

"Better to lose an arm," I said, barely.

Ricardo spat.

"Pain is good." I clenched my jaws tight to feel my will, to help me bear it. "It separates us from the body. It's the will that is important, the spirit. Nations and individuals are made . . . are made . . . are made by bearing suffering." The field softened behind a haze of pain. Ricardo forced my arm higher. I screamed; then regained myself. "There's a joy in suffering, in feeling . . . of feeling . . . my will accept this"—I whispered—"volun . . ."

"You're a shithead," Ricardo said, quietly, angrily, releasing my arm. "Or something. I don't know what you are."

Isaias ignored our dance. "How can you talk that way about the United States, Ernesto?" He shook his gray head in profound paternal misgivings. "You forget that they are our allies against Peron. You certainly sound like a Communist!" He looked about in the dusk: the bat, searching for agreement, for sound bounced back from the walls. "You know," the old man went on, "I understand the appeal of dialectics well. A youthful folly of mine, an early flirtation. But not a marriage. Never a lifelong commitment. That isn't the way for Latin America."

Why this talk of Marxism again? I hadn't said anything about dialectics. But he had heard it somewhere, an overtone to my words? an anagram hidden in my name?

Our audience had grown to thirty. All the people of the field had been drawn to us, our voices ringing excitedly in the cold air. The dusk hid the outer ring of faces. Only Paz Estenssoro, standing directly in front of me, and the six or seven right around us, were clearly visible. One or two of the soldiers nodded in judicious agreement with Isaias. The younger people—Ricardo, Helena, and the others—looked away embarrassed. (Good! It drew the lines between our generations more sharply.) One fellow, Roberto Soto, didn't look away. A plump man with a pencil mustache and a high pompadour, he wore a shirt ornamented with pink and blue flowery shapes, visible even at dusk. A young radical professor, jailed once by Peron, Soto smiled at me, a big grin, as if we shared a wonderful joke.

It got colder as Isaias went on. I pressed my hands into the pockets of my jacket, rolled the lint about with my numbing fingertips. Soto, I thought, must be very cold. One of the silent men took the pistol from his belt and pushed the safety catch on the grip back and forth, back and forth. (Where would it stop?) He walked outside our circle and, holding the gun with both hands, took aim at a tree. *Count to eight,* I thought. *Now gradually let out your breath as you squeeze.* The shadows formed around his legs like a long black coat. The shot: a sharp high sound. My shoulders shook involuntarily. He missed the tree.

Chaco gripped my arm, digging his fingers in. But I was glad for this danger. To speak the truth to the powerful, to risk their violence, was Gandhi's way. And if I could speak Gandhi's uncompromising words now, I would know that I believed them; it would make those words a part of my composition.

Isaias, deaf to the pistol shot, went on talking.

Paz Estenssoro interrupted the old man; he could see that no one cared about Isaias's youthful flirtations. "We are linked to the United States, but not only economically. We have a shared concern for the worth of the individual." His voice gained strength as he went, a wave rolling to its crest. He'd found the place in his text. "Surely you can understand that? We have a profound common heritage of liberal values, of faith in the electoral process. You must recognize that the United States has a greedy face, and a generous liberal face. We must speak to the friendly face, for we have a common way of looking. . . ."

I interrupted. "Of looting, did you say?" Soto laughed loudly. I was furious with Paz Estenssoro. Opportunist! "I think you're kidding us with these cartoon faces." I looked about me, not for support, but defiantly. But I saw nothing. It grew rapidly darker, and my anger made the world darker still.

Chaco, standing behind me and very close, put an arm on each of my shoulders. "Shut up, Ernesto darling," he whispered in my ear. "Please please please don't say one word more."

I couldn't hear. I wanted to stamp my feet hard in front of Paz Estenssoro. "It's stupid to need some point proven over and over, and criminal when it's proved by our people's suffering." I shook my spoon at him, splattering drops of gravy on his jacket. There was a rushing sound inside my head. Anger must be concentrated. Anger must be sublimated and formed into words. The powerful must hear the truth. That was Gandhi's way. "What you call the good face of the United States is just propaganda, the pleased smile on the jackal as it walks up to its dinner. You will end up a traitor to your people."

I had no right to say such things. (My pretensions became promises I had to fulfill, or become pathetic in my own eyes. More: they helped me find a way to fulfillment; they were the scaffolding for a stage, and costumes for a grand role. Others, seeing my stolen outfit, would expect something of me, require me to play a certain part. They spoke their lines to me. My response was as if already written.)

"Damn you damn you damn you!" Chaco hissed. His body hung from my shoulders like a weight. I shook myself, but he wouldn't fall.

Paz Estenssoro recoiled from me, his face contorted. He bent down, unspeaking, laid his plate and spoon on the grass, ran his hand over his hair. He looked about the circle, trying to make out faces in the dark. He ground out his cigarette on his plate, rose, lit another. It was difficult to see in the enfolding darkness, but I thought Paz Estenssoro was crying.

"I'm going to kill you."

I guess he wasn't crying.

He formed his hand into a fist.

"I won't resist," I said. "I won't hurt you."

"Damn right *you* won't hurt *me,*" Paz Estenssoro shouted. "*I'm* going to hurt *you.* I'm going to *kill* you." He looked towards the silent man who had shot the tree.

"You're going to die, dear, just like you want," Chaco said. He cried and stroked my shoulder.

Soto crossed over in front of Paz, separating us. He took my arm. Soto wore a lot of cologne on his hair, a cloud of alcohol and sweet spices, a sharp smell that in my dizziness seemed to have a harsh tinge of formaldehyde. I gasped. He put out an arm to stop Paz, and smiled engagingly. "When the time is right," Soto said, "Ernesto will be with us." This made no sense to me.

Gently, but forcefully, he pulled me backward, out of the circle. I thought

I had done well: I had *wanted* to smash my wooden spoon across the face of that traitor. *Yet I would not have resisted if he had attacked me.* And I had not moved toward my enemy, as I had in the bar.

My arm hurt where Soto held it. Paz looked away, talked with Isaias.

"You were very hard on my friend," Soto said wonderingly. "You acted as if he were responsible for the whole Bolivian Revolution."

I laughed at Soto's mistake. "He is." I looked away from Soto to get some clear air. "That was Paz Estenssoro, President of the Republic." I propped myself against the rough bark of a tree. I felt grand, though, naming our opponent.

Soto and Fernando laughed at me.

"Don't be silly, my friend. That's not Paz," Roberto said, smiling warmly. "Or I would certainly have grabbed you sooner! That would be stupid! That could be dangerous! You couldn't have thought you were speaking to Paz Estenssoro!" He looked wonderingly from me to Fernando, as if to ask my friend what sort I was. Fernando shrugged. "No, that's a fellow I know from the Ministry of Industry. A sub-sub sort. Paz Estenssoro has a long sad face, very melancholy, very soulful. I'll introduce you sometime."

From President to clerk! I sank lower on my tree. I had hallucinated an opponent. What sort of test was that? Yet my uneasiness about the MNR remained.

"Anyway, I wonder, if you're going back to town, if I might join you?"

Soto extended his hand to me. I pulled myself up. My arm ached; Ricardo had stretched every muscle thin.

"I'd enjoy talking with you," Soto went on, "and I'm sorry we haven't had a chance yet. Your intensity is very compelling, if you don't mind my saying so. I noticed it tonight, of course, and also at the cafes. It's as if your whole body were curved into a question mark."

He had discovered my own metaphor for myself. It pleased me.

Chaco laughed. I think he could see that I felt flattered. "Ernesto reminds me of a wolf who thinks he's a rabbit."

"He reminds me," Fernando said, "of Don Quixote."

"An unemployed actor," Chaco replied.

Fernando: "A despairing bandit."

Chaco: "A cheap gun that will explode in the bandit's hand."

Fernando: "A camel."

Chaco: "A whale."

F: "A cloud."

C: "A serpent."

F: "A dove."

C: "A ghost."

F: "A son of God."

C: "A seltzer bottle."

The two of them giggled and hugged each other, giddy with relief, returned to life.

"By the way," Soto said, smiling amiably. "I noticed that you and Fernando have very odd shoes. Is there a story?"

"There's always a story," Chaco said.

One of Fernando's shoes was a black snub-nosed boot; one was a brown wingtip with a pointy toe. They were the residue, Fernando explained, of Ernesto's last great business idea. Ernesto had figured that there weren't that many kinds of shoes in the world. All we had to do was buy up the odd ones for a few months, then form our holdings into the matched pairs that were bound to accumulate. "But," Fernando told Soto, "there's something very mysterious about market forces." The plan had concluded with heaps of orphan shoes, stored in his family tool shed in Cordoba. Our capital had been spent before we had found even one pair. Now, painfully, we wore out the inventory.

"But I don't understand," Soto said. "You have two matched pairs between you now."

We stood together looking at our feet. Soto was right. We each had a wingtip and a boot. That day in Fernando's garage fifty mismatches had made us blind with despair.

"It doesn't matter about the shoes," Fernando said. "None of them fit anyway. They're all painful as hell." And, of course, he winced accusingly at me.

We thanked Isaias, who stood by the bridge, saying farewell to his departing guests. He embraced each of us in turn, looking away from Soto's perfumed head. "You're just like your wonderful father," he said to me. "You say what's on your mind. You're a very harsh judge, Ernesto, like him. But you're young still. Time will soften you, as it has me, as it has me."

Roberto led the way back across the bridge. Ricardo and Helena stayed back together. I think he had his arms around her shoulders. (Some other kind of dance I didn't know the steps to.)

"She's pretty isn't she?" Fernando said wistfully, to no one in particular.

"I'd like to meet . . ." Chaco looked at me, his face turned to the side. He bit his lower lip, pretending to be abashed before my chastity. ". . . to meet . . . *someone!*"

"See you again," Isaias called out. And added, regretfully, his voice falling softly, "Ah, Thursday, I suppose."

Chaco sang:

> Men made plans, men had hopes.
> (Not that it matters. Unlucky men.)
> For the price of tin was falling.
> The words left their mouths, and fell to the ground
> Falling with the price of tin,
> Unlucky men.
> Their bodies grow light, their faces decay,
> And there's only one last rite to say:
> Seventy cents a ton.

My Bare Feet

He had been taken prisoner. (Soto's voice. The crystal had formed from layer after layer of translucence, thinner than the skins of an onion; then suddenly it had darkened to a different form of jewel. We walked within that jewel. Only the tips of the eucalyptus trees were visible, as silhouettes—those, and the mounds of earth that road-building machines had piled by the shoulders, like temporary fortifications. Soto's voice, and his darkness, moved beside me on the dirt road back to La Paz. His voice and his darkness and his perfume. Fernando and Chaco walked behind us. In this dark one didn't *speak;* a voice arrived—even one's own—severed from its author; it resonated in the crystal, floated up towards the treetops.) *He had been taken prisoner.* An investigation, you see? An investigation meant that they put some suspects in jail for a while. Or longer. Or the suspects disappeared. Brave friends came down to the police barracks to ask after one. Soto? No, never heard of him. . . . Every so often they took a man from his cell to a little room with a straight-backed chair. . . . He was in jail for ten days, and on the eleventh day the jail shook. Peron had been speaking in the Plaza de Mayo; dynamite charges had gone off near the rostrum. Gouts of water splashed from the faucet in the washbasin outside the cell, water red with rust shaken loose by the explosion. Soto had students who were political prisoners. They'd think he knew something about the people who had set the bombs. They'd want him to know something. Who knows what they'd think? They led some others out first, and after a few hours he smelled something odd. Pork, the guard said, smiling. Soto understood (he had burned his arm once lighting an oven): *They had other things besides straight-backed chairs.* Efficiency is a value to be cherished. The police wanted to show Peron how efficiently they worked to establish the facts. A burned body equals a thesis proved. Soto told the guard he had diarrhea. He did, but no one cared to investigate. He asked to go to the toilet. He pestered the guard every ten minutes, saying he had to go again. The guard became used to Soto's sudden needful departures and kept waving him down the hall to the toilet. Then, one time, when they thought he was sitting on the can, he walked out into the street, walked over to the Guatemalan embassy, walked now with his new friends on this dark road in the Bolivian mountains. The Guatemalan ambassador had driven him to the airport. The Guatemalan ambassador was a wonderful courageous person. "Someday," Soto said, "I must introduce you to him. He's gone back to Guatemala City. He's in the vanguard of their Revolution. You'll like him."

Soto spoke as if the exile world, and the ministers and subministers of several nationalist governments in power, circulated at a large party, and he was the host, making introductions for the people he liked.

"But we're not going through Guatemala!" Fernando's voice sounded urgent, insistent. "We're going to the leper colony at San Pablo." (His voice arrived from behind us, accompanied by the soft regular, painful fall of our feet on dirt and stones.)

Of course, Soto agreed. He wouldn't want to dissuade us from such good work. "It made a very strong impression on you, San Pablo?"

"Yes," Fernando said immediately.

"Yes," I agreed. It was very cold here after sunset. The chill made my outline sharper, concentrated my sense of self. An incitement to rhetoric. "The highest form of solidarity arises among desperate and lonely men." (I knew that I talked beyond myself; the words weren't mine to say.)

"Yes!" Fernando sounded defiant, as if disagreeing with someone. "Not among politicians!"

"Peut-être je m'accompagne," Chaco said.

A strong huffling sound interrupted the silence. A loud regular clangor, metallic about the edges, like a weak engine wheezing, straining along a grade.

"What's that?" Soto's voice went up an octave. "Do you think someone followed us from the party?" We all knew who he meant: the bogey man clothed in shadows.

"It's an animal creeping up on us," Fernando said. "I think it's a bear."

"Une chauve-souris," Chaco said.

"What?" Fernando sounded furious.

"A bat," Chaco translated.

"No more French, please, I beg you Chaco," Fernando said.

"*Et pourquoi non?*"

"What?"

"And why not?"

"Because I don't understand it. Because it's getting on my nerves. Because I'll break your skinny little arms if you do it again."

"What's that sound?" Soto asked again, clearly frightened. (How had he dared to walk out of that jail?)

"It's only Ernesto's strange way of breathing," Fernando said. "Peculiar isn't it?"

I gasped. The altitude was impossible. I resigned. My chest hurt too much. I gave up. But there was no one to accept my resignation. We continued walking.

"Ernesto has asthma," Fernando explained, his voice compassionate now, familiar. "He's had a very bad case of it, since birth almost. That's why he has to travel with someone. Someone must always be with him. Because of the asthma, I mean." (*I mean*—the phrase most characteristic of Fernando Who Wanted to Be Plain.) "Someone to give him an injection if he has a bad attack and can't help himself." Fernando sounded bitter. "Asthma is like a gun at his head. He thinks he might die every second of his life."

"So that's how you got out of the army?" Soto asked, indifferent to my soul.

"Yes, I used the asthma," I said. "Usually it uses me. I gave myself an attack by taking a cold shower. Fernando had to carry me home." It embarrassed me to speak of this small necessary duplicity. Had *I* already betrayed my country? I should have stayed and . . . and what? *Nothing to be done.* (What was the name of my work?)

My foot turned in a deep rut, twisting my leg. I fell forward into the dirt. "Damn!" A fork had stuck in my knee. I sat down on the road and undid my shoes, my stupid hateful torturous dearly bought shoes.

The earth, when I stood, was still warm from the day. It felt pleasant to stretch my toes, confined only by socks, out into the dirt. My knee calmed itself.

"You know," Soto said, as we got under way again, "talking to my friend at dinner, you reminded me of the Fidelistas." He sounded musing. "I think that despite your affinity for Gandhi, you share a certain viewpoint with them. What do you think?"

"A fiddleista? What's that?" The night wind blew sharply. I felt my lips moving.

"It sounds like a bug," Chaco said.

"It's a follower of Fidel Castro. You'd like him, I think. You'd like what he stands for. You should meet him."

"Who is he? A friend of yours?" A leader, I imagined, of some provincial party.

"Well, no, I don't know him. Not precisely. I know friends of his, I suppose. You really haven't heard of him? That's remarkable."

Soto said that Castro had been a student leader—and a gunman—at the University of Havana. "They all carry guns there, all the politicos."

"Ernesto would have liked that once," Fernando said, mockingly. "Before he discovered Gandhi. I mean, he used to believe in guns."

"Did he?" Soto asked, with evident curiosity.

"Yes indeed. When I was in jail in Cordoba, Ernesto came to see me. I wanted him to organize the high-school students against the Catholic education. He said he wasn't going into the street without a pistol. He was right in a way, I think. Not about guns, I mean. I mean *about politics being death.*" There was anger in his voice at this last judgment. Had I thought that then? And now? Should I imagine a smaller stage for myself, good done slowly, in particulars? What was the name of my work?

"La vie est absurde," Francisco said.

"Stop that goddamn it!" Fernando shouted.

"Weren't you," Roberto asked, "a little young for that?"

"No. Not to face guns. Fifteen years is old enough to know what your convictions are, and what is worth dying for. But not to kill. I was wrong about that." It was the willingness to die, I explained, that shamed one's opponent, forced him to see how he had failed his own morality, failed his nation, caused him to choke on his bad faith. My words rose towards the top of the trees, floated away. No one responded. The world came unknit. My words didn't reach out to any object. Perhaps, I worried, they weren't mine? My arm ached.

"Well, in Cuba," Soto continued, "they all carry guns." The student movement was divided into factions, factions supporting different ministers, supporting different parties, shaking down other students. "They fight among themselves. They're gangsters really. It's the national style." Castro had started as a tough guy. But he was different from the others. He had grown up, and now he was an uncompromising nationalist leader, the sort Ernesto would agree with. At least he was willing to die for what he believed in. After Batista's coup Castro had announced that he would fight for the Constitution. And, amazingly, he had. He had kept his word. In Cuba no one keeps their word! On July 26, during the carnival in Santiago, Castro's men came out from among the masquers and fired on the army barracks. "They were going to take rifles. So I've been told. And distribute them to the people in the city. There would be attacks in other cities. They'd occupy the radio station. I'm not sure precisely of their plans. A coup, I think. But you are like that, aren't you? That's why I thought of them. I mean, you believe in taking direct action now."

"Did I say that?"

"Yes. I thought so. Perhaps not precisely. No. Yes. In a way you did. . . . Don't you?"

"Yes. Yes I do." It was true, I thought, though I didn't remember saying it. Not violence, but new ways had to be found to move the masses, experiments all might join in, ways that showed a real struggle must be carried out now, not more exile talk. (Soto participated in my self-discovery, my self-creation, forcing me to play my part, the part he saw me in.) "Yes," I said, with increasing assurance (a surprise to me). "It's important to take action, not violence but real action. To begin something. And how did they do, the Fidelistas?"

"Oh, they were all captured," Soto said, with mild astonishment. "Most of them were tortured and then killed by the army."

Chaco laughed.

"Soto," Fernando said, "has offered to introduce you to a corpse."

"Well, you know, I'm not sure he's dead. I heard recently that they took him into custody, that he's going to stand trial. What a forum that will be for him! He's a wonderful speaker. Or so I've heard. I haven't heard him speak myself. Of course, I've also heard that one of his own killed him. Shot before capture, like a bandit by the police, as the saying goes."

"And do you know what all those young people died for?" I asked. More killing; work for stupid men. It would probably be rubbish. Like the rotten part of the MNR: renegotiating the terms with the imperialists. (But I had faith still that the militancy of the miners and Indians, if they were led by people of vision, like Nuflo Chavez, the Minister of Peasant Affairs, would prevail over that rottenness.)

"Well, no, not precisely. I don't know his program. I think maybe Castro's a Communist. Or his brother is." Soto stopped, turned towards me; a different inflection to his shadow, a waft of perfume mixed with the sharp medicinal odor of the eucalyptus. What did he hope to see on my face?

"It sounds to me," Fernando said, "like Castro's still a gangster."

Soto continued to look at me, for a moment, till Fernando and Chaco came up behind us. "Well, maybe he's not a Communist. Maybe he's a realist." Our footsteps began their soft plof plof plof. "I suppose that would be your opinion, Ernesto? He's certainly crazy enough."

I stopped to stare at his darkness. "What? Crazy enough for me, you mean? Crazy like me?" Soto made me laugh.

Fernando walked into my heel, hurting me, scraping my Achilles' tendon. Without thinking, I pushed him backwards.

"Excuse me," Fernando whispered.

Still, I liked Soto, though he was an obvious opportunist; he had a pleasing vitality, a generous animal warmth.

"No. Oh, no," Soto said. "Of course not. I mean that crazy people are the only ones with a chance of success in a situation like Cuba's. A crazy situation calls for crazy measures. Like my diarrhea. Sometimes being crazy is a form of realism."

"Like Hamlet," Chaco remarked.

"Shit!"

"What?" Fernando shouted, amazed at my voice.

"Shit. I said 'shit.' Yes I said it." I, too, was surprised by my voice. "I stepped in it. Shit." It was still soft and warm. I hoped it was cow stuff, not human, or some nondomestic animal.

"Feces you mean?" Fernando said joyfully. "Well you should pick it up carefully, and bury it. It will be a lesson for the villagers."

We stopped. I wiped my foot in the dirt. We had reached the outskirts of La Paz, the town of Obrajes. A glow came through the trees, golden, as from a flare, a continuous contained explosion. The trees looked molded in this light, as if they were made of some translucent material. I heard tinkly music, and the voices of drunken people. Gunshots went off very close to us. Soto and I leapt backward. A high voice, a woman's, shouted, "Halt!"

A few hundred meters from us two Indians came out of the trees. They wore woolen ponchos, black-looking, and carried old bolt-action rifles. I smelled the oil on the barrels and the sharp odor of powder.

Soto put his hands in the air, though no one had ordered him to.

"Damn," Chaco hissed. "They're not going to like me! They're going to kill us!"

An old man brought his face very near mine and stared at me. He looked my features over as if he were studying a picture, moving along my cheeks, across my eyes, down towards my mouth. His breath smelled foul, decaying matter, a corpse's. He didn't say anything. I was a dummy in a store. He turned his face to the side, inspected my mouth and torso. The other Indian, a young boy, pointed his rifle at us.

"Who are you?" the boy asked. His voice hadn't changed yet. It seemed a special indignity to be frightened by someone who hadn't passed through puberty. *Anyone can kill a man.* Our lives are more fragile than eggshells. Inside me was a precious runny yellow yolk.

"I believe in God," Chaco whispered. "I really do. I want to see a priest."

"We're men of peace," I said. The Indians wore caps with long ear flaps. The wool absorbed light and gave nothing back.

"And where do you come from?"

"From feeding ourselves," I said. "We were very hungry."

The boy's expression didn't change. "Could I see your papers please?"

I fumbled about in my shirt pocket for my Argentine identity card, a thick dirty piece of cardboard. The boy examined it in the weak unnatural light. Fernando stood next to me now, smiling, showing good will. Chaco stood next to him. He had one arm on Fernando's shoulder, and stood on one leg, the other leg poised behind his knee, like a stork. He sobbed without shame. He had lost control of his face, bereft child, as if his cheeks had melted. I looked around for Soto. He had disappeared, evaporated, beat it! I saw a darkness against one of the trees. That shadow, and Chaco's sobbing, triggered a panic in me. *Why had Soto run away?* I wheezed. The young one turned the card in his hand. He had a serious intent expression; perhaps he didn't know how to read. Perhaps he'd shoot us in a rage at not knowing how to read. And if they led us off to some field, what appeal would we have? Who would even know? *Anger must be conquered.* My catechism returned as a prayer. Blood soaking into the earth, streams of runny yellow blood. No! That violence must stop!

The older Indian bent over the card. His black poncho was tied with a brightly embroidered belt, and a leather bag hung down from a silver buckle on his belt. I recognized him. He sold furs in the square, half animal, my grandfather. He had a bright-red rash down the side of his face.

And he wore a wristwatch. How had he acquired a wristwatch?

I twisted my feet in the dirt, trying to get the shit off. The smell reminded me of mortality. The older Indian looked at my feet. He pointed to the boots I carried, and said something in Quechua to the boy. Perhaps he wanted the boots.

"He says," the boy said, "that he doesn't care for them either." He handed me back my card.

I laughed. Chaco put his other foot down. He snuffled the snot back into his nose, a child suddenly comforted.

"Yes," I said, "they're very uncomfortable."

The old man spoke again. The young one said, "He says he loses his balance if he can't grip the earth. He stumbles like a drunk. The stones in the city are too flat."

"That's it," Fernando said to me. "They're not used to pavement. There's nothing there when something should be. Funny to think of the smoothness of a thing tripping you up. The lack of an obstacle, I mean. Like being rich spoiling the personality!"

The old man spoke again, clicked, barked, made guttural sounds. Quechua ineradicable! A language of stones, pebbles in the mouth. "He says he'd like to look at your hand."

I held it out to him, happy with the repetition, a comic scene to write my mother. His touch was firm. I felt no moisture in his palm at all; it was almost dust. (You might have bathed in mine.) "I know. I have a rich fate awaiting me."

The old man spread my fingers out, to make the palm flat, and continued his study.

The boy translated. "He says he doesn't know about that. But you are what you say you are. A man of peace. A very ambitious and nervous one, he says. So we will walk with you through Obrajes."

I looked behind me. Soto hadn't heard the happy ending. He scuttled furtively from tree to tree. No one called to him. Let him decipher our parade!

The young Indian walked ahead, his rifle held in one hand. Fernando and Chaco walked behind. And the old man walked beside me, still holding my hand. A gentle way, Soto must have thought, for the prisoner to be led to his execution.

We came around the turn in the road. A neon sign of a golden rooster glowed in front of us, on top of a wooden shack. A man in a business suit staggered out the door, his arm embracing a police officer in an open brown tunic. They got into a car parked by the side of the shack. A woman, unsteady on high heels, followed. She fell forward, supporting herself with one arm on the hood of the car, and threw up. The lighting made it look like a play.

"Isn't that against MNR rules?" I said to the young Indian.

"I'd like to meet . . ." Chaco stared at me, his head to the side. ". . . HER!" He spoke boldly, defying my judgment.

Their putrid dance offended me. The Indians kept watch in the cold. The party bureaucrats, flaunting party discipline, drank in public.

The young boy stopped dead, fascinated. Perhaps he'd never seen a woman in high-heeled shoes. Or a woman stagger like that. Or throw up. His hypnotized voice told the old one what I'd said.

The old man lifted my hand and placed it lightly against his cheek. My mother's face, a thousand years from now. The erosion caused by the Ice Age. A lizard.

"He says," the boy said, still in his trance, "to feel his face. He says, we'll be here longer than the men in jackets"—the boy pulled an imaginary string running from his neck down his shirt—"the ones with cloth around their necks. He says, we're older than they are. We're as old as the mountains."

Perhaps he's right, I thought. There have always been lizards. "But those men are very old, too," I said. "The oldest profession: those who waste. Bureaucrats and prostitutes. They go on forever, wearing away at the mountains. You have to make sure they don't cheat you out of what you've won."

"Enough Guevara!" Chaco said. "They don't want to hear this! I don't want to hear this! No one wants to hear this now! Not from you!"

"What are bureaucrats?" the boy asked.

"Bosses. Overseers."

Reluctantly, he translated my words. The old man dropped my hand. Alvarados pulled at my sleeve. "Maybe Chaco's right. They don't want to hear such things. Not from us."

And Soto, the shadow, came out of the darkness. "Yes," he said, oracularly, "they wear away at the mountains. But look, the mountains remain!"

I looked up. Tall smooth darknesses, and many many stars. A parable. I couldn't read it.

Soto addressed his remark to the old man. The young one translated. One had to admire such a versatile flatterer.

The old man laughed, showing his nearly empty mouth, his teeth worn away to dirty brown stumps. His foul breath came out in little gasps, dominated Soto's putrid cologne. (What decay was it hiding?) "Well, perhaps," Soto said urbanely, as if we rose from a dinner party, "we should be getting back to town now. It's awfully cold."

The Indians nodded to us, and we to them.

Soto pranced away, a scampering motion that looked droll on him, his top part was so round and his legs so thin. He made me laugh again, though I was angry at him for scaring me. "I don't mind telling you," he said, "that I felt very frightened there for a while."

"Oh, you needn't tell us," Fernando said.

"Well," Soto said, unembarrassed, "who knows what they think? But you handled it beautifully, Ernesto. 'Men of peace,' that's just the way they talk. You saved our lives, I'm sure of it. It was very clever of you to take off your shoes."

We all laughed at him, at his inane stupid compliments.

"Guevara owed it to us," Chaco said, "after his performance tonight. But you missed his real stroke of genius. Dunking his feet in shit. Very Indian."

Soto laughed good-humoredly at our mockery. He had a high-pitched squeak of a laugh. "Well, why don't we all meet tomorrow afternoon, at the

Ministry of Peasant Affairs? I have a friend you should meet, the one Fernando says you admire, Ernesto, Nuflo Chavez." We agreed. I could not have been more eager.

Fernando looked at me quizzically, for he could see how much I longed for this meeting. Nuflo Chavez, architect of the land reform, was now my hope for the Bolivian Revolution, for the democratic Left. He was the leader of the peasant unions. I had seen smudged newspaper pictures of him marching at the front of the militias; a young man with famously bad eyesight, he walked carrying a machete. He, I thought, would speak the word of the peasant, the chaste and self-sufficient life of the villages, the word, like a knife, that would destroy imperialism. Nuflo Chavez, a ruthless man, Soto said, would contest Paz for the party's leadership. Nuflo Chavez, then, would be the land itself speaking, the rock showing through, not someone who spoke about the Indians, but someone who spoke for them, their union into a single force, as majestic as the Incas, and as ready for sacrifice. He would have work for me; and he would prevail. Chavez, I was sure, would be the leader I searched for. To speak with Chavez at the Ministry of Peasant Affairs would be to encounter the motor of the Indo-American Revolution.

Soto gave us each an embrace. "Good night dears."

Chaco asked if we could put him up for the night. We walked back together to our dirty room on Yanachocha Street. Soto waved us out of sight. "He's going back to that cabaret," Chaco said.

"He'll make many friends there, I'm sure," Fernando said. "Politicians to introduce Ernesto to."

My Enemies

The halls of the ministry got only a little light from a few small windows set high up in the walls. Long lines of peasants, Indians and mestizos, stood in each hall, up the broad stairwells, around corners, down the next hall, five stories of them, ranged two by two, waiting to receive certificates for land. There was barely room for the three of us to walk by, single file. Soldiers stood along the outside of the line, facing the Indians, their rifles held between both hands, like staves. The lines stayed next to the walls. They seemed subdued; patient; unexpectant. Once or twice people tugged at the rope on my pants, but they dropped their hands before I could turn.

Every hundred meters or so one of the militiamen stopped us, made us explain our business. The government was uneasy. This morning Paz had dissolved the radical mine board. Their infantile and extreme positions, he said, endangered the safety of the national revolution. They would bankrupt the country in futile gestures of defiance. Paz Estenssoro, I thought, stood now in the field of the dead, a dried bag coated with blood, waving in the wind. Chavez and the forces he led must take control of the Revolution.

The people in line didn't speak with each other.

The line moved along slowly, two by two. Many of the Indians walked barefoot; most wore sandals. They made a quiet shooshing sound as they moved down the corridor, a wave receding, receding.

Only men waited in line. They wore the hats of their regions, even here: colored wool caps of concentric circles or ridged patterns, and short-brimmed brown felt hats. The Indians looked sad; their long dour faces and ear flaps reminded me of unhappy animals, basset hounds. And the felt hats seemed cheap prizes won at too great a price from some crooked carnival. The halls were hot from the press of bodies, the lack of ventilation. The air stank with sweat and the foul breath of coca-chewing. The luster of the Indian clothes, which had lit the plaza like burning minerals, colored flames, looked sooty here, the ponchos grimed with dirt all along their intricate weaving. My stomach turned. I wanted to vomit.

Every so often, as we toiled down one of the interminable corridors, a peasant walked back along the hall the other way, carrying a small sheet of paper in both hands, his mouth turned down, his eyes absent, distracted. His face and clothing were dusted with a fine white powder. (The agrarian reform turned them into ghosts.) A round old man passed at my chest level. He held a ribboned staff in his right hand and the paper in his left. His cap was sprinkled with floury-looking stuff. He looked like a pastry.

"One more flight," Soto called down to me encouragingly. My friends stood on the landing above me, catching their breath. I rested a floor below them, chasing unsuccessfully after mine. The air here was too thick. To walk up to my friends would be like swimming through viscous distasteful muck.

I heard Fernando ask Soto how the government knew where each parcel of land would be. Voices floated down the stairwell towards me; the words, trapped in the gelatin, reached me like light from some distant planet, long after the event. I approached my friends and they suddenly moved on. Why didn't they wait? I would never reach them. Some geometrical paradox would defeat me.

The job was enormous, Soto explained, walking up another flight of stairs. They *didn't* know which land would be part of the reform yet. The landlord could appeal any redistribution order. He could object to the map-maker's surveying. He could (they turned a corner; I pursued) protest the decree to the local agrarian board. He could appeal the decision to the council of the National Agrarian Reform Service. Oh, there were lots of democratic safeguards. He could take the matter to the full council. He could appeal (we had to go down the hall to another stairway, and then up another flight. I stopped a moment next to two Indians in line. They stepped closer to the wall) to the President of the Republic, to Paz Estenssoro himself. "So they can't *know* what's available yet. Just one more flight, and down the next hall. My friend tells me that it will take about twenty-five years. So they're not giving out deeds to the land yet, just certificates that say that when there is land, the Indian is entitled to some. It gives the peasants a sense of participating in the reform." He disappeared from sight. I hurried along. My head felt light and my stomach very heavy, as if I dragged a wheelbarrow full of my nausea down the hall. Fernando's face, moving around the corner, looked back at me, his body already gone away. "What do you think of that?" Fernando's head asked.

"I want to vomit."

But Fernando had already disappeared, following after his legs.

I trailed Soto's high, amiable voice, a voice that accepted everything, a voice of good digestion. "Mostly what the government can do now is guarantee wages for hacienda workers, while this process goes on. That's a good idea, the minister thinks. Gives the Indians some money, brings them into the national economy. They'll start to want things like the rest of us, soft cloth, sturdy shoes. It'll be a boost to the national manufacturers."

I hated this; luring the Indians into history so the bourgeoisie in the city might grow rich. Chaco looked back at me, smiled sarcastically. He flapped his earlobes with his long finger.

"I want to vomit," I said.

"Of course," he said, and went off down another hall. Or the same one again for all I knew.

At the next corner a mestizo's head appeared above the line. He stood on top of a wooden crate in a work shirt and dungarees. In his right hand he held a thick black rubber hose. The hose ran down to a silver pump-motor by his feet, next to the crate. The motor chugged, a regular rhythm, ka-thunk, ka-thunk; and the bent spokes of the flywheel, like the legs of a creature that was all legs, spun around in an abstract pattern that made me seasick. I stopped to rest, staring at the flywheel, hypnotized by my illness. The two Indian guards we'd met last night came down the hall to the box, the next ones in line. (I must have passed them in my hurry.) The old man laughed to see me, sucking his lips in and out. The boy translated his clicks and wheezings. "He says, 'Everyone wants to join us now. It's Judgment Day!' " The old man extended his dry hand to me, and I bent (as I'd seen people in the square do) and touched it to my forehead, scraping it against my skin.

The man on the box put his hand on the old man's shoulder, stopped him.

They stood like that for a few seconds, neither one speaking; a mime. The old man opened the leather purse hanging from his belt and took out some new brightly colored bills. He lifted two misshapen fingers and waved them towards the boy—the bribe was for the two of them. The man on the box stuffed the money into his bulging back pocket and turned the old man by the shoulder, so he faced forward. Holding him like that, he put the worn rubber hose down the back of his poncho. The man on the crate said something, and the old man closed his eyes. The mestizo sprayed my friend's hair and neck. DDT; outside Cordoba I'd seen animals sprayed this way, to kill lice. A little of the dust settled on my lips. It tasted sharp, acidic, bitter. The man on the box gave the old boy a push forward and took the young one's shoulder. "You can go first," the boy said to me. He made a sour little face; for the first time he looked his age to me, a boy not yet through puberty faced with an unpleasant task. I shook my head no. The man on the box turned the boy's shoulder forward.

I tried to fix the old man's gaze as he went by me. But he walked past as if I weren't there; or he weren't. Anyway, someone had died. The mestizo put the hose down the boy's back; waited for his eyes to close; sprayed his neck and hair; world without end. No one asked for an explanation. Someone pushed your child's head under water; someone doused you with this evil-smelling acid. The event required of you as much or as little faith as baptism; and it was, plainly, just as inevitable. The particles of DDT caused my nose to clog. Snot wet my upper lip. I ran down the hall, unsteady on my legs, running to catch my friends, hoping to outrun the attack.

Chavez, the Minister of Peasant Affairs, the despicable hypocrite responsible for this ritual, rose from behind his desk to shake our hands. He was a short young man, a few years older than we, with curly hair and thick eyeglasses. He looked smaller than his pictures. His office had only a big desk, with a high window behind it. The light washed painfully against my eyes. A few revolutionary posters, threats against moneylenders, had been taped to the whitewashed walls. A bright unused machete leaned against his desk.

"I heard about your argument with Betancourt last night." Chavez's head bobbed from side to side as he spoke.

"Betancourt!" Soto exclaimed.

"Yes. Our revolution, our democratic procedures, are an experiment for the whole continent. But you look surprised? Perhaps you are a different man?"

Betancourt, I thought, leader of "the democratic left" of Venezuela. Another pathetic opportunist! (Supposing it were him.)

The minister, Soto said to us, was a leader of the radical wing of the MNR. He had led the fight for extensive land reform.

The minister smiled, delighted with himself.

"He presides now," a wheezing voice said, "over the DDT Revolution."

"Damn you," Chaco said emphatically. "Ernesto, this is Chavez now. The one with the machete. I don't want to be his enemy."

The minister stiffened and walked back behind his desk. "I don't think you understand all we're doing here. It's far more than a DDT revolution. Let me give you some of our literature." He reached into a drawer and pulled out a stack of smudged flyers. I didn't take them. He left them on his desk. Fernando, who disliked rudeness of any sort, picked them up and leafed through them. Ink came off on his hands.

"I think they'll give an idea of what we're up against. Some things are a little difficult to imagine from Buenos Aires." The minister's face disappeared, a little at a time, eaten away by light from the window. His ears were gone, and the brightness was moving in on his nose. "The Indian is a sphinx," he said. "He inhabits a hermetic world, inaccessible to whites or mestizos." He looked up towards the flaking ceiling. He sounded in a trance. "We don't understand his forms of life, the way he thinks. We call the Indian the masses, but we're ignorant of his individual psyche, and his collective drama."

Bits of sentences came to me. A soul. A symbol. Asleep. I formed the bits into ranks. You must find the gesture to reach deep into their sleeping souls. I spoke. "I want to vomit."

Someone kicked my leg, behind the knee. I stuck out a hand to break my fall, and half toppled onto Chavez's desk.

Chavez glanced at my hand as if it were unsavory stuff. "You're very young," he said. "The world isn't as easily understood as you think now. It doesn't always respond to the force of our desires. The Indian lives, the Indian acts and produces. But the Indian doesn't allow himself to be understood. He doesn't wish communication. Retiring silent immutable. He inhabits a closed world. He is an enigma."

Chavez must hear the truth! "You humiliate them," I whispered. My lungs fluttered.

"Please shut up now Ernesto," Chaco whispered. "I don't want *to go in back.*"

"I think we *should* leave," Soto said, with miserable false heartiness.

"Our intention, Mr. Guevara, isn't to humiliate anyone." Chavez's lips were huge, half the size of a normal face. His eyes glinted like machine parts. "You can't overcome centuries of oppression in the twinkling of an eye, just by willing it. I think you believe too much in the power of your own wishes, your own will. The Indians don't understand soap and water. We have no choice. We must attack the result of their ignorance. This way we kill the lice for them. We have no choice."

"I think I'm going to throw up."

"Damn him," Chaco said to Fernando. "Damn him. He won't shut up till he gets us all killed." He began to cry again. "My father was a pharmacist. My mother thought I was ugly. All of you think I'm ugly too."

"No one thinks you're ugly," Fernando said. He put his arm about Chaco's shoulders. His voice, too, sounded choked. "We just think you're a little funny-looking."

Chavez, the despicable piglet, would destroy the Indian villages; he stage-managed this farcical land reform that handed out pieces of paper that entitled you to wait till you died; he made the Indians' eyes go blank. "You treat peasants like rotting meat. You do this, you do that. What you do is keep yourself in business. Nothing changes. But you can't understand me, can you? You have no vision. You have no face." I reached out towards his glimmery head, which receded backward down a tunnel. I wanted to draw him back into the room. I had more to say. He must hear the truth! My fingers went through his cheeks. He slapped me across the face, his hand open, and the room shook into overlapping images. Anger must be *conquerated*. No. Not a word. I wanted to wrench his head off his neck! No! I must not! I would not!

I hung on his shoulders, unable to move. We fell down to the floor. I lay across him, my cheek next to his, panting for breath. My friends tried to pull us apart. But Chavez wanted to hurt me; he held me around the back and squeezed my chest hard. I threw up all over his face, green bile and DDT, mucus, and a few bits of corn from last night's gorging.

Fernando walked me down the steps of the ministry, his arm around my back and under my arm. When we reached the plaza he let me drop. I fell, like a sack, to the stones. The Indians walked around us. I might have been dying, but this accident didn't excite them.

"I've had it with this . . ." Fernando stumbled over a word. ". . . with this *shit!* Because that's what it is! I thought you wanted to write about the villages, on our way to our work with the lepers. I didn't know you were interested in this *cocktail* party!" He sounded as if he'd said "shit" again. "What's the point Ernesto? They're just politicians. They're not going to listen! Or do you just like *talking?*"

Chaco knelt beside me and, with the end of my shirt, in a strangely gentle gesture, wiped the vomit from my chin. He laughed. "A demonstration of nonviolence and self-control."

I pushed Chaco away, letting my hands flap against him, and sat on the stones with my head bent down, surrounded by my friends'—my enemies'!—legs. I didn't have the strength, or the will, to rise. "Why do you want me to meet these people, Soto? These bureaucrats!" My words came out in little gasps, an old man's voice. I panicked for breath, and heaved like a fish.

"What?" He looked bemused. After all, I'd just embarrassed him. "Oh, I don't know. I like my friends to know each other. You have an interesting point of view, Guevara. You're an interesting character. Perhaps you're right. I do want to see what you'll have to say. You have audacity. I admire that. I think one can learn things from you."

"Shit!" Fernando rarely spoke this way, and so, having succumbed, he gave himself over to it. "Shit. Shit. *Shit.* What a lot of *shit!*"

"I suppose," Soto said to me, "that meeting these people isn't very valuable to you." He was angry; he had remembered that *I* was the guilty party. "You seem to know what they have to say already."

"Go to hell." It was all the wit I could think of, or had the energy for. Why didn't Fernando prepare an injection?

"Well, no. I didn't mean it that way." Soto's voice became placatory. "It's not that you're wrong. But you speak as if you'd already thought of what you'd say, long ago, as if you'd already read this story. You seem to know what everyone's going to say before he says it. As if you'd already administered a land reform!"

"That's true," Fernando said, his voice full of musing wonder at Soto's perceptiveness.

"He's like an Englishman," Chaco said, smiling, giddy with escape. "They're so certain of everything."

"You see," Soto said down to me, "you're nodding now as if you'd already thought of this too." His head looked a hundred meters away, smiling pleasantly again, as if we shared a wonderful joke. "I thought you wanted to ask some people some questions. But you're not looking for answers. Perhaps you have answers?"

Soon they'd drag me off and put my head into a trough. "Please Fernando, I need an injection."

Chaco nudged me with his foot. "You think you can just vomit all the bad things up."

"That may be," Soto said. "But you're an extraordinary sort, Doctor."

Fernando spat. But he started back to our rooms to get the needle. "You *are* an interesting character," Chaco agreed. "You have to be carried from place to place like some mystic invalid who keeps falling into trances. Then you insult people who might kill us, and have to be carried somewhere else. You're better than an interesting character. You're a *dangerous* character."

I didn't say anything. I had run out of things to say. I had run out of breath to say them with. I had run out of Bolivian talk.

But the four of us patched it up. We agreed to travel farther together.

For I liked being *an interesting character*. It promised a rich fate; a good story.

Isle of Pines, July 1965

JULY 5

Rice and beans, and a little greasy chicken, one leg each. Ponco added some cayenne to the rice. On our trip to Ghana, Ponco had acquired this taste for hot things. Food a la Walter means mined with pepper.

I live in a fuzzy distracted state. Only the past tastes hot to me; the time here is absent; it comes upon me like bumping into a stone. I have entered deeply into this self-criticism; all I want to say now, all I am now, must be formed with the materials of the past. I lose consciousness here (where?). Or almost. I reached for some water to cool my mouth.

"No," Ponco said. The word sounded definitive in his growl, a desert not to cross. He broke off a piece of bread for me. I have to be reminded of the method for hot foods. I rarely eat them, for even mildly spicy things are bad for my asthma. But I didn't want to nag Ponco. He hates cooking anyway. (My nights are bland; his are fiery.)

He noticed my discomfort. "I'm sorry. No more hot foods?"

"I suppose not."

"And no taste for music?"

"No. My disabilities."

He took another forkful of rice, and didn't look at me. I felt he was working on a dossier, one that was more aesthetic than political.

I licked the grease from my fingers. Sometimes a fragment of this world (the real one?), the one which nourishes my body, keeps me alive for elsewhere, breaks through my absence. "Spicy chicken tastes good, though." I'll rarely have it again.

"Something bothers me," Ponco said, still without looking up.

I didn't say anything. I had heard him, but from a distance. My body was jostled by Indians on a small truck, people wrapped up in blankets. They looked like sacks with faces painted on them.

"You had four."

I came back to the table. Someone was criticizing me; that always focuses my attention. "Four what? Helpings? Limbs?" But I knew what he meant. I'd been expecting it.

"Brothers and sisters smart guy."

"Yes." I smiled. Strangely, it pleased me to be discovered. Hide and seek; peekaboo around the edges.

"You say. You were an only child. Or do I remember wrong?" Now he was playing with me. He *knew*.

"You're right." I got up and filled the pot with water, to boil for mate. For some reason, being discovered made me want to walk about. I was excited. I felt naughty and clever at once; a gay deceiver; my victims (who were they? my readers? my brothers and sisters?) should thank me for a good time.

"Wishes!" Ponco said when I was seated again. He smiled broadly, pleased with himself.

"I don't think so," I said. "We liked each other."

A weak defense. Ponco chuckled, a growly sound, low, ominous, the lusty laugh of a villain. "We know." He pointed to the back of his head. "Unconscious. Couldn't help yourself. You lied!"

"I guess." But that didn't feel right to me, much as I wanted to feed Ponco's delight. "No. I mean not exactly. It doesn't feel like that."

"Yes!" Ponco said, clapping both hands down against the wooden table. "We know! I remember. Someone showed you stories of the Revolution. You said no, not the way it was. You said, The only value is Tell the truth. Not make it pretty. Not heroic. Not, excuse me, even *interesting*. Accurate accounting. Balance the books. Not my way. Shame on me I thought. No writing for you Walter. . . ."

"But . . ." I interrupted him. I rose to get the boiling water for my gourd.

"No," Ponco said. "Stay." He walked to his room, and returned holding an open book. He stood in front of my chair, pointing out a passage to me. "Does the witness recognize the words?"

"Yes," I said. He was a very good-humored prosecutor. We both enjoyed ourselves. I had not seen him so happy in this confinement since we'd talked of Hilda together.

"Read them please!"

He pulled the book back before I could look at it. But I remembered. *We ask that the narrator be truthful, and that in an attempt to describe his contribu-*

tion he does not exaggerate his real role or pretend to have been where he was not.

"Let the record show," Prosecutor Walter said, "a quotation from his memoir was read by the witness." Actually, I hadn't said anything. "Not 'where you're not,' " Walter added for the jury, "but okay to murder a whole family?"

"But," I said, "this is different from what I meant then." I got the bubbling water and poured it over the brown leaves in my knubbly gourd. Ponco struck a pose by my chair, one hand on his lip, his head cocked to one side, his lower lip pushed out, one eye half closed. Confident dubiousness.

"I told you, before I wrote from the outside, recounting events, an observer. I wanted to say what anyone could have seen, a hawk's view, who did what to whom."

"No why?" Ponco asked. "Names. Dates. Miles marched. Soldiers killed. A movie with the sound cut off? No why?"

"You mean, *boring.*" I was a little hurt—vain, I found, about my first writing effort, my reminiscences of the Cuban Revolutionary War.

"A useful volume," Walter said, woundingly kind.

"A necessity for any library! Thanks. But these events, this writing, cuts into me. These events formed me. This is about how they formed me. The way I thought about them, the way I saw them, that's what matters."

"Poof! Brothers and sisters, good-bye! Didn't form you!"

"Well, yes. They were there. We were, are, important to each other." Were we? Are we? No, we're not. The truth is in the way I wrote it. I can say more things than I can write. Perhaps that's why Walter could only talk his stories, and when he could no longer talk, he turned to others' narratives. "But our, my, parents acted as if I were the only one, maybe because I was first and I was sickly. And I had—made myself have—many interests in common with them that the others didn't share. So I changed it to the way I felt about it." I sipped some mate, rolling the heat around in my mouth.

"Convenient!" he taunted me.

"It's not a story about them."

Ponco rasped rasped rasped. His laugh. "Not about you and women. Not about brothers and sisters. What is it a story about?"

"I don't know. It's about finding Fidel. It's about why I was ready to trust him when we met, ready for the expedition he proposed. It's about finding my work. It's about the project for Bolivia. It's about . . ." I looked up at Walter, smiling. "It's about me!"

Ponco put his arm around my shoulders, smiling broadly. "Good. Make it a good *story* then."

JUNE 18

Leftover rice for breakfast. I burned the rice reheating it.

"I'm going to write a book," Ponco said.

"I'm sure you'll be better at it than I am." Glutinous self-pity: I hadn't been able to write since our conversation yesterday. It haunted my hand. All that I left out, the smell of the people, the fear I felt on that truck in the Andes (no shock absorbers, every bump slammed my bones against cold metal), going downhill, around curves, bags and people like bags falling on my legs. Or something else, I don't know what, something lost. And why had I changed things, made Soto more amiable, more foolish than he was; why had I remembered (or had I)? constructed? invented? a Chaco Francisco more stridently askew than the man who sweated next to me on that truck (sometimes, for a moment, scared out of his whimsy)? He *was* thin. Soto was plump, with spindly legs. He did introduce me to many political men, or came along while I introduced myself. He did share interests that Fernando didn't, and drew Fernando's anger. But I have made him an initiator, when always I initiated myself. *Did* I? I have made him a petty devil. Why? Because I disapproved of his politics? (He went back when Peron fell, helped Frondizi take power, compromised from the start, without any vision but more compromises. My country's future became a jumble of nonsensical fragments. Peronists on the Left and Right, CP bureaucrats returned from exile by puppet generals.) Or have I changed him from poorer motives? To interest people? (Who?) To thicken the plot? To amuse, the way I'd entertain my parents, my best audience, orbiting their table? (I haven't thought of them so much in a decade!) Have I changed things without even knowing, my motives still dark to me? Am I serving some higher, or at least different truth, some near abstraction (self with extraneous matter rubbed away; a pattern already present). Or am I simply lying? *I can't bring them back as they were.* I want to pinch Fernando's arm. I want to see him wince, the skin between my fingers redden, the slight indentation left by my nails. "Owww! Why did you do that?"

"Do what?" Ponco said, recalling me to mineral things. Tables. Gourds. Burned rice.

"Nothing. I was thinking out loud."

He laughed and sipped some tea from a cup held between both hands. "You're just like your book!"

"Am I?" I said with what must have seemed startling desperateness. "Am I?" Perhaps that floating center, that little leaf carried this way and that by the river, was still intact! "Am I?"

"Yes," dear Ponco said, "it feels like you. Before you became you."

"Good." But I could tell from the unsettled feeling in my stomach, something rounder than greasy rice, that I couldn't go back to work yet. I wouldn't hit the target (get my man?). I needed the confidence that some force (another presence? History?) guided my hand, kept me from just lying, would make a false world, false word I mean, shake apart. (False world? Like this one: imperialism is a lying author.) Ponco went outside.

I went to my desk, this board

"Let's go for a walk."
Ponco sat tilted back, still reading *The Charterhouse of Parma*. "Good," he said, gracefully bringing his chair back to the floor.
"We can talk about the book you're thinking of. I'm sorry I was so distracted this morning. As soon as you said writing, I began to think about mine."
Ponco looked puzzled. "A book?"
"You said you were thinking of writing something. A memoir, I thought, though I don't know if you said that."
"A memoir?" Ponco, I think, smirked. Impossible! Ponco doesn't smirk.
"Yes. Are you smirking because I walk around in a daze here?" We strolled towards the ocean. I'd rolled up my sleeves and the tall grass tickled my arms. Ponco walked near the fence, playing a game, rapidly sticking a finger between the squares of barbed wire, in and out, while moving forward. Sometimes, because of his ancient gnome's voice, I forget how young he is.
"A memoir. Yes. Of the war. I wonder. Can I add magic wings to fly over the enemy? It once felt that way. It seemed nothing could touch us."
I looked down at my hands. "You can write it, I suppose, if you felt that way. I don't know. No one will believe you. They'll think you meant you felt that way. A metaphor!" New to the craft, I discovered simple things, like metaphors. And I felt that even my simple discoveries were questionable items. Could anything mean something else? "Anyway Walter, let's skip that sort of nonsense."
"Sorry. Didn't realize how you felt."
"Confused."
He lost his game, scraped his finger on a barb. He didn't suck it though, as if he were wary of his own mouth. He held the finger in front of him and stared at it. Now we were two men in a field on an island looking at our fingers. "At the table," he said, "you yelped."
"I imagined I was pinching someone. I imagined I was the person I was pinching. I was thinking of my friend Fernando."

"It hurt?"

"No. Yes. It's difficult to explain."

"We know!" Walter said with delight. He had looked his fill at his finger. We resumed our walk. "Fernando was a good friend for someone like you," Ponco—I forgave him—said.

We had reached the ocean. Ponco sat down in the sand and took off his shoes. He rolled up his pants in careful even folds. "I like where you write that your clothing was a vow," he said, standing up, smiling. "You—a dandy!"

"A dandy?"

Ponco continued to smile.

"You're right," I admitted. "My clothes defined my kind. You were bound to notice how I dressed, raise an eyebrow perhaps. And when you did, you lost face. You were concerned about petty things. I seemingly had no concern at all." A dandy; I had not thought of that before. It seemed a small gain in self-knowledge. My text revealed more than I knew, and what it revealed seemed true to me. A good sign?

"When I came to the mountains. A boy in a big hat. I was a dandy."

"No. I mean you seemed the most casual of fellows."

"A style, still. A casual style." He danced quickly on the hot sand, to the lip of the ocean, hurried mincing steps. He ran out towards a receding wave, and then, when it turned on him, scampered back. Out and back; another game.

"Look!" he said on his return. He pointed to his pants leg, where a little water had splashed up. "Have to change. My new style. Fastidious." A dry hiccup of a laugh. Had he looked at my journal? When?

We turned back towards the house.

"What did you mean a good friend for me? Or was that just another joke?"

"Don't misunderstand. I like him. Like me. He *used* to tell stories. And he can't hear. I can hardly talk." He stopped for a moment, remembering his voice, its gaiety. "He's clear about things. Big signs of his feelings. Primary colors. Clarity. You'd like that."

His game with the ocean again. He taunted me. And, like the ocean, I turned back, enjoying the play. "Go on." It was what I had wanted before, when I showed him my childhood—some talk about me. Though now it created a small worry in me. I had written me, and if I'd lied, were my lies, as I'd hoped, like some psychoanalytic symptom, an indirect way back to what was central? Had I, as I thought I wished, betrayed myself? Or was it just another story, one of so many possible, with me (whoever that was) excluded, outside, just another reader of an arbitrary epic?

"Very abstract. You are. One enemy. One opposition. Always. Primary colors. Or no colors at all, only outlines."

"Yes." He was criticizing me, but I was not displeased. I recognized myself. "Clarity. Yes."

Ponco smiled. "You lack certain qualities."

"Yes. It's necessary. To act."

He stopped by the fence. "And the shoes!"

"What?" We smiled at each other.

"First venture of the future Minister of Industries!" He laughed, a wholehearted mirth. His laugh had been a very deep sound when his voice wasn't. Now it sounded like the spinning flywheel of a machine. He showed his menacing teeth. I realized that I had only ever heard Ponco laugh wholeheartedly at his own jokes.

"It was like roulette," I said. "We always thought that the next batch of shoes would make it come out right."

"And the Indians!"

"Yes?" I enjoyed the game. The recognitions, though unkind (and how else would I have known they were genuine?), restored my confidence.

"You thought. They don't want raincoats. Ballpoint pens. Things. Material incentives. You thought. The workers want . . ." He paused, put his hands against the barbed wire. ". . . symbols. That's it. Rites. Communion with the spirit of the nation."

He was quoting a speech of mine! "You disagree?"

"Touchy!" He smiled, paused, thought. "No. It's all you. Same tune in a different key. You don't understand that, do you?"

"I understand it, but I can't hear it." I turned and started back to the house. Ponco watched the men working among the older trees with big metal shears, cutting dead branches. After a while he joined me, making swimming motions in the tall grass, hands together, then thrust out and apart: a breast stroke. It shook pollen loose, which I disliked.

"I was wrong." He'd swum up to me.

"Wrong?" No, I thought, you're right.

"Not young Communists."

"No?"

He smiled. His teeth are large, white, and even in front. I had pulled several in back. "It's an insane asylum."

"You're kidding. Planting trees?"

He nodded. "Patients. Work therapy."

"It looks," I said, "just like work itself."

"Work therapy. Work done by patients. Our theory: people *want* to work.

Communion with the nation." He studied my face. "Lack of same makes for alienation. Madness."

"You're lying!"

"Yes!" He smiled at my discovery. I thought I saw a spectral hand rise towards his mouth. He would spit on it, and wipe it on his pants. Or I wanted to see that hand. But that was long ago. "Work farm. Insane asylum. Prison. See?"

"Sure. A game. Find the similarity."

"Not a game. A poem. You inspired me." We'd come to the porch again. He picked up his book, sat down. "One more thing. Cornfields, near La Paz? That altitude?"

"Yes, Mr. Prosecutor. I'm pretty sure. I wouldn't lie about vegetables. Potatoes certainly. Many different kinds, big, small, blue and red skins. And I remember the taste of fresh corn in Isaias's stew. An Argentine specialty."

"Ah," Ponco said, a small hot gust of wind. "Do cook it sometime."

He went back to his reading, and I went inside to my board, my work, my work therapy.

Peru, September 1953

Their Silence

Dear Father:

I can't see the horizon; the slat sides of the truck narrow our view to disjointed strips of the roadside, the vistas enjoyed by penned cattle. But the sky overhead lightens, as if paint thinner had been added to a jar of black. It's black still, but finally I can, through the shadows, make out the darker smudge of these words in my notebook. All night I've wanted to write you about the curious fear that came over me this evening. I trembled with terror, like the first man to hear thunder; but this thunder was the absence of sound, the silence of the Indians who share the back of this truck with us.

Staying awake so long has, anyway, transformed my mood, given me the solidity of sensations, the purity of emotions, that come from not sleeping for a night. I remember that Mother said that these were the only times she felt as if she could write poetry. She had a name for this special state of mind: "the reward for vigilance"—for it was very important, she said, to see the process through for the full twenty-four hours; even a nap would cloud the mind, turn the clarity to headaches. (A strange name, as if her insomnia were guard duty on some imperiled frontier.) A morning after one of her vigils, she sat at the breakfast table in her bathrobe, cried over a newspaper article, laughed uproariously at a trivial song on the radio, spoke more intimately to me, and

A truck going the other way up the mountains on this narrow road just passed. Our truck pulled off to the side, and when I heard the oncoming groaning I stood up, gripping the topmost wooden slat with my hands. A heavy rope ran from the cab of the other truck to its back gate. Six Indian men hung on this line, their arms draped across it. I could see their faces for a moment, lit by our truck's headlights, round forms emerging suddenly from a nearly black backdrop. I shouted and waved my left hand. No one replied. Six scarecrow heads swung into my face with a rushing sound, and back, one by one, into darkness, like a fun-house device. Our trucks were less than a meter apart. Some of the Indians let their eyes pass over me, without expression; some had their eyes closed, like the oracle in Neruda's play. Our truck started up again. I fell backward onto a sleeping body, a rancid smell, like something curdled. Hands from inside a blanket pushed me off in rapid abrupt motions, like muffled punches. I leaned back against the side of the truck, my knees up in front of me. No one talks tonight, even if you fall on them.

The warm Indians are the aristocrats of this truck. (Fifteen or so share the flatbed with us, sitting against the side, or squeezed in between the burlap sacks and crates.) After the sun set they wrapped themselves in rough woolen blankets dyed in brightly colored stripes of blue, green, and yellow. They drew their covers up over their mouths. With their woolen caps and long ear flaps, they formed limbless rounded shapes, like those toys that, however you knock them about, always come back upright. As the light faded, Soto and I tried to speak with them. I smelled DDT on the man across from me, so I asked him a question about the bogus land reform.

Silence.

Roberto turned to the man next to him and made a remark about the cost of the ride.

Silence.

About the MNR.

Silence.

One of us speaks again, a friendly inquisitive banal voice.

And again.

A chill began. I pushed one of the burlap sacks aside to see the man opposite more clearly. His hands tied knots into pieces of red and blue string. A quipu, the Incas' record system. I said something about the cold. His eyes, a slit between his blanket and his hat, moved across my body without recognition, not even resting momentarily on my face. He undid his knots. It was no record, no remnant, just a hand fooling nervously with some string, a man training imaginary performers, putting himself to sleep. I spoke again into his silence. He didn't even show the mild bemusement of the auditor of a foreign language. We're far more foreign than that. We're landscape. His mouth under the blanket chewed constantly, slightly disarranging the folds of wool, like the creases of a masticating lizard's skin. I could not allow this silence! I demanded to know the reason for it. He said nothing. I was a bird cawing, a strange inedible soulless bird. A hand emerged from under the skirt of the blanket, pulled it down to his chin. The skin of his lip was brown and black, eaten away by coca and ground limestone. He stood in the center and spat over the side of the truck. Droplets splashed on my face.

"You're a careless son of a bitch," I said, brushing the spit off my face.

He looked down at me, the long green jaws, the scaly reptilian forehead and bulging eyes of a lizard. "The woman was right," he said, in the squeaky gutturals, the gnashing sounds of his species, "you don't know us." He flicked his long thin tongue towards me, then drew it back.

"I do," I said.

"You do not. What do you know about lizards? You should study natural history. Your place in the scheme of things isn't as big as you think."

"What are you talking about?" Fernando asked. "Are you talking to that guy?"

"Nothing. To no one."

The peasant fell backward, covered his nose; brought his knees up; sat.

"You sound," Chaco said, "like foreign tourists trying to meet girls at a social club." He was to my right. I didn't turn to see his face, its undecipherable punctuation. "You sound like you're reading from a phrase book. 'How many grots do you charge to give me a hernia, please?' 'Can you tell me how to turn myself into a bathroom?' "

"Probably," Fernando said, "they don't speak Spanish."

Chaco spoke French to the Indians in a high mincing voice, saying insulting things about their mothers and animals. He cackled at his own mockery, and Soto laughed with him. Soto's omnivorous amiability couldn't be long disturbed by a rebuke as mild as silence. "That's it," he said to Fernando, "they don't speak Spanish. Of course. That's it."

Their silence made my armpits damp; their silence was a sign against me. I felt as if I had no voice; my mouth was stuffed with dirt; no one could hear me. The peasants were stones; I wanted to shatter them. But my anger could hardly hide the fear that dissolved me. In their silence my worlds my words unraveled back past the present to nothing.

What terrified me hid behind the objects, the burlap sacks of leaves, the crates of Coca-Cola; it was another world another word not yet spoken; spoken and I'd shatter. The truck was too small, there were too many sacks and crates, there wasn't enough room, I was being crushed, I!

"Look at that," Chaco shouted. He had his eyes pressed towards the slash of roadside. We stared between the slats. A truck had overturned on the shoulder, its wheels facing us. There was a body in the cab; we could look down on the bloody face smashed against the side window. Along the road, near the back of the truck, lay three or four other dead bodies. It went by very quickly. They may have been stones. Or bags.

But it gave an image to my terror.

"Oh shit," Soto said, turning on me angrily. I could smell the sweat coming off him, even through his cologne. He'd been reluctant to get on this truck. "This one's not for us," he had said, as if considering something even he found distasteful. Our driver had drawn big eyes on his headlights, with arching eyebrows, and strung Christmas-tree lights over the top of the cab. He'd painted slogans on a board affixed to the front of the cargo area: FAITH IN GOD! ONWARD TO FINAL VICTORY! Antic humor, Soto said, wasn't what we wanted from a driver. And the slogans reminded him of the mottoes you see over the stone pillars at the entrance to graveyards. He knew it was foolish to be superstitious, but he was superstitious. He got a bad feeling from this rig and this place. The truck was parked in front of a quonset hut in a vacant lot on the outskirts of La Paz. The earth, dry as ash, blew all over our clothes. Fernando defiantly led the way into the trucking office.

The driver, resting in a chair tilted back against the wall, didn't inspire confidence in Soto. A fat man with a thick black mustache, he wore a leather vest and no shirt. "I don't trust fat men," Soto said, without irony. "And this guy drinks. I can tell." This was no way, Soto moaned, to travel on thin mountain roads. One mistake—and this fat guy's life, you could tell, was a string of mistakes—and we'd end up at the bottom of a gorge. I reassured him: Fernando and I had driven mountains just like these on a small motorcycle. It was perfectly safe.

For I wanted this trip. The Inca runners had moved from village to village on their mountain roads, roads zigzagged for grading, roads changing to small steps, stone stairways in the places of near impossible ascent. Their feet bled. They brought messages from the Inca. The trucks now formed the blood-stream of the villages. This fat man in a leather vest had plumes for me;

he was an Inca runner. There was, I said to Soto, nothing to worry about.

But Soto babbled on, not reassured, as the truck slowly, shakily, rocking from side to side, ascended a mountain out of La Paz. The driver, he screeched, was a maniac. He geared down, for no reason, when we were going up for Christ's sake. And look at the terrain! I stood, pitching from side to side, and looked over the edge into deep rocky valleys. Soto had a point; Fernando and I had never been in mountains or on roads like this. Perhaps they were the Inca's own! Built for a single running man! The drops were sheer, down cliffs littered with unused parts, huge stones left over from the week of creation, sharp slabs like the teeth of a prehistoric monster. We moved along the edge of a gorge with a jumble of stones at the bottom, a river of rocks. (A small animal, the size of a kitten—probably it was a pig or a pony—walked all alone along the rocks at the bottom.)

The turns of the road around the mountain went at acute angles; the driver should have inched around them, and even so he might have sent a back wheel into space. But he wasn't inching.

"Nothing to worry about," I had said to Soto, who was too scared, fortunately, to look himself. He lay with his legs out in front of him, pressed into a bag, bracing himself, his arms spread to each side, gripping the slats. The guy was certifiably crazy, Soto said. He speeds up on turns! He stops suddenly when there's no one there! He would tip us over like that, would drive too close to the edge, the wheels on one side would slip over, we'd fall down into the gorge like a boat smashed up against the rocks. "Shut up, for God's sake," Chaco said, not laughing, the muscles of his lips frozen into a wide circle.

After a while Soto drew his knees up in front of his face, relaxed his grip. But now, after those bodies had given a name to my fear, I heard his voice. His stupid panic was mine. I looked towards the indifferent, darkening sky. I wasn't chosen for a special fate. There were no special fates. The truck rocked a sack against my legs, like a leaden blanket, and I kicked it away as if it stifled me. The peasants' eyes had closed, oblivious of the danger. "God would take them when he wished"—the moronic will-less fatalism of the poor! Every time the truck shook I knew that it would oscillate farther, that it was about to tip over. I braced my legs as Soto had. I looked between the slats at the rocky slope of the mountain opposite us; there was not a meter of road between us and the edge. I looked back to the stony dark faces. I was being absurd! I counted my breaths to calm myself. This lacked all dignity, I was ridiculous. No, everyone else was stupid, we should get off, walk the rest of the way! I rose; I would bang on the cab, make him slow down. A jolt knocked me backward, and I jammed my arm reaching out behind me to break my fall, I went on falling, I couldn't stop imagining our fall, the truck upside down in the gorge, yet still hurtling downward, rocks raining beside us kicked loose by our wheels, our bodies spilling out like bags. . . . Relax! I remembered the breathing exercises from *The Hindu Science of Breath Control*. . . . I couldn't relax. I tensed my leg muscles to hold myself in the world.

I turned to Fernando. "Their silence drove me crazy. It's like a strange smell. It panicked me. I feel like I'm being buried alive, shouting to get out. But no one can hear me."

"A strange smell," Chaco said. I had hoped *he* wouldn't hear me. "Doesn't that panic ponies?"

Fernando nodded gravely towards me. He could hear how seriously upset I was.

"Their silence was severe," I said. "That's what I meant about a smell. It was present, palpable. It was as if they were *saying* that silence. I felt like I was going to die. And now every time this damn truck sways to one side I think it's about to tip over. I think it's because there's nothing I can do about it. I've got no control over things. I know that's crazy."

"Not that crazy," Chaco said. I couldn't see his clown's face, fortunately, his nervous lips making flickering shapes. "Soto was right about this guy, don't you think? He's a maniac racing some phantom no one else can see. And trucks go over all the time, you know. I heard about it in La Paz when I told people at the cafes we were going to take one. And you saw that one we passed with the four little tombstones behind it. They'd already buried the bodies."

"Shut up Chaco." Fernando spoke on my behalf, across my body.

But Chaco had more to say. "Guevara's a funny guy." (Was I dead? They spoke for me. They spoke about me.) "Shooting off his mouth to guys who might have *us* shot doesn't scare him. Trucks scare him. Trucks don't scare me anymore, Fernando. *He* scares me." He pointed his bony finger at my nose. "*He* wants us all to die—as a sign of our nobility. I think it would be safer, for his friends anyway, if instead of being nonviolent he just took out a pistol and shot the people he didn't like."

Fernando turned towards me, as if Chaco hadn't spoken. We had our cheeks pressed against the worn wood, facing each other. "That sounds like you," he said. "About control I mean. You like to be in charge, don't you. I mean like your football team of dangerous characters? And you find it hard to trust other people. But this guy has driven a thousand times through these mountains. I wouldn't worry about that."

"You're right," I said, hoping to reassure myself.

"I mean, their silence to all those questions was eerie. I felt it too, listening to you and Soto shouting at them. But it doesn't mean anything. We all think the world is talking about us, that it means something about our personality.

It doesn't mean anything. They just don't speak Spanish." Fernando had studied psychiatry. Behind his words I felt the sodden weight of certain clinical terms.

"Yes. My place in the scheme of things isn't that big. I feel all right now," I lied.

Chaco climbed over me. The three of them pressed together for warmth.

I put my leather jacket over my V-necked gray sweater, the one you and Mother gave me for my birthday, and I put my sports jacket, my largest item, over that. It split the seams. I hugged myself and repeated another verse of Gandhi's prayer, "I will conquer my fear." I imagined Gandhi walking towards the ocean. I must conquer my fear. Fear makes us slaves of the imperialists. Overcome your fear of death, and no one could rule you. He walks twelve miles a day, beginning far inland, to announce his teaching. (My heartbeat slowed.) Barefoot, dressed in a loincloth and a prisoner's small white cap, he has little knobs of knees, knots in a stick, too frail for his business. He will make his body submit to his will. (It calmed me to think his image, walking towards the ocean.) He walks away from the already known, from titles, from political parties, from the lying words of this world. He throws himself upon the Indian masses, and if they do not respond, he will die. The veins in his temples stand out as he waves to the people along the side of the road, fluttering his fingers like Chaplin. Parents come from their huts, sprinkle water on the road, smooth the path with long green branches. Some feel compelled to join him. They want to share in this gay inevitable progress, this defiance. And I, too, am drawn to him, as you are, Father. I feel more courageous in his presence. His figure moving forward delights me: Chaplin prancing down a city street, eluding the police as if by accident.

The symbol that will rouse the peasants is, I see now, not a thing made out of words, the deceitful speeches of impotent politicians. The Bolivian bureaucrats, the stinking opportunists of the democratic Left, are too craven for leadership. Our continent requires a leader's fearless actions; the will calls to the will, arouses it; an action will make these men and women—these rocks —rub their eyes in wonder and rise up and follow it, follow him, towards the ocean. This action

The time I can keep my hands out grows shorter.

These Indians, wrapped up warmly among sacks (and easily confused with sacks) wait not for a voice, an order, but for an action. His weak body walking; the will asserting how little the body, or life itself, matters. A people needs a call to a great sacrifice, to test itself to the utmost. I am more sure than ever of Gandhi's way, calling our people to a final suffering. They must suffer greatly (and they want to, even to die) in order to become a great people, single in purpose. They will die for an action, not words. But it must be something the leader does for *himself* first, by himself. Gandhi didn't preach defiance of the Salt Law, he violated it. He didn't recommend austerity like an MNR poster; he ate no better food than the masses, wore no better clothes. An action is true, you taught me, Father, if you can prove it on your own body. Only that action will compel belief in others. Paz Estenssoro, Betancourt, Chavez, Prio Soccaras, Bosch are men without courage, afraid to act themselves against imperialism. The democratic left is just talk, plans for others. The people lose faith, grow apathetic, cease to respond. The words, the deeds, the people live in separate houses. Where is the man whose actions could call them together?

I stopped for a moment to warm my hands, and fell asleep. *An Indian took a piece of paper and a ballpoint pen out from under his poncho. Chaco was right! He drew something on the paper and gave it to the man next to him. They passed it around the truck. I was afraid they wouldn't let me see it. But it was intended for me! Everyone looked towards me. He had drawn a picture of a hut, but with no doors or windows. A voice came from the house. A woman's voice, a woman moaning* —I woke with my heart pounding, afraid that it was Mother's voice. I could see her face, the moment before I woke, as I'd seen it looking down from my bedroom window the time you took her to the hospital. She squeezed your beard in pain. One of the Indian women moaned. My head and eyes ached. (Mother is right—a short nap, a dereliction of duty, and one loses the rewards.) I shook Fernando till he woke up.

"Are you all right?" I asked the woman. She sat near the cab, with two burlap sacks leaning against her shoulders. She had taken off her blanket and wore only a dark poncho. Her hair, in a long black braid, came from under her bowler hat. She rocked back and forth in pain. "Can we help?" Fernando said. "We're doctors." He pounded on my chest, put his ear to my heart. (I.e., "Doctors.") The woman moaned, ignoring us. Her face was lined all over, but not twisted as Mother's had been. None of the other people looked towards her. They had pulled their caps down over their eyes during the night.

Chaco woke when Fernando moved, and watched our mime. He smiled, raised an imaginary enema bag over Soto, and performed a charade irrigation. Soto slept on—the secret of such good digestion of life—his head slumped forward, shaken to one side sometimes by the truck's bumping.

"She's singing," Chaco said. "She doesn't need a doctor."

He was right. The moaning had become a cadenced sound. Her song was a few notes in a narrow range, repeated over and over. She had a deep voice. The sound moved forcefully through the cottony feeling in my head. The accent of her chant moved forward, or around, depending on where it fell. She rocked slightly back and forth, like a Jew at prayer. The truck too rocked, and wind whistled lightly through the slats; it all accompanied her song. The sun must have been at the horizon. I could see huts through the slats, as we came off the mountain, and hear roosters screaming shrill obbligatos. Her song buoyed me up, eased the strain in my neck and shoulders. A mournful tune, the few notes chanted slowly, the accents changing gradually. My body swayed against the potatoes in the sack. Chaco and Fernando smiled.

The sound, the light that washed over us now like a pale transparency, woke the others. Perhaps that was her task. They freed their hands from under their blankets, pulled back their caps from their eyes. They, too, swayed to her song. This motion wove us all together. The others joined her, the same low moan at first, the same few notes over and over, their bodies rocking back and forth. Sometimes the accents fell as hers did, sometimes not. It was a rushing river; you felt you could follow one voice as it moved forward in eddies, around rocks, over branches; but the sound of them all together was unchanging, changing always. Perhaps it was a saint's day. Chaco, ignoring all protocol, moaned too. One of the Indians smiled at him. (Impossible! What did *he* know about them?)

I turned to Fernando. "It's like the music for the dance we saw in La Paz, the same few notes, a simple thing, a chant."

"A few notes? No, it's not. That's the way you hear it. They're both really pretty complicated tunes." Fernando, too, began to sing. He smiled at me, encouragingly, tauntingly. *I* would think it was a tango. If I sang they would stop, their mouths dour. My limbs felt stiff. I hadn't had enough sleep. My mouth tasted foul, and the bitter stench of these people on an empty stomach, along with the constant rocking, made me nauseous. My body returned; enclosed me. I looked towards the road, the silver of tree trunks going by.

They sang the sun back into the sky. The sun I wait for, the leader I've written you about, will be, by his courageous action, the guarantee of the truth of the words of revolution. In his person the masses form a unity with the world, joined through his presence, the sun in their sky. His actions are the sign that cowardice will not shatter our unity; our world coheres, our work, our words will reach their objects; his acts weave the connection between the people, the words, and our deeds. I will find this man, this work.

My head really throbs. I wonder what you will make of all this!

An embrace from your
tired, hungry, cold, loving son,

Ernesto

Isle of Pines, July 1965

JULY 7

Ponco handed me back my pages over breakfast. *His* breakfast. Attacks kept me awake last night. I took only a little mate. The reward for vigilance: I'm exhausted; the room seems vague.

He giggled. "I see what you mean, 'you awaited *him.*' Fidel! The sun in our sky! I like that. Boom boom boom. Enter the god! Very mystical! Very flattering!"

"Not flattery. I really was as I say. So were many others. The nationalist leaders, like Paz Estenssoro, Bosch, Prio Soccaras, they had begun something, a move towards independence. But they couldn't complete it. Even to think of fighting the Yanquis they would have had to transform themselves, their bourgeois programs. They couldn't call on the people to fight. What I said was true in a way: they would have to be willing to die." I breathed shallowly. The room shimmered, bleached of color, losing substance. "We were burning with energy, a whole generation of us, disgusted with compromises. We wouldn't compromise with imperialism." I smiled, thinking of that purity, shining, without content. "We would destroy the whole world if we couldn't find something that satisfied that longing."

Ponco looked at me sadly, his head halfway down. "I know. I'm not a child. I was there." He tore off a piece of bread, and rubbed it in some jam. "You talk like someone's old man."

"I'm sorry. Of course you know. Perhaps my conception was a little . . . abstract, grandiose. Young. I didn't know the thing I was waiting for. I was sure I would recognize it, though, make whatever sacrifice was necessary."

Ponco smiled at me. "Free of this world's names. Without title. Without party. On an island. Without breakfast. I know who *that* is."

I shrugged, barely able to lift my shoulders. "I didn't know."

"Still." He looked down at his coffee cup. What was going on in that cup? "Yes?"

"The man who acts for himself." He got up rapidly, and walked into his bedroom. I waited. I was learning how to wait. Wait for Castro's help. Wait for inspiration. Wait for Ponco to come back.

He returned with Debray's book. I think he keeps a library of incriminating documents in there. He pushed it in front of me. His thumb occluded part of the paragraph, but I remembered it. "When Comrade Che Guevara once again took up insurrectional work, he accepted on an international level the consequences of a line of action of which Fidel Castro, leader of the Cuban Revolution, is the incarnation. When Che Guevara reappears, it is hardly risky to assert that it will be as the head of a guerrilla movement, *as its unquestioned political and military leader.*" Debray and I had worked on the book together. Walter knew that.

"Yes?" I scratched my ear. What was I meant to feel guilty for?

"See? The same story, different key." Ponco stood next to me. "MNR bureaucrats don't act for themselves. Gandhi acts for himself first. Et cetera. Action and politics." He held up one finger. Meaning, I thought, the unity of theory and practice, political talk, and military action. "That's you."

Ponco sat down again, drank some of that fascinating coffee. "Your letter. I wonder. It sounds . . . religious."

I laughed. "Coincidence of the metaphysical and the practical." I was kidding around. Ponco reminded me of other accusers. Fidel. My mother.

He looked baffled, stared at me, almost angrily. "Coincidence? Accident? Not physical?"

"No. I'm sorry." I realized I had borrowed his elliptical style. But to say that would be to remind him of his wound. "I meant that they all came together. This time. It must happen sometimes. What you call my religious urge, my psychology, and what needs to be done."

"That sounds religious too!"

"You too!" Breathing was becoming easier.

"Me too what?"

"You sound like Fidel. He said, 'The revolutionary who wants to become a saint.' I was. He said." I couldn't stop talking like Walter.

He rose again and went to his bedroom. What text would accuse me now?

He returned with a piece of paper and a ballpoint pen. He pushed the dishes to one side, and worked away, quietly intent, while I waited.

"Here!" Like a dream figure, he pushed the paper at me. A conglomeration of stick figures, and figures that looked like sticks. He could see I was puzzled. He came over to stand behind me.

"That's Fidel. On a big horse. That's the horse's tail. That's a sword. That's you. That's burning wood under you. You wear monk's robes. You can't feel the heat. Go on reading a book. You two divide up the world. Happy *coincidence.* Use it and it's yours." I turned to look at him, and he pouted, sticking out his lower lip, imitating Chaco. "You don't like my art?" he rasped. A whimpery tone was impossible for Walter. "I think it's profound." He tried to deepen his voice on the word "profound"; but his voice could go no deeper, and the word disappeared.

JULY 8

No word from Fidel.
Ponco worries. This morning he said, "Odd. Debray hasn't . . ." and then he stopped, afraid of his own dark conjectures. One expects promptness from Regis. Blue *lycée* notebooks with sharp theses. Before I came here I sent him to Bolivia to review our agreement with Monje, to locate sites. But his reports have not been forwarded to me.

Fidel is silent. Perhaps he is waiting for the July 26 speech to announce my intentions. Or

Or what will he announce?

Ecuador, September 1953

Guayaquil

Soto and Chaco went to Lima, to the apartment of a nurse I had known in Buenos Aires. Fernando and I stopped at the Inca fortress Sacsahuaman; no longer a fortress, but walls, large smooth irregular stones, closely fitted. Our archeological project lay in our friendship, unearthing again our common interests, repairing the fissures caused by my love of political talk.

"All this stuff about leaders, Ernesto. I don't get it. That's not self-reliance." We walked along the shady side of a wall that bulged in and out like a curtain. I pressed my fingertips hard against the cool stones. They had a message for me, a nourishment, if only I could press them strongly enough. The nail broke on my forefinger; the finger bled from the corner. A small but intensely painful wound. I smeared the blood against the stone, a light red trail mixing with dust; I wanted to leave my mark. Fernando looked at me, his head turned to the side. It embarrassed me. He reached into his jacket pocket and took out a small roll of gauze.

"I think you were right before," he said. "Good is done a little at a time. Not by violence. And not by leaders. But by individuals. I mean our first task is to make ourselves independent individuals."

I sucked on my finger, and said nothing. I didn't know what I truly thought. My thoughts were a tottery structure, not an active unity. This farrago about leaders, words, actions, these thoughts didn't form me; I didn't hold them; I only *entertained* them. But what might seal them to me? And why had I shown Fernando my letter? Why had I written my father? Like Betancourt peering about in Isaias's field, I needed the reassurance of others. I, too, stood in the field of the dead. Or worse: on the truck, writing home, I felt myself in the kitchen of my family's second house. I saw the wicker chairs, the cups of hot drinks from a height just above the table. I was a young boy, hurtling around the glass table.

I wrapped a bit of gauze around my forefinger and ripped it free with my teeth. A man in a dark-red tasseled poncho walked out of a hut halfway up the mountainside opposite us. He carried a staff in his right hand that glinted silver in the sun. An elder; when he instructed the children on planting, he struck them with the *vara*, inscribed the knowledge on their bodies so they wouldn't forget. He looked towards the top of the mountain. He *should* see stone terraces, low walls in regular layers, moving towards him down the mountain's face. The priest had given them instructions, brought by messenger from the Inca, given to the Inca by the sun. Good soil had been carried to the topmost planting areas. Now different foods might be grown, each crop happy at its own proper altitude. Ditches, sluices brought water up and down the mountain, to feed the terraces. No. He saw none of that. It was all no more. Only a few of the small stones from the terracing his ancestors had built. Why had they chosen such impossible places? They must have found exultation in the challenge of making the grand and difficult landscape accept them. They had mingled their blood with the land, made it theirs and the gods', and now they couldn't leave it. The elder looked up at the sun. It was twelve noon. The holiest hour. Still? I looked up too. The mountain bleached away. I stumbled on a rock and caught myself on Fernando's shoulder.

"I need to know more natural history," I said. "I don't know my place in things."

"What? I don't get it." Fernando kicked at the dust with his snub-nosed boot, raising a little explosion. "Well, I know mine," he said. "It's to learn about my continent, to live simply, and to do my work with the lepers now, a little at a time."

I stepped back a few feet and tried to run up the side of a stone wall. I imagined myself standing horizontally.

Fernando looked down at me in the dirt, indifferent to my achievement. "All your talk of sacrifice Ernesto. I don't get that either. You remind me of the Incas. Human sacrifice. I don't understand. Is that the unconscious of Latin America? That's madness! I don't want to rebuild the Inca Empire. I want to heal sick people, comfort them if I can't heal them. You know, you're not even an Inca, Ernesto. You're an Aztec. At least the Incas substituted guinea pigs."

"Oh, they offered the occasional human," I said. "For the most hallowed times." I spoke to the ground. Grit was embedded in my chin, and on my lips and tongue, mixed with gauze threads. I rubbed them off my tongue.

"No. You're an Aztec. You don't want the *occasional* human. You want hecatombs of sacrifice. You're afraid the sun will go out."

From the hard rocky ground I looked up at the sun. I forced myself to stare at it until it offered me a vision, until each ray stood out, distinct. Each one of us was a spoke of that wheel. Animals walked towards that center and spun about the sun—llamas, parrots, sheep, deer, owls, fishes, ducks, whippery wavery creatures formed from thin hollow lines, the vitreous bodies of my eyes. The sun had shown enough to me and forced me to close my eyes. My eyelids glowed red. I fell deeper into the ground. The sun with animals; the silver plate Montezuma gave Cortes.

"It's like the sacrificial stone at Machu Picchu," Fernando said from far above me. My prone position invited accusation. "You saw it and began to wheeze. It *excited* you."

"Don't be silly," I said. "It was the altitude."

But I lied. Streams of blood had risen for me from the stone, long, thick, nearly black threads, still steaming; veins that held the sun to the earth and brought nourishment to the god. Here comes the knife! We stared. We all felt it: at the moment of sacrifice the offering's blood became one's own, spilled out and coursing upward from one's veins. No. I wasn't there. *They* were united with the god, and through him with each other. Not me; even in imagination I was excluded from their communion at the stone, their song from the truck. I lay on the ground, with eyes closed, and picked small pebbles from my chin.

"You fell down panting across the stone. You wanted to sacrifice yourself."

"What are you talking about? That's not true." My body, subdued by the sun, was allowed to rise slowly to the surface of the earth. I opened my eyes. "I fell down, but I didn't fall on the stone."

"No, I guess you didn't." Fernando smiled at me, his curly head blotched with spots of sun. "But I'll bet you wanted to. I should have taken out my sacred Swiss pocketknife and offered you to Virachocha, the sun's father."

Instead he had taken a syringe from his knapsack and bent over me in the dirt, a few feet from the gray pole that yoked the earth and sun. He prepared my arm for a shot. Why am I drawn to places where breathing is impossible for me, my food so difficult to scrabble up? (But that's everywhere!)

"You know," Fernando said, no longer smiling, "I don't see what you find so wonderful about people suffering and dying. I think our work, a doctor's work, is to *stop* people from dying, not tell them what a grand and noble thing it is. I don't think it would be very grand, I mean, I don't want to die. I don't know about you. I really don't. I don't think you know what you're talking about."

I got up, brushed myself off. My arm hurt. It ached still from where Ricardo had impaled me on my beliefs. "The dinosaurs died," I said. "Big thunder lizards. All gone now. Death's not such a big deal."

"You're kidding," my bewildered friend said. He smiled at me in a warm openhearted way, shaking his blotchy head from side to side. He wanted to be in on the joke.

"Sure," I said, and returned his smile. (So eventually we would part in bewilderment.)

"And this Soto," Fernando said, as we continued our stroll round and round the walls. "I don't trust him, Ernesto. He's a careerist of the worst kind. He makes me feel soiled."

The stones lay together in an odd yet precise way, beveled to fit. How had they done it? Some stones were as large as houses, yet they had been lifted without draft animals or machinery. It was their *will* that had articulated their fortress, their will that upheld it until this time, their will that fixed our attention here, in rapt contemplation. What confidence they must have had in their leadership! Their labor, they knew, was the god's food, his delight, the community's life. Through the sun that fell on that man's hands, his hands became mine, mine his. "Soto is just a petty demon," I said. "You shouldn't take him so seriously."

"I don't. But *you* take him seriously. I think you're tempted by all the important people he talks about introducing you to. Paz Estenssoro, the Guatemalan ambassador, Arbenz, Fidel Castro. Who cares about such people? They're all like Chavez. They have nothing new to say. Our task is to make ourselves strong independent individuals, like those stones." Fernando's face lit with delight. He had found a resource to make his point plain. "Each one has a different shape, yet they all fit together smoothly. So they've endured a long time." He ran his finger along one of the edges. "No mortar," he said. "But earthquakes can't shake them."

I smiled too. Apparently the numinous stones were an all-purpose parable, skew to any particular point. But I knew, I always knew, what Fernando meant. Good can be done only a little at a time, without violence, like the careful building of this wall. And yet what was the use? There are calamities worse than earthquakes. Imperialism is a glacier, sliding down the mountains. What was the point of taking a rock from its path? And Gandhi's vision was more than individual good works. It was of an action, a symbol—without violence, yet as powerful as the sacrifice to the sun. Not the offering of others, but of oneself. Such a symbol would unite a people, make them into a nation of strong nonviolent warriors.

What action? What people?

I stood silently looking at the blank wall.

Fernando turned away, back towards the road.

In Lima there were letters waiting from my parents. But I didn't read them. I folded the light-blue envelopes in half and stuffed them into the side pocket of my leather jacket, the one with the zipper. "I understand about the nurse," Chaco said; his thin lips curled upward.

"There's nothing to understand."

"It was the time before your vows."

"Shut up, Chaco." I wasn't offended by his mockery. But I suddenly felt an impoverishment at the heart of my vow; not a strong will, but an incapacity.

No. I would not.

We took the bus for Ecuador. *Tumbes. Trujillo.* A woman dressed in black, with a black shawl around her head, sat in the back with four small quiet obedient boys in a line next to her. The children sat with unnatural stillness, their hands folded in their laps, the muscles of their faces drooping, the skin under their eyes sagging. The woman shared her food with us, cold tortillas with some stringy chicken. We gave her some money for milk. *Piura. Talara.* Roberto and Chaco played a game of cards with two country people who wore dirty white pants, and large shirts with red-and-blue embroidery, intricate Moorish-looking designs. The men had put a tall thin silver-colored box in the aisle for a card table. They passed around a bottle without a label. I took a drink. The peasants enjoyed themselves, laughing at my friends' mistakes at cards as if they were foreigners making riotous grammatical blunders. One of the men, a fellow with a long sharp face, hugged Roberto. "It's not really a card game," Soto said to me from out of this embrace. "It's a social program, a way to redistribute the wealth. I don't understand the rules. Chaco doesn't understand the rules. I'm not sure there are rules. Every so often this fellow here hugs me like a brother and says, 'I'm sorry, sir, but you lose. My six makes what we call *a happy set.*' Then he takes as much of our money as he wants." The other man handed me the bottle and I took another drink to celebrate their happy sets. It felt pleasant to be here with such amiable companions. *Talara.* The two peasants became angry with each other. The thin-faced man took a knife from a leather case at his belt and laid it on the metal box. The other man drew his knife. (I knew this tableau: "seriousness.") I took out the envelopes. My mother's spidery hand was as I remembered. But my father's handwriting made me uneasy. He had formed the address in the shaky block lettering of a child, nothing like his doctor's scrawl. I folded each letter into a tiny packet and put them both in my sports jacket's handkerchief pocket, way down at the bottom. Chaco stared at the knives, as if mesmerized, then put his head on Roberto's shoulder and pretended to be asleep. *Huaquillas.* A woman transporting chickens as a gift for her son in Guayaquil lent me a blanket. We shared a seat. She was plump, with a broad friendly smile. I put my feet up on the poultry cage, a neatly carpentered construction of light-colored wood and mesh. She had made it herself, she did everything herself, she said, since her husband died last year in a sawmill accident. She put her mouth near my ear and made a rumbling sound, air forced hard against the back of her palate. "Hear that?" she asked. "That's the saw. It means: Run the other way."

I nodded.

The bus rocked, and each motion itself made a hundred smaller motions. I swayed against the woman's side, and she didn't flinch back from me. I felt comfortable on the bus, cradled by the pleasant warmth of the liquor and my companions. The swaying induced a meditative state. I played strips of leather from my jacket back and forth, back and forth, through my fingers, a troupe of acrobats I trained. *Puerto Bolivar.* I had fallen asleep on the woman's shoulder, and woke to a tickling under my nose. She had put my feet on the floor, removed one of her birds from the cage, and snapped its neck. Its head dangled down forlornly, a thin line of blood trickled onto her lap. She made the rumbling sound in her throat, and with quick motions plucked the bird's feathers. (The chicken had been too dumb to run the other way.) I had a pile of feathers on my pants. Bad for my asthma.

Guayaquil. One foot above sea level.

In the mountains of Bolivia the air was so thin that I could not make my lungs work quickly enough to take in a sufficiency; breathing was a race. Here the air was wet, too heavy to lift, and when lifted it was thick with more than oxygen, with something unnecessary; the damp formed a scum in my chest. Our money had run out, redistributed without a plan on that silver trunk. We were trapped.

We lived in a small room by the Guayas River, close to the pestilence of mosquitoes and shit and worms and rats. Two new pilgrims joined us, law students from Argentina who felt they could not be lawyers. We shared our poverty to rent the room. There was one bed, where two people—Soto always, and the first other one to claim it each night—slept. The rest of us lay on the wooden floor, under a single sheet. (At first possession of the bed had been a simple scramble. But one night we awoke to Soto's screaming. He lay on the floor, kicking his legs up and down. I saw flames coming from his skin, and ran to throw my sheet on him. But it wasn't fire; it was fear. "I'm sorry," Soto said, smiling at us shamefacedly. "It's the rats. I'm terrified of the rats. I know it's stupid, but I am. I'm afraid I can't sleep on the floor." So we reserved a place in the bed for him. During my attacks the rule was bent for me also, and I, too, enjoyed the grimy bed. And attacks came frequently in Guayaquil. The air was a mold, something diseased that I took into myself, a fungus growing in the alveoli, till it choked me and I had to cough it out. The attack passed. My vigilant friends heard my stentorian metallic breathing return to normal. They reminded me of proper precedence. I returned to the floor.)

On the floor rats passed over our legs with light scratching motions that made Fernando want to vomit. We lay there naked, beneath a damp sheet, listening to the screams of fire engines, a long unpleasant whine. Boards crashed, collapsing nearby. In hell, fires burn when the flesh is already consumed. In Guayaquil, by miraculous dispensation, the houses of the slum burn despite the pervasive damp. (Beneath the fires, fueling them by transubstantiation, were streets covered with mud and fecal matter thrown up by the river.) Some part of the slum was always in flame, blocks of wooden shacks leaning against each other, burned to a deeper unity. The light ash and charred wood floated in the river. One evening I saw a man's corpse, half burned away on one side, carved by the fire like a side of beef, bloated to a hundred fluorescences of gray rot on the other side. Men with long poles tried to pull it to shore, but the corpse's cavity filled with water, and it sank.

We had no reason for staying in Guayaquil. We had no reason for leaving. Fernando and I had meant to go somewhere, to help someone do something about something. What was it? We had no energy for travel. We had no money. We lacked will. We needed rest. We stayed. Mosquito bites on my arm swelled to the size of walnuts. We needed rest. We stayed. I lay half under the sheet reading my mother's letter. *Dear Tete:* (Fernando, Chaco, and Gualo García lay beside me, asleep. It was early evening. But an empty day in Guayaquil exhausted us. . . . I watched a mosquito walk into Chaco's large ear. . . . Nothing to be done.) *Your reflections about "The Discovery of Latin America" are very interesting   But I wonder if Fernando isn't right and you're getting distracted by the talk of politicians   (Maybe their talk talk talk their empty pedestrian words are what has created in you this craving for something sublime, for Poetry, for great leaders whom you imagine speaking magnificent speeches from horseback and leading grand charges   But that's just your imagination Tete, that isn't politics, it's literature?* (The question mark didn't indicate a question, even a rhetorical one. My mother used punctuation rarely, and as the mood took her.) *I have always thought that perhaps you had more of a taste for literature actually than politics? But woe woe woe when the realms are confused! This talk of leaders isn't the sort of book I thought you had in mind when you left. Fernando is, though willfully plain-spoken sometimes, very perspicacious. He is much wiser and more undogmatic than his Stalinist mother by the way! Do please give Fernando my love and tell him what I said about him) Anyway you must learn to listen to what others have to say— sometimes they have things to teach you   Or you will end up like your father.* (She described me; she described herself. She always castigated most vehemently her own faults in others. I rubbed at a series of bites on my right arm. The skin came away in damp flakes, like wet cardboard. Clear sticky fluid coated my fingertips.) *Perhaps in the villages, there is nothing to be discovered. Nothing! At least entertain that thought for a moment? I say God forbid that our future should be a return to the stupidity, the human sacrifice, the slavery the mealy milching measly life of the Indians before the Conquest. By the Conquistadors, our ancestors! (Yes! I am their child, I don't deny it. And that is my inheritance from them, not to apologize. For God's sake Tete affirm yourself!) It is unfortunate that History moves in diabolically cunning ways.* (She didn't think it unfortunate. It mirrored her own contrary nature. It provided opportunity for drama, for saying something seemingly evil and shocking our cousins.) *But it does Tete! We may not approve of the cruelty of the conquistadors, but it is humanity's good fortune that they put an end to the barbarism of the Inca priests, and dragged the simple Indian masses halfway to the light of Reason! Yes, their Catholicism is just as dark and cruel and barbaric, But now there is at least the possibility of a free rational life in the future   It is criminal to look for guidance for our unhappy people in the Incas' thousand years of suffering! The Incas are the past! Let the dead bury the dead! The conquistadors and the Incas have nothing to teach us. Nothing Nothing Nothing   Listen to me! This is the twentieth century Tete! There's no refusing History, no going back. You can't refuse History Tete   It happens anyway   And your refusal is part of it   Your Gandhi (or should I say Tete your father's?)* (Having renounced coquetry herself, she easily recognized its ruses in others.) *was a man of strong but very limited vision, his blind spots may have given him the courage to face the cannon's mouth, but they were still enormous blind spots. He was a religious fanatic, and that's the most dangerous variety of madman. Thank God that Mr. Nehru (and you know what a coward I think he is!) knows that Gandhi's place is as a church for the simple at heart. In church the rational intelligent man pays his respects to nonsense and then he forgets about it and goes on about his business. Your Gandhi's spinning wheel is religion; "Eden"; something to keep the stupid poor happy, mystified, spinning away like the irrational geese most of them are. And still poor. Yes, Gandhi did do things himself rather than ordering others to do them. In this he is superior to most of this poor suffering world's leaders, its stinking Roosevelts and Churchills and Stalins.* (She was unbiased in her contempt. Contempt itself was her party; the Great Refusal of Everything. I rubbed away at the flesh on my arm till the blood and serum oozed up. Four bites had grown into my right arm's crop of walnuts. I put my shoes on and walked out naked to sit under some boards that were leaning against our shack. I had dysentery. Everyone in Guayaquil had dysentery. A warm rain poured on my body through the cracks in the lean-to. Someone ran to the river. I added my thin runny stream to the Guayas. There was still enough light to read by, and I sat in the stench with my mother's letter, liquid dribbling out of me.) *But is this constant activity always a good thing   The world needs leaders that can stand back a bit, who reflect, who can THINK RATIONALLY, who can plan the future for the masses, who are themselves incapable of the most elementary plan.* (Leaders should do things; leaders should stand back. My mother expressed her contradictions not by nuance or silence, but by whirling about, saying opposite things within a few sentences of each other.) *But one thing the poor suffering world doesn't need is more prophets, visionaries, more charismatic leaders, "suns in the people's sky." You sound like one of Peron's toady hagiographers   I'm embarrassed to quote that part of your letter to your father   (I know why you wrote him Tete! you feared what I might say about this religious nonsense!) I hope that you do not see your fate as following or being one of these irrational hypnotists? Think about Gandhi! For a man who walked away from all the world's honors he certainly managed to promote his name to everyone's lips   All his "sacrifices" were stunts, like his fasting where everyone could watch him. He wasn't denying himself food, he was gaining the mindless crowd's attention.* (I felt light. From diarrhea, from my mother's nihilism. I walked back to our sweaty sheet. The floor stuck to my skin.) *These selfless people (might I count your father among them!) give me a pain It's just a con job! Like Evita's (or your father's) "I make all these terrible sacrifices for you" Charismatic leaders are for religion—for slavery!—not the way to human freedom! Rationality and science are the way to freedom And it wasn't Gandhi's stupid ideas but his hypnosis that impressed the childish villagers. We've had enough of that In this benighted country! When he left the infantile villagers returned to filth! I know you think my notebooks are a little fad, a housewife's sad hobby? But you are wrong. I have the whole world in them! And I have many that are filled with clippings about Gandhi For I too was once taken with him (Taken in by him should I say? But I soon saw through him (you and your father always give yourselves over uncritically to things.) Gandhi's little stunts worked not because he reached into the soul (that ghost) of the benighted masses but because Indians are a stupid superstitious irrational people If they let him die, didn't do what the Holy Man wanted they'd get Bad Karma, which is some sort of curse like original sin or syphilis (They thought they'd be reborn as caterpillars) Superstition, that was Gandhi's stock in trade. When there were terrible earthquakes in India, he said it was because of Hindu oppression of the untouchables. Does that root out superstition? Does that help the few people capable of it to be rational autonomous individuals? After he died the morons all wanted to touch his corpse, they trampled each other to death trying to get to his body, to have that miraculous touch Just like Evita.* (Oh, she hated Evita most of all! And was that hatred untouched by the feeling good women have against whores, against those who are "willing to do anything" to make their way in the world?—A thought in my mother's style! Her letter, like any long contact with her, changed me, filled me with her sharp destructive energy. Chaco grabbed my hand. "No more. Every time I hear you scratch one of those bumps it makes my skin crawl." He rolled over again, turned his back to me.) *Gandhi didn't liberate the masses into rationality; he fuddled them. And they are easily fuddled! Your father has been "explaining" things to me. He's quite the Hindu these days, did you know that? (I feel like there's a silent conspiracy between you two to drive me crazy.) Your father says that Hinduism means "conscious shedding of attachments." By that your father means ignoring me. Tete, the truth is, I'm worried about him! He's been very withdrawn lately. I don't know if it has to do with your absence, but I think that perhaps it does. It is as if he were giving up. He won't even argue with me anymore. And I try to say deliberately provoking things to him! But he just lies on the living-room floor like a corpse. He says that whatever I think is fine, just fine. He doesn't mind. He has no desires, he has no opinions. It is very annoying. But I think that he took your leaving harder than you thought. He says it doesn't matter what he wants, he isn't going to live very long anyway. . . . It's enough to make me scream!) You and I, Tete, it is true, don't want many things. We have chosen voluntarily the life of deliberate poverty Gandhi recommends.* (Age, I was happy to see, hadn't robbed my mother of her makeup box, her powers of self-dramatization.) *But can we realistically expect this voluntary poverty from many people? They are too weak-willed and given to gluttonous mindless amusements But worst of all is this nonviolence business. That's where your Gandhi and I really part company. He preached nonviolence, but I think that he had just as much destructive energy as the rest of us. Enormous anger! He turns it inward. And he only does that—which is sick!—for the same reason others turn it outward, to make other people do what he wanted. It was just another way of being aggressive, by making people feel guilty. He reminds me of your father.—I think you're old enough now for me to say that to you* (Actually, she had been saying it to me since I was eight years old.) *He hurts himself so that others will see how they've made him suffer, will cry about him, will feel what rotten people they are So he will get his way! (I only wish that I could figure out what it is he wants now so I could give it to him!) Nonviolence is just another mask for his egotism. You can see, I hope, how his ideas of nonviolence were all bound up with his insane ideas about sexuality. I'm afraid that I have to speak frankly to you about this. Your Gandhi is a man who hates and fears women, who hates and fears sex, and who confuses violence and sex, as if killing and making love were the same activity. And because he thinks sex is sick he thinks violence is always evil. He wants to keep himself to himself. (I hope you are not embarrassed to hear me talking like this. I* have *been up all night, keeping watch on the frontier of Reason. That is the imperiled Frontier. But you can see how very much it would worry me to think of you following someone like this?) Not to touch (or hit) or be touched, because it was polluting?! He wants to be untainted unsmudged, women will befoul him! They'll make him waste his semen. You know that he practiced celibacy because he thought that keeping back semen would make him smarter? You know that Gandhi was making love with his wife when his father died. He felt so guilty that ever after that he refused to sleep with his wife She had to be punished for luring him away from his father! I hope it doesn't embarrass you to hear your old mother talking like this Tete! There are many things I could tell you about your father But I won't They're not the sort of things a child should know. But when I hear you talking about self-denial, about austerities, it terrifies me. You remind me of a nun! I don't want to see you growing up cursed with this same hatred of the body, this same hatred for women (Do you think that it is maybe bound up with your problems with your father dear? Have you considered that maybe you should see a psychoanalyst, someone who could help lift this curse from you? I don't mean to interfere, but I don't want you to have a barren life Tete!) Gandhi thought—listen to this! it's true! I have it in one of my notebooks!—that if he could remain celibate, while sleeping with a naked girl, he could solve the Pakistani question! This is the magical nonsense of someone who thinks his semen is all-powerful. Who thinks if he keeps back semen he'll be smarter. Semen in the head! He thinks his organ is all-powerful. He thinks that to have intercourse will kill the woman. Why! Because he thinks the woman will kill him, take his organ away! He is terrified of his own sexuality, his own violence, because he is terrified of women!!! Do you know what his assassin said I have it in one of my notebooks. "I believed that the teaching of nonviolence would emasculate the Hindu community." Now I will say something that I hope will shock you! His assassin was right! Gandhi stood before the British saying (Wait a minute, I have it somewhere)*

"Is this Christian, is this justice, is this fair play, is this civilization?" Do you know what would happen if we said this to a North American? He'd rub his head, look at us quizzically, and say "Hnnh?" Do you know how the police will react when you show them your nakedness dear? Do you think if you offer your body to the animals, the North Americans, they won't take it? We're their food! You make a big drama out of your anger, Tete. You ask yourself should you start a fight in a bar, should you hit an opportunist like Betancourt with a soupspoon. Tete, who cares? You should ask yourself why you make such a big drama out of it! By concentrating on your anger you don't have to look at what is going on all the time around you, the terrible slaughter of the innocents, the poor children. (And the masses are children, Tete! You must help them.) You have to do something (I don't know what But something) I think Gandhi liked being on the losing side He didn't want to win. Are you like that too? Are you sure you don't like Gandhi because like your father you want to be too good for this world, a victim, a saint? Gandhi should become a museum for tourists, a shrine for the poor (permanently poor if their little minds are so fuddled that they still visit shrines) and a vegetarian restaurant. Gandhi had one good idea in his life: What to do with shit!

Let us hear no more about him.

Dear Tete you cannot imagine how I long for one intelligent voice to converse with! Please, I beg you do not desert the party of Reason Most

people of all sorts—the masses! the masses!—are almost unbearably stupid!
They need strong rational thinkers to lead them—people like yourself! Affirm
yourself!

> *Much love to you my dear Child,*
> *Many Many embraces, from*
> *Celia de la Serna Guevara,*
> *"child of the conquistadors"*

My mother's company left me exhausted, exhilarated, angry, unprepared
for sleep; the caffeine, the dissatisfaction, had run from her veins into mine.
I lay rubbing the flesh around the row of large red bites—quietly, so that Chaco
wouldn't be disturbed. The pain, the activity, rubbing the flesh into moist little
gray balls, was a relief from the itching, a relief that hurt. My mother's activity,
ripping away at things, at an itch (for what? for recognition? power? for
change?) never pacified, never cured—that, too, was a pleasant pain; an active
tearing at one's own flesh that affirmed oneself through its being an activity,
its being one's own intelligence that did the world in, ripped it to pieces, even
as it ripped the self up with it. And these all seemed thoughts in her style. I
didn't want to think in her style.

My mother was a lucid armed sharp uncertainty, turning this way and that,
an uncomfortable body, unable to sleep, burdened with too much energy, more
life than this place could bear. She was a vivid splintering disorder, formed into
a collage only to splinter again. It was her art to make one feel during this
performance as if there were no possible activity except this endless criticism,
this tearing and laceration. *But she was wrong.* A housewife, she was bloody-
minded because she had never seen blood. (Where was her crowd, ready to
follow the leader who stood back and made important plans, the dictatorship
of reason, a leadership without an action—for action would open it to mockery.) Isolated, sitting in her kitchen, she could not see the dignity of nonviolence; excited by fantasies, she screamed for adventure, for blood. Her marriage
had made a squint to her vision; she confused her husband's sulks with the
exalted sacrificial actions that had united the Indian masses against imperialism!

My angry thoughts rocked me this way and that beneath the sticky sheet.
"Be still child!" Chaco complained. "Let us sleep!"

The next day, though, Guayaquil seemed my mother's state of mind, a
world covered in shit, destroying itself for someone's bitter amusement. Out-

side our room, mangrove thickets grew, half in the river water. Children played there, hopping back and forth among the tangled roots. The children played barefoot; worms entered through the soles of their feet. This morning Chaco found the carcass of a child by the root of a tree. He motioned me to come over, and with the side of his boot he pressed the child's thin cheek. Small white worms came slithering out of the corpse's mouth and nostrils. The child's feet dangled in the water, and the flesh slowly fell away, moldy bits of matter, shades of gray and brown, almost iridescent in decay.

"Squishy squishy squishy," Chaco said, smiling emptily at me. This was worse than the defeat he longed for. He looked like he was about to throw up. "Not the sort of world . . ." he said faintly, and stopped, as if to say, where one would care to go on living. And then, sadly, "where a person can take his shoes off."

I knew what he meant. I thought, angrily, there aren't enough antibiotics for these children, my mother's right. Was this what I avoided seeing with my talk about Gandhi and idyllic villages? Did I dream of apocalyptic changes in people's souls rather than see the work that as a doctor I had been given to me to do? *Yet Gandhi was right:* it would take a deep change for our people to learn even the principles of hygiene. *But he was wrong:* they also needed to wear shoes—even if they stumbled! They needed not hand looms, but factories to produce shoes. Then a doctor wouldn't do them much good? *I* wasn't what was needed. . . . And so my confusion continued around like my mother's sentences.

We walked by the docks. Men without shirts lined up for Guayaquil's only work, loading bananas from the United Fruit plantations onto the cargo boats. Bananas lay piled on the rafts near the ships, and in the warehouses by the docks; the place stank of bananas, sweet mixed with decay; green bananas, rotting bananas. (Bananas beyond repair were tossed into the river.)

After the loading crews were chosen, crowds converged on the riverbank, those who hadn't gotten work, and more men and women from the town. They chanted the name of the ex-mayor, Carlos Guevara Moreno. A charismatic man, my mother's voice said, a petty devil, a fraud who they believe will end their misery, bring jobs for all.

"The leader you wait for," Francisco said.

I was silent. My mother's voice had silenced me.

"Yes, Guevara," Chaco said, "tell us, how shall we know a true god from a false one in these thirsty times?"

Mo-re-no! Mo-re-no! Mo-re-no! They hurled the syllables out. Men and women pressed together, rushed towards the loading docks to stop the work.

Police formed lines by the boats, guarding the workers and the produce. The crowd stopped a few hundred meters away and chanted Mo–re–no! Mo—re —no!

"It's like a movie," Chaco said. "Regular performances."

An Indian in a dirty white shirt and no shoes, his hair cut into sharp lines along his cheekbones, like a helmet, taunted the police, running towards them, shouting, then darting back when they tried to hit him with their clubs. Then another man, a red kerchief wrapped around his forehead, joined him. They vied with each other. The kerchiefed one went too far, ran up to the police to vault their line. His feet went up the side of one of the policemen, as if he wanted to run up over his head. (Perhaps he imagined himself standing horizontally.) They both fell to the ground. One of the other policemen took out his revolver and shot the kerchiefed man in the head. The rest of the crowd gasped, a long intake of breath. They moved towards the wounded man, and then away, suddenly silent, like plants waving slowly in the wind. The other police formed a circle around the wounded man, trapping him in the circle of their legs. The policeman he'd knocked down, knelt and pulled on the wounded man's hair, to wrench his head off. The police, their revolvers drawn, stood around the angry man, and the dying man; blood poured from the man's head onto the kneeling policeman's shoes.

My body shook. This must not happen. Too much blood! Irrational, stupid. An open vein. There must be no more blood! I saw myself between the two men, kneeling, tending the man's wound. What did she know of blood? *She understood nothing.* I ran forward, towards the dock. Someone grabbed me around the chest and knocked me to the ground. The air left me like a shot.

Chaco's beak pressed into my cheek.

"This must be love," he said. He was crying. I could feel his tears on my face. I could smell him. Fear had made him stink.

I tried to throw him off, to rise.

"Be still child! You can't enter a movie." He hugged me harder. I gasped.

The policeman stood up, holding the red kerchief aloft, as if this had all been a game and this were the prize. The crowd moved off in every direction, down the streets, into buildings, into the air; a vision dissolving. They had done no more damage than a mist, a mist that bled, an opium dream, a demagogue's fancy. "The crowd lacks leadership," I heard Soto say to the nodding lawyers-who-couldn't-practice-law. Chaco wouldn't move off me.

I smelled things rotting, rotting wood, rotting fruit, rotting flesh. It was the smell of my mother's letter. It would rot my certainty if I let it, take away my vivid speech, the clear outlines of a vision of independence and chastity. I would not let it. Her mind was the joy of breaking glass, a harmless hoodlum's activity to no conclusion, to no purpose but the pleasure of the sound.

But I, too—lying under Chaco!—was going nowhere. We were going nowhere. A teacher who wouldn't teach. Doctors who didn't want to practice. Lawyers who wouldn't appear in court. Too good for this world? Too weak? Sheets of acrid black smoke filled the sky in the east. (Did we long for a leader who would never come, safe to long for because always absent? The leaders who spoke would always be judged wanting. *Where was my action?*) Fire engines screeched to rescue a building that couldn't be rescued. The fire engines of Guayaquil always arrived too late, appearing not to put out fires, but to take away the wrapped remains of bodies. And the crowds formed like this every afternoon after the crews were hired, and pushed, tumbled, chanted a magical name without magic, frenzied lovers of Moreno who had promised them jobs, Moreno who told them how to live, or anyway how to die, for him. (I heard her: They freely took on this voluntary sacrifice! This exultation of the will!) Taunts, screams, people eddying down side streets. Moreno—the name of a sporting event in hell. Mo—re—no! Mo—re—no! Day after day, world without end.

The last policeman left the dock. The crews returned to work.

Chaco let me up.

That evening, as the others slept, I dragged myself to the wall, by the window, and leaning against it, read my father's neatly typed letter.

Dear Ernesto:

I was very interested to read that you, too, are once more involved with Gandhi's teaching, and that you found your imagination of him to be a comfort during that foolhardy ride in the Andes. Perhaps it is a sign that you are meant to follow his teachings of nonattachment, and nonviolence (though I do not think you have understood his teachings yet in their full depth).

I, too, have been thinking of Gandhi's way, and even more have tried to immerse myself in the difficult tradition from which he comes. Since your departure I find that my activities here in Cordoba, the practice of medicine, the discussions of politics with your mother and her friends (as you know, I have no friends here) are of very little interest to me. Now it is as if these things occurred on the other side of a partition; soon they will, I am sure, drift away from me utterly. Perhaps I detach myself from life in order to ready myself for my death. I would not want you to think, though, that this turn of events bothers me. I am content with my lot. I want nothing.

To reduce one's wants, Gandhi taught, is the secret of contentment. All my life I have sought for this feeling of nonattachment, but my commitment to you and your mother have time and again pulled me back into the concerns of life. Perhaps your departure was a godsend to me, for it helped me to sever my last attachments to life. I do not engage in useless plotting in anyone's behalf, certainly not in my own. Each day I practice the exercises for breathing and posture from a book I tried to share with you in your childhood, *The Hindu Science of Breath Control*. It is hard for an old man to sit with his legs crossed. But I lie down absolutely straight, with my arms at my side, my palms facing upward, in what is called "the corpse position." I let my mind quiet itself. Your mother comes in at such times, to annoy me, often with worries about you. But I remain uninvolved. She seems to be standing at a great distance above me, and I can hardly make out her voice. It is as if I were already enjoying the peace of the grave. I see during those evening meditations that life is just a play of images, and not something for a man my age to take seriously.

You are quite right in your admiration of Gandhi's teaching, and its way of nonviolence. Your mother, of course, mocks me for this, wondering how I can eat anything at all, even vegetables, or wash myself, and kill microbes. It is not so comical as she thinks. It *is* a contradiction. We must do violence in order to live, but it is a beautiful thing if we can keep that violence to a minimum. Nonviolence is a very high ideal, for true aristocrats of the Spirit, men of intelligence and morality. To follow Gandhi, to be nonviolent, is a continual task, not something settled once and for all. Final victories are the imaginings of violent men; apocalypse; fiery consummation. Gandhi's way must be the will's slow patient work. It is a difficult path, and requires the utmost courage from those who follow it. One cannot experience that courage without the serenity of nonattachment. One must be attached to nothing, not even to one's family, not even to one's own life, if one is to have the courage not to take another's life when one's own is threatened.

Nonattachment comes from performing the correct action at each stage of our life. It does not come from following our particular fears and desires, but from finding our place in a much larger scheme, from understanding the stage of life that you find yourself incarnated in. One does not *choose* that state according to one's whims. One finds oneself there as part of a family, a profession. These circumstances, and not one's own wishes, determine to the last detail our conduct.

If one does this there is purity and clarity, not the muck and chaos of "personality." (Imagine, please, a provincial acting company making up its own lines, each actor doing what he wants, deciding to walk off perhaps during another's farewell speech!) It is like focusing a lens. Before the lens (the self) is focused, nothing is clear; the lens calls attention to itself. But once the impersonal cosmic drama is allowed to operate, the glass comes into focus. It is anonymous and self-effacing; nonattached.

Have you done this? I don't think so.

One cannot run away into the nonattached life. One must act selflessly, at the time dictated by one's place in the drama. One must pursue one's career in the appropriate way. (And what career, I wonder, could be more satisfying than the one I hoped you would share with me, that of saving lives?) One must see to the care of one's family. (I require no care myself, for, as I said, I have very few and very small needs. But your mother's case is different. She is attached to you deeply, misses your company very much, speaks of you often. But more than that—though she is too vain to admit it—she is getting old, Ernesto, and she requires your help.) One must raise one's own children. If one completes these necessary stages, these early acts of the drama, then one can be a true disinterested follower of Gandhi's way, the way of nonattachment and nonviolence. Have you done this? I don't think so. You have run away from your family, your profession, from your role. I think that lacks courage.

Your loving Father

And then, in an old man's writing—that shaky black script, that child's printing I had never seen before this letter—there was a message written askew to the rest of the page: "I am very tired. Please come home."

I fell asleep against the wall. My mind was dark, my limbs heavy. I dreamed of my father in a hospital bed, a long open ward. I was the doctor on call. When I went to examine him he grabbed me and hugged me, as if he wanted me to merge with him. I woke naked, in a small puddle of my own shit.

That evening Soto called a meeting. We had to get out of here. Each of us would contribute the clothing he didn't need, and Garcia would go to Quito, where they'd have use for the winter stuff, and peddle it in the street. A pile was formed on the floor, Soto's vicuna coat, some extra pairs of pants. I wanted to be rid of everything, my leather jacket, my sports coat, my shirts, my two pairs of pants, my underwear.

"The naked man in the empty room," Chaco said.

Fernando took back my clothes for me, surrendering only my sports coat.

A few days later we met to divvy up the money.

"Guatemala!" Soto said seductively. Sweat dripped from his sideburns and his mustache. Soto had a bad smell to him. (He rarely washed but each morning he poured more of that cologne on his hair.) Rolls of fat hung over his lizardskin belt. His chest was hairy, and he had large breasts.

"Guatemala," Soto repeated, as if it were a rich strange delicious fruit.

The other lawyers nodded at the delicacy.

"No!" Fernando shouted. It all happened at a great distance from me. Fernando's voice was high-pitched, almost crying. "We're going to Venezuela! Just give us our share."

"Venezuela!" Soto laughed. "How can you even think of it? Nothing's happening in Venezuela. Guatemala is the most exciting political event in our continent's history! A land reform expropriating the property of the United Fruit Company, a government committed, really committed to the goal of social justice, even if it means defying the North Americans! Guevara," he turned to me. I sat cross-legged, naked. Long light shit stains ran down the hairs of my legs. "You're fond of the word 'experiment.' Well, this is the most exciting social experiment in our century. This isn't like the opportunists of the MNR. Every sector of the population has been mobilized. Arbenz isn't afraid of anyone, not even John Foster Dulles!"

Ar-benz! I laughed. New syllables to hurl at the wall. I was a rag that had been soaked and wrung out and soaked again. I stood superior to an empty world. Or I was worthless. *I* was empty, and I wanted to be. Empty, naked, indifferent. Nonattached.

Fernando shouted, "Politics is shit! Politics is death!" He spoke quietly to me, reminding me of the time I'd visited him in the jail. Veins stood out in his forehead. "You said it, Ernesto. Politics is death. You were right! This talk is nonsense Ernesto. Good isn't done by Arbenz. It's done by many individuals acting independently, a little at a time." His voice pleaded, reminding me of intimate conversations, treaties entered into; friendship. "You were right, Ernesto!"

"Did I say that?" I couldn't remember. What did he want from me?

"Yes. Yes. You people with your talk, you don't know what you're talking about. Look." He pointed to his ear. But what he wanted to show us was an absence. "I can't hear with this ear. You don't care." He turned to me angrily. His hand formed a fist, and he pressed it hard against his own sharp cheekbone. "But I love sounds. I love music. Ernesto, you remember when I tried to teach you to dance? You wanted to show Chinchina how much you cared for her. I taught you the tango. And you got up at that night club when they were playing a rumba." He smiled at me, though he was crying now. He wanted to take me deeper into our past together, the bond between us, our vows. But I couldn't go *there*. "You made a stupid fool out of yourself. Because you don't care about music. You can't hear it anyway. Because you're so damn abstract. But I can hear. I love music. You never cared for it. I love to dance. You never could. You can't dance! You can't swim! You're so damn afraid of losing control!" He cried openly now, rubbing his sleeve across his eyes like a child. I had never realized, never wanted to realize, Fernando's anger, his resentment. I had admired him for his lack of bitterness, because, I suppose, I wanted him that way. He had admired me for seeing farther, admired me for saying things I did not now even remember saying, lines he had probably given me. "Look," he said, his strength gone, ashamed of crying, "forget it. I mean, I just don't want to lose another ear."

Soto laughed, the flesh of his breasts shaking. "You think you're the only one who's suffered in jails, sir?" He turned away from us and, with one hand, reached up to his left eye socket. "Look!" He held something up between his fingers. It was growing dark outside. I didn't look at the glass eye he held, but at the socket. My attention was fixed by that hole, a darkness within a darkness, a hole that entered into the darkness but didn't look out, a stony place. It fascinated me. I thought I saw a different shade of black, almost silvery. And a streak of red. (There had always, I thought, been something dead about Soto's stare.) "We mustn't be afraid," said the man afraid of rats. "We must see Guatemala," said the man who couldn't see. He turned from us and put the glass eye back in its socket.

I agreed. Fernando left the next morning for Venezuela. He was distant but calm when we parted. He embraced me. "Watch out you don't become a partygoer, like your friend Soto," he said. "A voyeur of revolutions!"

We were on a ship of the Great White Fleet, when I asked Soto about the injury to his eye. I admired him for not having mentioned it before, along with the straight-backed chair, respected his casual, insouciant story of his escape.

Chaco laughed so hard that spit came out in a little shower from his lips.

"You're kidding of course?" Soto asked.

"What?"

The two lawyers looked at me blankly, as if from glass eyes, smiling.

"I didn't lose an eye. I was just making a joke. You know, you're a doctor. I didn't think you could just pop a glass eye out like that? It was a childhood joke. You know, the way children will take out a false eye. I mean pretend to take out a false eye and put it in their mouth for washing." He showed me, with exaggerated motions. I remembered it from the playground, someone swishing his eye around in his mouth, drying it on his shirttail.

"But I saw it!"

"Saw what?" he said. He put his arm around my shoulder. "The eye I don't have?"

"You bastard." I hated him, not for tricking me (it must have been a deception I wanted), but for mocking Fernando.

"I guess it was silly," Soto said amiably. "But Fernando hasn't really lost the hearing in his ear, has he?"

"Yes. Of course he has. He wouldn't lie." (But then, I thought: he wouldn't be bitter either? We made others as we wished them. It was, as my mother said, a tricky world.)

"Well then, I guess that was really a little rough on my part. When you write Fernando again please tell him I'm sorry."

But I had seen it. The hole in his face, the empty socket, the greater darkness, the silvery shadow streaked with red. I had seen it.

Isle of Pines, July 1965

JULY 10

"Oh, good," Ponco said. "Guatemala!" His voice was the shimmer off desert rocks. He smiled broadly at me. There was something wonderfully full and welcome in Ponco's smile, and yet (so broad! too full!) something mocking and menacing as well. What could give the cat such pleasure, really, except the wounded mouse's last doomed erratic scamper? (The mouse! That's me!)

"You mean," I said, "that something's about to happen, don't you? Finally. You long for an *action*. Decisive. Something to thicken the plot." I meant that I—the younger I, still Ernesto—did. I wanted something to happen, a choice made by me, and yet inevitable, a fate; something irrevocable, my work, a name, a path I couldn't turn my back on. Ponco, I thought, must be remembering the note I left at the table several weeks (months, decades, pages) ago when I was setting out: an action: *I killed a man in Guatemala.* (As if it were a joke! Remembering that note, I felt ashamed.)

"Action? No." He smiled—impossible!—more broadly still, delighted with his world, his toy. (Who would have thought the mouse had it in him?) He turned his body towards me. We sat on the porch, looking at the tall grass pushed down by the wind. A storm was coming. Shelves of dark clouds sat on the sea. "Not action. Hilda!" A gasped "H" hitting a consonant; it sounded like a chant beginning. "Romance!"

Hilda. It might, I thought, have been the name of a storm. "I see your movie," I said. "You'll be disappointed. It wasn't like that."

He said nothing. With his right arm he made circular motions, thickening the plot, I supposed. The witch. He *smiled.*

And I smiled, too, thinking of those dear young people sitting in the dark parlor of her boardinghouse in Guatemala City, the weeks before the invasion. (In the kitchen, unknown to us, the Catholic cook, scandalized, listened avidly to our murmurous voices.) We met in *her* parlor always; we didn't have parlors; we didn't have rooms to attach the parlors to (Chaco and I, the last week before the mercenaries came—bombing the city, falling from the air—slept out on a golf course); we didn't have jobs. Hilda, an exile from Peru, a leader in the university arm of APRA, had a degree in economics and acceptable political credentials. (I had a useful skill, but no credentials; the Guatemalan CP was deeply sectarian.) The Revolution had given her work in one of its planning institutes. So we lived from her generosity. She provided fruit for me always, and gave me some of her gold jewelry to pawn for food money. It was, for her, an act not of charity, but of necessary solidarity with the exile community.

I perched on the edge of my overstuffed chair with its floral print of huge jungle blooms, as if that jungle threatened to engulf me if I relaxed my vigilance. Hilda sat sunk in her chair, her arms on the sides. She needn't be vigilant. She knew what she thought. (For it was my inner warring voices I was on watch against, those conflicts that threatened to overwhelm my faith in Gandhi and leave me speechless.)

Hilda was Ricardo's sister, the woman, as I had heard him tell his fiancée, "who knew many things." She had a slight sisterly contempt for Helena, that fiancée. "She's like a little dog," she said of Helena, "looking from face to face to see who will pet her. She has to have everyone's reassurance, everyone's agreement. Poor little animal!"

"And your brother, what kind of animal is he?"

She laughed, a slightly unpleasant, mechanical sound. Hilda had wit, a cutting wit, used purposefully. But not the light propulsion of laughter. "My brother is a bear," she said. "Hadn't you guessed?" Sometimes, she told me, she felt as if we were all animals, a continent of animals, not human yet. She saw it in our faces. Foxes, dogs—many many dogs. Wolves, bears, llamas, cats, sheep, ferrets, hawks. But no humanity. Not yet.

I was rapt at this bitter conceit of Hilda's. She had shown me, for the first time, that more inward part of her, where her thoughts and feelings joined and issued in images: almost-human souls trapped in animal visages. It was an intimate place, the place just before sleep, and her speaking of it marked a stage in our courtship.

Did she mean, I asked, that the imperialists were human, and we were underdeveloped? (And I? I felt Chaco patting my neck. I was a pony.) "The imperialists!" she said. "Don't be stupid!" Didn't I see? They weren't even animals. They were ghouls. They had no faces. Latin Americans would have faces when they acted, when they freed themselves of the ghouls.

She smiled, closed her thin eyes, shook her head to clear it of this poetic nonsense, closed that place to me.

Hilda was the origin of Ricardo's—that bear's—certainties; she had graven her beliefs upon her brother, her faith in the spontaneous revolutionary will of the masses. She had given him that solidity I so much admired.

But she was unlike him, too. She was quick, not playfully so, like my mother, but almost angrily. She wouldn't allow confusion or unmoored irony, which corroded one's ability to work. (And in her presence even Chaco grew more serious, willing to acknowledge that there was a question about his proper work that he, too, wanted answered.)

To error Hilda offered sharp immediate correction. I was drawn to that, to her stocky form in a short-sleeved dress with a brightly colored shawl over it, her hair drawn back into a bun, giving her round face a clearer definition. The woman prophet, the woman judge. "We were very serious," I said to Ponco. For some reason I felt compelled towards honesty with him, as if it were very important that he, especially he, have an accurate account of all I had thought and felt. "Not what you expect: fiery passion!" But that was wrong: there was passion, fierce in its way; not always for each other, but for our common cause, the defense of the Revolution, the defeat of Imperialism. (And that was wrong, too. For it was also *a passion between us.*) "It wasn't a tango, comrade. It was more like a seminar, a study group. Not what you think."

"Wrong," he said. "That *is* what I think." He pointed his long finger at me in quick jabs. I recognized Mr. Prosecutor. "Intellectual violence! Cold intelligent passion! Passion of the intelligence! We see!" He pointed to his own head. "Of the mind." He lowered his eyes suddenly, as if perhaps he'd gone too far with me. After all, I was. . . .

But no, not here on this magic island, where prisoners become young Communists become lunatics, become . . . enchanted princes, talking animals, the King of Argentina, avenging angels, words in Ponco's harsh transforming mouth. I wasn't *him*, that *name* ("Only your name could unite the guerrillas on the continent"), that giant costume I will once again reinhabit as if it were a *papier-mâché* dummy. For the moment here I felt a simpler thing, outside the sweaty costume of my fame, a person alone with his tastes, a few old habits, and his childhood. There was no going too far with *me*, I thought.

The rain began to come down in long transparent sheets, like wings. One of the wings beat against us, soaking us, and we scuttled towards the door.

JULY 11

"I want to tell you about Hilda." We sat at the table, and I sipped mate from my hollow tin spoon, my nubbly gourd. Ponco ate forkfuls of rice meditatively, as if it were more than food, as if it were the best, most involving amusement his world now offered. Ponco always gave himself over wholeheartedly to his pleasures. But rice! He must be very bored on this island. A thick book lay beside his plate. I couldn't see the title, but the cover had a picture of people being pushed aside by a train, a funny-looking train with a spherical engine. "I decided I can't deny you the satisfaction," I lied. I hadn't been able to write after our conversation yesterday. The sound of the rain against the window annoyed me. The feel of the damp annoyed me. The saliva in my mouth annoyed me. Really, I needed Ponco, his ear, his participation, his questions, his painful mean-spirited mocking insights. Otherwise the scene faded from me, the flowered print lost its bright colors as after too many washings. I saw the parlor under the waters of a deep river, the chairs and single wood table swaying this way and that, pushed by currents that dissolved them. Someone looked down into the river from its bank, but he saw nothing and turned away. I needed Ponco's participation to return my life to me. I wanted to know it immediately, to possess it whole; and it was in speaking to him that I regained its colors; it was my desire to tell him that made my memory work, that made things vivid. I couldn't wait anymore to write, and *then* have Ponco read the pages. I had to speak my story (and then return here, to my boards, to record the conversation). Without Ponco's questions I didn't know what it was important to talk about. Hilda's quick, decided voice? (It was her voice, high, rapid, unfolding a world, that I first loved.) Or should I speak of the Chinese cast to her eyes, the pleasant fullness of her body? Or of Nico's self-hatred, his abrupt motions, his constant, nearly odorless sweat making pictures on his shirts? Or of the CIA agents in the cafes, their dead, drawling voices taking a world away, their red cigarette packs offered as bribes for information on the city's crumbling morale. Or—or what might he lead me to discover?

"Good," Ponco said. He looked up at me, still chewing methodically. "The seminar on love."

I felt relieved. A topic. And then I felt, sadly, how much this damnable waiting has dissolved me. That *I* should be anxious for a subject! That I should need someone's responses, need to be set a topic! *I am a topic,* a revolutionary catechism, the unity of the military and the political, the struggle to begin *now,* the stroke that will arouse the masses and reveal to them that revolution is possible. My *name.*

But not then. And it is as if I were hurled back into the mood of that time, when one dispensation was fading, and I did not know from where revelation might come to me. Gandhi's words were the truth I had, and I held to him still, held to him hard. But he was only intermittently a vivid speech in my mouth (and mostly, oddly, when I spoke with Chaco). I heard in Gandhi's words my father's pathetic melancholy dirge of judgment, and wasn't pleased. And Gandhi's theses were corroded, too, by my mother's shards of uncertainty. The world Gandhi had formed, the sense he had made of things, fell about, like letters jumbled on a page. I could still make out the meaning, but where it had once been an unavoidable truth, the inescapable clarity of revelation, now I strained after it, as if solving a puzzle. Humanity, Gandhi said, had suffered terrible physical wounds, and one must not make it suffer more, no matter how right the cause. Blood soaks the earth, then, now, always in the name of justice. But justice, no matter how clever the dialectician's rhetoric, cannot come from blood. A violent savage man was no better than the wolf, the oppressor, the imperialist. Oppressed humanity must be the first to refuse the wolves' ways, to become true men, nonviolent warriors.

A catechism. I held hard. I believed him still. (Did I?)

"We studied Marxism," I said to Ponco. "We read the classics, and some of Lenin's pamphlets, *Imperialism,* and *State and Revolution.* Though Hilda disagreed with Lenin: she saw no need for central parties, new kings." Myself, a member of a Central Committee, I smiled. "I had read Marx before, of course."

"Of course," Ponco said, favoring me with one of his smiles. I understood. My tone was pompous—the student afraid he'd be thought ignorant. And he —of course—had joined Fidel, had acted, before he had theories for his actions, before he knew how to read theory, or anything else.

"The Argentine Communists were priests," I said. "They enshrined Marx. They interpreted Marx for the masses. And they compromised with the powers of the world, whoever they were at the time, as if keeping the church alive were the only value. They used their Marxism as an excuse for delay, for compromise with imperialism against Peron. The masses are not transformed by such dirty cleverness." I had thought of the young Communists at the university, lecturing us. I had remembered, too, my mother's dialectical flights at the kitchen table, her sleight of hand with the Cunning of History, evil means employed, like a conjurer's false bottoms, for good ends. *No,* my father said, severely; and I had assented. "But with Hilda, Marxism came alive for me. It was the Guatemalan Revolution. At first the party pushed Arbenz's government into more radical stands. They expropriated land for the peasants. Not just any land. Land from the United Fruit Company."

"Hallowed ground," Ponco said.

"Exactly. The Party seemed to stand guard at first over the integrity of the land reform. It was only then becoming clear that they and Arbenz would turn cowardly, that they couldn't take the last, the necessary action—that they would be ready once again to use Marx to justify cowardice and betrayal. They weren't the leadership I longed for."

"The Whore of Babylon."

"What?"

"My grandmother said. A Protestant."

"What?"

"The Book of Revelation. The Communist Party is the Whore of Babylon."

"What?"

Ponco shook his small head in strokes of weary disappointment. I was a man without significant culture. Mysteries were closed to me.

"The Communist parties in Latin America: the Church of the Revolution. But they betray the Revolution. They are the real Antichrist, the real Whore of Babylon."

"Oh."

"Protestants. We are. Revolution in the Revolution," Ponco said. That was the title of Debray's book. Was this rigmarole a joke about Debray? Or me? This waiting———

"Hilda," Ponco said, interrupting my dark thought. It sounded a gasp, a plea, as if he were afraid I'd forget my topic. "And Marxism."

"Yes. It was the times that let me see. And Hilda."

"Ah," he said, smiling in a most annoying way. Walter showed me a mouthful of rice mush. I didn't like his tone. I didn't like his smile. I thought —to myself—of Hilda. I would deny him the pleasure. (And being sure that I denied him something was almost as good, I found, as telling him.) Hilda found in Marx, I would have said, one message always: the spontaneous revolutionary will of the masses. She felt, as I did, that the Communist parties had only bridled the masses, held them back, as if, she would say, they were the head, and the workers no more than muscle. The Party made Marx's work hermetic, unintelligible. It was incapable of speaking the people's language. So she had turned to the nationalist groups, to APRA. It was the weakness of the

United States after the war, she said, that had given the nationalist parties space to blossom. (Our generation was a weed growing, before the gardener's hand regained its strength.) But the "democratic nationalists" were soon corrupted by compromises with imperialism. She, too, didn't now know where to turn.

So, for the moment, we studied. I told her of my plan, formed in Bolivia, to devote the next ten years to writing about the Latin American Revolution. (I thought this a necessary narrowing of my previous subject, my continent, my self.) I would travel for a decade, then go back to Argentina. I would also visit Europe—chat with Sartre—and the Soviet Union, India, China. I would . . .

Her thin eyes narrowed further, and looked to the wood floor. I found then that I did not want to disappoint her. But there was nothing, anymore, for us to do in Guatemala but wait. The beautiful Guatemalan Revolution, which we both loved, was endangered. And we would not be allowed to defend it.

So we studied together.

And Marx's work became a space between us, a field for play of a very serious kind. Each term—superstructure and base, vanguard and proletariat, surplus value and alienated labor—meant something more, something not sayable, a gift. Like a lover giving food, warm with her spittle, from her mouth to her lover's mouth.

What a thought! Not mine surely. I stared at Walter's mush mouth. I knew what his "Ah" had implied. And he was right. "That's rude," I said sharply. "Close your mouth!"

Hilda and I appropriated a world together; made it; this world, but re-formed, different. It *was* the world, in its truth. And it was (I know this sounds mad) Hilda herself; and it was a bridge between us, a copula. Made and remade. She said that everything in imperialism's lying order, its badly made-up story, caused Marx's vision, his truth, to be obscured, hid it, scrambled the story about, mystified us, as if the ruling class were the bad witch in the fairy tale. We were enchanted, dazed. And the trees, under spell, turned against us, blocked our eyes, scratched our faces. Her words, Marx's words, made clarity for me. "The MNR," she said of Bolivia, "is Bonapartist. It veers between the imperialists and the peasants. Because its power comes from the workers and peasants, it makes gestures in their direction. But only gestures. Because it must placate the imperialists, it always stabs the peasants in the back. The Indians you saw will round the corner of the stairs only to find another stairs. Or a drop into nothing at all." All so obvious. But it gave me a feeling of power over the world, this science, this order. I even understood Chaco's "Second

Talk on the Price of Beer," the way that, without a real revolution, inflation grew inevitably, a spreading stain.

You had to study and study again, though, so that things might be called by their proper name, so that the trees and the workers might be taught—no, they needn't be taught, they need only hear the words and the spell would be broken—that they might remember their true powers. But one must break the spell, re-call, re-form the true word, the true world, over and over. Arbenz and the Guatemalan CP would not speak the words, provide the leadership the masses required for that unremitting struggle against imperialism. They were afraid to say "United States"—("potato"!)—afraid to die.

And Gandhi? She *rejected* him. He tried to transform a revolution into a religious experience. He was a preacher. And he didn't even preach workers' taking power. He preached *reform.* He didn't prescribe doing away with the ruling class, just begging them to act more humanely. Gandhi didn't free India. What freed India was a Britain weakened by war and supplanted as the leading Imperial power by the United States. Gandhi had denied India the revolution that it needed, the revolution that China's masses accomplished. "He was," she said, leaning forward from her chair for this final damnation, "petit-bourgeois, the grocer's caste. And he had the notions of a petit-bourgeois."

"My father was a pharmacist," Chaco said. He sounded wounded. Chaco had definitely changed—one *could* wound him (or Hilda could)—and he, too, now wanted an action he could join himself to, a self that would act.

Myself, I didn't bother defining the doctor's caste. Chaco, I thought then, didn't understand the nature of these abstractions: impersonal, scientific.

But Marxism, I said, was rationality without poetry, without that which would rouse the masses to act. It denied what I knew to be necessary, the leader, the symbol which would unite us, which spoke of the needed sacrifice, even of one's life. Gandhi's words had a transforming music to them, a call. They promised not just a new social order, but a New Man, the self-sufficient villager, free not only of poverty, but of greed, of insecurity, of deforming anger, servility, the cringe left by colonialism. (I knew that Chaco required direction in his life. I looked from Hilda's angry face to his. I wanted him to believe in this vision, this man.) Gandhi's words spoke of an end to the terrible rhythm of violence, of revenge and vendetta that might disfigure humanity forever.

I could argue with Hilda as I never could with other critics of Gandhi, like my mother. For Hilda did not want simply to turn about lacerating herself. She, too, had a belief: that the masses did not require leadership. For sometimes the election would fall upon one man, and he would give voice to what was needed; and then it might alight upon another. All men could be prophets. The Revolution would come.

It was good to argue. And Gandhi gave us another subject, like Freud, to fight about. But it gave me, too, another voice. My head nearly burst from this dance that I was. I pressed one vision against another, Marx and Gandhi; both stood; both failed. I was between.

"There were usually four or five of us there talking," I said aloud. "Hilda, Chaco, Soto, one of his lawyer friends, and a Cuban, Nico, a follower of Castro, who had fled to Guatemala after the Moncada." I wanted to say that despite Ponco's smile, Marx was not a love poem. There were others present always. Things were not so intimate as Walter implied. (I was lying.)

"I don't know Nico," Ponco said. "Are you done with your rice?"

I pushed my plate towards him: new material for his meditative, methodical work.

"*Granma?*" Ponco asked.

"Do you mean did he go on the *Granma?*"

Ponco nodded, his lips curled upward in a smile, but closed. He was demonstrating politeness. He would not, I realized, this now fastidious man, this student of letters, have liked my telling him to close his mouth, criticizing his manners. "Yes. You knew. I meant *that.*"

And I had. I nodded back, ashamed of my momentary anger. "Yes. He died at Alegria. He ran behind me. I had just examined his foot." Why did I say that? How did his foot figure in the story?

"Fungh Ny."

"What did you say?" This time I really hadn't understood him, not even a word.

He swallowed, looked angrily at me, narrowing his eyes. I had reminded him again of his imperfection, his loss.

"Funny," he said, overly precise this time. The word didn't mean amusement.

"What?" I was distracted by an odd unrelated thought. My rediscovery of Marxism, the way that it made a shared space between Hilda and me, a country we ruled together, the deep satisfying involvement I felt in those talks in her parlor, the way the words joined us and allowed us to care for each other— it reminded me of something now—of telling my life to this short thin black man, my Ponco. "What's funny?" I repeated. I looked down at the table, away from his face, embarrassed. But I smiled.

"The way he held them. The few who survived the Moncada." He continued to lift forkfuls of rice to his mouth, dividing his phrases with bites.

"Went on the *Granma*. With him. Like losing. At roulette. And doubling. Your bet." He looked down sadly at his plate. No more rice. "How did he hold them? So many defeats. So many crazy plans." His face looked distracted, far away. His large brown eyes moved up and down following some inward play of images. (Pictures of a body falling—his? mine?—grasping for air, clawing the ground?) His thin cheeks, surrounding a voice barely there, a light scraping in the silence. He was lost in wonder—about himself, really. The boy who had come to the mountains. Or perhaps he wondered about his involvement in another mad plan.

"Nico loved him," I said, though I knew that explained nothing. It was, in a way, what needed explaining. But one could never get to the bottom of that. Infrastructure? Surplus value? The crystalline science could do nothing with *that* moisture. But it was passion in all its manifold and compound forms that made revolution. "And Nico hated him. And he couldn't speak of anything else." We sat in the parlor and talked of the defense of the revolution, of responses to the mercenaries already moving towards the border. How could the people be aroused to protect the Guatemalan Revolution? Nico thought my ideas of nonviolent resistance "diabolical." (If we were outside he would spit, his most frequent, most pronounced gesture of contempt, of damnation.) The government, Hilda said, must allow the people to act, to organize their own neighborhood committees for self-defense. Too late, Soto said. Too late. It was all empty prayer; parlor talk. Nico rose suddenly from the couch, knocking the bowl of fruit (bananas today) to the floor. His left arm punched the air. "Fidel would know what to do!" he cried. It was the jerking of an overexcited body, beyond Nico's control, frightening to watch. He was a large fierce-looking man. He had a broad flat nose, wide bones, and big veins that stood out on his neck and forehead beneath his light-brown skin. Anger made him taut, more sharply defined than those around him, as if he were outlined by flickering electricity, a man chosen by lightning, a man apart. "Fidel would know what to do!" Long welts, an irritable red, marked his cheek and neck: battle scars.

Chaco imitated Nico, punching more air, and humming "Fidel Is a Meteor / Fidel Has Big Plans / Fidel Is the Master / Fidel Is the Man." Soto laughed at the two of them standing next to each other, punching air together. Castro, he thought, was someone to be watched, a madman whose lunacy might be what the times demanded, might bring him to power. But Nico was someone to be laughed at, a person of no account. And Nico agreed with Soto's judgment; after all, *he* was not Fidel. His arm moved more and more slowly, as if the air had suddenly become thick around him. He opened his palm, slapped it against the side of his leg again and again, not softly, but with a hard sound, the sound of bruises, of damage being done. He sat, and looked down at his lap, silent. Fidel would know what to do. *He* didn't.

Nico and I sought each other out. He had seen battle. And though I did not condone that stupid pointless violence ("Oh, they were all captured," Soto said with mild astonishment. "Most of them were tortured and then killed by the police"), still, I knew also that Nico had knowledge that I coveted. He knew the depth of his own courage, the sacrifice he was prepared to make, his willingness to die. He had found the leader he longed for, and had recognized him, and been obedient to what he had seen in him. There was no mocking, ironic voice in his head, no sad, impeccable moralist, denying him the chance to declare himself, to act. I was sure that this gangster, this Castro, with his bloody badly planned adventures, was not the leader who would call the suffering people of Latin America to the great, the necessary transformation. He was a man with a red kerchief running towards a police line—as if he could stand horizontally! He was a failure, a charlatan—a lawyer! But I respected Nico, even if he was so obviously deceived in his love. For I wanted to have in my life his commitment, his courage, his faith.

And Nico, for his part, saw that I was not, like Soto, or the others, merely tolerant of his admiration of Castro. He felt the strength of my ambivalence, my refusal of his leader, and yet my search for someone like this Fidel, my search that was so much like Nico's own. I was more than merely skeptical. My contempt for this Castro was more urgent than that. I *might* believe in him, but I didn't. Why did I ignore, Nico wondered, Fidel's unmistakable grandeur? What blindness of soul! he said. If only he could find the right story to tell me! For Nico had to convince me in order to remain secure in his own faith.

As I, I felt, had to convince Chaco to remain standing in mine.

An odd dance. Nico and Chaco and I often walked through the city together during the last days of the Guatemalan Revolution. We did guard duty with the Youth Alliance throughout the morning, standing outside the tall stone posts and iron gates of the university, watching for anti-Communist saboteurs. But the daytime saboteurs were easily spotted: they were the single-engined planes, their North American markings painted over, that flew as they wished over most of the city. Guard duty meant witness, witness to the power of North America, to the final cowardice of the Guatemalan leadership, to the fall of the Revolution, to the death of the Indians' hopes.

One afternoon in June, a week after my birthday, a woman in a long blue-and-red skirt brought out to us a petition being circulated by the Young

Communists. It implored the Congress of the United States to desist from their aggression against Guatemala. I laughed at this craven inanity and passed it on to Nico. "Implore," he said angrily, "what does that mean?" He spat on the paper and handed it back to the woman. She wiped the spit off on Nico's own sleeve, and went back through the tall iron gates. One of the planes flew low over us. The roar filled my head. Nico took out his pistol and fired at the plane, leaping a few feet off the ground as he pulled the trigger, as if the extra distance would send his bullet home. I laughed. He was spitting at the plane with his gun. It all seemed far away to me. The city was behind a pane of glass made of memories and voices; people's gestures looked like a movie with the sound cut off. They seemed absurd. Nico's angry arrogant actions, spitting at paper, firing at planes. The plane itself. What did they mean? I couldn't quite remember. The only vivid sound was the roar of the plane, and that meant nothing. I felt very tired. (*Please come home,* he had scrawled across the bottom of his letter, in a child's unsteady hand.) My limbs made enormous effort to hold me up on the sidewalk. *That morning at Hilda's I'd received news of my father's death.*

The pilot waggled his wings, as if in friendly response to Nico's noise. Leaflets came fluttering down through the air, like huge light bird droppings dried by the sun as they descended.

"Look," Chaco said, "you hit it!" He picked up one of the leaflets and read it to us. " 'Friends of Christianity! Be sure that the liberators will execute all the Communists and their sympathizers! Vengeance will be ours for all that our nation has suffered from this foreign disease! Justice will be done! But to those who have cried out under the yoke of tyranny: We have heard your cries! Castillo Armas bears no anger against the Guatemalan Army, betrayed by a few of its highest officers! Surrender and you will face no punishment! Continue to obey the Communist tyrants and you will surely die!' " Chaco did not giggle as he read.

"Christianity," Nico said, and spat on the pavement. "There is no God!" He wasn't kidding. He said such angry things about God often, in defiant affirmation of His absence, His recalcitrant Bad Character. "No judgment!" he shouted. "No judge! Nothing! Nothing! Nothing!" Clearly these curses were meant to keep some danger at a distance; Nico violently shook off the waters of baptism. I do not know what crisis of faith Nico had suffered before he found the true word, the faithful one, Fidel. But some of the water had soaked him through; his speech was wounded with theological metaphors, accusations of soul blindness, of diabolism—and good news and greetings, too, of a messianic sort.

We walked by the Government Palace, on our way to Hilda's. That morning we had heard, and heard about, two twin-engined gray planes strafing the huge palace. Now rows of soldiers stood in front of the pillars of the long portico. More impotent witnesses. On the long uppermost balcony of the palace's right wing, men remounted machine guns. Chips in the gray stone ran the length of the balcony, from the morning's attack. They had fired back from there, while the soldiers hid under the portico. More spit. Ineffectual gestures; a rite; last rites. Only the masses could have saved the Revolution. But no one had raised the symbol that might unite them. Black drapery covered the palace's long windows. The forty cornices, rounded forms with spikes in their center that composed the top of the balustrade, all still stood. The palace hadn't been bombed, for Castillo Armas was certain he would come into possession of it.

Something crashed from above us. A tile clattered down near our feet. A young man in his undershirt on the long flat roof cursed and looked over the edge of the railing. Inwardly I heard his curses turn to screams. The army and the mercenaries battled now for bridges near the rail town of Zacapa, the link to Ecuador. North American planes had bombed that town, and the hospital in Guatemala City had been cleared for the wounded. The Federation of Labor sent loudspeaker trucks through the empty city, calling for blood donations. *What did she know of blood? Of the dignity of nonviolence?* Poor man, without friends, lying on the floor of the living room, with his hands at his side. Corpse position.

"It will all be over," Nico said, with great decisiveness, "if they get this close." But then, as always, he denied his own authority; his voice grew quiet, tentative. "I think," he added. His expertise, he admitted, was borrowed. He spread his fingers and pressed them into his neck. What would Fidel think? That was Nico's hesitation. Opinions could only be offered provisionally, until Fidel marked them valid. And Castro's confirming voice was far away, in a dictator's jail, on the Isle of Pines.

Is this leader, she asked, making men more themselves?

"Go away, Mother," I whispered. I wanted to silence these voices. They came without my asking, while the palpable world moved farther away, became spectral.

"What?" Nico asked. He bit his lower lip in anger. He thought I'd insulted him.

I smiled. I *would* insult him. (I watched from behind a glass. Did he have feelings? Perhaps by making him wince I could establish our reality for each other.) "Fidel would know what to do," I said. My mother played with the charismatic's name. The people of Guayaquil chanted it. Fi—del! As if it had some protective powers. Armed men moved out of the carnival crowd, towards the army barracks. . . .

It had no protective powers. They were tortured and then killed by the police.

"You're mocking me, I know," Nico said sadly, for it was a great sorrow to him that we could not feel the power of his beloved, the warmth. "But you're wrong, Ernesto. It's easy to mock. We're a generation of mockers." He turned accusingly towards the archvillain, Chaco, as if the source of derision were always in him. Chaco looked away from the accusation, humming to himself contentedly. He was, I knew, composing a song, another piece of his "cycle" on Fidel, little verses with titles like "Fidel Is a Mansion," or "Fidel Is a Soap," which he sang at inopportune times to torment Nico.

"But Fidel *would* know. I tell you Guevara—listen to me!—he is the most extraordinary man. Not only on the little island of Cuba. But in all the Americas. It's simply an accident that he was born there and not some bigger place! The rest of the democratic Left on this continent, they talk. They talk. Then they rest and talk some more. But Castro *acts*. History will show. He has *guidance*. He will liberate Cuba from that spider Batista. I know. I am certain. Absolutely certain."

Chaco smiled at me. Nico, Chaco said one night at Hilda's, frightened him, with this hagiography of a murderer. Who knew what it might incite him to do! "Nico frightens me, Hilda. But not so much as Ernesto, of course." He spoke his accusation directly to Hilda, who sat and looked at him quizzically. Who might ever know if he were serious? What *use* was such irony? "In the long run, in my opinion, Hilda, this Guevara will do more damage." But such mockery of me was rare now from Chaco. Our acquaintance had changed these last few weeks in Guatemala, as the city grew nervous and despaired, and had become a friendship. At night on the golf course he talked with me about Gandhi. And when I spoke he listened, with his face strangely calm (or so I thought watching him by moonlight). The absence of movement signaled a serious concentration for Chaco, the way Fernando's contortions had mimed the passage of his thought. Perhaps Gandhi might bring him singleness. As for Chaco's irony, Nico was now its preferred object. We stood and watched the palace. The men finished with the machine-gun emplacements and left the roof-balcony. Would they return, I wondered? I rolled up the sleeves of my sweaty shirt. It was hot here even in the late afternoon. I had slept in my clothes for days. My white cotton shirt had a sea-smell to it, and a moist feel.

"And you would be certain if you met him. You would see the light that is in his face, Ernesto. You would know then as I know. He is a fire in the field!

Nothing can stop him! All is consumed! He would take action against these mercenaries. He would leap at them. He says only an action will move the people, show them that a fight is possible!"

My words! I realized suddenly. His words. The longing of a generation. You'd like him, Soto had said; you share a certain viewpoint with him. Impossible! I could share *nothing* with such a man! He was a charlatan, a fraud, a killer, a gangster. (Was that my own voice, I wondered. Or that of a sad, stern, isolated moralist? I will not become you, Father. "Go away old man!")

"No," Nico said. He clapped his hands together, an engine revving up. "He is your age Ernesto. Or maybe a few years older. You would like him. He is manly. He wouldn't let the Guatemalan Revolution die without a struggle. That lacks courage! He would keep the idea of resistance alive for the future, even if we were to fail now." His hands thudded their approval.

But what action could Fidel or anyone take? Defeat was thick in the air of Guatemala City, like humidity before rain. The bad air was everywhere. The military would not allow Arbenz to arm the workers and peasants, so the Revolution's life depended on the loyalty of the Army, its only defenders. And the generals, Arbenz assured the nation, would remain loyal to him. The officers were his friends, his former students at the military academy. He had taught them how to read, a word at a time, each word a test of their worthiness. Poor Arbenz! The Party supported Arbenz's decision. The people must not struggle.

A North American aircraft carrier had anchored off shore near Puerto Barrios. The time for revolution was . . . not yet.

But Fidel, ah, Fidel would take action! Fidel would know what to do!

Fidel began each of Nico's thoughts. Fidel instructed him by word and example. Fidel accused him. Fidel had nearly gotten him killed. He had betrayed Fidel by surviving. He hadn't been courageous enough for Fidel. Fidel took risks. Fidel *acted*. Fidel spoke beautifully. Listen please, Ernesto, to this magnificent speech of Fidel's! Fidel knows what to do. History guides him.

Why haven't we heard from him? Why hasn't he spoken? This story fills his silence; entertainment between the acts. I continue telling the story of my past until Fidel speaks.

"You say the word 'history,' Nico," I said. "History guides him. But I hear the word 'God.' God guides Fidel."

Nico, furious at the mention of that Unfortunate Personage, spat an inch or two from my mismatched shoes. I pushed at the saliva with the flat end of my boot.

Fidel, he said angrily, *would* know what to do, by looking inside (as if that escaped theology). He was an instrument of history. Fidel wouldn't sit still (as if movement were a kind of election). *(He wouldn't sit here at this table, waiting for the end.)* He wouldn't sit still.

Nor could Nico. His motions were constant; abrupt; halted halfway; forceful-looking, but without purpose. He seemed angry always, a man on the point of striking someone. But he only struck himself. He beat his large fist against his leg, the side of his jaw; he pounded the heels of his hand together in a rapid motion that was frightening to watch, like a destructive machine, or a seizure. (How would Pavlov have explained that? I asked Hilda one evening, as if I were presenting Nico's case, as if he weren't there. And, as he sat on the couch banging his hands, he wasn't; he was lost in his painful ecstasy.)

Now he ran his palm through his long black hair, carefully straightened by him and formed into a high pompadour. He would not cut his hair, he vowed, until Fidel was released from Batista's jail on the Isle of Pines.

The feel of his hair reminded him, as most objects did, this grieving lover, of his heart's only subject. "And even in prison he struggles. He sends letters to guide our movement. Every day of his life Fidel fights. He needs struggle as you"—Nico turned towards me, the possible acolyte—"as you need knowledge."

What more knowledge did I need now? I wondered. What might return this world to me? What might help me move my sodden limbs one more step? What might help me breathe this bad air?

We walked away from the palace. My leg muscles hurt, cramped from last night's accommodations, the golf-course fairway. With every step my body complained from a thousand small places. I felt like a crumpled piece of paper.

Nico's wide white shirt reminded me of the smocks worn in grade school. We'd been gauchos—our heads shaved for lice—and had ecstatic knife fights. We made daggers from sticks, their ends burned black. A hit left a charcoal mark on your smock, where delicious blood would have poured from your torn skin. I risked my eyes running at them. I was fearless in my savage maneuvers. I had to make a distance between us, hold them off by the actions I might improvise that they were afraid to perform.

We headed towards the park, a little way down the avenue. I saw them then. The boy with the round lightly freckled face came first, a tormentor bribed with pieces of linted candy. Ernesto Banana, Banana Guevara, Banana Guevara, Banana Banana. They must not mock my father's name! (*You have his name,* she had written me. *You are what was best in him.* It felt like a curse.) They pulled me towards an iron basin, my tormentors, still with me, with me always, aroused to walk again by this shirt of Nico's, by my father's death, more vivid to me than my companions in the empty streets of Guatemala City. Why hadn't he protected me against them? Their legs surrounded me, trapped me. An animal, I writhed on the ground, straining for breath.

But he had protected me! He had taken the sickly boy, and with his magic regimen made him strong. Shazam, he said, tying the plaid scarf about my throat. He ran me through the streets until I could run no farther, until I had done my utmost. Together we charted my progress on the wall of my bedroom. The potter's clay figure brought to life by his love and longing. I became captain of the rugby team.

Only to be beaten down again. He walked along the sideline in the rain in that silly hat, watching them torment me. Why hadn't he stopped the game?

How childish, he said, to cry for your father's protection! At your age! "You're weak," he said, "your generation is weak."

Nico stopped in the middle of the street and looked at me, his face suddenly slack. He bowed his head, for he expected reproof. "Yes," he said, "we are weak. Most of us." *But not Fidel!* When he was fourteen Fidel had organized a strike of the sugar workers, a strike against his own father! And when he was eighteen he had walked all over the plantation, calling a public meeting, to denounce the old man. " 'You abuse the powers you wrench from people with deceitful promises!' " These were Fidel's own words; Nico could be sure that it was correct to speak them. So he shouted them. But there was no one else in the street to hear.

And Nico quoting Fidel was, Chaco said, the wind in the reeds, the sea in the background. Not unpleasant, and hardly meaningful. Like his pounding hands, another mechanical discharge of affect.

We had now heard bits of Fidel's speeches from every epoch—for Nico knew by heart pages of this wordy man's remarks. What heat, we wondered, did Nico find in this fat rhetoric? It was difficult for us to imagine warming ourselves there. This, Chaco and I agreed, was not literature, was not the sublime poetry of a true, an inspired leader. It was rant. How could someone be so moved by it? Chaco poked me lightly in my ribs, to share the joke.

But I was elsewhere. *My* father, I thought, had never deceived—not anyone but himself. *He* might more likely call a meeting to denounce me. Chalk letters on the big brown doors to the dining room. *This is what Ernesto Guevara said to his mother. . . .* A moral man, moving away from us into a perfect implacable justice, a quiet that was a continual accusation, the unanswerable accusation of defeat, for the failure of a man truly too good for this world condemned the world. And I, the one person this mistrustful isolated man had allowed himself to rely on, I had abandoned him.

Dearest Tete: Your father died yesterday on the floor of the living room. It was a peaceful end. Please, I beg you do not come home for the burial. By the time you receive this he will already be in the ground. And I am quite capable of taking care of myself. So don't insult me by returning! You have his name. You are what was best in him. You are Ernesto now. You have a book to write, a world to conquer for all of us.

Love, my darling Ernesto, from your mother,
Celia

"You see," the wind went on, moving through trees, over buildings, "nothing is more important to Fidel than truth. Nothing. Not his family. Not his career. Not his life. Nothing. Truth is his food. Without it Fidel would die. He wants nothing for himself but justice!" He was shouting again, and smashing his right fist into his thigh.

These charismatics, my mother said, always they want nothing for themselves! Nothing but absolute power over you! She was right, clearly right, sadly, unappealably right. Nico moved far away from me, behind the thick air, the air like glass. These voices! They sealed me off from the world, with their mockery, or their stern moralism.

Chaco placed an arm about Nico, to calm him. "Here," he said kindly, "have a cigarette." He offered him a red-and-white package he'd acquired at a cafe we'd stopped at that morning, before guard duty. Chaco made a game out of getting those packages, an amateur sport, for he himself didn't smoke. He sought out the North American "professors" without universities, the "journalists" who had no newspapers to write for. They flirted with each other. Chaco would smile, wink, encourage an agent to invite him over to his table, engage him in conversation. They asked questions about the city's morale (very bad), the army's loyalty (very questionable), the students' feelings (very strong implacable opposition to a certain country to the north. Know where?). Chaco spewed nonsense. "The Guatemalan people have chewed the food of nationhood." He nodded his head up and down earnestly, looking over at our table, where Nico grew taut with fury, and I, against my will, smiled fondly. "How can they spit it out?" For this little stew Chaco had garbled up bits of my thoughts and Nico's "Fidel Theology." "Do you know the taste of nationhood, sir, of real independence?" He flicked his large earlobe back and forth. His voice squeaked rhythmically, as if this were one of his songs. "It is bitter, but pungent, odoriferous, more vivifying than greed." He showed the agent the palm of his hand, as if delivering a benediction. The palm was puckered with lines, like my mother's, as if he, too, had put his hand over a fire. (I wondered how it had happened. I meant to ask him about it.) "The fruit of a tree," he said. Strange benediction; he began to waggle his fingers. "The fruit of *the* tree." The agent looked about, the businessman caught with a chorus girl. Bad for his career. He quickly slid a package of North American cigarettes across the table, the expected gratuity in these encounters. He didn't want to touch the madman's lined hand, those long thin fingers waving like worms.

Chaco wasn't the only one engaged in the cigarette enterprise. At meetings in the university, endless meetings, crowded, hot, meetings without plan, without hope, a long complaint, a shared anxiety without issue, I would see those packages here and there in the assembly, recognize them over my head on the balcony that ran the length of the room, held up for a moment, disappearing into pockets. Offerings of smoke rose to the gold angels on the high domed ceiling. It was hard for me to breathe. The red spots of a disease, I thought. Will the patient live? No one thought so anymore. The cafe was nearly empty this morning, the chairs still tipped over on top of the white metal tables. And the few students there spoke quietly of certain defeat. The Guatemalan Revolution was the grounds in their coffee.

Nico lit his cigarette. We took seats on a gray stone bench in a garden near the Government Palace. Pink and white flowers grew profusely all around us. (Someone, oddly, was still caring for them.) The sun went behind some clouds on the horizon. It would set soon. When it was dark the planes would come. The thought made me nervous. Some birds—could they be gulls? they had long wings—wheeled about the palace, and off towards the setting sun. Were they messengers bringing news of Castillo Armas to the General Staff? Or were they spies of some more far reaching conspiracy?—It was my anxiety, I realized, that made me construct whimsies about birds.

There was no one else in the garden. Last night the twin-engined planes had bombed near La Aurora Air Base, and then had moved on to attack the working-class quarters of the city. We could hear the fire engines at the meeting, a long wail above the speaker's voice, the beginning of a mourning. There were too many fires for the rescue crews. "We'll be safe on the golf course," Chaco had whispered to me, unsure and afraid. "*They* wouldn't want to destroy the golf course, would they?"

That morning the mercenary army had taken Asuncion Mita, El Progreso, and Zacapa. The rail line to El Salvador was cut. The battle had begun this afternoon for Puerto Barrios. If it fell, the city would be utterly isolated. The perfume of the flowers made it hard to breathe. The air was too thick.

A few men in dirty, worn clothes came to the Government Palace, a delegation asking for participation in the city's final defense. The nation longed for leadership For the leader who would act Whose actions would be a symbol A symbol that would Call the people to the necessary sacrifice.

Did I think that? My own thoughts came to me in bits, and seemed as distant to me now as the colors of the flowers, hidden by the glassy thick air. The palace was a picture postcard I looked at far away, in another country. My lungs hurt. But only a little. I don't need an injection! I won't complain! I won't have another attack!

The man I pleaded with was dead.

The delegation would be turned away. The workers must not be armed. Who knows how they might act if Castillo Armas were defeated, if they felt their own power? What might they ask for? What might they demand? They must be sent home, back to their burrows to hide.

Or to run away, if they could get their dog carts over the ridge. Yesterday Soto and the lawyers had left town. I had his farewell letter folded in my pocket, next to my mother's note. Hilda had read it to us the night before:

Dear Boys: I cannot see what earthly good will be served by your remaining in Guatemala. Clearly, this was a revolution before its time, an experiment that failed! I truly understand your affection for what Arbenz has attempted, and for the Guatemalans. But I don't see what purpose will be served by our remaining here to watch its death agony. Do you realize the risk you run? This is not your country! Ernesto, you were always a heedless man. I admire you for it, really, in a way. I don't expect you ever to take my—or anyone's!—advice. But Chaco! You are a more cautious and reasonable boy! Please don't be misled by other people's stories! You should follow my sensible example.

Anyway, I'm sure that Ernesto and I and Chaco will meet again under more favorable circumstances. Perhaps I will see you all in Mexico City.

Your comrade,
Roberto

This disgusted me, this talk of "the electoral way"—of compromises with imperialism and its lackeys.

Hilda smiled warmly at me. She had always despised Soto. She handed me the letter. "He thinks we're fools."

"Good. I wouldn't have it otherwise."

"He's not alone, you know," Chaco said, from the couch. "It's a general exodus. The Venezuelans left yesterday. And the other Peruvians, besides Hilda. And even Nico's comrades. The leaves have all fallen from the trees." He turned towards Nico on the couch. Nico looked uncomfortable, nervous, as if he were about to spring upon someone. (Himself, most likely.) Chaco's smiling mouth took over most of his thin face. "Why did you stay, Nico? After all, as Soto says, it's not your country. You have another struggle elsewhere, a leader to wait for. Are you, too, a heedless man, like our friend Ernesto?"

Nico turned to me. He waited, I felt, for me to give him my full attention, to look directly at him, even into his eyes. Or so I felt. It was difficult to see him from my chair opposite. We'd covered the windows with newspapers (newspaper that mysteriously fell to the floor each afternoon while Hilda was at work). The only light was a candle by Hilda's chair, and the pale, greenish glow from the radio dial. I found Nico's eyes (for I knew he awaited me); and when I did, he spoke.

"Because I am like Soto, Ernesto. Because I am much worse than Soto. Because I really am a coward. And I must not ever run away again."

Why did he need my look for his confession? I would not be his judge! My eyes slipped from his for a moment, to the small worn red-and-brown Persian carpet by his feet. I sipped some hot mate. No one replied to his revelation. But when my eyes met his again, he spoke:

The 26th of July. Someone at the assembly point had said they were going to the carnival as a reward for their training. No one had known the plan. Fidel, that is, hadn't revealed the plan till the last minute, when the arms were distributed. Nico had been given a .22. A .22! The man next to him, a fellow named Marcos, had looked at Nico's gun and said, "We're finished." Just like that! Everyone had known what he meant. Fidel had failed to get real weapons! Then the great plan had been revealed. It was to take the barracks to get army weapons for the spontaneous rising. But they hadn't had the weapons to take the barracks! Nico had used a .22 in practice. It wouldn't always knock a tin can over. Marcos said they were all going to die. He had shaken his head wearily. But he had gone. And Nico had gone. You had to trust Fidel.

Nico had stood on the highway, where he was told to stand, with his .22. Troop reinforcements might come down the highway after the main force had attacked the Moncada. He was to delay them.

They had come. Batista's soldiers had new Yanqui weapons. He hadn't seen the soldiers, really, only their guns. He had a .22! So he had run away.

Nico would not look away from me, or allow me to look away. He spoke very slowly, precisely, his hands lying on his knees. Nothing moved but his large Adam's apple. I knew that if I touched his white shirt now, even over his chest, it would be wet with his odorless sweat. I thought of Fernando's deaf ear, his hearing destroyed by a beating in a provincial jail. This is not your country! This is not your country! I thought of the smell of burnt pork in Soto's cell in Buenos Aires. They had other instruments besides straight-backed chairs! Clever Soto had escaped. Bodies found charred in fields outside La Paz, or dead in the backs of old taxis. The soldiers had come down the road towards Nico. He had run away. Politics. Who uses whom. People being held; or holding others; escaping; failing to escape. Tortured and then killed by the police. Too much suffering. Too much pointless suffering.

Nico, I had thought (for I wanted him to be so, a goal, an accusation to move me onward), knew the depth of his courage, the sacrifice he was prepared to make. And he did! He was a coward! And I? How would I have acted when the gun batteries pointed down at the marchers in La Paz? When Batista's soldiers moved up the street towards me? I was unknown to myself, to others, always unknown, pure potential; a child listening to stories, I might be any character in the tale—the hero? the coward? the great violinist? the Prince of Argentina?

Nico had heard the gunfire from the barracks. It hadn't been loud enough. There should have been more of it. Something had gone wrong. He had told himself it was all right to escape. Because he was a coward! Because he hadn't really understood the choice, no matter how many times Fidel had explained to them that in a real revolution you must be prepared to win or die. He heard Fidel's words. But he hadn't been able to imagine what they meant. Die? The soldiers had marched up the street towards him, carrying rifles with long curving clips. There had been torches along the highway for the carnival, black smoke had curled from the top of them. He had been able to see the weapons. They had had good weapons. Fidel hadn't gotten them good weapons. Not like those!

"You see," he said, "I tried to blame my cowardice on him! As if it were Fidel's fault that I ran away!"

And now Nico sobbed before us, not from grief or embarrassment, but from fear. He saw the guns again. He was still afraid. His body trembled all along its length. "Mother of God," he cried, "Fidel would have let us all die! The bastard! Someone should stop him now before he kills more young men!" He put his own large arms around his chest, hugging himself, rocking back and forth on the sofa.

We watched. It was unkind, but all of us watched the large man cry. He saw us watching and dragged his sleeve across his eyes. It was because he had been so scared, he said, that he had thought like that. He didn't think like that anymore.

He reached up to touch the ridges on his face and neck. "They're from a car accident," he said. "Everyone thinks they're battle scars." He smiled wanly at me. "I'll bet you thought that too, Ernesto?" He ran his fingers along their length, over and over, tracing his wound. "But I want you to know that they're not battle scars, because you're my friend, Ernesto. You understand the truth of these matters. I want you to know how I got them. I was drunk. In a car."

Why did he want me to know? So I might judge him, so that I might be the stern moralist? Very well. I smiled my tight-lipped smile. I did judge him. He was a coward.

Outside we could hear the sound of the explosions. The windows shook. I turned away from Nico, leaving him in darkness. "They're bombing near civilians now."

"Near *us*," Chaco said harshly. "*We're* civilians, Ernesto." The fingers of Chaco's right hand curved about his left wrist. To calm himself in crisis he often counted his own pulse beats.

But Nico's story frightened me more than the bombing—the slow implacable march of his voice. It spoke, like his hands slamming together, of obscure forces, beyond one's will, carrying one away.

"You shouldn't be embarrassed, dear," Chaco said to Nico. "You showed very good sense. Fidel *had* failed you. Here." He reached for the wicker basket of fruit—my fruit!—on the table in front of them. "Have an orange." He held it on the palm of his lined troll's hand. The orange seemed a thing from another world, a world filled with light.

"Don't call me 'dear,' you stupid clown!" Nico shouted. He slapped at Chaco's thin hand with his large paw, knocking the orange to the floor. "Just shut up! You don't understand anything! You don't understand about Fidel!"

The orange rolled slowly over to my seat. I put it into my jacket pocket. Later, on the golf course, our refuge, I would share its spill of light with Chaco.

No one spoke more. As the sound of the planes moved away, we went outside to see if there was anything we could do to help the victims.

Nico smoked without taking the cigarette from his mouth. I could see his eyes water painfully. A mild reproof, like his hand striking his thigh. He wanted this punishment. He had betrayed Fidel. What further punishment might he want?

I stretched my legs out in front of me. Another night on the golf course and they would never be straight again. "He's a bourgeois," I said, "isn't he? Castro? A plantation owner's son?"

And I? Child of the conquistadors? How might I affirm myself? Today the abstraction of class didn't seem impersonal; it stood accusingly against me, as if to say that all I could imagine to do was compromised from the start by the sullen nature of my imagination. (Or was I petit-bourgeois, because I would always contrive a way to escape the consequences of my imaginings?)

Nico waved my question about Fidel away, throwing the back of his hand outward, as if my inquiry were an annoying fly.

"You think that matters? That doesn't matter!"

To understand I need only hear what Fidel had told the Cuban Communists. Fidel loved truth. Fidel wanted justice. One had to trust that. One had to trust his hatred of injustice. It was real. If Marxism was the science of Revolution, as Hilda said, then Castro's movement would overcome its prejudices in order to realize justice. Fidel would unite all who could be united.

Nico paused to wipe under his nose. "Those aren't my thoughts," he said. "Those are Fidel's own. It's a beautiful truth isn't it?"

I laughed, though I knew that my laughter would pain Nico. I couldn't imagine his pain. I couldn't imagine, either, the Communist who would agree that faith in Fidel was more vital than the necessary truths of Marxism. "Unite all who could be united!" What magic in this Castro's personality allowed Nico to think this pointless tautology the ground of wisdom?

"Why do you laugh, Ernesto?" He blew smoke at me—maliciously, I thought. I looked up at the sun setting over the palace. A long point, like a sword, ran from the coat of arms that formed its central decoration. A ray of the sun was split by the sword. I struggled for breath. "Don't you see?" Nico said. "Fidel believes in justice. He will follow that wherever it might lead him. Even against his own father!"

Chaco laughed, stomping his feet up and down in the bleak delight of his despair over Nico, over this thralldom that had destroyed the black man's character. "Especially his father!" Chaco had chaperoned Hilda and me late at night, as we argued about Freud. "Of course, Nico. Especially his father!" Chaco's heels left round marks in the soft turf.

I pulled up some tufts of grass and chewed on them. Cool, but a little bitter. The food of nationhood. I thought of my own father, lying on the floor, his arms at his side. Severing his attachments to my mother and myself, preparing for death. I had abandoned him. *I don't know if it has to do with your absence, but I think that perhaps it does. It is as if he were giving up.*

I hadn't written back.

"His father," Nico said proudly, "his father is a real son of a bitch."

I spat out the grass helms. Why was there so much talk about fathers?

A barefoot Indian ran directly, intently, towards us across the grass, as if he had a message especially for our ears. Where had he come from? Had he been hiding behind that bush with the red berries? We stopped talking, amazed, and awaited him. He wore wide three-quarter-length pants with broad brown stripes, a bright-blue shirt with white squares woven on it, and a small straw hat with a red cord around the crown. He stopped before Chaco. Perhaps the message was for him. But then the man stood silently, staring unselfconsciously at Chaco's odd face. It was worth a stare. Or perhaps he'd forgotten his message.

"Take his hand," I instructed, "and put it to your forehead."

Chaco picked up the man's dirty hand and touched the stubby fingers to his face. The Indian looked away and pulled his hand from Chaco's weak grip. His lips closed tightly, making a sour pucker; he scrunched his eyes shut. "Why do you do that?" he asked. It was not his custom; it disgusted him.

Chaco smiled. "He told me to," he said, inclining his head towards me.

"Do you do whatever he tells you to? You can get in a lot of trouble that way. Unless he's your boss? But he doesn't look like a boss." He stared at me through half-closed eyes.

His look reminded me of the mestizo waiter at the bar in La Paz, the Indian guards outside Obrajes. This man turned me into a store dummy. He took his time examining me. My once-white shirt gave off a smell. My pants were stained with mud from our nights on the golf course, where my rolled-up jacket had been my pillow. I held the jacket in my right hand. It looked like a leather rag.

"He's our leader," Chaco said, continuing his joke on everyone. "We have to do what he says. We have to trust in his hatred of injustice. It is real. We have to trust his guidance."

"Well, he's not a very good leader if you ask me," the Indian said. "He should lead you all out of here, right now, before something bad happens to you, my friend. This is a dangerous street. This is a dangerous town. You should get out of here. You should get out of here right now. I think you need a new leader!" He laughed, and rubbed the side of his face with his hand. His thin eyes looked worried for Chaco, his lost nephew. "Follow *me!*" He ran off down the empty park path, down the empty street, out of town, getting smaller and smaller, another Indian off to feed the dying sun.

Nico rose suddenly, moved forward without waiting for us or even looking to see if we followed. Smoke trailed out behind him. We followed. "His father," he said, "is the worst man in Cuba! Except for Batista."

Fidel's father was a thief. He stole from everyone, even the United Fruit Company! On moonless nights he'd cut away at the forests, enlarging his holdings. Fidel's father had stolen deeds. Fidel's father had been unfaithful to Fidel's mother. He had fucked every woman in the province!

Nico pounded the heels of his hands together. Some ecstasy beyond joy. The pleasure (I imagined) of his imagining the coupling of Fidel's parents; poor child, all the body that was left to him was in watching the primal scene of someone else's parents. What selfless discipleship, my mother's mocking voice said. Or perhaps his pleasure was simply in remembering that Fidel had once shared such intimacies with him.

I turned from the loud sad spectacle. My father walked beside me, the opposite of all that Nico had said, a good faithful man in a silly hunting cap, the ear flaps tied up at the sides. What did he care what others thought of him? We walked by the slums near our house. He told me the story of Latin America, our unredeemed continent, the moral failure of its leaders. His hands balled into fists. But how could he do anything? How could he strike a blow at the United States? The United States, the land of rich unfeeling immoral men, imperialists who starved our people, cracked their skulls to reveal runny yellow yolks. It was easy to kill people. But that was something for weak people to do, ones without character, "Imperialists." A dirty barefoot child ran near the basin in the slum; I ran, I shouted something, it didn't mean anything, just sound shouted up at the sky. My father took my hand. He moved faster than I did, pulled me along. It was hard to breathe.

It was hard to keep up with Nico, to push through the bad air. Now he fluttered his large hands against his thighs, like a penguin. Each fluttering motion made my lungs move spastically in my chest. He walked faster, lost in love for Fidel's grandiose old man, his prodigious appetites, his fabulous larceny, his terrible betrayals. A mythic father for such a godlike son!

Why had he denied me my myth at the end, the one he had been chief author of? Did he want me to fail? I was crying.

And Nico's own family? Chaco asked.

Why did this clown remind him of his own mortality? He didn't want to talk about *that.* It wasn't worth talking about. He held his fists wide apart. He was a butcher's son. He was one-quarter Negro. He, too, had been a butcher. But that was before he met Fidel. What did that matter! It didn't matter. That was another life.

We came near the cathedral. It had a clock in each of its two huge bell towers, and one over its main entrance. (Our time on earth is transitory. How parched we are without the moisture of belief!) I pushed Nico along now, pressing my palm against his broad sweaty back. We were late for our meeting at Hilda's. It was past dinnertime, I said, and there would be some fruit at Hilda's. But most of all I wanted to see her. I wanted to have her embrace me in my sorrow. I wanted to embrace her.

Now Nico, the inexorable, wouldn't be hurried. He didn't respond to my weak touch, but stood, intent on the noise from the church. From inside the cathedral the bishop himself spoke, and large loudspeakers mounted on the bell towers broadcast his homily to the street. Arbenz's soul, the bishop said, was a withered black thing, like a bat. Arbenz and the Communists had wounded Christ, just as if they had stuck a spear into Christ's side.

A crowd of fifty or so stood by the high bronze doors, open now to the street. Candles glowed within the church, as if miming the setting sun. The last rays of that sun made the faces of the crowd look serene, peaceful, though the bishop spoke of blood. The women wore black. A few Indians stood off to one side. Catholics wagered on Arbenz's future instead of the afterlife, demonstrated the health of their political souls for the Ruler to Come. Cooks listened to the bishop and plotted our betrayal.

It was the duty of Catholics, the bishop said, to pray for the success of the brave men of Castillo Armas, avengers of the wrongs the Church had suffered. His men were knights of the faith. Castillo Armas was the cross and the sword.

"Castillo Armas," Chaco whispered from behind me, "is a banana shoved up the ass of the peasants."

"Why do they let that son of a bitch talk?" I shouted. My cheeks were wet. I cried for the Guatemalan Revolution.

Some people in the back of the crowd turned to look at us. Chaco put his palm into my back, and we walked on.

"They should kill the bishop," Nico shouted back over his shoulder at the crowd. His voice screeched and slid. "They should kill him! They should kill him!"

Chaco ran forward and put his arm about Nico's broad shoulders. "Shut up, dear!"

"Don't call me 'dear'!" Nico shook Chaco's arm, that stick, from his shoulder.

"Is that what Fidel would do?" I asked. "Assassinate him?" *I wanted to hear Nico say yes.* I was avid for it. "Would he have him shot?"

"Yes," Nico said softly, implacably, like a lover. "Yes. Yes." He could hear the eagerness in my voice. He went on, with growing sureness. "Yes. Yes, he would. Except that he wouldn't order it, Ernesto. He is not that kind of leader. He acts for himself first. *He* would do it. For it is just. The people should have their revenge. *He* would act *for* them, in their name, for justice!" His voice skidded about on the bishop's blood. The word "justice" was a sharp angry bird escaping from his chest. Nico, I remembered then, had never killed. He had run away. No wonder it excited him so!

"More blood!" Chaco said disgustedly, looking towards me, asserting our tacit agreement, our Gandhian certainties. But I was not thinking of that, in that way. I saw a man in a high gold hat, holding a shepherd's crook. I couldn't see his face. He stood by an altar. A dark man from the back of the church danced crazily in the aisle, hopping from foot to foot, shouting at the bishop, mocking his words in strange garbled parodies. But that mockery was not enough for him. He was not satisfied. He took a pistol from his belt and— before the multitude—shot the gold-hatted man. The image engrossed me utterly. I looked at it from a great height, as if from a theater balcony.

I had to tear myself from it to look at Chaco. His brows were quiet now, his features still, beyond mockery. There was no irony in his voice. He had a huge nose, little chin, thinning hair. I no longer thought him funny-looking, for he was my friend. But today I had to remind myself of my feelings for him, recall distantly his kindness. I could not now possess those, or any, feelings.

"Nothing comes of that, Nico." Chaco stared at me. He could see my tears. "But more blood. World without end. We don't require that Nico. Our continent has suffered enough."

Absently I nodded my agreement, my confirmation. The stern judge. Why did they want that of me? For truly I was still inside the church, watching the sacrifice, the necessary sacrifice.

Nico laughed at Chaco. I heard him from within my distance. There was no good humor in his laughter. It was his hands thwacking together in a new key, uncontrolled, gears slipping, grinding.

"I know what Castro would do, Ernesto," Nico said. He pointed at the air in front of him as at some confirming image. "Because I know that he himself has shot many many men." But then, the true Voice not present to assure him, Nico faltered. "I think. He never told me so directly. But I've heard it from many people. When he was at the university." Nico's own deep voice grew firmer. He stepped hard on the pavement. "He took risks."

"Of course," Chaco said mildly. He hummed to himself. What would Castro be in this verse?

For example, the head of the student federation at the high schools had boasted that he was going to take power at the university. He had been shot.

"Of course," Chaco said. (Perhaps "Fidel Is a Pistol.") Chaco tapped each hollow black metal lamppost, with its three round globes, as we passed. A satisfying clack.

We walked on. Nico looked towards me. The crowd was silent, dumbstruck by this man's act. And some moved forward silently to take the gold hat from the dying man. Would they bury it? Or offer it to the dark man?

"And someone shot Manolo Castro, State Secretary of Sports, a most corrupt man." Nico turned his head to the side, as if he had said something very sly. Coyness was odd on his large face, an adult in children's clothing.

"Mais certainement," Chaco said. "One Castro kills another. Who would not appreciate such irony? *C'est délicieuse."* But clearly Chaco, one-time connoisseur of ironies, didn't. His voice was thick with disgust.

A jeep raced through the empty street towards us, and, at the last moment, swung in a wide arc to the other side of the road. FEDERATION OF LABOR was painted in black block letters on its doors. Four or five workers in dirty undershirts sat on the backs of the seats, shouting "Go home Yanquis" at the shuttered buildings. One of them fired a pistol in irregular rhythm at the sky.

"Your Castro," I said giddily, "is a gangster." It wasn't a judgment; only a description; another verse for Chaco's song. I didn't care about Castro's murderous qualities. No, more than that: I wanted them, I wanted Nico's litany to go on. These spectral corpses made me feel peaceful. I breathed easier. I wanted the hecatomb to mount and mount. Death, dying, dead. They were just words, after all.

Nico laughed richly, as if my apparent insult had given him the greatest pleasure. The dark formed around him now, as if shading itself to his tone, slowly absorbing him. "That's just what Fidel says now! The regime, he said, which could not impose justice, permitted vengeance. The blame lies—listen to this Ernesto!"

He was right. I wasn't listening. Castro's words bored me. This would be more justification, more Castro rant. I wanted the savagery itself, the list of suffering bodies, held or holding others; escaping; killed. Across the street from us one of the Guatemalan soldiers threw his rifle into the road and ran into a shuttered shop. The shopkeeper had nailed boards across his windows. That morning the artillery commander at Chiquimula had fled to the Panamanian embassy.

"Listen," Nico insisted. "Ernesto you must listen! 'The blame,' Castro said, 'lies not with the young men who desired to make a revolution at a moment when it could not be done. Victims of illusion, they died as gangsters. Today they might be heroes!' "

Chaco stopped. We walked in the middle of the road, for there were no cars in the streets anymore. Chaco's body shook with rage. I had never seen him so angry before. With Gandhi's vision had come the possibility of judgment, of outrage. He took Nico's broad shoulders with both of his hands, and made Nico face him. "Now you listen Nico! You listen to me! Do you hear what garbage you're repeating as if it were the word of God? Revolutionaries are gangsters at a different time. Thugs are embryonic revolutionaries! Don't you see, Nico? It's just killing. He kills now for the people, you say. The people deserve revenge. You sound like that flyer of Castillo Armas's! You sound like that bishop! Castro's just another priest offering a sacrifice! Hilda's right! Revolutionaries have become priests to the people." Nico twisted this way and that, but Chaco, surprisingly strong, would not let him go. Bits of Chaco's saliva clung to Nico's clothes and face. From my grief, my distance, behind my voices which severed me from the world, I watched these two odd men in the street, and wondered what they were so excited about? No one had really died! It's only words.

"But Hilda's wrong, Nico. It's because the people won't kill. They only watch. They aren't transformed by that, only shocked into silence. Castro lifts himself away from you by all this killing. He kills, you think, but you ran away!" Nico, bewildered by this madman, looked imploringly at me. I could see the cords in his neck. They were just a show. As Chaco had once said, You can't enter a movie. And who would want to? I had no desire to interrupt them. Nico saw my indifference. He turned back to his accuser.

"You ran away, not because you're a coward, but because you're better than he is! It's all just killing, killing killing. And that's all that will ever come of it! Not justice! Just more killing! Ernesto's right, Nico. *You* should listen to *him*. We don't need more death. We need to change ourselves."

Chaco released him.

It was *Fidel*, Nico began after a moment, who had rallied the people in Colombia when Gaitan was murdered.

We walked on. If Nico had been shaken by the clown's outburst, then clearly a rapid repetition of the magical name was the remedy.

Fidel had been there for the Pan American Conference. Peron had paid for the Cuban Student Delegation, for Peron had known that *Fidel* would stand up to the Yanquis.

Nico looked about in the dusk. He took longer strides; he wanted to be sure he was a good distance ahead of Chaco.

Then, when Gaitan had been shot, the people had gone wild. A spontaneous outburst. "The sort of thing," Nico said over his shoulder to me, "that Hilda talks about."

And it had been a real uprising. Police stations had been blown up! Shops had been looted!

Yes, I thought. Yes. Go on. Get to the deaths.

Fidel had gone on radio. He had said his own name. Fidel hadn't been afraid to say his own name. He had called on the people to revolt. And the people had responded to his voice. And Fidel himself had fought.

"I have heard," Nico said, "that he killed thirty-two people himself."

Chaco stopped again, stood with his hands on his own cheeks, pulling them downward, curving his mouth. "I want to throw up," he said.

But I, *I* wanted these deaths. They felt a barrier to my grief. As if I could bury his death in so many!

Nico went on and on in the dusk. More rant delivered in reverent tones. Something about marching towards death. Smiles. Supreme Happiness. Great Joy. On their lips. The Call of Duty.

I couldn't concentrate on it. Nico's churchy tone, Castro's empty rhetoric, always sent me far away. And my lungs hurt. I needed to sit down. I needed a shot. I couldn't keep up with Nico.

Nico stopped. We formed a little line in the empty street. "But I failed him." Perhaps he would cry?

"Of course," Chaco said. "Of course you did, de—" He stopped himself theatrically, putting his hand across his own mouth. "Of course you did, *Nico.*"

A smile of joy on their lips? Why? They looked like zombies going into that dark land. When he raised the gold crown they all might die. But they smiled. They wanted it. The call to a great sacrifice.

"Do you need a shot?" Chaco asked, touching my arm lightly. "You're wheezing badly." I had taught my friend to give me the necessary injection.

"No," I said, though I did. I wanted to collapse in front of Hilda's chair, have her tend me.

"Do you want to hear my song then?" He looked beneficently on both of us, and spread his arms like a crooner. "It's called 'Fidel Is a Horse.'"

"No!" Nico shouted furiously. He spat on the pavement in front of Chaco's shoes.

"No," I said. It was dark now. I couldn't see the globule of spit on the pavement. The air felt moist. The rain was coming down hard on the roof. "We were at Hilda's."

"What?"

I had spoken aloud, interrupting his reverie as well as my own. Ponco sat beside me reading his thick book.

"I'm sorry," I said. "I forgot where I was." I sipped some mate. It was cold. And Ponco had cleaned up the dishes.

"Me, too," Ponco smiled amiably. "I'm on a stove boat. The captain's grand, but he's not trustworthy. He has odd ideas."

What boat? Did he mean me? I half clung still to the skirts of my story. He showed me the book jacket. *Moby Dick*. Men, their faces disfigured by fear, leapt into the sea from a small boat. A shadow menaced them from behind. A vengeful railroad train? In the ocean?

"You should read it," he said. That growl—it was indeed a voice to give orders in.

"I don't like North American books," I said. "Too crude. It is North American, isn't it?"

Ponco smiled and nodded at me.

"What's it about?"

"It's about . . ." He paused, staring at me openly, as if he were trying to read some hidden word in my face. Or perhaps he wondered what my response would be if he risked a sally. ". . . it's about whales."

"I'm not interested in whales."

Ponco said no more, but went on staring, no longer smiling. It was like a small sun gone down. What sad message had he found in my features? I allowed him this silent interrogation, casting my eyes down at his book jacket. I could see now that this shadow was a whale, not a railroad engine. Do whales, I wondered, eat flesh? ("Fidel Is a Captain"? "Fidel Is a Whale"?)

"Perhaps," Ponco said, at the conclusion of his study, "you should write down what you were dreaming about. Hilda?"

"No. Not precisely. No. Yes. Perhaps so. In a way." I was fuddled, still walking the empty terrified streets of Guatemala City, waiting for the attack to begin.

I went to my board. I couldn't yet stop to write down all that came before. I had to go through with it, to its conclusion, the paratrooper I killed. *I killed a mercenary in Guatemala.* A man who needed killing? Yes. No . . .

Yes.

Guatemala, June 1954

A Dark Room

I heard the radio playing from behind Hilda's door. It was the Voice of America (*their* America. We were static on the airwaves, a noise between the true articulations, their civilized speech). The announcer indifferently crumbled the Guatemalan Revolution. Four thousand dead. Castillo Armas promised more bombing of the capital. The city would suffer, he said, until Arbenz and his Communist agents capitulated. (The city would suffer for decades after, until the end of time. Until Yon Sosa and the guerrillas liberate Guatemala. *It will come.*) The mercenaries claimed the rail junction to El Salvador, the railroad town of Chiquimula. And this evening Puerto Barrios celebrated its freedom from Communist tyranny. White flags hung from the windows. Church bells chimed; they would ring their joy all night long.

Guatemala City was cut off, its connection severed. Betrayed. Its hands empty at its sides. In corpse position.

We entered. I couldn't see anyone there in the dusk. Perhaps Hilda had left the radio playing and fled, gone into hiding. Our friends had all fled. How would she leave a message for me? I gasped for breath.

But she was there! Sunk deep into her large chair. I saw the outline of her calves first, by the pale green light of the radio dial. The candle was out. Or it hadn't been lit yet. She didn't rise to greet me.

There was nothing to do. We argued about what to do. Outside we could hear the drone of the planes; the bombs dropped near the air base first; and then, like rolling thunder, they came forward. I lifted the corner of a newspaper page that we had pasted over the window, and saw the red spots, the fires. There weren't any fire engines tonight. A large explosion shook the glass, and a giant column of fire with a corona of black smoke tongued the air on the edge of the city. They had hit an oil storage tank.

"We must act!" Nico implored us from the couch. There was a sobbing sound to his voice, a fear, a longing. "We can't just sit here. We have to fight. We have to keep the idea of resistance alive."

No one responded. He looked loony, banging his hands together; and his words seemed more pointless discharge, another heavy thwacking sound.

Hilda had let her long black hair down and was braiding it slowly. I could see her hands as they moved towards the green glow; too intimate an act, I thought, for others to witness. "The government came from above," she said. "It was never the people in power. It was only Arbenz, *a friend* of the people." But her pronouncements lacked the stonecutter's force; her voice was hollow. She wasn't judging really, but letting go, accommodating to loss. She undid the braid, and slowly began to braid her hair up again.

My lungs felt a little better here, for the moment, though the room seemed very stuffy. I sat down on the couch with my companions. Perhaps I only needed to rest. "They haven't struggled," I said. There was a jagged metallic aspiration to my words, the asthmatic's overtone. It was a clear formulation; it had logic; but it was very distant—and it was hardly mine to speak. "They haven't been transformed," I said slowly. My grief closed about each word, engulfed it. Gandhi's thought disappeared from me. "They haven't become men yet."

Hilda laughed. "If you can keep your head when all about are losing theirs . . ."

". . . and blaming it on you," I said. "If you can trust yourself when all men doubt you . . ."

". . . but make allowance for their doubting too." Her voice grew high and solemn when she recited poetry.

And this was our favorite poem; it was pass and counterpass of a small secret society; it was a way we had found each other one afternoon a few weeks ago as I lay struggling for breath on the couch. I had wanted very much for her to know me, to think well of the direction of my life. Something she had said reminded me of "If," and I had said a line or two of it to her. And she had finished it; for she, too, had once memorized it, taken heart from it. (It was, she said, a favorite poem of Gramsci's. He became a part of our curriculum.) And "If" became a sign between us, another field of play.

The glass shook. The bombing moved closer to our neighborhood.

"Do you want to hear my poem?" Chaco asked. His voice had a tremor. "It's a song really. It's called 'Fidel Is a Horse.'" His fingers, as if by their own will, moved slowly towards his wrist, and the repeated comfort of his own pulse.

"No!" Nico shouted.

"No," Hilda said. "Please. Not now." It was too painful, she said, to think of us sitting in the dark, squabbling, while the planes destroyed the city.

We sat quietly, counting our rapid pulse beats, drawing our painful breaths, listening to Nico's anxious empty assertion. Thwack. Thwack. Thwack.

Then Chaco spoke, his voice quieter now, not nervously playful, but insistent, chastened by Hilda's rebuke. Hilda was right, he said. There should have been mass struggle.

The tremor was gone from his voice. As once with me, the thought of the masses in motion, of action that all might join in, the symbol raised—the feeling that by imagining its necessity one had already joined in the struggle —all this brought courage. There should have been, he said, the kind of struggle Hilda and Ernesto both talked about. But not more killing. She was wrong about that. Our masses would not kill. Killing only made the revolutionary powerful, turned him into a priest. It should have been as Ernesto had said: noncooperation.

"Nonviolence!" Nico turned to shout the word contemptuously into Chaco's big ear. "Listen, Chaco!"

We thought a quotation from Fidel—that Horse—would follow. But Nico said nothing more. Listen, he meant, not to words, but to the sounds of the explosions destroying the workers' houses, terrifying them back into their burrows. I thought of Hilda's brother's milder lesson, raising my arm behind my back till I stammered with pain. (My muscles felt that still, a spectral discomfort.) I saw the windows of this house explode inward, the harsh wind slamming us against the light-pink walls.

"Nonviolence!" Nico shouted over the roar of the planes. He spat on the carpet.

A small old woman stepped suddenly through the swinging door to the kitchen. She was dressed in her best long black wool skirt, to greet the invaders. "I saw that!" she screamed. "You filthy pig! You disgusting man! And I heard what you've been saying all these nights!" She came forward quickly into the room, as if she had little uneven wheels beneath her, and stood fronting Hilda, her palsied head rocking back and forth. "I saw what that black man of yours just did!" She pointed towards Nico, a tiny bony hand from under her black shawl. How did she dare? But she thought her righteousness, her rage, would protect her. "You are animals, filthy filthy animals! You are disgusting people! Only this poor Catholic," she said, pointing to me, "is a good man. The rest of you should die! You are bad people! You are Communists! I've told the right people about you! They'll come to get you! They'll kill you! You should die!" There was ecstasy in her final words. She saw our blood.

No one spoke. She was an apparition, she was Death itself, the sour-milk woman, the bad witch who waits in the cellar to bite your head off. Her shrill voice, her small black figure, barely visible in the dark, made me bring my arms against my sides. Hilda pulled her brightly colored shawl about herself.

The cook scuttled back into the kitchen, as if that were already liberated territory, where we couldn't follow.

Nico rose, without speaking, and walked to the front door. Hilda put on her long green knitted coat. We went out. (Despite Death's accusation, we felt ourselves held securely in the palm of our youth, that sweet stupid unending vitality. What bad could happen to us?) We would check on blackout violations. We would be witnesses.

The Argentine Embassy
Guatemala City,
Guatemala

Dear Father,
This is the last letter I will write to you, even this way, in my thoughts. (Tonight I am waiting for sleep on the floor of our embassy's main reception room.) For to write to you I need to imagine your angry answering voice. And I have done what I can to silence your voice inside me, just as it has been silenced in the world.

But let me tell you the story of that death.

When we left Hilda's the planes were no longer dropping explosives, but they still made passes over the city, a darker shadow against the night sky, a black shawl over a black dress. The machine guns had been silenced, and the planes flew slowly, at lower and lower altitudes, surveying their domain. We could see the bottoms of their wings in the fires from the bombings. The city was dark but for those fires, and a monstrous glow of light from the cathedral. Perhaps, we thought, it too had been bombed.

A few other students, in small groups for mutual protection, wandered about as we did, and we joined together, drawn towards the fire in the cathedral. There were about thirty of us. We passed each other the bleak rumors of the day. The delegation I had seen enter the palace that afternoon was not from the unions. They were army officers come to arrest Arbenz and take over the government. They themselves had then been summoned to the office of the U.S. ambassador, and arrested. Castillo Armas and his masters would not be cheated of their victory. The Cabinet, the army staff, Fortunoy—the head of the Communist Party—had fled. There was now no government in Guatemala.

When we neared the end of the street we saw through the stained-glass windows how a thousand candles prayed for Castillo Armas's arrival, implored God that the land might be returned to its rightful owners. And more light: joyful searchlights beamed from the balcony around the bell towers, protectors of the cathedral, guides for the planes. The bells began to ring, slowly at first, a heavy clang, a mournful sound.

"Look," my friend Chaco said. He stood with his right foot up near his left knee, balanced on one leg. Chaco pointed past the right-hand bell tower.

I followed his finger. Paratroopers floated through the night sky, lit by the glow from the church and the sharp lights sluicing up at them. We were all quiet, transfixed by this vision of a new angelic order, this coming hell on earth. Have you ever seen such a thing, Father? (But I forgot. You won't reply to me anymore.) It was peaceful, their slow floating, the white silk moving down through the thick beams of light, the burning city silent except for the departing planes, and the bells that chimed now in higher faster peals of joy and welcome. It looked, as everything had that day, like a distant image, unconnected to me, as if I were just hearing about it, the story of the fall of a city that Fernando might have told me long ago. (Perhaps this, I thought, was what you meant when you said that from your meditative posture on the living-room floor you looked upon life as a play of images? Had I assumed your distance, your death? Was I sentenced by you to spend the rest of my life behind this glass, walking around like one of the already dead?)

My lungs clanged and wheezed. The paratroopers had brought more bad air with them. The other students moved away from me.

Ten or twelve apostles of the new order had already fallen to earth. In irregular ranks they came towards us, down the wide boulevard. They wore suntan-colored uniforms and high leather boots. They all carried automatic weapons. I felt the way my Cuban comrade, Nico, had. I couldn't take my eyes from their rifles, the long blue-black barrels.

The students cursed the soldiers in shrill voices. Bastards! they screamed. Whores! Pimps!

It was more spit. I heard the inward-falling roar of the fires burning a few streets away. People ran shouting in the parts of the city we had just left. Their shouts were anxious, calls without responses, a bewilderment of cries. Where would they run? They had lost everything, even their future.

Nico took his gray metal pistol from his belt and held it up before everyone like a chalice. The students were silenced by it: a knife that cut their voices away. Nico waved the pistol about in the air and screamed and screamed, not even a curse, it didn't mean anything, just screaming up at the sky.

"Don't do that dear!" Chaco said sharply. He meant to calm Nico, and spoke to him decisively, as one might to an anxious patient, as both you and he have often spoken to me. For the sight of that gun in the air would surely draw fire on us. The other students moved backward, behind Nico, washed there by fear, yet held by their fascination. Something terrible clarifying bloody might happen here on this ground. (They formed an audience, just as Chaco said. Nico would be their priest.) Now Chaco shouted at Nico, "Please dear, please please please please don't do that!" The medical student had seen blood. He knew its sources.

I seized Nico's hand, forcing it down. He was a coward, Father. And like all cowards he could only make pointless gestures. (How could a man strike a blow at the United States? How could you do anything, Father, but make gestures?) Nico didn't know what he was doing, and he would accomplish nothing, and get us all killed. Because he wanted to die. That was the funeral procession in his voice the night before. He had sentenced himself to death because his comrades had died at the Moncada, and he had survived his foolish leader's foolish plan. (How stupid you would think his Castro, Father!) Good, I thought, then Nico should die. But he shouldn't bring death to these others, to Hilda, to Chaco, to the shocked innocent students standing behind him.

The gun came away in my right hand, as if Nico had passed it to me; and Nico ran into the dark. He would not, he had sworn, run away again. But he couldn't change. Now he knew his nature. (But I? I was still unknown, Father, always unknown, pure potential.) The gun felt heavy in my hand, as if it were a test to lift it up, to point it outward, to hold it steady.

The mercenaries came towards us, past the low white rectory building, nearly to the edge of the cathedral. With my left hand I clicked the small metal flange on the butt of the gray pistol from red to blue. But the gun still pointed outward. The man in front walked casually, like a large complacent townsman out on a stroll for a June evening, his belly full from a good dinner. About six feet tall, he had a broad chest. His features were still in shadows, but I thought they had an Indian cast to them. There was a cool breeze that night. The sweat chilled on my skin as the breeze passed over him. Me, I mean. (For I stared at him that intensely.) He would smile as he looked about. Those who march towards death with a smile of supreme happiness on their lips. His smile disgruntled me, gave me a sour pain in my gut. I loathed him then as I had never hated anyone before.

I clicked the safety catch from blue to red. I have often wanted to kill, Father, though since I have been a follower of Gandhi I have actively bent my will against that violence. This time, when you and Gandhi were weakest in me, I had a gun in my hand. It might have been another time. It might have been another one of imperialism's thousand servants. But it would have happened. I was, as Chaco said, a faulty pistol, waiting to explode in someone's hand.

Should I have asked them, Father: Is this Christian is this fair play is this civilization? Mother was right. They wouldn't understand. Their faces were Latin, but their cruelty, their stupidity, their rapacity, the money that bought them and set them floating dreamily in the sky and put them in motion towards us down the avenue, that was North American. They were Imperialism's creatures. Inwardly I saw their faces: identical round smooth things, the features little polyps, barely formed; they had no ears—well-designed things: they couldn't hear people scream. Father, listen to me: *Our nation is not one family! No reconciliation with these creatures is possible!* My rage, my hatred, my desire to throw myself upon them tore apart all the atoms of my body; my fury dispersed me into my elements; I streamed forward towards them. Dear Father, I thought, I can't please you anymore. You are gone now. I can't harm *you* anymore with my anger.

I aimed my pistol at the first man's chest, gripping it with both my hands. Just as North America had set them walking towards me, past the edge of the cathedral, so, I felt then, some equal and opposite force had set me here, where one street joined another, facing them. I know now that it was an illusion, that there was no election, all just molecules thrown together by chance with opposite valences. But I felt then as if I were concentrated to one blow, that I could in one stroke make the world mine again, the true world that Hilda's words had revealed to me, that was our place of play, that was Hilda. "Are you a Communist, Ernesto?" your friend, old man Isaias asked me in that field. He was shocked at that thought. The United States, he said, is our ally. We have a shared concern for the worth of the individual. Wasn't that stupid, Father! Criminally stupid! You taught me in our walks about the city that the United States is a callous top-hatted magician turning dead people into round gold coins. They are our enemies, Father, now and forever, yours and mine. They destroyed the Guatemalan Revolution as if they were crumpling the page of someone's story. They condemned the Indians to death, death from parasites, death from cold, death from hunger, all for a few more gold coins. Am I a Communist, Father? I, child of the conquistadors, plantation owner's son, petit-bourgeois? No. I'm not. Not yet. Nor are those who, like Fortunoy and the Guatemalan party, call themselves Communists, but only talk, sitting around their glass kitchen tables—and so betray the masses. But I could change myself. It was given to me to act. I could bind Marx's truth to me.

And then, Father, I heard your voice: *Is someone dying here? I'm a doctor. Can I help?*—as if you were bewildered, set down in a strange place. (The street faded from me, and I fell inward to our private theater. There were only our voices now.) You saw what was happening. You became angry. *By what right is this thing done, Ernesto? This Indian has thoughts of his own, a family, a small pain perhaps in his back from his fall. He wants to learn to read the newspapers. He has a history of his own, Ernesto, a way of seeing things, particular, and so invaluable. You're like a fatal disease to him, son. Is that what you want to become, is this the grand career you dreamt of, that you left me for?*

I listened to you; my thumb flicked the safety catch from blue to red, back and forth, click-click-click (where would it stop?). I couldn't let you take this opportunity from me. For it seemed then a chance to declare myself finally, beyond any possibility of second thoughts. I felt, Father, that I must act, that I could, if I acted, silence your voice, all that obstructed me. I could, by doing this, make myself single, become this action only, beyond your commentary. I could break through the grief that sealed me off from the world. (For I miss you terribly, Father. I mourn you constantly.) So I begged you to help me. You, I pleaded, must help me now to silence *your* voice. You knew that I was a knife, Father, and that I could never become a doctor in your way. You must accept that now. But with your help I could be a small story in the fall of the city, a tale that might one day awaken another. (A book, she had said laughing, you'll make a story out of yourself!) I stammered to you then, broken sentences! A story. The fall of a city. The continent needs. A surgeon's knife.

"Don't, che!" Chaco shouted into my reverie. He didn't sound scared. He, too, was angry. Something awful was being done. He had found courage, my Chaco. He had transformed himself. I envied him, Father. "Dear che, no! Only more blood will come of that! Only more violence! Only more death until the end of time! Please please please please stop now!"

But what did he know of blood? He, or any of them? We might stop, Father, be nonviolent warriors. But they would then kill us all indifferently. They would never limit their greed until we destroyed them utterly, crushed their heads. I slammed my foot down on the pavement, smashing one underfoot, and not blood but a milky-white juice ran from it, like sperm. My chest shook. A harsh wind took me over and made my body tremble. *No,* you said, *you must not tremble. Remember* The Hindu Science of Breath Control!

I brought my other hand up to steady the pistol. *Count to eight,* you said helpfully. You became my ally, Father, in the death of your voice, your moralism, your hopes for me. *Count to eight, now gradually let out your breath as you squeeze. Make that tin can dance, Ernesto! Remember how we did it? Well, make it hop now!* The man we were going to kill passed near the front of the cathedral's high stone pillars, the huge molded bronze door with its reliefs of suffering bearded saints. I felt a warm flush on my skin, like a blanket. My back and chest were covered with sweat.

I could see his smile now.

Why should he live, Father, when you are dead?

The trigger jammed against my finger, and that small halted gesture jolted my body. The safety was on. I flicked it off. (I had an intense feeling for that small piece of metal. I felt as if it were in my mouth, on my tongue, like a sweet involving taste.) The sweat made the ball of my thumb slip over the flange. This small necessary motion required enormous concentration.

Was the safety On or Off? Is someone dying here? I fell towards him in sudden discontinuous clicks, as if our two images were coming together. Are they only words, I thought, as I pulled the trigger through, Death, dying

Dead. The man grabbed his chest, scrabbled at it, as if to pluck his heart out, and fell down. His hands went to his sides, already empty; in corpse position. I wanted to go forward now, to comfort him, to care for him. Poor man! The other soldiers formed a circle around his body, blocking him from view, their rifles pointing towards us. And then, Father, the strangest thing happened to me (perhaps you have heard of such a case?): the world lost all its colors. It was black and white, like a piece of newspaper held to a window, or a film negative held to the light. I was terrified! I looked this way and that, as if there were someone in the crowd who could help me. Hilda and Chaco stood near me. They too had been drained of color. A hysterical symptom, I thought, trying to calm myself with the magic of clinical names. The magic failed. I panicked, certain that I'd driven myself mad! I tried to run forward to the wounded man. I knew that if I touched him I could return the color to the world. I wanted knowledge, the knowledge that should come to me from killing him. And to gain that I needed to touch him. I had to go forward before the soldiers walked away and the body disappeared.

But Chaco held me back. He pulled at my shoulder, dug his fingers into my upper arm, and his grip was surprisingly strong. One of the mercenaries fired towards the crowd, sharp rapid high sounds, ping! ping! ping! The students scattered down side streets, back towards the gates of the university. Some screamed as they ran. Hilda stood behind me and yanked on my shirt. She was crying.

Chaco shouted, "Damn you che!" and flung his arm from me. He held his hand towards my face. He had been shot in the hand, a bullet that would have opened my shoulder. Blood covered his beautiful lined palm, dripped slowly off his thin nervous fingers. That blood on his hand was a suddenly vivid color in my black and white world. The other hues trooped back, organized themselves around that sight, like cloudy chemicals forming in a developing tray. Chaco screamed. "I can't move my fingers che!" The high sound was like the beginning of one of his silly songs. He put his arm around my neck for a moment, patting me, gentling the pony. My neck felt sticky, wet with blood from his hand. Then he slid to the ground. He'd been hit again in the side of the head.

I knelt to him. With the corner of my white shirt, I wiped the blood from his cheeks, as he had once gently wiped the vomit from mine. I wanted to ask him what it felt like to die. His pain belonged to me! There was so much blood! My shirt was soaked with his blood. It should have been my blood!

His body twitched for a moment, like a momentary convulsion, and was still.

Chaco Gives Up the Ghost

"He's dead, Che," Hilda said, quietly. "There's nothing more to be done." She pulled me up by the arm and towards the side streets. "He was right!" She laughed hysterically as we ran, a series of trilling sounds broken by sudden gasps. "He was right! You *are* a dangerous man!"

It was so hard to breathe! My lungs scalded, tearing at themselves. My friend, the one who could give me my injection, was dead, and I was responsible for his death. My legs wobbled. I wanted to fall down, but Hilda held me up, her arm under mine. We ran down the dark side streets, though no one pursued us. I had become a pilgrim, an exile, a refugee like the others. I needed a place to hide.

Well, Father, good-bye. I have moved into a world so strange to you that your moralism won't reach into it; I can't conjure up your response within me. You helped me in this, Father; when I called on you, you sacrificed yourself. I'll mourn for you always, for our walks, for your instruction, for your ruined work on me. But I must take leave of you. I can't go on talking to no one, Father, and I no longer hear you.

We are not one family. Imperialism has corrupted the national bourgeoisie beyond the hope of final redemption. They will always turn against democratic nationalist governments, as they deserted Arbenz. The very best elements of the national bourgeoisie may begin, but they can never fully carry out the transformation of our society. For that would cause conflict with the imperialists. To struggle with imperialism they would have to call on the people. And the people, once united, might want an end to the privileges of the bourgeoisie. The bourgeoisie becomes Bonapartist; impure; a contradiction that cannot maintain itself. They lure the people forward with empty promises, and then stab them in the back for the imperialists. So, the struggle against the Yanquis and the oligarchies must be direct, total. We must not hide our goal, the final defeat of imperialism! If the Communist parties are not ready for that conflagration, they will be destroyed in it!

I must sleep now. Thirty of us share the floor here. We're on a list of Argentines wanted by the new Guatemalan government, a very comprehensive list put together by maddened cooks, and with information bought with cigarette packages. Person has granted us asylum, and the ambassador has very kindly found blankets for us. Strange world, where Peron protects me (as the police kept the crowd from attacking Celia). But one must use what allies one can in the fight to build socialism and destroy the United States' power. (So long as Peron opposes the United States the workers will trust him!) This is a world sharply defined indeed, but not by your moralism· or Mother's *trompe l'oeil* dialectics that tear up everything. (*That* is just breaking glass.) *This* is the world of politics.

I embrace you, old man,

your son,

Ernesto

Isle of Pines, July 1965

JULY 12

Ponco emerged from his room, walking with a rapid determined stride, his eyes on the floor, a man with a mission. He shook his head from side to side. But I already knew the bad news.

"Tsk, tsk, tsk," he intoned metronomically, each click coinciding with a turn of his small head. He sat down at the scarred table, his lips pursed around a sour taste, and made a show of not looking at me as he squared up his papers, my chapter, tapping their edges with the tips of his fingers. We didn't speak for several minutes. I sipped some lukewarm mate.

"I knew him," he said.

I nodded agreement, and looked down at my hands. I felt as ashamed of what they'd written as of many of the other, more spectacular, things they'd done. The hide-and-seek feeling was gone, the game over. I was a furtive little boy caught out in something dirty.

"An amiable old man. A decent old man. A good old man."

I nodded. What a fine time the prosecutor was having!

"A little quiet, though. We met in the office in Havana. True?"

I nodded. "True" in Walter's voice was bedrock, irrefutable.

"He was a little portly. He had shaved his beard. Just a gray mustache left. True?"

I nodded. He'd got his man.

"Your own father, Che!" He paused, meditating how to make the crime more horrible for the jury. "I liked him."

Walter's father had run off during his childhood. And mine (I had always felt) was the quintessence of fathers, the principle of patriarchy itself. The very thing missing in Walter's life. Of course he would be drawn to him.

"You go too far. Your father. He lives."

Perhaps Walter was right; I had gone too far. And yet it had come to me, one sentence following another, with the clarity of the intuitively right, like love or a winning strategy. But how could I justify it? That I couldn't snap the thread, had to follow it, the unbroken skein of words a sign of the story's rightness? His death was just *there,* the next piece of the story. But that wasn't justification, only tautology. We're here because we're here.

"Che! I know what you're going to say. It felt that way. You took leave of him by your action. Of his world." Walter still hadn't looked at me. I watched him do some more headshaking. His cheekbones are high and prominent. His skin is stretched very taut. I felt that if I scratched it with my fingernail I would tear it, like a piece of fine thin paper. "Good-bye," he said. The harshness, the minimum possible sound, words made out of pain; they were a poem on the word's meaning: farewell. Walter's voice was made for saying "truth," for saying "good-bye." "And I know what you might not say. You wanted him to die. *You. Wanted.* You wanted to have done with him."

"He had cancer," I said. "He was operated on. I didn't return home. We had died for each other. He survived the cancer."

Ponco placed his hands on his temples, and vised his head—our mime for psychoanalysis.

"But Freud had it wrong," I said. "And so do you. I didn't kill the mercenary instead of my father. I killed my father inside myself so I could kill the mercenary. You see?"

Ponco shook his head no, but wouldn't look at me.

"Freud had it wrong," I tried again. "We don't see the state, the enemy, as our fathers. Our fathers, inside us, the family, they work for the state, you see? We must uproot them first."

Ponco shook his head some more, slowly, his head half turned towards the door, away from me.

I gave up, and stared at my hands on the wood.

Ponco looked over at me finally, but I looked away before our eyes could meet.

"What audacity!" he said to the wall.

It is a favorite word of Fidel's. My genius, he would say of himself in exalted moments, is the extent of my audacity. Revolution is audacity and more audacity. The word is his most effervescent praise for others, for an inspired stroke, for an imaginative attack.

I looked up at Ponco. He had turned towards me, smiling broadly, welcomingly. We laughed, and there was all collaboration in our laughter. We'd once been cellmates. We were in on the big joke. I remembered the evening in Fernando's tool shed, among the thousand mismatched shoes. We chimed together.

And I did not yet know how deeply collaborative we were.

"There's a problem," Ponco said, taking one of my sheets out. "Not with your patricide. Worse." He placed the sheet on the table between us, and pointed to one of the paragraphs. "Remember, Che. He's a . . ." He placed a long thin finger against his cheek. ". . . a sensitive man."

I read:

We had heard by now bits of Fidel's speeches from every epoch—for Nico knew by heart pages of this wordy man's remarks. What heat, we wondered, did Nico find in this fat rhetoric? It was difficult for us to imagine warming ourselves there. This, Chaco and I agreed, was not literature, was not the sublime poetry of a true, an inspired leader. It was rant. How could someone be moved by it?

I looked up at Ponco. He stroked his lip with the back of his thumb. "I see what you mean," I said. "But I change my mind later in the story."

"Sure," he said, smiling at what he found to be a weak obtuse defense. "But put something in *there*. He's a *very* sensitive man."

"All right. I'll think about it." I started to take the piece of paper up.

"No. Wait. Consider this." He took out another sheet and placed it next to mine. There was a paragraph in the center of the page, neatly written out in tiny block letters:

(I know the answer now: we could not feel it because we had not heard him speak. We had not seen him before an audience, in the plaza, in the kitchen of a sympathizer's house, sitting in his caravan of jeeps, in the middle of a dirt path, with countrypeople gathered around him. We hadn't seen him take their gestures, their doubts, the hesitations and secret thoughts they expressed by the movements of their bodies, the looks on their faces, the unspoken words of their hands, and give them voice. The moment suddenly transformed, a communion in his words—for one's anxiety marked a desire, and that desire, if one had the courage, was lawful. He was voice. He was permission. But we hadn't been there, yet. We didn't know.)

I was stunned. Words fled from my mind. (Into Ponco's?) I pulled on the edge of my beard, until it stung, to take possession of myself again. "Did I write that?"

Ponco smiled, and there were, I swear, new depths of delight in that smile. My astonishment, my bafflement, was immaculate praise. What virgin fields of joy did he see opening before him? A new career? A different, more intricate sort of lying?

"No," I said. "Of course not. *You* wrote it. Of course. I meant that it is very good. Very good indeed. It sounds a great deal like me."

He stuck his lower lip out in a silly disappointed pout.

And I was lying. It didn't sound a great deal like me. It sounded, I thought, exactly like me. It was uncanny. He had stolen something from me—my soul? my style?—and so I felt I had to cheat his accomplishment slightly, in order to keep a patent on myself. (I heard my mother's witchy voice, as if it were coming from Ponco's small black face, "It was like a strong wave buoying me up, buoying you up, because I felt *I was you.*") Funny business. Ponco's words made me anxious, as if Ponco had inhabited my skin, guided my hand. No, I mean as if I had guided his hand. (Quite a collaboration! As deep as killing a man!) I gasped for breath, in short wheezes. "Yes," I said, trying to sound judicious. "Very good indeed. Almost me. Perhaps I'll use it."

But it wasn't almost me. *It was me.*

No doubt the dizziness was an attack starting. I went back to my room, to lie down.

This afternoon I sat with Ponco on the porch. He read his book on whaling. I stared out across the high grass, down to the now calm ocean, lapping in short precise waves, practicing its regular stroke. My pain, too, had subsided; my breathing was a little more regular. And my mind was empty. I just stared, my face slack, the long field moving inside my head without obstacle.

Why hasn't he spoken, "the voice of permission"?

I looked over at Ponco, for no good reason, my head just turning in the slight breeze, like a stalk of grass. He was staring at me. "Fidel," he said.

How did he know! "Yes. Why haven't we heard from him?" I saw a crowd of four hundred thousand people in Havana. Fidel stands alone on a high wooden platform. The stage is enormous, so that he might look isolated and vulnerable. He is alone with the masses. (The sharpshooters are on another platform, beneath him, hidden in the scaffolding.) Behind, in the crowd and on the sides of the plaza, there are towers of crisscrossed wood, to support the huge black loudspeakers. Fidel talks. But I can't hear him. I can feel the mood of the crowd. It is October of 1962. The Soviets have abandoned Cuba. They ordered their ships to retreat. (We saw a North American film of it: A radio message. The wake of white water of a turning ship.) Their technicians have picked up the weapons already in place as if they were the vacation toys of bored tourists. Fidel must comfort Cuba in its poverty. The crowd is filled with anger, lassitude, and a sullen fear. This last month they have been ready for invasion, for sacrifice, even for apocalypse; instead there is the dull ache of the embargo, the humiliations of a minor clown's role. Fidel must enter their emptiness—his emptiness—and then he must rise out of it and raise them with him. Start a pratfall—and then, as they exclaim with rueful self-hatred, "That's just the way I look," he must catch himself in mid-careen and turn the near-fall into a dip, a glide, the most graceful tango. Having shared his clumsiness, his self-criticism, they can then soar with his grace. Fidel has done this before— by logic, by cajolery, by surprising metaphor that turns brittle earth into a dove's wing, he has moved them from desert places. He points, he jabs at the crowd, and a low hiss forms, a wave receding over rocks. I know that he will pick up that jangle and resolve it for them into a new harmony, the next paragraph, a richer, unexpected chord. (*That* series of metaphors sounds like Ponco, if you ask me! Or whomever Ponco sounds like.) Fidel stares up at the sky, as if for inspiration. A smile just barely lifts his lips. (I know that he is pissing into a rubber bottle strapped to his leg.) He looks out at us. He has found his inspiration. He raises his hands over his head and shouts something to the crowd. But what? *I can't hear him.*

"No," Ponco said, recalling me to the worn wooden porch. "Not *now.* In Mexico. Our story." But I felt the anxiety in Ponco's voice as well. Why hasn't he spoken?

"Ah. Mexico. *Our* story." But my mind was still an empty space with grass waving in it.

"What was it like?"

"What? Mexico?"

"Meeting Fidel," Ponco said, exasperated. "The man. Who might. Call the People   The Words   The Actions   From their separate houses. I like that. I see three little houses."

"Ah." I made a sniffle of a laugh. Three little houses. But I couldn't think of anything to say.

Ponco brought his chair legs down with a crack. He was beginning, I thought, to reach his hand forward to shake my shoulder. But he stopped himself, drew it back. It was not a gesture we would either of us have been comfortable with. "What did the room look like?"

"Ah," I said. "The room." But then it did come back to me. The kitchen of a wealthy sympathizer. (Ponco had written that!) Maria Antonia. "A lot of people standing around waiting for him. There was a big black pot on the stove. Spaghetti. His favorite. There were guns all over the room, pistols on the kitchen table. Rifles leaning against the wall." I stopped. The grass grew up in my mind, ripened, turned brown, scattered its seed.

"Ah," Ponco said, after a while, mimicking me. "Let's try another question. How did you come to be in the room?"

"I was working as a doctor in an allergy ward, an assistant, and doing some experiments of my own. On cats." I studied Ponco's face, to see if I might produce a tremor of surprise. He had been right this morning when he had said that he knew what I'd say. So I wanted to say something now that he wouldn't expect. "Little pussycats. You know. The dear furry creatures."

"Yes," Ponco said. "I like to eat their livers. And their little pink tongues."

I shuddered. "I paid a peso per cat. They brought them to our apartment sometimes. If Hilda got to them first she would pay them the peso to release the cat. Then the kid would capture it again, and bring it to me at the lab. I've always been unlucky in business."

"Ah," Ponco said, smiling (as if to say, All Cuba knows that). "But lucky in love."

"Certainly." I stretched my legs out over the porch steps. It was a hot clear day. I liked the feel of the heat on my legs. "Hilda is a very remarkable person. She found a place to hide me after I shot the man, then went back to her house. The cook had been a dedicated woman. She had betrayed Hilda. The mercenaries were already there to arrest her. And they wanted me, particularly. There had been informers in the crowd that night. The cook was shocked. I was such a good Catholic!"

"All your talk of sacrifice and self-denial! You sounded like a nun!"

"I suppose. Hilda wouldn't tell them where I was, so they took her off to jail. I made it to the embassy the next day. She had been very good to me. And she had owed me nothing. I admired her character."

"But Che! What about love?"

I was then still a nun, I thought (but wouldn't say). Hilda and I were affianced by then. But I could not wholeheartedly make love to her. Was it that most common form of degradation, the Argentine macho unable to take the woman he respects? (I could imagine her at a meeting of the Central Committee more easily than in my embrace.) Anyway, the Gandhian prohibition was still in force; every time I reached out to her the world broke into shards of anxiety. "Talk of love isn't for people like us," I said to Ponco. "Hilda felt that, too."

"I know: 'Our vanguard revolutionaries must idealize their love for the people. They cannot descend with small doses of daily affection to the terrain where ordinary men put their love into practice.'" He smiled. At me. At his feat of memory. "Once a nun," he said.

"Always true to the vows," I said. I was amazed. At this odd continuity in myself (if it was real? I would have to think about that). At the length of the speech for Ponco. And that he had memorized so many bits of my work. And why? I could not believe that it was simply admiration. Ponco was a very complicated man. This wasn't appreciation; and it wasn't simply mockery, either. Perhaps it was to help him duplicate my style!

"No music," he said. "No women. No fun. 'No life outside the Revolution.' "

I was lost in wonder at Walter. This was not irony. It was some more profound, some angrier interrogation.

Though his next question was innocent enough. "How did you live, Che? Before the Revolution. Before Fidel?"

"In Mexico? I did odd jobs. Then Soto found me a contact who gave me the hospital job. Soto said it was to keep me till Castro arrived. He was very determined that I meet Castro." Having killed a man I found I could work again as a doctor. Yet the work, like making love, felt distant, difficult, not my own. I, too, was waiting for something else—perhaps this Castro.

Soto had found us almost immediately after we arrived in Mexico. He came to Hilda's boardinghouse, holding a bouquet of roses. When she saw him standing in the doorway with the flowers, Hilda broke out in laughter, as if her mirth were some sort of terrible allergy to roses. There was always something a little mechanical about Hilda's laugh. And the extent of her hilarity here only magnified that industrial quality, the machine become diabolical, spewing out small metal parts mixed with cookie dough, beyond control. She rocked back and forth. Little flecks of spit appeared on her lips. She hiccuped with laughter.

Soto stood there bewildered, holding his flowers before him, but talking from the start, talking all the time. "I know you thought me a coward," he said. "But time has proved me right, hasn't it?" He looked at Hilda, not knowing what to do with his offering. He handed me the flowers.

I dropped the flowers on the floor. Hilda, overcome, sat down next to them.

"I heard you put it to them," he said, trying a different tack. "I heard you raised a banner. I heard you kept the struggle alive. And I heard Chaco died." Soto, too, was mechanical: a flattering machine. The last remark had come out in the same tone as the rest, as if Chaco's death were something I should be proud of.

"Yes," I said. "Chaco died." That was the only part of his litany whose truth I was sure of.

"Nico said . . ."

"Nico wasn't there. Nico ran away."

Hilda tittered from the floor.

"Yes. Well. Perhaps it was the right thing to do? You can't do for others what they won't do for themselves."

Hilda put her hands in front of her face. She gasped for breath.

I couldn't reply to Soto. What would Chaco have said? I couldn't hear his voice. I couldn't imagine it then.

I couldn't imagine it now. (As if, being responsible for his death, I had also killed my ability to envision him.)

"Hello," Ponco said, waving at me from his chair.

I was grateful for his greeting (though his was not a voice for hailings).

"Before Soto came, I covered the Pan American Games," I said, recalling Ponco's question, "for Peron's Latin News Agency. I sold books door to door. I worked taking photos with a Guatemalan who had fled with me. A frail, short guy. We met on the train. Penniless defeated man. Hilda and I called him Shorty."

"Yes," Ponco said, no longer smiling. "I knew him, Che." I felt how all good humor had suddenly fled from Walter.

"Yes. Of course." Why, I wondered, was Walter so angry at my forgetting? Did it make him inconsiderable? "We had a racket together. 'What a beautiful baby,' I'd say to some strolling couple. Shorty would walk by casually, and join me. 'Yes. Beautiful. Beautiful. Even my child wasn't so beautiful as yours. It's hard for a father to admit that.' Hard indeed! Shorty was nineteen, and he looked a sickly fifteen. 'I wish I had a picture of my Somoza when he was younger to show you. But it never occurred to me. What a mistake! Time passes so quickly, and snatches us all away. Trujillo was so pretty then. And now, frankly, he's revolting-looking! So bulbous! And even my memories of him have crumbled. My wife says so too. Soon time will have eaten Peron's pretty face away, and left only the current version, a disgusting fat thing!' "

I stopped suddenly. Did Caceres say such things? Or am I making them up for him? As my voice speaks, it makes his uncertain, supplants it. "He was given to bizarre imagery," I said, as if criticism proved the object had existed before me. "I suggested a simpler style to him. But Caceres was so shy he had to speak in that flowery way. Playing a part released his tongue. Anyway, then I'd point out how fortunate it was that I was a photographer, and for just one peso—"

"The cost of a cat," Ponco said.

"—I would photograph their beautiful child."

"No," Ponco said, definitively, as had most of the couples. "I don't think so. I'd rather have a nice delicious cat."

"Yes. We did very little business."

"But lucky in love," Ponco said. "Caceres's love. For you."

"Yes."

Adversity had made Caceres and me good friends. He had wanted to come with Fidel. But Fidel had thought that would be one too many foreigners. (And, he had said to me, wasn't Caceres a little small?) As soon as we won, Caceres had arrived in Cuba, with his cardboard suitcase, and stayed at my house in Havana. I gave him what advice I could about guerrilla warfare, and sent him for more training. But I didn't see much of him. I'd find him at home, studying Indian languages, eating chocolate mixed with cinnamon and nuts. "That's bad for you," I'd say. What would he reply? Time seems to deny me voices today.

Except for Ponco's. "Juliao," Ponco said, "dead in Brazil. The student group in Ecuador. Caceres in Guatemala. Blanco captured. Isolated. Dying of fever in Peru. Masetti, in Argentina. He was ours, Che, trained by us, and he never even killed a soldier. Turcios Lima dead. De la Puente dead."

Truth; good-bye; and naming the defeated; the bleak work Walter's voice was fashioned for. But why was he doing this? From his own anxiety? To see how far he could go with me? Or to make me shudder, killing some cats?

"We will win," I said. "Rising all over the continent. They cannot fight that way. Here and in Asia. We will create one, two, three, many Vietnams."

"A good phrase," Ponco said, and he sounded genuinely thoughtful and admiring. What odd changeable moods inhabited this small man! "You should use it. In the speech for the Tricontinental."

If I ever am allowed to give it, I thought. I moved down a step, to have something to lean my back against. A cat in the sun. "We will win," I repeated, as mechanical in my way as Soto or Hilda.

"Who made the world?" Ponco said. "God made the world."

I understood. My words had been catechismal. A faith. Our faith? I had no other audience now. I needed Walter's agreement. I needed *Ponco*. "Caceres wasn't vigilant enough," I said. But I disliked the sound of my voice. It had the flat, acrid tone of self-justification. "He was betrayed by school friends who knew his plan. I told him not to trust anyone. He was too trusting." Shy, he had looked at me on the train from Guatemala until I'd spoken to him. He shouldn't have spoken to strangers.

"Too trusting! That won't be our problem!"

"I have a lot of pictures of him." Why did I say that? "He liked having his picture taken." What sort of justification was there in that? As if he knew he was going to die?

"Ah," Ponco said (for it was *our* problem). "Pictures! And did you write a poem for him?"

It was, I thought, an accusation. But of what? That I turned defeated comrades into poems, pictures, stories? That I sacrificed them for my art? What madness! And then I recognized poor Ponco's condition—it was the moody self-hatred of a man unhappy in his love, in love half against his will, and struggling with the delicious poison. And I—our cause—the poison apple, that love.

"And when I'm shot you'll write a poem about me."

"Or you about me," I said. Ponco's voice had not been bitter.

"To excite others," he said, "so the business can go on."

"Yes," I said. We were on the edge of a precipice, skating together.

"Good. Someone should keep up our end. But I don't write poems. I used to tell stories. Now you tell a story. The room," Ponco said. "Fidel. Remember?"

The room: it sounded like a stage setting. The place the deed was done. And that felt right to me. "Soto had found Nico with the Cubans. And he brought Nico and Raul to see me—to encourage me to meet Fidel."

"He thought you'd insult him!"

"No. I had acted like a Fidelista. Shooting that man. So everyone thought. And, for myself, I knew that I couldn't really go back to the practice of medicine. What *could* I do? Perhaps this Castro knew? And Raul and I agreed on things politically. Hilda and I often ate with the Cubans, at their boarding-house. They were waiting for Castro to be amnestied. They were a very mixed group then, very different tendencies. Castro's instructions had been to unite all who could be united. I remember that I spoke there once of seeing the struggle in Latin America in the international context. The Bolivians, I said, should have asked for Soviet aid to build their own smelter, make themselves independent of the United States."

I remembered I had half risen from my seat as I said it. It was like my uncertainty in making love. I could see the truth of what I said, but I couldn't attain to it, not yet. There was still a prohibition, nausea, the hangover of all I had once thought. As I had spoken, I had seen a factory rise up in the middle of the Indian villages, taking the place of the church. High black smoke-stacks, covering the praying people and their water with black ash. Was that what I wanted? Yet through that smoke I glimpsed a different shape to the world.

"They should, I said, sell the tin to the Soviets. And some of the Cubans were shocked. I remember one of them took me aside, and said, 'Batista made a thousand concessions to the Yanquis to hold power. We will make a thousand

and one and take it away.' The revolution purified things, of course. But after meeting these people I didn't expect much from Fidel."

"Fi—del!" Ponco chanted. "I like the way your Nico used his name. Said it so many times. It became a nonsense word. Like a kid saying 'spoon' over and over. Till it becomes hollow. And floats away. Empty sound. Might mean anything. Like Che."

"Yes. I thought Fidel would be another empty fraud, like Moreno. But in other ways the Cubans were a very different group from the student radicals I'd known. Rawer. They had escaped death. They had been in jail. Both the fanatics, like Nico, and the opportunists reminded me of what Chaco had felt about the Bolivian Indians. Intensity from an unknown source. Who knew where it might take them? Most of all I felt they wouldn't calculate their actions. They might suddenly run away, as Nico had. Or they might charge the guns. The inspiration of a great leader is like great wealth. They might carelessly squander everything, even their own lives. But they wouldn't calculate."

"Raul."

A name, I thought, like farewell. "No. Even Raul. He's shrewd and mistrustful. But he believed utterly in Fidel. He was sane within the larger madness. But always within it."

Ponco smiled. Why, I wondered, did that formulation bring him such particular delight? Did it describe one of us?

I rubbed my backbone against the edge of the step, just for the pleasure of it. A very old cat. My mice were now dream things, memories. "I remember after dinner once, Ricardo—*our* Ricardo, not Gadea —came over to me. He was very thin then, even more than he is now, and he moved in an abrupt way, as if he were ashamed of his natural grace. He grabbed me by the shoulder. It hurt."

"Do you think," Ponco asked, "he's afraid he's a Travis?"

"What? A what? Are you serious? I don't know. You may be right." It was an odd thought. And what did it matter really? "You read too many stories," I said.

"I've found a new activity," he said, "a substitute."

I thought, at the time, that he meant interrogation.

"Why did he take your shoulder?"

"He said, 'The continental traveler! The hero of the Guatemalan Revolution! Nico has told us about you. Endlessly. Frankly, we're all sick to death of hearing about you. Do you know a lot of things, as Nico says?' Yes, I said, I know a lot of things. Just like my wife, I thought. 'I'll bet you do! I'll bet you know how to read aɪ write.' I thought Ricardo Morales was a little mad."

"He is," Ponco said.

"Well, I said, 'Yes, of course I know how to read and write.' That was a mistake. 'Of course you do,' he drawled. His grip on my shoulder tightened. 'Of course!' He pointed to me with his free hand, showing me off to the others. 'Well, I don't! So why don't you teach me?' Once, he told us, he had seen a bandit just arrested by the police. Ricardo had been bringing in a herd of beef. He stood by the barracks door, listening to the officers taunt the bandit. The police were educated men. They, too, knew many things. And the bandit had said, 'Oh, gentlemen! If only I had known how to read and write, I would have destroyed humanity.' Ricardo laughed in that mirthless way of his, as if bitterness itself were his favorite food. That was his ambition, he announced. To rid the planet of its stinking lice. Present company apparently included. He dreamed, he said, of a hare looking up one morning in an empty field. I took a copy of *The Civil War in France* from my jacket pocket. I told him he needed to know Marxism for a project like his. 'No,' he said, 'I know all about Karl Marx, from Fidel's letters.' For Fidel had sent lectures from his cell and they had formed study groups around those documents. 'Anyway,' he said, 'I know what Fidel knows about him. And that's enough. I want something I don't know the end of. Like a story.' "

"Smart man," Ponco said. "I always thought so. He'll join us." I could hear the relief in his voice at Ricardo's imagined assent.

"Yes. He will." And I, too, was pleased, thinking of that thin, lined, bitter face, looking so much older than its years. I thought of how he came to be with the 26th of July: After the Moncada, Fidel had fled to the mountains. Ricardo had taken him in, for no reason. He envied bandits and Batista said Castro was a brigand. Castro was found in Ricardo's hut, unshaven, covered with mud, asleep on the floor. The lieutenant who discovered him bent over Fidel, holding him down. He brought his cheek close to Fidel's, and whispered in his ear, "Don't give your name or you'll be shot." Fidel and the lieutenant had been in the debating club together, at the university. So Fidel escaped to stand trial. But the soldiers burned Ricardo's house down. And the same lieutenant had put Ricardo's right hand on a rock and smashed it with the butt of his rifle. (There was no debating it: Ricardo had harbored a brigand.) Ricardo followed them down from the mountains, to the prison. He waited there till he could make contact with survivors of the Moncada.

"So you found a story for him."

"Yes. I borrowed a detective book from one of the other men, and taught him from that, every night for a month."

"I know," Ponco said, his face alight with joy. "Ricardo was my teacher. The book was torn by then. He had the alphabet you'd drawn on the back leaf. He kept it in his breast pocket. A charm. It makes me . . ."

"My grandchild," I said.

"No. I was thinking: your father's great-grandchild. That nice old man."

I saw Ricardo in the mountains, at the beginning, when there were only eighteen of us, already defeated, without a chance. (Or were there fourteen? Or twelve? I sometimes count. But someone is missing. Or counted twice. There are other needs being served here—like a man enumerating his lovers, confused by guilt, longing, and his vision of himself.) Ricardo walked up to a large man watching some cattle in a field. I heard him say, "Do you know how to read and write? Don't lie to me!" The big peasant looked at Ricardo's rifle. Then he picked Ricardo up, though Ricardo is a very tall man, and sat him on the back of one of the cows. Ricardo laughed, and shouted, "You're a stupid . . . ventriloquist!"—using the most preposterous-sounding word that he could remember. He got down from the cow, and kicked the man in the backside. Then he put his arm around Joaquin's shoulder. They walked off, a little ways ahead of us, and then a little ways more, Ricardo cajoling him, insulting him, flattering him, till we were ready to make camp. The two of them squatted down, and Ricardo took out his detective novel. It still had its green cover then, with its lurid picture of the woman in the short black negligee.

It was a racist North American novel, full of gooks, spics, and niggers. When we had a mimeo machine later on, Ricardo duplicated passages for our classes. I remember that the book began, "I had just come out of a three-chair barbershop, where the Agency thought a barber named Dimitrios Aleidis might be working. It was a small matter. . . ."

And even as I recalled the words, I heard my uncanny collaborator's spectral voice. " 'It was a small matter.' When R. needed volunteers he'd say, 'The Agency needs an operative. It's a small matter.' You know, we made up heroic exploits for Dimitrios Aleidis. How he had come to Cuba to join Fidel. Etcetera."

That serial, I remembered, was mostly the work of my young friend, Walter of the high unquenchable voice. Much like his stories of himself, but with Aleidis substituted for Walter.

"R. and I," Ponco said, "are the only ones in Cuba who know the whole plot of that detective story." He smiled, seraphically.

But I wouldn't give him the satisfaction of asking.

"All right. I'll tell you the murderer. It was." And he made a muffled noise into the back of his hand. "You know, Che, Ricardo shared your pleasure. Using pussycats to shock people."

Found out, so easily!

"He'd cook them up on a Bunsen burner. Make new recruits eat a piece.

I told him how much I   And my whole family   Enjoyed their little livers and tongues. Thus our Friendship."

I laughed and sat looking out at the ocean, and thought of the water covering the field, lapping up over my boots, my legs, ridding the planet of its vermin.

"Fidel."

That name, recalling me to my memory work, and suddenly there were no more images. It was too hot outside, that's why I wanted to drown the world. I was sweating under my arms. My pants clung to my thighs. You'd think this remembering was hard work. I pulled myself back into the shade of the veranda. "I don't remember what was said." For today, I thought, was no good for voices. "But I remember how I felt before he arrived."

"Yes!" Ponco said. Clearly, this was best of all.

"I thought I was angry with myself. I had killed a man for little reason. Or too much for my own reasons. What I'd written my father was bravado. I felt guilty for what I'd done. I hadn't left his world. And I was confused. I was not the sort of person who could have done such a thing. Then what sort of person was I?"

Ponco made a sound of agreement, a long grating sigh.

I looked off into the sun. "And I remember an odd thing Castro said to me when we met: 'I've been waiting for you.' "

Ponco clapped his hands together. "And?"

I didn't speak for a while. Looking at the sun had made me a little woozy.

"And? How did it *feel?* Meeting him?"

I stared out at the long grass. The sun scythed it straight across, like a plain fact. Once again the grass moved inside my blank mind. I saw the room at Maria Antonia's. Someone entered. "It felt . . . it felt like I was suddenly part of a drama."

Ponco clapped and clapped and clapped. Was it the word "drama"? Was I supposed to bow?

"Don't speak," he said peremptorily, though I had no thought of speaking; I was entirely vegetative. "Don't say   Another word." He left his thick book on the chair and went inside. I sat and waited for him to return with some new sheaf of accusing documents. What might they be?

For half an hour the sun slowly rounded itself to a single color. Ponco's doll's-head popped out from the doorway, startling me. The rest of the body didn't follow.

"Is it true you saved his life. In Mexico?"

"Yes."

"Don't tell me about it!"

He disappeared. The sun grew larger, achieved a more coherent form, and it, too, disappeared. Ponco didn't return.

Or come out for dinner. That night I saw the light on in his room. I knew that my collaborator's ban on speech still applied, so I didn't disturb him.

JULY 13

He emerged in the morning, after I had been at the table for an hour. He walked a slow shuffle, a tentative step, holding some pages again, but this time apparently uncertain of his accusations. He looked weary, as if accusing me (the substance of our romance) wore him down. And he had shaved his wispy mustache. (It had never amounted to much.)

He sat for a few moments at the table, running his palm over and over on his hair, just touching the top of his curls. "Here," he said, handing me the papers. He smiled wanly, not sure, I thought, of my pleasure in his work. But why, suddenly, did it matter to him? Before, the barb of the accusation had been its own delight.

AN HISTORIC MEETING

A Play in Two Acts

BY

"Travis" Tulio

"A pen name," Ponco said. He had risen from his chair, and come over to stand behind me, bending towards my shoulder. He was not the sort of author who would be reticent in offering guidance to the reader. "It's like a *nom de guerre*. Perhaps you need one, too. Make you freer in talking about yourself."

I saw his point: it was a different sort of battle, a different sort of secrecy. I paused, thought. "Che," I said.

"Sure. Right." But Ponco had lost interest in that line of attack. He wanted me to read on.

Act One: Ernesto Guevara Smokes a Cigar with Fidel Castro

Scene: The house of Maria Antonia, a wealthy sympathizer of the 26th of July Movement, and of Fidel Castro, its leader. We are in the kitchen, a large room with a big stove. There is an ornate kitchen table of heavy dark carved wood. A big black iron pot of spaghetti sits in the middle of the table. Another pot sits on the stove. There are dirty cups and dishes scattered on the table, and several handguns. A machete hangs from the back of one of the strong-looking chairs. Rifles lean against the stone walls, which have been painted a light-pink color. Seven or eight people occupy the room, some sitting in chairs pushed back from the table. One man stirs the pot, making the plot thicker. One, a blond man, squats by the wall, cleaning his rifle. A tall black man stands, combing his long hair out of a pompadour, parting it in the middle so it falls down the sides of his face. It is not clear from any of this activity if dinner is going on now, is just over, hasn't begun yet, or was over long ago.

There is a large window right behind the kitchen table.

A lull in the conversation. An air of expectancy.

[Fidel Castro enters. He is thirty years old, light-complexioned; six two; solidly built. He has shiny, wavy black hair and a mustache. He is assured and graceful in his movements. A hush falls as he enters.]

"How can a hush fall?" I asked. "You just said there was a lull in the conversation."

For a moment the quick man didn't reply. He looked as Neruda must when he has been drinking and someone corrects his grammar. "It felt that way." He leaned back from my shoulder.

"You weren't there," I said, responding to the mockery. "Not that I remember, anyway. What do you mean it felt that way?"

"I *was* there." Ponco leaned forward again, pointing to the page on the table. "*There* there."

"Ah."

"Besides, the story needed it."

"Yes," I said. "We know about *that.*"

"I'll change it. 'A deeper hush fell.' Or: 'Within the silence the heart of the silence was revealed. The intake of breath. Hands suddenly still.' All right?"

His voice, I thought, sounded younger: faster shifts within that sliding gravel and dirt. This writing, I realized, was the new activity he'd found, the substitute for reading too many stories. (Perhaps mimicking my prose style had released a voice in him.) I read on:

[Castro crosses the room and stands at the head of the table. Every face follows him. He is brought a plate of spaghetti by the tall black man whose hair comes down to his shoulders.]

CASTRO: My favorite!

NICO: Welcome home, boss! Now I can get my hair cut!

CASTRO: You look good, Nico! Strange, but good. (*They give each other big hugs and kisses on the cheek. All of the other men come over and hug him.*)

[*Castro sits at the head of the table in a big wooden chair. He eats the spaghetti in a few seconds, as if he had inhaled it.*]

NICO [*pointing at Castro admiringly*]: This *blanco* eats like a *negro!*

[*All laugh.*]

CASTRO: Well, I haven't had any spaghetti in a long time! [*He is brought another plate, and he eats and talks at the same time.*] Listen! Have you continued our propaganda work?

RICARDO (a tall thin man with a severe lined face): Yes. Ten thousand copies of the *Manifesto* have been sent to the underground in Cuba. By the way, I can read it now!

CASTRO: Congratulations, Ricardo!

RICARDO: Thanks. It is due to the efforts of a man called Ernesto Guevara, a doctor. He killed a mercenary in Guatemala. He is our kind of guy. Nico will tell you all about him, until you beg him to stop.

NICO: He is very courageous, Fidel. He has his own ideas. You'll like him, Fidel. I like him, Fidel.

CASTRO: Nico, don't use my name so much. It loses all meaning. I feel like I'm floating away. I don't know who *I* am. It's like saying "spoon" over and over. But I'm the spoon!

[*Nico says "spoon" over and over while everyone listens.*]

NICO: I don't get it? [*He turns to the others.*] What does he mean, he's a spoon?

[*The others all turn away from Nico and towards Castro.*]

CASTRO: Never mind, Nico. We must see to it that another ten thousand copies of *History Will Absolve Me* are printed up for Pais in Santiago. I am more sure than ever, comrades, that ceaseless propaganda work is the heart of the revolution. Propaganda of words, soon to be matched by propaganda of deeds! Ricardo, now that you read and write, take a note for Pais. "Dear Frank: Show guile and smiles to everybody. Don't be so abrasive with the other parties. We must unite all who will be united and neutralize the rest. Follow the same course we followed during the trial: defend our point of view without wounding others. We will have time later on to trample underfoot all the cockroaches. Accept all sorts of help. But remember, trust no one. Signed, Fidel." Read that back to me.

[*Ricardo has been sitting in a chair next to Fidel, with his hands on his legs. He has stared at Castro during the preceding speech without moving.*]

RICARDO: Signed, Fidel.

CASTRO: Thank you, Ricardo. *[With evident sarcasm]* With such men how can I fail!

RICARDO: You give Frank good advice, Fidel. But maybe you should say more about what our point of view is.

CASTRO: Our point of view is: We will unite all who will be united. Our duty is to social justice alone. All will save themselves if they save their principles. From the deepest dregs of corruption will come, more purified and clean, the ideal redeemer. Sacrifice is now our only duty.

NICO *[heartfelt]*: Thank you, boss! I understand. *[He bows his head.]*

CASTRO *[pats Nico's head and puts a strand of spaghetti in Nico's mouth]*: Good, Nico. Remember: we will unite all who will be united.

RICARDO: But shouldn't we say a word or two more about what we are uniting for? More about our principles. About our goals.

CASTRO *[exasperated]*: I liked you better before you knew how to read and write!

NICO: I understand, Fidel! We will re-establish the Constitution of 1940!

FELIPE *[the blond man who leans against the wall, cleaning his gun]*: We will get rid of the North Americans!

JESUS: We will build a socialist state in Cuba!

[They all look to Castro.]

CASTRO: We will unite all who will be united!

JUAN: We will link ourselves more strongly with the liberal values of the United States, our shared concern for the individual!

MARCOS: We will realize the dreams of Marti!

ALMEIDA: We will realize the dreams of Chibas!

FELIPE: We will realize the dreams of Lenin!

NICO: We will realize the dreams of Thomas Jefferson!

FAUSTINO: We will realize the Moncada Manifesto!

[Each grows visibly uneasy as he hears the others shout. Each looks about from face to face angrily and then with growing bafflement, exchanging hostile and bewildered looks with the others. Then, like plants slowly bending towards the light, they resolutely look away from one another, and towards Fidel, the sun in the people's sky.]

CASTRO: We will untie all who will be untied!

[The others start to nod, and then their gestures of agreement halt, grow confused. Marcos's hands, extended with palms up and fingers open, are suddenly palsied. Felipe's arm is half raised in a clenched fist. He looks up at it, realizes it is the wrong arm, and slowly withdraws it.]

CASTRO *[senses the confusion in their gestures, the hesitations and secret thoughts they express by the movements of their bodies, the looks on their faces, the unspoken words of their hands, and gives it voice, resolving that jangle]:* I goofed! We will unite all who will be united!

RICARDO *[looking towards the floor]:* Sounds like "spoon" to me.

Something nagged at me. "Resolving that jangle"! Were those my collaborator's words or my own? Had Walter sneaked into my room?

Before I could ask him, Walter pointed towards that part of the page, and smiled. "I'm making fun of myself," he said.

Of himself? It was the part he had written for *me* yesterday!

"Read on!"

And, imagining that might solve these mysteries, I did:

Scene Two: Same room, many plates of spaghetti later. Two men lie on the floor snoring, one man has his head on the other's chest. One man is passed out across his arms on the table. Castro is dictating more instructions to Ricardo, who now takes them down, with great difficulty, on some paper.

Raul Castro enters, with Che Guevara, a young unkempt doctor, his pants held up by a rope, his leather jacket in shreds.

Ernesto looks about himself warily. He trusts no one. He takes in the room, and stares at the men eating spaghetti and talking.

GUEVARA: I feel like I'm in a play.

TRAVIS TULIO'S VOICE *[from off stage]:* You are!

"Do you think that's corny?" the real voice of Travis Tulio asked from behind me.

"Yes," I said. I found I was indifferent to Walter's feelings, the "Travis." "It's ridiculous. It's terrible. It's stupid. It serves no purpose." Not, frankly, that I could see the purpose of the rest.

"I'll cut it," he said decisively, apparently unhurt and steeled to the awful act. He reached over and drew a thick pencil line through that section.

[Raul Castro enters with Ernesto Guevara. Castro stares long and meaningfully at Guevara.]

CASTRO: Come. Sit by me. Have a plate of spaghetti. I have been waiting a long time for you! *[There is a note of mystery to Castro's voice; fortunes told. He sounds like Che's mother.]*

GUEVARA [as if mesmerized, walks towards the table]: You have?

CASTRO: Yes. Since I first heard of you, I had the feeling that we would have a lot to say to each other, a lot to do with each other, a lot to accomplish. You understand?

GUEVARA [clearly baffled]: No. I don't think so.

CASTRO: Have a plate of spaghetti. [Guevara, still mesmerized, sits by Castro.] Good. I heard about your argument with Paz Estenssoro, the MNR leader. You were right! He is a traitor to his people. You were entirely correct in telling him off. A man who has the courage to do that is someone I could work with!

GUEVARA [increasingly baffled, and looking as if the perplexity is causing him some pain]: You did? He is? I am?

CASTRO: Yes. Sartre thought very highly of what you said.

GUEVARA: He did?

CASTRO [examining Guevara quizzically, as if he were a store dummy]: Are you all right? Of course he didn't. I don't know Sartre! [Castro smiles broadly.] Let me say this from the beginning. [His face becomes serious, and he leans towards Guevara.] I have nothing to offer you but constant struggle, unending struggle. We will keep the spirit of the Moncada burning with an armed struggle. It will raise up the Cuban masses. It will show them that a real struggle is possible now. Propaganda of the deed. There will be a revolution in Cuba from top to bottom. Is that your cup of tea?

GUEVARA [His body stiffens; he snaps his fingers in front of his eyes, ending his period of hypnosis.]: And the North Americans?

CASTRO: Don't worry about that. I am all the names of rebellion in history. I am Mussolini, Marx, Hitler, Lenin, Napoleon, Julius Caesar. I am one with the world-historical process. I am married only to the Revolution.

GUEVARA [no longer baffled, and growing increasingly angry]: And the North Americans?!

CASTRO: The North Americans! The North Americans! You're just like Raul! You both talk of nothing else! You're obsessed with the big whale, the North Americans! Listen: We will unite all who will be united to make the revolution! Now is the hour of the furnaces and only light should be seen!

GUEVARA [shouting]: And the North Americans?

CASTRO: All right, damn you. If they won't cooperate, I'll throw them off the island! There! Is that all right with you? You have my word!

GUEVARA [extending his hand]: They won't cooperate! I will join you!

CASTRO: Good! Have a cigar! They're helpful for asthma.

[He hands a cigar to Guevara, who is unfamiliar with the object and holds it at a meter's length. He watches Castro, to see how it is disarmed, and duplicates his movements. Both men light up.]

Curtain for Act One of
AN HISTORIC MEETING,
A Play by Travis Tulio

[A placard appears in front of the curtain: LUKEWARM ORANGE DRINKS WILL BE SERVED DURING INTERMISSION.]

Ponco leaned forward, his head right over my shoulder. "Well?"

Was he serious? Did he really want my (or anyone's) opinion of this nonsense? Then I remembered his light last night; he had not slept in order to produce this pastiche. I might offend him. (One is, I had learned, strangely sensitive about such matters.)

"It wasn't quite like that," I said.

"Of course not." Ponco busied himself at the stove, lit the charcoal, started some water to boil for coffee. "This isn't a story where things simply are as they were. This is . . ."

"Art," I said, smiling, hoping to deflect his annoyance, and any further discussion of his work. "First time tragedy, second time farce. Karl Marx said that." But why, I wondered, did Walter want to make us all ridiculous?

"Karl Marx," Ponco said, from the stove. "The theater critic?" He measured some coffee grounds for the water. "So? What was it like?" He didn't sound angry, merely curious.

I thought.

Ponco came over with his coffee in a blue pottery mug.

"We talked," I said. "He did introduce me to smoking cigars, by the way. How did you know that? He said they were good for asthma. Mexico City has an air drought. I wheezed throughout our first meeting."

"Fidel thinks cigars are good for everything. If you had had leprosy, he would have told you that cigar smoke was good for that. What did you talk about?"

"We talked about everything. Our ideas of revolution, of socialism, of the need for sacrifice, personal and national, to form the New Man of our continent. We talked about the Vietnamese victory at Dien Bien Phu. I said the United States would never allow the elections mandated by the Geneva Accords. I had the feeling he agreed with me. But you know, Walter, I'm not sure that he said so!"

I looked over at Walter, and realized we were both shaking our heads, in rueful unison. We smiled.

"I had never met a man so curious, so utterly given over to conversation. He loved ideas. And yet his abstractions seemed very palpable to him, like characters in a book. I could feel them. He always looked for the practical within the metaphysical. He wanted to know what might advance his work, and he would search anywhere for that, plunder all culture for insights, military tactics, metaphors, rhetorical tricks. We didn't agree on everything. But he seemed to me someone of tenacity and modesty. He was the best element, I thought, of the national bourgeoisie. Nothing more than that. His inclinations were socialist, but he was not yet a thoroughgoing Marxist. He wouldn't be able to carry the revolution through. There would be a further struggle, with Raul and myself on the Left. Other leaders might have to supplant him, to carry the revolution forward."

Ponco pointed to me. "Now," he said.

"Perhaps," I said, but it wasn't something I wanted to think about. The small nickel pistol raised from the breakfast plate. "And his plan! His plan was mad, Walter!"

Ponco held the cup before him, with both hands around it, and smiled and nodded. I knew what he thought: one madman speaks of another. A loony-bin Napoleon, confiding to the doctor that so-and-so is crazy to think that she's Joan of Arc, here in nineteenth-century France.

"It *was* mad. To land on the coast of a heavily defended island and spark a rising with a group of eighty men! And he announced the time of our landing in advance! To show the people he could be trusted! That's madness! But I was schizophrenic in his presence. I knew his plan was crazy. I knew that his class viewpoint was limited. But I also felt something very different. I felt a limitless possibility. Hadn't the Vietnamese defeated the French? Impossible event! And I felt that I could no longer avoid declaring myself. The struggle would be a stage, however limited, in the fight against imperialism, against the Yanquis who had destroyed the Guatemalan Revolution. It was like the cigars," I said, and, as if in delicious illustration, I took one from my shirt pocket and lit it. "They're no good for asthma. I *knew* that. But I smoked them anyway."

"You became Che," Ponco said, nodding slowly. "For real."

And though I didn't fully fathom his remark, it seemed right to me; I nodded in agreement. "When I spoke to Fidel my guilt fell away. Or rather, I discovered something about myself harder to acknowledge than guilt: that I didn't feel any remorse, really. About killing that man. That confused me. But it was undeniable. I had killed a man, the unthinkable thing for the doctor and the doctor's son —the so-called Gandhian! I had been a fatal disease to him, as my father's voice had said to me, and I didn't regret it. I didn't think anything about it, at least not while I spoke with Fidel. Fidel was amplitude, Fidel was sweep, Fidel was permission, Walter, you were right about that. He spoke of a grand historical movement, of necessity, of wrong turnings that were needed for the march to find its way. And it all seemed far more than the personal, than petty morality. Killing a man was a mild indiscretion in the larger wave of history. It all seemed a huge staircase, and one's ascent was inevitable."

Ponco made a sweeping motion with his hand. He had very graceful hands. They looked like the wings of a circling bird, rising, rising, rising. And then I thought of his little playlet. No staircase there. Just a game of chutes and ladders. What if all sense to history was arbitrary; just farce?

"I was mixed up by it all. Thinking I felt guilty had been an anchor to my personality, a touch of home. There had been confusion for me in killing that man. But there was a deeper confusion in realizing that it didn't matter, provided I went on with my new business. So I held on to what I knew a little while longer and I joined the expedition as a doctor."

"Permission!" Ponco said gleefully. "I knew it! Read on." He picked up some more pages from the table and handed them to me.

ACT TWO OF
AN HISTORIC MEETING
A PLAY BY

Travis Tulio

Act Two: Che Kills a Man

[A shadow is seen in the window behind Castro. "Che" Guevara rises from his seat, takes a pistol from the table. He fires through the window. Glass shatters. A man screams. A body falls.]

CASTRO *[looking at Guevara as if he were mad]:* What was that? You've shot the gardener!

CHE: No. It was somebody sent to assassinate you.

CASTRO: No! Really? How did you know?

CHE: I could see him fooling with the safety on the gun, pushing the flange back and forth, back and forth. He couldn't decide whether or not to kill you.

[Castro gestures, and Marcos and Almeida, without further words, go outside to examine. They come back dragging the body of a fat man in a blue business suit. They drop him on the floor and stand by the corpse.

Marcos squats down by the corpse and takes the fat man's wallet from his jacket pocket. He looks through it.]

MARCOS: It's true. Che's right. He's one of Batista's agents. *[He takes some bills from the wallet and puts them in his back pocket.]* For printing expenses. *[Marcos and Almeida hoist the body up again and bring it to the kitchen table. They put it in a chair next to Che.]*

CASTRO *[to the corpse]:* Have some spaghetti. I've been waiting a long time for you.

[Everyone gives a macabre laugh.]

THE CORPSE *[in a toneless voice at first, but with growing petulance]:* No, thank you. The dead don't eat . . . spaghetti.

NICO *[to Che, with evident admiration]:* You didn't think! You acted instinctively! You're one of us!

[The others look at Nico, critically. What right does he have? He ran away! But they look with acceptance on their new comrade, slapping his back, etc.]

"That's true, in a way," I said, though I didn't know why I should offer Walter satisfaction. (He was staring at me when I looked up, reading my face as I read his words.) "I felt that I couldn't go back after killing that mercenary and watching Chaco die. Back anywhere. I couldn't return to Argentina. I couldn't return to practicing medicine. The world had vomited me up. So these people—most of them had killed, too—these people became my new family, my group, my world, others who had acted with only their own sanction, others who couldn't go back."

"Precisely," Walter said. "My feeling exactly." For after all, he, too, had made that crossing. "Read on!"

The growl of command! I read:

CASTRO: Nico's right! You will make a great fighter, Guevara! So what do you think of my plan?

CHE *[he holds up one hand, with the cigar in it]:* On the one hand, it is hopeless, crazy. *[He holds up the other hand.]* On the other, I think that the will calls to the will, arouses it. An action like that might make people rub their eyes in wonder, rise up and follow it. *[His hands balance and waver in the air, first one going up, then the other.]*

CASTRO: You'll never make things balance. You have to decide. You have to jump in. The leader acts to free himself first. The leader must act. I like the way you put things, though. Let's talk metaphysics.

RICARDO: Metaphysics? What's that? Not physical?

THE CORPSE [*laughing amiably*]: It's physical, yet not physical anymore. Like me. *I'm* metaphysical.

CHE: The will, I think, asserts how little the body or life itself matters. The symbol will arouse the sleeping soul.

THE CORPSE: Not mine, that's for damn sure. You've put it to sleep beyond the call of symbols. I'll show you. Give me a lit cigar. [*Ricardo puts one in his mouth. Nothing happens. After a time the cigar goes out.*] See?

CHE: We must call the people to a great sacrifice. A nation finds itself in acts of collective sacrifice.

CASTRO: Yes. The leadership by its actions can show how little material things, even life itself, matter. It is national dignity that is essential.

THE CORPSE: The hell it is! You people don't know what you're talking about. Making corpses and being one are very different things. And *thing* is the operative word here, let me tell you! Life isn't a material thing that doesn't matter. It is an immaterial thing! A spiritual thing. Very precious! And all gone in my case, damn your eyes!

CASTRO [*to Che*]: We think as one! I knew it. We must call the people to a great sacrifice. In a great sacrifice they will become a great people, single in purpose.

THE CORPSE: I made a great sacrifice! I'm single in purpose all right. I'm getting nicely stiff.

CASTRO: You shut up! You're dead!

THE CORPSE: Not a very kind way to speak to the dead! Don't the dead have rights?

CHE: Don't the living? The revolution is for the living!

THE CORPSE [*truly agreeing*]: I see your point. Well, the two of you are really some pair! I think you'll make many more corpses together!

[*Guevara and Castro laugh, a deep, lasting, collaborative laughter.*]

Curtain of Act Two of
AN HISTORIC MEETING
A PLAY BY
Travis Tulio

I was sure from that "collaborative" that Walter had been in my room. "You've read my journal."

"No. But I'd like to." He took it, or pretended to, as if I had meant a compliment for his inventive intuition.

I didn't say anything more. He'd read my mind, he'd read my journal. What did it matter? That was the feeling Travis's little effort left me with. What if history was just plain stupid?

"Hilda must have hated him," the *farceur* said. "Taking you away to Cuba. Endangering your life."

"What? No. You don't understand her Walter. She didn't hate him. She wanted to *join* him. She wanted to go with us. Not because I was going. But because of him, because of the cause."

Walter laughed. At me? At Hilda? At all of us? He laughed alone this time. I wasn't sure of his laughter anymore.

Cuba, 1956-57

From My Journal

11/26/56: Nico and I stood on the long wooden dock at Tuxpan, in bright sunlight, with most of the men around us in our new olive-green uniforms. We stared at the *Granma*. My hands pricked with dread, as if they'd been asleep for a week. We had a good long look. "It's happening again, Che," Nico said finally, in a choked voice. "He's gotten us a twenty-two." His large brown eyes filled with water, and he made no effort to hide his face from the others. "Cover your face," I said, worried about morale. "No," Nico said sulkily, a child having a tantrum before bed. Nico is a coward, but I saw his point. The *Granma* is fifty-two feet long, a white pleasure boat with a sporty prow and guardrails made from shiny chrome. It is a plaything made for eight amiable people, not eighty-five men with arms and supplies.

The boat was too small, but we had to use it, we couldn't wait to purchase another one. Fidel had spoken. Fidel had spoken in radio broadcasts, in newspaper interviews, in clandestine leaflets distributed throughout Cuba. THIS YEAR WE WILL BE FREE MEN OR MARTYRS! I heard Pino, the fat captain, tell Fidel that the clutch needed fixing. "No time," Fidel said. Pino took off his cap and ran his hand through his unwashed black hair. He was shirtless, and his large breasts hung down. There was a north wind blowing, he said imploringly. Soon small-craft warnings would be posted. (And ours was certainly a small craft, a too-small craft.) With his right forefinger, Castro tapped the end of his brown mustache, miming thought—for the matter had already been decided. He pointed the forefinger outward, the barrel of a gun aimed at the captain's large hairy chest. "We leave today," he said.

For we have to make good on his speeches, interviews, leaflets, his *promise*. And men will be waiting at Niquero on the thirtieth with trucks and supplies for us. The troops must be there for that meeting; it is crucial to his plan. We are to take Niquero and advance towards Manzanillo. At the time of the landing, the city network, under Frank Pais, will rise in Santiago. Then a vaguely defined but overwhelming apocalypse has been revealed to Fidel, of sabotage, agitation, and general strike. (Pais met with the leadership in Mexico City to dispute this vision. His skin was sallow and hung in folds near his neck, as if his diet were irregular, his weight constantly changing drastically. The time was wrong, he said. His networks weren't ready. Castro tapped the end of his mustache. Pais was overruled.) So we must go through uncertain weather, on a small boat with a bad clutch, to a fortified coast that has been notified—by our leader—of our arrival. To show our good faith, Fidel said, to show that Fidel Castro and the Movement of the Twenty-Sixth of July can be trusted by the people. *This year,* he has said, we will be free men or martyrs. This year: we have one month left. We must make good on his dare.

Caceres, who had trained with us, came down to the dock to make a last appeal to Castro that he be included in the expedition. No, Castro said, Guevara is enough. The force mustn't be internationalized. It must appear a Cuban national movement. Caceres helped us load the long white wooden crates of arms, and the heavy black boxes of ammunition and medical supplies. Fidel had done all right on the weapons: two anti-tank guns, fifty-five Mendoza rifles, three Thompson machine guns, forty light hand machine pistols. Caceres stumbled on the uneven wood of the gangplank, and a crate containing the oil-covered parts of a machine gun slammed into my stomach. I bellowed in pain, a wordless sound. Ricardo, standing behind me with an ammunition box, laughed. "Che never curses," he said to the men behind him. "What strong will! He should have been a priest." No, I thought to myself, a nun. I caught my breath, and looked up at Caceres, his face abashed and sad —for he was both clumsy and unchosen. The sunlight poured down behind him into the harbor. Then I looked at our small white boat, surprised by the sight of it, as if a piece of doll's furniture had been put in a sitting room. I wondered how many of these weapons would ever be fired? For it was like Castro to be careful about many details—the training under General Bayo, a veteran of Spain, had been excellent—and then to overlook one matter, and that one the essential.

After the loading, Caceres embraced me, and I returned his hug, pressing his head into my chest. But my thoughts were elsewhere, on the storm to come, the small-craft warnings, the small craft. Caceres had looked gloomy throughout the work, disappointed by Fidel's refusal. But his step as he walked away from us had a buoyancy, and I saw him look over his shoulder at the boat and smile.

Three other Cubans who had trained with us gave one last look at the ship and walked away after Caceres, unwilling to risk any more on such a mad plan.

11/27/56: Since the time Nico spoke to me on the dock yesterday I don't think he's said another word to anyone. This morning was calm and bright: a good omen, we thought, for the weather reports had been wrong, and Fidel had— magically—been right. Nico walked to the bow carrying a bucket of seawater with careful, slow steps, as if there might be a shortage soon. He sat cross-legged, facing the ocean, with the bucket beside him. Methodically he soaped his face and head till he produced a thick white lather. It looked like a curly judge's wig. Nine men stood around him in a half-circle, watching, but he took no notice. He had moved away from us, behind that invisible barrier that makes it impossible to warn the prince of the traitorous plots, the poisoned swords. He shaved his cheeks, and with long slow strokes of his straight razor he shaved off his now-curly hair. He carefully washed the razor off in the bucket after each stroke. A wind came up and swayed the prow. A small red line opened on the right side of Nico's scalp, and grew in size, a flood pouring through a town. "You've cut yourself," Marcos said in a thick voice, as if out of a daze, hypnotized by the decided motions of Nico's long gleaming silver blade. Marcos took one of his dozen white handkerchiefs from his pants pocket, and held it towards Nico. Nico ignored it. The seawater, I thought, must have stung in the cut, but Nico didn't show it on his face. The cut will scar up from the salt, like his other "battle" wounds. I stared. Light gleamed from his large expanse of scalp, blue pink black brown in the sun, a streak of red that was welling and widening; the colors blended and shimmered like the rainbow formed by oil on water. "An ornament for the prow," Marcos said, the spell broken. He tucked his handkerchief away in his pocket; he had them hidden all over his clothing.

Nico's little ritual struck me with the force of a poem, an immediately apprehensible yet surprising gesture added to the lexicon. He meant that he was ready to die.

11/30/56: The wind that cut Nico's scalp grew in density and ferocity. The good omen was proved false, the storms began, and I lost my stomach for the enterprise. The first men started coming to me in my capacity as medical officer. But I couldn't find the box with the antihistamine tablets. Fidel gathered on the deck those of us who could still stand up, and we sang the Cuban national anthem. He had constructed a compelling image for himself: his men defying the storm, roaring back at the waves. But by the second verse the rain began, hard whipping cords; suddenly our clothes were as wet as if we'd dived into the ocean. High waves lifted over the prow. The sea turned black. Faces began to twist and melt. Men vomited over the sides, clinging to the chrome railings, or threw up on the deck, the wind spraying their vomit into their faces. Someone shouted that there was a leak below, that water was flooding in.

As we bailed the ship, the big metal buckets going from hand to hand, I held the pail for a moment and threw up in it. So had many of the men around me. I received a bucket filled with seawater, other men's vomit, bits of cracker, sausage, and green bile; I added my own. There were twenty of us working in uneven lines, on a deck eight feet wide, bringing the water up from below. Pino's orders contradicted Roque's, his second in command; Roque's orders were askew of Almeida's, our group's officer. It was impossible to see an arm's length through the sheets of rain. The sun had gone out. The lines never got straight. The pails moved about frantically in the dark. "That's my own puke again," I heard someone behind me say. "I recognize it." The buckets were just being passed around without being dumped. Water crashed over the deck in huge fists, a man slammed into me, and I fell backward onto someone's chest. The metal pail was knocked from someone's hands and hit the side of Almeida's small head. He shouted for me to help him. But I couldn't get out from under the body lying across me. My arms felt weak. Slop from one of the buckets splashed over my cheek. I turned my face to keep from choking on my own vomit and sputum, and threw up the little food bits I had left onto Almeida's jacket. I prayed as I threw up, as generations have before me, "O Lord take me now!" Ricardo, groaning somewhere to my left, added responsively, "If only it comes now! If only it comes now!" We sounded like acolytes.

But it didn't come then. It will come too late; on land. If we ever find land. The boat is too small for the waves. At high speeds the clutch slips; in the storm accurate steering was impossible. We have gone days off course. And Roque, a man as fat as the captain, panicked. The boat was overloaded, he said, too heavy. That was why it was taking water. He had the men toss many of the heavy automatic weapons overboard.

During the last moments of the storm, after the rain had stopped, the air turned heavy around me. I writhed with an attack, my legs stuck straight out, rigid with pain. The other men, my comrades, were terrified by the spectacle and drew away from me. Only Ricardo came near the odd fish flapping on the wet deck, near the bow. "Do you want a shot?" he asked. I had trained him and the others in first-aid techniques, shown them on my own arm how to give injections. But I shook my head no this time. "I can do it with my good hand," he said, as if I had refused him because I feared his clumsiness. I couldn't explain then that I didn't want to start using up the epinephrine yet, that this attack was bad, but that things might get much worse. Ricardo squatted down next to me anyway, not touching me, but watching. He looked curious, not particularly sympathetic. He stroked his thin lips with his thumb meditatively, a thoughtful pathologist. The mild pink flesh of his lips grew bulbous, breathed in and out. Ricardo watched. This was what he had come down from the mountains to the courthouse for: new sights, strange spectacles, and revenge. I think he really does despise humanity.

The attack means I won't be much of a combatant for a while, so I exchanged my new semi-automatic weapon (given to me because I was the best of Bayo's students, the best marksman; I could make things hop) for Ricardo's old bolt-action rifle. Because of Roque's panic there will be a shortage of automatic weapons. He was wrong, too. It wasn't the weight. The water had come from a broken pipe in the toilet. The desperate bailing and the jettisoning had been unnecessary. But the weapons are gone now.

Today the sea settled itself after its attack. But my stomach feels the same, I can't tell the difference between my nausea and my constant fear. Bayo said that terror would be one's companion throughout the war. The most dangerous thing a guerrilla can do, he said, is to let the fear lead him, let it make him fight at the wrong time, *let his fear be a dare to him,* a challenge to his manhood. *(This year we will be free men or martyrs!)* The first rule of guerrillas: don't attack unless you're certain of victory. Guerrillas can't afford to lose a battle. The army can; it has many men to spend. The first lesson: learn to run away. Manhood, Bayo said, is for the rich. (But across the chessboard his mistakes came from his inability to refuse an offered pawn. His large hands, with their old veins, would hesitate for a moment, then take the fatal gambit.)

It was Bayo, square-faced, dispassionate gentleman, who convinced me that victory over Batista was truly possible. (But then what had I thought before? What did I think I was doing when I joined Castro?)

We lived in ten separate apartments scattered over Mexico City, as protection against police raids. Bayo had gone from apartment to apartment, giving us theoretical instruction, and teaching us how to clean and reassemble our weapons. A stocky fastidious exacting teacher. Then he had found a ranch for us, six miles long, ten miles wide, covered in part with jungle. There we followed an improvised series of exercises that Bayo's deep slow authoritative voice made sound magical, certain of success. We learned to shoot pistols, rifles, machine guns; how to make bombs and destroy tanks; how to spot aircraft, and where on the fuselage to aim; how to march through jungle without being seen—forced marches with full pack, running till we could not go on running, crawling, lying still, five ten fifteen hours a day. He would not relent on his regimen until we knew how much pain we could stand, until we collapsed, dizzy from the strain and the grandness of our mission. He lectured on strategy in guerrilla warfare, how to harass an enemy, bewilder him, attacking with a circle maneuver and stepping away, then leading the army into the next group, a tactic called "the minuet."

Guerrilla warfare, Fidel had said, in a voice of mild, distant consideration, would never succeed in Cuba. The honor of the Cuban people would be revolted by it. But Bayo had convinced him that no other method was possible for such a small force, that honor, too, was for the rich. (Fidel's objection was strategic: that "Cubans" would be revolted by it, not that *he* was.) And Fidel's gifts as a leader had so impressed Bayo that he had wanted to join us. I had thought that if Fidel could convince such a strong-willed realistic man . . . but that was before I saw the boat.

And Bayo had not been impressed with Fidel at first. They had met in a bar in Mexico City. Bayo, a Cuban but a veteran of the Spanish Foreign Legion and the Spanish Civil War, had been an instructor at the military academy in Guadalajara. Soto, knowing of Fidel's need, had found him and arranged the meeting. Fidel had spoken at length of the Moncada attack. Bayo asked how the men had been prepared for their roles. Not at all, Fidel said smiling. Bayo had pursed his lips, but said nothing. What, Fidel asked, did Bayo do now? He ran a furniture factory. Did he like it? No, it was not to his taste. Would he be interested in something closer to his old line of work? Bayo, judiciously, said that that would depend. So Fidel explained—at length—the dimensions of his revolution to liberate the oppressed. Bayo said he would be interested—at a salary of eight thousand dollars. But wouldn't he be interested, Fidel asked, in a glorious expedition to free the fatherland from the yoke of an ape's dictatorship? No, Bayo said. He had been born in Cuba in 1892, when it was still Spanish. He was not a young man. His parents had left for Spain when he was six. He had no memories of Cuba. He would be interested for six thousand dollars. Would he be interested, Fidel wondered, for two thousand?

"You've always been a gangster, you dumb stupid bastard. Your plan stinks. Your idea is impossible. I've had a thousand conversations with young fools.

They have a few drinks and dream of overthrowing Franco, Somoza, Trujillo, Perez Jimenez, Peron, Carias, Odria, Stroessner, Rojas Pinilla, and our own— your own, I mean—Batista. But their words are like our cigar smoke." His large hands rose, miming smoke. "I'd be interested," he said, "for four thousand dollars."

"I'm not drunk," Fidel said, tapping his mustache. "It's a deal. Will you take it in monthly installments?"

That was equitable.

And after such doubts, Bayo, at the end, had wanted to join Fidel! My stomach ached. And I realized, as I looked over the bow, that I had heard the story of Bayo's negotiations only from Fidel, heard it only after Bayo offered to join us (and had he? I had heard that only from Fidel, too).

I have Bayo's rules in my new notebook (where, I wonder now, did I leave my old notebook, my old life? and why?). The pages are filled with diagrams of tactics, the ink already dissolving from the seawater that has washed over our small bow. I am chief of staff (for I was Bayo's best student) as well as medical officer. —What vanity! Pride, nausea, and fear: my companions till the end. The old man outside Obrajes was right: I am a nervous ambitious man.

The radio receives, but doesn't transmit anymore. No one knows how to fix it. Today, as ordered, Pais began the rising he did not want in Santiago. Courageously, loyally, he had followed Fidel's instructions. A few men clustered below deck, near the set, and passed its words back to us, and above, where I stood looking at the sullen ocean. The customs house has been set on fire. Political prisoners have been freed from Boniato jail. Dozens of policemen and soldiers have been killed. Batista has suspended civil rights throughout the province.

Everyone, Fidel said, after assembling us on deck, should be cheered by the news. The 26th of July has many followers capable of striking blows at the dictator, willing to make the supreme sacrifice for the Movement. But I think we all felt (though would not say, for we are tender of each other's morale, and to see the extent of one's own fear on another's face might be devastating) that it was only another big mess. The actions don't coordinate with our arrival, because we haven't arrived. We're still at least a day from the coast. And we were meant to land at Niquero, where trucks and supplies wait for us. But Pino says he can't find Niquero.

12/1/56: Each day brings new disasters, comic calamities, farcical presentiments of doom. The only omens anyone trusts anymore are bad ones. Last night we headed in for the coast, looking for the Cabo Cruz light. We must make land soon, for we're about to run out of food, fuel, and water. All night long the boat went back and forth along the coast, searching for the light. A wind sprang up, buffeting the ship. No stars were out. Roque climbed to the top of the bridge tower to get a better view of the coast. The tower slanted beneath him, he tripped and fell overboard. Ricardo, standing with me by the rail, turned his back to the sea. "Let the son of a bitch die," he said. "The boat is too heavy. And he's too fat. We can spare that shithead better than the machine guns he cost us."

Towards morning we found Roque, barely conscious, but still alive. He's lost some weight; but we've lost another day.

Castro seems to me now like a badly coordinated careless giant. He is something more than merely ambitious, and he is never anxious. If I close my eyes this evening I see him towering over us, somewhere off the bow of an absurdly small white boat. He looks a god of the sea, huge, powerful, charismatic, smiling at something we cannot see off in the distance. He is as heedless and unworried as a child, and as unknowing of what he does. He tosses us about, hardly noticing what happens to the tiny figures; he flings us here and there like toys, knocks us over, throws a few more of us into the air.

12/2/56: We've run aground. A salt-marsh swamp, Pino says, near a place called Belic. At least he hopes it's near Belic. He hopes it's near shore. There's no moon, and it's impossible to see ahead through the tangle of vines and mangrove branches. They are like cross-hatchings that lead to deeper shades of darkness.

12/7/56: *I'm alive*—the song my mother's fingers sang as they drummed on the glass table. When I look at my comrades' bodies, sprawled on the ground in filthy clothing, I wonder why we don't say that to each other after every sentence, after every word of every sentence. Or perhaps we do, and until this moment I haven't had the ears to hear this endless assertion. We're alive, we all chorus, we're alive. It's our achievement. That is the music I'll hear now in our voices, whatever doleful lyric we recite.

They found us on December 5 at four in the afternoon, at Alegria de Pio, three days' march from where the *Granma* had run aground. On Castro's orders we had thrown most of the extra supplies—the remaining heavy equipment that had escaped Roque's panic, the explosives, extra ammunition boxes, food, and medicine—into the muck of the salt marshes. We couldn't get them ashore; we couldn't survive on shore without them. The black boxes half sunk into the marsh, as if the swamp couldn't believe our folly and wanted us to reconsider. The area around the boat looked like the careless giant's picnic ground.

A fighter plane flew over the yacht, and we jumped into the swamp, up to our knees in thick mud. It was night, and impossible to see through the tangled low branches of the mangroves and the thick vines that grew between them. Ricardo, walking in front of me, carrying his rifle with both hands over his head, tripped over a mangrove root and grabbed at a vine with his hand. His rifle fell into the marsh. He screamed, and one of the men behind us fired a shot. I heard Almeida cursing him. The creepers have thorns that ripped the skin on Ricardo's good hand. I stopped and bandaged it as best I could. The air was humid, unpalatable, dense with mosquitoes. You couldn't swat them away, your hand just moved through the indifferent swarms. They got into your nostrils and mouth. Immediately little walnuts formed on my arms and neck. But the worst thing about them was the sound, a continual low fretful annoyance. The men just ahead of me looked like wraiths, animated by the sin of their past lives, unable to stop marching, a purgatorial march (as if, if they just kept marching, they might get out). Our sins or his? I could hear the splat of men farther down the line falling into the mud and cursing. Why can't my lips form those words? (It's all too vivid to me. When one of them names an act, a part of the body, an excretion: I see it.) Behind us the shadow of a naval frigate moved towards the yacht. It fired towards the shore, several kilometers away. The roar shook the vines back and forth slightly, like the strings of a monstrous piano. More planes passed overhead, drowning out the sound of the cursing, the mosquitoes, the squish of our boots sinking into the mud. It wouldn't be long, I thought. It was hard to breathe the damp air. I tried to concentrate on breathing, to keep away my terror. It was hard to push through the thick wet paste of the marsh with one's shins. I tried to concentrate on the difficulty of taking the next step. My boots had filled with sandy mud. I tried to concentrate on the difficulty of lifting my feet. "The swamp," Nico said quietly. He hardly spoke anymore. He meant we would die in the swamp. Men dropped their knapsacks, their canteens into the slime, to make walking easier. "Don't throw away your rifle," Marcos shouted, passing on a message from Castro. He had tied one of his handkerchiefs around his head to keep the sweat from his eyes; it was the brightest thing in the swamp. "The only thing worth holding on to is your rifle."

"No," Ricardo said from behind me. "Your shoes." We knew what he meant: for running away.

After three hours' march the tangle of branches let some light through. The ground grew sandier and firmer. Men lay down for a few moments on the damp beach. But we had to hurry onward. The white yacht, clearly visible in the dawn, marked our location. A B-27 appeared and flew over the boat, to the shore at Niquero, ten kilometers away, and then back again, looking for us. Castro's plan—his new plan—is to move directly to the Sierras, and then make contact with the city network. He is sure we can establish ourselves among the peasants there, find food until the city sends aid. We had never, he said, intended to topple the dictatorship at one blow but to launch a revolutionary campaign that, with agitation and sabotage, would culminate in a general revolutionary strike. He told us this with great certainty, as if the past weeks had never happened, there had been no boat too small for the seas, beached a few miles from shore, plainly visible to the aircraft, no broken clutch, no missed meeting at Niquero. We had always meant to run aground in a swamp near Belic and throw most of our supplies overboard. You always sound so certain, Chaco had said to me as I lay on the stones in La Paz. But I am a pony of certainty compared to Fidel the Horse. *He is a man without a memory.*

Three more days of marching, in from shore, to dusty earth and low thick gray-and-brown scrub. When someone fainted we called a brief rest. But the planes continued flying overhead, and we had to move on. Some countrypeople ran out from their hut and told Almeida that they would offer a prayer for us to the Virgen de Cobre.

"What's that?" I asked.

A theological debate ensued in my squad:

"A black virgin," Almeida said. "It's made of wood. It was found in the bay by Indians, before the Church came to Cuba. A miracle." Almeida has grown a skimpy black beard. His small brown face is surrounded by streaming hair. He looks like a cartoon that forms a face no matter which way it's turned.

"Horseshit," Ricardo said. "It was placed in the bay by the Archbishop, for the Indians to find."

"Shut up, asshole."

And I saw a mound of steaming dung, an anus. I believe too much in the power of words, magical oaths, to give one's word—as if the oaths were a solid fort that one lived inside. Not Fidel! He doesn't inhabit his formulations; he is the motion between, the verb itself.

The 5th of December. We had walked through the night, following along the edge of a cane field. Towards dawn, few of the men felt they could go on. Every few minutes the whining would begin somewhere in the line, comrades begging the squad leaders for a rest period. Castro, at the center—the most protected area (though wherever he is, is called the center)—ordered a halt at daybreak. We made camp in the thickets at the edge of a dense wood. Across a wide dirt road were the cane fields of Alegria de Pio. The long curved leaves dangled down from five-foot stalks, leaf over leaf, a light film of dust coating the green leaves near the road. The sharp thin lines of the leaves had the clarity of a line drawing in a children's book. (The reward for vigilance!) To the right of us there were more woods; and beyond the rows of cane an open field of short brownish grass sloped down to more thick brush, palm trees and hardwood. The sunlight and hunger made me woozy. The air felt like a thick scratchy blanket. I passed out, and slept through the morning. Towards noon Marcos woke me, to tell me a dream. The sunlight hurt my eyes, and I closed them as I listened to his deep slow voice. We were marching through a swamp, he said, Fidel sounded very sure of himself giving orders, but he didn't really know the way out. The swamp was hundreds of miles long—Marcos could feel its length in the dream. Che knew the way out, but no one would listen to him —yet. Marcos went on with his recitation, but as he spoke I dozed off again, his words mixed with the pain the rocks were causing my back and I inhabited his dream. My body ached all over as we walked through the swamp. The swamp was alive and malign. The mud made a loud heavy droning sound as it sucked our boots down, trying to keep us there. My heart was beating rapidly, and I awoke to the great noise of planes circling over our hiding place; brightly colored Air Force piper cubs, yellow, blue-green, like streamers thrown into the air and carried about by the wind. Men in olive-green uniforms—my comrades, I remembered now—ignored the planes; they stood by a field of sugar cane, cutting pieces of thick brown-and-green stalk and sucking on them. The planes came in at lower and lower altitudes. Still unsteady on my feet, I set up a first-aid station, to treat the men's feet. My last pair were Nico's, huge blistered things, tormented by his new boots. Grayish-brown fungus grew over the sores. I cleaned and bandaged them. It was four o'clock in the afternoon. I know, because when the firing started I looked at my watch. I had been leaning against a palm tree with Nico, after treating him, eating half a sausage and two crackers—the day's food: I said something to him about the sausage, but the words were absorbed by the drone of the planes. (Hear that whine? It means: Run away.) Anyway, Nico wasn't much of a conversationalist; no more stories of Fidel. The firing began—so many explosions seemed solid, like a curtain falling. The shots came from all over, from the woods, the cane, the sky, the earth. Bits of bark showered from the trees. The bullets, I thought crazily, were chipping the world away. Nico began to bawl. I lay prone. Why? Once, long ago, I'd been taught to. I heard someone shout, What time is it? What time is it? and I looked at my watch. But I was the one shouting.

Almeida ran back towards us, down the edge of the road. There were little puffs of dust near his feet, where the bullets landed. Another comrade came up from the other direction and dropped a black box of ammunition by my feet.

"Pick it up," I ordered from the ground.

"Fuck yourself," he said. "That's all shit now."

He ran towards the cane field. I left my medicines behind and picked up the box of ammunition. I followed him towards the cane. Nico grabbed his boots from the ground and ran after me.

"Where's Fidel?" Almeida shouted over the awful din of the firing. "Where's Fidel?" He ran down the path towards us, lifting his legs up suddenly very high, as if the ground burned his feet. Did he think he could skip away from the bullets? "I can't find Fidel," he shouted. He wanted orders. I shook my head—no, I hadn't seen Castro, no, I didn't know what Castro's orders were, no, I didn't give a fuck about Fidel—and ran towards Marcos. He was leaning on his knees in the middle of the path, firing a machine pistol. Nico screamed, "God save my life! God save my life!" I turned, surprised at the sound of his voice after so many days, and saw that he'd been hit in the face and chest at once. He held a boot out towards me, and blood poured from his mouth and nose. As I stupidly reached out towards his boot I too was hit, a sharp pain in my chest, and wetness on my neck. I touched my left shoulder and looked at the blood on my hand, red rich stuff, unbearably bright, beautiful in the sharp sunlight. I was dying. "There is no God," I told Nico, and held my bloody hand out to him. Nico vomited thick clots of blood, and shouted, "They have killed me!" It came out with a wavery sound, as if he were under water. But the water was his own blood in his mouth. He fired his rifle at the sky again.

I fell on the ground near Marcos. "Oh shit," I said. "I've had it. The stupid fuck has killed me."

"It's nothing," he said, before he looked at me. He went on firing. Then he turned, and I saw in his empty eyes that I was a dead man.

All the firing was from the woods. I looked this way and that down the tree line, and saw some comrades sprawled in the grass. I thought they had been killed in their sleep, and that seemed especially awful to me—as if they'd been cheated of something. The soldiers had moved up on us, and we hadn't heard them because of the planes. I fired towards the trees with the greatest passion I had so far felt in my life. I couldn't see them, but I wanted to kill as many of them as I could. I wanted to kill some of them. Even one. I wanted to set the wood on fire, the shore on fire the island the sea the continent on fire. But the old gun I'd taken on the boat was a piece of shit, and jammed after two shots.

Marcos was no longer next to me in the dirt. He had left me to die. I wanted to have a good death, and remembered a story that I'd been read as a child, about a man freezing to death in Alaska. I saw myself leaning against a single pine tree in a field of snow, the open field, watching flakes come down in the sunlight like motes of dust. Why weren't there any of my tracks in the snow? My boot marks were filling up with new snow, and it would all be as it had been before, as if I'd never been! I hadn't accomplished anything! I started to say a favorite poem of my mother's. Time blots me out, as flakes on freezing bodies fall/I'd like to kill that stupid bastard/I see the whole round world with every animal and every flower and it's all one big pile of shit, a big big big pile of shit/and every leaf and every branch/is shit too, and you're a stupid shit, and there's nothing that I like at all. Come down and carry me away O avalanche! Baudelaire (was it Baudelaire?) he was really a stupid shit, living in his mother's house, waiting for his mistress to sneak up the back stairs, Fernando was right, he didn't know what the fuck he was talking about. Somebody on his knees near the cane field shouted, "We surrender! Please don't kill us! We surrender! Don't kill us! We're like you! Please don't kill us!" And Ricardo, already in the cane behind him, shouted so everyone could hear him, "Shut up you stupid cowardly fuck! Nobody surrenders you piece of cow dung!" I was already dead, I didn't want to surrender, I wanted to fire my rifle more, I wanted to kill some of them. Raul Suarez crawled towards me from the edge of the woods, and I saw his body jerk upward as a bullet hit him. He reached me and showed me his chest, a black stain in the middle of the dust on his shirt. He started to rip the shirt open, so I could examine him. "Don't," I said. "I can't do anything for you. I have no medicines. I'm dying." And he was going to die, too, the poor bastard, another of the giant's casualties. Six or seven spectral pilgrims crawled past me towards the cane, and Suarez joined them, abandoning me to my recital. I turned the page to a poem that had solaced Nehru in jail. A lonely impulse of delight/Drove me to having my face shoved in the dust the mud the muck the shit/I balanced all brought all to mind/The years to come seemed waste of breath, what the fuck is he talking about? he doesn't know what he's talking about either, poets are a useless bunch of pricks, Fernando was right, I should have gone with him, and not that one-eyed charlatan opportunist liar with his fake eye, this was the blood I saw in his eye, my blood. I touched my neck as if it might suddenly have magically healed. My hand came away wet. It felt very hot there. A waste of breath the years behind. That was true. A voyeur of revolutions. I wished I'd killed more of them. Any of them. It was all wasted time. Gandhi was a joke! I wanted to kill those soldiers more than I wanted anything. Except my life. And I wanted that so I could kill some of them. I wished I'd killed more of them in Guatemala.

Ricardo came towards me from behind, from out of the cane, on his belly, pulling his long bulk forward with his hands and forearms the way Bayo had taught us. What kind of animal was Ricardo?

"I'm dying," I said. I thought he wanted to have a better look at my death. Another theological debate ensued:

"Stop praying," he shouted angrily.

"I'm not praying."

"Yes, you are, you bastard. I heard you saying the rosary. You're a coward, Che. I thought you were a Communist. I thought you were an atheist. I thought you meant the things you taught me. But one small bullet wound and you start saying the rosary."

"Two wounds," I said. It was important he get it right—my wounds were my last, my greatest, my only accomplishment. "And I wasn't saying the rosary. I was reciting poetry." I was dying. Soldiers we couldn't see were scattering the field with bullets as if bullets were seeds. It was important that he get it right; it didn't matter at all.

Ricardo stupidly stood up and pulled on my shoulders. He ripped the skin further, and I could feel more blood come out. He wanted to kill me! Then he lay down again. "Poetry! You're worse than a coward. You're a faggot bastard asshole."

"Fuck you," I said. "Everybody fucks your mother. Especially Castro." How could he talk that way to me? "I'm dying," I said.

He smiled. "Not yet." He stood up again—he would get killed like that! —and dragged me a few feet towards the cane, by my legs. I couldn't feel anything anymore in my shoulder. He got down next to me again, putting his face close to mine, and ordered me to crawl the rest of the way. Bullets kicked up dust just behind us. "You stupid Argentine scum, if you don't move I'll bash in your sick little chest with my rifle."

This must be love, I thought—and I meant it. Ricardo's affection astounded me! The feeling of rescue flooded me. We made it to the cane. The soldiers still hadn't come out of the woods towards us. They fired furiously into the cane, but they couldn't see us clearly anymore. Suarez pushed his hand in my face. His thumb was gone, blown off. "Use a handkerchief," I said to Marcos, who always had one. I reminded him how to bandage a wound. Airplanes came in low and strafed the cane field behind us. Almeida shouted,

"Where's Fidel? Where's Fidel?" like a bird call. He wanted orders on what to do next. I couldn't see Almeida through the leaves.

"Fuck Fidel," Ricardo mumbled.

I saw a fat comrade try to hide behind one of the cane stalks. I saw a man lying on the ground with his fingers to his lips shouting, "Silence! Silence! Silence!" as if it were the noise that was killing him. I saw a man bleeding from his face, who took off his belt and tried to tie it to the top of a stalk, to hang himself.

I moved on my belly towards the last rows of cane. I shouted for Almeida and the others to follow me. The men had to be moved quickly, before the planes returned and strafed the cane again. My chest stung as I crawled, but not with the profound pain of before. Suddenly the field to my left exploded into high flames and thick black smoke. I choked on the air, rolling over on my back and kicking my legs out from the strain. If you can keep your head and all about you are losing theirs and their hands and their faces and their lungs then you're a stupid dumb fuck who doesn't know what he's doing and you deserve to die. . . .

"Shut up Che! You've prayed enough! You're making me puke!"

I crawled again, until I had to rise and lead the men, running across the open field into the woods beyond. I knew as I ran that I wasn't going to die. In the woods Marcos bandaged my neck, while Ricardo watched, drinking in my winces. The wound was close to the shoulder, and much less serious than I had at first thought; so I wasn't ready to become a recitation yet. With me were Raul Suarez (badly wounded in the chest and hand), Almeida, Ricardo, Marcos, and Benitez. We walked farther into the woods, until night came, and slept piled on each other, nourished by the smell of blood and feces and sweat; exhausted; defeated; ecstatic. Mosquitoes blanketed us, attracted, I thought, by the blood.

"Can't you do something about that sound? You're wheezing like a broken machine."

"What sort of machine?" Benitez asked innocently. Older than the rest of us, a veteran of Spain, he was also the most convivial. He loved conversation.

"A toilet, Benitez, you stupid Spanish shit. What the fuck does it matter what kind of machine?"

This morning I counted our resources: two canteens, the rifles and pistols. Two packs, mine and Almeida's, but no food. Marcos has only one shoe. I counted the men over to myself, as if their names formed a poem. There was joy in looking at them. Blood covered Ricardo's sleeve—my blood; and blood mixed with dirt dried on my chest and fell away in big flakes. Suarez's hand looked already infected. Almeida had ripped his shirt sleeves to bandage wounds, and the tatters hung from his arms, making him a scarecrow. In the distance, somewhere else in the woods, I heard the crack of a few shots. "Army patrols," Ricardo said, "shooting stragglers." He sounded as if the image gave him pleasure. (After all, he wasn't among them.) Benitez advised against marching during the day, to avoid the patrols, and so I might rest from my attack. So we remained in the wood, and I made these notes.

"Good," Ricardo has just said. He has come over to my resting place, where I lean against the rough bark of a tree. He is six feet, half a foot taller than I am. From his shirt pocket he takes his new pair of metal-rimmed spectacles, and holds them over me. "Write more," he says. "Blind the world!" It was while learning to read that Ricardo acknowledged his need for glasses. He thinks that the little letters, so difficult to decipher and make yield their names, have robbed him of his once-perfect vision. He's squatted down next to me while I write, and cleared the leaves away. With a small stick he's drawn the alphabet in the dirt; an obscure mockery of my writing. Hearing the scratching, Suarez woke up screaming, and Almeida put his hand over his mouth.

I see now that, giddy with my returned life, I've made the battle sound funnier than it was (it wasn't funny at all). From survivors' stories the business of war finds new recruits.

As we wait for nightfall the army might come upon us; if we move through the woods we might run into one of the patrols. The men sit rigidly, their heads down, immobilized by anxiety. Or they lie on the ground, in corpse position, not even twitching in their sleep. If I could look into their minds—how I wish I could!—I would find them equally still in their dreams, afraid that if they reached out a hand for that lovely glass of water it would shatter, and the army would discover us. Our once-new olive uniforms are covered with dirt and excrement. I cannot take my eyes off this raggedy army, their chests moving in and out in small spasms. I find I can hear the music most intensely when I watch them. *We're alive.*

12/8/56: I led the men out of the woods last night, and towards (I hope) the Sierras. Perhaps the others will follow Fidel's plan (though he might have another plan by now), and find their way to the mountains. If there are others.

For food, we took handfuls of grass and chewed on them. I stuck a few holes in a can of condensed milk. Each man got a little of that, measured out in the end of a vitamin capsule, and a few sips of water.

"Castro's dead," Benitez said, licking his lips, as if he'd just finished a greasy meal.

"Shut up," Ricardo said. He was furious. Benitez had spoken the worst blasphemy, the only desecration that Ricardo recognized. Once he had been the first to curse Fidel, but now he could not bear the thought of Castro's death. So many sacrifices had made Fidel holy. What did Fidel matter, I wondered? This business was over. And yet he did matter. It couldn't be over. It mattered more now that he be alive than it had when one could almost sensibly have had faith in him, love for him, loyalty to him. Fidel had to be somewhere in the mountains, ready to lead us into new disasters. We all felt it, even the atheist Ricardo. By the deaths of so many comrades Fidel had taken all our soul stuff, all our brains and courage, into his keeping. We thought we might be, felt we had to be, stumbling towards him, our mouths stuffed with bitter grass. Who could really believe that if this discredited leader were still alive the Revolution might move forward?

And yet we did believe that.

12/10/56: "I'm never taking my boots off again," Marcos said.

We walked through thick scrub, tearing at it with our hands, to get to the ocean. (My plan is to keep the ocean in sight, on our right hand, to make sure we are moving towards the Sierras.) There was too much moonlight—the army might spot us. There wasn't enough moonlight—we kept stumbling, and falling on our faces over the roots and rocks in the field.

When Marcos spoke I realized that for five days I had been carrying Nico's boot in my pack, that I'd taken it from his hand in the field, as he'd coughed, vomited I mean, his life up.

Another theological moment:

"Here," I said, handing the boot on.

"A miracle!" Benitez exclaimed, as if I'd just now materialized the shoe.

"Try it on first," Ricardo said, ever the doubter.

It fit.

"A miracle," Benitez repeated, this time triumphantly.

"It's not the kind of world," I said, remembering a friend, another casualty of the struggle against imperialism, "where a person can take his boots off."

"More of Guevara's Marxism," Raul Suarez said. He was feverish now, and rarely spoke. I think he felt that as a doctor I had failed him, that if I had looked at him instead of reciting poems I might have saved him.

"Not more of his Marxism," Ricardo said disgustedly. "More of his po-etry."

"I don't care," Marcos said. "I think Che's right. I'm not taking off my boots again until Jesus comes back."

No one asked why I hadn't given him the boot before.

12/11/56: I asked Marcos what the Sierras were like.

"It's like the movies," he said. And then he added, nonsensically, or making all the sense in the world, "I'm hungry." He is a big man, and the hunger seems hardest for him. But I cannot allow another adventure like yesterday's. We had come near a palm-wood house on the shore. There was music playing inside. If this was a celebration, I thought, it would be best not to show ourselves. The peasants would announce our presence all over the area, simply for the joy of gossiping. But the others wanted to eat. I went with Benitez towards the house. The music stopped, and a man said, "And now let's drink to our comrades in arms, whose brilliant and courageous exploits . . ." We ran back to the brush. The men complain often, but I can't risk another sortie. Yesterday has made the world ominous to me, the trees might betray us.

"Yanqui movies," Marcos said, remembering his subject. "About the Wild West. The Sierra Maestra is large estates run by foremen. The foreman's job is to keep the peasants from planting little plots of coffee trees on the unused land. If he sees a peasant's house he burns it. Sometimes the countrypeople can't take it anymore, and they wait for the foreman and shoot him in the head. The Rural Guard come for the peasants. They make examples of them. They tie people to trees and flay their skin off. Then they take the peasants' land."

"The countrypeople don't make examples," Ricardo said, smiling—a very disagreeable sight. "We don't expect the shits to learn." We were very lucky to have Ricardo with us—if only he wouldn't smile!—as he is the only member of the Movement from a peasant background.

"Benitez," I said, "give me the can of milk." It was time for the day's ration. But Benitez had turned the can upside down in his pocket, and the milk had dribbled onto his shirt.

Ricardo raised his hand beside Benitez, as if he were going to strike him on the head. But he stopped his arm in mid-motion and turned away. He knew that Benitez could bear denunciation or a blow, but it would be torture to him not to be spoken to. Ricardo has an instinct for a man's weakness, his fear, how to punish him.

No one spoke to Benitez for the rest of the day.

12/14/56: At night, land crabs scuttled about our feet, among the red dirt and saw-toothed rocks near the shore. We stomped them. "A massacre," Marcos said proudly, holding up one of the slain by a claw.

"The first great rebel . . ." Suarez said.

". . . victory," Ricardo said, finishing the thought for him. Suarez's head lolled to one side, and he had difficulty remembering the end of his sentences. Ricardo had to hold him up on the march.

Suarez was wrong, though. It turned into another defeat: wide-winged observation planes fly over the shoreline; a fire was out of the question. So we ate the gelatinous parts of the carcass raw, and it made our thirst monstrous. The canteens are utterly empty.

I took the tiny pump from my vaporizer and sucked up rainwater from the declivities in the rocks. This yielded four or five drops for each of us, shared out in the eyepiece of the fieldglasses. There is a foul taste in my mouth. I feel like my tongue is rotting.

So I allowed a further folly: Benitez and I approached another shack. As we neared the door we saw a uniformed man, clearly outlined in the light from behind, a silhouette in the window, with an M1 rifle.

Benitez thinks the army has scattered patrols among the peasant families, expecting that we'll look to them for food. So there's no possibility of help from that direction. To enter one of their houses would be like playing Russian roulette.

12/16/56: Small planes fly over the sea to our right, saying unintelligible things through loudspeakers. Almeida and Benitez, veterans of the Moncada, say that the planes are calling for our surrender. But if we surrender we'll be slaughtered.

We moved farther inland. Walking on the cliffs would leave us too exposed, so we must pick our way among the rocks, between the high paths and the sea. If the army finds us, we'll be trapped.

I look from face to face for reassurance, to hear the song of our survival. No one has the strength to walk anymore.

12/18/56: "I can't stand it," Marcos said. "I'm going to drink my own urine." His puffy face suffused with pain. Tears would have come to his eyes if he'd had the moisture for tears.

I see no choice but to risk contact with the peasants. There is a shack near the road here (Puercas Gordas, Ricardo says). It's a tottery wood-frame thing, with a small sagging porch. No windows on the side of the house, and no metal chimneypiece. It looks poor enough. A small child in a dirty white shirt and shorts has run into the house, screaming at the sky. I think she has spotted us in the low gray-and-brown brush where we're hiding on our bellies. There may be soldiers inside. But I see no other choice. Almost none of the men are willing to go on. We must throw ourselves upon their mercy.

12/19/56: *We're alive.* And they know that Fidel—that was what they call him—is alive too. It won't be easy to kill him, the father said. Fidel is an honest man. He always did what he said he would do. He said he would come this year, and he had. (Jesus Christ, I thought. He was right!) The radio says Fidel is a bandit (they are very proud to have a radio). But they know there was a family who gave his men some pork, and Fidel paid them for it. The rich lie about Fidel. (Poor Fidel! the mother said. She was a thin woman, with a deeply lined face. I couldn't have guessed her age. She sounded as if she were speaking of one of her own children.) The man said he and his friends would take us to him. But the highways were heavily guarded, and we must leave our shirts and our weapons behind. He is clearly terrified, and yet, against his better judgment, wants to help Castro. I know the feeling!

We left the rifles, and Suarez, there. The families in the mountains passed us from hand to hand. Each countryman seemed to know a safe place where we could rest and find some corn and a little meat. The next man took us farther into the mountains.

12/21/56: Castro was already talking when we got to Cresencio Perez's small farm in the valley. He came towards us shouting, where were our rifles? where were our fucking rifles? There were eight or nine comrades there, and one new man, Comrade Acuna, a peasant missing his top front teeth. He must be very courageous to have joined us under these circumstances! We are not a prepossessing group! "You stupid sons of bitches," Fidel went on, by way of greeting. We met in front of Perez's shack, under some palm trees; a flat dusty yard. At the sound of Fidel's cursing everyone stopped. No one embraced us. We had abandoned our weapons, Fidel said. That was criminal! We should be punished for that, we hadn't paid for our error yet. The price we *should* have paid for abandoning our weapons was our lives. Our arms were our one and only hope of survival if the soldiers had found us. (He looked well, I thought. He had already grown a full brown beard.) We were criminals, he said. Worse than that: we were *stupid.* Standing around him in the chalky dust, we stared at him dumbfounded, exhausted from our last long march to the farm. The countrypeople—Perez and his son (our lost guides), and several local families —were all there watching our humiliation. We looked at the bare ground, like children. Castro had no right to say such things! He had nearly killed us all! And yet I felt the hot shame rising all over my body.

He led us into some woods, a distance from the house, where we made camp. He said nothing else throughout the night. The men with me passed out on the ground. But Castro didn't sleep. I would wake during the night, and I saw that some of the others did also—as if his presence troubled our sleep, made us fitful. And he would be sitting there, watching us, but not looking from face to face. He had led seventy-four of our comrades to their death, and now he sat in judgment on us for hiding our guns! Our guns hadn't been very useful to us so far! We were defeated, for Christ's sake! (And then my mind, like my uncomfortable body, would twist about: He was right. We were defeated, but there was no one to accept our surrender. Batista's army would murder anyone who surrendered. We should have held on to our guns. —But why? So that more of us could be murdered in our sleep, or while eating a last piece of sausage? My mind was trying to accustom itself to the full hopelessness of our situation.)

As for Fidel, he sat and looked at us.

In the morning, as the sun rose, and the men tossed this way and that, wanting to sleep some more, Fidel stood up. Suddenly we were all awake. "We are in the Sierras," he said, lifting his arms high above his head—and, without volition, my eyes looked upwards towards the indifferent sky. (And my nose smelled Fidel's acrid odor.) "The days of the dictatorship are numbered!"

What nonsense! The man is insane! We were all going to die. I began to recite poetry again. Fidel went on talking, in a high excited voice, as if he were addressing a crowd of thousands (and perhaps in his imagination, his megalomaniacal imagination, he was), speaking of the help we'd gotten from the Sierra peasants. We must learn their lives. The foremen who hound them, and steal their land, and destroy their shacks. If you can make a heap of all your winnings/And risk it on one turn of pitch and toss/And lose/And lose Nico, and Raul Suarez, and Chaco. But Chaco wasn't his responsibility. No, he was the North Americans'. And never breathe a word about your loss. That didn't seem Castro's style, not breathing a word. He'd breathe a lot of words, explain it away. The loss was really a victory; my mother's magic; the dialectic. The peasants worked in the plain fifteen days, he was saying, gathered a few pesos, bought salt and a little fat, and then returned to their coffee trees. They will never have enough land of their own to live on. The Agricultural Bank gives only to the rich. When the Rural Guard pass a countryman's house, they take what they want, a fine chicken perhaps. (I'd like a fine chicken!) The merchants cheat them. There are no doctors in the Sierras, no schools. That will be our life. We will join ourselves to them. If you can talk with crowds and keep your virtue,/Or walk with Kings—nor lose the common touch,/We have entered the Sierras (he said), people had accepted us, buoyed us up. (I saw the silhouette in the peasants' window, holding a rifle. The army, too, lived with the peasants! The voice drinking the brave comrades' health—who else had joined him in the toast?) In the rigors of the march, the sacrifices to come (there was a true word, I thought, touching the painful scar near my neck), we would be made to conform to our new medium, to the life of the countrypeople. Our rough city edges would be worn away. He went on:

He went on.

And on.

He spoke of the time when more peasants would join us, like Comrade Acuna, of the help the countrypeople had given us, of the fear they had already overcome—because they had seen we were willing to keep *our* word (his actually), to begin the struggle, at the sacrifice of our own lives. (That word again! I looked at his eyes—they stared off over our heads at the foliage beyond. Our own lives, I thought. Or other people's.) If you can bear to hear the truth you've spoken/Twisted by knaves to make a trap for fools. Why the recitation? Because I didn't want to believe anymore. (I looked about me: many of us had beards now—like a religious sect.) Had we known, really, how enormous the odds were when we set out from Tuxpan, known that of the eighty-eight men standing on the dock in the sunlight in their brand new uniforms, seventy-two (or -four, or -six) would die? Which of us had the imagination for so much death? Did he? Oh, he did in his way, but for him it was only one moment in some grander airy construction, the bodies sublimed into a stately thing, a snowflake in stone, the heights of Machu Picchu. And that wasn't real death, at all. And lost and start at your beginning. We would not fail them, he said (I wanted breakfast. My stomach twisted painfully). The Revolution was for the countrypeople.

He went on. He shouted, he cajoled, he whispered, he kicked the dirt with his boot like an impatient horse. He had tossed us into the air, as if we were inexperienced riders, and most of us had come down broken. This was the man who had led his forces against the Moncada, and one unit had gotten lost in traffic, so the rest had died or been captured and hanged by the neck from the bars of the cell while their families watched. This was the genius who had bought the little boat to bring us to Cuba, a toy boat so small that most of our weapons had been thrown overboard to keep it afloat. Our precious weapons! Whose fault was that? We could not fail them, he repeated. They felt that already. They trusted us. Now we must prepare to strike our first blow at the army. The boat had landed in a swamp, three days late for its rendezvous, twenty miles off course. And then he had led us by night into an ambush. (Perhaps they had followed the long leaves and chewed husks from the cane we'd sucked on. Perhaps a guide—one of the trusting countrypeople—had betrayed us. Perhaps no betrayal was necessary. Our beached white boat made our location obvious. And he had told them we were coming. ("Fidel keeps his word," the peasant had said. So he was right to tell them? Impossible! I must think of another poem to recite.) Seventy-four(?) men captured and killed. Nico was right, poor bald Nico. Yours is the earth and everything that's in it. Nico is in it now. Harden ourselves for battle, he said again. Or I wanted to hear it. My heart beat faster with expectation. I hadn't managed to obscure enough of his words! I saw again the grand circular motion of his hand that evening in Mexico. What did deaths matter? The Movement swept all before it. It was inevitable. It must begin now.

No. Horse manure. He's insane. Horse manure to be dried and used as fertilizer. But I longed for battle. If I do accomplish a brave act, I thought, it will be because I am led by a lunatic. I surrender my life now. (But, again, there was no one to accept my surrender.) We did not, I thought, have a chance of surviving his "plans." And yet the schizophrenia I had first felt when I had met him and he drew his plans in the air before me was on me again; and on all the others. He is a madman, and we cannot possibly win. And yet that silence, that night vigil, waking on the forest floor to find him still squatting there looking off into the distance, that voice that came out of the dry place of our defeat, the loss of our weapons, the wreck of all our hopes, and then spoke of—victory! Impossible! And yet, I believed—or half believed, or half of me believed—that voice. Why? And why do the countrypeople believe him, believe us, help us?

He spoke, according to my watch, for two hours more. I finished all of the Baudelaire, and was halfway through the Neruda poems I knew.

1/11/57: Acuna, in the stillness of the woods, began to shout that he'd thought our camp would have plenty of food and water, and real anti-aircraft defenses. Now planes chased him, and he had nowhere to hide, no food, and no water. Almeida calmed him. But the next day the gap-toothed bastard sneaked off back to his home, taking his rifle with him.

1/15/57: The countrypeople bring news of the deserter Acuna: He boasted to his village of his activities with the guerrillas, the battles we've fought, etc. A neighbor betrayed him. Captain Rosellos has beaten him, shot him four times, and then hanged him.

As political officer, I spoke briefly this evening on the lesson of Acuna's death: the value of cohesion, the uselessness of trying to flee individually what is now a collective destiny.

Ricardo rose from the circle and clapped his approval. (But he clapped very slowly. Meaning?)

1/16/57: The Magdalena River after two days' march. Fidel ordered that I give target instruction. The attack will be soon.

The men then washed while I lay by the side of the river, a lizard in the sun. I didn't want to lose my sweat, not yet, before the battle. The smell of my body gives me a sense of security, comforts me. Marcos made a critical remark about my stink, and I said that the torrent would be too strong for me, the shock too much for my chest. "You could still wash," he said.

I stretched out in the sun and pretended not to hear. The overlapping sounds of the river, the single note become many, become one again, mixed with my body odor, and upheld me, as I floated towards the sky.

1/17/57: We marched along a narrow rarely used footpath in the shady woods, following machete slashes that a peasant (Melquiades Elias) made for us. He has slashed the side of trees and broken the brush where the path was over-grown. It comes out on a hill overlooking the La Plata barracks and the river. Throughout the afternoon we kept the barracks under surveillance. The main building is a long one-story wooden rectangle, with a white zinc roof. Two small storage huts are on either side in front. Construction of more storage space is going on, piles of wood lie in front of the barracks, and ten or eleven men work without shirts, their chests exposed. A boat came into the inlet, soldiers landed, others went aboard.

Somewhere between this hill and the barracks there must be guardposts. But where? There is only one way down to the barracks, and if we cannot keep them from giving the alarm it will be impossible to attack.

We pulled back into the woods to let two soldiers on horseback pass. They had a prisoner, tied about the chest and waist with a thick brown rope; and they pushed him ahead of them with their rifle barrels. The peasant, a thin fellow in a dirty green sweater, cried that he hadn't helped anyone. "I'm just like you fellows," he said—and I remembered our comrade shouting this at the soldiers from the cane field. This was, finally, the most basic of pleas—that we are all the same, all embodied beings; held by or holding others; escaping or failing to escape. What horseshit! The scream of the misty inane, of idealism, "not the particular interests of the proletariat, but of human nature in general, without class, the man who belongs to no class, has no reality, who exists only in the realm of philosophical fantasy." (I have been using the *Manifesto* for our political instruction classes.)

The Rural Guard, thoroughgoing creations of Marx, were having none of the peasant's immaterial philosophizing. "Shut up you shithead, or I'll whip you."

"I'm just like you fellows," the peasant repeated, sobbing.

"I'm tired of this boring fuck," one of the guards said. He shot the peasant through the head. The man fell to the ground, and one of the soldiers got down, undid the hemp rope. He took a piece of cord out of his pack and tied the corpse's hands behind his back, though he wouldn't be using them again until the Day of Judgment. He dropped the hemp rope next to the dead man, and left the body with its feet in the La Plata River, its face turned up towards the sun.

We couldn't bury it, since they might return.

Soon after this, Ossario, one of the most notorious foremen of the region, a fat man in a wide white shirt, appeared on the path, riding an unhappy-looking mule. A young black boy rode behind him. Marcos shouted from the woods, "Halt in the name of the Rural Guard!"

"Mosquito," Ossario said in a slurred voice. (He has provided us with the password; now we need only find the guardpost.)

Fidel came out of the woods, with Marcos and me. He told Ossario that he was an army colonel investigating the slovenly work of the Rural Guard. The rebels should long ago have been liquidated. Fidel's uniform was torn and dirty, and I couldn't imagine that the charade would work. Ossario said nothing, only stared soddenly at Fidel. His thick hand ran up and down the folds of flesh near his chin.

Fidel was able to interpret Ossario's gesture. Something was wrong with the picture: our unsoldierly beards. "I've been in the woods after them for weeks," he said, explaining the hair. He kicked the corpse's chest, pushing it a little farther down into the river. "The Guard is fucked up. Worthless."

Ossario agreed. He looked down at the path, to acknowledge that he spoke with a superior. He was so drunk that I thought he'd fall off the mule. The Guard, he said, spent all their time in the barracks. They were afraid to leave. They ate and farted but they did nothing but go on useless walks right outside their own quarters. Ossario got down off the mule, and took mincing unsteady steps around it in the dirt, peering between his fingers, to show how very meek the Guard were. All the rebels must be destroyed! he shouted. And he— Ossario—could do it himself in a few days! But the Guard couldn't. They were useless scum. They didn't understand the peasants. Since the rebels had come to the mountains the peasants were acting disrespectfully. He had had to beat two of them just this morning. But the Guard let the peasants talk back. Ossario stood with his hand on the mule's flank. The mule was panting for breath. The foreman stared at Fidel, a worried look sliding slowly across the fat of his face. He was becoming suspicious again. Had he seen the men in the shadows of the leaves?

Castro laughed at Ossario with rich appreciation. And then—perhaps carried away by his role (he so loved an imposture), or perhaps to quiet the drunk's suspicion—he placed his foot on the dead philosopher's nose, and crushed it with a crack.

I thought Marcos would puke.

Fidel went over to Ossario then and the two murderers engaged in a cannibal tête-à-tête. They talked of what they would each do to the rebel leader if they caught him, and I saw Fidel, quite unconsciously, I thought, touch his balls when he heard Ossario's plan for them. The black kid smiled at all this. I thought from his expression he'd figured us out, but the smile was a wide warm one; he seemed to be enjoying the fat man's final disgrace. He got off the mule nimbly and came over to me by the edge of the woods. He wore a large floppy hat woven from dried palm fronds; his pants were tattered in the leg. Ossario, busy making an imaginary feast of Fidel's balls, didn't notice the boy's escape. The kid pulled my shoulder, and I bent over so he could whisper in my ear. "I know who you are," he said, in a high excited voice. I tapped my pistol in its webbing. "No. Don't. I was on my way to you. I knew that Fidel was still alive, no matter what the radio said. They can't kill him." He said this with great satisfaction, as if he shared in Fidel's immortality. "He has been sent by God to liberate Cuba. I want to join you. You must let me. I will be one of your bravest soldiers." I put my finger to his lips to quiet him, and he grew instantly restless, like a bridled horse. He must love to talk.

I heard Castro invite Ossario to come to the barracks with us, to take the soldiers by surprise, show the world how unfit they were. I saw Ossario point to a small thatched lean-to among some palms on a hill just below us. The guardpost! We hadn't seen it in all our reconnaissance!

Ossario laughed, thinking of the Guard's humiliation. Here, Fidel said, give us your shirt. One of us will wear it. Look, we'll tie you up so you look like a captured rebel. And the fuddled man allowed Marcos and me to tie him up, using the dead man's rope.

After we had his arms tied (there was just enough rope to go around his fat belly and do the job), I stuffed one of Marcos's handkerchiefs in his mouth and held it in with a piece of cord, which I took from the philosopher's hands. The tied twine cut into Ossario's lips, and he whimpered. He looked up at me, surprised, a dim panic spreading through his rummy fog. He realized finally that he was a dead man. No doubt he wanted to say that he was just like us. "Terrible to die," I said to Marcos, "with your mind so unclear."

Marcos shrugged, indifferent to the joys of ratiocination, the consolations of philosophy.

Ossario's scream was muffled and came out sounding like a fart.

The staff withdrew to the woods to discuss whether to proceed with the attack on the barracks. I was in favor. Marcos was unsure. If we failed we'd be out of bullets. Was it good strategy to make an attack whose failure would finish us? I said that it was time to begin.

"What would Bayo say?" Ricardo asked, smiling at me. He meant to mock me for being more precipitous than our teacher would have been (and I had been teacher's pet).

"He would say that we cannot win without firing a shot. You can't balance these things forever. You have to choose a place, and begin."

"You just want to kill some soldiers," Ricardo said. He put his arm around me from above, and stared down through his metal-rimmed spectacles. I was his semblable, his brother. "Well, so do I," he added. "So do I."

"Yes," Fidel said. "Che is right."

I was given Ossario's broad white shirt with big pockets. It made me look like a boy, and it stank disgustingly from his sweat—nothing like my own sweet elixir. Deprived of my smell, my comforter, my protective shield, I panicked. We loaded the fat man on the mule behind me, and I rode down the rocky path towards the Guard's hillock. The rest of the men walked in the forest. I could see them moving among the thick green foliage.

"Halt!" It was a young voice.

But I would never be able to deceive him. The shirt's smell was making me sick.

"Halt!" he repeated. Perhaps he was as afraid as I was, peeping through his own fingers.

"Mosquito!" I squeaked finally. "I'm bringing a prisoner in." I entered the little hut of palm fronds and held my pistol in the guard's mouth. He began instantly to weep. Ricardo came from the woods and tied him up. (If the guard had been willing to sacrifice his head he would have saved the barracks.)

The guardpost gave a good view of the barracks. We waited for night. There was a full moon. The ocean looked particularly peaceful and welcoming. One of the soldiers came out and took a look around. It was a hot night, and probably uncomfortable inside. The boy picked up some leaves and put them behind his ear—a pathetic attempt at camouflage; it made me fond of him. I was eager, but waited for Fidel's beginning. The boy had a placid look on his face as he turned towards the river. Fidel opened fire with his automatic weapon, and the soldier fell shouting "O Mother!" Another soldier ran from the barracks, without his shirt, not towards his wounded comrade, but trying to get behind the building where he would be safe. I saw his legs and chest, but the overhanging porch roof hid his face. I hit him on the second shot. His rifle fell to the ground, bayonet first, and remained stuck there. All the men began to fire towards the building then, and I ran down the hill, as if the hill itself were carrying me forward, pushing us towards the soldiers, shooting my rifle as I ran. Were others running with me? Had an order been given? But the hill pushed me onward. Camillo was with me, and Almeida. We reached the flat area, and a group of palm trees. I hugged the sharp-edged bark, crown on crown, and panted for breath. Almeida shouted for the Guard to surrender, and someone replied from the window with a burst from an M-1. Crespo and I threw our hand grenades but they didn't explode. Raul Castro threw a stick of dynamite, and this, too, didn't go off. I took a can of kerosene from Crespo, and felt myself moving forward, certain of what to do, moving as if I were drawn by the fire I was about to set. What if a bullet struck the kerosene as I cradled it in my arms? I saw my hands explode in flame, and myself running forward, holding my burning hands up into the night as if they were candles. Marcos came with me, but he withdrew as the bullets from the barracks hailed down around him. Camillo, too, went back. The firing made an awful din, high sharp sounds. Benitez and I reached one of the outlying huts and threw kerosene on the pile of lumber. It ignited, and the upreach of the flames was my heart's desire realized. One of the soldiers ran out of the barracks, and I shot him in the chest. Stupidly, he ran into the flames and fell there, making a disgusting smell.

From behind the flames and through them we fired hundreds of rounds. The others joined us. The barracks was being wiped out by our bullets. Benitez noticed that there was no answering fire, and he and I entered the main barracks, firing as we went. The long wooden room was filled with smoke; my lungs fluttered. Soldiers lay on the floor screaming. Men stood with their backs to us, and their hand in the air, shouting their surrender in every direction, as if it were a prayer, and we were the angels descended to answer it. "Why wouldn't you let us surrender?" one of them screamed at me angrily. "Why wouldn't you let us surrender?" He said they'd been shouting it for half an hour.

"We couldn't hear you," I said weakly, and I ran through the door into the moonlight and the better air. *I had done my utmost.* The fire had burned down. I wasn't sure that I had told the soldier the truth. Had their voices been drowned out by the sound of our rifles, or the force of our desire, the blood beating in our ears?

No casualties on our side. Four soldiers dead. Five wounded. Eight Springfields. A Thompson sub-machine gun. A thousand rounds. (We had used five hundred.) Cartridge belts, fuel, knives, clothing, some food. A few soldiers had apparently escaped by boat during the fight. The prisoners were angrier at them than at us.

We set fire to the rest of the barracks and withdrew up the mountain, into the woods, carrying their wounded. Under Fidel's orders I used up much of our medicine caring for their injured. Ricardo and Raul wanted to kill the other prisoners, but Fidel released them (except for Ossario, who had been executed by Raul when the battle began). A captured guerrilla, Fidel said, is always killed. A captured soldier is freed. Our men will never surrender, and the soldiers will know that they can always save their lives simply by surrendering. Morale will decide this war, not numbers.

"And," our new comrade, the young black man, said—not the least hesitant about offering his opinion in our council—"if we let them go like that, they'll realize what total shit we think they are as fighters." This view made many of the men suspicious of Walter. But he seemed to me an immediately likable fellow.

I spoke more with him on the march back to the Sierras. His name, he says, is Walter Tulio, but perhaps that is a lie—or story; for his tales about his life all seem a little far-fetched. He has held more jobs than seem possible for someone his age (and he is unclear about what his age is). But I felt that he only meant to entertain. I spoke to him about our politics, the goals of the revolution, and had another theological discussion, explaining to Walter the difference between Divine Election and the leader thrown up by the masses and embodying their will. He looked at me very seriously, though he was clearly uninterested in my abstractions. He said he couldn't see the difference between our two views. When the people speak it with God's big voice, he said, as if he were a university professor dialectically reconciling our positions with a Latin tag. He gave me a broad smile, pleased with his cleverness.

"How old are you?"

"Nineteen."

"You're lying," I said. "You're twelve."

"What does it matter? I know what I think."

I looked at the green-and-brown mountains, my new home. I thought of the young boy outside Fernando's cell, ready to go into the streets if only he had a pistol. "So what do you think?" I asked fondly.

"I think Fidel was sent by God, to free Cuba."

Again, he listened to my explanation. Then he spat on his own hand, wiped it on his pants, and began to tell me about his time working as a baker.

1/18/57: We continued our march into the more inaccessible zones of the Sierras. A grim and contrary army came forward to meet us: the peasants were moving down towards the coast, with their household things, chairs, pots, pans, strapped to their backs with leather cords and hemp. I stopped a young man carrying a table. "Table Man," I said, "what's this about?" But he didn't want to talk. I wouldn't let him go, and he was terrified, kept trying to look at the sky, to peer up around the edges of his table. "Planes are coming," he said finally. "If you keep us here we'll all die." An army corporal and a foreman had told the peasants to leave the zone; the Air Force knew the rebels were in the zone, and were going to bomb it. The man had told the soldiers that there were no rebels here. But if you questioned the corporal the foreman hit you with the machete handle and said you were a liar and a rebel sympathizer.

I told him that the soldiers were deceiving him, that no one knew of our presence in this zone. It was a way to get them off their land, so the foreman could take it.

Yes, the people had thought that at first, and hadn't left their homes. But the attack at La Plata had come just after the corporal's visit, and they had all heard about it. We had killed fifty soldiers and burned their barracks. So there were rebels in the area, and the army knew about it. The bombing story was true.

There was no point in arguing with him. I let him go, reminding him that anyone who cooperated with the army would be killed. At that he put down the table, by bending backward till its feet were on the ground. He asked me to undo the thongs on his chest. "I'm sick of carrying it," he said. It belonged to his father. The boy's name is Rolando, and he wants to join us.

Fidel made another recruit: Moro, who had a whole houseful of goods on his broad back. He will be a powerful addition. "Between them and you," he said frankly, "things can't get any worse."

The Sierras,
May, 1957

Dear Fernando:

I'm sending you some pages from my journal, so you can see how things are with me, how things have changed—and yet how little I, and what I have been looking for, have altered. It is only that I see now that it was in all that I forbade myself—in the violence that is within me, the violence that every day makes and marks our world—that all that you and I sought has been found and fulfilled. Yes, our people must become a great people, single in purpose, treasuring their dignity more than possessions, more than life itself. But it is not, I see now, passive suffering that will accomplish this transformation but active suffering, the violence of armed struggle. The will calls to the will, arouses it; an action will make our men and women rub their eyes in wonder, and follow it. But that action cannot be the leader's martyrdom, his taking more suffering on himself like Saint Sebastian or Saint Gandhi. It must be like the action of the leader of the Cuban people, Fidel Castro. The leader must himself begin the armed struggle, the violence of revolutionary war.

Before the coming of the violence the peasant cannot imagine a change in his life. His world is infrangible. The Rural Guard is a fact to the countrypeople, like the weather, or a large stone in his field. He knows that the foreman and the soldiers will take what they want, his chickens, his house, his land, a part of his crops each year. There is no point in pleading with the soldiers. They have no more mercy than the rock. So the countryman has turned his violence inward, turned his will against himself (as I did, in my way, with Gandhi and his austerities). Perhaps if the right words are said to the Black Virgin, perhaps if the right penance is offered, crawling the steps of the cathedral on one's knees, then the weather will relent. The Guard never will.

But the War begins! At first the peasants cannot believe that we will win. They flee from us, a band of poorly dressed, badly armed rebels. But we win victories. We overrun the army's barracks. We come like fate, we appear as lightning appears, too terrible too sudden! And the countrypeople's disbelief and fear turn to admiration and a desire to help us, to join us, to participate in the work of liberation, the violent overthrow of the dictator. Fernando, there is nothing more beautiful than this transformation, when a man weighted down by the repeated miseries of his life, taught by endlessly recurrent humiliations that no change is possible, that he is worthless, a mere object without power, something to be worked and then when no longer useful (and how soon that is) thrown aside like *shit*—when such a man finds that with a rifle, with Fidel's leadership, he can strike a blow at the oppressor, and for the first time feel himself powerful, a member of the march of humanity. And if the peasant cannot join us directly, then he becomes part of the bloodlines of our support. He stops the slaughter of his animals, saving them for our bad times. He becomes used to bombardment, to machine-gunning, and he builds shelters for himself and his family. When the army arrives, he packs his household goods on his back and flees from the zone with his cattle, leaving only his shack. And the soldiers—enraged at their impotence against us—burn the shack to the ground. When the army leaves, he returns. He rebuilds. His hatred against the army grows concentrated, pure; he has a will to conquer. How terrible that is, and how necessary! I am glad that our enemy is powerful, that our struggle will not be the meaningless musical chairs of a coup d'état. For it is through long struggle and sacrifice that men are transformed.

It is violent action that forms the New Man. It is violence by which he throws off his despair, his passivity, his sense of inferiority. He becomes a free man by killing his oppressor. Gandhi's actions were milky work. The Indian masses didn't strike hard, killing blows against the British. Dread still squats in the Indian heart. They still feel themselves weak things, incapable of resistance, acted upon, suffering their history, not making it. (The untouchable still rings his bell as he boards a bus, lest some Brahman be polluted by the sight of him!) How else but by violence was the New Man ever formed? How did the Incas inscribe their word on the tribes they found? With hardness towards themselves, and with the necessary cruelty and violence. We must become efficient cold selective killing machines.

And we have! We have struck more blows against the army than I have been able to write to you about, we have overrun outposts at Altos de Espinosa, and the barracks at El Uvero. All of the army's isolated barracks, their forward positions have been closed, from fear of us. And an army cannot advance without its point men.

Soon they will mount a counteroffensive. And we look forward to it! For each battle not only strikes wounding blows at the dictatorship, it hardens our forces, and ties us ever more closely to the peasantry. The guerrilla nucleus grows used to the life of the countrypeople, the easily infected bites of the horseflies that drop from the macaw trees (I tell the men not to scratch, but they disobey; dirt gets into the bites, and abscesses form); we grow inured to days without food. In some of the long nights we spent in the mountains,

Fernando, I thought that we had gone hungry. But we had no notion of hunger, of having neither food, or the certainty that one would ever have food again. Hunger like that really wearies one. And it is the everyday experience of the countrypeople. (There is no train home from here!) Violent acts cut one off from any return to the cities, to normal life under the dictator. And the people would not trust us if we had not taken that ineradicable step. We live with the people now, as they live; the War forced us to share their lives. We have become part of the peasantry.

Their lives must change. They need shoes against parasites, vitamins, decent clothing, machinery to work their land with. This will require industry. But I see now that all that I hated—the "diabolism" of manufactured things—comes not from industry itself, but from the terrible perversion of it by the Imperialists. They starve the great mass of humanity to produce immoral luxuries for themselves. The Imperialists have twisted the people's achievements, and they have chained up the people's power, thwarting the world to come. But industry itself is good, it is not the work of the bourgeoisie, but of the great masses themselves. Industrialization is the glory of the workers; it is their will in its ineradicable continual efflorescence. The workers of the world will juggle the instruments of industry and science as so many playthings. They create and destroy in the endless activity of their will, their violence. For it is violence that makes the world, Fernando. There is violence in opening the ground for planting, in building a factory, there is violence in the surgeon's knife, there is violence in the revolutionary's gun. Through the activity of the revolution I have been able to overcome my blindness to the beauty of industry, to join myself to its spirit. Through the revolutionary war I have joined myself with the fruitful violence of the world, made myself one with it. Violence is not a demon to be wrestled with. It is the thread that knits us together, that binds flesh and blood into one compact. The guerrillas are bound up with the peasantry through the War—and the peasants and workers are themselves the upsurge, the violence of the world. That upsurge is life. I will not mind if death surprises me on this island, if I know that my funeral dirge will be beaten out in the staccato of machine-gun fire, in new chants of war and victory.

Our violence is not like theirs. Theirs is demonstrations; they want sacrificial victims, scapegoats: the man chosen at random, killed to terrify others, turn them to stone, make them afraid to come out of their burrows. Their work is not violence, but terrorism, torture, that dirty thing. We want to destroy their terror theater, destroy the enemy utterly, not keep him in a subhuman condition so we might torment him for our amusement. We want to transform the world so that there are no more oppressors and oppressed, overthrow the ruling class, not replace it, do away with rulers and ruled forever.

I had thought that our suffering, freely accepted, would shame the soldiers, our country's tormentors. But the soldiers, like the mercenaries in Guatemala, are just instruments of the Imperialists. And the Yanquis cannot be shamed. They drink our pain. They are the stomach of the world. They know only how to eat and vomit and eat again. How I long for a time—not far now, I think —when the soldiery of North America will appear directly on this island, on our continent, when we will be able to strike direct merciless blows against the United States itself.

I see now, Fernando, what I found in Gandhi: his ideas are the last, most concentrated, most seductive snare of Imperialism. The Imperialists, and their deceitful culture, had succeeded in shaming me. How could I think well of myself? I was a native boy overawed by the moral achievements of Europe. I was not able to live in that resonant edifice. (And Argentina offered only its hideous, deformed masculinity.) So I turned against myself. Gandhi was the form of my self-accusation, my self-hatred. And more: he was my way of outdoing them, of being more saintlike, of making myself shine more purely than the European, taking on more pain than even the most ascetic figures of the Imperial cultures. But their "morality," I see now, is only the mask of exploitation, the lie told to pacify the oppressed, make him ashamed of his own drives, his own violence.

Yet Gandhi served me well. Sometimes, Freud says, one must put an obstacle between oneself and one's beloved, a wall, a trial, a sword. Against that wall one's unsatisfied desire grows stronger, passion swells to a flood. Behind Gandhi's word my own natural powers were pent up, until they were too strong to be enclosed, until, in a street demonstration in Guatemala, they broke out as if against my will. But my act wasn't against my will—*it was my will*, my violence grown strong. Fidel and the Revolution have helped me, as they have helped the Cuban people, to acknowledge that violence, to acknowledge my own will.

I am political officer of the group, and I shall use this letter as the text of my talk tonight. So, you see, you too, old friend, will be participating in our revolution.

> A warm embrace,
> Ernesto "Che" Guevara

—I'm called Che now. The perfect name: an empty sound that might mean anything, that anyone might fill in as he wishes!

Chaco is dead. He died very honorably, fighting the Imperialists in Guatemala.

P.S. Did I mention that I'm married? A fine woman, an activist of APRA, my wife's name is Hilda Gadea. And I have a daughter, born just before I left for Cuba, also named Hilda.

From My Journal

5/23/57: A notable day: I received a canvas hammock. I don't think that since childhood I've been so happy about a gift, felt the same sort of simple warm involvement with a thing. These canvas hammocks usually go to those men who have already made burlap ones for themselves. That's a precaution against the laziness, the slackness about tasks that is our worst enemy. Then when the city network manages to get some of these beautiful canvas things to us, they are distributed only to those who have already made and used the burlap ones. But the lint from the burlap infuriates my lungs, so I've been sleeping on the ground. Since I didn't have a burlap hammock, I wasn't entitled to a canvas one. Fidel noticed this vicious circle and himself intervened to award me one of the canvas prizes.

Today, too, we ate our first horse. The peasants in the group were revolted by this cannibalism. Joaquin, Ricardo, Ponco, Rolando, and Moro all at first refused to eat their ration of meat. This was clearly the greatest crime in their eyes that the guerrilla could have collaborated in, and they treat Manuel, our butcher, as if he were a murderer. He had cut the horse's throat, and by the time I got there it had fallen over, and was pouring its blood onto the grass. Ricardo had squatted down a few meters away, watching the ceremony.

"It's a pity," Ricardo said, as the blood flowed out, "that you can't take a bite from an animal, and have him live and grow it back."

"What?" I was stunned by the quantity of blood that fell from the horse's neck, and formed a pool on the ground. And I was surprised that Ricardo's imagination would run to whimsy—though I suppose it was also a vision of continual cruelty.

"The way you work a man," he said.

"Ah." He was more poet than I supposed.

"It's a badly designed world," he said, rising. He walked to the grass where the blood had pooled, and put a finger in. He brought the finger to his mouth, as if he meant to suck on it. But then he jumped back from his own hand, and shook the drops off; the horse's blood was cursed stuff.

I went to touch the horse's flank. It gave off a great heat at the end. The heart beat faster and faster, then more and more slowly. Its big eyes looked as if they implored all creation, the palm trees, the grass, the bright sky, and then went glassy.

Eventually the countrypeople came around, from hunger. It was our first meal in more than a day. Several of them took their dishes off under separate distant trees to eat alone.

It is a fibrous gamey meat, sweeter than beef.

Today, too, I wrote the following poem:

FIDEL IS A HORSE
for Chaco Francisco

The mare lies in the long grass; and the thick grass, blown
by the wind,
scratches her flanks.
Her foals lie beside her in the dewy grass.
Docile mare, big-eyed mare.

But if the mare forces you against a wall with her flank,
slams you suddenly with her side,
or kicks you with her legs,   hits you even a glancing blow
with her hoof,
then: a tremor like rippling water runs the length of your body
your heart like a shot strives to break from your chest
your mind fails   your will
fails   your legs are paper & bam!   they crumple!

But if you are hungry in famine time, in slack season
in the dead months when there is no work at the mill
She will give up her body to be your meat.

The hound master sees the mare asleep in the tufted grass.

The hounds are sent. They bound across the field, they fly at her
legs, she is rising too slowly! She has not
been vigilant! They are on her!

The thick purple lips spread back on sharp teeth, they gnaw at
        her heels,
She struggles to rise, her colts twist their necks in terror,
The hounds dart their heads searching out the thin of the leg, the
        bump near her hoof
They desire to bite down there, break the tendon there, hobble the mare,
bring her down and fall on her flanks, rip the flesh from her flanks.

But the bleeding mare rises! The raging mare moves back, rears up &
down on the heads of the yelping dogs, crushing the hounds' skulls,
the thick bones.

The mare licks her foals clean with her tongue.

But the hound master waits; the field is not safe,
& the mare has no home & the foals have no home.
Hurry! Do not pause to lick the colts clean of the dogs' blood!

The mare runs to the mountains;
she climbs the rocks, stepping lightly with long legs, lifting them high,
nudging her children's flanks with her head, hurrying them on.

There are fields of sweet grass in the mountains.
(But the colts must learn: no fields are open fields.)
The hounds desire the mare's thin legs, to bite near the hoof,
break the tendon, hobble the mare, bring her down, and fall on her flanks.

The mare sleeps now with her eyes open. When the sun rises in the
        mountains
The mare bends her legs under her, throws forward her weight &
stands. Her ears are straight back 'gainst her head.
The mare shakes sleep and heat from her soft mane.

Riders of the mare: hold tight to that long mane,
stay close to the mare's strong back, as ancient riders lie
flat, hug hard to the backs of their horses, nourish themselves
as they ride drinking blood from wide veins in the necks of their horses,
never dismount, move ceaselessly, elude all pursuit, mount and rider
one creature, one life,

hold tight that tangled mane, grip strongly,
or you will die in the dead months in famine time
in slack season when there is no work at the mills,
& the mare will go astray in the mountains, and the colts will
                                have no mother,

Grip strongly! And you may ride the mare where you will,
you people,
and the land you move across will become your land,

by her motion.

Isle of Pines, July 1965

JULY 16

Ponco came into my room, to return my pages. I sat in front of my board, staring at the tall grass and the ocean. All still today, like my imagination.

He showed me that he had underlined some phrases from my letter to Fernando. "For the Speech," he said. "On Vietnam. The Call."

If, I thought—as he did—*I'm allowed to deliver it.* But that isn't to be spoken, not even between us. I looked down at the underlined phrases and saw more dares that I had made myself, further scaffolding for the part I wished to play. I had not then had the right to speak such things.

"Jack London," Ponco said inexplicably to me. Perhaps he simply intended to change the subject from the one neither of us had mentioned: *Why hasn't Fidel spoken?*

"What?"

"Alaska. The story."

"Ah." Ponco stood beside my chair, but I continued to look out the window. The light turned the small waves translucent at the bottom, the mild wind dusted them with snow at the tops. O avalanche!

"I like the part about me," Ponco said, still trying to attract my attention.

"Good," I said. My mind felt empty, tired, as if writing had meant pouring out its contents, returning an empty shell to the present. "I had been worried you might not like it." A lie. I hadn't given it a thought.

"No." He smiled. "I like reading about me. Young. A believer. Before I lost my faith. To an agent of the devil. Atheist. You."

I returned his smile, but could think of nothing to say.

"You should write a book about me."

"My next project," I said ruefully. It seemed a cruel joke on Ponco's part —as if to say the time on this island might stretch out until . . .

"And I'll write one about . . . you."

"Oh." That round emptiness was the circle of my mood. I couldn't locate the target of Walter's irony.

He reached from behind my chair and started to turn the pages of my old water-soaked book, the one covering my years before Cuba. He thought in my absence to have a more intimate look. I held his hand. It felt light, as if the bones were hollow. Perhaps our Ponco will take flight one day!

"Sorry," he growled—apology was impossible in his tone. "Did you remember to say that I was a very curious fellow?"

JULY 17

Each day passes now without word, and without words. Ponco accompanied me towards the ocean, object of all my empty stares. I stopped, for no reason, in the middle of the field, balancing my palm on the tips of the tall drying grass, letting them tickle my hand.

"No writing?" he asks.

"No. The story seems over to me."

"What about the rest?" he asked. "The building of socialism."

It was very hot. Sweat already formed under my armpits. "Not my work anymore," I said. I remembered a speech I'd given with Fidel, after the missiles had been taken back. My memory of before—myself, deaf, in the crowd below —was false.

I had been on the platform with him. I, and no one else, not even Raul. And his speech had been a failure. It had reminded me of my parents' kitchen, the provincial stage of that master dialectician, my mother. I could hear her intonations in Fidel's voice that day, as she turned a staff into a snake, interpreted craven compromises as heroic acts, tried to make us accomplices to the mysterious cunning of history. That day his voice was like hers, it lacked a certain energetic confidence; we were all in a little town in the mountains of Argentina, just guessing about the big doings in the metropolis. (Who could say if the words had the same meaning for us that they did for Churchill and Stalin? The fashion might have changed, and we wouldn't have been notified.) He lacked conviction; he'd failed, remained a commentator on events, not an actor. The nation was diminished. Four hundred thousand people waited, looked up at Fidel and me. Behind the crowd and on the sides of the plaza, there were towers of crisscrossed wood to support the huge black loudspeakers. A field opened beyond the towers. Children, a few inches high, were back there, running about, kicking multicolored balls the size of marbles, while the adults talked. To my left were the pastel buildings of Havana, and you could already see in them signs of decay, broken windows, chipped cornices—the destruction the government had allowed to happen. (To give back the life and money drained by the cancerous city, Fidel would say—but not when he was in Havana—to let Havana die so that the countryside might live.) To my right, past a boardwalk, a metal railing, and a thin strip of beach, was the ocean. That day it was dark, choppy, and there were masses of black clouds on the horizon.

But it was still sunny in the square. I talked on. The sun was dull but constant, and we had all been there for hours, sweating. It should have been good for us—like drunks in a steambath getting out our bile, our defeat, our anger. But the feelings were bottomless. Their sweat rose towards me, a thousand different smells, blending to an overwhelming perfume—dirt, fear, soapy cotton, grease, humiliation, longing. They were a jungle, a swamp, a rank hot smell, a stagnant inlet. So many of the countrypeople (brought in by the Party Committees in huge schoolbuses and flatback trucks) wore white smocks and loosely woven light-tan hats that they also looked a cloud filling the plaza, a cloud with raggedy edges stretching towards the ocean. I felt that I looked down at the sky itself from above. Cloud, swamp, jungle, ocean—why not a flock of birds, gulls, blackbirds, bright green-and-red parrots, all mixed together in Fidel's aviary? Or the sun? . . . Or the very source of all metaphors? . . . etc.

Or why not a field of radishes! Or of stones! That's the way they responded that day.

I jiggled up and down in spasms, a nervous excited speaker, a man dangling on a wooden platform a hundred feet in the air. (And my bladder ached. I had to piss. I had a rubber bottle strapped to my leg, and a tube running to my penis, but I was too embarrassed to urinate with a few hundred thousand people watching. I just couldn't make the flow begin.)

Fidel, as always, was another verse. He and the crowd were an old married couple, comfortable, altering each other to fit, annoying and forgiving each other. (Except for the ones he's divorced, across the barbed wire in this field, in jail.) Like a married man he isn't ashamed to piss, to use the bottle strapped to his leg.

Fidel and the crowd are, he likes to say, two parts of a tuning fork, the waves from the one making the other tine shake. But there was no oscillation today. He had already spoken, and he hadn't done the trick. They were still sullen. I was speaking again, Fidel standing by my side, strangely still, absolutely still. And his immobility was so striking that it destroyed my speech. Everyone looked towards him. The son of a bitch was upstaging me by doing nothing at all! So I gave up, leaned forward, pressing my hurting chest hard into the sharp edge of the podium, raised my arms high over my head, shouted, "Ever Onward to *Final* Victory!" letting my voice rise high on the last word —too high: I screeched. Spots of the crowd answered me, but only spots. I, too, had failed. The despair drifted up to my nose, black acrid stuff.

But as the mild sound of the crowd died away, Fidel leaned across and in front of my body, towards the microphone. I could smell him strongly. His shirt was drenched. For the last week he's been drinking rum and beer steadily, eating yogurt (with cherries) to coat his stomach—a Bulgarian custom. He gave off a heavy pungent boozy smell. In a low harsh voice, a stage whisper (audible in Miami), but the more intense (as he calculated) for the seeming restraint, he added to, or revised, my conclusion: "*Ever* Onward!" And then again, in the same whisper, but diminished—a man going down a road—"*Ever* Onward!"

He didn't wait for a response. He drew himself back as if recoiling from something, pivoted on the heel of his fancy black boot, turned his back on the crowd. The whisper, amplified a thousand times, still echoed from the speakers at the back as he turned. His immobility, his silence, his sudden sharp motion to the microphone, the loud whisper, the quick turn (Fidel too had abandoned them!), it riveted their attention. Except for the children, kicking their balls in the back, there was a great stillness.

Then the people shouted, a few at first, the Party members no doubt, the Revolutionary Defense Committee men, but then more and more joined, their voices chased after the departing man, arched towards the platform, gulls rising from the ocean after feeding, a few and then many, until the sky was white with them, repeating "*Ever* Onward!," gathering and rising above our heads. The field of white stones revealed itself as a flock of silent birds, waiting for the word to come to rise and fly. The sound died away, the last wing gone into the sun and out of sight.

How I admired him! If he sold Coca-Cola, I thought, they would be drinking it now on the Ho Chi Minh Trail! He is the master manipulator, the man of the intricate particular rhetorical skills for constructing socialism. His music builds the walls of the cities. I had said, Battle and final victory: peace, release, rest. (My theoretical journal: *Final Point!*) But Fidel was marriage, daily trials, long sacrifices, begin again, it all must be done over. *Ever* Onward! He sliced towards the microphone with his whisper, and left me out in the cold —an affair. As Ponco said, He'll be the stay-at-home. That day he had made it a way of dividing the world, and he had taken the better, the more noble part for himself. Could he see it that way now?

"No," Ponco said, recalling me to our open field.

"What?"

"You're right. It's not your work." We faced the ocean. A mild breeze cooled my sweat. "I liked your poem."

"Good."

"A love poem." He smiled, but I couldn't rise to the challenge or even feel the sting of his mockery. We walked closer to the waves. "Has Fidel seen it?"

"No. Of course not."

"I think you should send it to him." I heard anxiety shadowing his voice. "I could give it to one of the guards."

Guards? I thought. Who are they guarding? The young Communists? The mad people? The prisoners?

Or me?

JULY 23

Walter was gone when I woke up. Off on a walk, I thought, or to get supplies in town.

He returned without food, but with a sheaf of papers in his hand. Unfortunate harvest? He smiled coming up to the porch, where I had appropriated his seat for some more convenient ocean-staring. I had not seen *that* smile before from the virtuoso of that expression. There seemed both fear and expectation in it.

"News from the Inca," he said. He stood before the porch, in the sunlight, with the ocean behind him, as I had stood once, disfiguring a picture of him, rubbing him out. What was he doing to me? Anxiety scrabbled in my chest. Why did he hesitate to give me the documents, to come forward and give me the papers he held in his right hand?

There was a report from Debray:

Ramon:
Fidel's instinct was right. Bolivia is the location for the guerrilla, and this is the most opportune political conjuncture. Monje, Chairman, Central Committee of the BCP, told Fidel in talks in Havana that the country is ripe for

rebellion. They would need only ten thousand dollars to get under way. Fidel has provided the money. Fidel did not mention your participation as political-military leader, or the continental scope of the rebellion, but that will, of course, only make the process of recruitment, within and outside Bolivia, that much more rapid.

SUMMARY:

1. All possible electoral remedies have been exhausted. The entire population considers General Barrientos's election to be a charade. The first of the necessary conditions has been fulfilled: "When the forces of oppression come to maintain themselves in power against established law, peace is considered already broken."

2. Recent developments, along with the electoral charade, make several strata ripe for movement in our direction, once the guerrillas appear:

   a) Even the remnants of the pathetic Agrarian Reform have been liquidated. The army has returned both land and peasants to the previous owners, who have slithered back from Argentina.

   b) Lechin, the old union leader of the miners, was arrested as a deliberate provocation. The Trotskyites responded stupidly, by calling a strike. The well-disciplined miners occupied the mine area.

The miners' position at first looked strong. They had a miners' militia already organized; some (though out-of-date) arms; a radio station to propagandize with; dynamite; detonators; expertise; control of the tin.

But: They remained in their liberated zone, the area around the mines. They did not go on the offensive. They waited to win a few concessions from the government—for their leaders said that the time for insurrection was . . . not yet. Once again the miners' leadership forced them to relearn your propositions on the necessity of guerrilla warfare—at the cost of their lives.

The army waited. The army cut the road to La Paz. La Paz is the source of the miners' food. The mines themselves are in rocky soil, twelve thousand feet above sea level. The land produces stones. There are a few communities of Aymara Indians, who raise potatoes, and dry llama meat.

After a few weeks the miners began to run out of potatoes and the dried llama meat the Indians gave them.

The army waited. The army didn't need the ore from the mines right away. It had U.S. loans.

After ten days the miners ran out of milk for their children, meat for their families, medical supplies for their infirmaries. They had no cough medicine left for their silicosis. Each man wanted to tear at his lungs.

The army waited.

The miners remained in their liberated zones. How often must your theses be proved and re-proved! They were afraid to leave their wives and children to the army. The miners had no military-political leadership. The miners' militia guarded their homes.

They did not become what you have shown they had to become to survive: a guerrilla army.

The army waited. The generals, the North American advisers, met in bars, drank toasts, smiled, set the hour of the miners' massacre.

When the soldiers came the miners hurled dynamite at them. It had worked for their fathers against the decrepit guns of the old army, a decade ago. But it did not work against machine guns. It was ineffective against airplanes, against the weapons and tactics the army had received from the United States.

The Bolivian Rangers, elite force of jackboots, trained by the United States, surrounded and destroyed the miners. Mines were bombed from the air. The miners' windowless wooden barracks, laid out in neat rows, made easy targets for the planes. And the bombs only incinerated the people; the mines themselves are safe underground. Nothing of value was lost. The smelters are in the United States and England.

The army occupied the zone, went from house to house, dragged the families of the militants into the open field and murdered them, men with their women and children. A common grave was dug for their bodies.

Your theses were proved again:

An insurrection, spontaneous, and without military-political leadership, cannot defeat a modern army trained and armed by the United States. The miners learned last year that the victory of 1952 will never be repeated.

Now they are in mourning, in despair.

But your theses will be proven:

Your appearance will transform that despair into a realistic hope. "It is not necessary to wait until all conditions for making revolution exist; the insurrection can create them." Your appearance will make them see the new possibilities their violence can create. The miners now realize that an insurrection in the mines will be effective—as you have written—only as the last stage of a guerrilla war against the army, a war carried out in the locale you've named, in the countryside, far from the army's sources of supply. As you have argued, the objective cannot be reform, coexistence, or a liberated zone that allows the gorillas to decide the hour of the people's death. The objective must be state power, final victory for the oppressed over the imperialists. The only instrument for this victory is guerrilla war.

The miners' blood has set the stage for your arrival, for the appearance of the guerrilla. Once again your theses will be proven correct!

Onward to Final Victory!
Danton

Ramon:

Despite Danton's doubts I strongly suggest the ranch be in the southeast. It will be easy to construct storage caves. The ranch land itself has plenty of water. The vegetation of the region is thick. If we move north we can travel to Vallegrande, through a mountainous and heavily wooded area. Difficult for the army to follow. From there on the woods become sparser. If we move south to Argentina the terrain is similar. The farm is in a canyon between the Serranias de las Pirirendas and the Serranias Incahuasi. "Ask me my name and I will respond with geography." (You see: Ricardo, too, has learned some poetry! Please pass that on to Walter.) The ranges join up farther south and become the Salta range in Argentina.

Ricardo

Ramon:

Tania has told Monje that we will only establish a base here in the southeast, and then move into Argentina. Monje is suddenly very protective of his sphere of control, the time isn't ready for rebellion, the Party must have more complete control of the Bolivian operation . . . etc. He is a coward.

But I once again strongly suggest that Bolivia be our first goal. Monje's original report to Fidel—that the conditions are ripe here—is accurate. And from here we can coordinate with Brizola in Brazil, and Bustos and the others in Argentina, Lobaton and Gadea in Peru. Monje has already assured Fidel of his support for a guerrilla movement—and this is before he could know that *you* will be the leader. Surely that will keep him from turning tail!

A farm has been purchased, against my advice, in the southeast.

Advantages: close to Argentina

                   easier to survive in the initial stages

                   defensible positions, jungle, rivers, etc.,

                   as described in Ricardo's report.

But it is far from populated zones, and the region itself is sparsely populated. We will have to bring in everything ourselves.

But if we succeed in supplying ourselves we could stay here forever. It will be very difficult for the army to discover us, or attack.

But it will also be difficult here to sink roots into the peasantry.

Conclusion: this could be, if you O.K. it, a kind of base camp, and the group could move out from here for operations elsewhere, then return to this area, where virtually impregnable camps could be built.

Danton

Buenos Aires,
April 1965

My Dearest One:

Sometimes I think we can no longer confide in each other directly? Or could it be that we never did! Perhaps we have always spoken with such maddening indirectness and irony? Perhaps we have always misunderstood one another.

But that's how it is now isn't it? So I have to decipher your letters as if they were a document for one of our family meetings over the newspaper! What is their *true* story? Who did what to whom? We speak through masks!

But I can't talk that way anymore. I don't have time. I *have* to *get* right to the *point.*

It's madness, just complete utter lunacy, that when there are so few people on the island of Cuba on the continent on the planet earth who have our knack for planning that we should all go cut cane for months. I'm sure there are lots and lots of fine cane-cutters people who are very *happy* doing that kind of thing. You should be organizing their labor, not doing it yourself. Is that why you dropped from sight? As you said? To cut cane? I can't believe it?

And then you write about serving as manager of a factory for five years! There are many people who can manage factories Tete. (Excuse me, but I named you first, before the crowds did. I am your mother after all, so you must excuse me?)

It's crazy for you to cut cane for months, but it is absolute total lunacy for you to go manage a factory for five years [*For that is what I had said I was going to do. To confuse those who monitored my movements. To obscure the nature of my dispute with Fidel.*]

When your trip abroad went on and on, I asked, Will Ernesto still be minister? Who has decided in this struggle—for I could smell that there was a struggle—that led to your foolish plan?

Well, you're no longer minister, you're going to manage a factory! That is a waste of your enormous ability! This is not your mother speaking! It's an old woman, a sick woman, a woman who has dedicated her whole life to the triumph of rationality, of socialism [*I remember, sadly, that I laughed at this point, certain that she could not be very sick if so much of her old paint box were available to her.*] And this old woman wants to see the triumph of reason, the triumph of socialism!

If you manage a factory will you be doing the most you can for that cause, for my cause?

If for some reason you cannot work in Cuba anymore, then there's Algeria, where Mr. Ben Bella would be happy to have your advice in organizing the economy. There's Ghana, where Mr. Nkrumah would welcome your help. Vietnam, where you would be warmly welcomed I'm sure by Mr. Ho Chi Minh and General Giap. Yes. You will always, like me, be a foreigner, a stranger in every land. That's your fate

And then, typed after the last paragraph:

Dear Ernesto (I will never be comfortable with that slang name, son): Your mother died yesterday evening at five o'clock, May 1. She has been complaining of fatigue for months, and I had been anxious for her to see a doctor. But she had refused, as she always has, saying that it was nothing to be concerned about. I think that, ever since the operation twenty years ago, she has been living as if in expectation of this event, suspected then that it had come, and didn't want to know about it herself, or have us worry. When she began to lose weight I insisted on her going to Stapler's Sanitorium. Three days after admission she was asked to leave by the management! The owner told us that the presence of the mother of a famous Communist leader could well ruin their reputation! I think this event gave her some of the most profound joy of her last days. We found another place for her, also in Buenos Aires.

The pleasure of cursing the manager at Stapler's was to be her last. She came out of her final coma only long enough to smoke a cigarette. I took the cigarette from her fingers, still burning. As you can see, she didn't finish this letter.

When she first went into the hospital I tried to reach you in Havana, but you had apparently left strict orders that you were not to be contacted under any circumstances. Your friend Soto says it is a tactic of yours when you are having a dispute with Castro. By your silence, apparently, you usually get him to come around. Soto, by the way, has been very useful, and very kind during the weeks of your mother's hospitalization. And he has agreed to take these letters to Cuba, and to see that they reach you, wherever you are.

You can see from your mother's letter how very much your work meant to her. She was always very proud of you. Your ways are not mine, admittedly. I am not sure that one does not do more good for the world, as your cousin Alvarados said to me, a little at a time. But you have done what you thought best, and perhaps you are right. Your mother, certainly, thought so.

Love, son,
your father,
Ernesto

JULY 25

My inclination now is to organize the Cuban nucleus, and begin a sort of training operation (for us and for the native forces) in either the Congo or Vietnam. Meanwhile, arrangements can proceed in Bolivia. But I will have to see what the situation looks like from Havana.

I was packing up the manuscripts this morning when Ponco came into the room. I had laid them out on the unfinished board, like a subject for dissection. They made several neat piles.

"What shall I do with them?" I wondered aloud as he came in.

"You could give them to Fidel," Ponco said. But that idea seemed to make him sad. "For a book."

"No," I said, responding, I thought, to his sadness. "They're too incomplete." I had lost all interest in these things. I had resumed my position within the large costume of my fame. My name. I wanted to begin operating the levers, making the feet move, working the machinery for the voice. My mind was already in Bolivia, and the many steps that must be taken. My anxiety had fallen from me, my waiting was over, my work beginning. I had no more interest in myself as a subject for reflection, the subject of—the hero of—a book.

"I'll take care of them," Ponco said, quickly, a gravel slide. I thought I detected a suppressed greed in his voice. He picked up the piles, and placed them neatly one upon the other.

"You'll be my archivist."

"What?" His mind seemed to be on ordering the manuscripts. "I'll see that they find a safe place."

"That's what I mean. Archivist. He's the man who minds the records."

"Ah. Yes. They're in good hands," he said. "A safe place. I'll be your archivist."

But as he said it the word suddenly sounded a little ominous.

JULY 26

We spent the afternoon by the radio, the last day here, listening to Fidel's speech. There was a comfort to being so much in the provinces, so far from the platform. I could leave the room to take a piss, I could make myself a cup of mate. The speech went on till evening, and the only light in the room was the green glow of the old radio on the scarred wooden table.

Fidel read my farewell letter to the Cuban people. "Other lands claim the help of my modest efforts. I can do what you cannot because of your responsibilities at the helm of Cuba. The time has come for us to separate."

"A divorce," Ponco said. "How sad." He brushed imaginary tears from his large eyes.

"Let it be known that I do so with a mixture of happiness and pain. Here I am leaving my purest hopes as a builder, and the dearest of those who are dear to me . . . and I am leaving a people who accepted me as a son. This is like a knife cutting my spirit. But to the new battlefields I shall carry the faith you taught me, the feeling that I am fulfilling the most sacred duty: fighting against imperialism wherever it is. That comforts me and heals my wounds."

Etc.

The reading made the culmination of the speech.

Ponco had his head down, resting on his crossed arms. "Nice job," he said, as if he'd just woken from a deep sleep. I thought I heard a craftsman's appreciation buried within his growl.

Dates

<u>1966</u> The Tricontinental Conference meets in Havana, with delegates from Third World countries—and movements in rebellion—on three continents. They inaugurate the Organization for Solidarity of Latin America, Africa, and Asia. (The Third World must share more than its poverty; it must share in liberation or death.) Ernesto Guevara (not present) is "honorary chairman." In Peru, Guillermo Lobaton and Ricardo Gadea (the brother of Ernesto Guevara's first wife) gather up the scattered fragments of the guerrilla movements, to continue the war in the mountains. Lobaton is killed by the army. In Ghana, Nkrumah is overthrown by a right-wing army coup. The leadership of the Guatemalan Communist Party is arrested and then shot. Leonel Brizola, governor of Rio Grande do Sul in Brazil, flees into exile in Uruguay; he prepares a guerrilla front for his country. Douglas Bravo, a leader of the Venezuelan guerrillas, is expelled from the Communist Party. Codovilla, head of the Central Committee, reaffirms that the Party will follow the line of peaceful coexistence. ("After all, history is not our pet. Right now, talk of armed struggle is premature.") Mario Monje, leader of the Bolivian Communist Party, meets again with Fidel Castro. He reaffirms his intention to cooperate in a plan to establish a guerrilla base in Bolivia. Castro provides another twenty-five thousand dollars for the Bolivian Party to use in promoting the Bolivian Revolution. Fabricio Ojeda, a Venezuelan guerrilla leader, is captured by the army, with many of his men, and then shot. Joaquin, Ponco, and Ricardo—veterans of the Cuban Revolution—go to La Paz, to organize men, supplies, and support networks for the Bolivian guerrillas. Mao Tse-tung encourages Chinese peasants, workers, and students to rebel against Party bureaucrats, revisionists, and all those—however highly placed—who have taken the capitalist road. The Great Proletarian Cultural Revolution begins. Regis Debray, the French theoretician, returns to Bolivia, to continue his research on the best terrain for a guerrilla base. A huge piece of land is purchased in a canyon in the semitropical southeast of Bolivia. Coco Peredo, a young Communist militant and taxi-driver, rents a warehouse in La Paz. Supplies are bought or smuggled in, taxied

to the warehouse, slowly moved to the farm. In Guatemala, Turcios Lima, and most of his men, are killed by the army; Cesar Montes becomes leader of the guerrillas. The United States begins the long intensive bombing of Hanoi, North Vietnam. The people of Hanoi dig holes in the streets to hide in. North Vietnam protests to the world its civilian casualties.

II

THE DIARIES OF THE BOLIVIAN CAMPAIGN

Isle of Pines, May 1968

MAY 1

My plan:

1. Separate the papers into neat piles. (My mother said I was incapable of neatness, I would always be a careless slovenly pig. *I* said *she* would never stop drinking. *She* was wrong. *I* was right.)

The documents: His journal from the campaign. My journal from the campaign. His journals from before. The notebook he left behind with Hilda. The manuscript of his life that he wrote on *this very board.* The other men's diaries. (He told everyone to keep a daily record. He said it was good hygiene. Why? I think it was some idea of Gandhi's—a vow left over from Che's adolescence. Anyway, most of the men didn't write much in their journals, they never got the habit. They would do it only every so often, as a way of imitating *him.*)

2. Spread everything out on the board.

3. Put the piles of paper in order, the papers within each pile to be arranged by date. Get a view of what I have to work with. Look through everyone's entries for September, etc.

4. Make one long account of it, covering all the details.

5. Decide which details *matter.*

6. Decide how to tell the story in its final form. For whom am I telling the story? To make them do what? Or some other question? (It's on the tip of my tongue, it's in the part of my vocal cords that I don't have anymore. I can't put it into words.)

To make them weep!—that's one answer. Or to make them vomit—that's the answer my own body gives me over and over.

MAY 2

His room—mine now. His board—mine now, too.

When I first returned here I slept, as before, in the small room across from the kitchen. I thought he would walk out of his room in the morning, holding a sheaf of papers, the next installment of his less than honest—or more than honest—story of his life for me to read. (What might be on the ghost's pages?) But the specter never came to the table. And I couldn't sleep in that room anymore. I can only sleep here, in *his* room, on *his* cot, with *his* brown blanket. At night I play with the blanket edges, running them between my fingertips the way he did even as a man. (The athletes he trained—they were *us!*) And I work at *his* board, a piece of wood over two sawhorses, with piles of papers spread out on it, the same scene I would see when I sneaked in here before.

It's the board over the two sawhorses where they put his body, outside the laundry shed in Vallegrande. I have a picture of it tacked to the wall, next to the ocean view and the framed unreadable poem. A photographer stands over his corpse, his right hand pointing towards Che's poor chest. (So there must have been another photographer, not in the picture, taking the picture.) A Bolivian general holds a rag to his face. But he doesn't look like he's protecting himself from a bad contagious odor. He doesn't look like the body really *smells*. The general just wants to show he finds the business distasteful; he's gentry, he's particular. (Jesus, do *I* think *his* body *didn't* smell?)

His body *there* becomes this pile of papers *here*. And the no-smell from his papery body makes me want to puke.

I just went out on the porch and threw up on the grass, a yellowish pool of bile from my stomach, and the remains of a few pieces of bread I tried to eat for breakfast. I find it hard to swallow food. I take a few bites and gag. I can't *order* the food to stay down. Some things, Che, *are* beyond our will! If I do manage to make myself swallow something, I throw it up half an hour later, decomposed, like a corpse. I don't digest anything in my stomach, I just bury it there for a few minutes. I thought the difficulty swallowing meant the cancer had come back. (I *knew* it was cancer eight years ago, though the doctors lied to me about it. And I knew it would come back. Every time I have swallowed for the last seven years, I have felt my spit sliding down around little obstructions that I knew in my heart would grow until I eventually choked to death. That was another bond between Che and me. We *both* thought we were going to die every second of our lives.) But the doctors last month said no, it wasn't cancer. I couldn't eat, they said, because I was "upset." (But they might be lying to me again?)

All of the men volunteered to stay at the top of the ravine and cover the withdrawal of the main force towards the river. He had said it would be certain death. And he chose Inti, Urbano, Nato, Benigno, Dario, and me. *And we were the ones who survived!* After the battle, we waited till night, and broke through the encirclement. The soldiers at the edges of the ravine had grown inattentive, tired. They had already captured Che, taken the prize, the red kerchief. They thought the game was over. Why worry about us? Where was the glory in capturing us?

We killed four soldiers. After that we walked fifteen days through hardwood forest. The trees protected us from planes. The peasant who sold us food also sold our position to the army. The food was only some handfuls of roasted corn, but I could eat them. The army surrounded us again in the forest, but we got out. The sentinels were careless, talking with each other, not even holding their rifles when we came upon them. They thought the war was over. Inti led us into the Mataral region, to Casas Viejas. (We knew Che had intended to make Inti the leader if we succeeded in establishing a Bolivian center, so he was the leader.) We bought some food there, paying a lot for some scrawny chickens. But I could eat them, too. No problem! In November we went east towards the Cochabamba–Santa Cruz highway, trying to avoid the army—if they had asked us, *we* would have told them that the war was over! They caught up with us near La Cabana, and Nato was wounded in the spine. He couldn't move his legs or control his bowels, and he was in terrible pain. He asked me to shoot him so that the army wouldn't get him.

We went southwest of the highway to get away from the army, then north. There were good people in that region, followers of the MNR. They hid us, gave us new clothing. The other men worked on farms, pretending to be laborers. But I am a black man, and Bolivia doesn't have many blacks. And Che had taken lots of pictures of all of us. Now the army had his knapsack and the pictures. I would be easy to identify. So I hid all day in a tunnel they dug for me, moist-smelling, with crumbling sides and thousands of insects. Chicken-wire-and-stick gratings, covered with leaves, hid both ends—two exits for my burrow, for escape. For weeks I lived like a mole, underground. I pretended it was my grave, I practiced being dead, and I gnawed my pork strips alone in the dark, with the smell of decomposing things and wet earth filling my nostrils. But I *could* eat. (I was *happy* to eat. It was the day's big amusement. Not that the social life outside was much; we hardly spoke with each other anymore.)

The peasants got a lightweight green truck for us and we rode on the flatbed into Santa Cruz, our legs stretched out like farmworkers. We took a plane to Cochabamba, a little thing with two propellors. (I hated it! I thought we'd die! Before, I hadn't been afraid of airplanes. But Che had.) Parts of the city network were still intact there, and Inti knew how to reach them. They hid us in their apartments. But I'd been in a tunnel for weeks, underground, already dead. I needed to see some people. So I took a little stroll, and got a bad haircut from a talkative fellow with mottled skin. And I had a lemon ice in a little white paper cup. It was fine. Very tasty. No trouble drinking it.

The dissident Communists, the ones who had broken with Monje and the Party, got us dark jackets, heavy mufflers and caps, and white knapsacks for the trip to the Chilean border, to Sabaya.

The magistrate in Sabaya was a rat, he suspected something and telegraphed the army. But they couldn't get to us: there were no landing fields for their planes. And, like an answered prayer, it began to rain every day, a cold endless deluge, the final onslaught of the waters. On its way to extinction the world became mud. The army couldn't get its trucks into the mountains.

The way out was terrible. The rain turned to snow as we walked higher through the pass, towards Chile. The ground was mud that froze around our feet. I had never been any place so cold, and please God I never will be again! The wind sliced through my jacket and scarf. I thought my bones were ice and might shatter. The wound in my thigh ached like a stone inside the flesh. We didn't speak to each other anymore except about necessary tasks or directions. It was as Che had written about the men of the *Granma* marching near Belic: we felt we were in purgatory, and perhaps if we just kept marching we might get out. Whose sins had put us here? Ours or his? We were the extension of Che's body. But it wasn't like the *Granma* and Fidel. Che was dead! I looked at the snow and thought of Che's first wound, and the white field he had imagined for himself to die in. This was it. (I was already inhabited by scenes from his memory!)

All this time we hadn't had much to eat, and what there was we had to pay dearly for, to greedy, frightened peasants. But I ate greedily too. Roasted corn: I could eat it! Pork rinds: I could eat them! Lemon ice!

We made it across into Chile, to Arica, unsure of what would face us there. You felt in the mountains that you were moving from desolation to desolation, that nothing good could await you. The Bolivian government might have asked for help from the Chilean Army. If they had received it, then the mountains might be filled with troops waiting to surprise us.

But the people came out of their huts to greet us, to cheer us. The Mayor of Arica is a Communist. I drank the hot rough liquor they offered us—I could hardly stop drinking it!—and I ate some salted beef.

The government in Santiago gave us forty-eight hours to leave the country —we were like lepers who might spread their contagion. Allende arranged for our passage to Tahiti, where the ambassador met us. We had pork again, very tender, cooked outside on a spit for hours with a sweet sauce. On Friday, March 1, we flew to Paris. I began to have some difficulty swallowing food. I felt like my throat had pebbles in it, little circles of pain. By the time we got home the pebbles had become boulders. I would stare at my plate and acid would wash into my stomach, a hand would form to throw the food out of my belly, giving my insides a squeeze as it went. I couldn't eat anymore.

I had lost maybe fifteen pounds during the insurrection, maybe more—it was hard to hold my pants up at the end. I probably lost ten pounds more after Churo, during the escape. But I have already lost ten pounds since Paris. I now weigh a hundred pounds. If I go on like this I'll float away! I don't want to kill myself, and in truth it doesn't feel as if *I'm* doing it.

He is. He has stolen my appetite. He has stolen the rest of my life. What do I have left to look forward to? From now on *my* life will be to tell *his* story. I can see the days to come: I give a talk to a group of Young Communists who are doing volunteer work in the orange groves, telling them how important the spirit of sacrifice was to Che, how he taught that it is through sacrifice that we are unified with our comrades and the New Man is formed. I will meet with Yanquis here to cut cane, and tell them of Che's sense of internationalism. I will dedicate schools named after him, and launch literacy campaigns. (They should use the detective novel. But I wouldn't suggest it, for I see signs that the Revolution is losing its sense of humor.) Each October 8 there will be a memorial rally for me to address. I am going to hide out here, underground, already dead, from the almost daily festivals of the Year of the Heroic Guerrilla. It hurts me to talk. I'll shame myself, croaking in public like a rusty machine. No wonder I want to vomit all the time! It isn't acid inside me. It's my hatred of him. I want to vomit him up! His body has become the food I eat! He almost killed me—that's what I want to scream at meetings of Young Communists and innocent cane-cutters. He almost killed me! I curse him, but when I do the curse comes back and withers my own body.

I can't even say that. I'm not allowed to hate him. I feel woozy and the bad feeling makes the room grow dark. (Or maybe it's the lack of food.)

I don't understand why I'm not allowed to hate him. He nearly killed all of us—all but five! (Inti stayed behind to lead the Army of National Liberation —consisting of Inti Peredo, sole proprietor. Inti is inhabited by Che's dream, and like all the others who tried to be his body, Inti will die. I give him three months at most. He's under his own curse, too, doubly guilty—he survived both Che and his own brother.) *The strange thing is, we didn't try to survive.* When we volunteered to protect him and the others we expected to die. Should we feel guilty that we were lucky and outlived him? We shouldn't. But we do.

He nearly killed us all! There were plenty of times after it was already clear that the business was over, that we didn't have a chance of success, when most of us could still have gotten away if he'd led us out into Chile or Peru. We could have come back here to our island, rethought our plans. But he wouldn't consider it. Fidel would have given it up as a bad business, retreated, and thought up another plan—though Che was right, Fidel would have pretended that the new notion had been the only plan all along. But not Che—he had to live out his first idea, his words engraved in stone. *He* wouldn't *allow* us to escape. He wouldn't *let* us live!

I know: I love him and I hate him, and that's why I'm "upset," that's why I want to vomit. That feeling of mixed-up love and hatred—it reminds me of Che's family, the one he wrote about—or made up—here, on this board. They didn't know if they wanted to caress each other or hit each other. They must have wanted to puke all the time! They must have walked around their big house doubled over with nausea.

He almost killed us all! If I could hold on to that *fact,* I could simply hate him and maybe eat something. But hating him makes me feel heavy and sad. And thinking that he wanted to kill me, when I loved him so, that "upsets" me, that drives me crazy. I know I shouldn't take it personally. But why did he choose me to guard the retreat from Churo if he thought it would be certain death? I did love him. Maybe if I could simply hold on to that fact I could eat something.

In a way he *did* kill me. He sentenced me to this, turned me into his talking gravestone, my memory a movie theater with continuous showings of his life story, his many miraculous discoveries. I'm his "archivist."

He almost killed me! Why should I feel guilty towards him—and not Nato, whom I shot in the temple with my own gun? Why do I feel as if *I* failed *him?*

MAY 3

Move on to step four.

Bolivia, 1966

SEPTEMBER

From My Journal

9/7/66: La Paz, Bolivia. Notes for the beginning of a book:

These are the things you need if you have the will to make a revolution: *canned foods, sacks of corn, men, cooking utensils, leadership, lard, good sturdy boots, a government without legitimacy, hungry powerless people, radio equipment, canvas, padded jackets, courage, woolen caps, hammocks, accurate maps, a compass, courage, machetes, guns, ammunition, men.*

I've forgotten something.

9/9/66: The air in La Paz is very thin and sharp; it makes me feel lightheaded, and as if my skin were stretched very taut. Yesterday Ricardo passed out on the sidewalk in front of a movie theater. It made him angry at everyone. (I'm sure now that he's afraid people will think he's a Travis.) The miners, Ricardo, and Che. A name for the Bolivian Expedition: The Revolution of the Weak Lungs.

OCTOBER

From My Journal

10/15/66: More disguised comrades from Cuba. Cadres recruited from the BCP. We wait together at the farm. Ricardo in charge. Four men pretend to be pig farmers and employees, and are building outhouses on the property. Also under construction: a corral, a kitchen garden, a henhouse (we have a few hens, and a rooster who screams at any hour of the day or night—only by chance does he announce the dawn). The rest of us hide in this little shack with a corrugated tin roof—the only real building on the land. Its walls are made of halved tree trunks daubed with mud. The many chinks let the wind through. Thirty men place their sleeping bags close to the stove at night, warming themselves. In the morning almost all of us wake with stiff necks.

NOVEMBER

From Guevara's Journal

11/4/66: Ernesto Che Guevara died in the street-fighting against U.S. Marines in Santo Domingo, one of those insanely opposing soldiers with sticks and stones. His handwriting in hotel registers proves his death definitively this time. (For he has died many times before, in Argentina, Vietnam, Cuba, the Congo.)

Adolfo Mena, a Uruguayan businessman, arrived today in La Paz, where the thin air hurts his weak lungs. Mena is middle-aged, with deep worry wrinkles on his high forehead, and thick black eyebrows. He wears heavy glasses in severe tortoiseshell frames, and slicks his thin, graying hair back in the manner of Robert McNamara.

11/5/66: The air is too thin here, it will not support me. As I walked along the square I was seized by a kind of vertigo, as if the air itself had let me drop and I was falling and falling through an enormous empty space, with nothing to stop me from falling forever.

Instead, I arrived at the Hotel Austria Bar, a retreat of frosted glass and red plush opposite the Government Palace. This time, with my businessman's gray suit, my immaculate though scanty coiffure, and an authoritative stare through my glasses, the mestizo waiter seemed happy to serve me. I looked rich and used to command. As, in fact, I am.

The waiter snapped open the cap of the beer bottle for me, and, because of the altitude, foam gushed up. I grabbed at it with my hand, as is (or was) the custom. "Money will come to you," one of the men at the bar said, smiling. He was a colonel in the Bolivian Army, and wore sunglasses despite the bar's dim lighting, giving him an insect look. "You bet," I said, and turned away. No more staring contests with bugs for me; my anger has found more appropriate means.

The red plush of the bar has worn away to frayed cord in places, like the Bolivian Revolution itself. The bar and I are both the worse for the wear of history. One beer, at this height, makes me tipsy—a fact that my Gandhian vows kept me from discovering before.

I toddled back to my hotel room, unmolested, a man of peace still, although a nervous, ambitious one. The only older Indians who show themselves in La Paz after the curfew are specters, ghost dancers. The government wishes not their visible presence but their silent labor. And the only posters on the walls are of half-naked women carrying rifles: movie advertisements. I shouted angrily at one of the begging boys who had risked the police in hopes of a coin. He didn't run from my rage, or turn away; he simply stared at me and began a long racking cough. I was angry at myself really. It was stupid to go to that bar, stupid to show myself, the equivalent of a staring contest.

Tomorrow, early in the morning, Mena is to be driven from La Paz to the guerrilla base in the Nancahuazu region.

11/6/66: Jorge, my driver, has let his hair grow while at the farm. Thick black curls stand out on all sides of his head, like a bushy hat or a hidden animal. His mustache, though, has grown less profusely. There's a little space, right below his nose—the very deep indentation of his lip—which is completely empty. As we talked he kept taking his hands from the wheel, smoothing down the wings of his mustache, touching under his nose, to feel if anything had sprouted. (I mentally christened him with the *nom de guerre* of Mustache.) He thinks, as he's been told by Tania, that I'm an old man, a Cuban Party official, come to survey the arrangements. He spoke with me as you might with an old man, polite chatter, but with the air of being slightly more knowing about this business than a member of an older generation could be. Mustache talked a good deal, which made him a good companion for a car ride, though it might be a strain later. The ones who talk a lot continue often, out of fear, when they have nothing more to say, driving everyone mad. Jorge gestured when he spoke, a cause for worry in the present, because he insisted on taking his hands from the wheel, poking them in the air or at my shoulder. (Airplanes frighten me; I don't like cars or trucks; my theory of guerrilla warfare is the work of a man who can't stand any means of locomotion other than his own feet.)

I made old-man's talk back, fleshless, banal. We were chatting on this way as we drove, talking of the prospects for guerrilla war. It was hard to speak with him about it. He was eager for the fight, and knew all the formulations, but he didn't really feel how the formulations were earned. It was difficult to talk, too, because there was a loud rattle from the metal doors and the Plexiglas windows of the jeep. You had to shout everything.

"I suppose," I said, "a great deal of secrecy is necessary to make sure you're not discovered in the early stages."

"What? Oh. Yes. Absolutely. Before the center is firmly established is the most dangerous time for the guerrilla. Perhaps you know what happened to Masetti's group in Argentina? They were discovered before they could establish good contacts with the peasants. So they were destroyed before they began engagements with the army."

"Yes," I said, abstractedly. "I've heard that. It's important to learn from past mistakes." I turned away. I didn't want to talk of Masetti with him, not yet. (I switched his name back to Jorge.) He sounded like a rich boy: he spread an air of unreality on whatever he talked about. We were on a bumpy road that ran near the edge of cliffs, high above the Nancahuazu River. The seats of the jeep were raised up off the road, and I could sometimes stop the talk in my mind, and let myself wander with the last light off the water, hear the splash of the river—or imagine it—as it moved hard over the rocks.

It was near evening. There was a moistness in the air that made me anxious in my chest. How will my asthma treat me here this time? The canvas top of the jeep was down to make room for the crates of guns brought from the warehouse in La Paz. (Not .22s!) I felt a chill on my neck and buttoned up my long Russian coat, pulling the felt collar about my face and lips.

Jorge was saying something like "Some say there are elements left."

"Elements of what?" I shouted.

"Of Masetti's guerrillas. Still operating."

"Oh. You sound very committed to the guerrillas yourself," I said, though he didn't; he didn't sound like he knew what he was talking about. (The basis of a first commitment is a very good imagination, so that you can at least dream the dangers you are entering. I need a battalion of dreamers?) "Will you stay with the guerrillas," I asked, "if the Party doesn't support them?" My hands were touching my wrinkles as I spoke now, crawling through the ravines of my forehead, scurrying through the wiry vegetation on my eyebrows, acquainting myself nervously with the new map of my face. My old face was there and not there; peekaboo around the edges. I'm not comfortable in disguise; I hate being old.

"I don't know if I'd stay then," Jorge said, alarmingly taking his hand from the wheel to open his palms into the air and turn towards me. His eyes are deep-set, and they looked troubled by my question. "I'm not sure. For myself, I'm certain that this is the right course eventually. But Monje, the Party's first secretary, says one must be sure to pick the right time to open hostilities, that's just as important as the rightness of your course. Otherwise it's just suicide, and you help no one. And only the Party can decide when the revolution is on the agenda. That's what Monje says."

"I think," I said, "the time is very auspicious now, here in Bolivia. The miners have learned that if they stay by their mines, in fixed positions, they will be bombed into submission. The government and the army are the same, and they rule for imperialism. Guerrilla war is clearly the only possibility for liberation." I had forgotten, as I spoke, who I appeared to be. My hands reminded me that I was an old man. "I think," I concluded, "one creates the right time: by beginning." In my disguise my words had none of the authority my name would have given them; spit bubbles; lacking my presence, they were merely rhetorical.

"*You* do?" Jorge said, looking away from the road, and smiling condescendingly at me. He thinks I'm an old man! And Jorge is a bit of a brat, in my opinion. (I wondered what his class background was. I must keep up my charade, I reminded myself, till I know him better, have sounded his commitment more.) "Well, we—the others from the Party and I—are waiting for Monje to declare the Party's position. I think," Jorge said, "I will go along with the Party. When I became a Party militant I committed myself to their discipline. And we all respect Monje. He's a very clearheaded man."

"Is he?" This was the reverse of what Debray had reported to me. He called Monje "lacking in clarity, weak, and vacillating." But Monje hadn't known I'd be leading the undertaking. I wondered what difference that would make.

"Yes," Jorge continued, "very intelligent. And a warm good person too, very sincere. He's the one who recruited me into the Party when I was at the university, and he made me editor of the Party newspaper. I feel very close to him."

I said—because I was momentarily jealous of Monje's hold on the boy, and because I wished to test the potency of my name on the other Party members (and why had Tania allowed Jorge, someone of such weak commitment, to know so much of our plans? what if the Party backs off now?)—"Jorge, I'm not what I seem. My real name isn't Adolfo Mena."

"It isn't?" Jorge turned from the wheel again, to smile expectantly at me. He clearly liked secrets—perhaps that was what Tania played on to interest him in us. A good tactic with intellectuals: they like to be in the know.

"No. It's Ernesto Guevara." And, I added, to heighten the effect, "I'm Che Guevara."

"What?" Jorge said, without surprise, still smiling expectantly. I had made my revelation in a quiet voice, to increase the drama. He hadn't heard me over the rattling.

So I shouted, bringing my mouth up to his ear, my gesture turned idiotic by repetition and volume, a silly joke carved in stone, "I AM CHE GUEVARA!"

Jorge let go of the wheel to grab my shoulder, squeezing it hard to see if it was real. We sluiced towards a cliff edge. He slammed on the brakes, no hands on the wheel, and we parked halfway in the air, our snout stuck out into nothing. A convincing demonstration of the power of my name. We crawled out of the jeep through the back, over the wooden gun crates. We hid the crates in some shrubbery, covering them as best we could with dirt and branches, and walked the rest of the way to the farm. I stumbled often in the dark, but Mustache's night vision was good. He was a strong walker.

11/14/66: I've sent the men out in small groups, as explorers. From what I've seen, and what they report, it is hard to put together a coherent picture of the area. It is as if they were reporting to me on the individual landscape of their dreams. A semitropical area, but with little water. Areas of abundant vegetation, wide-leafed plants, jungle that opens inexplicably into fields of low grass, grass that turns to fields of stone, stones that end in tall cliffs that overlook the Nancahuazu River or one of its tributaries.

The rivers flow from the mountains that surround this valley, running down the mountainsides only to disappear for miles, and then reappear suddenly, almost as torrents. We are in a canyon between the Serranias de las Pirirendas, to the east, and the Serranias Incahuasi, to the west. They meet to the south and become the Salta range in Argentina. The peaks of the mountains look like different planets, one bare of growth next to one covered with snow, and the next green all year. They incite my imagination, as if I could step from peak to peak, planet to planet, back to my native land, to Argentina. For once the guerrilla is established here that will be our next goal.

The land is covered throughout with grayish trees and a ground cover of prickly plants. To the north of the farm the mountains are covered with hardwood forests, and at the edge of the northeast corner of our land lie the sometimes sandy, sometimes extremely rocky banks of the Nancahuazu River. The river is broad and turbulent in most places, dangerous to cross. (In other spots it narrows to a creek.) The river runs through rocky inclines, very steep ones. The men move along the beach; the beach narrows away to nothing, and to continue to walk the men must climb carefully—very carefully, Ponco says —along the cliff sides, or hack a path through one of the deep wide ravines that run from the river, long slashes in the mountainside, as if someone had poured acid all over it, ravines dense with vines, spiny crawlers with cactuslike leaves, sharply serrated. All of the men's hands have lost a little flesh, grabbing the vines for support. And as we walk into a ravine our feet scare up swarms of mosquitoes, dark clouds of them.

11/20/66: Days of construction, and exploration. We've spent the last week continuing our reconnaissance of the area, looking for places to build the permanent camps—places with access to water, cover of vegetation, raised areas for observation posts. We've mapped out several. The men enjoy the explorations, take pleasure in using their bodies. And so far the Bolivians and Cubans are getting along well together.

The Bolivians, like Jorge, are openly uncertain of their commitment to the insurrection. My name sways them to the brink—!—but they still await Monje to announce the Party's position; they'd rather not break Party discipline.

For the moment we're staying in the brush, not far from the Tin House, and usually we bring our supplies from there in the evening. It reminds me of when I'd play at camping as a child, in my parents' back yard.

Last night a heavy rain forced us out of the thickets, for we don't yet have canvas tops for the hammocks. (The people in the city network always find it hard to appreciate how important a piece of canvas can be out here.) I spent the evening in the Tin House by the fire, getting sheep and cattle ticks, glutted with my blood, off my arms and legs. You stick the still-hot end of a match into them till they shrivel up: you must be sure to get the head or it burrows in deeper. (Possible metaphor for speech.) I reminded myself of my mother some nights in the kitchen, poking, or trying to poke, at the flies and mosquitoes with the lit end of her cigarette. "Psst!" she'd say. "My aim is uncanny! Pssst! Psst! Die now mosquito!" But she never got any.

DECEMBER

From Guevara's Journal

12/10/66: Three camps completed, each several miles from the farmhouse—though the nearest one, called Bear Camp, is on a hill overlooking it. Construction is finished on the defensive trenches and the brick bake-oven for bread. I've overseen the construction of showers made of muleskins (the skin, stretched taut on sticks, has holes punched in it; a partner pours water through), and Ricardo has taken charge of constructing an amphitheater of split logs, with a lectern—for speeches on tactics, daily lessons in Quechua. Also under way: operating tables for the doctor; and latrines. We have completed more than a dozen observation posts overlooking the camps, the Tin House, the trails, and the river. Lines have been laid for radio communication between the camps. Marcos has drilled the men in defensive maneuvers and in setting up ambushes.

12/17/66: Tania came to the camp today, accompanied by the liaison to Peru. She can travel freely over the whole countryside, without, she assures me, arousing suspicion. (Though from now on I have ordered her to remain with the city network.) She's gotten herself a job with the Ministry of Information, collecting native songs and stories, going to Indian villages, tape-recording their chants. She says she's done a little of it already, interesting work, though all their songs are mournful. (Ponco said, "Well, they don't have much to rejoice about.") I was impressed by this useful coup, this job with its built-in cover, but she said it was minor magic. She's also arranged a job with a radio station in Camiri, her own show, broadcasting advice to the lovelorn once a week. This will be a perfect way for the urban people to remain in contact with us, through nonsensical coded love letters that she'll read on the air. She had to convince the station manager that she knew about radio work.

Once, I remember, several years ago, I was talking with her and Joaquin about such things, admiring her accomplishments. They had just returned from preparing the ground for Masetti. "It's simple," she said, "you play upon their idea of what a woman is, of who you are. You do it too," she said to me, "in your way. You let them make you into an idol, then show them how they can placate you, win your approval, be like you."

Joaquin said, "Playing on people like that would make me feel dirty." He pursed his lips as if sucking something sour. It looked funny on such a big man. His face is in broad slabs, a huge thing, but it used to be very expressive in its way.

She didn't act insulted; he had been working with her for a while; it was allowed between them. "It doesn't bother me, Joaquin, you know that. I live far back in my skull." She pointed to the middle of her head and grinned at us, crossing her eyes a little, and smiling. She had a pleasing, antic way of making faces, very appealing. She didn't brood about what happened to her. Like cartoon figures, or Venus, she could go through any disaster and be restored, whole, in the next frame. Perhaps that, I thought, is what gave her face such an appealing vivacity, such lightness.

The same quality, though, made you want to do something with her (and then, sometimes in anger, to her) that would matter to her, touch her, get a real response, leave a mark. I had first met her in East Germany; she had been my interpreter. Her parents had been Communists, refugees from the Nazis who had fled to Argentina. It was a bond between us; we shared childhood stories, and made mildly ironic remarks (initiated by her) about the Party bureaucrats I was meeting, for the most part men with sullen unpleasant faces. She made one feel intimate with her, and yet there was a line that was not being crossed, a distance between you. Of all the people I've known since the Cuban Revolution, I always felt that she was least impressed by my fame. That fascinated me. But perhaps that isn't the way she is; perhaps that distance was something she devised to interest me, something she used. She had me arrange a scholarship for her to study in Cuba, and then offered to help me in the Masetti project.

She continued, "I take it all in from far away, Joaquin. It doesn't reach me. I laugh at them, the truth is. They think I'm this. They think I'm that. What do I care what they think! They think I'm a pin-up. An easy lay. A reckless woman, a helpless person. Whatever. What do I care what they think? I use their image of me for our work. There's always something in it, a little point that I can ride in the direction I want to go. Do they want to help the helpless? Be strong to the weak? Do they want to fuck me—ignite the cold woman? Or act really dirty with the sensualist? Or do they want to cure the crazy—that one is more popular than you'd think!—calm down the hysteric? It remains their image, not mine. I'm far away from their hands, their eyes, their words. Taking it all in, getting what I want. I don't care." She smiled. She had her hair down that evening, and several buttons of her green blouse open. (I disapproved; I was attracted.)

"Anyway, comrade," she said, "it's the same in any case. The truth is, I've learned, that others always decide who you are. You're just playing a part that they need for their production, their play. And they're doing it too, strangely enough, for each other, though they don't know it. I wonder where the director has gone? I know that sounds adolescent. I know it's an adolescent feeling. But it's true too, and I can't outgrow it. I can't forget it, and I can't outgrow it. It's funny having the feeling that I should be so happy play-acting. But if there's nothing real, then knowing you're play-acting makes it better. I'm like a great actor who doesn't care that his wife is having an affair." She puffed her chest out, and curled her mustache ends. "He decides he *wants* her to do it, wants to be jealous, so he can play a great Othello. He knows that everyone's wife is unfaithful, after all, his, yours"—she looked at me—"but he knows that he's different from you, he can use it. At least this way I have my little joke on everyone. When I'm doing something in our cause, all I worry about is if I have enough script to get me through the scene." She laughed. She was bringing an intensity to her speech (her bit of dialogue?) that suggested she was willfully making an embarrassing revelation. It was hard for me to see what was so awful about what she was saying. I guess it did seem a little adolescent. But it mattered to her: she looked as if she were doing something shameful. "You say to yourself: I know what I'm doing. And because it's secret you feel that it is all yours, you have an inside, you are someone. You think to yourself: I know why I'm doing this, I know how it will bring about the world to come. And *you* don't." She looked at me, at Joaquin, and back again, and once more this way and that, this way and that. "I read somewhere," she said, "in Fanon, I think, that when people are tortured it can drive them crazy. But the ones who are really harboring secrets, they never go mad. Even when they put electric currents through them. They bite down on their secret. They know why they're there. The torture is really traumatic, he says, only if you don't have information to hide. Then it's all so unjust. Why are they doing this to you when you can never satisfy them! It's good to have our secret project. Most people aren't so lucky. They have nothing to hide, they have no *real* secrets." She opened her arms rigidly to the two of us. Her face was willful, her features sharp. The attraction I had felt was transformed by now; she made me feel queasy, gave me a dry feeling as at a clinical demonstration.

"Most people," she said, "most people have no secrets. They're spread open to the world."

This evening we were sitting near my hammock. She was wearing fatigues, her black hair in braids. She had a little green spiral notebook in front of her, but she never consulted it. I asked her how Monje had responded to our apparent change in plans, to my arrival here.

"He goes this way and that," she said. "He repeats what he told Fidel, that the Bolivian Revolution must be run by Bolivians. But he needs Cuban money. When I mentioned your name he promised twenty of his best men for the struggle in the mountains. That's what he calls it always. Mention the word 'guerrillas' and he talks about mountains. He's got mountains on the brain. He told Fidel that he'd follow you anywhere. But I got the feeling that if it were dangerous where you were leading, he'd want to follow from pretty far behind. Then, after making his promise, he talks vaguely about insurrection in the mines again. Or in the city. He says the rest of the Party is against beginning the armed struggle 'in the mountains' too soon. They're afraid of the crack-down, afraid of being outlawed from the next election. They're afraid of being thought of as bed-wetters. They're afraid of a lot, frankly. I did as you said and arranged a meeting for here. Perhaps seeing you will clarify things for him. And anyway, we've recruited the most militant members of the Party. The two brothers, Coco and Inti, they're the best of them. And Jorge is all right. But if the Party turns against you, it will be up to your personal magnetism to hold them."

"And the correctness of my position."

"Yes," she said smiling. "That too. Absolutely. But be crafty when you talk with Monje. You can bring him round if you do it right. Be wily as a serpent, gentle as a dove. Don't define him out of things. Let him think he's a very big part of your plans. He's got a sizable ego. He's got to be flattered a lot, always, made to feel the important man, central to everything. And he's pretty clever too. He's been around awhile."

"And Moises Guevara?"

"He holds down the Peking line among the miners. He's split with the CP about their foot-dragging. Very ardent for the armed struggle. Debray likes him. Moises is working-class. That counts big with Regis. Ricardo met him, though, and says he's a silly troublemaking prick. If we have his support Monje won't touch us. Debray hates Monje. Thinks he's unclear and deceitful. But it's the lack of clarity he hates most. He thinks everyone in the world but you is insufficiently *clear.*" She sat up straight and set her lips in a thin tight line.

With one hand she smoothed down an imaginary Debray mustache. "No compromises for him."

I said, "You'd better close down the warehouse. It's more dangerous than it's worth now."

I met with El Chino, and talked of his plans for Peru. We talked standing, very close to each other, because of his difficulty seeing. He seemed overwhelmed by my presence, effusive as always, hopping back and forth, as if drunk. A small vital man, he squints constantly, despite thick glasses, giving his eyes a Chinese look. A problem with an optic nerve; progressive myopia. "I share your vision of a continental revolution," he said, incongruously, for it was hard to imagine him seeing anything very clearly. He wants to send twenty men for training. "The best opportunity in the world, they'll consider it an unparalleled opportunity."

He'd stay with us for a training march, then go to Cuba and talk the situation over with Fidel. I'd see that the Peruvians got twenty rifles. After we're well established he could send five more men for my "unparalleled" training. We must not internationalize the struggle too quickly. He wanted a photo of me to show the boys in Peru and drive them crazy.

He thinks de la Puente was infiltrated and betrayed. And he believes some of de la Puente's guerrillas are still operating, but he's not certain. I think this is like Jorge's conjectures about Masetti—the need for the immortality of rebellion becomes a ghostly belief in the immortality of rebels.

We had our first batch of homemade bread.

SUMMARY:

1. We'll finish our work on the camp and fortifications (pits with pointed sticks for the most part), then move north to threaten Cochabamba, Santa Cruz, and Sucre. Take control of the railway line from northern Argentina.

2. We will threaten the Gulf Oil pipeline. This will force the imperialists to send troops to defend it.

3. Divided into small bands we will hit several points north of the river.
   While the army is still dispersed we'll retreat back towards camp, and our fortifications.
   If the army follows, we'll kill them.

4. The zone is sparsely populated: harder to organize but easier to defend. Food will be a constant problem here.

But the army will have difficulty operating; and we know the terrain.

We must have stable lines of communication, and supplies of food. The Party's support is essential. With it providing supplies, doing propaganda work in the cities, spreading news of our victories, and sending recruits, we can and will stay here a long time.

5. Hostilities will begin when we're well established. Not before fall of 1967.

12/23/66: Today the men finished work on the supply caves and lined them with canvas. Radio equipment (the transmitting unit), spare clothing, photos, passports, lists of urban contacts have been stored. The caves were covered over with wire gratings, logs, then camouflaged with dirt and bushes.

12/24/66: The mosquitoes are thick at night, and very annoying. I still have an allergic reaction to their bites; they swell on my arm to the size of walnuts. So I've appropriated the only mosquito netting for my own hammock (fortuitous conjunction of power and need). Poem on mosquito netting?

On the radio: a strange piece of advice for the lovelorn of Camiri: "And for my good pal: keep watch! Your lover with the Italian name is on his way to you." This means that Mario Monje, first secretary of the Bolivian CP, is coming to the Nancahuazu camp.

12/25/66: We were gathered in the amphitheater when he arrived, digesting Christmas dinner—roast pig, nougat from Spain, beer and cider. I was leading a session of self-criticism. In the last few days there have been fights between the Bolivians and the Cubans, especially Ricardo, who has been leading the vanguard group. Many of the Bolivians—Chingolo and Coco among them— say he's too harsh, makes them work too much, shows favoritism to Cubans. But many of the Bolivians (I suspect Chingolo) are slackers. It's a bad sign against us (I was saying), for even the shadow of nationalism must be banished. The only nationalism for a country under imperialism is socialist internationalism. So I was saying. (I had to be vague; I didn't know if the Bolivians involved were lying.)

I was speaking from my place on the logs, my words rising into the cool evening. I could hardly see the men's faces, causing a lazy infatuation with my own voice. "You have no nationality anymore except the liberated territory directly under your feet." At first I wasn't glad to see Monje. His presence could only draw these apparent contradictions more sharply. But that would be good for us, after the initial difficulty: it would purify our forces.

I got up from the log and went over to him. At another time I would have stood up, but waited for him to come to me. That would have been better for the men to see: we must rely on ourselves only, not on outsiders. But I needed the Party's support in the cities, for agitational work, supplies, cadres. And I wanted to bridge the gap between the Cubans and the Bolivians. So I walked over to him.

"I am Che Guevara," I said. I still had a balding forehead and gray hair; I was barely recognizable. Monje and I clasped hands, and he looked down quizzically at mine, for one expects a stronger grip from a warrior. I'd barely touched his flesh. His hand was tender, a bureaucrat's, but his grip was firm. His face, only dimly lit now, looked round and plump, with small eyes, slight black beard, and he wore a green cap that was too small, perched high on his head. His clothes were the same fatigues we all wore, but fresh-looking compared with ours; more of a costume, I thought. He looked uncomfortable, kept hitching his shoulders back to make things fit. He was a young man, about my age.

"Guevara," he said, "I am honored. We must talk. When I get my breath back, that is. That was a long walk for me." He smiled. The men were all looking at us. Monje's unstated question—Why are *you* here?—was in everyone's mind.

"Yes. We must talk." I started to squat down.

"But we cannot talk here." His voice was deep but not overly resonant, a sincere effective voice for small gatherings, for committee meetings.

"Why not?" I said (though I knew).

Monje gestured very slightly with his arm, indicating the men watching us.

"Anything we say can be said in front of them. We're together in this now," I said, though that was not yet clear. "It is liberty or death for all of us."

"Yes. I know. I understand. I appreciate that fact deeply." He smiled a little at my speech. A politician's admiration for a gesture, tempered by the fact that it was at his expense. "Still, I think we should talk alone. We might both feel freer, find it easier to curse at each other a little."

I agreed. We walked over to the round brick bake-oven, near where my own hammock swung between the trees. It was a clear night now, a little chilly, with many sharp stars. There was a fire going in the oven—fresh bread for the morning—and the flame gave a low steady reddish light to our bodies. Monje squatted down, as countrypeople do, low on his haunches, flatfooted, with his ass up against his ankles, the body balanced, self-contained. Were his parents peasants? I didn't know his class background. That made me feel off balance.

I sat as he did, opposite him. We might have been about to draw figures in the dirt between us, discuss the weather, the crops.

He gave me a cigar, lit it with a square silver lighter, then lit one for himself. His hand flared before me, and his troll's face with its little black beard. His features were in the shadow of his peaked cap; his eyes were a deeper darkness in the darkness of his face.

"I needn't tell you," he said, "that these cigars are Cuban. A present from Fidel, when we last talked this matter over." He puffed for a moment, circling the cigar end in the lighter's flame. "Your name wasn't mentioned then. Or at all, until quite recently."

"I'd like to make clear now," I said, "that I am here in my name only. And my intention—to realize my ideas—is mine alone. I don't want to damage relations between the Cuban and Bolivian parties."

He made his cigar glow for a moment, not speaking, illuminating a silver ring on his finger. (A wedding ring?) "I am here," he said, "for the BCP, to begin with you a discussion, a serious discussion, on the problems facing the Bolivian Revolution. Before we begin that discussion, I must say that the Party cannot be committed to any specific scheme."

This was already a betrayal. He had promised to commit men to the struggle. But I didn't say anything about his duplicity. I needed his support. And you have to be careful with bureaucrats, they have enormous vanity. "And I want you to know, before we talk, that I intend to begin the struggle with those here with me now, with whoever remains with me. We want your participation as political head of the guerrillas, subordinate only to the military chief. For the moment that is me."

"Well, we have a lot to discuss."

"What I said was clear."

"Yes. Oh, yes. It was clear. The Party thinks, though, that there must be a Bolivian head of the revolution as long as it has a Bolivian environment."

"I will be military chief. There will be one command." I wanted to define the positions sharply. He would have to confront it and eventually change. I would not allow the Party to control the guerrillas.

"The Party," he said, "must direct the guerrilla movement."

"I understand," I said angrily. "You will supply the ideas from the city, and we will supply the dead in the countryside, in 'the mountains.' No. The guerrilla movement is now the vanguard of the class struggle. It is the people in uniform." The Party, if I allowed it, would compromise our goal: continental revolution. I was sure of it. They want the guerrillas to put pressure on the national ruling class, then call them off if a good deal can be made, if they'll share power. But the guerrilla is the only instrument that can smash the army, and without that no socialist revolution can stay in power in America. "One form of struggle is primary if the aim is revolution. Guerrilla war. There must be a single command to the struggle: the guerrilla chief. The guerrillas do not merely create the conditions in the city for a coup d'état. Quickly won and quickly lost. The people have not struggled, they have not shaken off their passivity, they are not transformed. And the army remains. The imperialists will share power only for a moment. The guerrilla struggle is the method for class struggle throughout Latin America, for making the Continental Revolution. We will win."

"Bolivia is not Cuba, comrade. Our country is strongly nationalist. You will not be able to unite the masses unless the Bolivian Revolution is also a nationalist revolution, and has a Bolivian head."

"You know, Monje, the imperialists see you rolling your little ball of twine across the field, saying, 'Everything on this side is Bolivian and belongs to me, and everything on the other side belongs to Guevara.' And they laugh. Because they know that the whole field is theirs. And as long as you talk like that it will always be theirs. Something called the 'Bolivian Revolution' cannot be won. They'd strangle this country to death: *you have no port.* They'd organize the petite bourgeoisie against you. They'd have you overthrown. It's a joke, a running joke, already on its way to a plane into exile. If we do not struggle on many fronts, in Africa, Asia, and Latin America, we cannot win. We must divide the forces of imperialism, here, and in Brazil, in Peru, in Argentina, Colombia, Uruguay, Ecuador. We will make this continent another Vietnam. They cannot fight like that, here and in Indochina. We'll bleed them to death. The Revolution must be continental. Once we make that clear, once you help us make that clear, the people will understand. You must share my vision."

I was gesturing with my cigar as I spoke, and by mistake touched the lighted end on my own wrist. I yelped.

"What?" Monje said.

"Nothing. An accident." We paused for a moment. The pain was good for me; it distracted my mind from my anger. I cooled off, but my anger had left me exhausted. Monje was scratching himself through his beard, over and over. My words were annoying flies. Or maybe he was being bitten by mosquitoes. Lenin's phrase came to mind: If you want to know what the bourgeoisie is thinking, don't listen to their words, watch their hands. And a phrase then came to my mind, I don't know from where: If you want to know what you're thinking, watch your own hands in dreams. I wondered what Lenin would have thought of that? . . . Clearly I was tired.

"You haven't heard me out, Comandante." That was true. We had both been talking very quickly, exchanging slogans. Though I did not expect to hear much from him anymore, perhaps he would come around now that my stand was clear, now that he saw the possibility of continental revolution. We *would* go ahead without him. If the Bolivian Party didn't support us they'd be swept away. His voice slowed down. "As the head of the Revolution," he said, "I will be better able to secure our relations with other groups. I can secure the support of the Communist parties throughout the continent. You have spoken of how important it is for the work in the cities to complement the guerrilla groups in the mountains. I think I can secure Venezuela's support for Douglas Bravo. Codovilla is a friend of mine."

This was more crap. "You are certainly welcome to try. But it won't work. For Codovilla to support Bravo is for him to support an insurrection in his own party. I am sure I will be able to unite the revolutionary forces of the continent." I didn't need him.

"You seem very certain of your powers," Monje said, almost sarcastically.

"I am sure of the correctness of my ideas. And I am willing to risk my life to prove that they are right." I tried to talk more slowly, too. But I wanted to get this over with. I wanted Monje to leave. I could tell we'd never get anything from him till we won victories. This whole conversation—though I'd given nothing away—made me feel unclean. I felt as if my bowels and ass were straining, as if I were trying to defecate.

Monje said, "I will resign my position in the Party, secure its neutrality, and bring cadres with me."

He would be of the Party and not of it. I needed his cadres, but he'd find a way to make us dirty, to compromise us. It wasn't worth that. "Your resignation is up to you," I said. "But you're just protecting the good name of the Central Committee members who should be denounced for betraying the struggle if they don't support us. It's a vacillating position. They should be condemned for their crookedness. We must make our position clear. Time will decide who is right. Our task now is to unite all who will be united to make the Revolution."

"That is another point," Monje said, calmly, as if he didn't care, or didn't notice, that I'd insulted him. "We think your force is attracting all the heterodox elements, the pro-Peking groups, the Trotskyites. You've been negotiating with the renegade Moises Guevara. As political chief of the guerrillas I can give the force a consistent line. I will keep out adventurers and provocateurs. And infiltrators. We will follow the Party line and have their cadres."

For a time I said nothing; I was weary and anxious at once; I wanted to be out of this. Monje again lit his cigar, and I imagined I could see the expression on his face, a look of hurt, and great anger. But I had nothing more to say. "These polemics are for the rich. I will unite all who will be united to make the revolution. I will be the chief of the guerrillas."

"Comandante, I must ask if your stand is subject to bargaining?" Monje, too, sounded nervous, as if he'd done what he had to do, and wanted to leave.

"No." He knew it wasn't. It never had been. This was all *shit.* I wanted it over with. "I am the chief."

"Then we have no more to discuss. I must take this opportunity to tell your men that whatever my personal feelings may be—and I admire you very much —they will not have the support of the Party, and they will be breaking Party discipline by staying here."

Monje rocked forward and heaved himself up quickly. I, too, stood up, but my right foot had fallen asleep and my leg crumpled under me. I half fell to the ground. Monje caught me and pulled me up.

"Thank you."

"Think nothing of it."

Neither of us wanted to look the other in the face.

We walked back into the camp. My bowels were heavy still.

We gathered the militants together in a semicircle by the lectern. There was a lantern on the table. The Bolivians looked like young boys. My comrades from Cuba, who stood farther off in the shadows, had all entered the country disguised as old men. Seen together like this we look odd, something indefinably off about us that annoys at the edge of consciousness; find what's wrong with this picture; it was as if some of us were wearing putty noses, or ears, or chins. A family of normal sons and a clownish group of fathers.

Monje said, "The Party cannot support the guerrilla movement. As a matter of Party discipline, the militants must leave with me."

The men, their faces softly illuminated by the lantern, looked at each other and at me. I said nothing and made no sign. A fair test: it would purify our forces. Jorge shuffled a bit on his legs and ran his hands over his face. But no one else moved.

Monje spoke again, resonantly, "As the first secretary of the Communist Party of Bolivia, I am ordering all Party members, as a matter of Party discipline, to leave now, with me."

Not one of my chicks moved. They looked over at the cooking fire where Ricardo was making a big tin pot full of coffee. Their ears were filled with talk about me, Fidel's praises, which we'd just heard on the radio, their own dreams of glory. And something more, I thought: the beginning of a commitment whose end was not clear. My position had been the correct one. It had held them.

Jorge said, "I'm staying. Victory or death." He needed to spit in someone's eye, a gesture to ratify his decision.

One by one the men repeated the statement.

Inti concluded the circle, very sad-looking, as always. "It's victory or death," he said, fabricating a little benediction of his own. Inti, tall, stooped, reminded me of a minister. Or an undertaker. "They make it that way. We cannot share power with imperialism. We cannot, we will not, share this world with them."

Monje turned towards him and stared. "If you ask me, Inti, it's you that makes it that way. Right now we can breathe and carry on our work. You're going to put a stop to all that."

Then, clearly, he regretted speaking. He worked his lips nervously, sucking them in and out, looking at the ground. "Well," he said finally, in a calm voice, "you've won their hearts, Comandante. I hope Jorge and the others are more obedient to your orders, to this commitment, than they were to the Party's. And you may find that the countrypeople don't know your name as well as Party militants do." He smiled, and everyone else smiled as well, relieved. "This is a historic moment, isn't it?" Monje said. "The beginning of this great enterprise?"

"Yes," I said. "Let's have a drink."

Ponco poured rum into the tin cups, and I personally gave each man his drink. I raised my cup. "This marks the beginning of a new War to the Knife, the Continental Revolution, the liberation of our continent. Our lives, the lives of any man among us, mean nothing, nothing when compared with the importance of making the Revolution, the deeds of revolution."

The men raised their glasses and we all drank down the sweet burning liquid.

Coco said, "Let's have another."

So we did.

Later, by the fire, after Monje had left, we tossed in the dregs of rum, making little hisses and flicks of flame. Ricardo served up the coffee. Camba said, "We should mingle blood." He extended his wrist and made a light cutting motion across his vein with a finger of his other hand. "It would show that we're all comrades, and that when one man's blood is spilled, so is everyone's." Camba is the youngest of the men. His face is thin, his eyes intense, his movements angular, jerky. Maybe he was drunk on the rum and the beer from dinner.

"We don't need rituals to prove that," Joaquin said paternally. "It's true."

Camba said, "I think the Party's position is disgraceful. Monje is going

back on his word to us. I think he should be killed, and his blood will serve
as an exemplary punishment for his vacillation. We could follow him right now
and shoot him in the head, or we could have someone in the city do it." He
made a pistol with his finger and shot himself in the head. "Pow."

He still wanted a blood ritual; Monje's blood this time. His desire to kill
Monje, a party leader, a comrade, proved his commitment to me, to the others,
to himself.

Several of the men, though, nodded. I was surprised to see Mustache
among them. I suppose they felt abandoned by the Party at a time when
individually they each faced great danger.

"No," I said. "The Party will support us at some point. Once they see that
we will win."

Tania agreed. "Yes. Che was right. I hadn't seen it before. This way the
Party won't be a brake on your actions. And when you win victories the Party
will support you."

From My Journal

12/30/66: I am sad. Today I am very sad. There is clearly some problem with
my friend's, our chief's, character. All this talk of purity! Who cares about
purity? Only saints and crazy people who wash themselves over and over.
Gandhi! He should have compromised with Monje, made some deal. Or lied
to him. Or best of all, gotten men from him, taken Monje on the march with
us as "political chief" and killed him. Not the way that Camba said, to make
an example. That's like Che, more purity crap, making examples to the world.
No, it should have been sneaky, the way Fidel would have done it. Why does
Che have to draw the line, be right, appear before everyone as an example, with
clean hands, get us in bad difficulties?

I spoke to him about it. "You should have made a deal with him."

"There was no deal possible." He looked angry at me. He's changed; he
doesn't want a "devil's advocate" anymore. Or any opposition. But I am his
friend, so I went on.

"You got angry," I said, "you consigned him to the flames. All right,
he is no *revolutionary*, yes, I agree. But you could have lied to him. You could
have let him think more highly of himself. You could have neutralized
him."

"No, that would have muddled the situation. This way our stand is clear
and sharp. Tania agrees with me."

"Who knows what she thinks!"

"We will be an example to be emulated, a rallying point. Everyone knows what we stand for."

"I could have stood the ambiguity."

"No. By making our position clear we'll attract better people, ones who are truly committed to us. The situation will organize itself around us. We will ring like a bell."

"Ding-dong!" It was all I could think of to say.

Che laughed at me, and walked away.

That was our conversation. It made me sad. It makes me scared, too.

From Guevara's Journal

12/31/66: I laughed this morning to think of my conversation with Monje. It should have gone:

Guevara: I spit on you.
Monje: You're a fool.
Guevara: You're a coward.
Monje: You're an adventurer.
Guevara: You're a worm pretending to be a snake.
Monje: You're an invalid pretending to be a hero.

But then, this afternoon, I had a troubling conversation with Inti that was far from comical. (Inti is a profoundly serious young man, perhaps a little melancholy. I like him. I will make him political commissar over the Bolivians, to settle the uncertainties and doubts that are bound to develop about the line we are following—once the worm of hunger starts gnawing in their guts. There is nothing like hunger to improve the workings of the critical faculties. They will wonder if guerrilla warfare is mass enough, or is it adventurist, or is Guevara simply a madman. Once we win victories and gain recruits it will all seem clear to them again. But for the time of uncertainty and anguish, Inti can provide the necessary clarity, the necessary discipline.) Inti thinks that Monje knew—from conversation with Debray and Coco—that I would never agree to relinquish leadership of the guerrilla to the Party. He came with that demand, knowing it would force a rupture and leave him with clean hands, as if he'd tried to make a deal. That's why he wasn't disturbed by my insults. There had been no hurt on his face; I'd imagined it. I needed him but he didn't want anything from our conversation.

This was especially troubling: Monje's reports to Fidel and Debray had been crucial in our decision to come to Bolivia (whatever we may have thought of him personally). He had described Bolivia as ripe for rebellion. Inti thinks this was a ploy to get Fidel's money.

But Inti says that he himself is unshakable in his conviction that ours is the right course, and that this is the right time to begin. Victory or death.

Isle of Pines, May 1968

MAY 6

Even then I knew it would become a story!
September 7: "Notes for the beginning of a book," and "A name for the book of the Bolivian Expedition: The Revolution of the Weak Lungs." I didn't think of writing a book in Vietnam or in the Congo. But in Bolivia, it seems, I knew from the first. (I don't remember *knowing*—yet there it is in my journal. I kept thinking of titles!)

Again the dark of the room closes around me! Did thinking of titles, of making a story—was that evil? How stupid! *I* didn't kill *him* so that I would have something to tell! I didn't kill him at all! *He* nearly killed *me!*

Anyway, his mother knew first. It's in the manuscript he wrote before we left for the Congo to train the men. "You'll make a story out of yourself."

He said once that I reminded him of his mother!

No more today.

MAY 7

The *worst* thing is: sometimes it makes me happy. I look at the piles of papers, his, theirs, mine, the photos from U.S. magazines, the new pile that I'm making by copying out sections from their journals—and I'm filled with joy. I wish there were a mirror in this place: I want to dance in front of it! It's mine, I think, it's mine! That's a terrible thing to think! To be happy for his—I can't write it!—for his *death*—isn't that what it means? Not "*it's* mine"—but "*he's* mine"!

I didn't kill him! *He* almost killed *me!*

MAY 8

I'm thinking of my conversation with him after Monje left. Why did he speak to Monje that way? To be pure? To make an example?

In his manuscript he said that *they* made examples of their victims. They were terrorists. What if *he* made an example of *himself*? Was he a terrorist, with himself as victim?

He wasn't his only victim. Just five of us escaped. Five!

In the book I was reading on this island last time, a thousand years ago, when I was a child, the mad captain threw his sextant overboard. He wanted to read his boat's position from the stars. (What's a sextant? Some way of finding out where you are? I need a dictionary.) Why does he do it? Was it like Che with Monje? (In the book it was called *"dead* reckoning.") The captain wanted to make it hard on himself. (But it wasn't just himself he was hard on. The whole boat went down. Only five survived.) So he could feel it was himself only, *his* will, uncompromised, shining purely, like a flare. Hilda was right. Purity makes bad politics. Like Quixote. Ahab. Bad politics but good stories. I think Che would have liked it better if we hadn't used rifles! They would have had fancy weapons, and we would have just our will and the purity of our motives. (He hadn't changed! He still hated technology!)

Talking like this means no dinner tonight. I have to punish myself, send myself to bed.

Bolivia, 1967

JANUARY

From Guevara's Journal

1/2/67: In the late afternoon, after a day's work cutting trails, I gathered the men in the "amphitheater" for Joaquin to talk to them about Masetti. I wanted to reinforce my speech about the difficulties to come, the trials we would face;

I wanted the men to have something to test their green commitment against.

Joaquin stood stiffly by the lectern. He is a huge man, with arms like steam shovels. He stared straight ahead as he spoke, not even looking from face to face. Public speaking must make him uncomfortable; and the mobility I remembered in his face has been gone since his return from Argentina. The only motion he made was the bobbing up and down of his giant Adam's apple.

It began as a lecture, in his deep paternal voice. "Before the guerrillas are established among the people is the most difficult, the most dangerous time for them. We must all be very careful that we are not seen, or that we have a good story for whoever sees us. This is what happened to us in Argentina: we were discovered before we could begin killing the soldiers. The zone we operated in didn't have enough people. It was poor. And that made it difficult to get food.

"The first thing our commander, Jorge Masetti, did, when we arrived in the mountains of Argentina, was to issue a proclamation of our existence, of our strategy, and our goals. He wanted the people to rally to us. He wanted to make our stand clear. This was a mistake. Before we were ready to face the army, the army knew all about us. Many people did come to join us, dedicated people, good people, people who were eager to fight. I remember a boy named Growald. He had his toenails extracted so they wouldn't become ingrown and hobble him on the march.

"But we never really saw the army. There were no victories. The guerrillas began to turn on each other." Joaquin's eyes were unfocused, sunk into himself; he wasn't looking at any of us; he wasn't talking to us anymore. He had told the story many times, he was telling it again. The images were made to pass through his mind and he tried to feel nothing. To feel nothing, he had to be far from the images. His face, I noticed, was covered with perspiration, but he didn't touch it. He wouldn't, or couldn't, move his hands; they lay by his sides. I wanted to wipe the sweat from him.

His voice became slower and slower, as he tried to keep from sinking into his dream, his nightmare. "There were fights constantly, just constantly. Men began to talk about whether guerrilla struggle was the right course. Maybe it was elitist or adventurist. Maybe we had begun too early. Maybe we should have prepared the ground more. Masetti should have stopped such talk; he should have been stronger. But maybe he had doubts himself, too many doubts. Everyone thought of a reason. The boy Growald was tried for lack of morale. That wasn't the answer. He was tried for being too critical, for spreading dissension. I didn't understand that. Everyone was doing it. And he hadn't stolen food from others. The tribunal was undecided. But Masetti ordered him shot. I was ordered to carry out the sentences. I didn't understand it. But I did it. The boy died shouting, 'Long live the Revolution!' "

I sat on a split log, part way up the hill, sucking on my pipe. It was out; it tasted stale. But my hands felt too heavy to light it again. I tried to remember what Growald's face looked like, then realized that I'd never seen him, only heard about him from Joaquin. But I knew people like him, boys who at first are so ardent for the armed struggle they have to show it in some way, having their toenails extracted or their chest tattooed, or doing some ritual, like Camba's. But this need just shows how weak their feeling is. I had even killed a boy like that. He had strangled a policeman in the city, without help, then walked to the Sierras with the man's gun. Later he committed a rape, telling a peasant girl that he was Che Guevara, the doctor, and wanted to examine her. He begged me to have him buried with his uniform on. I couldn't allow that. And he, too, died praising the Revolution.

"From then on," Joaquin said, "everyone knew that going on was pointless. But we went on, marching around. Our radio was broken. We had no contact with the outside. Masetti, our commander, became withdrawn. No one could speak to him. He didn't speak to anyone, only gave orders, that's how it was. Men began to desert. The army caught the deserters, and got information from them, and shot them. The army sent infiltrators to join us and lead us into traps. The army infiltrated our city network. They sent soldiers dressed as peasants into the zone, so they knew all our movements. We were betrayed constantly, over and over. Three of the guerrillas were captured when they surprised our camp. Some of us escaped, but without any food. We went deeper into the jungle. Three died of starvation. I saw this. We were so hungry that I saw men eat fruit that caused convulsions, and they ate it even though they knew it caused convulsions. That is how it was. Masetti and I were the only ones left. He left me one night and went deeper into the jungle. I wouldn't follow him there—a wild place, with jaguars, and vegetation so thick that you couldn't see the sun. It was a way of killing himself. I'm sure of that. He wanted to die. I made my way back into Bolivia, shooting monkeys and birds for food. I was the only one that escaped."

The men nodded, or stared at the ground, or looked very grave, suitably impressed. Stiff little masks of mourning; they were tempted to break into smiles. A sham, a false internal dialectic, a failure of the imagination. At the mention of each difficulty they said to themselves, Would I act like that? I would never act like that! And then it was as if the difficulty had been overcome in fact as well as in fantasy. Their pride in themselves increased proportionately. They were ready to face the next problem with their new pride, certain now that they wouldn't give in to it. Illusory, suicidal dialectic.

My limbs, too, were heavy with grief. I and Joaquin (he was heavy too; he continued to stand rigidly by the table), we were the only ones moved by his talk.

1/7/67: I send the men out each day in small hunting parties, for birds. This will train their eyes. The farmers (Jorge, Coco, Aniceto) purchased additional food in Camiri.

Groups from the vanguard (under Ricardo) cut more trails for escape. We now have trails on both sides of the Nancahuazu River.

1/8/67: Our neighbor came to the Tin House to talk to Jorge again. (Jorge has a full mustache now. Still nothing immediately under his nose. But he leaves it alone. I think I'll call him Jorge.) Our neighbor is a very nervous fellow, Jorge says. Ran the brim of his black felt hat through his fingers, over and over, with great dexterity, turning a wheel. "He has a long nose, and a thin face that slopes backward, the nose is like the tip of a pyramid. He's got long flowing black hair that he combs backward. And he's missing his two front teeth. His teeth are all rotten and brown. He reminded me of some animal, but I couldn't think of the name of it."

"A ferret," I said.

"A hawk," Ponco said.

"A fox," Inti said.

"A bloodhound," Camba said.

"Please go on," I said.

"Well, I didn't invite him in. I didn't want him getting too chummy. He stared at his shoes for a while, asking if the shooting was good, how the game was running. He said, 'There are certainly a lot of hunters, a lot of men with rifles around here, a lot of hunting going on, unh-huh, unh-huh, unh-huh.' He said 'unh-huh' over and over after every few words. And in between sentences he would whisper things to himself very fast.

" 'Yes,' I said, 'we often have friends up to hunt. I told you we would be using this place as a hunting lodge for our friends, as well as doing a little farming. Don't you remember?' He was very oily with me, very obsequious. I acted like he was a piece of cow dung that I didn't want inside, so he'd know his place and leave us alone." Jorge paused, to see if I approved.

I smiled. "Go on." Jorge was a good mimic.

"Algaranaz said, 'Unh-huh, unh-huh.' He was drunk, I think. He smelled boozy and rank. And he was leaning up against one of the door jambs as if to steady himself. While I was talking he started sinking down. He stopped turning his hat and gripped it till his knuckles were white. He braced himself against the door, and stared at me. We were only a few feet apart. He said, 'I know you're not a hunter.' His eyes were going unfocused; I thought he was going to pass out. 'No, I know what you're doing, unh-huh, unh-huh. I know a lot of things about you.' He started whispering again while I stared at him, dumbfounded. 'I know a lot more than you think I do. And I'm willing to collaborate in the cocaine business, unh-huh, unh-huh. The cocaine business, isn't it? Isn't it? That brings in a lot of money, doesn't it? You have to be more even-handed with your gains. We're not all as rich as you are, you know.'

"I told him he was crazy, and just walked away. Left him in the doorway. After a while I saw he had clamped his hat down really hard on his head and walked off."

I instructed him to tell Algaranaz that we'd be happy to have his "help with the farm," his advice on "how the game is running." Offer him a small bribe, and add that if he makes any trouble for us at all, if he goes to the police, if he tells anyone, even a friend, you'll find out about it and you'll have him killed.

I know Algaranaz's type well, and we're in no real danger. The peasant farmer who has done all right for himself, a shrewd, cunning man. A mixture of short-lived belligerence, petty daring, and deep subservience. Courage enough for a little blackmail, a little black-market dealing, but not enough essential dignity to see how petty his schemes are, that he's just about as badly used as the poorer peasants, his occasional employees. The small landowner's vanity is immense. But it's just vanity, not pride. There's no way for it to become revolutionary anger. The oppressor sits in his heart, a fierce fat little god, and exhales dread. Algaranaz has no character except what he apes from the class above him. He tries to make out his idol's words, but when Algaranaz speaks them they appear all mangled, comical. He knows he sounds like a clown, and he hates himself for it. So he takes revenge on anyone more powerless. Greed, resentment, and dread are the substance of his little life. Jorge's contempt was just the right tactic to remind Algaranaz of his place. The threat will be enough, when coupled with a sweet little bribe, to take care of him completely.

From My Journal

1/11/67: Three days ago Jorge Vasquez paid the bribe to Algaranaz. Today three policemen came to the ranch to demand a bribe for themselves as well.

The bug felt the touch but jumped in an unexpected direction. Algaranaz was more daring than Che thought. Or he couldn't help boasting.

We had to pay the bribe to the police. Soon the whole countryside will be on our payroll, and we won't have to make a revolution. We'll order them to become Communists, and fire the ones who don't.

Does Che, I wonder, underestimate the courage of the petite bourgeoisie? He has too many theories, sometimes, to see what's right before his eyes. But it's hard anymore to talk about these things with him. I'll save it for my book, *My Comrade, Che.* (Or perhaps, *My Difficult Comrade, Che.* Or, *My Pig-headed Comrade, Che.*)

From Guevara's Journal

1/14/67: Coco returned from La Paz, where he'd gone to get the recruits from the youth wing of the Party. I met him in the Bear Camp, overlooking the farm. He was still wearing his business suit, a thin blue fabric, worn through and too small for him. His black shoes were dusty from his walk, his face, usually so amiable-looking, was red, angry.

"I got them all right. As planned. Then *he* popped up at the bus terminal."

"Who popped up?" I said. "Slow down."

"Monje," Coco said. But he didn't slow down. "He was waiting at the bus by the door, by the bus to Camiri. He stood right in front of the door and said, 'I won't allow you to take these men with you. They're Young Communist militants, and they're under Party discipline. I can't allow them to go with you.' You know, as if it wasn't his idea, but a Party decision that he had to carry out. Well, two of them said they were going anyway, they didn't give a fuck about Party discipline. They were good kids. They were brave guys. One of them said he was a Party member, and wanted to remain a Party member. One of them didn't say anything at all. He was too confused. I thought he was going to faint in the middle of the bus station. He would have been a big help! Monje said that if any of them went with me on the bus he was going to give their names to the police, and tell the police all about them. I couldn't believe that! I had loved Monje, you know, and he would kill us all! I said, 'If you do that, I'll kill you. I swear to you, Monje, that Inti or I will kill you.' But I had to leave the men with him, and get on the bus, didn't I? I didn't have any choice, did I? I just couldn't take the risk of his informing on us. The whole thing upset me a lot. I have to sit down. Why did he do that?"

What *is* Monje's game? First his offer to Fidel, and now this. His duplicity? Or perhaps even Soviet pressure?

Kill him?

Kill Algaranaz now? As an example?

Too late for that.

1/15/67: This evening a disastrous session of criticism, self-criticism. Coco's report has made the Bolivians edgy. They wonder why the Party is so adamant? Is it good sense? Betrayal? Power politics? A reading of history on a level they are not yet initiated in? They are picking at a scab.

The talk soon degenerated further. Benjamin, a serious young medical student from the city, part of Ricardo's vanguard group, said Ricardo is playing favorites. (I have the vanguard group staying at the Bear Camp, keeping watch over the farm area.) "He makes Bolivians do all the shit jobs, all the carrying, all the cleaning up."

Ricardo was sitting near Benjamin, his long legs sprawled out. He did not defend himself at first, or even seem to notice, but remained relaxed, hardly moving. No one spoke. Ricardo said, "Benjamin, stop whining."

This stupid response infuriated Benjamin. As if against his will, hypnotized, he got up and walked towards Ricardo. He didn't know what he was doing, he was so enraged, his anger pushed him forward, like a wind, until he was facing Ricardo. He shouted, nearly screamed, "You told me Bolivians aren't worth shit!" Benjamin was shaking.

Ricardo ignored him, turning away slowly, and looked at me. "I punished some of the Bolivians, Che, because they showed disrespect towards me, and towards you, Che." He paused (as if he were trying to decide whether to break some slight to me or protect me; or perhaps for invention), "They called you . . . they called you a pompous fuck."

Benjamin emitted a screech, "That's a lie!" His body leaned towards Ricardo in a little weaving motion. Then an extraordinary thing happened: Benjamin spat at Ricardo, but just as he was spitting, Camba put up his palm and caught the spit in his hand. He wiped his hand off on his pants, and gave Benjamin a sweet understanding smile.

Everyone looked over at me. I was inappropriately smiling, too, at the unexpected grace of it. I ordered Benjamin to sit down, and talked a little of the difficulties of waiting, of the unity we would find once the march began. But I spoke cursorily, quickly, I couldn't wait to dismiss them. Such petty difficulties make me nauseous. At that moment, despite my smile, I despised them all.

From Camba's Journal

1/17/67: Ricardo is a stiff arrogant brutal courageous temperamental prick. I respect him but I hate him. He smokes a pipe and looks down at the end of it, so his eyes are together at the end of his nose. He wears thick glasses too, so his eyes look huge and watery. He has long thin fingers that he curves over the bowl of the pipe, and he moves very gracefully. Not like me. The way he moves is very smooth and attractive. Then he stops, like he's remembering something, and becomes all jerky, the way I am.

From Guevara's Journal

1/31/67: *Monthly Summary.* Monje's actions cloud the picture. We cannot expect support from the Party until we win victories.

The soldiers and police may soon tumble to what we're up to, no matter what bribes we pay.

We will sooner than expected have to enter the nomadic phase.

We must form the guerrillas into a nucleus of steel.

The arguments with Ricardo, and between Bolivians and Cubans, show that more speeches from me will not help.

Only shared hardships can now speak.

FEBRUARY

From Guevara's Journal

2/4/67: Tania, in complete violation of the instructions I gave her, has come to camp. I did not think that such carelessness and disobedience were characteristic of her! There is always the possibility she was followed. If she was, not only will the army have found us, but our liaisons will be trapped here with us. She brought Debray, who will be the contact with Cuba, and Bustos, the Argentine liaison. They will be followed, Regis says, by Moises Guevara, bringing six men that he has recruited from the mines.

2/5/67: A few groups of soldiers, small patrols, have been seen here and there near the Tin House, nosing about, even as far as the river. What are they looking for? and why? They are like some progressive disease, the first sign red spots here and there on the patient's arms, legs, trunk.

Jorge and I: aristocrats still. I misjudged Algaranaz. (My mother's contemptuousness for people who were "not our type.") Or Tania?

2/6/67: The patient presented another symptom: reconnaissance planes flew over the zone today.

From My Journal

2/8/67: A group of thirty soldiers approached the Tin House across the open fields in front, and from along the riverbank. Pacho, one of the former miners, who was with Ricardo in the vanguard, disobeyed orders and shot one of the patrol. Ricardo struck Pacho across the face with the handle of a machete, and ordered the immediate retreat of the vanguard group towards the base camp, where Che was, with the main body of our men.

A messenger from Ricardo preceded the vanguard. He arrived at the main camp, sweaty and out of breath, and told everyone to prepare for complete retreat. Che was enraged by Ricardo's orders. He pushed his chest out as if he were having one of his attacks. He dictated a message to me for Ricardo, that "wars are won with bullets." He ordered the vanguard to return to Bear Camp and set up ambushes in the established locations.

He seemed exhausted by his rage, and conducted his meetings with Bustos on Argentina while lying in his hammock. After that he began a chess game with Debray.

It is all *too fast*. I am stunned.

From Guevara's Journal

2/9/67: I told Debray what a useful tool a pipe is for a guerrilla. Shreds of tobacco, cigar ends, can all be used in a pipe. I began to wax lyrical about my own pipe, engraved with names of battles in Cuba. "A pipe and a pair of boots, that's all a guerrilla needs, Regis. Make a note of that for your book. With them he has a feeling of contentment—that's the pipe—and security—that's the boots. With decent boots he can flee from danger, he's the master of his fate."

Debray, usually a note-taker, was hardly listening. He was jumpy about the coming battle. But he played well, as always.

A poem to my pipe and boots?

From My Journal

2/9/67: If it was too early to engage the army before, why is it right now? We could have withdrawn, given up this project. The Party is against us here. The reports, both on the Party and the landscape, were wrong. And the miners Moises brought with him are crap.

Che's temper. Che's pride.

No. *This time he was right.* We are here. The time to fight is now. You can't balance these things forever. Our violence will change the political situation, the Party's attitude. I hope.

From Coco's Journal

2/10/67: My first battle.

Our ambush was by the river. After they walked into it and we opened fire we shouted, "Long live the Army of National Liberation! Long live free Bolivia!" At first I was so nervous I was firing my rifle as quickly as I could. Then I remembered what Che had said and husbanded my ammunition, picking my targets. When I did that I could hear my own voice, and I wasn't really shouting our slogans—I was screaming them in a high-pitched voice at the top of my lungs. I could hear the other men from both sides, and some of them were screaming too. "Surrender, soldiers! We don't want to kill you!" And: "Join us! We are your brothers!" I think it was my own brother, Inti, who was shouting that. He sounded calm. He always sounds calm. How I admire that!

Their lieutenant was in the middle of the river, and that was where he was wounded. I think I shot him, but I can't be sure. (Ricardo put his arm around me afterward and said it was me.) The lieutenant kept on shooting at the mountainside where our part of the ambush was. I saw him hit someone and heard a scream. It was Moro, I guess, wounded in the arm. The lieutenant managed to get to the riverbank, but then he was right in range and the bullets really started to come down on him. He did a strange thing: he raised his hands up, as if he could protect himself that way, as if they would keep off bullets! He was wounded in so many places! He died by the river, his body half in and half out of the water. Some of his men followed him forward, and they died too.

From My Journal

2/10/67: After the battle, Inti, one of the best of the Bolivians, was delegated by Che to speak to the captured officers, offering the major in charge a truce for the entire zone, "if you would be willing to stay with the guerrillas to guarantee it."

The battle had a curious effect on me. I felt my heart opening towards the captured men, not with pity, but as if it were a radio station! I could receive their thoughts, broadcast by their nervous mannerisms—and the major had a lot of tics. I was seeing things *from* their eyes. A tall sad-looking fellow with a mustache offered the major a truce if he would stay in the zone to guarantee it. The major laughed hollowly (I was sure his laugh had slowed his progress in the army). He tried to think of something to say to this bizarre offer. What did *he* care if there was a truce? And why did this sad-looking fellow think the major's presence would guarantee anything? As if General Barrientos thought the major was the Holy Infant! He did not! The major twitched—he was finding it hard to come up with a reply. He was uncomfortable and scared. His clothes were wet. He thought: I wouldn't want to die in water. Then he laughed again, thinking: As if your skin could feel clammy after death! For a moment he saw—*I* saw, I saw *him* seeing—the image of the lieutenant's body lying half in and half out of the water. It made the major shiver. I don't want a truce, he thought, I just want to be very very dry and very very far from here! The lieutenant's body looked soft. The river was carrying the blood from a thousand wounds. It looked as if the river were killing him by draining his blood. But it wasn't the river. It was these people, this tall stooped man, that black man staring at him now in a way that gave him the creeps. That stare made him shiver more. (It was funny thinking his thoughts, thinking that *I* gave his body that tremor.) He pressed his right arm against his side, to try to stop his shaking. It was getting out of control.

The major looked at the guerrillas. They looked at him. I smiled, and he shuddered, as if I'd been considering how he'd taste. There were ten or eleven of us standing around the edges of the clearing, drinking coffee. That reassured him for a moment, and he stopped his shimmy. Coffee is innocent enough. Then the earthquake began again. As if you couldn't drink coffee and then shoot someone! So they drink coffee, what does that mean? Something silly went through the major's mind: Socrates drinks coffee; Socrates is a man. We're all men because we drink coffee. So what? Men shoot each other too. (He touched his cheek, which had joined the dance of his body parts.) After they fool around with us, he thought, they'll shoot us. They don't have prisons to send us to, they're guerrillas. So they'll shoot us. The one who's talking seems like a nice enough fellow, though. But so dour-looking! Who can tell what crazy people think, how they'll act. And these are crazy people, who wait by the sides of rivers to kill you! "I retire from the army next week," the major said. "I get my pension. It's a good pension." He laughed again, a little repeated hiccup of a thing, tee-hee, tee-hee, tee-hee. The dour fellow—Inti, they called him—didn't smile. He never smiled. Story of my life, the major thought. Perhaps laughing was a mistake? "Well, I mean, unless you fellows overthrow the government. I guess that would be the end of my pension." I wish that nigger bastard would stop staring at me!

Camba, thin with intense eyes under very heavy brows that grow together over his nose, walked to one of the prisoners, a private. He put his arm around him in a friendly way. "Hi," he said, and gave the soldiers a big smile. "I'm called Camba. It's my *nom de guerre,* you know. I love having a *nom de guerre.* You'll never guess who I really am. I want to sing you a song I've just made up." And he began to sing:

> We can put you in the river.
> We can put you in the stream.
> We can put you in the mountain.
> We can put you in our dream.
>
> We can put you in the river.
> We can put you in the deep.
> We can put you in the mountain.
> We can put you all to sleep.

The song, I thought, didn't have much tune, but Camba chanted it in a very cheerful engaging way. The soldier, though, didn't appreciate the humor of it. He had fainted after the first verse. Camba finished the song anyway, on the ground, kneeling beside the ranger, cradling his impassive face between his hands.

Inti ignored the singing. When it was done he turned to the captain. I think Inti's stare made the captain nervous, but *he* had his answers ready. "I'm a Communist. I only entered the army a year ago because the Party ordered me to." The captain clearly thought of himself as a very clever guy. He had read a lot of books. He was sure to rise faster than the major. And he didn't have an idiotic-sounding laugh. He was proud that he thought more quickly, was a quicker, better liar than the major. But wait—the major might believe him! That would be a disaster! "In fact," the captain added, "I have a brother studying in Cuba." That would prove to the major he was lying; he didn't have a brother, only five sisters, everyone knew that and made fun of him for it.

Inti said nothing. The captain thought that maybe he'd made a mistake. There had been rumors about Cubans. But maybe there were no Cubans here. Maybe they didn't like Cubans! As long as he'd been in the army there had been rumors about Cubans.

"We are here," Inti said, after a time (I knew how they felt listening to Inti: you could die in those pauses. Or be shot.), "to liberate Bolivia from Imperialism."

No one said anything.

Camba brought coffee and plain rolls for the prisoners. While they ate, Inti talked more of our goals. He spoke slowly, sincerely, almost sadly. I saw his eyes rest for a moment on each face, and then (he hadn't found the face welcoming) he would turn to the next. The captain flushed. He had felt suddenly silly eating his roll. What a stupid thing a roll is! It tasted heavy and dry inside my own mouth. The captain looked about nervously, and saw that the others, too, looked down at the ground when Inti glanced at them. The captain became angry at himself. Shit, he thought, that's the ground he was trying to put us under.

"Our quarrel," Inti said, "is not with you, but with those who sent you, the rich men who plunder our country." If I were the captain I would have understood that—theoretically. But if I'd been wounded? The captain looked over at the wounded men being bandaged by the guerrilla doctor, a dark man whose own arm was bandaged in a black sling. Would a wounded man, the captain and I wondered together, understand that it was nothing personal? We left out the dead altogether. They definitely wouldn't understand.

"Soldiers," Inti said, "remember you are our brothers. If your superiors force you to fight, come ahead and don't be afraid. We won't do anything to you if you throw down your arms, raise up your hands, and shout that you surrender. We won't harm you then, as we are not harming you now. You will be released."

The captain, clever man, saw the drawbacks to this offer. What if your superior sees you surrender, and he gets away? Things could go very badly for you when you got back to your outfit. Especially if your superior resents your cleverness and your masculine but musical laugh. Besides, a battle is like a natural disaster. (I was sure this had been the captain's first. He would remember it vividly as fragments of color and light and wetness and heat, and each fragment still terrified him.) It wouldn't have made any sense not to fire at the enemy, even if you thought his cause was just. It would be like a rock refusing to participate in a rockslide! Unthinkable!

Inti offered the prisoners a chance to join the Army of National Liberation, to join in the glorious work of freeing Bolivia from Imperialism's stranglehold.

No one spoke.

During the silence, army planes bombed the area. The soldiers fell to the ground and clung to it, sure that their stupid officers would kill them by mistake. (They would have too, if they could have bombed more accurately.) The explosions were more than a mile away, in the river, but the sound was enormous, deafening. Freddy, one of the guerrillas from Moises Guevara's group, grabbed Inti's arm, and shouted something at his face. I couldn't hear it, but I knew from many such incidents in the past, many men surprised by their own fear, what he was saying. He shouted that he'd been promised a safe camp, a place that would have defenses against air raids. He thought that if he shouted his resentment loudly enough, someone would be forced to protect him. Inti took Freddy's hand from his arm.

The bombs raised spumes of water and shattered rock. The tips of the spouts were very beautiful, just visible over the foliage.

After the bombing, Inti told the major that he could recover his dead the next day if the burial party returned stripped to the waist. "We won't take your uniforms," Inti said, "because it's cold tonight. But we have to keep your boots and watches and cigarettes. The army will give you others. But we don't have anywhere to get them at the moment. I'm sorry, but we'll need those things." I helped Coco and Camba collect the various objects. I felt like a bandit, and smiled towards Ricardo.

The soldier that Camba had sung to stuck his hand in his pocket. "Wait a minute. I had ten pesos hidden in a cigarette pack." He must have been ashamed of fainting. He needed a way to show some daring.

I laughed. "You're a courageous son of a bitch, aren't you? Shows what happens when we're nice enough to sing to you." I could see from his eyes that he had trouble following my words. He flinched at the sound of my voice.

"I told you we were too easy on them," Ricardo said, laughing too. It is an awful thing to hear Ricardo laugh! "Here." He handed the soldier ten pesos.

The soldier reached out slowly to take it. And then, ashamed again of his cowardice, said, "I'll bet it's counterfeit."

"You know," Ricardo said, taking off his glasses and cleaning them on his shirt, "Ponco's wrong. You're not courageous, are you? You just don't know where you are or why. You never have. And you never will. Turn around." Ricardo put on his glasses. The soldier stared at him. Ricardo had fat-looking eyes behind those lenses. "Turn around, you little bastard!" The soldier turned and Ricardo kicked him in the ass, knocking him to the ground. "All right.

You can go now! And," he said to the man on the ground, "you can tell your superiors how the guerrillas tortured you, but you didn't give them any information. As if you ever had any to give!"

The prisoners walked off to the river, singing barracks songs—so loudly that they couldn't carry the tunes. They were surprised to be alive, and they wanted to show anyone waiting in ambush that they weren't guerrillas. For a little distance some of the men followed after, a raggedy army, abusing the soldiers in raucous voices.

"Good-bye! Do come again! We can use the boots!"

From Guevara's Journal

2/10/67: The final result: three 60mm mortars, sixteen Mausers, one rifle. Two radios, boots. Seven deaths, fourteen unwounded prisoners, and four wounded. But we didn't manage to get any food.

Departure is now extremely difficult for our guests. We will have to get them out of this zone. I received the impression that Debray was not the least bit pleased about this when I told him; though, once again, it did not affect his game.

Clearly we were betrayed. We should have been able to stay here a long time. But by whom? Monje? Algaranaz? Someone else?

Too many candidates.

In any case, I miscalculated somewhere.

From My Journal

2/10/67: It is unbelievable! Che simply goes on playing chess with Regis, and listens to radio reports about us. (Barrientos announced that there are no guerrillas . . . that they exist only in people's imaginations. . . . Then: that an unknown group with automatic arms treacherously attacked a group of soldiers who were surveying a road . . . that the nation must join in a fight against local anarchists with money and arms from Castro's communists . . . that the nation must prepare to defeat the guerrillas led by Ernesto Che Guevara, the Cuban bandit and adventurer.)

How do they know already that Che is here? He did not show himself after the battle. Someone has talked! But who?

And why does he not see that it's time to go? It's time to get a move on. It's time to hit the road. I told him that. He waved me away and went back to playing chess with Debray, that old young man, that young old man. But it is crazy to stay here now! Did that little bit of bloodshed exhaust him? After the wolf eats a little it goes right off to sleep. But we were once used to much bigger meals than those few soldiers!

Or is he angry at himself because he made a mistake? (That is his usual behavior under that circumstance. Like his father, lying on the floor, hands by his sides.)

Did he make a mistake?

MARCH

From Guevara's Journal

3/2/67: Radio battles. Phantom battles. The Bolivian radio announced that there are five hundred guerrillas. But they are already completely surrounded by two thousand soldiers, and the encirclement is closing in. They are being attacked from the ground, and by napalm from the air. Ten to fifteen guerrillas have been killed.

3/6/67: Debray and I spoke of the miners, Moises Guevara's men. Inti has just told me of Pacho's disobeying orders, and Freddy's disgraceful outburst during the bombing.

"These men are dregs, Regis."

"Yes. The pro-Peking miners wouldn't cooperate with Moises in the end. They have their own line, that there must be more preparation before hostilities begin. Moises enrolled unemployed miners, and personal friends. He promised them money and comfort. These men are of unknown political background, except for Simon Cuba, the one you're calling Willy. They are weak. The most important support for a guerrilla is his ideological conviction. Moises's men lack ideology. They joined to escape poverty. Except for the miners like Willy, and the middle-class Communists like Jorge and Coco, there is the danger that recruits will see the guerrillas as a way out of poverty, a good job with a chance for rapid advancement. Then, instead of appealing to them politically, Moises told them you might be here. It was effective. Your name was another big come-on. But as I say—and I'm sure you'll agree—it's no substitute for ideological conviction. Militants from the BCP would have been better."

"I thought you hated them. It was you who were in favor of collaborating with Moises." I was enraged with him. But the only thing I could think about was how calm he was. When he was delivering an analysis his face became impassive. The rest of the time he tied his hair in knots and was ready to leap out of his skin.

He said, "I've changed my mind."

"You know, Regis, every time something happens you're sure it couldn't have happened any other way."

"Of course." He was chewing some meat from the plate in front of him. It got on my nerves.

"Then it turns out the next thing has happened some other way than the only way it could have turned out. And you have a perfectly coherent, very convincing explanation about why it happened that way instead, and why it had to happen that way, and couldn't have happened any other way, and *should* have happened that way." Regis was smiling at me, and smoothing down his mustache. It was so *characteristic* of him that I couldn't help smiling, too. I like Regis, really, though he's a little frightening; I think he has an interpretive mania.

He's very vehement lately about how useful he could be outside.

3/8/67: The radio brings us some very good news: Barrientos announced that military missions from the United States, Argentina, Brazil, and Paraguay have arrived to study the guerrilla movement, and to make joint plans for combating it.

Radio Havana announced that Hoan Bich Son, Chief of Mission for the NLF, has declared that the armed struggle in Bolivia is "a stimulant for the South Vietnamese Revolution."

From My Journal

3/8/67: Che thought the Barrientos and Vietnamese statements cause for a celebration. The struggle is already on its way to being continental. The U.S. will begin by sending advisers and end by sending its own troops. We are creating another Vietnam. He had rum distributed—though he presided over the party from his hammock. He won't get out of that fucking hammock except to shit. I'm surprised he doesn't just open his fly and piss from there, too. Anyway, we were drinking, to ourselves, to Vietnam, to solidarity, to the Continental War of Liberation, to whatever, when Chingolo suddenly started to sputter and spit his rum out all over Coco's shirt. "What's wrong?" Coco said, instead of "You stupid bastard," which is what I would have said. Coco is a considerate person, better than most in my opinion, and slow to anger. I like his full, smooth face.

"I don't know," Chingolo said, "but suddenly the rum started to taste really funny. It wouldn't go down."

"An omen," Camba said in his squeaky voice, not loudly, but there was an unfortunate lull, so everyone heard. "Definitely an omen." Something will have to be done to straighten that little prick out about how it's not O.K. to say out loud everything you think.

"You know," Ricardo said, "you guys . . ." He paused—I think he was about to say "you Bolivians" and corrected himself. ". . . you guys with omens are full of shit. Omens don't mean anything to me. Ranger corpses, those are my omens."

It was enough to make everyone laugh nervously.

Che had more rum distributed.

Why the fuck won't he get up?

From Guevara's Journal

3/9/67: News from the vultures: the corpses haven't been picked up. The army is afraid of us.

3/10/67: Coco reported to me about the army's attack on the Tin House, which he watched from the Bear Camp observation post. From the sound of it they used a full division. First they softened up the empty house with mortars and aerial bombardment, blowing up the outhouses, the corral, the vegetable garden, the henhouse, the few hens, and the rooster. "The rooster," Coco said, "screamed and screamed."

"Every scream," Ricardo said, "will be counted as a casualty and added to the number of guerrillas killed."

After decimating the poultry, the army retreated.

On the radio this evening General Barrientos announced that the guerrillas have been exterminated.

From My Journal

3/11/67: Fireworks! But the sound has cured him of his disease. He rose up and announced that we must leave the camp, drop off the visitors, regain our contact with the outside. We will need supplies for the battles to come. He gathered the men together. The war has begun. We are the Army of National Liberation.

THE ARMY OF NATIONAL LIBERATION

Aniceto	Marcos
Camba	Miguel
Che—called Ramon	Moro
Chingolo	Pacho
Coco	Pombo
Dario	Ricardo
El Rubio	Rolando
Inti	Tuma
Julio	Urbano
Leon	(Regis Debray)—called Danton; contact with Cuba
Loro	
Luis	(Bustos)—contact with Argentina
Nato	Joaquin
Pablo	(Tania)—liaison with the city network
Pedro—also called Pan Divino	
Ponco	Ernesto
Raul	Freddy
Victor	Moises
Willy	Negro (El Medico)
Eustaquio	Alejandro
El Chino—combatant and liaison with Peru	Paco
	Polo
Antonio	Braulio
Arturo	Eusebio
Benigno	Serapio

From Guevara's Journal

3/12/67: The march begins. I had the excess supplies stored in the caves we've prepared: arms, bullets, documents, photos, film, books, dollars, cameras, tape recorders, typewriters, clothing, blankets, the boots we took from the soldiers, medicine (the epinephrine for my asthma). My plan is to draw the army out of the zone, and, when necessary, circle back to Nancahuazu to retrieve the medicines and other things as needed.

From Coco's Journal

3/12/67: When Nato and I unwrapped the radio for broadcasting messages from its protective canvases, we discovered that it had been destroyed by water seepage. I told Che. He said nothing, but his jaws tightened, and he looked over my head. I think it must be a serious problem for us.

From My Journal

3/13/67: We are making a diversionary move to the north. On the way out we passed the as yet unburied bodies of the soldiers killed in the ambush. A Bolivian ranger wears a black beret, jackboots, a leather belt, light-green sunglasses, and a brown-bordered white neckerchief tied with a silver loop. The vultures, in tearing at the flesh, have turned the shirts and neckerchiefs to rags. (Imperialism and the War of Liberation have turned the soldiers to garbage.) Most of the corpses, lying in the mud, still wore their black berets and sunglasses. The flesh left here and there on the top of part of the body and face was black and puffy. The Bolivian ranger also wears pants stuffed into his boots, so their legs had been protected. Or wasted. The vultures couldn't get at them. But the river could. Bits of very white waterlogged flesh had come loose from their clothes and floated downstream. I could see it stuck here and there among the rocks.

3/15/67: We've lost the way, encountered some steep cliffs, and been forced to double back. We should be south of the Rio Grande. You wouldn't think it would be hard to find such a large river!

From Guevara's Journal

3/16/67: Inti and I have tried a few talks with the peasants in the region near the river. Unsatisfactory comedy. We don't frighten them certainly, but we don't impress them much either. They listen, and hang their heads, and listen, as impenetrable as stones. Or they reply evasively, as if they hadn't understood our goals. But they'll sell us food—if the price is right. (So many minutes of playing catch per piece of candy.) The answer is more victories: our violence will give these stones ears.

There has been one exception among the local peasantry, a man named Honorato Ispaca, who lives near the river. He invited us into his home, a thatched hut. There was little light, and a great deal of smoke inside. On the floor a child clutched his stomach, and moaned, a high breathy sound, terribly plaintive. Ispaca, forgetting his visitors at the sight of his son, left us to kneel by the boy's head, so he might pray.

The boy told me that an animal jumped around inside him, and that every time it jumped it hurt him terribly. His face was down to bone, his eyes enormous. Blue and red and green candles had been placed by his head—the work of magical curers—and white candles by his feet, from the church. He looked already dead. Candles burning like this during the day for their magical effect, a father kneeling near his son's head—it reminded me of my childhood, when the light had lain on me like a heavy weight. There was a pungent pine smoke that stung my eyes and made the air thick and difficult to breathe.

An old man sat in a wooden chair near the boy's head, opposite the father, chanting words in Quechua, rocking back and forth. Behind his words, a light accompaniment, I heard the strongly rushing waters of the Rio Grande. A cooking fire burned fitfully in the center of the room, and smoke drifted out slowly through a hole in the ceiling. Four women in wide bright overlapping skirts leaned above two metal pots on the fire. They looked up when Inti and I came in, then returned to their stirring, wailing along with the man's chant in softer voices. Three more young children in dirty white shifts stood near the women, staring at us. One of the little girls, about six years old, carried a baby in a black-and-red blanket tied to her back. She talked to the infant, describing the skinny strangers. In a corner, a whole litter of black kittens mewed and crawled over each other. The air was heavy with smoke, pine resin, sweat, and the smell of the river.

Ispaca, kneeling, spoke. The child had become ill because of a quarrel he had had with a man nearby. The man had loaned him some money for drinks at a festival, and when Ispaca had grown sober again, he couldn't pay his debt. He had dreamed of the man a week ago. The man had come to him in his field and said, "You owe me an ear of corn, a new ear, and you haven't paid." Ispaca had said, "But I don't have it." The man said, "Yes, you do." And when Ispaca had looked down there was a new ear of corn in his hand. "Now I'll take it," the man said, "whether you want to give it to me or not." That corn had been his son's soul.

Ispaca sobbed, holding the sides of his own face. His enemy must have gone to one of the men who know such things, and had him put an animal in his son's stomach.

From his chair the old man stopped chanting to listen to Ispaca and nod in agreement. "There was an owl hooting all night," the old man said, smiling, as if he were gratified by the bad omen—for it made sense of things, displayed a coherence to the world, however unfortunate for Ispaca's son.

"And a dog barking," Ispaca added, though he—thank God!—didn't sound pleased at this confirmation. "Five of my children have died," he said, "and it was always this way beforehand."

These stories sickened me. There was, I told him, no magic. His son did have an animal in his stomach, a worm. It might have come in food, or it might have entered through his son's feet, because the boy had no shoes. Now the worm lived in his son's stomach, and everything they fed to the boy the worm ate. That's why he was so thin.

But they didn't feed him, Ispaca said. They were trying to starve the animal.

The old man smiled at me, happy to offer instruction. What I had described was exactly what a sorcerer would do. He would leave a piece of corn on the road, a piece with a blood spot on it. When the boy stepped on it the spirit of the animal entered his stomach. It would live there till it killed the boy.

He grew emphatic in his lesson, delighting in defeat, in the sorcerer's triumph, in the implacable vindication of his story—the boy who lay beneath him moaning.

Only someone who knew more could save him. But the old man had never known that to happen.

My disgust became palpable in my stomach. The way the old man twisted my words, made them congruent with his magic stories—it caused an animal to grow in my stomach. I felt nauseous. They must be forced to enter the twentieth century, to give up these stories that reconcile them with their humiliations, their children's deaths. I said again that the worm would not kill the boy. It was not magic. It was a real worm in his stomach. We had a medicine for it. (A real worm? I thought, hearing my voice rise towards the hole in the ceiling with the smoke. What would that prove? The worm that grew from the corn no doubt had a physical body, indistinguishable—had one ever seen it—from the worm our medicine would kill. Their stories had many entries and no exits.)

I sent Inti for El Medico. A black man, his entry startled the household. The women placed their heads together over the pots, then returned to their stirring.

El Medico gave the boy a white liquid. The boy retched emptily, his body flopping like a desperate fish. The women stopped stirring, and stared at us angrily. They wailed more loudly, more sharply, to curse us forever. The old man spat on the floor, in the dirt.

The worm, El Medico explained in his musical voice, can't stand the medicine. It would come out through the boy's mouth.

Which it did. El Medico pulled it gently, several meters of long white flat flesh the texture of rubber, jointed in segments, streaked with the boy's blood and bile. The women screamed at this obscene vision.

The boy lost consciousness, and the women instantly became silent.

El Medico said that he had only fainted, that he would wake soon and would be all right. It was, as they could see, only a worm. It was good fortune that the worm's head had come out first, El Medico said (for demonstration purposes, since we could not be certain), for if the head remained the worm could grow a new body inside the boy's stomach. Now he would crush the head; the worm would die; the boy would live.

El Medico found a small rock, and did the deed with his boot. I could tell from the old man's face, his lips drawn up into a toothless death-mask smile, that the talk of a worm regrowing its body had made an impression on him, an unfortunate wrongheaded one. It had given him another confirmation of his hobgoblin world, a new possibility for evading us. The worm that regrows itself would be another room to his dark construction, the Indian's endless tomb.

Our magic was greater than the sorcerer's, he said, sucking his lips with satisfaction.

"No," I said, wanting to spit his bad taste out. We had no magic, I explained. We had medicine, made by workers in factories. The tapeworm was a natural creature, like any other animal. Like their pigs. But what would that mean to him? Natural? He knew of no discredited supernatural. They had only one world, this one, visible and animated by unseen powers. I felt as if I were pushing my meaning up an impossible incline. Their minds were a maze of dark walls that my sentences might wander in, lost forever. Or worse, my words might be transformed (by magic!) into parts of the prison. His world was as coherent as mine, included as much. There was no word that I might speak that he couldn't translate to his own satisfaction, and so avoid entering history. He needn't even argue with me. I said "workers" in "factories"—and he heard of new magicians from unknown hells.

We would have to batter our heads against this maze's walls until they broke, and light and air rushed in.

If the children had good food, I said, then they would be safe from worms. If they had shoes then they would be safe from the small white worms that he had seen come from children's mouths. They didn't need men who knew, they needed shoes. The children didn't have shoes because all the wealth of Bolivia, all its tin and oil, go to the United States, just as the little money they earned from their crops went endlessly to the men who sold them seed and tools.

"You made the worm's soul go into something else? An animal?" He was thinking of Jesus, whose spell sent demons into swine, ruining someone's family. (Every soul went somewhere. Nothing was wasted—or the avalanche of death would be too terrible.) And what were pigs but familiar domesticated demons?

The air was too thick in the hut. My lungs closed painfully into fists.

Ispaca followed us outside into the clear but moist air. He was grateful for our help. I felt that he had understood the things we'd said. I told him that he could help us by telling his neighbors of what we were trying to do for Bolivia. And he could help by giving us food, so we would be strong in fighting the rich people's army. And by not cooperating with the army when they tried to find out from him whether we had been there.

". . . from us?" he said, for his fear suddenly only let him stammer out a fragment of his thought.

He need only tell the army, no matter how they threatened him, that he knew nothing about us.

He brought himself under control. "Whatever I can do," he said graciously, "I'll do."

Gracious, but tautological; it bound him to nothing.

El Medico told him to see that the boy had something soft to eat when he awoke.

I gave Ispaca some money to raise hogs for us. This will implicate him and convince him that we will return. I told him that if he helped the army he would punish him.

The army will tell him that if he helps the guerrillas they will kill him and his family.

Time will tell which way he jumps.

For now we will head back southeast, towards Gutierrez, a town on the main road from Camiri to Santa Cruz. There we can pass Debray, Bustos, and Tania back to the city.

From Coco's Journal

3/19/67: On the march today I walked with my brother. "Inti," I said, "you remember during the battle?"

"Remember what?" A long sentence for him.

"I want to tell you something. I was so scared that I pissed in my pants. I don't think I'll make a good guerrilla."

Inti stared at me for a moment. He is very quick-witted, I know. What does he think about in those silences? "That's nothing," he said, "I shit in my britches."

"Come on," I said, "you're saying that to make me feel better."

"No. I really did. Big soft wet turds and shitty liquid in a stream, it started coming out all at once, I couldn't control it. As soon as they started firing at us. And all the time I was talking to the prisoners about liberation and our fight against imperialism my pants were full of shit. I thought everybody would be able to smell it."

Moro came up behind us with his arm in a sling. He was a big strong man who had joined Fidel during their Revolution. Later he had become a doctor. I was carrying his pack for him. It was heavy and the sun was terrible. He must have overheard us. "That's nothing. The first time I was in battle in Cuba, I shit my pants, and pissed, and I swear to god, snot came out of my nose. I was leaking from every hole in my body."

"See," Inti said, "the Cubans do more of everything than we do." He didn't smile, but I'm sure he was joking. It's better to make jokes about those feelings than to let them fester.

"No, really. When I'm nervous I snort. When the firing started I began to snort really hard. When I felt the snot on my lip I thought it was blood. That's when I pissed in my pants, because I thought I'd been wounded in my face. When I felt the wetness in my underwear I thought I was bleeding there, too, that I'd been shot in the balls. That's when I shit in my pants. Every one of the Cubans has some story like that. Even Ricardo."

"Even Che?" I asked.

"Even Che, I suppose. I don't know. I've never asked him."

From Guevara's Journal

3/20/67: We have run out of dry corn and powdered milk, and the peasants we've contacted haven't been very forthcoming.

To get anywhere we must hack our way through jungle growth that is like a wall. There have been several faintings among the machete wielders.

From Camba's Journal

3/21/67: Buzzz Buzzzz Buzzzzz. The mosquitoes are always in our ears, on our skin, sucking our blood. Soon all I'll be able to hear is that sound; it will fill my whole brain. That's when I die. When my head is one big red mosquito buzz, all my blood gone, replaced by buzzing.

From Guevara's Journal

3/22/67: Today: monkey meat, bitter and fibrous—a day of good hunting. Yesterday: dead fish from the backwaters of the river.

3/23/67: In camp Tania played the tapes she had made—Indian voices singing, telling stories, chanting. It caught me up again in the web of my youth, the repetitive chords (or so I heard them), the slow mournful syllables, the sequences chanted over and over and over.

On the march I told Tania of my time in Bolivia after medical school, of watching a dance on the main square in La Paz—for I found that that was my most vivid image of the Bolivian Revolution—and of my truck ride through the Andes. Those were the first times I had heard music of the kind she had played for us. I had wanted then to submerge all I was in their steady song, be woven up and transformed by the repetition that rocked back and forth, high and low, like a loom's shuttle. I had thought the sound wove the Indians and their world together into an indissoluble whole—thus their immobility: they could no more move than a piece of a tapestry could change its shape or position, a woman become a city. They sat indifferent to the jolts of the truck, the danger, the stink, or our words. "But that's what's slowing down our development now. They still think everything is as it is forever. The stones, the trees, the landlords, the soldiers—all facts of nature, immutable. They're all stoics. They've forgotten how to protest, how to rebel."

"Unable to rebel!" she said, laughing. "But, Che, they had just made a revolution! It's easy to mistake them. But their life is really one long slow rebellion against their rulers, their conquerors, a quiet, steady, implacable resistance. They haven't fought again as they did in '52. But they haven't had the leadership for that. Within their own lives, though, the resistance is still alive—they rebel constantly. Like *their* Christianity. For centuries the priests have been trying to impose a nice Christian servility on the Indians."

"Haven't they succeeded?" Coco asked. "Each of the villages has a house the Indians have built for the priest. And they feed him from their own stores. They kneel down and beg the priest to accept the food that their own families need."

"Nonsense!" Tania said contemptuously. She was quite capable of a peremptory gesture of instruction, striking the children with her *vara,* if that was what the role called for. "The Indians here scare the priests to death. I met this young priest, in the town where I made the tape I played you, a nice guy, didn't even have a beard yet, a very sweet face. And he was confused, lonely, helpless-looking. He said he talked to them and talked to them, and the Indians listened in absolute silence, perfect immobility, like the Indians you rode with, Che. That silence is an icy indifference, a coldness beyond hatred, just as you described, where you don't even exist for them anymore. He said his words began to sound absurd to him. His voice echoed emptily in the big barnlike church. He felt he was going mad from their silence. Alone, he had found himself repeating the catechism over and over, something he hadn't done since seminary, to remind himself what made him. But it didn't work. Nothing in the village returned his speech to him. His gestures didn't find any response. His words became empty fragments of sound, floating away in all directions. He said he was even starting to hear voices. But the Indians, he said, already heard voices. Every element the priest told them, the Indian voices took and twisted about. The priest baptizes a child, and the Indian mother takes him away immediately after paying the priest and has a curer take a mouthful of rum and spit it all over the baby."

"A baptism of fire," Camba said, "after the one of water." Single file, we walked down the thin path the *macheteros* had prepared for us. The heat was thickening the air.

"Exactly," Tania said to him, "you think like an Indian. And after the priest performs a burial, the whole family goes up and starts kicking the coffin. They want the dead man to be furious with them. They believe in resurrection, all right. Immediately, the body comes back covered with dirt, to sour milk, and with a syringe, to suck blood. They don't want Mr. Corpse coming to take them to the land of the dead for company. They kick him to show they're not his pals anymore."

[I want to kick his corpse. I want to get his syringe out of me. I want him to know that I'm not his pal anymore and to stop making the room dark.]

"The priest said he spoke to them about Christ, his love and his mercy. The Indians listened attentively and ignored Christ completely. They think Christ must have been an Indian. Because the Jews—that means rich whites with tails—crucified him. They don't care what the priest says, they can't see the value of praying to Christ, the sweet powerless bastard couldn't keep himself from being nailed to the wall. They only worship the saints, who are store dummies they've got dressed up in their idea of rich people's clothing, lace tablecloths and dried fruits on a string for necklaces."

"But the saints they worship are still white people," Coco said, not combatively, but trying to think the thing through. *"Rich* white people."

"In the churches they are, yes. But when the saints come to them in their dreams they don't look white. They look like Indians. They speak Indian languages. And the saints told them to put my friend the priest in a deep hole with some dry turds and only give him enough corn and water for a week—enough to keep him alive. And, of course, they did it. But the police can't find out who did it, because the whole village did it, nobody did it, the saints told them to do it. It may not sound like much. . . ."

"It doesn't," I said. My lungs had begun to ache. I had a hard time getting the words out. "It sounds like mumbo-jumbo, or practical jokes. They'll have to leave all that behind if they're to understand their position and become revolutionaries."

"It got to the priest, though," Tania said. "My friend couldn't stand it anymore, the silence most of all, because he knew that as his words fell through that silence they were twisted, bent to the Indians' needs. *That* was their rebellion. And what was that ungodly need? My friend abandoned his church to the Indians after the turd treatment. They could do whatever blasphemous thing they wished there. He said they drank real blood, menstrual blood, on the altar. But he was a little odd by then. He went there twice a year, to say Mass—because the Archbishop made him do it. Why syringes? he wondered. They made everything barbaric, ugly, dark. 'You can't make savages into Christians,' he said, 'you only make Christianity savage.' He was leaving right after Mass."

"Tania," Ponco croaked, "don't you see? We're the priests, this time. We're the white people." And he wheezed an unhappy laugh. For if they thought white people were devils, what might they make of him?

"For the moment we're the priests," I said. "Till they join us." I could feel that Ponco had spoken against his own will, from a presentiment he could not deny.

"Yes," Tania said, "for the moment. The main thing is that *they will join,* for their spirit is already bent to resistance. They need only be shown how to rebel, how to fight for their land."

Later, in camp, I took Walter aside to speak to him about morale. It is all right to speak critically with Tania and me. But he must be more careful that others—like Coco and Camba—don't hear such talk.

Isle of Pines, May 1968

MAY 10

Can I change things? I review his words, our talks about his own writing. He made his brothers and sisters disappear, his father die of cancer. Because it *felt* that way. Can I change things—depending on how *he* felt to me, how I felt about him?

What about *history?*

Can I change his words? I know how to mimic his style.

He took *me* aside to speak about morale—I'll leave that in. It was very unfair and I felt the world a little unsteady underneath my feet, a hole had opened, for I had just been speaking as he sometimes did. But I'll leave it. People will know that I'm giving an honest account if I put in something so wounding to my vanity.

Do I want to hurt him?

MAY 11

I spent a very bad night, playing with my blanket edges, but not sleeping. Not eating, either. (Weight remains at about ninety-eight pounds. Maybe that's why I sleep so much.) I am *sure* I don't want to *hurt* him. (I'm keeping him alive. I'm giving up my life to keep him alive, telling his story. Isn't that enough?) The only change I've made so far is this: once he said "jerking off," and I have taken it out. It wasn't *like* him. Sometimes, I think, we are invaded by the souls of other people, the ones around us, and our voices sound like theirs. (When I was with him it was easy to make myself sound like him.) But it isn't really ourselves then, and the true picture of a man would leave it out. (Of all the people I have known, he was the one most himself all the time, as if he were protected against our migrating souls, behind some glass.) Not much will have to be changed. He wanted to have his gesture pure, have it ring out clearly. *I could help him.* I'll show what's already there more clearly. I read somewhere: the statue is already *inside* the stone.

No. I have no right to alter anything.

Bolivia, 1967

APRIL

From Coco's Journal

4/3/67: My feet, and those of a couple of comrades, have begun to swell up. Edema from malnutrition, Che says. I poke at them sometimes at night. My finger sinks right in. Ponco showed me his feet, and they're the same. "See," he said, "watery flesh, fleshy water." We've worn through our boots, they're just scraps of leather.

I walked with Ponco. I think I have a lot to learn from him, but he doesn't talk much to me, or to anyone, I think, except Che. He asks me questions about my past, and listens very intently. And when he does speak he's very funny, very sharp. His voice is raspy, a low growl. They say he was operated on for cancer. He has known Che for more than eleven years, and they seem very close. He is the only one who talks alone with Che, and once I even heard Ponco shout at him. I wish he would talk more to me about his experiences. But he doesn't like to tell stories about his life.

Today the sun was so hot it was cracking stones. I don't think I could have gone on if it weren't for Che's example. He is suffering from asthma, but he doesn't complain.

From Guevara's Journal

4/4/67: Four of the men have come down with malaria.

4/5/67: We will continue to move southeast towards Gutierrez.

4/6/67: Tania is sick with fever. Malaria. A bad case. I can see it not only in the puffiness and redness of her face, but in its unformed quality. In the time before her illness her face would have this unformed look also, just after waking —as if she had to shape it by an effort of will, remind herself of who she is, what she is supposed to be like; sometimes I felt she could give it any shape she wished. It reminds one that she is an agent. But now her face has that look all the time; slack; her muscles are weak; her will is weak. The heat is hard on all of us; it is impossible for her to bear.

And Debray is scared. He skitters about. He demands (not asks) to be taken into the guerrilla as a combatant. Half an hour later he talks of how useful he would be on the outside; the necessities of struggle demand that he return to Cuba; he describes a safe route. At each turning he has precise reasons of great clarity and insight. Perhaps his mind can work at the service of any goal. (What provides the goal, then?) He must go. He has a journalist's credentials, and there are few soldiers near Muyupampa. If he hasn't been betrayed, his cover should keep him safe. A necessary risk. Bustos will go with him, with messages to Argentina. Tania is another matter; she is too valuable; we must find an absolutely safe route for her. But we have to get Debray and Bustos out before more soldiers arrive in the zone. And Tania and the other sick ones are slowing down the march.

From Coco's Journal

4/9/67: I walked with Joaquin. He moves slowly, but stands upright though he has a fever. Debray is very thin. Each day he seems to grow thinner. He walks with a stoop, though he is not carrying a full pack. We were all silent for a while. Then Joaquin spoke very rapidly. "Don't you see Regis? It didn't start out for me as an idea. When I joined Fidel I had few ideas except trying to survive. There wasn't much to eat. I looked after a few cows. I knew Fidel's men would kill us if we collaborated with the army. The army would kill us if we helped Fidel. Some days the army would come and take some of my cattle. Some days Fidel would come and take some. I wanted to live. Sure, I despised Batista's men. But it wasn't just Fidel's speeches that made me join the Movement. It was also the feel of the weapon Ricardo handed me, the wooden stock slapped against my shoulder, the recoil of my weapon, and the way it shook my chest. It was the possibility of doing something about my feelings. I had no words for it."

"Later there were words, Joaquin, don't forget that. Or how would you have known whom to point the rifle at?"

"Yes, that's true, Grandfather. Later there were words, oh my, were there words! Around Fidel there are always plenty of words. But you're right. I came to understand what the feelings I had meant in my world. There's room for words. There have to be words, too. But that isn't the way it started for me. When I listen to you, I don't know. Can it start out as *thinking?*"

I didn't say anything. I thought of my father's house in La Paz, the big dining room with its carved wooden furniture, the portraits. It had begun as thinking for me.

From Guevara's Journal

4/11/67: Near Iripita. Set up an ambush on both sides of the river. The ambush was eight men from the rear guard, on both banks, and a reinforcement of three from the vanguard. The soldiers tracking us advanced with little caution, exploring the edges of the river. A few of them walked into the wooded area, and ran into Braulio and Pedro, before reaching the main body of the ambush. The firing lasted a few seconds. One dead, three wounded, four escaped back down the river. El Rubio was found wounded. His gun was jammed, and at his side was an unexploded grenade with its pin pulled. Inti, who found him, said his legs were still twitching. He was unconscious by the time they brought him to camp. I knelt by him in the dirt of the clearing, and put my hand hard against his chest. He was still alive, breathing faster and faster, shallower and shallower, his heart moving more quickly, his body giving off heat. It is the way a lamb feels, or a horse, the rapid respiration, the life coming and going, going so rapidly beneath my fingers, as if, as he died, he were moving backward from man to animal to matter.

Later, Debray, moved by the event, asked again to be incorporated into the guerrilla. He meant well. But I couldn't take any more of it. "You have no experience. You have little endurance. Ten city intellectuals are worth less to me as guerrillas than a single peasant from the region. The peasant doesn't know dialectics but he knows geography."

"Well, until you have a little more success in recruiting peasants, perhaps a few city intellectuals will have to do." He must have been very angry at the way I'd spoken to him, to come so close to criticizing me.

"You have your point." I was jumpy about El Rubio's death. Debray's eyes showed that he did not mean what he was saying. Or so I think. He would change his mind in a few hours. I wanted to make it easy on him to leave. I wanted him to leave.

"You have your point. As always. But it wasn't criticism of you that I meant. The peasant wouldn't be any use to me in the city. There are messages that I must get to Fidel about the Bolivian Party. I need you to set up support committees for the Bolivian Revolution. Speak to Sartre and Russell in my name. It will be difficult enough for you getting out of here."

"In any case, I should stay with the guerrillas. Every man matters now."

"But do you want to?"

"My personal preference doesn't matter."

"I am putting an end to this discussion. You will return to Cuba. Give my messages to Fidel. You can have the child you've been talking about with Elizabeth." El Rubio's death had made Regis think of that; for the last few hours we had been talking about my children, about his desire to become a father. "You'll make a good father. You'll give them clear standards to measure themselves against. Let's not talk of it anymore."

Still, there was something impressive about Regis. Each night, nervous as he was, exhausted as we all were, he would sit and go over a manuscript on the Latin American Revolution he was carrying in his knapsack, revising, getting it right.

We learned from the captives that Gutierrez is occupied by the army. We cannot risk leaving our contacts there. We will move south towards Muyupampa, and look for a spot there.

4/13/67: We continued southwest towards Muyupampa, to put some distance between ourselves and the army. It is imperative that we find a safe place for the visitors, our contacts with the world beyond this canyon. It is particularly troubling that Tania disobeyed orders—an inexplicable lapse of judgment on her part—and came back to the camp. We must regain our links with the city network—and what might be suitable for Debray will not do for her.

4/17/67: We spent the day in camp, resting. The canned food has run out.

Tania put her arms towards the fire, catching her sleeve in the flame. She did it very slowly, so everyone could see, but no one did anything about it. She just stared at her burning arm, with a dazed expression. Moro grabbed her and with his good arm pushed her to the ground, rubbing her sleeve into the dirt till the fire went out. The doctor looked at the arm; she wasn't badly burned. No one said anything.

She began to scratch herself with her nails, running them across her cheeks with a nervous mechanical motion. She was mumbling something to herself. Her nails began to dig into her skin hard, the blood rising under them, turning up furrows of some rich red earth. This time she was screaming, but not from pain, I think: wailing and crying.

I went to talk with her, to shut her up. There would be food to eat soon, I said. Her fever would get better. She wouldn't have to march long distances anymore. I was going to leave her with Joaquin and many men. She knew Joaquin was a good man, our comrade from many struggles. They would stay near here, safe from the army. We'd drop off Debray and Bustos and then rejoin Joaquin. She'd feel better soon. Joaquin would find a safe way for her to leave while we distracted the army. The doctor would take care of her now. She'd be feeling better soon, her fever would break. She would be on her way back to the city.

She became calmer, she apologized. It was not *her* talking, she said, but her fever.

It was her own fault, I thought, but did not say. She should never have come to the camp again. Debray could have found his own way there, as he was supposed to. She had disobeyed orders and common sense. Once the army found the camp, we had to get them out, wander about until we did, or be cut off from our support.

Why had she come?

I gave Joaquin his orders: Stay in the zone. Make a show of strength to keep down the army's mobility. Wait three days while we go towards Iripita to drop off Debray and Bustos. "After that, if we haven't returned, remain in the zone, avoid any head-on fighting, and wait for our return. It will give the sick a chance to rest." We were standing in the sun, a distance from the camp, in a field of tall grass. It made my head ache. Sweat glistened all over Joaquin's forehead. He looked past me as I spoke, his eyes glazed, his mouth open. The sun, I thought. It makes him look vacant, distant. He didn't even nod in agreement.

We parted. I led the center group out of there. I couldn't wait to put some distance between us and Tania and the other sick ones.

And now to get Debray out, away, gone.

4/19/67: We will continue to move south, to divert the army from Joaquin's group. And there will be a safe town for Debray in that region, perhaps Lagunillas or Muyupampa.

4/26/67: A coded message from Havana. We tape-recorded it and played it over and over to decode it. Dark news: Brizola's group in Brazil is finished. They were decimated by bubonic plague, and the few remaining ones picked up by the army.

Monje has met again with Fidel and announced to him his full support of the guerrillas. He has requested more money for operations in the city. Should it be given to him?

One almost has to admire Monje's audacity. Ponco was right, I should have killed him when I had the chance.

Or is he responding to news of our victory at Nancahuazu? We are still the darlings of the airwaves. It is possible that the Party is coming around to our point of view. I must get a message to Fidel of our needs and how to contact us. He must oversee the Party's good faith.

4/27/67: The Chilean radio station reports that U.S. military advisers have arrived in Bolivia.

<u>Another Vietnam</u>

From My Journal

4/29/67: Guerrilla strength is estimated by the radio to be three hundred men.

That means there are 257 phantoms. There are thirty-three human guerrillas with us, and ten with Joaquin. So far there has been no contact between us. The liaisons to Argentina, Peru, and the rest of the guerrilla groups already in operation or that Che hopes to form are here with us, trapped. Tania, our contact with the city, is trapped with Joaquin's group. Debray, our liaison to Cuba, is with us. The radio equipment is broken, and there's no way to broadcast to Cuba.

We can only listen.

Listen to the Meeting of the Tricontinental Conference in Havana. Fidel read Che's message from "somewhere in the Americas."

"The solidarity of all the progressive forces of the world towards Vietnam is similar to the bitter irony of the plebeians coaxing the gladiators into the Roman arena. It is not a matter of wishing success to the victim of aggression, but of sharing his fate: one must accompany him to death or victory. Vietnam must not be abandoned.

"We must ask ourselves, How shall rebellion flourish? We have said for quite some time now, The struggle in our America must achieve continental proportions.

"The beginning will not be easy. All the oligarchies' power of repression, all their capacity for brutality will be placed at the service of their cause. Our mission, in the first hour, shall be to survive. Later we shall carry out armed propaganda, in the Vietnamese sense: that is, the bullets of propaganda of the battles won or lost—but fought!—against the enemy.

"The great lesson of the invincibility of the guerrillas will take root in the dispossessed masses. The galvanizing of the national spirit. Hatred as an ele-

ment of the struggle, a relentless hatred of the enemy impelling us over and beyond the natural limitations that man is heir to and transforming him into an effective violent selective and cold killing machine. Our soldiers must be thus; a people without hatred cannot vanquish a brutal enemy.

"How close we could look into a bright future should two three many Vietnams flourish throughout the world with their share of deaths, and their immense tragedies, their everyday heroism, and their repeated blows against an imperialism impelled to disperse its forces under the sudden attack and increasing hatred of all the people of the world.

"Our every action is a battle cry against imperialism, a battle hymn for the people's unity against the great enemy of mankind: the United States of America. Wherever death may surprise us let it be welcome, provided that this our battle cry may have reached some receptive ear, and another hand may be extended to wield our weapons, and other men ready to intone the funeral dirge with the staccato singing of the machine guns, and new cries of war and victory."

(Prolonged applause.)

A nice piece of work. Vietnam must not be *abandoned!* His favorite word. Forlorn word! We played the radios very quietly at night, deep in the forest. The glow from the dials was the only light. (Now is the hour of the radios. . . .) We had to lie on the ground with our heads near the speakers to hear.

Afterward no one said anything.

From Camba's Journal

4/30/67: Last night I had a dream. We were on a high mountain together, Che and I. The air was very thin at the top of the mountain. I felt woozy in my dream. There was a little crust of blood inside my nose (I touched it with my finger as he was talking and brought it out to look at). We were above the timberline. The earth was red and dry. There was snow on nearby peaks. It was very quiet, the only sound the whoosh whoosh whoosh of the wind moving around us. Che was pointing out the countryside to me, saying that from this mountain we could see four of the countries of the continent at war. "There's Patagonia," he said, "and that's Babylonia, and that's Folderol, and that's Pompadoodle." (They were all funny names. I can't remember them exactly.) "See, Camba," he said, "they're all turning red." And it was true; the ground down there was oozing blood. When he finished pointing out the different countries, he said, "See, there's a hill that looks like a dinosaur, don't you think?" And he pointed to a hill that had an egg-shaped bulge in front of it. That was the dinosaur's head. And on its trunk there were long thick bulges, columns of red and green. Those were its legs. I could see it. Suddenly we were standing in front of the hill. It was a giant green-and-red lizard with a man's face. The face was craggy, like a mountain, because it was a mountain, and bearded with a very wispy black beard. It wore a funny green cap. It said to Che, "You think you can eat me, young man? You want to try my tough salty meat?" It had a woman's voice—very deep, but a woman's voice. It laughed, a little high-pitched trill, like the nervous major who we captured. Then it swept its tail across us. The tail had sharp scales on it, sharp as razors. And they were so sharp, and moved so quickly, that if he cut you, you wouldn't feel anything. (I don't know how I knew this, but I knew it in my dream.) I looked at Che, and his face was covered with blood. I started to scream, and put my hands to my face, because I wanted to know if it was covered with blood too. But Che took my hands away from my face. He said, "Be quiet, Camba," and put his arms around me. "Don't worry, Camba," he said. I was crying, and he rocked me in his arms. It was nice being held and rocked. That's when I woke up.

I never got to feel my face and find out if there was blood on it.

Isle of Pines, May 1968

MAY 15

But why did Che separate himself from Joaquin? From that time on we nosed about the countryside, looking for him, like an old dog with a cold. The army blocked our way to Joaquin—without even knowing what they were doing—and we wandered off in another direction, telling ourselves that we would join up later on, that Joaquin's group must go this way, too, until the reports of their losses began to come on the radio, and we couldn't tell ourselves that anymore.

At first the army was amazed—how could we strike at them from so many different places? They couldn't *imagine* that we had separated into two groups. But the division made us weak, and it trapped Tania, our contact with the city. Watching Joaquin and Che talk together in the field of tall grass, I had thought that this was a minor tactical decision, leaving the sick with Joaquin, giving them a chance to rest so we could make a rapid foray towards Iripita and drop off Debray. But look at what he *wrote:* "I couldn't wait to put some distance between us and the other sick ones.

"And now to get Debray out, away, gone."

He was a sick one himself—weak-chested, he could hardly breathe most of the time! That's why he separated us from Joaquin, that's why he couldn't stand *the other* sick ones. He wanted to put some *distance* between himself and them! He wasn't like them! He wasn't weak! He was a doctor who hated sick people! (And, now that I think of it, that has been true of almost every doctor I've ever known.)

Drawing the lines; he was always drawing the lines with that sharp mind of his. The line between him and weakness, between him and dirty compromises. To make himself pure he had to put more and more things on the other side of the line, weak things, hypocritical things, *things that weren't like him.* And Debray? Why the rush to get rid of him? Did Che have to say that Regis was not like him? After all Che's years of battle and sacrifice? Impossible!

But why did he leave them with *Joaquin*—Joaquin, who had *the look.* Joaquin's face when he told us about Masetti—Che wasn't the only one moved by Joaquin's speech. I was *terrified* by him. I couldn't take my eyes off his Adam's apple, the only thing moving in that huge slab of a face. Joaquin's eyes looked straight at NOTHING. And then Che and Joaquin standing in that field, that damnable, open field. (No field is an open field if you yourself are standing in it, you yourself with your desire to die.) "He looked past me as I spoke, his eyes glazed, his mouth open. The sun, I thought. It makes him look vacant, distant. He didn't even nod in agreement."

The liar—he knew it wasn't the sun that did that to Joaquin's face. He knew what it meant. Surviving your friends can be like a disease, an *acid* blackness inside your mind, and you push back against it as long as you can, pretending that nothing is wrong, though you are more and more tired each day, and it spreads inside your limbs, your throat, your eyes, and whispers and whispers and WHISPERS a suggestion to you that you should take yourself off this planet as rapidly as possible. His friend Nico had that look, telling his story of the Moncada in Hilda's parlor in Guatemala City. The symptoms of the condition: the limbs won't move, the face inert, the Adam's apple grown big, and the spit so heavy that it won't go down without a major effort. The slow march in the voice, taking Joaquin away, taking us away. The need to have someone else's eyes to receive your confession, until the case is so advanced that you can't even *look* at anyone's eyes. Che *knew* that Joaquin had a bad case. Why did he leave him in charge, turning the rear guard's march into a funeral procession?

Did he have to draw the line between himself and Joaquin—show that he wasn't like him, that that wasn't his problem, he didn't feel guilty?

When Che had first begun discussing his plan with Fidel, his plan for the continental revolution, many Vietnams to save Vietnam, Fidel said that Che had sent many people to prove *his* theory of guerrilla warfare, his theory that the time was transformed by beginning the struggle, and they had died, and Che felt troubled. He couldn't stand to live when they were dead on his account. (On his account: they were down in the shopkeeper's books, under Che's name: he owed them.) Che had to prove his theories were good, that the others had died from their own mistakes. Or Che had to die himself, to appease his guilt. Maybe, Fidel had said, Che wanted to die.

—I'm having trouble with my spit. It feels like liquid metal. It doesn't want to go down. *There are things that Fidel can say about him that I can't even write.* (Or Fidel *could* say them. Not now, not anymore, not during *The Year of the Heroic Guerrilla.*)

I had thought, as Che had said, that this "analysis" by Fidel was crazy talk, perhaps an evasion on Fidel's part. He didn't want to offend the Soviets by supporting Che. But now I don't know. *Now I want to see Che's face, his neck.* Did he show signs? Nico, Joaquin, Che: survivors.

Inti, too; but he is probably dead already. He had one task left to do that would allow him to delay his having to die. He had to return to Honorato Ispaca's house and kill Ispaca for betraying Joaquin's group to the army. Inti had that look at the end. He had survived Che, he had survived his brother, Coco. He turned back from the border, the bobbing piece of flesh caught in his neck making its difficult way up and down, poisoned knowledge that he couldn't swallow, couldn't spit out.

And *me?* I wish there were a mirror on this island so I could see what I look like. I'm glad there isn't. But how can I escape the shadow forming inside my body, like a second black body, growing more solid every day, until it will demand that I be split open so that *it* can walk about?

Can I escape by telling *his* story? That was Che's first thought, coming here—wait a moment, I have to consult his manuscript—that he would write his way free, "rewrite himself instead of sacrificing himself and his comrades." But I'm not rewriting *myself,* sacrificing myself, I'm writing *him,* his story. I'm sacrificing my life, though, to writing it. Maybe I can pay off my debt to him by telling his story. What debt? I don't owe him anything!

My weight remains the same, at about a hundred.

MAY 16

Can I change things? Can I add things? I feel now as I did after the first battle: that I know what people were thinking, what they would have said *if* they had spoken.

I want to mix my labor with his, not just record things, but write them. (Do I have the right?)

Bolivia, 1967

From Guevara's Journal

5/8/67: Benigno came on the run from the ambush, his long legs flying down the path, to report the unexpected arrival of our first journalist. He had come riding past the ambush on the dirt road to Muyupampa, ten kilometers from our camp, his mule led by a peasant guide. Marcos had detained him. The journalist had said he was looking for us. Marcos awaited my instructions.

The men worried that this meant that the army, too, was close to discovering us. But journalists, I told them, are far more persistent and perspicacious than the soldiers will be. ("Sure," Ricardo said. "We don't shoot at them.") In the middle of the Cuban war, when we were fierce implacable ghosts to the army, eluding them, striking as we wished, Jorge Masetti, working for an Argentine newspaper, had found me, his compatriot, for purposes of an interview. And a writer from *The New York Times* came to the Sierras to see Fidel. Raul marched twenty men—we had only about thirty then altogether—down a grassy hill in front of the reporter and Fidel, but far enough away so that the visitor couldn't make out any faces. Then the men scurried about behind the scenes, climbed to a different hilltop, and Raul marched them down again. Each time they came into view Fidel made up the name of a different column of the Rebel Army, and the newspaperman scribbled it down in his spiral notebook. The notebook contained a battalion's worth of spectral guerrillas. ("How many in a battalion?" Coco asked, afraid that important instruction was passing him by. "I don't know," I admitted. "A lot.") When the notebook became a newspaper story we seemed to the world to be a substantial presence, a possible victor over Batista. Men came to join us. We became a substantial presence, a possible victor over Batista.

I sent word that this reporter might come ahead. Soon El Chino emerged through the thick overhanging leaves, leading him down the thread of a path that the men had cut. The journalist, still on his mule, sat erect under a white pith helmet, with a black camera strapped around his neck, batting at the long leaves with a regular motion, as if he were a prince waving at a crowd. He had an imperious face, with a long straight nose (his mother, he told us later, was English, his father Chilean). His large brown eyes moved about rapidly, though he didn't turn his face. His straight upper body swayed slightly—from inscribing a circle of fear on the air.

The peasant boy walked behind, smiling, patting the mule's rump. He had on a wide palm-frond hat that reminded me of young Walter's headgear when he had arrived on the back of Ossario's mule. Ponco stared intently at the boy, as I have seen him doing often these last weeks at captured soldiers. He smiled tenderly (perhaps a little narcissistically).

El Chino, too, was smiling, somewhat abstractedly, for his concentration was fixed on the slim path ahead of him, which he could barely make out. Chino carried a sub-machine gun, and wore a brown policeman's cap with his uniform. He had admirably even white teeth, which he takes very good care of, an example to us all. With his thin eyes inside their slight folds of flesh his expression had menace to it.

"Hello, gentlemen!" the reporter cried out when he discerned us through the trees. His tremulous voice was full of false heartiness, for he knew the guerrilla's character from army propaganda, from Marcos's peremptoriness in seizing him on the path, from Chino's toothy grin—if we suspected he was a spy we would kill him and leave his body for the vultures. As it turned out, Wolfe (our reporter's name) had no political commitment—his party was that of sorrow, those who weep for the sad, inevitable fate of humanity. Greed and curiosity had made him intrepid at the start of his adventure. But now he saw the unspeakable face to face, and peeked out bravely (but for his slight swaying motion) from behind walls of anxiety.

"Hello!" Coco shouted back, naturally gregarious. Coco wants to be a part of all our encounters with the peasantry, too. Despite their lies, and their past evasive nonsense, he always has an appetite for new conversations. He was pleased to have a visitor. So were we all. Wolfe was contact with the outside, however tenuous, and he signified that we were news, a big story, the sort worth risking your life to get. We all smiled welcomingly at him, with what must have seemed to Wolfe the frightening cordiality of cartoon cannibals saying hello to dinner. Many of the men wore dirty green camouflage suits, and long leather boots that we'd stripped off the Rangers—reminders to Wolfe of our darker thoughts. Reminding him, too, that the army might come upon our camp as he sat and talked to us. In the middle of that battle he might be slaughtered indifferently with the rest of us, unable to establish his press credentials.

Wolfe brought his camera to his eye. That showed courage, I thought. Or perhaps he did it to make a reassuringly familiar gesture; to hide himself, or to show that he had power, too—he could take our image. He tensed his knees against the mule's sweaty flanks. I looked as if through his long lens at my men sitting in the little clearing, leaning against trees. They were skinny, clearly hungry and weak. Some men's cheeks were hollowing, and Benjamin, the former medical student from La Paz, looked positively cadaverous. I shook my head no, broadly, so El Chino might make it out. Ponco shook his head, relaying the message. Ricardo echoed Ponco's motion at closer range. El Chino saw that and jerked the reins, making the mule shift about and shake Wolfe. Through his viewfinder Wolfe must have seen the guerrilla camp suddenly disapproving of him. "No pictures," El Chino said. "Please. And you should get down from your mule."

"Are you hungry?" Ponco asked the boy.

"Yes, starved," Wolfe himself replied nervously. "We're both starved."

"Who the fuck asked *you?*" Ricardo shouted. He, too, was nervous.

"Shut up, Ricardo," Ponco said. "These people are our guests."

"I've been traveling with the army for the last few weeks," Wolfe said, looking away from Ricardo. "There are troops now in Gutierrez." He wanted to show how cooperative he could be, but he wasn't sure whom precisely to address his remarks to. So he offered his information and his good will to the air in front of him. "I've been looking for you people for ages." He told the assembly his name then, and that, as we would see on his credentials, he was a reporter for Time-Life.

Chino held the papers against his nose and nodded to me.

Traveling with the army, the Time-Life reporter said, had been terrible. They drank polluted water with insects in it, and ate cold C-rations. The soldiers were irritable (strange word, I thought; it made them sound like cranky children), ready to leap at each other's throats. (Not like our happy family, we all smiled back at him.) "They're terrified of you. There's fear in all their faces."

Flattering, and probably true. They didn't know that we were momentarily divided in half, or that our radio transmitter was broken and our city liaison trapped with us. They didn't know of our difficulties making peasant recruits. All *they* knew was that we killed soldiers when they didn't expect it.

Wolfe laughed—perhaps because we looked pathetic considering our reputation, perhaps (after all, we did have guns) to hide his own fear.

"Why do you laugh?" Ricardo asked. "Don't you think that the soldiers *should* be scared of us?" Ricardo laughed himself. That disagreeable sound was the worst test Wolfe would face with us.

"Of course they should!" Wolfe said, taking a step backward from Ricardo's hilarity and into his mule. "War is a dangerous business." The mule snorted.

Wolfe changed the subject. Our food was very much more delicious than the sickening C-rations that the North Americans provided for the soldiers. He spooned up some of the disgusting lukewarm lard-flavored water—mixed with a few handfuls of beans—that Ponco had fetched for them.

"Tell the soldiers about our food when you get back to them," Ricardo said. "If you get back. Maybe they will join the Revolution for its *cuisine.*" As he said this last word he turned to Ponco for approval. After all, Ricardo's vain look said, he, too, read *literature.*

Wolfe's face was a light bulb being switched on and off. *When you get back. If you get back.*

Wolfe continued with his story, as if by establishing how he'd gotten here he'd prove that he was who he said he was. He had begun looking for us months ago, in November, at the first rumors. (November? I saw the men look at each other, wondering: What rumors? Who had spoken of us? Monje? Someone here with us now?—I must speak with Tania when we rejoin Joaquin.) He had begun searching north of the Rio Grande. When he had heard on the radio about the first battles, his guide had deserted him. But Paulino, a brave young boy, had led him down the Camiri road. He pointed to Paulino, a boy no more than fifteen years old, who leaned against a tree with Ponco. Paulino looked disconsolately at the soup. He picked out one of the beans with his finger, and wiped the scummy water off on his shirt before eating it.

"I've come a long way," Wolfe said, "to interview your commander."

Wolfe, I suspected, had already recognized me. I was skinnier than my pictures, and the ends of my hair were gray from my old-man's disguise. But it had mostly grown back, and my brown beard was full again. I was recognizably myself. Yet Wolfe would never dare mention my name—dark magical powers resided in that syllable; I was King of the Cannibals; it was taboo to say it; my men would rend him for the profanation.

"I am the commander of the guerrillas, Che Guevara," I said, stepping forward from among the men.

"But you're so thin!" Wolfe exclaimed. It was involuntary speech. People come to feel that they know those whose pictures they have so often seen in the newspapers. One becomes like a figure in their dreams, something they are often given to look at, that speaks to them obscurely, though they have no control over it. They come to have a proprietary feeling towards the image— they feel they deserve, at least, a reassuring continuity. So they're distressed when one changes. Wolfe's squeak was different from a friend's concern. It was more intimate.

"Mr. Wolfe," I said, "it will be a pleasure to give you an interview. In return I would like you to accompany two other journalists who I'm afraid have preceded you, Mr. Regis Debray of Maspero Publishers in France, and Mr. Bustos of Argentina. I would like you to take them back to Muyupampa." Wolfe was happy to be accepted by us, but deeply sad to think that we had already been discovered by the press.

"Of course," he said wanly.

"I would like a favor: I would like to have a few rolls of your film. I used to be a photographer myself, and it's very hard for me to get film now. And I would appreciate it if you'd distribute a communique of ours to the Bolivian newspapers. It will be no risk for you." Of course I had many more vital messages about supplies to get to the city. But Wolfe couldn't be trusted with the name of a city contact; the army would suspect him for a while, and follow his movements.

Wolfe agreed to all I asked.

We left my men to get news from the guide, and Wolfe and I went off a little ways into the forest for our talk. "You needn't worry for your safety while you're with us," I said. "No harm will come to you here, you have my word on that. You can say absolutely anything you like to me. Let's have a good open honest talk together." I wanted Wolfe to be someone it was possible to talk with, I wanted to make him a little more courageous.

But, as it turned out, Wolfe didn't require my reassurance. Once he took his small tape recorder from his knapsack, and set it whirring, he changed utterly. He became a reporter, a contentious, all-too-knowing man, quite able to hold his own.

Interview of Che Guevara by Michael Andrew Wolfe

WOLFE: Mr. Guevara, when you talk in your "Message to the Tricontinental," of turning this continent into another Vietnam, aren't you talking of an unparalleled reign of violence for this continent, an unprecedented suffering for its people?

GUEVARA: They suffer now, Mr. Wolfe, less spectacularly perhaps, but just as inexorably. In this country, where we are now talking, few tin miners live beyond the age of thirty. When they enter the mines as young men they know they will die near that age. If they don't enter the mines, they have no work and nothing to eat. So they are forced to kill themselves. Each year more children die in Latin America of curable diseases and malnutrition than all who died at Hiroshima. There is already a war going on against my people. Now we are going to fight back. We are going to make the sacrifices necessary so that our children may have a different life.

WOLFE: But the war you speak of means that many of those miners won't live till thirty, or twenty-five or even fifteen. And many of their wives and children will die as well.

GUEVARA: The struggle will be long and difficult. But none of us should hesitate to offer the necessary sacrifice. If we fight here, and in Asia, and in Africa, we will win. The Revolution will be continental. All of Latin America will rise against the United States. And then the Revolution will become worldwide. The people of the Third World do not want to die. But they do want to live freely, and with dignity.

WOLFE: The War in Vietnam has shown that the United States, too, is willing to make sacrifices. They will not allow the victory of a Communist Revolution. Bad as you say things are here, they could be far worse. Now the people have potatoes and beans. They work. They read the newspapers. You know what I mean: they're alive!

GUEVARA: They read the newspapers! I can see that that would seem a supreme pleasure to a journalist. But seventy percent of the Bolivian people can't read. In any case, the United States can't kill all of us. They aren't all-powerful. The world situation, the balance of powers, means that they cannot use their nuclear weapons. People's war will defeat them. The Vietnamese are teaching us that. We must not abandon Vietnam. We must fight alongside it. The revolution will be on three continents. It isn't in the interest of the United States to fight all the world's people. Such a war cannot be won. It would drain them of their sons and their resources. Such a war would barbarize their country. The people of the United States would not accept it. If their rulers demand it, then they will rise against those rulers.

WOLFE: You have great faith in the people of the United States.

GUEVARA: (No response.)

WOLFE: But isn't there some other way, some way of less violence for our continent, less suffering and death?

GUEVARA: No. The imperialists will not allow any other way.

WOLFE: But who are you, who is any man, to choose this for our people, this magnitude of suffering?

GUEVARA: We do not choose it for them. We begin the struggle, and so show the way the fight must be carried out. We offer it to the people. If the people do not join their efforts to ours then we will not win. But they will, and we will win. Right now the people of Bolivia suffer history. We will give them the chance to become agents of history, actors. We perform the actions that history demands of those who would step on to its stage.

WOLFE: How can you say that "history" demands anything? Don't you interpret "history" as if it were an oracle, a god? Isn't it *you* that demands?

GUEVARA: (No response.)

WOLFE: *Comandante Guevara, perhaps you would like to explain why, at the last moment, when you were surrounded in the Churo ravine and you asked for volunteers to cover your retreat, and all the men volunteered, you chose, among others, Inti Peredo, whom you thought the best of the Bolivians, destined to lead the war of national liberation here, and Walter Villamil Tulio, captain in the Cuban Army, a very decent fellow, your closest friend, and the man who loved you most in the entire world?*

GUEVARA: (No response.)

WOLFE: Isn't it true that in the terrible violence that you are now engaged in, you do the very things you say you're fighting against? After all, I've been with the Bolivian soldiers. They are just young men who couldn't get any other work. They are terrified. They don't want to die. And they aren't the imperialists.

GUEVARA: You are right. They are only the unknowing agents of imperialism. But we must first kill the specters of imperialism, so that the United States will then be forced to send its own soldiers, as they have in Vietnam. We will defeat them as well.

WOLFE: You kill as the army does. And in your book on guerrilla warfare you speak of the necessity of using terror against the countrypeople, to keep them from aiding the opposition.

GUEVARA: Their terror and our violence are not the same thing. Our violence will help the countrypeople shake off their passivity; it shows them that they might act. The army, on the other hand, mean to terrify the peasantry, to keep them from acting, to turn them to stone.

And no countryperson would help the army of his own free will. We must at least warn them not to cooperate with their oppressors.

WOLFE: That is not very clear to me, Comandante. I think it means that you both threaten the peasants.

GUEVARA: We didn't construct this situation, Mr. Wolfe, but we must all live in it. We are none of us bad enough for this world. Our movement thinks this: If we are to win our liberation we must make ourselves into killing machines. Effective, violent, selective, and cold killing machines.

WOLFE: My God, that's monstrous! Can you hear what you're saying?

GUEVARA: It is the image of what's necessary. We are trying to become what History calls for. It has been very good speaking with you, Mr. Wolfe.

Here is the communique you promised to distribute for us, and the two colleagues, fellow journalists like yourself, who are most anxious to leave with you. Good-bye, and you may leave whatever way seems best to you. We must continue our march.

STATEMENT OF THE NATIONAL LIBERATION ARMY OF BOLIVIA

Our national resources have served, and are still serving, to make foreigners rich, leaving us Bolivians a terrible wound in our side, and the worm of hunger gnawing at our guts. This is why we fight, and why we ask you to join us. Our country or death!

I found my talk with Wolfe—empty though it was—enjoyable. As for the content of the thing:

GUEVARA: Exploited masses Class struggle Imperialism Armed struggle Historical conditions Liberation *Violence*
WOLFE: Conscience Sadness The Cruelty of the World The Vale of Tears Pity The Human Condition Misery *Horror*

It wasn't much! But I cannot argue with my comrades, cannot talk even that freely with them. I can only listen and give orders. (The distance between me and the men is, of course, now a tool of my work.) And the peasants evade and look down; they cannot really talk to us yet. When they have sometimes spoken it has been, so far, shameful nonsense. In time, of course, our victories will change them, and they will have the courage to argue with us. But for now I am surrounded by silence.

Wolfe reported that Muyupampa, too, has soldiers in it. Debray was informed—for it may increase the risk to him—but he insisted on making his departure. Very well!

I am left with one troubling thought: how had Wolfe known, several months ago, before we were established, long before a battle where I carefully did not show myself, that *I* was the commander of the guerrillas, a celebrity worth the trip to speak with? Even Monje would not have known. I must interrogate Tania when we rejoin Joaquin.

We will move back north, towards Joaquin's group and the rendezvous.

.   .   .

5/10/67: The scouts report troops in almost every direction. We cannot remain in the appointed area.

5/12/67: The army, without knowing the trouble it causes us, has pushed us north, towards Ticucha and El Meson.

5/13/67: Shortly after we set up camp near El Meson, a column of sixty-five soldiers was spotted, and I ordered an ambush put near the river. The advance column of the army was led by a man with two bloodhounds. I shot at the first and missed. Inti fired and killed the guard and a dog. I immediately ordered a retreat, and as we withdrew the army exchanged fire with us. Rolando was fatally wounded.

Poem for Rolando? Rolando, carrying his father's table on his back, fleeing Batista's army. "Between them and you," he had said, "things can't get any worse."

From My Journal

5/13/67: A story about Rolando? His small slim body reminds me of children's stories. Once upon a time . . .

From Coco's Journal

5/13/67: Rolando, wounded in the neck, died. I liked him best of the Cubans. Besides Che, of course. But I admire Che rather than like him. It's a different feeling.

From Guevara's Journal

5/14/67: The smell of the soldier's blood marks our location. We will have to leave completely the area where we were to rejoin Joaquin. We will move back towards the Nancahuazu camp. The army patrols and staging areas will force Joaquin back in that direction as well.

5/15/67: We have continued moving north, looking for signs of Joaquin's group, but without success. It has been slow going. For the last two days we have been short of water. Game in the area is scant. Today Inti killed a big black bird: thereby we shall save supplies. There is a reserve now for two days: dehydrated soup and canned meat.

·   ·   ·

I recorded a message from Fidel and have laboriously replayed the tape for decoding. The message: "Kolle, speaking for the Bolivian Party, said that Monje had confused the Party's Central Committee by saying that the operation was only on a national scale. I made clear the continental dimensions of the struggle, and the strategic place of Bolivia. Kolle asked to speak with you, to discuss their participation in the operation. He seemed staggered by the idea of a continental movement. He leaves immediately for the zone. I think something can be done. He wants economic aid to pay for training for his cadres."

I talked over this latest development with the men. Our victories, I said, are having an effect. But it is deeds that matter from the Party, not words.

Inti is skeptical that there will ever be deeds. He thinks the Party is only interested in Fidel's money, and that they will never make contact with us, blaming circumstances.

Time will tell.

5/17/67: Today Monje was interviewed on Chilean radio. Coexistence, he said, is for the United States and the Soviet Union. Thermonuclear powers must avoid war. But Communists must not give up on the war against imperialism within our countries. That is why the Bolivian Party gives its wholehearted support to the guerrilla movement in Bolivia.

Inti now doubts his own skepticism. And Coco thinks we should choose someone to return to the city, contact the Party, and arrange for incorporating their cadres.

That, I said, is impossible. It would be certain death for the messenger, and too great a risk for the rest of us if he fell into the enemy's unkind hands.

I cannot have the men dreaming of a possible escape into the cities for any of us. They must realize that we stand or fall together now; here; there is no life for any of us outside the Revolution. Victory or death.

From Coco's Journal

5/18/67: There was nothing to eat today except some lard-flavored water. We sat in the darkness of the forest, listening to the radio and drinking the stuff. Barrientos admitted that there are Yanqui advisers. The Chilean station said that the guerrillas are forcing the cities to take defensive measures. The U.S. has sent more helicopters, napalm, planes, arms, and another contingent of Green Beret advisers.

Che was pleased by this, and of course I am too. I guess we are doing very well. But all those weapons! I saw the forest in flames and helicopters landing on the road near here, and I was scared.

From Guevara's Journal

5/19/67: The men showed me—by their slow pace, slumped shoulders—their reluctance about walking today. There hasn't been enough food for the machete wielders, and none at all for the rest of us. The solution is to set a better example.

René Doré has been arrested. The radio said that Doré was a mastermind of the revolution, a bloodthirsty guerrilla who led many ambushes against the Bolivian Army. A thoroughly bad character, Doré, in Cuba, had feasted on delicacies while Guevara directed mass executions in the Havana city square —for Doré's amusement, presumably.

"A movie villain," Inti said.

"No," Ponco said, "more like a comic book." As an illiterate Walter loved cartoons. They were his only stories.

"I can't go any farther," Benigno said, indifferent to the proper medium for my portrayal. He has to carry one of the heavy guns.

Doré, the radio said, was captured in the woods as he hid trembling behind a tree. Bustos, too, was arrested, and Wolfe. As it turned out, then, it was the army that no longer believed in Wolfe's credentials. But he at least will soon be released.

How did they know about Bustos and Debray so immediately?

5/20/67: Nothing to eat today but more lard soup—without the additional beans. We are nearing one of the food caches. The situation will indeed be desperate if the army has discovered our supply caves.

5/21/67: Doré became Debray today. In the last two days he has been transformed from co-leader to political commissar to intellectual author of the guerrilla movement—to mere combatant. Today, along with his proper name, he assumed his real position: courier. It is easy to imagine that each of these demotions represented many hours of the torturer's work, beatings, bullets fired in the dark, electrodes on Regis's genitals, etc. I heard Ricardo elaborating some of these educational methods to his group, to add emphasis to my points about the necessity for cohesion and the dangers of falling into army hands.

In Debray's case the torturers failed, for they must have begun with the grand story they wanted, and revised only very reluctantly, marking the revisions on Debray's body. The admission they desired was that he, and we, are Castro's agents. Debray denies all still, and says that he was a reporter. By now he is probably in a coma from his beatings.

Our messages to Fidel, about the Bolivian Party—and the ways, under his supervision, that they must show their good faith by resupplying us—are lost.

5/22/67: Bear Camp, Nancahuazu. The army had been to the camp, which gave us some bad moments. Their footprints were everywhere. The board for the latrine had been smashed, and the cooking site covered with dirt. As I walked through the camp I could feel the emptiness form in my stomach.

But the caches were untouched! We had eight cans of milk—a stunningly good breakfast. And we ate the last of the dehydrated soup, and the canned meats. We have still more lard in the caves.

Tuma, our scout, reports that the soldiers have occupied the little farm and trampled the corn.

From Coco's Journal

5/23/67: A small patrol of about twelve soldiers came down the river, picking their way among the rocks, and fell into our ambush. Marcos shot the lieutenant, and we all called for their surrender, but they went on firing. I shot one of the soldiers, who fell on the rocks, and then rolled into the river. Most of the soldiers ran away, but six were captured by the rear guard of the ambush, as they ran directly towards our guns. One of them fell on the rocks as he tried to escape, and he broke his leg.

We assembled our prisoners near the river. "Let's not fuck around with them this time," Ricardo said. "Let's just kill them." I don't think he was serious. He asked the major what his last wish was. The major spat near Ricardo's foot. I thought Ricardo would hit him, but he just laughed and touched the spit with his boot, rubbing it along the gray-and-brown rock.

"I want my body to be given to my men to bury," the major said. The major had a broad face. His nose looked out of joint, like a brawler's. "So that it can be taken back for a Christian burial."

Ricardo stopped smiling. He doesn't like to talk about Christianity. "Why do you say that's all you want? Are you an idiot? You *look* like an idiot."

"I don't want the same thing to happen to my body that happened to my dead comrades." The major seemed very angry. I suppose that was what he did with his fear.

Ricardo was too furious to speak, so I told the major that he was wrong, that the unburied bodies weren't our fault. We had made it very clear to the officers that they could come back the next day, unmolested, to get the men's bodies. But the officers had left their men to rot.

I said this loudly so the other prisoners would hear.

"You are savages," the major said, just as if I hadn't spoken. He was making me angry, too. I saw how he must have gotten into a lot of fights.

"You're a lucky man," Marcos said. Marcos was covered with sweat from the battle. He perspires more than the rest of us, and he has to wipe himself dry or he breaks out into a bright rash. "In the Congo, when the guerrillas kill an enemy, they rip open the skin of the dead man's chest with their long knives. And they pluck out the nut, the man's heart. Then they eat it. Perhaps, if you aren't more polite, we'll let our Congolese friend work on you." He gestured towards Ponco, who stood on one of the rocks by the river, smiling in the sunlight. "Do you have your long knife, Ponco?"

"You betcha Ponco have long knife," Ponco said, dancing from foot to foot gleefully. "Man look very good. Very good fruit for Mponco. He skin and eat mighty quick now!"

"You disgust me," the major said to Marcos. But his voice had the jitters. It was obviously a joke—or so I thought—but Ponco's performance had scared him. I think it must have been that very strange sound Ponco makes.

"You not disgust Mr. Ponco," Ponco said, smiling with delight. "Delicious Thing You Are." He walked across the rocks to the major, batting his eyelashes. This was too much for the major, who took a step backward, and started to fall from his rock. Marcos grabbed him by the shoulder, and the major screamed at his touch—a little high-pitched sound. Everyone laughed at him. Ponco then talked to the other prisoners in an ordinary way, about troop locations, and began collecting the food from their knapsacks. I think they liked the way we had made a fool of their major.

Later I asked Ponco whether what Marcos had said about the Congo was true. He said yes, that the Congolese soldiers did sometimes eat the dead mercenaries' hearts. Che had been horrified, of course, and tried to teach them better manners—to show more respect for the dead. But the Congo people said that *their* way showed the most respect. They didn't waste anything—they acquired the soldier's courage by eating his heart. If you ate a lot of hearts you were sure to become a great warrior.

I told Ponco that I didn't think his story would usually have bothered me so. But I had been thinking of the man I'd shot leaving a trail of blood on the gray rocks, as he rolled over them into the river. I could taste the salty blood on my tongue, and I felt nauseous.

Ponco said that he understood how I felt. During battles he sometimes had that same strange taste in his mouth, like his saliva had turned to blood. But he could see the Congolese point of view. At least they made it a personal matter. The imperialist forces, in the Congo and Vietnam, dropped bombs whose metallic hearts fragmented to a thousand slivers. The bombs didn't ruin property, but the slivers entered soft things, like bodies. The fragments were coated in plastic, so that X-rays wouldn't show their location. The victims hemorrhaged and died.

It was the waste of a good heart, Ponco said. The pilots couldn't even see their victims, let alone lunch on them. Ponco thought it was better to taste the man's blood. He thought it was too bad we couldn't develop an appetite for their hearts.

I don't know. I saw what he was saying. But I thought, as he talked to me of those sorcerers' weapons, *Dear God, what are we beginning here?* I thought of the rum I drank in this camp many months ago, when we toasted a new Vietnam in Latin America. Is that what we want for our continent? I saw our villages on fire, and I felt a sliver of smooth metal enter my chest, moving towards my heart, something no X-ray could see.

And later, when I thought over the battles I'd been in, I thought that I would rather have been flying an airplane myself, and killing soldiers I couldn't see—from a safe distance!

But Che is right. We are doing what is necessary.

From Guevara's Journal

5/24/67: We seized a few loads of toasted corn from the soldiers, and some sugar and coffee. We also took their boots. Ours are worn through by the combination of the damp and the rocky terrain. The leather flakes away far more rapidly than I had expected. We also exchanged our rags for their fatigues.

According to Marcos's interrogation of the prisoners, the army is encamped on the grassy flat hunting plain, half burned away now by their napalm. We will move north. I had bottles filled with lard from the caves for the march.

I think it is likely that Joaquin's group will have moved north also.

5/25/67: On the Bolivian radio station today it was reported that Michael Wolfe, an admitted guerrilla, and Guevara's liaison with Chile, had hanged himself in his cell, using his own belt.

Apparently Tania was right; it is better to have a secret.

.   .   .

5/27/67: The solid foods were gone, and the lard soup made everyone sick. Fortunately, yesterday we came upon a small farm, an adobe house, with a sewing machine. We bought some roast pig, chicken, squash, and corn, all at the usual outrageous prices. Coco, Inti, and Ricardo had a few empty conversations with the merchant farmer.

From My Journal

5/27/67: I listened to Coco, Ricardo, and Inti talk to the farmer we encountered, an old man in a thin dirty sweater and a soft brown felt hat. He had glittery eyes that kept darting about, and a quizzical ironic expression.

He welcomed us as great bandits, the greatest in memory, great bandits with special powers.

"What?" Coco said, as if the man had poked him. "We aren't bandits."

The man laughed amiably at Coco's comic attempt to confuse him.

We were the best bandits, he said again, the greatest bandits. We paid for what we took from the poor. (And it was certainly true that we had paid him very well for the corn and squash he had sold us—enough money so that he wasn't so poor anymore!)

"But we are not bandits!" Inti insisted. Inti sounded like someone had struck him hard. The two brothers were like Che: *everyone must get things right:* No opportunity for instruction should be lost.

"But of course you are great bandits!" The man was still amiable, despite the brothers' attempt at deception.

After all, he said, if we weren't bandits why did the army chase after us? And why did we carry guns? It was because we wouldn't join the army! All the other bandits had joined the army by and by. It was so much easier to join the army and steal from the peasants that way.

He stopped suddenly, and looked off into the forest. Maybe he worried that he'd put ideas in our heads.

Inti insisted that we were guerrillas who fought the army because it stole from the peasants. We would help him and the others to set up tribunals to judge soldiers who stole. And whatever sentences the peasants decided we would carry out with our rifles.

"Yes?" the man said musingly, stroking his lip. He was relieved that he hadn't inadvertently convinced us to rob him.

There was a bandit, he said, who had set up as judge over the army. In the thirties. He couldn't remember the man's name, but he thought that his wife probably could—she remembered everything. He had known a woman once who people said had slept with that bandit, the one whose name he couldn't remember. He had joined the army eventually.

Coco said that we would never join the army. We would fight until the guerrillas became a new army, made up of all the people of Bolivia. An army that served the nation.

"Yes?" he said. "That would be nice." But he had lost interest in Coco and Inti, for they distorted the basic fact: that we were bandits.

Coco asked if he would sell us some chickens, and named a very high price.

"Some chickens? No, we can't. We have very few ourselves."

Ricardo, who didn't mind being thought the best, the greatest of bandits (with special powers, whatever that meant), laughed, alas, at the man's refusal. He said, "But you've already told us we could simply take your chickens if we wished!"

The man looked at the ground. Ricardo's laugh has that power.

"But," Ricardo added, "we are very great and very good servants of the people. We do not *take* from them."

Che was disgusted by all this talk. He named an even higher price for the chickens.

"Yes," the man said to Che. "That's very good. Just as I thought, you are very even-handed with your gains."

Che wheezed angrily at the man's stupidity.

"I am sure the army will never catch you if you are even-handed like that. Everyone will protect you. Everyone will hide you. But if I were you, sir," he said, looking directly into Che's eyes with an expression of blunt hard speech, "I would be very careful of the people around me." He glanced quickly, meaningfully, at Inti and Coco, who had tried to fool him before, by denying that we were bandits. "There's a saying, you know, 'Killed before capture, like a bandit by the police.' You understand what I mean? Those around you. Do you know their hearts?"

Che gave some money to Coco to give to the man, though Che stood only a few feet from him. It was clear that the old fellow made him uneasy. He instructed the man to buy some pigs for us, and said we'd be back in a few months to pick them up. This was to keep the man honest. Soon, I think, we will be the largest pig-raising corporation in the region.

"That was good," Coco said, as we took our food into the forest to rejoin the rest of the center group and eat. "He liked the idea of the tribunals." Really Coco was trying out the notion that the man had liked that idea; he didn't know what to think.

Ricardo laughed, and there was great misfortune in the tune.
Che looked sick.

But not as sick as he was about to be. We ate the man's food too
quickly, and it mixed up with the lard in our otherwise empty stomachs.
Nato belched like a cannon shot, and everyone laughed. Benigno started to
fart uncontrollably, like a pot bubbling. Soon everyone was belching
and farting. "An organ concert," Che said. But we were all too busy to
laugh.

Marcos suddenly pulled down his pants, waddled one step away from the
rest of us (for privacy), and squatted down. Diarrhea and vomiting became the
fashion, and the leaves and small green plants and vines were covered with our
shit.

When the concert had concluded, we gathered up our things for the
march. Che wove little circles, stepping first right then left, with tiny unsteady
steps, and then he fell to the forest floor. For a moment the will left our bodies,
and we stared at him, as if he'd died; or we'd died; or both. He had passed
out.

Benigno and I made a hammock to carry him in. Even unconscious he
animated us, drove us forward. He was our will. He was like a little god that
we carried from place to place. And then, after we had set up his shrine for
a few minutes, someone would interpret his mute body, like an oracle, and we
would move on, wandering farther north, in the direction we'd divined he
wanted.

I could see that Che, even though unconscious, was shitting in his pants.
I turned his face to the side—in case he vomited, he wouldn't choke. Julio and
I and Marcos and Benigno carried him, though we were of uneven heights.
The poles hurt my shoulders, and the others', too. But none of us would
surrender the burden to anyone else—as if it were an *honor*. We continued
north.

Che recovered after a few hours. It was—if you want my diagnosis—the
combination of the food, the asthma, his asthma medicine, and *being thought
a bandit*.

From Guevara's Journal

5/28/67: I've returned to my feet, though I still feel lightheaded. And my
stench is disgusting, even to me. We must find water for washing.

JUNE

6/1/67: In the evening, as we ate more lard soup, Benigno, our machine-gunner, operated the radio. He has long thin fingers, and turns the dials in small motions, with wholehearted concentration, as if he were some new species of man, part flesh, part technical apparatus. Which didn't improve reception. The only clear channel was domestic. A reporter asked Barrientos what he planned to do about the bad situation in the mines. "The government," Barrientos said, "will keep faith with the nation." We inferred from this that there is new trouble in the Altiplano.

Willy said that the miners had already been planning another strike at the time he was recruited by Moises for the guerrillas. The miners wanted to coordinate their actions with ours, and had waited eagerly for reports on our activities. While he was still there, the party had regularly taken up collections, supposedly for the guerrillas. (Willy would like, he said, to hold that Party member's face between his hands now. For, of course, he knew now that none of the money had reached us.) In some of the mine shafts the miners had set up shooting ranges—so they would be trained and ready to join us when the fighting reached their area.

At first the news cheered the men. But then their smiles were haunted by the taste of lard on their tongues. We are unable to contact the city, unable to get supplies. If we cannot reach the miners before the army moves against them, our isolation may rob us of a great opportunity. And the only news of us the miners will have is the static on the airwaves, between the lies spoken by the Bolivian announcers. They will have to form true words from that static.

I began a night march towards Ipiticito.

6/2/67: We took the town of Ipiticito this morning at first light. The town is perhaps ten adobe buildings with bright tile roofs of blue and red, very inviting when the sun first struck them. The hillside around the town is worked-out gray dirt. The farming has moved on, farther up the mountainside. In the distance behind the town were the green high hills, thick with growth, that we must cross to get to the Rio Grande. Here and there on the hillsides were a few thatched-roof huts—the peasants who must feed us.

I had the townspeople gathered in the main square—a rectangle of beaten-down earth without decoration. I told my men to show their rifles at every house, so the inhabitants can tell the army that they were forced to attend our meeting. We gathered seventy-five townspeople in all, most of them very old, no likely recruits. The young people, one woman informed us, had fled when they heard we were coming, afraid they'd be pressed into service with us, for they assumed the guerrillas had the habits of the government road gangs that sometimes come through here to collect laborers. The old men of the village wore soft gray felt hats, and the women wore the derby-looking things (as if they were almost, but not quite, British bankers), thick woolen tops, and layers of skirts with red and blue checks. They all seemed to be unhappy to be standing out in the already bright sunlight.

I spoke of the general state of the country, and the coming miners' strike. I predicted that once again, at the orders of his imperialist masters, Barrientos would try to bomb the miners into submission. All Bolivians must join together to stop such slaughters. The wealth of Bolivia should be shared by all Bolivians, not given away to North Americans.

One of the men, in a sweater the color of grime and worn wide pants held up by a rope, cleared his throat to speak, a long racking sound, like a small rock slide. The others moved away from him, afraid of his phlegm, or his audacity. The rubber from their sandals made a slight shooshing sound as their weight shifted. "But Bolivia," the man said in a high voice, "has no wealth."

In any case, the man had no teeth, and I had difficulty understanding him. As I stood dumbly, Inti answered him, from the side of the crowd. "Yes it does. But the North Americans pay Bolivian soldiers to take it from us. That is what we are fighting to stop."

"But the radio says there are people with you who aren't Bolivians. That man isn't Bolivian." He pointed at me with a bony finger, and a sour expression twisted his mouth, such as it was. Coca-chewing is an epidemic of lip and tooth disease for these people, producing a variety of spots, growths, and half-eaten areas.

"Yes," Inti said, seriously, slowly, "North America has many enemies. All the enemies of imperialism must join together to fight it."

"I know why there are foreigners," the man said. He rolled what there was of his lip in upon his gums, in a parody of a smile. "It's because Bolivians aren't worth shit, that's why!" He wheezed a laugh that started him coughing for a minute or two. No one spoke. We stood together in the hot sun and listened to the old man cough. "We can't do anything for ourselves," he said when he could speak again. "We're shit! We're helpless!"

There was a shroud of whispers woven in the crowd. They were shocked at the man's foul language.

"No," Inti said, patiently, sadly. "If we join together we can defeat our enemies."

I spoke again. Many many countries, I said, were ruled by North America and kept down in poverty. All of these countries must fight together to free themselves. Every defeat of the North Americans, in any of these countries, would help to free their own country.

They had probably heard, I said, of Santo Domingo. I told them that I had been there, and that it was in a country like Bolivia. The people there had wanted to have a better life. And the North Americans had gone there and killed many countrypeople because they had wanted to work their land together, for themselves.

They had heard of the Congo. I told them that I had been there, too. The people wanted a better life for their children, and the North Americans had gone there and killed many countrypeople, like the people of Bolivia, because the people of the Congo had wanted to work their land together, and use their mineral resources to build their own country.

They had heard of Vietnam. I had been there. The countrypeople were like those in Bolivia. And the North Americans . . .

As I said "North Americans" an old woman in the crowd shrieked, a sound like a knife on a grindstone. She beat her hands in panic on the back of the man in front of her, who didn't turn around.

I smiled at her. Yes, I said, the North Americans went there and killed many Vietnamese, because those people, too, had wanted a better life for their children. But the Vietnamese have fought back against the North Americans, and were still fighting. With our help the Vietnamese would defeat the North Americans. And in time the people of Santo Domingo, the people of the Congo, and the people of Bolivia would all join the Vietnamese in their fight against the North American imperialists. If Bolivians wanted decent medical care for themselves and their children, if they wanted schools, and even universities, for their children, if they wanted to work the land together, if they thought the money made from Bolivian tin and Bolivian oil and Bolivian labor should be shared equally by all Bolivians, then they would have to fight the North Americans, and those who worked for the North Americans, like General Barrientos and his officers. That was why people like myself, from Argentina, and people from Peru, and from Cuba, had joined with Bolivians.

No one spoke. The heat was heavy on me, and my stink was very unpleasant. For two days I have had only leaves to wipe my own feces off my body. Whichever way I fly I cannot escape my smell. I stared emptily at the crowd, and dreamed of finding enough water for a thorough washing.

I called off the meeting and sent the vanguard ahead under Ricardo. Most of the townspeople scurried back into their houses. But a few stayed to talk with us. No one approached me—perhaps because I had scared them, or perhaps because of my bad smell—so I stood about the edges and listened to the others.

A few men were gathered around Inti.

"But we work our own land now," one of them said.

"Yes," Inti replied. "But you owe most of your crops to the men who sell you seed and tools and cloth. You have nothing left for yourselves. After the Revolution, if you shared the land, the nation could provide you with tools, with tractors and new and better seeds. You would have much bigger harvests."

"I wouldn't *want* land that belongs to *all* of us." He bit his lower lip in fear, and looked about himself from under the brim of his hat. "I won't say any names, but there are people here that I don't like. I don't trust them. I want my own land. My family and I will work it, as we do now. You know," he said, without turning around this time, "not everyone here is a good person. Some of the people in this village . . ." He was puzzled. How might he express their inexpressible evil? "Some of them smell bad."

I went over to where some people spoke with Benigno, our machine-gunner.

"Where are you from, sir?"

"From Cuba."

"Cuba? Where's that, sir?"

"In the Caribbean."

"What's that?"

"It's an ocean."

The man turned and said something in Quechua to the fellow next to him. Perhaps he was ashamed to ask Benigno what an ocean was. "Ah, I see," he said, after his friend replied. "And where is your ocean, sir?"

Benigno curled his long fingers into fists with frustration. He couldn't think of what to say. "It's near . . . It's near North America, near the United States."

"Ah," the old man said. "So the United States is North America! I see!" He clapped his hands together and smiled. "The Kennedys!"

And the old woman whose scream had been such a satisfying tribute to my rhetoric, asked, "What is a North American, sir? I'm glad to say I've never seen one. They must be very bad spirits, very powerful! The ones who have needles! The ones who want our blood!" She looked over at Ponco, who was talking to a child. Perhaps North Americans were like him, people with dark skins. "I don't want you to make them come here. Please don't make them come here and kill us!"

.   .   .

A few more women stood around the outskirts of the square, next to the shady wall of one of the houses. They were afraid to speak. Coco asked one of them if she had questions. She looked down at the ground, embarrassed by the attention. But another woman said, "What's a university, sir?"

"It's a place where high-school students go to study."

"What are high-school students?"

"Those who have finished secondary school."

And then, naturally enough: "What are secondary-school students? Where do they come from?"

"They come from you yourselves," Coco said. The woman looked about herself, at the three other women standing near her in their long skirts and hats. She laughed, but I could not tell if it was a laugh of confusion, or mockery, or embarrassment.

But the other women grew brave: "Where is the Congo, sir?"

"It's a country in Africa," Coco said.

Camba laughed. He had come up behind me.

"And where is Africa, sir?"

"It's across the ocean from Bolivia."

Of course, the next development was inevitable.

"What's an ocean?"

That was a hard one. There weren't even lakes in the region. Coco's round troubled face grew blank.

The last of the women in the group had found her voice. "Where is Vietnam?"

Camba stepped forward before Coco could speak. He hopped from foot to foot, like a child eager to give the right answer. "In Asia," he said.

"Asia?" the woman said. "Where is Asia, sir?"

Camba turned to give me a sly smile. "Over the mountains, there," he said, pointing past my shoulder at the hills beyond. "A thousand days' walk."

I had had enough. I felt dizzy from our lack of water, and my own smell. My speech to these people, when I heard it now, through their ears, became a dark maze of words where either the Indians, or I, were lost. The names of places and things unknown to them: my text might have crumbled around those sounds. Or perhaps they had put new thoughts in those places—dark-skinned creatures, Poncos with syringes. From those new nouns, new sentences must have taken shape, with a meaning I couldn't imagine. If I could have looked into their minds, and heard my words as they had understood them (*if* they had understood them at all), I would have made no sense to myself.

I would see a man standing in a dirt square, a man with my face, and he would be barking like a dog.

We got information from them about the nearest route to the Masicuri River, where we can get water for washing. They had none to spare, for they carry back only enough drinking water for two days at a time. They also told us what they knew of the army's movements: a lieutenant had been through the week before, and had claimed that they had the guerrillas encircled.

But this report was not the end of our prizes: we also got some potatoes, and a small yellow truck belonging to the Bolivian Petroleum Company. One of the drivers had returned to the village to visit his parents. When he had heard we were coming, he had fled to the woods, abandoning his vehicle. Spoils of war.

We loaded some of our packs onto the truck, and sent it down the dirt road towards the river, with Marcos driving, wearing Chino's policeman's cap. We will cut our own trail through the forest.

On the march Inti suggested that we try another line with the peasants in this region. They already have land. We must promise them local reforms. One of them had told Coco that the bridge over the Masicuri needs repair. For years the authorities had made promises and done nothing.

Inti is right, of course. But I could not reply fully: that to offer that kind of help we must establish ourselves in a zone. To do that we must find Joaquin, for until we win the peasants' trust we need more men, and more supplies from a support network. Right now we have none of those things.

Eusebio, one of the Bolivian slackers, said we shouldn't talk about cooperatives, we should promise them their own land. Eusebio is a poor worker, and of weak political understanding. Inti explained to him the goals of the Revolution, but I felt that he understood those no better than the townspeople had understood the geography of *our* planet.

6/3/67: The directions they gave us were wrong. The road does not lead to the Masicuri but ends at a forest.

I have a special contingent of flies buzzing around me, which seems to amuse Camba. He is becoming a little unbalanced—from thirst, I think, though he has been unpleasantly odd from the first.

I sent out scouting parties to find the right direction to the river, and I established an ambush.

From Camba's Journal

6/3/67: It was hot in the bushes by the side of a dusty road. I watched the red ants walk over my boot. I meant to kill some of them, and I lifted my other boot, and then, when I was about to bring it down, I stopped. The long thin trail of red was a way of seeing my blood move in my body. The ants are veins that connect the plants, the animals, and the people who live here.

A truck came down the dirt road. Two soldiers were asleep in the back. Marcos said they looked so comfortable he didn't have the heart to kill them. We let them go by. The next truck came, *and no one was asleep in the back,* so we threw grenades. The truck formed a big red flower that hurt our ears. The explosion shook the ants from my boot, severing the blood line. A bad omen! (But I will do as Ponco told me, and not speak of it to anyone.)

From Guevara's Journal

6/4/67: The scouts have found an encampment of farmers who say they live on the way to the river. I sent the truck up ahead, and had the center group follow after.

From My Journal

6/4/67: The village was six thatched huts and a lean-to, where they store tools and sacks—and where one family also lives. Inti was the speaker. Perhaps he could convince someone to join us. He told the assembled families about the Bolivian Revolution. As he talked, children—their heads wrapped in long dirty white rags—ran about examining the men. (Maybe the people here think the sun is bad for children.) There were only—or even—two young men in the crowd.

At the end of Inti's talk Che stepped forward. "Now is the hour of decision," he said to the thirty people, mostly old men and women. "Bolivians have a chance to make history. The whole world is watching what happens here in Bolivia."

This received the usual deep well-like silence, the silence we might all drown in, the silence of the grass growing over our graves. An old man hobbled forward, clippety-clumpety. He was very thin and pigeon-toed—the perfect recruit. He wore one of their dirty sweaters, woven from dust, and the usual felt hat. He held Che's shoulders and looked up and down his thinning body. Then he raised his own skinny arm, gestured to two young men—the only young men there—and they walked off, a small parade, into their hut.

Che looked stunned with remorse and anger, like a jilted lover.

After the dramatic departure the countrypeople talked with us in a surprisingly open friendly fashion. I drifted from group to group listening to the conversations.

An older man with a pleasant face and large bulging eyes talked with Coco. They stood in front of his hut (it looked, to me, like piles of hay baled together). He said that he had heard all about us from the people in Ipiticito. They had told him that we had come to establish a reign of justice.

Coco nodded uncertainly, his head half palsied by doubt. Reign? An odd word. Something out of an old story. Where could the man have learned it? The syllable sent a shadow across Coco's kind smooth innocent face; he sensed that confusion was about to swallow him up.

"And you are all chaste?"

"Chaste?" Coco said. Another odd sound! "Yes, we're all *chaste.*" Coco was tasting ashes in his mouth. Whose?

Ricardo laughed at this, a high, loud, rapid, breathy sound—and, as always, a very unpleasant one. Three or four people in the area stopped talking until Ricardo finished making his noise. "Yes," Ricardo said. "We're chaste. By necessity."

I thought that R. had been in a terrible rush to add his bit, and I wondered again if his "necessities" were the same as mine and Coco's.

"Good," the man said. "That's very important. You must not marry, or even lie with women until you are victorious."

Ricardo threw his arms wide, as if he were about to laugh again. Fortunately this time he just stared up at the bright blue sky and smiled.

Apparently they are all part of the same sect (Adventist, they call it), for Inti was receiving similar marital advice from another old man. "You must not marry," he said. He shook his tiny fist towards Inti, and rubbed his dirty right hand along his thigh for emphasis. They seem to have the idea that we all have June weddings planned. "You must not get married or drink or smoke until you have brought about the New Law." There is a ritual. We're the priests, though we don't know the rules. And if we make a mistake it all might go awry. The women would become whores; the men would have to take pigs for wives. One misstep (and we didn't know where we were walking) and we'd bring about hell on earth.

Inti, too, was confused. He showed it by looking sadder still. "We don't drink or marry," he said after his rumination. "But we do smoke."

These people are incredible, I thought. Once you start talking to them you have to answer their questions; you try to think as they do: they take some part of your answer, misinterpret it, and lead you further afield; soon you're made over in some foolish costume from their dream closet.

"Well," the old man said thoughtfully, his hand moving more slowly against his thigh, "not everyone agrees with me about that." He brought his fist up to his mottled cheek, and rubbed away the wrinkles. "But you should at least try to give it up."

"It's very hard to get tobacco," Inti said, his voice full of mourning for his lost pleasure, his lost life. "Anyway."

The man slowly—reluctantly, I thought—took a worn leather pouch from his belt. "Here," he said, "you can have some of mine. It's hard to do what's right, I know. And life offers us so few pleasures."

The old fellow looked abashed. Inti had made a stunning move, hinting at what he wanted—the old man's tobacco—yet not asking for it. He had forced the fellow to share the treasure; he had won the game (though he hadn't known he was playing).

The man took Inti's scarred hand and poured some brown leaves into it, tobacco mixed with twigs and dirt.

Marcos, meanwhile, repeated Che's promises to a group—one man, several women—by the lean-to.

After the Revolution, Marcos said, the people would have an army of their own, one that served them.

"After the Day of Change," a man said, "we won't need an army." He sounded frightened—maybe of contradicting Marcos, maybe of armies, maybe that in our ignorance of the proper procedures we would screw everything up and they would have to eat garbage and walk around on their hands. "All men," the worried fellow said, "will follow Justice."

"Yes," a woman said. "Tell us when the Great Day will come, when the Good King will return, and drive the Bad King away."

"When?" Marcos said. "What?"

I knew that Marcos, after a manful struggle, would soon *go under*.

"The Day when we will follow Justice, when our King will come again, when we will all be in our proper places once more, when it will all begin again."

This seemed like nonsense to me. But Marcos did what he could. The Day would come, he said, when we all worked for it, when all of the people joined us in fighting the soldiers.

Marcos smiled, thinking he'd done well.

"No fighting!" the woman said angrily. (We were going to make a mistake. We were going to muck up the ritual. Everyone would have to wear mittens on his feet.) "There must not be any fighting. There must not be any killing. That is a sin." She shook her head back and forth, instructing the boy.

No fighting! What, I wondered, had she thought our rifles were for? But we were in their dream now, and who could tell what we looked like there? Maybe our rifles looked like hats in their dreams.

Anyway, she said that we didn't need to kill. When we all wanted it the bad world would end. There would be a Day of Change. Those who were at the bottom would be at the top. The first would be last, the last first. We would all be in our proper places. Everything would begin again and nothing would ever change. Every day would have enough evil. World without end.

She had a singsong voice as she repeated some very old verses. I thought different pages of the prayer book had got mixed together. It sounded at first as if the words were so old, and so often said, that they didn't have any meaning for her, just a tune she recited to herself as she went about her business. But as she went on, and Marcos's pained face seemed to contradict her, her anger and her conviction grew. "The King will return," she concluded furiously. "And each day it will begin again. We will be in our proper places."

The Revolution, Marcos said, trying once more, would happen only when they helped us to bring it about. (His voice wavered as he said the word "Revolution." King? he must have thought. Proper place? What did they think he meant?) The Revolution would happen only if the people made it happen. We would have to kill the greedy ones who stole all of Bolivia's riches and wouldn't share.

The sweat had already sprouted on Marcos's broad forehead, the way it does in battle—the rancid-smelling sweat that is dangerous to him. And I detected another odor in my vicinity: Che was near my shoulder. I stepped to one side, so I could see his face as he listened.

The woman was saying again that there must not be any killing. She was a broad woman, wider still in her many-layered blue-and-red skirt. She wore several shawls around her shoulders. And she wanted to throttle Marcos. The lady was the killer!

The Change would happen when all truly wanted it, wanted it in their hearts. Her voice broke in anger.

"No," Marcos said. His voice was weak, his face drawn and pale, until the spots came out and mottled it; he was no match for her. Marcos said that we had to do more than want it. There would have to be many battles against the army that protected the rich. The people had to join the guerrillas in fighting the army. And when we had defeated the army, then the people would take power. They would have their own government, and their own army. Then we would make a just world where all would be equal.

Marcos, too, I thought, sang an old song.

The woman no longer looked at Marcos, but at the high fields over his shoulder. "When all truly want it," she said, "then this world will end. There will be a Day of Change. Those who are lost now, the hidden ones, will be first then. And we will all have our proper places."

Their singing, Marcos and this woman, didn't mesh into a harmony—not one I could hear anyway. If they had both sung at once they would have canceled each other out (maybe canceling us out at the same time) like cross-hatched lines. Their two voices speaking at once would have made a blackness, a silence.

Marcos took a step backward into the lean-to, away from the final inexplicable unarguable assertions, away from the sun of her anger and misunderstanding, which was making him sweat so. He took a handkerchief from out of his jacket, and brushed the sweat from his forehead. The handkerchief was smudged and soiled. Marcos needs a Day of Washing, so it all can begin again, each day with its own evil. Each of Marcos's linens is a memorial to a hard day's march, or a battle. (If only we had the eyes to see, his pocket linen forms the record of our campaign.)

"Who is the lost monarch?" I asked one of the other women, one who I thought had a nice round face and mockery in her brown eyes. "The hidden one."

She stared at me. Maybe it was my color, or my odd voice. She shrugged her shoulders under her sweaters and shawls. "I don't know, sir," she said, looking at the ground. "What is a monarch?"

"A king," I said.

She went on looking at the dust by my torn and shredding boots. "Could you tell us about kings, sir?"

I had the feeling she didn't really know what the word meant—this thing that they all waited for! "A ruler," I said. "One not chosen by the people. He forces them to follow his orders."

"He will wear a fringe of red wool," Coco's dietary adviser said, for the rest of the countrypeople had come up around us. "He will wear it over his forehead."

"Why?" I asked.

"I don't know," he said. "Because he does. He is afraid of nothing. Their horses don't frighten him."

"Whose horses?" I said. "Why would he be frightened?"

"I don't know," the man said. His hand rubbed his leg. "And I told you, he *isn't* frightened."

"He is not a living man," Inti's friend said. "He is different. He can't die. He is already dead. He is a man wrapped in white, hidden away, already dead. His head is like gold."

"And he will become our ruler," the woman who had fought Marcos to a draw said. Usually women weren't so outspoken. "After he has fasted for three hours."

"For three days," another woman said.

"For three months," the small man said.

"You must come barefoot and bear a load if you want to see him," the battler said.

"A load?" I asked. I knew then that they were speaking of Christ, but they had made him over as an Indian.

"To show you are his servant. On your back."

"No," the man with the bulging eyes said. "On your head."

I was sure they were making this up as they went along! They couldn't agree on anything. I looked at Che and each word seemed like a poison added to the air. The upper part of his body made a small circle.

"You must fast a month before you see him."

"For three months!"

"A year!"

"He has a coat made of the soft skin of vampire bats."

This didn't sound like Christ!

"And a coat of hummingbird feathers that shine in the sun."

"For a month before he becomes our King there will be a great feast. We will drink for a month."

"For three months."

"He will see that llamas are given us. For eating."

"He is very even-handed with his gains."

One of the men kissed his two small fingers and flung them up at the sky.

"Why do you do that?" Coco asked.

"I don't know."

The others went on speaking, adding to his glory, whoever *he* was. It gave them pleasure to multiply his luxuries.

"He has a huge house, made of stone, not like our houses. He and his sisters live there."

The women laughed, and looked at the ground. (I thought for a moment that there was something suggestive in their laughter. But that was impossible.)

"When he goes out men from his clan bear him in a huge chair, its legs covered in gold. Or they run with him cradled in their arms."

"We have come," Inti said, slowly, deliberately, sadly, "to put an end to kings. You work now to feed the rich, your lives are wasted in work so that the rich might have gold legs on their chairs."

"Then kings are bad things?" one woman said, suddenly docile, confused, yanked from her reverie.

"Yes," Inti said. "You yourselves must rule."

She looked around her at the small man, the other women, then turned away from us all, disappointed.

I watched Che during all this noise. He looked worse than Marcos, as he huffed and puffed, his eyes narrowed with anger and strain. "You're the King," I said. "Sometimes we carry you." He, too, turned away, disappointed.

They gave us some corn and directions to the river.

From Guevara's Journal

6/5/67: Again their directions were wrong! The truck overheated on a dirt road to nowhere, and we hadn't any water for it. Camba, without speaking, got up next to the engine, pulled down his pants, and, standing on his toes, urinated a tiny stream of drops into the radiator.

Ponco applauded this striking improvisation.

But none of us had more than a few drops of urine. We all added a little, plus two canteens of water.

We marched farther north, until the truck ran out of gas.

"Can't piss gas," Ponco said.

Isle of Pines, May 1968

MAY 19

There were other old men who stared at Che, in other villages (and he stared back). "The old man had a maze of broken blood vessels around his nose." "The old man's lower lip was eaten away by the coca and limestone disease." "A senile tremor on the right side of his face, which looked like a message, something obscure, contradicting his words." "Glaucoma. He pressed close, but he couldn't see my face." And: "I've seen him before. That cold look. He would have spat at me—if he dared."

What if I combined them into *one,* the one who held Che by the shoulders, and walked off with the two young men (the last young men we would see for a while)? Sometimes they seemed like one person, like they had one thing to say, one song, and they had scattered the parts up and down the mountains. A song called: "Please please please sir leave our village." Or: "We can't help you sir." I wrote some of it down, and some of it I remember:

When we fought, in the Revolution, we thought we were getting something. But when we looked down there was nothing in our hands.

I have many enemies. Why do I have to go out and look for someone to kill me?

You hear that whining? I saw a man once pushed into the blade of a big saw. You hear that whining? You want to push me into the saw.

The army came. They wanted my sons to be soldiers, so I'd be all alone. I had to hide my sons.

All you can hear is your own blood in your head, your own life.

I kill you, you kill me. That's history.

MAY 20

He meant that the old man with the cold look reminded him of No Legs, from his childhood.

I am the only person in the world who knows *that,* and if I died, the knowledge would die with me—*the thing that he wanted to say.*

No Legs—the beggar who spat on him as a boy. I could *show* that. I could say that the old man who held his shoulders "had a maze of broken blood vessels around his nose, and something worse than winter in his eyes. He would have spat at me—if he dared."

I could . . .

Can I?

MAY 21

I can't spend forever balancing this. I have to make a choice. I have to get back to my work.

But it would be *right* to make it one speech. It felt that way by the end.

One single speech from all their lips: One word: *No.* Or: *Farewell.* (They, too, had a voice to say farewell in!)

After Inti spoke Che stepped forward. "Now is the hour of decision," he said to the thirty people, mostly old men and women. "Bolivians have a chance to make history. The whole world is watching what happens here in Bolivia."

This received the usual deep well-like silence, the silence which we might all drown in. The silence that fertilizes the grass growing over our graves. An old man hobbled forward, clippety-clumpety. He was very thin and pigeon-toed —the perfect recruit. He wore one of their dirty sweaters, woven from dust, and the usual felt hat. He held Che's shoulders and looked up and down Che's thinning body. He had a maze of broken blood vessels and something worse than winter in his eyes. Then he said:

"I kill you, you kill me. That's history."

No.
Then he said:

"Look, I'm missing a finger on my hand. See? I was drunk one day and working in a mill. You hear that whining? No? All you can hear is your own blood in your head, your own life. I saw a man once pushed into the blade of a big saw. You hear that whining? You want to push me into the saw."

No.

MAY 22

"I'll tell you what history is. You talk so much. Sometimes they come and kill a few of us. Once we went off and killed a lot of them. They had rifles. The miners helped, they had dynamite. We blew the soldiers up. That was good! I liked that! It made me feel better. Then we worked our land. After a while the soldiers came back in new uniforms, and they killed us and made us leave our land. We didn't like that so much! When we fought we thought we were getting something. But when we looked down there was nothing in our hands.

"Look, I'm missing a finger on my hand. See? I was drunk one day, and working in a mill. Most men lose something working—even their lives. My wife died after she gave birth to my youngest son. My first son died from a fever. Most of the children don't grow up. Now you want them to go off and kill soldiers. Do you think the soldiers won't fight back? You want my children to make history. I kill you, you kill me, that's history. Why do my sons have to go out to look for someone to kill them? Can't they find someone here?

"It's hard to stay alive, impossible to stay in one piece. See? Look! See? I'm using all my wits to stay alive. I'm thinking all the time. I watch my step. I try not to make enemies. I try not to let my enemies catch me off guard. I saw a man once pushed into the spinning blade of a big saw by an enemy of his. The sound of a big saw makes your guts flutter up and down, it makes you want to run away. It gives you a headache, like someone turning a nail in your head. It becomes everything inside your head. You don't have any past. You don't have any name. Just that sound in your head, like an ache. You can't reason with it! What screeching! My friend forgot where he was, and his enemy pushed him into the saw.

"I don't want to be sawed up, so I use my willpower. I try to remember my name, even though the saw makes a big noise. I control my anger. I figure out when it's a good time to plant. I try to say the right things when the soldiers come. I use my brains. God gave me a good brain, so I use it. They wanted my sons to be soldiers, so I'd be all alone. I had to hide my sons, I had to find good places to hide them, and make good excuses for where they'd gone.

"When I was young, like the boys with you, we were at war with Paraguay. They wanted some of our land for cattle. I didn't like them taking something that belonged to us. I went and fought them. We killed a lot of them every which way. They killed a lot of us. I don't know who won the war. *I don't have any cattle.* That wasn't using my brain. That was stupid.

"You hear that whining? You don't? That's because all you can hear is your own blood in your head, your own life. That whining is the saw. Someone is always happy to push you into the saw, to get land for cattle, to win freedom, for the honor of our country. Someday they'll defeat me. My will will be too weak for me to go on. Someone like you or the soldiers will want to push me and my sons into the saw and I won't have the strength to resist. The saw will have sharp blades. It will cut us in half like that, rip us to pieces! All we'll hear will be the whining. Eeeeiiieee! you won't even hear us scream. Little animals will come and lick our blood. We won't mind. Good for them! But I'm not going to go off and walk into the saw, say, Here Mr. Saw, why don't you cut off my legs, or make a nice meal of my head. That would be stupid! I'm not stupid. That's why I'm still alive."

Then he raised his skinny arm, gestured to two young men—the only young men there—and they walked off into their hut.

I had a nice dinner tonight of chicken with rice. Not too spicy. Spicy foods don't agree with me anymore (and I'm afraid of airplanes). But I could eat it.

I think I'm meant to help out in the writing, help say the things he wanted to say.

Who am I kidding? Only *he* could grant me that privilege. And *he* left me to die.

Bolivia, 1967

From Coco's Journal

6/8/67: The Masicuri River. We bathed in small groups, all through the late afternoon and into the night. The long trees over the river were thick with balls of leaves at the top; the white light of the full moon was softened by them as it flowed down onto our bodies. It was like being in a huge room. The water was cold. Che was in my group, and I could hear him clanking near me. "He sounds like a motor," I whispered to Inti. Camba overheard. "A motor shouldn't get wet," he said. He sounded genuinely worried, as if Che really were a motor! Che's breathing became more labored, more and more mechanical-sounding, but he went on splashing himself. The water was thick with cold, the cold was like a color you could drink with your skin. Feeling it on my legs and balls was like drinking a color. Sometimes, after a difficult time on the march, or in battle, the way things look is very intense, I feel like everything, the trees, the river, is alive, as if it might be about to speak with me.

In the morning we did laundry. Marcos has dozens of handkerchiefs! He washed each one individually, very carefully. Ponco went over to Marcos by the riverside, and held the linen up to his face. He said that each handkerchief was a story that he could read.

Planes moved above the trees, the drone fading and returning.

Che ordered a march northwest, towards the Rio Grande, where we will look for a crossing.

6/14/67: We walked along the riverbank until this evening, when thickets, tangled so tightly that they formed a wall higher than a man, blocked our way. We could cut through the thickets, or cross the river. Che decided to cross, but the raft-building group couldn't find suitable wood.

I went with a small party, under Marcos, to look for peasant families that might have a boat. Suddenly the rocks behind us exploded into fragments. The enemy had set up a mortar tube across the river. Marcos remained calm, and we fired back, while retreating towards Che and the center.

Che ordered an ambush set up on our side of the river, and sent a party to cut a trail for our retreat, parallel to the Masicuri, but farther into the forest.

The army never crossed the river towards us.

They are on both sides of the Rio Grande. Che says that they will expect us to go back south, towards the Nancahuazu, but we will continue moving west, along the riverbank, looking for a crossing. Che has an instinct for thinking the way the army does. (He said once that for as long as the war lasts the army and the guerrillas are part of the same organism.)

I worked for a while as one of the machete wielders, hacking at the tangled bank. It was part woody material, part thick green vine that ran in and out and all through it. I copied Ricardo's motion, raising the long blade and my arms across my chest and high above my head, over my right shoulder, then swinging down from the balls of my feet. But I was not so strong or graceful as he was. Sometimes the blade nearly bounced back from the vines. I felt their strength working against mine, as if they didn't want to be cut.

We made our way through. Che says we're near Ispaca's house.

From Guevara's Journal

6/18/67: Ispaca came running out of his house to meet us, not by way of greeting, but to keep us away, to ward us off. And yet he did not have the courage to tell us to go away. He stammered. He looked down at the ground. He pulled on his black hair. His first words—when he could get them out— were that the pigs had died. He had cared for them, he swore, but none of them had lived.

I tried to calm him. I told him not to worry about the pigs. I asked after his children's health.

The boy we had cured was fine. He was very grateful. But otherwise things were very bad with his family. The little girl, the one who talked all the time, she had died. And the infant that she had talked to—describing the world, I remembered, and its skinny suspicious characters—she had died, too. The sorcerer had taken them, Ispaca said. It was punishment, punishment for his son's being saved by us. And then the pigs had died. Who knew what might happen next?

I gagged hearing Ispaca's story, as if his words had physically caught in my throat. He wouldn't look me in the face. I felt that he himself didn't believe the nonsense he'd spoken, that there was a deeper shadow than superstition behind him, forming his words. I asked him if the army had been there.

He didn't speak, but looked off towards the bright sky. He ripped some strands of tall grass from the ground, and threw them aside. A light breeze picked them up and carried them towards the river.

I repeated my question.

"Yes," he said. The army had been there.

Had they harmed him or his family?

Yes, he said, they had. Then he laughed. Yes, they had *harmed* them.

I promised that we would avenge whatever had been done to him.

No, he pleaded. He didn't want revenge. He didn't want anything. He simply wanted to be left alone.

Then he stared at the ground, and I think an inspiration came to him. The army, he said, they had killed the pigs, thinking that they were meant for the guerrillas.

Possible, I thought, but unlikely. Still, I wouldn't have thought Ispaca would have had the courage, or the desire, to steal from us—unless he were desperate.

But there is simply no way to get to the bottom of their tangled stories.

I asked if he could spare us some food. Of course we would pay well for it.

Please, no, we needn't pay. We could take whatever we wanted.

He meant: we needn't pay for it, if we would only leave quickly, leave him alone.

He gave us directions to a turbulent but shallow crossing. He said again that he was sorry about the pigs.

6/19/67: The cold waters of the Rio Grande are now to the south of us.

Monje, on Chilean radio, announced the Party's total support for the guerrilla movement, the people in arms.

The interview had an unsettling effect on the men. The possibility of help makes our isolation more palpable. And for the militants, Monje's speech held out the possibility of reconciliation with that majestic (if, in the case of Bolivia, mainly imaginary) organization, the Communist Party, the church to which they had thought they might dedicate their lives, and so align those lives with the grand march of history. The guerrilla, not the Party, they realize now, is the forward point of that march in Latin America. But their old loyalty, and the nagging sense that the Party might still triumph over us in the end, made them anxious for a reconciliation. After all, the keys of the Revolution had been entrusted to the Party; Lenin had established its inevitability; so perhaps it would inevitably be the ultimate leader and master of the Bolivian Revolution. (And the Party had the support of the chief socialist power of the world.)

I sat on my canvas ground cover, at some distance from the men. I could see that Jorge was excited. Jorge has hair all over his face now, but not a lot of it, and he played with the ends the way Debray used to (or, if he is alive, still does). Jorge was certain that the Party had been won over to our line by our victories, as I had said they would be. Monje, whom Jorge had once been ready to murder, had redeemed himself in his eyes—in part because Monje had shown himself adaptable to changing conditions. (What Jorge would previously have called unprincipled.) Adaptability, Jorge thought now, was a good Machiavellian trait, a necessity for the Modern Prince—and perhaps there was a criticism of me in this. Jorge is alert, and he senses how desperately we need the Party's help.

Coco chimed with Jorge in excited agreement—Monje had been won over.

Monje had also spoken of the situation in the mines. It was clear from his words that the leadership was now chasing after the miners, who were far more militant than the Party, more fearless, and already galvanized by our actions. The miners are about to strike. This will be a heavy blow to the government. If, to save face with them, Monje has deceived the miners into thinking he has contact with us, is helping us, then his actions are criminal, he is a traitor, and no punishment would be too severe. He is leading them into a trap. But if the Party does supply us with men, in the next month the situation in Bolivia could be immediately transformed.

If only we had more men! The peasants have given us nothing, and so far show a profound incomprehension of our goals. It will take many more victories to win them over. For now the cadres must come from the cities.

But I remain firm that no men will leave the group to go to the city. I am far from certain about the Party's sincerity. Monje seemed to me a thoroughgoing coward. Yet perhaps Jorge is right. Monje could not know of our separation from Joaquin, and how desperate things may soon be with us. Perhaps Monje now thinks the Party needs us far more than we need them.

From Camba's Journal

6/22/67: Abrapa was a little settlement in the valley, ten adobe houses. Once it had been a big ranch, but all that was left of that time was a high brown wall with a scalloped center. The wall went across only one side of the village, and had a tall wooden door in the center.

The villagers waiting behind the wall wore white wool smocks with a line of red thread near the waist. They looked like angels. Maybe they wore white because we had come on a festival day. There were signs of celebration. A big wooden board on two sawhorses had been laid before we arrived with thick clay plates of cold pork, chicken, tortillas, potatoes, corn and beans.

One of the villagers, a portly old man, danced forward to welcome the center guard. He almost sang his welcome! We must sit down! We must have some food! He had been waiting for us for a long time!

"How could he have known we were coming?" Inti asked his brother.

Coco shrugged, but I had overheard, so I told them how the ants connected us to the animals and to the Indians. The Indians could hear us in their blood.

The brothers turned away, because they don't like me.

The food looked awfully good!

The portly man held his short arms wide. Since he had first heard of us, he said, he had had the feeling that he and Che would have a lot to say to each other. "You understand?"

Che stood open-mouthed in the hot sun. There were small stones all over the field in front of the houses, not as if they hadn't cleared the field, but as if they had gone out and gathered stones to spread around. Che, standing among this harvest, looked slack, as if the man's statements had hit him across the chest with a pole. Ponco, standing next to Che, started to smile, and then laugh like a child—a child with no voice—as if we were all his toys. Everything had been placed here to entertain him, made up for his amusement.

Che didn't say anything to stop us, so the rest of us went and took the food with our hands. We were hungry. There had been no food for days, and we had had a hot dry march from the Rio Grande.

The other people in the village, the old people and children (for there are no young men in the Bolivian countryside), stood about as we ate, not speaking, silent white birds. We grabbed at the food they offered us, pushing each other aside, overturning the plates.

"Why are you so quiet?" Benigno asked one of the little boys. Benigno is a tall man, thin, but very strong, and handsome-looking.

"Pastor Barrera speaks for us," the boy said, pointing to the old man who had been waiting to talk with us. "He is our mayor."

I put a bottle of clear liquid to my lips, some of their liquor. Che shook his head no at me, so I put it down. Maybe the food was poisoned!

"Pastor Barrera is a generous man," Coco said, chewing pork rapidly.

"Maybe it's a trap," I said. "Maybe we're being poisoned." I was passing on what Che had told me.

"Shut up asshole," Ricardo said. Ricardo hates me. He hates everyone, but he hates Bolivians more and he hates me most of all.

After we had eaten, and arranged for food to be taken to the rear and vanguard groups, the mayor asked Che if he might talk with all of us.

"How does he know Che is chief?" Inti asked his brother. The Indians bewilder Inti. They are like a long march in the hot sun, so long, and so hot, that the world wavers in front of his eyes.

Coco shrugged. I knew that the mayor knew that Che was leader because he had seen Che control me with a shake of his head. The mayor saw that our bodies are connected to parts of Che's body. But the brothers had been rude to me before, so I didn't explain.

I wish I didn't know these things! They make my head swell, and they make everyone hate me.

Pastor Barrera raised his right hand behind his ear. Everyone in the village grew quiet, as if he had put them into a trance. They are all connected to *his* body. "Look," the mayor said loudly. He walked over to a big rock by the side of his house.

"An Inca rock," Che said. "Six-sided."

"Where's the rest of it?" Inti asked.

"End of the empire," Ponco croaked. "Bits and pieces."

Pastor Barrera said he would roll away the rock, and under it there would be a book.

He pushed the rock with one hand, but it was an enormous fellow, and of course it didn't move. He made pretend grunting sounds, while he reached under it, and his hand came out with a package wrapped in an embroidered piece of cloth. There were red and blue and green threads in the cloth, and other colors, more than I could count.

Carefully, he unwrapped the cloth, and took out a book, worn, with a torn brown cover, and pages half falling out. The countrypeople laughed and applauded. They had seen this trick before; it was an old favorite. A little boy was so delighted that he punched my leg.

"I can read this book," the mayor announced. He smiled directly at Che.

Che stood holding some of his beard in his hand, pulling on it. He didn't smile back. The upper part of his body swayed in a little circle. Maybe he had eaten too fast.

"I believe you," Coco said to the mayor.

The mayor asked if we didn't want to hear him read?

Coco nodded. Coco is kind, but really he is like Inti and Che. He doesn't realize that the Indians are the only ones who know the secret doors in the forest that lead out of here. Coco just humors them—to get their good opinion for us—as if they were the children.

The old man opened his book, and held it at arm's length. "A specter is haunting Europe," he said in a ringing voice, "the specter of Communism." Pastor Barrera's eyes had many wrinkles around them, and his nose was covered with broken veins. He looked alight as he read to us.

The people of the village applauded and laughed.

"You've been reading Marx," Che said, with genuine admiration. He had let go of his hair, and he stood steadily again. I wish men respected me as they do him!

The mayor told us that a Communist had given him the book many years ago, when he was a boy, during the Revolution. And we were Communists, too. And we had come to hear him read from this book, just as the first man had said we would. We had come to see if he had truly learned to read, to see if he had made himself ready for the Day of Change, for the Revolution.

The man's small face lit more brightly still with his deep satisfaction in himself. He had passed his test.

The countrypeople smiled. They were proud of their mayor.

The Communist had told him that if he studied the book carefully he'd understand many things. The Communist was right. The mayor did understand things!

Che, too, beamed with satisfaction. At last he had met a reasonable man. The way had been prepared for Che, made smooth for us.

The man held the book to his face, half-covering his pocked lips. He smiled coyly from behind the dirty cover. I thought he looked like a picture I'd seen, a Japanese girl hiding behind her painted fan. In a sly mocking voice he said, "I don't really know how to read."

More tricks! Che put his fist in front of his face. He looked like the man was about to hit him, and he wanted to ward off the blow.

Did we want to know how he did it? the mayor asked in a high rapid voice. His eyes darted about my *comrades* (hah! really they hate me). Che looked over the mayor's shoulder.

"Yes," I said, though I shouldn't talk. I'm not connected to Che's soul. "How?" I thought it was a good trick.

He smiled. He had gone to a class after the Revolution, and they had heard the book read aloud. Then they had talked about it. And whenever he had had a job outside the village, or in Santa Cruz, building the roads, he had taken the book with him. When he had heard someone on the job say things he agreed with, he took the book out and showed it to him. He always knew which ones it would be safe to ask, for the Specter meant for him to learn, and it protected him.

"The Specter?" I asked. I knew that the man's talk made Che unhappy, but I knew, too, that he had things to teach us.

"The Specter of Communism."

Inti laughed in a melancholy way. He sounded like someone who had lost a lot of money.

The mayor would go off with his comrade, away from the bulldozers, behind the mounds of earth, and they would read a little of the book. He kept a special marker with him.

From out of the book's pages he held up a small blue wand, and the villagers applauded.

"A ballpoint pen!" Che said. He hadn't wanted to speak; his voice sounded like a cry, something struck from him by the pole that had swung into his chest before, when the man had said that he had expected us. Ballpoint pens must have special powers. (I will ask Che about it later, though I know he will despise me for asking.)

The ballpoint pen was the mayor's *special marker.* If he heard a friend read a part he especially liked, he had him draw a line next to it. When the mayor met someone else who knew how to read he'd show him the passage with the line next to it, and have him read it. In a few years the mayor had the best words written in his heart. Now he loved to say them out loud to everyone.

The little boy gave my leg another blow. They liked to hear him read aloud, too.

"There are," the mayor said, "many very true things in the book."

Che's face came alive again. He shone at the man, amazed, uncertain, delighted by his words. A dog had started to talk to him like a human being! "After the Revolution," Che said in his high, kind voice, "everyone who wants to will be able to read, so they can understand things for themselves." When Che speaks of the future he always sounds soft and sweet, as if he were caressing it.

The mayor smiled warmly at Che. But there was, I thought, something crafty and mean in his face, too. He was testing us. "Sometimes," he said, "one book is enough to make a man understand."

Che agreed. He turned to Inti. The people, he explained, need only be given a hint. A few words about imperialism, about the necessary struggle, and the circumstances of their lives teach them the rest.

Inti and Che like to please each other by repeating the things they already know.

The mayor explained that after a man understood things he didn't need books anymore. The whole world was like a book to him, and he could read God's thoughts.

Che's face fell. He looked sick again; the man had turned back into a dog and peed on his leg. Che couldn't see that he and Pastor Barrera were saying the same things.

But Pastor Barrera didn't notice Che's disappointment. He said that he knew from what the radio had said about us that we would understand things. And that was the main thing—to understand things. For we all became like the rocks in the end.

The crowd nodded sorrowfully.

"No," Inti said. He spoke up to the sky in that sorrowful way of his. Inti is like Che—he can't listen, not even to an angel. "We don't agree. We must act also. There are accounts that must be settled." Inti is the most intimately attached, because he is connected to Che's soul. He can be Che's mouth.

Accounts to settle? The mayor was shocked. Crinkly lightning came from his eyes, flash! flash! flash! I put my hands in front of my face, to keep from being burned. My hands smelled of pork.

The lightning drove Inti backward.

I held my hair up with my hands to show the mayor that I had understood him.

"Things are never really settled," he said angrily. "They must go on over and over forever. THAT IS WHAT THE BOOK SHOWS!"

The people of Abrapa looked at the field of dust and stones. Why would anyone dispute with Pastor Barrera?

"No," Che said. He turned away from the mayor, towards the people. "The children of your village," he said, "die from diseases that could be cured. . . ." He stopped and pushed his chest forward, for his lungs hurt him.

The mayor's hands formed into fists at his sides, and the thick veins stood out on the backs. "You don't understand," he said. He was disgusted. We had called ourselves communists. He had thought that we had come to hear him read. We had deceived him. "Look!" he said, his voice patient again. "You and your men are all worn out."

That was true, I thought, looking about me. Our skin was covered with dirt and cuts. Moro's arm was in a sling. Many of the men looked like paper cut-outs about to fall to the ground.

We had marched down the road into the village, Pastor Barrera said, and we were hungry. The food was already there for us, waiting. We ate something at their table, and then we marched away. They had set the table for they had known we were coming. They knew that we would leave. They knew that we would come back again, so they had a table always set for us. We said, Accounts must be settled with the rich! And the countrypeople thought we were the Messiah. And we made the Revolution. The people were living in their village again. It had begun all over. Someone marched into their village covered with dust and hungry, and he said, "The time has come for us to settle accounts with the rich!" The way for redemption was to follow him. And he was telling the truth! The mayor himself could feel it in his words, he could see it in the saviour's face, for it would glow as ours did. So he and the others followed him.

The saviour was coming. He walked down the road towards us now, into their village. He ate at their table with his men. No, he wasn't there yet. He was about to come into their village. The mayor could see him on the road, walking with his men, raising a cloud of dust around themselves as they stamped the ground in fury. He was always about to arrive. He was always right at their big doorway. He was about to say, Accounts must be settled. He was always eating with them. No, he wasn't. He and his men had just gone. They had always just left the village, just this minute, they were on their way down the road. We could get a glimpse of them. Look at all that dust! The saviour comes over and over again. Everything must happen over and over again. NOTHING WAS EVER SETTLED! THAT WAS WHAT THE BOOK TAUGHT!

Pastor Barrera, mayor of Abrapa, bobbed his head up and down, in profound agreement with himself. His head was barely attached to his neck, like a doll's head on a spring.

Many of the heads in the crowd, men and women and children, went up and down, too. I tried to make my head go the way his did, with a palsy. I wanted to see things the way he did; it would mean that I wasn't here anymore, in this terrible valley, so far from home, outside this adobe house—but far away from here, in a better place. I would inhabit all the bodies that he had named, *that were all my own body,* and it would be impossible for the soldiers to kill me, for they would have to kill each and every one of my bodies at once, and some of them were already, and some of them were not yet.

The mayor told Inti and Che that if they lived as long as he had—but I think he was really only a few years older than Che!—then they, too, would understand things. He had thought that they were *communists* like himself, and that they knew that it was first one person's turn, and then another's. But no, apparently they couldn't see that. He was sorry—and he did sound deeply, sadly regretful; he was giving us some very bad news—but he was now certain that it was impossible for us to understand things. It was our time to do our violent work, as he had once done, so we couldn't be like he was now, standing at the side, watching, seeing things clearly. We had to think that it all *mattered,* that it was done once and for all, that it *settled accounts.*

Slowly, ceremoniously, making gestures as broad as a priest's, he took the cloth from the top of the rock and wrapped up his book again. He took the bottle of chicha from the table and sprinkled a few drops on the package before putting it under the rock.

I was thinking of a carnival I'd been to once in La Paz. There was a huge barrel, bigger than a room, turned on its side, and dozens of us stood inside it. The barrel spun around. It was hard to keep your footing, and if you fell over, other people would trip over you, or you might fall over them. But maybe it was our feet moving around, stepping this way and that to stay upright, trying to settle accounts, that kept the barrel moving!

I thought of our long march, up the Rio Grande, and back to Muyupampa, and back to Nancahuazu, and then up to the Rio Grande again, and it was like being in that barrel that went round and round; everything did happen over and over, the heat and the starvation, and the vines we had to rip away to keep our balance, they were all the side of the barrel. But you couldn't just get out, for the people in the barrel and the barrel itself would roll right over you. We would have to get everyone to agree that accounts couldn't be settled; then we could stop at the same time. But they wouldn't believe we would do it, they would think it was a trick to make them stop dancing as fast as the barrel and fall down so we could laugh at them. So I would have to get off alone, the way Pastor Barrera had, at just the right time, so the barrel wouldn't crush me. I would have to learn when the right time was.

Pastor Barrera was speaking with Che still. He told Che that he must have visions of his own, ones that comforted him and his men. Che looked away very rudely, pretending not to listen. His breathing got worse and worse, grinding away, like it was grinding up his insides, and when it was all done there would be no Che left.

The mayor, wanting to be friends, said that he and Che were alike, that they were both connected to the very center of things, both in their proper places.

"No," Che said. It was hard for him to speak. His words came out like a slight breath of wind, the merest thing. But he wanted things to be clear with the old man, with the people of the village. *He wanted to settle accounts.*

Pastor Barrera was furious. He recoiled a step from Che, and tripped over one of the small stones. He put out his hands for balance, and he looked so much like a plump little angel that I thought he would float away.

The people of the village gasped, and in fear the little boy hit me again.

I went to Che and put my arm around his shoulders to help him keep his balance. "Why does he hide his book under a rock?" I asked.

"What shit," Che said with weak anger. He must have been very upset, though, for he almost never curses.

I told him that if he wanted the Indians to stop talking he should cover his ears, and I showed him how.

From My Journal

6/22/67: After the little set-to with the village leader, Camba had put his arm around Che, half holding him up. Che made that animal sound, almost a groaning, but deeper and more metallic, that means a ferocious attack. Camba let him go, and put his hands over his own ears, not wanting to hear Che's breathing. Che's illness scares the men—it scares me—like a sick parent's. Che scrabbled the inhalator out of his shirt pocket, and sucked on it. He tossed it aside—used up I suppose—but the machinery of his lungs was oiled, and slowly grew smooth and quiet again.

The mayor ran to where Che had thrown his inhalator and grabbed it up. He hid it away under his white shirt.

An old woman told Che that he should be more careful. Throwing things away like that was dangerous, they might fall into the hands of sorcerers. He should have things that had been close to him like that, as close as his hair or fingernails, destroyed, burned up, so that the evil ones couldn't get at it.

Che said nothing.

Pastor Barrera was all right though, she said, as if Che had been worried. He was a good man. He cured the sick by reading parts of his powerful book to them, the one he had read to all of us from. It was a great honor. He would take care of Che's things.

Che walked away.

I listened to Camba, who spoke with the mayor. "What are specters?" Camba asked.

Specters were the body of all the actions that others perform for us that we should perform for ourselves.

Camba nodded, though I could make no sense of that, any more than his earlier speech. It sounded very *philosophical*. I wish Regis had been here to explain it all.

But the next bit was very unlike the Sorbonne, I think. "At night," he said, "the specters come from the river and watch over the fields for us. During the day the village worked for them. We are their specters, you see, and they are ours."

"Like shadows," Camba asked. He annoys the men—myself among them —but I don't think he means harm.

The mayor nodded. And he warned that if we didn't show our gratitude to the specters, if we didn't leave anything for them, they would use their syringes. While we slept they would come and take our blood. They would put that blood inside themselves, and then they would come and take our place during the day. We would die and go into the river, and could only live by night. We would be specters.

Camba listened intently. When the man was done he took out his notebook and wrote something down.

"Are you planning a book?" I asked.

"I'm making a map," Camba said, and smiled at me. It was a cringing smile, as if he were afraid I'd hit him. He is a coward and knows that most of the men despise him.

Che had recovered fully by now, and had taken the camera from his knapsack. He took pictures of Marcos and Moro standing by the table we had found set for us, and then asked for some of the countrypeople to come forward, and have their pictures taken with us. I can't see what good these photographs will do us. We can't develop them, and if we could, we couldn't use them for propaganda, since they would only help the security forces punish the friendly peasants. Yet in every camp, and in every village, Che takes pictures. (An old habit, he said, the last time I asked. And I added, "Memories of what time will *destroy.*" He didn't think that was very funny.)

Anyway none of the people of Abrapa wanted to be *shot* with us. Che explained to them how the camera worked. Most just stared, and the rest of them looked positively horrified. In some way I didn't understand there was a syringe in there somewhere, or something just as awful.

The little boy I had seen smashing away emphatically at Camba's leg demanded that we make a picture right now. Che said that the pictures couldn't be developed for a long time.

"Developed?" the boy said.

Che, the patient teacher, began a lecture on how pictures were developed, but the boy had lost interest and returned to hide behind his mother's skirt.

Camba walked over to some countrypeople, including his little boxing partner. People in pictures never age, Camba said. It was medicine against the specters.

Use it once and it's your own, I thought. But Camba had goofed. The townspeople gasped, and the mother put her hand on the child's head, to reassure him.

Our special helpers, Camba went on, the ones that could lure the pictures out from where they hid in the camera, they were far away, in the cities. For the pictures to be seen, everyone in the village had to work with us for the Revolution. Then we would all go down to the cities and have the pictures developed. Only when everyone here worked for it would there be pictures to see. The pictures would show that they had been for the Revolution at the very beginning, when the army pursued us, that they had *recognized* us, before everything changed.

Che looked unhappy at Camba's talk. But Camba had gotten the knack, and with his inducements the woman with the little boy came forward to have his picture taken with Che. Moro, his sling off, took the snapshot, and then we moved east, towards the village of Morroco.

From Guevara's Journal

6/22/67: Abrapa was another disappointing encounter. The countrypeople refuse to comprehend what we offer them. I feel their resistant will in each response, in each story they tell about us. And Camba continues to be a difficulty, even going so far as to pander to their evasive magical thinking, their dream talk. But we are not a dream; and by entering their language he enters their long sleep, the sleep that we must awaken them from or die. Even Ponco does not yet see how their incomprehension, and worse, their twisting of our words into millennial fantasies, bandit stories, could lead to our defeat. He smiles at them.

I am troubled, too, by my own anxieties, which I allowed to overtake me in a most unpleasant way. Camba's nonsense convinced one of the mothers to have her son's picture taken with me, "so he might be revealed as an Angel at the time when everything is different" (different, they insist, and yet somehow the same). I sat up on the table, and Camba posed the child on my knee. I put the last cigar in my mouth, to make a prop for the photograph, and put my hand on the child's head. A rambunctious boy, he was very light on my leg. He had a large nose for such a small child, and had had his hair shaved off, perhaps for some curer's ceremony. The down of his head was sweet against my hand. He was a leaf, too thin, with a slight protuberant belly, and deep circles under his eyes. Probably he wouldn't live long.

Moro held up the camera, and the child began to squirm. His mother threatened him, but he wouldn't stay still. I held his head harder with my hand, and he screamed. His head was like an eggshell in my palm, and I felt how easily I could have crushed it. I was angry. I didn't feel well; my breathing was easier, but still unsteady, and my stomach churned from the feast that had been here for our arrival. But there was a more than unsettled feeling arising from my bowels, a feeling that was erotic, and very ugly, the feeling of power that I had over the doomed little boy, almost as if I wanted to hurt him, to squeeze his head, to make him cry. It was all the more disturbing in that it had followed so closely upon the tenderness that I had just felt, or thought I had felt, for the boy. Perhaps the tenderness was a mask. Or perhaps both feelings were of a piece, a desire for control, for the exercise of altruistic power over another, and gratification for oneself; if one couldn't help, then hurting would do as well.

They refuse our gestures towards them. Nothing we do is understood. Our love, so far, is impotent. And then there is the great anger that comes in each of us when our love is misunderstood, rejected. I wanted to make contact, to be recognized, if not as a benefactor, then I would strike that child, that woman, that stupid old man, hit them hard across the face, wake them up!

Moro, his arm fully healed now, took the picture. The mother took the crying child away. We bought some food, mostly dried salted corn, and the little meat that was left. I insisted on paying. We began our march east.

From My Journal

6/23/67: The one who told us that everything happens over and over had a point. An hour's march from his town, the organ concert began again, a chamber piece compared to our last recital, but it still left us weak.

From Guevara's Journal

6/25/67: Extraordinary news! The Chilean radio reports that a mass grave has been found in the Nancahuazu region, with sixteen bodies in it, men women and children, an entire village, executed by Barrientos's forces. The government, of course, denies the executions, denies the mass grave, denies that any bodies were found.

From Coco's Journal

6/27/67: Fifteen kilometers' march today. The forest was thick; Che says we cannot use the woodsmen's paths; so our trails have to be cut for us by the machete wielders. Vines that tangled into the branches made it slow going. And the hills were very steep. At one point, Marcos and Benigno both fell and rolled over with their packs, until trees stopped them. Marcos had a big bump when he rejoined us, and was unsteady on his feet for a while. Benigno was angry at Camba, who had jumped over him as he rolled his little way downhill.

In the afternoon we left the forest for a settlement of four thatched huts. A cry went up from the village as we came out of the forest, a sad sound, like mourning, and some of the inhabitants were seen running away from us into a field of tall corn. We ran after, waving our rifles in the air, to bring them back. Camba is right; they are like little animals.

"The mass grave," Ponco said, in that ominous voice of his. He meant what we had heard on the radio—that was what had terrified the peasants.

Still, most of the animals were friendly, if shy, once they overcame their fear. Their mayor—a middle-aged man with broad features and short gray hair named Calixto—sold us food, but didn't speak much except for the negotiations about price. A military commission that passed through here last month had named him mayor, so it is possible that he is one of theirs. Another peasant told me that the commission had made a list of all the inhabitants, and had taken photographs of the area, and of every house. Che says this sounds like the Yanqui advisers.

"Thorough," Ricardo said glumly.

At dusk two pork merchants in broadly striped gray-and-brown serapes arrived at the settlement. I was surprised by how clean their clothes were. When I felt underneath their shirts I found two pistols. Che was furious. He is worried about infiltration and assassination. Inti, who had interrogated the merchants at the vanguard post, should have uncovered the weapons. But Calixto said that he knew both men, that they were traders from Postre Valle—so there was no harm done. Calixto is a very nervous man, and as he talked with us in his house, he skittered about touching his things—the gourds that hung from the ceiling, his one tin plate, his hoe, his sewing machine.

"For sending and receiving messages," Camba said.

I laughed, but then I worried that Camba might actually have meant it. He has been saying more and more strange things lately.

Calixto stroked the top of the black sewing machine with a hand curled up like a claw. Frightening-looking—for a moment I really believed the peasants were part animal. Arthritis, Che said, and offered Calixto some cortisone, a medicine for it.

Calixto declined, but he offered us some coca, which he said was good for his pain, for all pains.

Che accepted the offer. I turned to Ponco, showing my surprise. "It's for his asthma," Ponco said to me. "He's running out of epinephrine."

At the word "coca" all the men in town, even some of the younger ones, came from their hiding places, in the houses, the woods, and the corn stalks. The stuff is far from rare, but I think they all wanted to be part of the ceremony, the initiation.

Che placed men from the center all around the perimeter of the settlement. And the rear-guard and vanguard groups remained in ambushes some distance away, at the approaches to the village.

In the middle of the dirt floor Calixto put a kerosene lamp that made a soft pleasant light. Che's breathing was a grinding sound that filled the whole hut.

I felt cold sitting on the dirt, and a little feverish. It had turned chilly at dusk, and I had worked up a sweat chasing down the people from the settlement. I hoped the coca might help me too. I'm worried that I have malaria, like Tania. I don't want to be a burden to the group. Maybe the coca could help me carry on if I get sick, the way it does the Indians.

Near the opening a woman in a broad red skirt with a blue zigzag pattern on it, like regular bolts of lightning laid one upon another, rolled out corn meal on a long board. A small cooking fire glowed between some rocks. I could smell charcoal and the smoke stung my eyes. There was a big black cooking pot on the fire. Guinea pigs ran about on the floor, eating green scraps.

Calixto filled one of his clawed hands, like a little scoop, from a leather bag that hung by his waist. It had the same blue zigzags on it. He sprinkled some chicha on the leaves, and thanked the Benefactor for giving them coca. (I wondered if the Benefactor was the fellow with the coat made from the skin of vampire bats.) He bent our heads back and poured the dull green leaves into our mouths. Calixto had a gentle touch, like my mother's when she fed us something special from her own hands, even when we were teen-agers. It was funny to feel a man's hands against my lips like that, feeding me.

Calixto instructed us: the first time we should chew only as much as our human benefactor's hands could hold. He took some for himself, and passed his leather bag to an old man with a face like a rotting apple, dirty, spotted with darker browns and reds. The enamel on the old man's teeth had decayed away to a black color, and his upper lip was pitted, as if a little animal had been gnawing at it. Other men took leather bags from their own waists and passed those around, too.

A young man with a familiar face gave us some limestone shavings in a small gourd, to mix in our mouths with our leaves. That really made my saliva flow with an acid bitter taste! I was thinking about my stomach when the old man said something to me about my visions.

"I'm sorry," I said. "I don't understand." I was too nauseous to attend to him. I thought I was going to throw up from the bitterness. Unable to help myself I spat on the floor. "I'm sorry," I said again, wiping my mouth with my sleeve. But several other men spat; a little rainstorm of droplets fell on my hands and thighs.

When I came back to the hut, the old man was saying that Bolivians didn't have visions like ours anymore, because they hadn't fought for a long time.

Calixto smiled. He said he didn't remember his father's ever having been much of a fighter. (Neither is Calixto. Every feature of his face says coward. How could he ever leave his house, his gourds, his sewing machine? Even as he spoke to the old man, his eyes glanced over his possessions, his precious things.)

Still, Calixto had to agree with his father. We must have a powerful vision, for there were many soldiers, and they hadn't been able to catch us. "In fact," Calixto said to the pork merchants, "they have killed a whole lot of soldiers, a bundle full." He sounded proud of us. Maybe, I thought, he wasn't such a bad sort.

One of the pork merchants nodded, and the other followed suit. Their faces looked yellow—fellow sufferers, I thought, sick from the coca.

"Yes," Calixto said, smiling at the merchants in their identical clean serapes. We had killed a whole bundle. A lot of soldiers. We had "covered the soldiers' faces in blood."

He dragged his claws across his cheeks, to show the blood flowing down.

Calixto's father, the old man with the apple face, took another leaf of coca for himself, and pushed it with his tongue to the side of his cheek. He mashed his gums together.

His mouth was disgusting-looking! My heart started beating awfully fast, like it wanted to run away from my chest. I put my hands over my ribs to keep it in.

Perhaps, Calixto added politely, we didn't want to talk about visions?

Che didn't say anything. He doesn't like their foolish talk. And the coca hadn't helped him; his lungs made a clamor; he was still having trouble breathing.

Another man said that to speak of our vision might give away its power.

I was about to say that there was no vision, but Calixto's father had the floor. In the world of vision, he said, all that happened here was as nothing, was empty.

"You are all specters," Camba said from just outside the doorway, "hobgoblins. Ghosts."

The men at the table looked horrified, but they nodded their agreement. "I see," one of them said.

Calixto opened the fingers of one of his hands. His face was in agony. "I couldn't do this without coca."

Calixto passed the fingers of his clawed left hand through the now wide-open fingers of his right. If a man was fortunate enough to have a vision, and kept it in mind, then nothing could harm him.

He was speaking to the other men in the circle, because, I guess, he thought we must already know this.

All the things of this world would go right through us, because our real bodies were in the world of vision, and this stuff—he clasped at his precious table, the gourds that hung over our heads, the lovely woman who made tortillas, as if he were angry with them—this stuff had no substance in the place where our minds and our real bodies were. That was why, during the Revolution, the best fighters hadn't been killed by the army.

"Yes," Camba said seriously, "they were already dead in this world." He smiled and looked intently at the Indians.

They nodded. Either he understood them or he was an expert to them—he lived in the world of vision. (He certainly does live in his own fantasy world.) The bottoms of the men's faces, their teeth and mottled lips, were clear in the kerosene light. Their eyes and foreheads were in shadow.

Che turned slowly towards Camba, and gestured for him to come over. When Camba bent down to speak with him, Che slapped him slowly, hard, across his skinny back. Camba coughed and fell forward onto his hands. It looked like Che was burping him!

One of the men across from me pushed his felt hat back on his head, so I could see his eyes. Their best fighters, he said, had been killed by traitors, as they played with their own children. The man looked furious, for his right eye was streaked with a bloodline.

Traitors had killed the best fighters, he said again, angry at these betrayals. The fighters had been enjoying themselves with their families. They had thought they were safe. They didn't have their visions in mind.

The young man with the bowl of limestone shavings turned his face away from the table and the lantern light, embarrassed by this old-people's talk.

Then he asked to see the twigs that we used to push the soldiers' bullets aside. The boy had a small round pleasant face, like an old friend's. It glowed with curiosity and expectation.

Che told him that we had no twigs. Che's voice was so weak that though I sat next to him, I could hardly hear him. The circle leaned towards Che. They looked like shadows waving on the ground, when a tree shakes in the wind.

One of the shadows made a voice. We had dreams, he said, that told us when the enemy was present. We could read the insides of animals, and we understood the patterns of the clouds.

Calixto leaned into the lantern light, and smiled at his friends, the pork traders. They nodded their agreement. As the night went on they looked sicker and sicker.

The people here knew that we had suspected the traders at first, and wanted to scare them a little.

Che said that we had no dreams, and no omens but our own cunning and the help the countrypeople gave us.

The young man interrupted. How did we put the soldiers to sleep so we could sneak up on them and cut their stomachs open?

Ponco leaned towards my shoulder. "We're exasperating the boy. We know about fucking and we won't tell him."

The rotten-apple-faced man put another leaf into his mouth.

"We don't put them to sleep," Che said, in a whisper.

"Except permanently," Camba added, "with our guns."

The boy was disappointed. "We've just told him," Ponco croaked into my ear, "that men and women are exactly alike." His voice tickled me, and I laughed. Everyone stared at me, leaning into the light. *Their* faces looked like goblins'.

One of the goblins said that we had invisible cars that ran on magic fuel. That was how we got over the countryside so quickly, appearing where the army didn't expect us, surprising them, and *killing them all.*

Camba laughed behind me. His laugh was a squeaky sound, a coward's laugh. But he didn't say anything, for fear of Che.

"They have white liquids to make the sorcerer's worm crawl from your stomach."

"There are two of him," a man said, pointing to Che.

"And he has rings that make him invisible."

Che held his fingers up near the lantern, to show that he didn't have any rings. They shrank back from his hand.

Che has scars on the back of his hand that I hadn't noticed before. I looked at my own hand, covered with scratches from tearing away at the vines, but Che's were different, more like teethmarks.

"They have farts," the young man with the limestone said, "that are like thunder and lightning."

I was reminded of my mother's rules: it was *rude* of them to talk like this, to call us "they" to our faces. But we wouldn't give them the satisfaction they wanted—so they just ignored our denials, and talked about us as if we weren't here. It was a spooky feeling—I felt like a specter.

I thought the boy was just joking about the farts, but no one laughed. I felt sure that I knew his face; whose was it? It was like having a hair stuck in my throat.

A raspy voice, speaking Quechua, said our leader had a strong special smell that put people to sleep.

This was too foolish, so I didn't translate it for Che.

Che put his hands over his ears, and they all grew quiet.

The only sound was a badly led army of mosquitoes that charged the lantern a few at a time and were sizzled up. Their unburied corpses surrounded the light. The young woman went on rolling out the dough. A small breeze blew a flurry of ashes, and each flake turned slowly in the wind over the fire. It was very beautiful. I walked around in the wrinkles on the old man's face, and slid across the young man's smooth cheeks. I wiped away some dirt on the back of my hand with spittle, and watched the blood flow through my veins. I felt pretty good. I wasn't hungry, and I felt like I could walk all night. The coca will help me keep up with the others if the fever comes again.

I liked watching the woman by the fire, too. Her hands had long fingers that fluttered in the air like a bird's slowly beating wings. She squatted down over her work, and showed the outline of her thighs through her heavy red-and-blue dress. Maybe seventeen years old, I thought, she wore her hair in black braids.

With her right hand she grabbed up one of the squealing guinea pigs and bashed its head against the pot, gutted it, and threw it in. She wiped her hands on her dress, and went back to her board.

I haven't had a woman in more than nine months! But I had hardly thought of them either. I have thought mostly of the pain of my own body, and if I have dreamt of anything it was of having more food. But now I wanted this woman very much! I liked watching her arms move rhythmically back and forth over the corn meal. I wanted to be the corn! I even felt stiff—a miracle! I thought my cock had died long ago. (The village will have to build a statue for the miracle of my cock!) I looked over at Che's face, afraid that he had seen me staring at the woman, and knew what I was thinking. But he looked emptily at the apple-faced man who stuffed another leaf into his hole. I wondered if Che and Tania had made love in our camp? Camba smiled at me from the opening. I think he knew what I was thinking!

Calixto detached a bone-handled hunting knife from his belt, and I thought he, too, had seen my lust for his daughter. I wanted to reach out to hold his arm, but it felt like there was an enormous distance between us, and I could never get across it. I remembered a story from school, about how first you would have to go half the distance, and then half of the half, and so on. So really it was an infinite distance. That was how it felt to me. Calixto held out his clasped hands with his knife in the right one; the knife gave a blue shine in the lantern light. He cut his left hand at the webbing between the third and fourth fingers. Blood welled out slowly. He brought the cut hand to his mouth and sucked his own precious red fluid.

I thought I was going to throw up.

"Here," Calixto said to me, in a goblin's hoarse voice, "give me your hand." He held the knife towards me, point down. "The blood will make you stronger."

I held my hands together between my knees, and curled my body over them.

The young man with the limestone shavings told me not to be scared. He gave me a dour disapproving look.

With coca, Calixto said, a man can stand pain. He can walk through snow barefoot. The Spaniards couldn't do that! Even before there were saints the Benefactors had given coca to the Indians. That was why the priests didn't like it. It was a bond among the Indians. It made them forget their place!

"Boy," Calixto said. And the boy who had spoken of our farts took the knife. It was Paulino—the one who had led Wolfe's mule, hundreds of miles from here! Paulino, smiling mockingly at me, cut himself with the knife, and held the bloody hand towards the cooking fire. He wanted the young woman to see it. She looked at his hand, and smiled fondly. His blood dripped down to the dirt floor, and hit a wet patch, where someone had spat, mixing the white foam and the red.

"My future son-in-law," Calixto said proudly.

My hands felt cold. I prayed that that didn't mean I had malaria.

Calixto and Paulino, like terrible birds, sucked blood from their own hands. Calixto spat a glob of blood into his other hand, and mixed some brown leaves up with it. He shoved the bloody mess into his mouth. I thought again that I would throw up, and shut my eyes.

After a time I felt small stones falling on my head. I opened my eyes to Che, his legs crossed, drumming his fingers on the heel of his boot. My head hurt. Most of the countrypeople had left.

"You can't sit still," Calixto's father said to Che. "You are a very uneasy man."

"Because you have such big plans for us," Calixto sighed. "And we cannot do them for you."

To my surprise Che and Ponco both laughed, one low and breathy, one a harsh rasp. "A nervous ambitious man," Che said to Ponco. I didn't understand. Why didn't he show any anger at Calixto or his father? Che and Ponco's laughter reminded me how long they have known each other, how much they have already shared. I felt excluded and a little sad.

Che got up and we left. We made our way into the forest, on the trail that had been prepared for us by the vanguard group. I pushed my tongue towards my teeth and felt the tip of it disappear. It reminded me of what Calixto had said when he passed the fingers of one hand through the other, that the things of this world just passed through the man who thought of his vision. Where had the tip of my tongue gone? To join the specters!

I told this to Che as we walked along in the dark, and we laughed together. I told him of my feeling that I could walk on their faces and I asked him if the coca had helped him at all.

A little, he said, for the pain, but it couldn't free his lungs, it couldn't help him breathe. Still, he thought it might be useful for numbing the mouth for dental work. (Sometimes the peasants let him work on their rotting painful teeth.)

Near morning we slept—or my comrades did. My heart smashed at my chest, asking to be released, and I had to stay awake to keep it from getting away.

From My Journal

6/27/67: We made camp in the forest outside the village, a few kilometers from the corn. Che's breathing hasn't improved. He is our center, our lungs, and his metallic clanging makes the air seem thick around us.

In the morning I said to him how surprised I'd been that anyone had seen us pissing in the truck's radiator.

Ricardo asked, in his dainty way, what the fuck I was talking about.

I said that the piss must be the truck with the magic fuel the Indians had spoken of.

Che agreed that that made sense. And clearly they had heard about Ispaca's boy, and the worm, though that, too, was some distance from here.

"They have one ear," Camba said. We ignored him, so that he might calm himself. Yet he is right, for it does seem that way. In each village they seem to know of things that happened hundreds of miles away. (*It seems that way* —the very thing Che had said about the lies in his life story.)

"And they knew about our farting, too," Camba added.

"And the smell," Coco said. Then it was clear on his sweet plain round face that he wished he hadn't mentioned that.

"What smell?" Che asked.

Coco told him that someone the night before had spoken of a magic smell, a smell that put the soldiers to sleep. Coco is the only one of us who really commands Quechua.

Che laughed, hiding his face behind his tin coffee mug, embarrassed to remember his smell.

"Who are the two Che's?" I asked, to change the subject.

No one could answer that.

Coco amazed me when he said that the boy who had cut himself was Paulino, poor Michael Wolfe's guide. His face had been too far from the lantern for me to see clearly.

I was afraid that the young men would have fled by this morning, and that I wouldn't get a chance to speak with Paulino. But Che had posted guards to make sure no one left the settlement.

From Guevara's Journal

6/28/67: Ponco has renewed his acquaintance with Paulino, Wolfe's guide and Calixto's future son-in-law, the boy who performed the self-mutilation. Paulino's fiancée, Calixto's daughter, informed him that the "pork merchants" are frauds—one of them is a lieutenant in the army.

The center guard surrounded Calixto's house, and told the spies that if they came out immediately they could avoid being shot. The officer, a tall sallow man, stumbled out, as if he'd been pushed, sobbing piteously. He made a nice spectacle of himself for the countrypeople! He is a second lieutenant, not with the army, but with the police force. The other man is a teacher in Postre Valle who, the lieutenant said, had *volunteered* for the assignment. If true, that willing complicity was a disagreeable sign. It was a bad sign, also, that Calixto and the others went along with the charade. The army is having success in working on their fear.

Ricardo was for killing them, of course. I was surprised when Ponco agreed with him. He said that the lieutenant had violated the articles of war. This bloodthirstiness bespeaks an unusual degree of anxiety on Walter's part. *(Che, they had made fools of us!)* I decided to keep them with us for a while, then send them away with a warning about the rules of war; they were out of uniform; spies.

As punishment, we took their pants.

I was in a forgiving mood, for Ponco has convinced Paulino to act as messenger for us. His mother wept at the idea, but Paulino was adamant.

I decided to trust him with messages to the Party, and ways to contact our agents in Cochabamba. This is a crucial moment in the country's history. I must have the necessary men in the field to take full advantage of the coming miners' strike and the shaky situation of the government in La Paz. Perhaps, too, I can get the medicine I need for myself. I have also entrusted Paulino with messages for the city to transmit to Fidel. Fidel must oversee the activities of Monje and the Bolivian Party in spending his money or we may never get the necessary men from them. The Party and the city network can set up way stations for us where we can obtain supplies as we pass—guerrilla department stores. I have marked some possible locations on the map.

Help now could be decisive.

From My Journal

6/28/67: Che told me of the messages for Paulino, and the guerrilla department stores. Che has big plans. ("He is the master / He is the Man." Would he, I wonder, like to hear a few verses of his friend Chaco's song?)

Our interrogation of the army spies reveals no sign of Joaquin in the area, so we are heading farther west, towards the forest. To the east of here is only jungle that the countrypeople never enter. There is a certain kind of vine there, Calixto instructed us, and if a man steps on it he will wander in the jungle, lost forever. "A pointless place," Calixto called it.

From Guevara's Journal

6/30/67: While listening to the radio tonight we drank some coffee—"gift" of Calixto's household. (After we discovered his cooperation with the army's ruse, I allowed the men to take from his house without payment—but there wasn't, despite his fears, much to take. It is the third time we have used the coffee grounds.) Good news: Barrientos had banned the BCP, the POR, and has arrested militants from the Party and from the MNR. According to the Chilean radio some of these militants have already been shot.

"Yanqui efficiency," Ponco said. And in that voice he can make efficiency sound like a euphemism for a death sentence. Which it often is.

The Party has no choice now but to forge an alliance with us.

The Chilean announcers also speak of more Green Berets being sent to Bolivia, and of the use of napalm—both of which La Paz unconvincingly denies. It seems certain now that the North Americans will intervene here in strength.

After the news Camba insisted on singing a song for us. The men shrank back from him, expecting some new display of his instability. Instead it turned out to be an amusing thing, about a revolt of the vegetables against the gardener.

There was general good feeling in the camp. Coco, Inti, Jorge and the other militants are pleased that the comrades they left behind—the ones who were shot—are also sharing the risks of revolution. And, of course, the increased North American involvement is good news.

From Guevara's Journal

7/1/67: The radio is rife with rumors of deals and counter-deals. Two more parties have withdrawn from Barrientos's government, demanding that the Communists and MNR militants be freed, and legal status returned to both parties. Clearly the minor parties are trying to curry favor with us, believing Monge and Kolle's statements that the Party and the guerrillas are comrades. (Once again History is made when people act on misapprehensions, lies, and myths. Yet their actions have real consequences!) The Peasant Union has warned Barrientos against forming an alliance with the Falange.

The Barrientos government continues to disintegrate. If only I have a hundred more men when the miners finally deliver their blow! That would be the end of Barrientos! Seldom has the possibility of the guerrilla as catalyst been so clear!

The messages I gave Paulino will alert our allies to the necessary measures. This will make the decisive difference.

On the march, deep in the thick forest, Camba shared another verse of his vegetable epic with us.

From My Journal

7/2/67: Camba sang us into the little settlement, repeating the last few days' worth of verses—but all out of order—and adding one about a pretty but stuck-up tomato. Che's spirits were good today and he enjoyed Camba's tuneless singing. But I don't trust Che's mood—not because it is bad or good, but because he usually doesn't *have* moods. He *shouldn't* have moods. He surrendered his rights to them long ago, when he assumed his empty name.

The small settlement—perhaps thirty square brown thatched huts—had a huge church, white stone and adobe with a sloping roof, and a scalloped front piece. The land in front of the church was bare dry earth, worked out long ago. Green hills rose behind the building; some plots of corn and the runners of potato plants spotted the small terraced fields of the hillsides. These people,

I thought, had to walk a long distance to get to their work. Why do people make their lives so difficult?

Why did I?

We gathered up twenty or so from their huts with our insistent invitations, asking them to join us in the church for a talk. I held my rifle in front of one man, explaining to him that now he could tell the army we forced him to come to our meeting.

He looked at the ground, sourly. "Do you think the army will care *why* we talked to you?"

Most of the ones we found were older men, and women in black derby hats. But there was one young fellow, of a possible age for a recruit; he was very skinny, with large brown eyes.

The church's interior was a cave, with no seats. There were high tall windows near the wooden altar in front, but they were nearly black with smoke and dirt, and let in almost no light. Some green boughs had been scattered on the stone floor. Every fifty feet or so on a raised platform against the wall stood a clothing-store dummy. His costume had been painted on, but across his shoulders they had placed bright pieces of cloth. Silver and gold thread in the cloth absorbed the light from the dozens of candles that burned before each saint. The Indians had placed strings of dried berries around the dummies' necks, and from the center of the strings they had hung little round mirrors.

"You are in their hearts," Camba said as he and I stood in front of one saint. I think that was a good guess—he has the knack of understanding them. Camba stuck his tongue out at the mirror.

I didn't like that. I felt uneasy even being inside a church—my stomach was queasy; maybe I was profaning something. I don't believe in God anymore (do I? what will I say when I know I am dying?), but I still believe in profanation, or my stomach does. And now that I don't believe anymore I feel I don't belong in a church. The Indians' piety, dark and thick, hung all over everything and seeped into me from the green boughs, the expensive cloth, the grotesque dummies. Each candle flame was a tongue sticking back at Camba and me, a tongue of flame from hell. (I still believe in hell.)

The skinny fellow came over to the saint we stood near and crossed himself. He gave Camba a sniff, like a dog's examination, and returned to the back of the church. It was funny, because the kid gave off a terrible stink himself, like compost, or a body decomposing. He carried a hoe, and stood in back by the big door, like a guard.

Some of the other Indians crossed themselves by a favorite store dummy, or peered into the mirrors. "To see the state of their souls?" I said, and Camba smiled approvingly. As the Indians walked about, they lit more candles, and muttered brief prayers, just the way my mother would. The church blazed with white candles. But the dark that gathered under the high roof was too great for the light. The church was like a night sky, with many many stars, but no moon—pins of light, but still a dark place.

Inti spoke, and the villagers quietly knelt on the floor in front of him, as if he were a priest come to perform Mass for them. He was barely visible from where I stood in the back, by the side, holding my rifle, just a tall shadow. He spoke of local conditions, the need for new tools to work the land efficiently, of new kinds of fertilizer and seeds. After the victory of the Revolution, he promised, when the villages formed cooperative ventures, they could work the land with tools paid for by Bolivia's national resources. They could even have tractors!

Whatever they were.

He asked for questions, and some of the Indians crossed themselves.

Che spoke then of the need for violent revolutionary action against the army. The Imperialists used the army to rule over Bolivia. They oppressed the people and stole from them. If the people worked together with the guerrillas, we could defeat the army and the Imperialists. Then the people would have their own army, and their own government.

As Che spoke the skinny boy hopped about excitedly by the door, leaping up on one foot, with the other tucked up behind him, then bringing that hidden foot out at the height of his jump, to land upon. He went up and back behind the Indians with that crazy hop, his hoe on his shoulder. It looked like a parody of an army marching.

The boy had on a white shirt with big wooden buttons, and as he hopped about, and Che talked, he took the shirt off. His skinny chest glistened with grease. Maybe he has a bad chest, too. All the time that he jumped about he talked to himself in a loud, rapid voice. Sometimes he pointed his hoe like a rifle.

I thought that he must be a little mad fellow that they all took care of.

Che spoke of the necessary battles we had won already—with the people's help. My mad friend said "killy killy kill, die die die"—helping Che along. Then he said—I think, for he spoke very rapidly in a garbled mixture of Quechua and Spanish, shouting some syllables out and swallowing the rest—something about the Sheep and the Goats, and the Last Judgment. Everyone would get up again. Everyone would come back, good as before. "Where's your arm?" he asked. He was very excited. "Where's your leg? Have you lost it? It will all begin again! *It will be all right!*" He screamed this last promise in a choked voice, strangling the words.

He reached out his hand to some imaginary playmate. "I am the Resurrection and the Life!" he said. So I supposed then that he hadn't been listening to Che at all, but was remembering some things he had heard the priest say. I supposed Che was too far away, half in shadows, the fellow couldn't hear him. And the boy spoke all the time anyway, he couldn't be listening to anyone, couldn't respond that quickly.

But then Che said, "We must not abandon the miners, we must not abandon Vietnam!" Che's words had a breathy sound, a halo of aspiration around them.

The mad boy howled, "abandon Abandon ABANDON! Don't abandon Me! I'm drowning, I'm drowning, I'm drowning!" His voice had a piteous choking sound, not of drowning in water, but in the darker stronger current of his confusion. I thought of my mother, late at night, very drunk, touching my face, and trying to recall my name, and I felt tears starting up behind my eyes.

The people on their knees bent forward towards Che and back towards the half-naked boy, not turning towards him, just making a slight motion of their heads, like corn waving in the wind. No disrespect showed on their faces, no sly smiles—no expression, really, at all. They were stones. Or turnips.

Che stopped for a moment, brought down by the mad chatter, or the indifferent audience. The boy stopped, too. Che and he faced each other, though I don't think they could have seen each other's faces. The boy smiled towards Che, drawing his lips all the way back savagely, a dead man's grin.

Che spoke of the people helping the miners now, in their time of need, by helping the guerrillas fight the army. If the army wasn't stopped they would slaughter the miners, kill them to protect the North Americans' profits, profits that should be spent for the good of the Bolivian people. The people of Bolivia must make sacrifices now to defeat the Imperialists' army and build the nation. We must cut off the hands of imperialism in Bolivia.

The boy said that the army had blood on its hands, the blood of—and then there was a garbled sound that I thought was a name, maybe Christ's.

The people nodded.

The army, he shouted, had bloody hands. But he had the truly bloody hand, the hand with the true blood on it.

He held his hand in the air and waved it about.

He had a bloody hand. He was a bloody man, he had a bloody hand, and he would have revenge.

Che stopped again. Could he hear what the boy muttered in the back? Should I stop the boy? I don't know why I hadn't thought of that! I felt somehow as if it were a deeper profanation than Camba's tongue if I were to restrain this boy, if I were to lay hands on him. There was a forceful circle around him. And besides, I think I wanted to hear what he would say. But I came to my senses, and started to move towards him.

"No," Che shouted, and I thought he meant me. I went back to the wall. Maybe he thought it would make a bad impression if we expelled by force someone that the town took care of.

Che spoke again of their having an army and a government of their own, one that served their needs instead of oppressing them.

He was having trouble breathing—he is desperate for medicine—and thrust his chest forward to ease himself. Cruelly, the boy thrust his own chest forward, and imitated Che's sound, for Che's lungs were making an awful metallic racket. But it sounded almost musical from the boy's mouth.

"If we want our liberty we must take it, we must fight for it with our own hands!"

My young friend shouted his mad poem, he was a bloody man, he had a bloody hand, and he would be revenged.

The boy spat into his own hand, and held it up. I guess that was supposed to be blood. Nobody but Che and Inti and I looked at him.

We must not let the Imperialists steal the wealth that belongs to all Bolivians. We must not let the Imperialists steal the tin miners' lives.

Che paused, trying to suck up air. The boy no longer talked along with Che, but listened to Che's breathing. Then he shouted that they were poisoning the air.

Che looked rapt, entranced.

The boy went on talking, saying that he was the way.

Che looked at the peasants and said, "You are the way!"

I felt the whole world shake, the walls become liquid, for I felt Che was *playing* with the mad boy.

The boy went on muttering to himself, conjugating redemption, I am the way, he is the way, they are the way, we are the way. Who made the world?

"Imperialism," Che began with a grinding sound. It was painful for him to speak so loudly, such an expense of breath.

The boy wailed at that response, making a high meaningless sound, less coherent than an animal's cry.

Che stopped. "Thank you," he said to the Indians.

I thought I heard the boy shout, "Leave me alone!" But it might have been something in Quechua.

On the way out the villagers bowed in front of the boy and held his hand to their foreheads. Maybe he isn't crazy but some kind of holy thing. Or maybe they think crazy boys are holy. Sometimes the boy spat on his hand before he touched it to their foreheads.

Anyway, we did leave him alone, moving back towards the east. I had some things I wanted to ask Che, but he didn't want to talk.

7/4/67: Morroco. My friend Paulino has been returned to his village by the army, over the back of a mule. I asked his mother to show me his grave, so I might put something on it, but she refused. Anyway, what words could I have said over his grave? Poor Paulino, his curiosity, heedlessness, and friendliness reminded me of . . . me. Poor Paulino, poor us. Poor *me*.

Calixto offered us some pork, a bribe to keep us away from the village. When Che moved towards his house anyway, Calixto began to sob. He got down on his knees and grabbed Che's legs.

We took the pork.

As we walked off Calixto shouted after us in a whining voice, "You must not judge us too harshly, sir!"

"No medicine. No men," Che said to me.

Camba overheard. "No Paulino," he said. "No wedding."

7/6/67: We moved along the rocky shore of the Florida River today, and were forced to climb a steep cliff that overlooked the river in order to move forward at all. The cliff had a narrow overhang that others before us had used as a path. It was smooth with their steps.

Benjamin, as usual, fell behind. He was the skinniest of my comrades. Lately he had grown dizzy on the marches and held us up. Three days ago we found him sitting by the side of a path, resting his head on his arm. And two days ago he wandered off, dazed, and stood a few feet into the brush. Today, by the time we noticed him he was far back down the cliffside, senselessly fooling with the cloth ties of his knapsack.

Ricardo shouted at him. Benjamin's head jerked upward, moving with a loose snap, like a puppet's head. He made his way towards us with infuriating slowness. I wanted to kick the son of a bitch, for I knew that Che didn't like being near the river.

Che sent Benjamin ahead of us, so we could keep an eye on him.

Benjamin nodded with empty eyes. We pressed ourselves against the cliffside, and he made his way to the point, in front of Willy. Each day Benjamin, walking with trembling, jerky, unnatural steps, looked more and more like a cloth construction. He had to will each movement. I admired him for the effort, though I didn't like him. Anyway, there was nothing I could do for him. I didn't have any food to give him.

Che had Willy carry Benjamin's knapsack. Willy, a miner, is stocky and strong, and walks with a roll, in a stiff-legged way, like a sailor on the earth. I watched Che take him aside two days ago, and tell him to keep an eye on Benjamin. But Willy and Benjamin hadn't cared for each other. Benjamin was very proud, and complained less than other comrades, but his distance, and his arrogance, made Willy dislike him. So Willy was always rolling ahead of him, like today.

Che let Benjamin get about fifty meters up the path in front of Willy before we started after. We walked along for a while like that, picking our steps very carefully, moving upward. I was afraid. The path was narrow. And it was dangerous to be exposed this high up against the side of a cliff.

Willy was telling us—telling Che, really—the story of his life. I've heard this happen many times before, here and in Cuba: during the march one of the men would walk with Che, telling him something embarrassing, some failure, some terrifying regret. Always they spoke in a quiet, urgent, yet slow way, like our progress along the cliff. Che is of us, and yet outside us, like a confessor or an artist—anyway we thought he would know what to do with our sorrows. I suppose Che is the way his own father was; he is our judge. We could leave him confirmed in our own lives—as if we'd read our own biographies, and the author, even if he hadn't thought we were good people, had at least come to a just estimation of our sufferings.

—I must ask Che if he noticed this, too. *(I never did.)*

Willy was talking about his father. (Everyone but me has a father to talk about—an endless subject for stories.) Willy's father was a union leader in the mines. "I was a little bastard," Willy said.

"Me too," I said. Che looked over his shoulder at me, and wrinkled his brow.

"I mean," Willy said, "that my father and mother weren't married when they made me."

"Me too," I said. I lied. I didn't want Willy to feel embarrassed; I wanted him to go on with his story.

I needn't have bothered. Willy wasn't listening to me. I looked down past the edge of the path at the broad rolling river beneath us. I felt dizzy then, and squatted for a moment. Ricardo kicked me. I stifled a scream, and it came out like a peep—insofar as I am capable of a peep. I looked up; we had much higher still to go along the cliff.

Willy's mother was an Indian. His father was part Indian, part Spanish, and part black. Willy thought that the more races you had in you, the more different kinds of misery you could have.

"One is enough," I said. For misery, I meant. But Willy wasn't listening to me.

Willy's father hadn't wanted to marry his mother. She had tricked him with her pregnancy with Willy. Willy didn't know where his father had thought he was going! But his father had thought he had something better in him than being a miner. Willy's father would hit Willy and the other children casually, but he beat Willy's mother more seriously, all over her body—because she had trapped him. He acted like she was the reason Bolivians were poor! Or like Willy was—it was his fault for being born!

Willy's father had lived long enough to see his son go into the mines because he was a union official and he didn't have to go down the shaft as much as the others. But when the strike came Willy's father became the loveliest man alive, and he gave all his extra life back.

Willy turned to Che, so I could see his face, sweet and sad. He looked like he wanted to stroke Che's cheek.

I knew from that mild sweet look that Willy's father wouldn't live till the end of the story. (Besides, this was Bolivia; most stories have a lot of doomed characters.)

During the strike, Willy's father had gone everywhere, talking to meetings, keeping up people's spirits, seeing that food was shared, organizing the militia units, even helping to drill them. And what did he know about drilling a militia? Nothing! His father was a little guy. Willy was himself half again as tall as his father. And he was shorter than Che, and Che wasn't that tall, was he? But his father had been strong then!

Willy turned to us again and smiled. We inched along the side of the cliff. I put one foot down slowly and placed the other one in front, in a nice straight line. There was no room for error!

Willy's father had been lightning, darting everywhere. He had a large head, like Willy's own, with curly black hair, and his father's head bobbed up and down when he was excited, like a crow's. The small birds try to peck at the crow's eyes, and he snaps his head back at them. Well, Willy's father had been like that when someone at a meeting raised an objection to what he said. He snapped his head at him and tried to smash his words. The man's words were an annoyance, a danger.

I was sure now that Willy's father wasn't long for this story, because Willy sounded too sweet about the son of a bitch. Dying makes a person lovely. I had even remembered my uncle as a witty man for a while after he died—for about thirty seconds.

I looked down at the river, and at the rocks on the other shore. The trees were thick just beyond. If you jumped into them they would certainly catch you and hold you up! What if soldiers appeared out of those trees down near the rocks? We were like a series of targets strung out along the side of the light-brown cliff. The scouts said that couldn't happen, there was no sign of the army in the area. (But the army had helicopter transports now, huge buglike things. We had seen one lay soldier eggs onto the hunting plain near the Nancahuazu.)

Vertigo pulled me towards the edge again, and I squatted for a moment, but I got up before Ricardo could walk over my back.

The miners had been destroyed, without a fight. All the drilling with the militia and the prehistoric guns was a joke. They never fought. They couldn't leave their homes their wives their children. (Willy had no wife, no children. He wasn't going to let happen to him what had happened to his father! He was *chaste*. I saw why it was a necessary discipline to bring about the Day of Change.) The army starved them. For a long time there was only a little dried meat that the Indians gave them. But no milk for the children. And no cough syrup. Che could imagine what it was like for the miners without cough syrup!

That was true, I thought. Che could certainly imagine that.

The men called the cough syrup "oil," because their lungs wouldn't work without it, so that they just coughed and coughed and ripped themselves open from the grit, until they bled. No one knew where to go, or what to do, and every time they took a breath they started a cascade of coughs, ripping pieces of the lung away. Little flakes of flesh mixed with the blood and speckled their lips, like chipped paint.

The Party had said they would settle things, and Willy's father had repeated the Party's words. And that was wrong. When Willy had gone to jail he had hated his father for that. But what was the right thing to do? Until he had heard about Che's plan Willy hadn't known what to do, either. Anyway, his father had paid for his mistake.

First the planes were small in the sky, and harmless-looking, but they grew with their sound, until the roaring filled Willy's head until he couldn't think anymore. The army had bombed the miners' barracks. Bombs are furious things! Willy had been terrified. His father had everyone hide in the mines because he knew the army couldn't risk destroying them. But Willy had been so scared that he had run about outside, not knowing what he was doing, just screaming up at the sky, and the earth and the rocks and the wood from the barracks had all leapt up at him! It was a miracle that he hadn't been killed!

As soon as the army had let them, the miners had surrendered. Then the helicopters landed outside the mines and spewed out soldiers. The soldiers fired into the mines and dragged the miners' families out of their hiding places. Willy's father was taken into an open muddy field outside the barracks, where they pushed him to his knees and shot him.

Willy was arrested because he'd been everywhere with his father. He had had to watch the executions. A lot of men had been shot, union leaders, and miners, and people who had had nothing to do with the union. Most of them had been shoved into a big hole, still alive, and all the soldiers fired into the hole. The miners looked like a bunch of maggots on a piece of meat, crawling all over each other covered in blood. But *they* were the meat!

Willy's father hadn't screamed, he had died bravely. He just gave his life back. Willy's mother was dead now, too, killed by a punch in her stomach. She had gone to the political police to ask for Willy. That was a stupid thing to do! So now this fighting was all Willy had!

Willy was furious at his mother for looking for him, for getting herself killed. Poor boy, he was right about one thing: we were his family now, such as we were. No life outside the Revolution.

Willy had been brought from his cell so he could be shown to his mother. They had held him up and beaten him for a while, and his mother had cursed the police. They had been hitting Willy in his face and he had once been very handsome—before they flattened his nose.

He was still a good-looking man, I thought, especially when he smiled. But perhaps his mother had been attached to the face he'd been born with. Mothers are like that—when they're sober.

I tripped over a piece of rock and fell. I clung to the stubbly ground with my hands, trying to dig my fingers into the stone. My nail bled, and I brought it to my mouth and sucked on it joyfully. I thanked God for sparing me!

"What are you mumbling?" Ricardo said. "Are you losing your mind like the vegetable singer?"

I rose and brushed myself off, laughing, for there was no point to the brushing. There was dust, I thought, all over my dust. "No," I said. "I was praying."

Ricardo *laughed*, that ugly sound. He thought I was simply lying about prayer, for he didn't know I had read Che's version of him at Alegria de Pio. Probably he didn't even remember that time himself.

"I was reciting poetry," I said.

Ricardo accepted that with a nod—he has a taste for literature now himself.

We continued on. We were finally going downward. I would have run to the bottom, but I was too afraid of falling. Willy's mother had cursed at the police, and hit one of them on the side of his head with her fist. That was a stupid thing to do! But they were spoiling Willy's good looks! And that was the only thing she had liked about him.

Willy's voice became slower and more urgent still; and I knew we had come to the point of the story, the reason he was telling it to Che. It wasn't his father. It wasn't the miners' massacre, or his discovery of Che's strategy—the necessity of guerrilla warfare. It was the policeman hitting his mother.

The policeman had hit his mother once in her big belly. His mother had struck the policeman because she didn't want Willy to be ugly; or dead. And with Willy's father gone, he was the only one to support the family.

I thought, You must never hit a policeman. He thinks it starts a relationship between you; it's a policeman's idea of romance.

His mother had been pregnant, so when the policeman hit her—*pow!*—it had killed her. Willy watched the blood flow out of her middle, staining her skirts. He tried to get free of their hands to go to her, but they held him and went on hitting him for a while, absent-mindedly. They didn't seem to notice what they were doing to him anymore, once they had started *her* bleeding.

It must have been a rare treat for them, I thought, to hit a pregnant woman.

His mother had gagged and fallen to the floor, and her face went white. Willy could have closed his eyes, maybe he should have closed his eyes, but he hadn't. He had watched the blood pouring onto the cement floor till she had died.

And *that*, I realized, was his embarrassment, I thought, his *sin*, that was why he had to tell Che *this* story. In all the blood, the stuff that had come up from the miners' lungs, or out of his father's head, or been smeared in the hole full of dying miners like maggots, it was his mother's blood that had held his attention. Willy had seen it when he shouldn't have, and he hadn't turned away. But why was that so terrible? I thought of my own mother, her head fallen into a plate of beans *I'd* cooked for our family. Maybe he had wanted her to die? Pow, Willy had said, too loudly, with too much satisfaction. I felt sick.

It was where the blood came from that was so awful, Willy said. She and his father had made love together, and *that* was the blood that poured out onto the floor. Willy thought of how his father had used to hit her, too.

Had Willy wanted to hit her? To be on his father's side? Like Che's mockery of his mother? It didn't make any sense to me. But then, why should it?

The police made Willy mop up the blood.

We walked on together. I felt crappy. I think it was remembering *my* mother.

"I think," Willy said, "that we must all have stories like that to tell." He pointed back to the men of the center group strung out along the cliff. Willy spoke slowly still. "Your own story," he said to Che, "must be like mine."

Che smiled, but he didn't respond to Willy. He was having trouble breathing.

"No," I said for him. "His story isn't like yours. He had a gentler life."

Willy pointed backward towards Che's rifle.

"He's a self-made man," I said. "Like Rockefeller."

Che ordered us to go forward more quickly, so Willy didn't turn around again. "Ah, Rockefeller," he said to the air in front of him. But I don't think he knew who I meant.

Who did I mean? The man from the cartoons, top-hatted, turning our lives into gold. The One Who Owns the World. The metal rabbit the poor dogs chase. I noticed Benjamin, on point, wandering from the trail. His head was down, he staggered about, lurched towards the cliff, and then towards the air. Che ordered Willy to run forward and pull him back. But as Che spoke—just as if Benjamin had heard him and was so proud he would rather die than be helped—he made a single abrupt movement, like someone had yanked his string, stepped onto the air with one foot; and tumbled forward.

For a moment I thought of those cartoon cats that can walk on air awhile, until they look down, realize where they are, and fall. But this was no cartoon. I entered Benjamin's body, and fell with him, a slow spiral, down into the river. The blood pushed up to the top of my head as I fell and it felt like it would pour out through my ears. My hands went numb.

Benjamin's gun dropped to the side as he fell, and arched down to the river glinting in the sun—he had kept it clean. A pound of feathers and a pound of human being fall just as fast. It's a law we will repeal after the Revolution. Benjamin didn't scream. The men stood on the ledge and gaped at him, thinking, What does this silent sign mean? They probably felt numb with his blood, as I did. We were short of men, even scrawny ones like Benjamin. That made us all keenly empathetic.

I knew that Benjamin couldn't swim, for when we had crossed the Rio Grande he had clung to my arm.

He was still conscious when he hit the water, and when he came up he beat the surface of the river. But the river pulled him under. Willy ran the rest of the way down the side of the cliff with his quick stiff steps. (That scared me! If Willy fell, that would be a real loss.) He shed his pack and boots by the side of the river, and dived in. But Willy didn't know how to swim either, and an undertow pulled him out in the wrong direction. It took all of his strength to save himself and make it back to the thin line of rocks.

Benjamin bobbed up once, and then disappeared again under the river. His arm came up through the water. "You see," Ricardo said, "I told you Bolivians aren't worth shit." Benjamin's hand flopped from the wrist. Ricardo *laughed.* "Look," he said, "the nice boy is waving good-bye to us!"

I could live without Ricardo, I thought. And then: *I couldn't live without Ricardo!*

In camp that evening Che gave a speech about Benjamin. Admittedly, he said, Benjamin was a weak and inept guerrilla. (And, Ricardo's lips said to me, an asshole. I think Ricardo takes Benjamin's death as a special vindication granted to him by the god of war. How dare the boy have spat at him? Sometimes Ricardo's vengefulness blinds him, for Benjamin's death brings us all closer to the edge.)

But, Che said, Benjamin had had a strong will. And his will had sustained him long after his body had given up. Benjamin's intelligence was hard, unsparing of anyone.

That was true, I thought. He had been a sharp-toothed demon in our sessions of criticism–self-criticism, listing all his own faults scrupulously. And then all yours.

Benjamin, the story went on, had joined the guerrillas because his thinking had shown him that guerrilla warfare was the only strategy for making a revolution. And only a revolution would save the lives of most Latin Americans —not another doctor. Benjamin could not *know,* and yet not act on that knowledge—despite his physical weakness. He couldn't live a contradiction. That deserved our admiration.

He was unsuited for guerrilla life. But we should have taken better care of him. Perhaps his comrades sometimes felt Benjamin was judging them too harshly, and that he had no right to judge them at all. But it was his deep morality and his pride in himself that had led him to join the guerrillas—and it was tragic that these should be the very qualities that had separated him from his comrades.

That would not do. Every man must be the care of every other. Each man is his brother's teacher, and keeper . . .

And guard, I thought. I smiled at Che, who did not speak this last word. Maybe he didn't even remember where this had all started! Maybe I remembered his own words better than he did! (Then I remembered too that, though Che suspected I had read his journal, he didn't know for certain, so I stared into his brown eyes guilelessly, no longer smiling.)

This eulogy of Che's, I thought, like the one I wrote for Paulino, was as much for Che as for Benjamin. Pride, moralism, intelligence, physical weakness, and the inability to live a contradiction—who did that describe? The forces that sustained Che, that made him our leader, also separated him from us. Was he pleading with us then, that in his weakness we might look after him, if he couldn't get more medicine and needed our help? Maybe all speeches over the grave aren't about the body—no body in this case anyway —but about the speaker. He names the qualities he's most attached to—fatally attached!

Che didn't seem to notice my stare. The other men all looked properly abashed and moved. I think they were, for Che's pleading voice *had* been very moving. (After all, he was pleading for himself.)

Che distributed the last ration of black beans to bolster the men's morale.

From Guevara's Journal

7/7/67: I had not been attentive to Benjamin, not to his condition in general (I wished him gone, really), to the animosity he had generated among the other comrades (none of whom cared for him), or, finally, fatally, to his location on the path on the day he drowned.

I wasn't listening very attentively to Willy yesterday, either. I heard a narrative punctuated by blows, the miners' massacre, the policeman killing his mother ("pow!" Willie shouted, waking me from my reverie), but I was thinking of our encounters with the Indians the last few weeks. I saw again the knife that Calixto had held, cutting the webbing between his fingers. I thought of the old man, Calixto's father, stuffing the coca leaves into his mouth. His face was all mouth, a toothless puckered hole, and the wrinkles of his skin were a landscape to dreamwalk, a thousand ridges and valleys. We moved on his face, and as he chewed coca the ground beneath our feet shook. I and my men fell forward towards his lizard's mouth. We scrabbled at the ravines in his cheeks to keep from falling in, but one by one we failed and fell. We would be chewed up with the brown leaves and blood, ground down, spat out. (I looked towards the river and felt the damp rise from it along the cliffside, weighing down my lungs.) The Indian chewed us up. We'd be spat out in some new shape, reborn, with thunder and lightning farts, magic rings on our fingers. "Che" stood in front of a group of kneeling Indians. Grease covered his thin naked chest, grease that protected him against bullets. He held his right hand up before the Indians, and blood welled onto his palm from the webbing between his thumb and first finger. *I am the bloody man,* he said, *I have the bloody hand, and I will be revenged.*

It made me laugh, a laugh that almost made me fall over. It was then that Ponco noticed Benjamin, and I shouted to him.

From Coco's Journal

7/7/67: Today we captured another slat-sided truck, once again the property of the petroleum company. Benigno stepped out of the ambush and pointed his rifle towards it. The driver stopped, or I would have shot out his tires and sent him into a ditch.

Che was glad to have the truck. "A welcome gift," he said.

"They're right," Ponco said. "Everything returns. Nothing is wasted." Ponco laughed. His dry laugh is full of sorrow. Ricardo asked if Ponco thought the truck still had our piss inside.

Anyway, the truck will carry our knapsacks for a while.

Che is having a lot of trouble walking, yet he continues without complaint. *And so will I.* (I don't think anyone has noticed my night sweats or trembling, not even Inti.) We will move south towards where Che says Joaquin must be. We ordered the mestizo driver of the truck to march with us. We will let him go at the next village.

From Camba's Journal

7/8/67: The center entered a settlement of ten thatched huts around a big empty dirt square. One part of the square faced a large adobe church with a brass bell on top of it. Brown paint flecked from the church walls.

Dozens of white bodies ran from the church, back across the dirt to their huts. Dressed in white, they were like a plague of rabbits. Ricardo was so surprised to see them scurry that he drove the truck with our knapsacks on it into a ditch. The big back wheels spun in the air, and the truck slowly slid forward.

The Indians were very shy, too, like rabbits, and stood by their huts, not saying anything, not even to each other. The women just peeked from behind the entries. And their silence was immense. They wouldn't talk to us, or come out to get a better look, the way they do in most places.

Che didn't say anything about gathering them up for a meeting. He doesn't want to talk to them or *hear* them.

We worked in shifts at getting the truck out. When I stopped pushing I stood back to look at my comrades, struggling in the sun. Ricardo and Benigno jostled each other, trying to brace themselves against one wall of the ditch and push upward on the radiator. Tuma lost his balance and fell over. Tuma looks like Che, same long face and brown beard, the same sorrowful eyes. I saw that he was Che's double. Tuma curses everyone in his high voice, especially Ricardo, because Che *wants* to curse Ricardo. Everyone was angry with Ricardo for getting us into this.

I wanted a drink badly. It was very hot. I had a terrible taste in my mouth, like something rotting.

Willy went on pushing alone as Tuma scrambled up. Willy feels bad about Benjamin's dying. (No one liked Benjamin, but they like me even less.) The veins on the side of Willy's head stood out; then they broke, and blood streamed down his cheeks.

Then everything was all right again.

But we weren't making any progress on the truck. When we stopped pushing, the truck slid farther down into the ravine with a heavy sigh from the rocks and dirt, and more cursing from the comrades.

None of the Indians laughed, though we were a funny and pitiful sight. It was like they were made of glass, and lived in painted glass huts. The ground was a big pane of glass. The bell on the church tower might be glass, too. If they rang it, it would shatter into a thousand pieces, and the fragments would pierce our hearts. "I hope they don't ring the bell," I said.

"What the fuck are you talking about, asshole?" Ricardo asked. "Why the fuck would they ring the bell?" Ricardo was angry with himself because this problem was his fault; he had squandered our truck, and everyone cursed him for it.

I bit my arm and of course I wasn't glass. Ricardo wasn't glass. I saw that we *didn't belong* there. Ricardo's curses were stones, and the beads of sweat on his cheek were too thick, like gravel. If they fell, they would shatter the glass earth.

I went over to help push, so we could get out of here before we destroyed everything.

"Forget it," Che said. "It's a lost cause."

I laughed, because of course in the world to come he will be the Saint of Lost Causes.

Che and Coco talked with some of the Indians who stood in front of the church. Coco had ripped the brown pants he had taken from one of the prisoners, and his leg bled.

Coco asked the Indians to help with the truck, and they stared at him.

"I think they speak Guarani," Coco told Che. "I only know a few words of Guarani."

In Quechua Coco asked about the best routes to the river. He made an up-and-down gesture with his hands, like water flowing.

The Indians made some gestures back.

"They understand him," Ricardo said, "when they think it will get rid of us."

We marched off, abandoning our truck.

But now the dust on the path was glass. And when we entered the forest again the green stuff, the endless green stuff that crawls between the trees, was glass. The machete wielders shattered some of it so we could move towards the river. When I grabbed a vine it felt cold and solid, and when I ripped it it broke in my hand and sent icy green shards to the ground. If I stepped too heavily the earth broke in long spidery lines. I could see the jagged edges we had already made. The Indians of this region hate us because we are too heavy, and our steps destroy their world, crush the vegetation, shatter the ground.

I tried to speak with Che about the problem we're having with the peasants. We don't belong here, so we will just break things wherever we go. Che should give this up and march to a different country that isn't made of glass. Che could take us all back to Cuba with him.

But Che didn't want to speak with me. He said we would have more water when we reached the river, and waved me away. But I wasn't asking for water. I was trying to tell him something.

Che doesn't like me. That was what killed Benjamin. The lines that link all the comrades together, that had tied Benjamin to the rest of us, were broken by their hatred so he fell off the cliff and drowned.

Now they hate me.

From Coco's Journal

7/9/67: We continued moving back towards the Rio Grande. Che says that Joaquin must have remained in the south. We cannot expect immediate help from the party anymore, so we must rejoin Joaquin. With our full numbers we can at least make some demonstration to coincide with the miners' strike. That could be decisive.

My night sweats have gotten worse. I still haven't told anyone about them, not even my brother. As I walk, I say a prayer with each step that they will go away. I don't want to be left with one of the peasant families.

I will keep up. Che labors under far worse burdens, and he is always among the first.

7/10/67: This morning Barrientos again announced that he will keep faith with the nation. A joke repeated over and over, Che said, begins to sound like a threat. This afternoon we learned again what imperialism's lackeys mean by keeping faith with our nation. Barrientos had not waited for the miners to strike. He had ordered the Air Force to bombard the barracks in Catavi. The Argentine station says that the army occupied the mining area, smashed the radio transmitters, and killed eighty-seven, including women and children.

Che said this is a temporary setback for us, but it will mean much faster progress for the Revolution in the future. The miners' union, the Party, the Trotskyites, and all progressive forces will see that aid must be concentrated on the guerrilla movement, that there is no other way.

We had never, Che said, thought that there would be a quick victory. It will be a long arduous struggle throughout the continent. But it will now be clear to all that only a mobile force dedicated to the destruction of the army and the establishment of socialism can unite the people and make the Revolution in Bolivia.

The other Bolivians, even my brother, were grief-stricken. Especially Willy, of course, who knew many of the miners who were killed.

I feel angry and abandoned, as the others do.

7/11/67: To increase cohesion in the group—I thought—and to help us overcome our sadness about the miners and the lost opportunities, Che put an ambush on the little road leading to Abapa. A column of twenty soldiers—still stupidly using the already cut paths and the roads—fell into it. We killed four of them, and the rest ran away. I am sure I got at least one of them myself.

We withdrew immediately into the forest, our spirits considerably higher. I got ready to withdraw from that camp, but Che said that the army would not have the morale for a counterattack, so we needn't leave the area.

At dusk the firing began. At first I couldn't believe it, but the sharp sound of the bullets convinced me! Chunks of the trees flew at us. Mortars shattered the forest to our right, and they were moving up towards us. The sound of their bullets popping and whining seemed to come from everywhere. We were all terrified. Eusebio screamed. It was like being trapped in a cloud we couldn't see our way out of.

Che stood up in the center of the camp and rallied us, pointing the direction the attack was coming from, and the way we would retreat. Benigno fired back with the machine gun, making a big racket, while the rest of us gathered up our things as best we could. "Retreat, too, is a kind of battle," Ponco said to me very calmly. But I couldn't understand him then; it just seemed like empty syllables of sound. And now it just seems like retreat to me!

And retreat was what I wanted then! The sooner the better! But I think Ponco wanted to help me calm myself.

Even as he spoke Ponco was hit in the thigh and fell down next to me. Inti and I picked him up and dragged him from the area while the rear guard covered our steps.

Throughout the night we moved up a hill. Next morning Tuma died from a mortar fragment near his neck. He was an old comrade of the Cubans and looked a lot like Che—but he had a terrible mouth, even worse than Ricardo's though not as vicious, more like high spirits.

From My Journal

7/13/67: He has changed directions. We are moving northeast, towards the jungle, that "pointless place" that even the Indians won't bother with. This is madness! We cannot establish ourselves in a zone where no one lives.

At the beginning of the day I hung on Inti's shoulder, but I let go of him and dragged myself forward to question Che. He said nothing. Of course he is sad about Tuma's death, as we all are, and about his own miscalculation on the counterattack. But to me it feels worse than that. Despite his brave speech about how relying on our own resources will give a new depth to our commitment, and how the massacre of the miners clarifies the situation, what it all really means is that we are alone. We cannot reach the Party, and they have made no attempt to contact us. The city network too—if it still exists—has been ineffective in reaching us, supposing it has tried at all. Our contacts with Cuba and Argentina—if they are still alive —are in Bolivian prisons being questioned by CIA cowboys. And we have no idea how to rejoin Joaquin. The Indians don't understand our goals, or misunderstand them, which is worse.

Camba marched with me in the afternoon, holding me up. In a desperate shocked voice he said he had to tell me a theory of his. ("Theory" was a strange word for him to use, like the Indians saying "reign.") His "theory" was that Tuma was Che's double, his shadow, and that he had acted out Che's desires —such as cursing Ricardo. (I don't know about Che, but I had wanted to curse R. for his carelessness.) What did it mean, he asked, if Tuma died? He sounded worried, unsure.

I shrugged, but I needed his arm and couldn't walk ahead of him. Stupid man! It's hard when I'm around him not to think in the crazy way he does.

What does it mean?

Nothing. Che will have to do his own cursing, I suppose.

My thigh burns, but Moro says it is a flesh wound and will heal rapidly.

Isle of Pines, June 1968

JUNE 10

And it did heal, though the rough lizardskin on the outside of my thigh stretches painfully tight on days like this one, dark days, before a storm. It did heal, but Che hadn't withdrawn to that pointless place in order to speed *my* convalescence.

And the jungle *was* a pointless place, an awful place. The air was damp and hot and thick, like having a piece of wet rubber pressed against your face. After the first few steps of the morning's march our bodies were covered with sweat, and our faces had a dull red color, like boiled meat. My body was dissolving—or just rotting—a sickening continual dizziness. I could see why the Spaniards—or so Inti told me—had thought the air in the jungle carried disease.

But really it wasn't the air that carried disease, Inti said, it was the mosquitoes and other insects. I could believe that, too. They were everywhere, the biting stinging boring things, on the plants, in the trees, up our asses, ticks, spiders, chiggers, ants, mosquitoes, red-and-brown things even Inti didn't have a name for. The mosquitoes smelled my blood and hung thickly around the drippings from my wound, an ooze tainted with red. The chiggers worked hard, too, boring into my flesh. Inti told me that the chiggers didn't want blood. They turned our tissue to liquid, and supped on that liquid. The chigger bites —Inti said—swelled into hard lumps that itched fiercely. That made me laugh, for his pompous slow tone instructing me reminded me of the little schooling I had ever had—because, of course, it was *obvious,* we all *had* those lumps, we all *knew* what itching the bites caused. Inti tried to sound disinterested as he taught me about the "flora and fauna" (I didn't even know it was called "flora and fauna"), scholarly and distant. But all the time my teacher's hands scratched furiously at his arms and legs, just like the rest of us.

Anyway, *the insects* didn't need Inti's instructions. They knew their business, and chipped away at us, day after day, taking little bits of our flesh and blood and tissue-become-liquid. We were intruders, just as Camba said. They wanted to make us disappear. "At least if we were dead," Marcos said, "we wouldn't itch." The insect bites irritated Marcos more than the rest of us, because he had very thin sensitive skin. Each day his face looked lumpier and sadder—almost as lumpy as Che's, whose body was covered with walnut-size bumps. But Marcos was wrong; the jungle didn't want us dead, it wanted us *gone,* like the toad I watched the army ants devour till it had never been. The jungle wanted to incorporate every part of us into itself, wasting nothing.

We stuffed our pants legs inside our boots to keep the insects out, but our boots were falling apart, and the insects got in through the cracks in the leather, and crawled up our legs. Our bodies were mottled and gashed where we had dug furrows into our flesh.

And there was nowhere safe to rest in the jungle, nowhere that wasn't *after* us. The spiders and ants were everywhere, and the plants had long thorns, thin and sharp as needles, hidden inside their leaves and on their stems. The outer edges of the leaves had poisonous spines. When we marched we innocently brushed against the plants and their scratches erupted into long red painful rashes.

And walking in the jungle made the inside of my head hurt, it made a kind of painful fuzzy sound in my head, a staticky sound from the buzz of the mosquitoes and flies near my ears, from the lack of food and water, from the *senselessness of everything.*

Inti told me that the jungle *wasn't* senseless. He had studied botany (which is plants, or "flora") and biology (which is animals, or "fauna") in college (which was far away from the jungle). He knew things about the jungle, and he tried to take our minds off our pains by teaching us about it. He tried to show me "the intricate harmony" of the place, how a tree with feathery leaves and long thorns "lived cooperatively" with red ants. He tore off a branch and displayed the ants clustered near the bottom of the leaf. The ants lived at the base of the thorns, and ate sugar sweetly provided by the glands at the stems. The ants were "partners" with the tree: it gave them food, and they protected the tree, by cutting away at the vines that attacked it, by eating insects that wanted to devour it, by biting any larger animals that brushed against its sheltering leaves. They even patrolled the perimeter of the trunk, and gathered up seeds scattered by other plants, seeds that might grow into competing plants that could block *their* tree's access to the sun. (They were patriots, these ants.)

Inti pointed out a tree that looked to me like a man twisted in agony. There had once, he said, been another tree there, but a vine had grown up around it, and strangled it. The vine had taken root, and grown thick as a tree. The twisted shape we saw was the vine. (The tree had rotted away, had *disappeared.*) Now new vines curled about this vine-become-tree, and by and by would take *its* place. (As the bourgeoisie had replaced the feudal aristocracy, as we replaced the bourgeoisie. Count on it, I thought, there will be further revolutions.)

I stuck one leg behind me and leaned over to listen to Inti's many many many lectures on the ants. He showed me "leaf cutters" walking home from a demolishing job with little bits of greenery in their mouths. A meal, I thought. But no, they didn't eat the leaves, they buried them in special underground chambers. Delicious fungus grew on the green bits, and that was what the ants ate. Fungus and mold grew everywhere, tangles of thin white fibers like spiders' legs in a jumble. Mold grew on the surface of my bandage, though Moro cleaned and changed it every day. Mold sneaked inside the telescopic sights of our rifles, and ate away at the protective coating on the lenses. And one night it grew on Eusebio's eyes, and in his nose, on the bodies of some insects he had swatted as he slept (for his hands moved even when he was unconscious). When he felt the mold holding his eyes closed, Eusebio thought he had died, and he screamed and screamed until Moro decided on the prescription for hysteria, and hit him.

But on with the lecture: Inti showed me army ants, battalions marching in close-order formation (all that hup-two-three shit, Che had called it when we watched the new Cuban Army drill). They cleared the ground before them, scouring it clean, attacking a fat red toad who waited one moment too long before jumping away, sinking their pincers into his stomach and eyes, pushing him over, devouring him utterly. One minute there was a pile of ants moving forward towards a toad, towards a lump of flesh, then there was a little mound of ants, and then there was nothing. (I saw it when I closed my eyes that night. I was terrified of *going away*, terrified that my soul wouldn't die, but would be spread out among a million army ants.)

The ants were nomadic, marauders, bivouacking during the nights, then setting off on a march at sunlight, leveling some new piece of ground. They rested three weeks at a time. "Their bite is fierce," Inti said—though we all knew that, too. The Indians, he said, had used the soldier ants to suture wounds. When the "doctor" squeezed the ant's body, its jaws clamped the flesh, closing the wound. Then the body was pinched off, making a "stitch." "If you were an Indian," Ricardo said, "your thigh would have little ant jaws hanging from it."

Army ants, by the way, form their lines by smelling the ant in front of them. (Every ant was the care of every other, the one forever in his nostrils, the one who smelled him. What revolution could use *that* metaphor?) Inti smeared a little of our useless bug repellent on the branch in front of their line of march. The odor disrupted their close-order drill—about the only thing the stuff ever did accomplish—and the ants milled about confusedly, tripping over each other.

The maddened ants swirled about in a daze that looked like the inside of my head. No matter what Inti said the jungle had no harmony for me. "No species dominates or grows too large," he concluded. "Each holds one of the other species in check. Each has a place. The jungle forms one big organism."

"A giant toad," Camba said. "I feel like I'm in the intestines of a giant toad."

But more than that I felt like I was inside a fire. The fuzziness in my head was the continual high-pitched crackling that I was sure you would hear if you lived inside a fire. The sharp leaves ripping my face, the thick vines that rubbed against my wound and inflamed my leg, the poisonous red trail left by the spines of a serrated leaf I had brushed with my hand were flames licking at me, the fire of hell that burns but doesn't devour.

It wasn't as noisy as I thought it would be in a jungle, really. The sound of our boots crushing the loam and thick ferns, the mosquitoes' buzz, Camba's high unmusical voice singing his little song of the vegetables, that was all the noise there was most times, except for the blessed days when we heard the chattering of a monkey swinging overhead, and held our breath, praying that Inti or Benigno might shoot it for our dinner. It was quiet enough sometimes to hear a rustling sound from the ground near us, the lady of the jungle giving a little shaking to her garments. "Ants," Inti said. The other insects made the leaves rustle as they leapt from their homes, running away from the indifferent implacable marauders. The rustling sound was the jungle in panic, it was the insects screaming.

A few Indian families, the advance guard of an MNR project to settle the wild places, still lived inside the fire, though the center guard of that march had never arrived. The government had brought the families here, helped them clear a little land, given them some seed and tools, and then—more than a decade ago—had abandoned them. The government in La Paz (where was that?) had been overgrown by Yanqui mold, they had long ago given up on this brave project in favor of other projects, like resettling Switzerland with the profits from the cocaine trade, the money from the mines, the bribes from the oil companies.

The peasant families lived in houses made of thin pieces of wood lashed together with vines and copper wire and string. We ate that month by stumbling from family to family, following the smell of the man in front, resting during the night, and marching during the day. Often there was three days' march between families, between meals. And they couldn't spare much, just some potatoes. We paid them well—though it would be a long walk for them to be able to spend our money.

They told us not to eat anything in the jungle, no matter how good it looked. The jungle, they said, wouldn't help us. The demons filled the fruits with poisons. There were certain terrible trees inhabited by devils; we must not even stand under them, for if the rain washed their sap into our eyes we would

go blind. (I looked to Inti and smiled.. But he nodded. *There were such trees!*)
The jungle was filled with the cleverest of demons, and we must be constantly
vigilant not to be deceived by their tricks. This man had seen a sorcerer's
caterpillars sent to eat leaves while he watched so he would think the leaves
were safe. But they had twisted up in his stomach and nearly killed him. He
had shaken and sweated and vomited for days.

"Cyanide in the leaves," Inti said. "There are species of caterpillars that
have adapted so they can eat such things."

The settler just stared. After all, what did this add for him? He still couldn't
eat the leaves.

"What about the monkeys?" Coco asked. "Surely we can eat them?"

"If your brother could kill them," Ricardo added dourly, by way of criticizing Inti's shooting.

The settler was horrified. How could we think of such a thing! Were we
like the ants? he asked. Would we eat anything in our path? To kill a monkey
was evil, the devil's work! The monkeys were the souls of children not yet born,
souls on their way through the trees, on their way to becoming human.
Couldn't we see that they had human faces?

We could, of course. But we were hungrier than the settlers.

Some days we passed through parts of the jungle where huge leaves grew
overhead, like giant ears, and kept the ground dark. Nothing grew too thickly
there; we only had to push the lianas away to move forward, and kick the snaky
vines with our feet. Other parts of the jungle we had to tear our way through.
The machete wielders went ahead of the main group, hacking at things, but
they could only mark a path for us, not make one. And the jungle had nearly
grown back around the marking before we could put our feet down. In those
parts of the jungle they used the machetes like long fingers, not cutting things
but picking the material up, tearing it away. And we finished the job with our
hands, ripping at the vines as we went, pushing into the thick tangle of leaves,
and feeling it close behind us as we stepped forward into more long leaves, and
thick poisonous vines that tore back at the side of my thigh and my bandage.
(Once, at night, I saw Eusebio, asleep, exhausted, but with his hands swimming
above his head, pushing dream leaves aside, tearing at fairy vines.) The crawlers
grew in a dense pattern like a madwoman's senseless weaving. What was she
weaving?

A net.

Why did he do it? It felt to me like despair and confusion. His. Mine. We
couldn't find Joaquin as long as we stayed in the jungle. We couldn't make

contact with the city network—that is, if *they* were trying to find *us*. But the army couldn't find us there, either, we were safe. *And I think Che was suddenly afraid of the army.*

We had inflicted bad losses on the army, we had shaken the Barrientos government, we had begun to bring the Yanquis into the conflict, just as planned; and we had only taken a few losses ourselves. (Rolando, El Rubio, Tuma, Benjamin, from our group.)

But we didn't need to take many. *In eight months in Bolivia we hadn't made one new recruit.* Every one of our dead was a weight attached to our waists dragging us farther under the water. If we didn't make new recruits we would drown. We could kill a hundred soldiers for every one of us they killed, but eventually they would put another hundred into the field, and kill just one more of us, and then, by and by, there wouldn't be any of *us* left. We would have killed two thousand soldiers or so. *And we would have lost.* I ran through the sad mathematics as I marched, trying to hold on to numbers that scurried off into the buzz in my head. It was a way of marking time, keeping my mind off the terrible itching, the hot pain of my wound, my swollen feet surrounded by rags of fabric and leather. (I was one of the fortunate ones; I had a pair of the new boots we'd taken off the last batch of Rangers. U.S. boots, Vietnam issue, they let more water in through the drainage holes and fabric sides than they released. Mud clung thickly to the lugged rubber sole, adding extra weight to every painful step.) And being in the jungle was a way of marking time. But I didn't know what we were marking time for? Until what? I ran through the figures again, trying to get my courage up to speak to him.

Two weeks went by in the jungle, and there was little to eat—mostly mealy potatoes from the settlers. Sometimes, on the best days, Inti or Benigno bagged a monkey, a fibrous bitter thing that we grilled on a spit. At first they *were* difficult to eat, almost human-looking, but after a few days in the jungle they looked less and less human.

There wasn't much water. The settlers carried it into the jungle, for the only natural water was in stagnant pools covered with green slime. As we stared, black clouds of mosquitoes drifted up towards us, like our own unhappy fears.

We got weaker. Coco, when he was asleep at night and couldn't help himself, moaned. During the day, though he tried to hide it, his body shook. I told Che, who had Moro treat him as best he could. Anyway, Coco stopped getting worse, though he didn't get any better.

After the second week there were faintings, almost every day, from fatigue, malnutrition, and dehydration. And sometimes I had to be carried.

Che's asthma grew worse, too. After a week in there he had no real medicine for it. Bad as the jungle air was for all of us, it was worst for him. He could barely suck the air in through the rubber mask of humidity.

Half the entries for his journal for this time are about his lungs, and the lack of medicine:

I have been injecting myself several times a day in order to be able to walk at all.

And:

My chest is on fire. I feel as if the air is burning up inside me.

And:

Today I tried a 1:900 adrenalin solution prepared from collyrium.

And:

All the adrenalin solution is gone. I have been into the sedatives.

And:

Today I finished off most of the painkillers, keeping only a small quantity, in case of wounded.

And:

The last of the sedatives are gone. I have been injecting myself with novocaine. There will be nothing left for tooth extractions. And it didn't work worth a damn.

And:

To my shame, I used more of the painkillers; there will be very little for the wounded.

And:

Julio and Benigno carried my knapsack today. Until this attack passes I am good for nothing.

etc.

Why were we there?

I heard the jungle chattering and roaring, even when it really wasn't making any sound at all. I just expected it would, and, as my hunger grew, my expectations made me dream those sounds. It was the fuzz in my head, that static on the radio that obscured more static, growing louder and louder.

The vines would twist around and within me, and live off me, and then I would die, and they would take root.

The ants that bit me were really protecting me. They would put me in one of their deep chambers, and bring me leaves to eat, so I would survive and they could continue to bite me.

The trees I saw were once colonies of ants, grown thick. They ate everything in their path. If you brushed against the ants they would become vines, vines made out of ropes of ants, sewn together by their own strong jaws, and strangle you.

The stories Inti told me (not stories, *facts*) all ran together like the jungle until they made no sense to me. The jungle was a sign—but of what? Of too many things; it didn't make sense, or it made too much, or one idea kept changing into another and then, before I could hold on to it, it crumbled away. The jungle was a giant toad. The jungle was *bureaucracy*.

Why were we there?

We straggled from one little settlement to another, several days' march between each, from nowhere to nowhere. We would never find Joaquin this way. We would never build a base among the peasantry. *We would never get enough to eat.*

During the second week, at a criticism–self-criticism session, *Eusebio expressed a doubt.* It was a little muttered thing—in a tangle of his usual whining about Ricardo making him carry more than his share, Marcos having insulted him, etc. But despite our fatigue and the fact that we were only half listening to him, we heard it: *we had begun too early.* Inti silenced him with a long slow speech about the victories we had won, about the guerrilla as catalyst, creating enormous instability in La Paz, etc. But *this* little doubt was *a sign* I *could* read. It meant that there were in all the men other reservations, growing as quickly as white filaments of mold, doubts forming inside their tongues. Inti might quiet them now, make them see the inevitable wisdom of what Che had done (but where in this waste *was* the wisdom?), yet like the growth of the jungle itself new doubts would spring up, stronger someday, breaking through the vines of discipline, demanding expression. I could see their thoughts in their hesitant steps. Julio stumbled over a crawling vine: that meant: *guerrilla warfare is too elitist.* Benigno and Pacho pushed each other: that meant: *guerrilla warfare is too adventurist.* Eusebio started to stumble, and grabbed at a piece of prickly vine. He held it in front of him, smeared with his own blood, fascinated: that meant: *guerrilla warfare should not have begun until we had prepared the ground more.*

Che hardly spoke. He listened to us at meetings, and in camp. And on days when his lungs would allow it, he smoked his pipe, and nodded at Inti's remarks. Usually he sat a little ways off from the rest of us, surrounded by his silence like a heavy blanket, like a circle of solid air—what I had felt around the crazy boy in the church, a lifetime before.

At the end of our second week in the jungle, physical fights broke out. Ricardo hit Eusebio, the stocky, whiny Bolivian with doubts. Ricardo had hit other Bolivians, like Pacho, before. *But this time Eusebio hit him back.* They were both too weak to do any damage. Inti hung across Eusebio's arm, and Moro—risking his own newly healed arm—threw himself across Ricardo's back. They hung on each other's bodies like vines, and then they all went tumbling to the ground, looking like some four-headed jungle monster. No one had the energy for *real* fighting. But this four-headed thing lying in the mud was another sign I could read.

When we started marching again I hit Ricardo across his shoulder with my cane, and he turned around. He looked savage, one lens of his eyeglass had shattered in the fight. Then he made out that it was me, and he smiled. I said a short prayer that he wouldn't, but he laughed.

"You asshole," I said. I was furious with him for fighting.

"I'm sorry, asshole," Ricardo said. He brushed mud and bugs off his uniform. "But I can't understand what you're saying. You sound like you have a very bad sore throat." Then he laughed some more.

Finally I made *the impossible suggestion.* I waited on the march until Che was behind the rest of us. He was shaking from the effort of breathing, and he looked like he couldn't even tear at the vines, only lean against them until his weight broke through the tangle. I stood aside, on the trail, watching him, and when he came past me, I held his arm to stop him. He hadn't seen me, and he jumped away, as if I were a snake. He tripped and fell into a plant with sharp leaves.

I helped him up. His body vibrated from the strain.

The others trudged forward, disappearing behind the green curtain, and we were soon completely alone. We stood under a plant with leaves five feet across, like a ceiling, in our own room of the jungle.

I was a snake. But I had to speak. *I suggested that we give up the struggle in Bolivia.*

Is that why he left me behind at Churo to die? Because of that?

I said that it wasn't too late to make our way out of the jungle, and to the northwest, into the mountains. We could march into Chile. There we could make contact with Cuba, and so find a route home.

Che stared at me, his eyes angry, his chest thrust forward.

I crushed ferns under my foot, delicate things, fidgeting like a boy embarrassed before a teacher.

Our retreat, I knew, would be a disaster, a blow to morale for every movement on the continent. In the world, maybe. I saw a news photo of our getting onto an airplane, a flight back to Cuba. CHE GUEVARA DEFEATED, FLEES WITH HIS BAND OF MEN BACK TO SAFETY! It was a picture that would *destroy* us, *destroy him,* a group of hollow-faced men, dressed in rags, covered in dirt, their arms, hands, faces, crisscrossed by nicks, cuts, scars. The men had difficulty struggling up the metal stairway to the plane. A black man, leaning on a cane, had to be supported by his comrades.

We had left the Congo, given it up as impossible. But this was different; the Congo for us was an anonymous venture, a training mission. Guevara was Che now, and all that the name meant: Objective conditions are ripe in Latin America. The guerrilla's blow will reveal this, will clarify the situation, will ring in the air and gather the masses. One two three many Vietnams to save Vietnam, to destroy Imperialism once and for all.

My flesh crawling with uninvited animal life, I reviewed this catechism as if it were written on Che's furious face. Che's name, Che's face, was a promise, a strategy, a faith. If we left Bolivia the faith would crumble, the name grow ordinary, the face dissolve. And he would be Ernesto again (and I would be Walter). I didn't want that. I didn't want to do that to him.

But I didn't want to die either.

Che stared at me savagely, like the curse he would never utter. His labored loud metallic clanking terrified me. I was afraid of what his anger might do to him, what I might have done to him by speaking. I *knew* how much more isolated I had just made him feel.

"Joaquin," he gasped, by way of cursing me.

He meant that we must rejoin Joaquin, that we must not abandon him.

He waved me ahead of him, and I walked forward, leaning on my staff, digging it into the mulch near a fallen tree trunk covered with ticks and chiggers. A thousand brown-and-black bugs, a battalion of them, charged from the rotting wood, like the log was giving birth to them, throwing them out into the world. Why? What great force cast them out? It made me think of firecrackers going off in Havana, sparkles of light poured from the center of the explosion, one circle following upon another. I stared. Where was the very heart of the wood where all the insects came from?

"Retreat, too, is a kind of battle," I said, afraid to turn around, to face him again.

He pushed me forward, hard. I fell, and stuck my hand on the log, to stop myself. My hand sank into it up to the wrist. It was an army ant bivouac, that was what the insects had been running from, the "great force" that cast them out. I could feel their pincers closing on my fingers, their stingers entering my palm, and it hurt terribly. But I didn't draw my hand out immediately. I wanted to punish myself for speaking to Che, for suggesting retreat, suggesting we abandon Joaquin. For betraying Che. Finally I took my hand out, and ants crawled all over it, and hung down from it. I shook them off, and pounded them dead.

In a few moments my hand was swollen with painful lumps.

JUNE 11

His first notes begin a few days after we entered the jungle. There were entries of miles marched, his difficulties breathing, medicines tried, and some distant, brief remarks about disputes in the group, problems maintaining morale, praise for Inti, the leader to come.

Then:

. . . that knife as it came down to cut the webbing between Calixto's first finger and his thumb, the tenderest part of his hand. As I watched the blade come down into the light from the lantern, I could feel in myself the mild but pervasive effects of the coca we had chewed together. And I knew then that Calixto watched his own body suffer from a long distance. Even the sharp blade slashing into his own flesh would occur for him as if it were all happening on a movie screen. The knife, the hand, the welling blood were all part of a distant drama. Even his pain would be only another actor, flat, clear, distant, almost a memory.

And we, too, are only spectacle to them. How can we make them enter a spectacle?

Those were the notes we saw him scribbling each time he called a rest period, while we wrote nothing ourselves. We were too tired. We were too confused. We would not know what we had seen, what we had done, until he told us *why* we had done it. The different parts of our sentences would have gone off in different directions, like ants that had lost the scent of the ants in front. (Once, the day Ricardo struck him, I saw Eusebio fill a few pages hurriedly, and I wondered what vicious things he was saying about that bastard. Now I have his diary and I know: *Dear God,* it says, dear God, please save my life, dear God please save my life, dear God please save my life, Dear God please Save my Life Dear God Please SAVE

MY LIFE dear God, over and over in a large shaky hand for pages and pages. Then nothing more.)

The next day Che wrote:

And yet they move, they move constantly—repeated actions, like obsessed things, without thought, without change. They work tilling their fields— chewing coca—pushing in seeds—chewing coca—harvesting potatoes—chewing coca—coca gives them strength, numbs the pain in their shoulders, places them above the dissolution of their bodies—spectators to their own lives, from an arctic distance.

They are filled with an icy energy, without heat, electric—and they follow the wires endlessly. These Indians aren't a fire that blazes across the field, consuming everything in its path, gathering to one enormous conflagration. They follow the thin copper bands of their lives as electricity does. They couldn't live outside those bands, and so they run the pattern already laid for them, the threads in a weaving whose design has long been known—till their hearts stop. And in this cold all the turns of their life, that maze, are clear to them, clear and infrangible. They even see the pointless death that awaits them and all the generations to follow. But they cannot imagine a way out of this maze—any more than an electric current could dream of leaving its wires. Everyone moves along this path, yet each of them is far away, as if watching, utterly still.

The coca makes their hearts pound like imprisoned things, and reminds them that beyond the unchangeable confinement of their poverty there is only another confinement, that life itself is a prison. This world of theirs, perhaps they can imagine it being shattered, like a construction made of ice, but it cannot be molded. Life is coca solid, coca pure, coca clear. The world is a Bible text from the mouth of God. Not one iota of it will ever change.

But this is no different from what we faced in Cuba. Why even pretend that the dried green leaves are an important obstacle—they are only a symbol for some darker thing that I cannot yet name. For we have brought the violent event that should have woken them from their chain-step somnambulance; yet they do not respond. I feel in them something deeper than sleep. (Or perhaps they dream while awake.) In any case, they watch. We remain a spectacle. They observe us, as Calixto eyed the knife, glinting in the soft lantern light, moving down towards his hand. Their life is a story that someone reads to them. You cannot change a story once it is already written. Or it is a play; and it would be rude to stop a play just because the actors pretend to be in pain;

or dying. (We will get up and walk again, the mad boy shouted. How could we shout back that we won't? They would hear it as only another line of dialogue.)

Then there are many more entries about his problems breathing, and the different substances he injected.

JUNE 14

His birthday. He would have been forty today. Then he would (he said) have to have given thought to leaving the guerrilla. If he had lived till now, maybe he would have agreed to our leaving, and we would still be alive.

(What a strange thing to have written. *I am alive.*)

I took the day off, in honor of his birthday, and started to walk down towards the ocean, through the field of tall grass. My thigh ached, as if the bullet had made a hollow space, a tunnel in my leg. When I got halfway down to the beach, the ocean glimmered invitingly in the distance, indifferent to my limp, asking me to dance back and forth with the waves. I began to sneeze. I told myself: *I* am not allergic to pollen! I even shouted aloud to the other specters who lie in ambush in this field. But saying it aloud didn't make any difference; the field still wavered in front of my watering eyes.

I knew what *that* meant—so I came back to this little house, and our board.

It is different (he wrote) *from what we faced in Cuba. Some darker force resists us here. It is as if, when we came to Cuba, the peasants were empty-handed. We came, and they looked down, and we had placed a powerful tool in their hands. Here they turn aside, they evade us, as if their hands were already full. Yet I cannot see what it is they have; it is present to them, but ghostly to me.*

They do not listen to our story, and certainly they refuse to take their place in it. Instead they make one of their stories out of us.

But their story is nonsense, evasions, the twists and turns taken by coward-ice! Perhaps cowardice, their deep soft cowardice, is all that we have fallen into —nothing darker or more mysterious than that! The magic rings, and cars, and thunderous farts, are all so much cowardice. The Indians put us above them, supernatural, so that they can retreat back into their burrows, and yet save their self-respect. How—they can say to themselves—could they dare to join us, or even to help us? For we have the magical protections—the ones that they have imagined for us—and they are just Bolivians, they are just . . . shit. So they are wise to watch us.

And we die.

1) *I cannot yet see a way to use their magic stories against their cowardice. To agree to magic powers—and invite them to share in them—would only eventually retard the Revolution's development. But in every speech I must stress my own physical weakness, the asthma, etc. Thus: Even the weakest of them can be terrible. (And so my childhood fantasy might be realized: my asthma given to me as a sign.)*

It was amazing to us then: each rest period, as we lay in our hammocks, or on our ground covers, our *tablecloths* where we were the food, we looked over and wondered, wondered what he was writing, wondered how he *could* write when we had to bend all our willpower just to suffering the jungle.

I see now that *he* was the static in my head. *He* was what didn't make sense. We had given all our soul stuff, our will, into his keeping, and he had wandered into that pointless place; that didn't make sense, and so our world didn't make sense. Since the first battle I had a special radio; I could tune in the thoughts of the men we captured. I didn't pick up Che's thoughts; he was the air the radio waves moved through. Now that air took my words and turned them into buzz. And behind that buzz there was only more buzz.

That static was the place he had told me about in his note to me here, a hundred years before, on our dinner table. That time was the thin band of white, the time between the frames on a motion-picture film, the time when he didn't know what to do, when his stomach was upset and the world a jumble. *But now it was our stomachs, too.*

Daily fights broke out among the men. Marcos hit Pacho again, with the handle of his machete, breaking his nose. (Pacho, hit so many times, was beginning to look like a prizefighter—a losing one.) One day Camba sang, and Eusebio screamed at him to shut up, and then began to weep.

Che meted out punishment as necessary, and restored discipline.

But his thoughts were elsewhere.

Should we call attention to their cowardice?
Is it cowardice?
Chaco's voice: "You want to say no to History, but your no is just another note in the chorus."
That no is the shadow, the darkness that resists us: They want to say no to History.
They must take our instruction, we must show them what I learned in Guatemala, when Chaco died, that all the time, behind their backs, history goes on, wears away at them, takes their children, corrodes their bodies with

the acids of work and malnutrition. History destroys their way of life, unravels the pattern of their weaving.

But we cannot shout at them to wake them into history, for they won't even hear us, won't shout back at us. They will live their refusal in their stupid dogged unending repeated unchanging suffering. They will live their no to History in the twisted stories they tell about themselves and us, the ones that make a spectacle of us; their myths and magic refuse not just our action but History itself. Their refusal is their constant work, the sacrifice of their own lives.

"The last shall be first, and the first last, and it will begin again. Each day has enough sin. World without end." And the Marxist, with his *Manifesto* beneath an Inca rock, said, "It all returns. The Messiah comes over and over again."

That is their dream, the dream of an over and over again, an end to history, to linear time, the dream of a circle of endless recurrence. Marxism is the dream that history itself has of its own ending, the Revolution, the expression of its always unsatisfied desire for rest, a fiery consummation. But that is not their dream. Theirs is Gandhi's dream, the dream of those who would refuse History, the dream of jumping over history and back to the past, to their way.

But their way is endless suffering!

And what was *our* way, those months, but endless suffering? Che, unable to suck up enough air to live on, sat and wrote those *philosophical theses* in his journal.—And by that time I could not have counted consecutively, without mistake, to a hundred! Yet Che wrote. Flies laid their eggs in scratches on Marcos's and Camba's legs. Maggots hatched out and burrowed under their skin. They screamed in agony as the maggots crawled inside them. We had to cut slashes in their arms and legs to burn the white things.

Meanwhile Che continued his line of thought, his new line:

Clearly the Indians despise us, despise what we represent to them. I am an ambitious man. I see now that they are horrified by that. I have a bloody hand that offers them change, progress—the things they have bent all of their imagination to refusing. Ambition which had no place in the Inca way. The Inca—that is the deepest shadow of their dark implacable resistance: the Inca way: recurrence, stability, without progress, without change. Everything in its place, changing only to begin again as before. The King over all, keystone to the arch. Ambition is a threat to them. They wish their life to be a continual recurrent task—the only thing settled once and for all is the rules of the game.

*"Final victories are the imaginings of violent men; apocalypse; fiery consumma-
tion. Gandhi's way must be the will's slow patient work. It requires serenity,
and that comes from finding one's place in the larger scheme." That was the
Inca way; and that is the darkness, the opposition to History that we confront
here. Even they hardly remember the meaning of their words. The fag-end of
Empire—they only had a garbled sentence from the center, the god who spoke
from afar, the Inca. The Conquest crumbled that world. And then the modern
world fell like an atomic bomb on the rubble that was left. Only the imperfect
memory of already broken fragments is left. They want to take their place in
an endless recurrent pattern. We must offer to restore, to remake that pattern.
We cannot drag them into the modern world, but we can lead them into it,
if we offer it in the image of their desire.*

*They refuse the Revolution as the progressive consummation of History,
the History that jolts and jars and finally destroys them now. We must offer
them the Revolution not as an end to work, not as rest, but as shared work
that will never end, shared continual suffering. Now they are the pointless
sacrifice, wasted by others, by the imperialists, in the name of a progress that
never comes and that they do not desire. They want, and we must offer them,
the chance to sacrifice themselves not once and for all, but continually.*

Around this time, our third week in the jungle, Che began to speak with
Camba alone. They walked together, or sat to one side in camp, talking in low
voices. Che listened intently, his chest thrust forward, his head bent towards
our loony bird's chirping. Camba, I saw, read to Che from his "special notebook," the one I'd asked about, the one where he recorded "maps"—the
Indians' "secret paths" out of the forest. Those were the paths Che now
wanted to follow, or bend into his new directions. They continued talking until
dusk, when the bats came out of the trees, and Camba heard the disgusting
whirring sound of their wings. Bats horrified Camba. He sat frozen with terror,
unable to talk.

*Socialism, and even industrialization, as the continual sacrifice of ourselves,
as a way to honor the ancestors whose land this is, by our shared labor.*

*Their past refuses us if we seem like a continuation of the awful present
that wears away at them now, that wastes them meaninglessly. Their dream
is recurrence. So we must join that past to the future we offer them, leaping
over the present. The Inca way has resisted us as it did the conquistadors.
Gandhi was right! They do not want History, Western civilization. It was all*

*contained in my first dream, the notebook I kept with me, The Discovery of
Latin America.*

JUNE 15

Almost every day on the march through—or was it around?—the jungle,
Camba sang to us. The melody wandered about unsteadily, as we did. Sometimes Camba stopped in the middle of an old verse and simply started a new
one. And sometimes he began a sentence and then sang nonsense syllables, as
if he'd suddenly become a baby again. Or he would bawl out some imperious
need.

So we couldn't sing along. But we generally enjoyed the performance.

The song was about a garden full of vegetables, happy with their vegetable
existence, and the Chili Pepper, who wanted them to revolt against the gardener. I have put the verses together as best as I can remember them:

> The Chili Pepper sang:
>
> You will all go into his pot
> You will be part of his stew
> You think you are rooted forever,
> comrade vegetables,
> But you're not! You're not!
>
> The Vegetable Chorus sang:
>
> What pot? What stew?
> Someone's crazy here—
> And we think it's you!
>
> The Celery sang:
>
> Mr. Chili, look at me,
> And admit the fabulous beauty you see:
> I'm so green, so leafy, so tall
> I could never bend, I could never fall.
> Drinking up rain, putting out leaves,
> Sending down roots, choking out weeds,
> Putting out leaves, making up seeds,
> I'm far too clever to fall
> For your story,

I'm far too clever to fall
Into his stew!

The Chili sings:

Says you!
Mr. Celery. Says you!

The Carrot responds:

I'm rich, I'm rich,
I own all the dirt
All the dirt all around
I own the whole garden
I'm deep underground
With leaves up above
I'm rich I'm rich
The sun sends me its love
I own all the sunlight
I own all the rain
Your talk of rebellion
Just gives me a pain!

The Chili sings:

Stupid petit-bourgeois carrot
It's someone else's lessons you parrot!
The gardener has a special kind of garrote
For skinning un-class-conscious carrots.

For the Red Pepper knew better, knew better,
The Chili Pepper knew better, and he sang:

Oh, you think you're rooted forever
But you're not, you're not
Oh, you will be part of his stew, Oh,
You will go into his pot!

The Vegetable Chorus sang:

What pot? What stew?
Someone's crazy here—
And we think it's you!

But the Chili Pepper sang:

Friend Vegetables, he sang,
Comrade Vegetables, pay heed

("I'm hungry!" Camba suddenly shouted, interrupting his own song.

No one said anything for a while, as we tore at the vines. After about five minutes Ricardo spoke, "So are we all, asshole, so are we all." And that closed the complaining. Camba, as the Pepper, sang again.)

Comrade Vegetables pay heed!
I have been sent to you
In your hour of need!
Study History Comrade Vegetables!
We are not free, Comrade Vegetables!
We are owned, bought and sold,
We must leave this garden
I implore you—Be bold!
We are owned by another, this garden he owns
He cleared it of weeds, he cleared it of stones
He has stock for a stew and meaty soup bones
Now he wants *us*—he won't leave us alone
So it's into the pot when he thinks we're full grown,
When we're tasty and juicy and all he desires,
It's into the pot, and onto the fire!

("I have a feeling," Coco whispered, "that this has an unhappy ending."

"Bolivian stories," Inti said, echoing a thought I had once shared with him.)

Think of our fathers, think of our mothers!
Where are they dear comrades?
Nig glub fig pick poo nig nig nig

("Camba couldn't think of a rhyme," Ricardo said, flaunting his critical abilities. "The asshole.")

I hate this vegetable existence, don't you?
I want to be free, touch the sky, move around
I can't stand the feeling that I'm half buried in ground

—But you are, said the Carrot,
And what's wrong with that?

I want to roam widely, see the world, hear its sounds
I don't want to flavor his stew—
Do you?

—Oh, don't be silly, said the Celery
No one can touch me
I'm leafy and green
I'm lovely and tall
It's easy to see
God loves me best of all!

—You're crazy, Mr. Chili, said the Carrot.
The garden's the world,
There's nowhere to go
There's nothing to do
There's nothing to see
And nothing called "stew."

The Vegetable Chorus sang:

Wise up, Mr. Chili,
We're not crazy like you
It's ordained
It is written
We're telling the truth
There's no pot in our future
And nothing called stew
And if there was
Well, just what could *we* do?
We're just Vegetables!

—I'm so pretty (sang the Tomato), I'm red and plump
And juicy, too

—You'll be delicious, said the Chili
In a stew, in a stew.
Oh please join me Comrade Vegetables (begged the Pepper that leper)
Or we'll all go into the pot
Where it's hot

We'll all go into the stew
Even you,
Little Tomato!

—I'm wise (sang the Potato)
I'm deep and profound
I've leaves up above,
While I live underground
I'm old and I'm dirty
But my brain is still sound.
You're a hothead Mr. Pepper,
We old ones know better
The garden doesn't need a revolution
The Vegetable World changes
By slow evolution!

—You've a hundred eyes, said the Pepper,
But you don't see a thing!

—I'm too pretty, said the Tomato,
I'm round and I'm firm, and I'm so full of juice
That's acid and witty;
I've too much life to cut loose!

The Potato sang:

I know of the sun, and I know of the earth
I'll be here forever, for a thousand rebirths
I just want to grow, send out runners and roots
I've no need for a rifle, for gun grease and boots!

The Celery sang:

No salad, no stew, no dinner, no soup!
I'm too singular, veined, not part of a group!
I'm too good for a movement,
My head in the air, naturally quite aloof!

—You're so hotheaded! they all chorused,
Saying good-bye.
You're a fool or a Communist,
And you surely will die
Squashed like a nick pook blg foop nig nig nig
Leave us alone! We're happy like this!

And if we're not, well, we're not,
It's our lot
And so what?
This is the way it was long meant to be
Vegetables are for gardens, they're not meant to be free
(Whatever that is!)
We hate you, Chili Pepper
Go die, Chili Pepper
Get squashed, Chili Pepper
Drop dead, Chili Pepper!
But most of all, Chili Pepper
Shut up and leave us alone!

We'd all be killed if we pulled up our roots!
We can't leave now, we've too many shoots
And who ever heard of a tomato in boots!
Leave us alone Chili Pepper!
Shut up Chili Pepper!
You're crazy!

So the Chili Pepper,
That leper,
Went off all alone
He strapped on his knapsack,
And picked up his gun
His fight was a long one
With unquiet nights
And days on the run
The Chili Pepper went off all alone,
The Chili Pepper left home all alone

Good luck Mr. Chili!

Camba keened the farewell, as if he hadn't much hope for the rebellious ambitious vegetable, the poor sad lonely doomed little red pepper! It would have brought tears to the stoniest heart—if our bodies had had the moisture to spare for tears.

As a joke one day Marcos said, "There's something wrong with your political line, Camba. If the vegetables are the workers, then *they* clear the ground, not the bourgeois gardener who owns the land. Inti better have a talk with you and straighten you out."

Camba stared at Marcos, bewildered. He didn't sing for several days, and we all missed his little ditty. To the extent that we could hold on to its silly world through our weakness and fog, it had refreshed us, it let us imagine ourselves in a cartoon, or at least in a nursery, somewhere far away, where such songs might occur, and children might listen. So I asked Marcos to apologize to Camba, and Camba began again one day, in the middle of a line, like an engine starting up, "Nig bloo bloo plig nig, the Celery sang: . . ."

The song was called "United Vegetables vs. United Fruit."

JUNE 16

The Inca versus the Conquistador, the Inca against the Imperialist, the Inca versus History. The Inca is the empire without history, static, settled, immutable. And within that stillness life was filled with meaning, their work joined them each to each and to the godhead. (Of course they had a history of conquests—but one within a fundamentally unchanging structure. So we, too, must give them our new territories—of industry, of the tractor and the factory —in an image that rings with the truth of their past.) Our mistake has been to offer them new words, what is called progress, the ability to enter history, the very acid they have bent their will to neutralizing.

Instead: a rebellion against history. Against imperialism. One that will end history, though not for a long-promised rest or even "prosperity" but for suffering. Not an immediate or even a progressive end to suffering, but the re-establishment of a meaning for their continual suffering, a meaning that they can find now only in broken fragments. They long for a messiah who comes not once but over and over at every moment, the pattern of recurrence that they dream of in their stories, that they wish to make of us, that they have instructed us in. They will sacrifice in a battle against the present, for a future that they can think will be the past made perpetual, that will be a continual meaningful suffering. The God of Liberation is a God of violence. But he must also be a God of sufferers.

That shared suffering is the vein of blood that ran like a road through the villages, forming the body of one giant Man. Their work, their suffering, made them part of that One Man, that God who was imaged in the Inca. It was not release from work, but shared continual work, not rest, but continual sacrifice of the self that joined one with the community, that makes the community, that makes it One Man. So it is, too, with Communism.

She spoke of the return of the just king. The King who will return is the form of the Inca remade by us, the king of the return. The God who was imaged in the Inca will be the One Man we offer them, the Internationale. Lenin, Stalin, Mao, Fidel, and . . . Inti perhaps. Or one of their own, unknown yet.

We moved north, as a feint (and to get medicines for Che), and then back south, to search for Joaquin again.

Bolivia, August 1967

AUGUST

From Coco's Journal

8/14/67: The time in the jungle was hard for me—for all of us. The chloroquine Moro gave me helped, but the jungle still made my tissues so watery that I could hardly stand. And the heat turned the watery flesh to steam; my face melted away; now I'm so thin that I look as dour and lean as Inti. The Revolution has made us into brothers!

But the jungle was hardest on Che. At night, in our hammocks, we heard his lungs strain and wheeze like a piece of creaky overburdened machinery. They tried to wring the water out of the air, as if it were a moist rag, to find something for Che to breathe. *But Che made the necessary sacrifice:* going into the jungle and staying there, despite the pain it caused him, until we had confused the army, thrown them off our trail.

And it worked! It was like the ground had swallowed us up. Today we surprised the soldiers completely, appearing out of nowhere, and taking the town of Samiapata.

The town is on a branch road, a mile south of the highway. We drove up slowly, in the bus we had seized this morning back near the sawmill. (We had left the real passengers under guard with Che and the center at our command post there.)

At the intersection there was a police booth for two or three men, and a gray wooden refreshment stand with a table in front, and a fading Coca-Cola sign leaning against its legs. (I looked forward to having a Coke.) The police waved us to a stop at the intersection. I saw three or four soldiers lounging by the stand, and threw the metal flange on my pistol nervously. The piece of metal felt comforting, as if my own blood went through it; the pistol has become a wonderful part of my body.

We got off the bus without incident, hiding our weapons under the jackets we'd taken from the passengers, and we moved to the outside of the officials, pushing them to the middle according to Ricardo's plan, like beaters in a hunt. One soldier gave me the evil eye when I bumped him with my elbow, and called me a clumsy son of a bitch.

Ricardo, at the center of the circle, raised his arm, and we pulled out our weapons, pointing them inward at the crowd. The bald-headed soldier who had cursed me said, "I'm sorry," in a choked voice.

"That's all right," I said, and I pushed my gun barrel hard into the very small of the bald man's back so it would hurt him.

We had surrounded them! The police and soldiers were stunned. There were no more guerrillas, the radio said, and if there were, they were far from Samiapata. But then, suddenly, there we were! The Revolution had burrowed underground, and emerged like an old mole, covered with rotting leaves and dirt, blinking, its big teeth bared, outside their wooden refreshment stand.

Pacho and Aniceto stood guard over the prisoners, and the rest of us rode into town on the bus. I was disappointed that there hadn't been any Coca-Cola. We dropped Chino off at the Infant of Prague Pharmacy, a white building with a statue of the Holy Infant on a little piece of mosaic sidewalk in front. Samiapata is the largest town we have seen in four months—a dozen paved streets, sidewalks, even a movie theater.

The army was bivouacked in a long adobe building that had once been the town school. One of our prisoners from the highway, the second lieutenant with the bald head—and a bad head-cold that made his tongue thick—identified himself before the door of the school, and ordered their surrender. He started to stutter, probably from fear, but I thought it might be a trick, and put my pistol to his temple. He bit his tongue right through then, and a thin thread of blood trickled down his lip, a vivid red. I laughed to see how scared he was, and that made it worse for him, and he started to choke on his own spit!

They let us in. Julio gathered up their arms, munitions, clothing, and blankets and loaded them into the bus. I made the officers undress. Their underwear was so clean and white that I couldn't take my eyes off it. Probably they thought I was queer!

A private who was just coming to from his last-night's binge lay on the floor, pretending to sleep. But I saw him put a hand out and move it towards a pistol near his pillow, so I shot him in the head. His legs twitched under his brown army blanket, like a child who doesn't want to go to sleep. (I had hated to take my afternoon nap, and used to beat my legs up and down like that, to annoy our governess. It made me laugh again to see him do that. I thought the maid would have liked to put me to sleep in just that way, with a bullet through my forehead.) The bald lieutenant screamed, "He was only looking for his glasses! You've murdered him!" But I think he was lying.

I telephoned the sawmill, and told the center that the town was now secure.

Julio went through the street gathering up the townspeople for the march back to the police booth. They were afraid of us, and very reluctant to come. But they were afraid not to. As we went I looked into some of the houses, adobe rooms, sometimes with a charcoal stove to cook on, and I wondered what it would be like to live in this town, to trade with the mestizo peasants and Indians, to marry some young girl who would become one of these fat old women. But I can never have a life like that, any more than I can have the life I was raised for, and not only because my people wouldn't have me back, but because I've changed. I can see it in the fear of the people we shepherded to the police booth, fear that *I* caused. Sometimes I feel split in two, and when one half of me sees the things the other half does he is bewildered, and I am bewildered. Nothing in my life prepared me to be a fighter—a murderer, the lieutenant said—but I think that can happen to anyone, for there are times when the whole world leaves its jobs on farms and in banks and goes off to war. What bewilders me is the joy I feel sometimes, the surge of agreeable power that overcomes me. I was *right* to lift and fire my pistol into that boy's forehead. It felt good to see his legs kick up and down, the last convulsive involuntary motion that he will make on this earth—*and I made him do it.* And when the lieutenant screamed in terrified disapproval of the man he saw before him, I was deeply pleased.

Knowing that about myself where can I go live?

It was noon by now and very hot in the streets. The buildings wavered, for I have trouble focusing my eyes when I get hot. I put my hand on Julio's arm, so he might lead me back down the little branch road to the main junction.

Soon Che came, with some of the center guard. He rode the mule that Benigno had found for him yesterday. Che can hardly walk, because of the asthma, but the medicines Chino was getting would soon remedy that. Our leader would be whole again.

Che had Inti speak first. Inti stood on the refreshment-stand table, and he talked with a lot of feeling about the international situation, but he looked unsteady up there, and I found it hard to concentrate. I wasn't sure if he was off balance, or if it was my eyes—from the fever or the drugs—and that worried me so much I couldn't concentrate on what my brother was saying.

Bolivians must join other oppressed people of the world in their rising against the United States. (I wished they had had Coca-Cola. Our governess used to give me Coca-Cola when I was sick, and I suppose I still think of it as a cure-all, even for malaria.) Our blow now, Inti said, could be decisive in defeating Imperialism and gaining our liberation.

More than a hundred people stood on the asphalt in the hot sun, and the light made parts of their bodies look to me as if they were under water. When Inti spoke they stared at the road, like kids in a classroom who didn't want to be called on.

Che spoke after Inti, still sitting on his mule. He had trouble forming his words, and sometimes wheezed for a minute at a time between his sentences. I was sure his body was shaking this time, and not my eyes.

He spoke of the miners' massacre. Bolivian soldiers had pulled the triggers. But they worked for the United States. The United States was like a ghost, a specter, living off of our labor. It sucked the blood of Bolivians, using our own soldiers like syringes. And it turned our blood into gold coins, like a magician.

Barrientos and the other generals worked for the United States. The generals were weak-willed slaves who weren't fit to lead. The Bolivian people themselves must rule. And the revolutionary struggle would form the Bolivian people into a nation of heroes, men of strong will, fit to govern themselves.

They could see, Che said, that he himself was not a physically strong man. They could hear the trouble he had speaking, breathing, they could see that he could not even stand. And as a child he had been even weaker. Other children had mocked him, bullied him, tried to make him do their bidding, just as the United States bullies Bolivia. But the people of Samiapata could see, too, that even a physically weak man could rebel, and that if he did, if he fought for the nation, then he gained in power. Now Che was no longer afraid. Now he was a man who caused fear in others.

Ricardo pushed the lieutenant, the sick stutterer, towards me, and I pushed him back with one hand, like a ball. I heard a sharp sudden intake of breath in the crowd when they saw this, as if they thought we might kill him for our sport. But I could tell, too, that they liked what we were doing. I thought again of the sudden upsurge of giddy pleasure I had felt when we took our guns out and surrounded the police. *We were weak, but we caused fear in others.*

Bolivia, too, Che said, could become a nation of heroes, a nation without fear, an independent nation that caused fear in others. A nation was the body of one Giant Man. That Man was brought to life by our acts of sacrifice. When one of us suffered for the Revolution—and we were all ready even to die if that were necessary—it filled the veins of that Giant Man with life. When all of the people of Bolivia joined together in the many acts of war and sacrifice that were necessary for liberation, then the Man who was Bolivia would awaken.

Awake again, he added.

The battle was never-ending, the battle was always our constant work, now and in the future, providing through our repeated acts of sacrifice the blood that flowed in the body of the Giant. As long as we worked for each other, building socialism, the Giant lived, and watched over us, and protected us.

Each Bolivian had a place in the life of the nation, in the body of that Giant Man.

"They can live," Ricardo said to me, "right up its asshole." Then he realized he was talking to one of the "they," and added, "Most of them."

But I was trying to understand what Che was saying so I ignored him.

Each Bolivian had a place in the body of that One Man. And when the Giant awoke again and walked, we would have achieved our liberation, and we would be worthy to be part of his immortal life.

The townspeople nodded along with Che. When he paused to take breath —or try to take breath—they stared at him, waited avidly for his next revelation. I saw them feel with Che in his difficulty, saw their belief in him in the curve of their bodies towards his offering. Maybe they realized that what he said must be true, for he suffered so much pain to tell it to them.

Anyway, they were fascinated by Che's speech in a way they hadn't been by my brother's.

On the way out of town I marched with Jorge, behind the bus filled with our wonderful new supplies. I asked Jorge about Che's ideas, for Jorge is the smartest and the best-educated of us.

I said that I thought Che had described the community we had discovered in battle, that would be built by all of us in the fight against Imperialism.

Jorge looked at me as if I were mad, shaking his head from side to side like a panicked animal. "Ghosts!" he said, sounding angry with me, like a spoiled child. "Giants!" he whimpered. "What kind of asshole are you?" I put my arm around him to comfort him as we walked. But he went on whimpering, and then sobbing. I wanted to hit him to make him stop.

From My Journal

8/15/67: A very bad day. When we reassembled by the sawmill Che went through the cardboard box of medicine, looking for his asthma medication. He went through the box twice, saying nothing. His hand formed a claw—for he suffers now from arthritis—as he pawed over the vials, packages, little metal tubes, plastic containers. Squatting on the ground he looked a desperate thing, tearing at meatless bones. *Why would he let us see him like this?* I have never before known him to lose control in front of the men. The noise of the saw grew in my ears, between my ears, terrifying me. I couldn't take my eyes off Che's maddened face as he discarded the medicines, throwing them into the dirt, and then picked them up and dropped them into the box, only to throw them aside again one by one. El Chino had gotten the painkillers we need for the wounds to come, but nothing for Che's asthma. And medicine for Che was the reason we had come so far, risked so much, declared our presence in this zone, near a main highway. Soon the air will rain troops down on us.

We left the highway and moved back into a region of thick growth, the upper edge of the damned jungle where he had us wander for a month. We are moving southeast, back to some of our old haunts. Che thinks Joaquin may have picked up our trail there.

Jorge continues to cry, little sobs like bird sounds. He turns his face away whenever I look at him.

From Guevara's Journal

8/18/67: Without our knowing it a company of soldiers came upon us from their side of the Florida River. We are just fortunate that they are so badly led, for instead of waiting until morning, when they could have launched a devastating attack, they began firing immediately.

There was only a crescent moon; we could hardly make them out among the thick growth on the other side. We withdrew in the darkness, away from the bank, back into the forest, and the bullets scattered about as we went, covering a wide area. From the firing we could tell that there were many soldiers, but the forces were shadows to each other, and we both shot without direction.

Eleven knapsacks were left behind in camp, medicine, binoculars, my copy of Debray's book with the notes I use in our teaching sessions, and the tape recorder. Aniceto was shot in the chest, Raul in the neck, both fatally. We dragged them through the forest. Pacho was wounded in the leg. Ponco counted three thick shadows by the riverbank, army casualties to our meager returning fire.

I marched the men along the trail we had left, despite the risk. When the sun came up Jorge was missing, having lost his way in our retreat. He will certainly catch up with us.

At first light we buried Aniceto and Raul, both good men and old comrades. Surprised in camp—the sentries were criminal in their negligence. I will investigate to find out which are responsible and see that they are suitably punished.

8/19/67: Julio continues to display amazing effectiveness as a forager—though I am not sure he always deals fairly with the peasants. He has found me a mare to ride. (Without the horse I would have to be carried.) The mare is a docile animal, of a pleasant gray color. I think we will be good companions. Of course I named her Rosinante.

No sign of Jorge. It will soon be clear to him that we withdrew through the forest. Unless he was wounded he should join us by nightfall.

Tomorrow I will make my decision on whether to send a group back to the Nancahuazu to get medicine from the supply caves. The risks are great, to the men I send and to the rest of us if they are lost, but as it is I cannot long continue.

From My Journal

8/19/67: Che is wrong—if I didn't know him better I would say he was deceiving himself. Jorge wasn't wounded, he didn't lose his way, and he won't be catching up with us. I myself saw him scamper down the riverbank when the firing began. And Inti saw it, too, though he hasn't said anything either, for fear of demoralizing the men. It's a bad sign when a man as dedicated and ideologically formed as Jorge deserts.

8/20/67: Rosinante the mare grew recalcitrant today and wouldn't move despite Che's sweet entreaties and stern reminders of the necessity of sacrifice. Che brought his whip down across the mare's eye, opening a gash. Blood dripped down on the lid.

Nothing was said, though everyone in the center group saw. I took Camba aside before he could speak.

8/21/67: Another unhappy day. Che has sent three men—Julio, Antonio, and Arturo—back to the Nancahuazu camp to get medicine. His plan is to move east to Morroco, and then double back to rendezvous with them at Ispaca's house.

The risk is enormous, and all the men feel it. These are all good men (he could not send others, for they would certainly desert), and their loss would be a severe blow, one we would not likely recover from. —Yet Che must have medicine, we can all see that. His body trembles as he stands.

So we walk a knife's edge.

From Guevara's Journal

8/21/67: Our move into Samiapata has brought its own trail of unfortunate consequences. The government has taken new measures: U.S. advisers are now spoker of openly on the Bolivian radio. Martial law has been declared throughout the country. At another time this would be good news, rushing us towards an inevitable crisis. But now we do not have enough men to put in the field, and will not for the foreseeable future. The balance of forces is in their favor.

Not a peep from Monje or the Communists.

From My Journal

8/22/67: On the way to Florida. Che brought everyone together tonight for a talk. Pacho, he said, is recovering well from his wound. But the men are familiar with the problems we face: lack of contact with the city network and the miners' groups, lack of recruits from the peasantry. And Che himself is very ill; he is—he said—"no more than a human carcass." And the episode of the mare proves that at some moments he has lost control. That, he promised, "would be modified." But our situation is a difficult one. The problems must weigh squarely on all of us, and whoever does not feel capable of sustaining them should say so now.

No one spoke.

"This is a moment," our leader said, "when great decisions are made. Guerrilla war gives us the opportunity to become revolutionaries, the highest level of the human species. And it allows us to graduate as men."

I had a thought then—that I knew what the diploma looked like. Rolando,

Aniceto, Raul, Tuma, El Rubio—all recent graduates. I looked up at the forest ceiling, thick and green.

"Those who cannot reach either of those two stages should say so now, and they will be permitted to leave the struggle."

No! I thought, even his craving for purity wouldn't allow that! No one must leave—the risk was too great for the rest of us. I was sure he must be lying, and that possibility—a sea change in him if true—was itself unsettling.

The sun was setting, filling in the blanks between the leaves with darkness. Che dragged his heel in the dirt. It was hard for him to press down with enough force to make a mark; his leg shook like a piece of paper.

The men knew what this line meant. Inti crossed over to Che first, and then one by one the others crossed over, myself included, each saying that he wished to continue, country or death.

On the other side of the line with Che, in the promised land of continual sacrifice, Eusebio said that he would go on, but that Moro hadn't been carrying his own knapsack. Moro had put his knapsack on the mule that was meant to carry firewood. This wasn't fair, Eusebio thought, since Moro's arm had long since healed.

"You're a stinking little liar," Moro said—and most of us *are* little in comparison with Moro. "Or worse. Maybe it's another hallucination, like the ones you had in the jungle." Moro made tiny swimming motions with his hands, the kind Eusebio had made in his sleep a few weeks ago, tearing away at the vines in his dreams.

"You shouldn't talk that way to a comrade," Benigno instructed Moro. He has a thin delicate voice, like his hands. "And you do slack off in work sometimes. I've seen you. Maybe you think you're too good for work now that you're a doctor." Benigno said there were other slackers, too. Pacho, for one, hadn't carried his fair share, even before he was wounded.

My stomach felt sour. A stink rose from the bodies of the other men. Something rotting.

Pacho spat. His spittle landed right on the line Che had, with such difficulty, drawn for our edification. "You're a liar, Benigno. Maybe you're the one seeing things."

Che looked savage in the half-light. The shadows covered his face, like a ghost beard that grew in between his real beard. "Enough!" he said. His voice was a low harsh sound—like mine. Then he "modified" and regained control of himself.

"There are two things being debated here," he said. His voice was slow, his anger plain to all of us in the precision with which he marked each word.

The men flinched from him. "Two things of very different categories. One is whether we have the will to continue the struggle. The other is a matter of little grudges, internal problems of the guerrilla. This kind of petty dispute wrests greatness from what should be a major decision."

I smiled, just raising my lips, not showing my teeth, as he does sometimes, as his father did before him. He was saying, I thought, that we didn't have enough sense of history, for history requires ceremonies to mark—or make—its crucial junctures. *This* ceremony wasn't working out. We were supposed to wed our fates, and it didn't seem like we had formed a true marriage. We were already bickering.

Camba, who can always be counted on to make matters worse, suggested again that we mingle blood.

Che's face was dark, but I could swear that he stroked his lip as if he were considering the loony's suggestion. "No," he said, finally. But we would slaughter the mare, Rosinante, for meat.

Moro, doctor and butcher, led the mare away from us, into another part of the forest. When the horse screamed, everyone looked at Che, and went on staring at him as the terrible high whinnies became weaker and weaker. This was a real sacrifice for Che, since now he will have to walk—and he can barely stand up.

We had a low fire and cooked the meat, some for now, the rest to be taken on the march. Che dished out tonight's portion personally.

But it was just horsemeat, I thought.

And I didn't see anyone writing a poem.

8/22/67: Che's asthma worsens. Whatever else we are doing on the march, gathering wood, talking together, we listen for the sound of his breathing. He has turned us into his parents!

8/23/67: The radio announced a combat near Monteagudo. One dead, they say, Antonio Fernandez of Joaquin's group, whom we called God's Bread because he was of such sweet good temperament. (When you die you get your real name back.)

And a report, too, of a guerrilla deserter captured by the army. A vigilant patrol came upon a man bathing in a stream, who claimed to be a peddler traveling to local religious festivals to sell his goods. The army patrol interrogated the bather from the banks of the Florida River and were about to go on, satisfied with his answers, when the man in the river raised his arm to brush away an insect, showing his forearm and the back of his right hand. His extremities were covered with deep scratches, and the observant major knew that the marks meant that the man had had to tear his way through thick brush with his bare hands. These marks are characteristic of the arms of the foreign bandits. When the deserter then tried to run away from arrest he was wounded.

As we listened to the radio several of the men looked at the backs of their hands, as if maybe they, too, had been thinking about leaving. But the signs of their commitment were already scratched into their bodies. (Lenin was wrong. If you want to know what a man is thinking, don't listen to his words when you draw a line in the dirt. Watch his hands as he listens to the radio and dreams of deserting his comrades.)

From Guevara's Journal

8/24/67: More news of dead from Joaquin's group. But this time no names were given so it may be a lie. I am like an amputee who continues to feel pain in his missing limb.

Jorge is lost, captured by the army. It is a dangerous loss, for Jorge knows the names of many of our city contacts. The men all thought of this. But I pointed out that Jorge was of strong ideological conviction. He will not cooperate with the army, and will certainly be killed (this last thought, particularly, seemed to cheer them up).

8/25/67: The radio gave a report about the taking of our supply caves, with details so precise that it was impossible to doubt the truth—they described the location, the construction of the grating, and the contents. How could they have found them? Someone must have talked. But who? Jorge? One of the men sent to camp? Julio? Arturo? Whoever it is must be punished.

From My Journal

8/25/67: Now Che is doomed, sentenced to suffer his asthma for an indefinite time—for another foray into one of the larger towns is out of the question after our move on Samiapata; they are all closely guarded, surrounded by the army. Che said, without thinking, "It is the hardest blow they have given us."

I thought of our dead comrades. And others, too, had this vision. "Rolando," Ricardo said to me. "Tuma. Aniceto. Raul. Those were hard blows."

But we were being sentimental. Che's survival, his wholeness, matters more than any of our lives. He is the crucial one, for we have given our soul stuff into his keeping. He is our head. He must have medicine.

From Guevara's Journal

8/26/67: Two deserters from Joaquin's group, and Jorge, were exhibited to the press. They all said that Debray had been an active combatant, killing many honest and courageous Bolivian soldiers. The three of them were heartily sorry for what they had done, misled by foreigners. The guerrilla leaders had lied to them, promising a camp with air defenses, good food, and a chance to rob the countryside. Instead they had faced starvation, and had been bullied by Cubans. The guerrillas would not keep any of their promises, for they were no more than common bandits.

Jorge's voice in this sour chorus of betrayal was a blow. My good name has no magic at this distance, against their torments. And what other cooperation might he have offered them already?

Debray showed great nobility, saying nothing.

From Coco's Journal

8/26/67: Camba came up to my brother on the march today, with a message that he wanted Inti to give to Che. He said that his physical condition didn't allow him to keep on going.

"Pustules," he said, "like red flowers. You can't see them, but they're there. It's a kind of leprosy."

Inti didn't ask if Camba was embarrassed to show his legs, or had invisible pustules. "Why don't you speak to Che yourself?"

"He will never let me go," Camba said, sounding very sad. "He likes my singing."

Not knowing what to say, Inti laughed. And suddenly Camba laughed, too, a few seconds after my brother, like someone doing an imitation.

"There's no future in this business anyway," Camba said. He sounded like a young employee, anxious to find a company that had room for advancement.

I told the story to Ponco. He laughed—his merriment sounds so sad and dry. He said he could see Camba's point. Che has been talking a lot to Camba, listening intently to our loony bird, learning the paths through the forest. (I didn't understand what Ponco meant.) Maybe, Ponco said, Camba can teach Che how to sing his verses on vegetables. (Ponco said that Che is tone-deaf!)

Later Inti heard Camba speak with Che.
Che was furious. He accused Camba of cowardice.
Camba whimpered like a struck dog. "I don't have a stick," he said, like

a disappointed child, *"a big stick."* (Inti said Camba might have said "big prick.") Then Camba wailed, saying over and over that he didn't want to die.

Che was disgusted. He made Camba walk ahead of the others with him and Inti, and then, when the others couldn't hear, he promised to let Camba go soon—but not immediately, for Camba knows our route to Joaquin, and our possible rendezvous at Ispaca's house.

Camba laughed. "There is no route to Joaquin," he said. "I've seen the maps. He's not on them anymore."

Inti wanted to strangle Camba when he heard him talk like that.

But Che spoke soothingly. When we reached Joaquin, he said, Camba could go. It would be better for everyone if he did go.

Che made Inti promise not to tell anyone of his promise to release Camba.

From My Journal

8/26/67: Coco told me of Che's conversation with Camba. Soon everyone will know. And this will put ideas in their heads. (Does he really intend to let Camba go? Impossible!)

The loss of the caves, the imperiled city network—for Jorge knew many of our contacts—the losses, real or fictional, to Joaquin's group, all have put morale at a dangerously low point. We must be on guard against deserters. (I think Pacho and Eusebio are likely candidates.)

From Guevara's Journal

8/27/67: Now Eusebio! "I won't leave now," he said. "You can trust me, Che. That would be cowardice. But this goes on forever. There's not enough food. My feet are all cut up. I want you to say that I can go in six months or a year, depending on our situation."

What cowardice! But I promised him what he wished.

My word didn't satisfy him. "Florida," he said. "Abrapa. Morroco. The peasants hate us. We haven't involved the masses. The guerrilla struggle has no mass base. We should try to get away."

"I will not tolerate such talk."

"My feet are in terrible shape," he said again, to distract my anger. "How much more must we walk today? Why won't Moro help me? I worry about my family. The deserters will have given our names. What will they do to our families? . . ."

He went on in this disconnected way. I walked ahead of him.

From My Journal

8/26/67: Abrapa. The board on its trestles was still there, but covered now with empty plates, a few rinds of meat, pieces of broken crockery, bottles on their sides. The army arrived here before the Messiah returned. Again.

Che had organized a troop to gather the people up from the fields and mountainsides where they run at our arrival.

But this time it was unnecessary. As we came through their huge doorway Pastor Barrera and two other men bowed to Che. Other villagers peeked out from their huts at first, and, if they saw us looking, they, too, bowed or blew kisses up at the sky. After a few moments they joined us.

The mayor once again had something to show everyone. He went to his big rock and with his theatrical flourishes took out a little package, wrapped with a cloth embroidered with red and blue squares. Slowly he unwound the cloth and held a small white object aloft.

It was Che's inhalator!

"Everyone here knows what this piece of you has meant to us. You are a man of great power and great knowledge, and we are all grateful that you left some of your power with us. Everyone knows the feats this part of you has accomplished, for it has cured many of us, and kept us safe from harm. Thank you." He smiled and showed the holy relic to everyone, turning it in the air, saying, "We have kept your trust. We have kept this part of you safe from the army, no matter what they have done to our village."

I watched Che's face to see his nausea form. But his face was untroubled.

Forty or so people nodded their agreement with the mayor. Had there been so many people before? They came to us now like birds to grain.

Inti addressed the crowd, speaking of our battles with the army, and the need for all Bolivians to help the miners in their struggle. Bolivia's treasures must be used for Bolivians.

The townspeople looked away from Inti, up at the green hills and beyond, at the sun, dreaming their dreams. This was not the food they had come out for.

When Inti was done one of them said, "Sir, we have heard about the Giants." We had gone among the villages, teaching that there were Giants in Bolivia. And we guerrillas knew the way to make the Giants do what we wanted. We knew how to offer the soldiers' blood to them.

The man took off his brown felt hat, and bowed his head. He kissed the tips of his fingers and shook them up towards the sky, then smiled at Che like a coquette—one that hadn't taken care of her teeth, for they were jagged mountains worn down by an ice age of coca.

And Che returned his smile. Their nonsense didn't dismay him anymore; it even seemed to please him, make his breathing lighter.

We ourselves, he said, the guerrillas and the people of Bolivia who fought for liberation, all those who struggled and sacrificed for the Revolution, were the Heroes who lived within the Giant. When we worked and sacrificed together then our blood ran through the Giant.

"How do we know what the Giant wants?" the man asked, meekly turned into a child again, I thought, by this story.

"The leader of the Bolivian Revolution will speak for the Giant. And that leader will come from the heroes of the Revolution."

The man nodded, taking in this new information, but it didn't make him happy. He ran his hand through his hair. "Sir," he said, looking at the dirt, "does that mean you won't let us see the Big People?"

These peasants, I thought, are just like Che, only interested in their own spiritual development!

The Bolivian nation, Che said again, repeating his lesson (re-forming it, I thought, as he repeated it), its people and its land together, were a powerful Giant. The heroic acts of the Revolution would awaken the Giant. You could not see him, but all who worked for the Revolution would feel the Giant's power protecting them.

This was the grain they wished—and as he spoke more villagers came from their huts to join the crowd. There were even young men among them.

"How will we know the leader who speaks for the Giant?" Pastor Barrera asked. I felt a new compliancy in him; he wanted to cooperate, to offer the right question.

"Those who claim to lead Bolivia now, like Barrientos," Che said, "are dead men. Barrientos is a stone. You cannot see yourself in him. You will know the true leader of the Bolivian Revolution because you will see your face in him. Each of us is already in the leader, as we are in the Giant. He will speak for us and for the Giant."

The townspeople no longer fidgeted like prisoners when Che spoke. They stared intently, as if his difficulty breathing, the odd way he carried his chest, were filled with necessary information for them. But I looked at our men around the edges of this crowd, and Che's strange words were like a pain in their bodies. Ricardo's head shook from side to side—not in disagreement, more like a tremor, a palsy.

Che thanked the people for keeping his inhalator safe from the army. He reminded them that they must never speak of us to the soldiers.

The mayor nodded solemnly as if being given a sacred mission. He wrapped up the piece of plastic, sprinkled chicha on the cloth, and hid it again beneath its rock.

From Coco's Journal

8/26/67: The courageous fellow who had asked Che about leadership took me aside in the evening. "There are things," he said, "that we haven't shown you yet." He wanted to be friends, conspirators even. We went back to his hut, where he unwrapped another precious object. I could hardly see it in the dark smoky air. (Since my illness I, too, have a little trouble breathing.)

"What is it?" I said.

"We drink from it," he said, "at festivals. When we're alone."

It was a skull! A bowl had been attached to the top of the skull, and a nozzle came out of its clenched teeth. I could swear that the bowl was made of gold.

"Is it a Spaniard?" I asked. I thought it must be very old, hidden away at the time of the Conquest, protected despite torture. I was pleased to think that he trusted us enough to show it to me. (Though gold was useless to us—as he might have calculated for himself.)

My friend shrugged.

"Or a troublesome soldier?"

He shuddered. That was impossible! They would have been killed for that!

"A priest then?"

He smiled.

They offered us food later, and wouldn't take our money.

Isle of Pines, July 1968

JULY 1

I see now. He was trying to make a *seam* between our world and the Indians'. Now he himself was—*is*—that seam. But he could not make the join heal together then, no matter how hard he clamped down—like an army ant!—with the teeth of his intelligence. If the words were the ones the Indians listened closely for, then the men grew uneasy. Maybe, some of them thought, Che has gone as mad as Camba.

Che wouldn't talk to us anymore; he wasn't interested in explaining, or couldn't. What we thought didn't matter. Even our allegiance didn't really matter. He didn't need us, or not for very long. His *plan* didn't involve us.

Bolivia, August 1967

From Guevara's Journal

8/27/67: A message from Fidel, in code. But we have lost the tape recorder, so we can't replay it and translate. This god speaks now in a garbled voice, from afar.

Some of the men thought they understood a phrase or two from the oracle.

"Don't sell any more milk, a hug, Fidel," Ricardo said.

"Don't see any more of that ilk, my love, Fidel."

"Don't be a piece of silk, you mug, Fidel."

Etc.

It was the first laughter in weeks.

But there was uneasiness, too. It reminded us all, again, of our isolation. These words half understood, like the peasants themselves, were a barrier we couldn't fling ourselves against. We were somewhere else; put to bed in another room. A dark one.

8/28/67: The army reports three killed in the Nancahuazu region. From the descriptions, it cannot be doubted that these are the party I sent out for medicine.

From Coco's Journal

8/29/67: Morroco. Calixto's village. This time, too, a larger crowd than before, more than twenty people, women, children, and a few young men. Curiosity now overcomes fear and their angry grief at the loss of Paulino.

Calixto said, "You know how to make the Giants do as you wish. As only a Hero can." He stood in front of his hut, near the cooking fire where his daughter had bewitched me. He was authoritative; it all made perfect sense to him I guess.

Again Che said that the Revolution joined land and people into a Giant, ready to walk again among the liberated nations of the world. The Revolutionary struggle would make the Bolivian people into heroes, joined to the life of that Giant, part of his immortal life.

A woman in the back cackled. "You don't look like heroes," she said. She had a sly mocking smile that I had seen before. Could this be the mother of my beloved? She had a round smooth face, and a body made round and smooth and enormous by her skirts and shawls. This was what I had to look forward to as we grew old together!

That made me laugh, the idea of our growing old! Anyway the coca energy was gone from my body, from my prick.

"If you had eyes to see," Che said to the doubter, "you would know that we are indeed heroes."

"And so you have come to tell us what to do," Calixto's father said. They are all still angry, I guess, about the boy's loss.

"The Bolivian people themselves will decide what to do. The leader of the Revolution speaks for the power of the Giant. He will come from among the Bolivian heroes. And he will be someone you recognize."

"We know," Calixto said. "We have heard. He will know what is in our hearts."

A light rain began to fall. My body felt hot. I thought steam would rise from my feverish skin, taking more of my flesh. Already I am even thinner than Inti.

"Yes," Che said. "But you will know, too, what is in his heart. You will see yourself in him. His heart will be a mirror in which you can see yourself, for he will be from among you."

"From among us?" Calixto said. He looked around him at his twenty friends, standing uncomplaining in the rain. "From among us?"

"But we're garbage," the sly woman said.

"I see her point," Ricardo said to me. He doesn't care anymore that I am Bolivian. His huge eyes swam towards my face from behind his thick glasses.

"Fuck you," I said.

Che told them all how they might become Heroes.

From My Journal

8/29/67: One of the men Che had chewed coca with before took me aside. He showed me a heap of stones behind his house that had a small crockery vase on it, a household shrine. The vase had a picture faintly outlined on it that looked like a man in a flowing robe with a sunburst behind his head. "Look," the man said. "His ashes." He looked up at the sky and blew a kiss from his fingertips.

"Whose ashes?" I asked.

"I don't know," the man said. "But they're very powerful."

"Why do you blow a kiss to the sky?"

He shrugged.

"Ah," I said.

We were getting to be pals.

"Who stole your voice?" he asked.

"I sacrificed it," I said, "to the Revolution." I thought to add, Now the Giant speaks for me. But my theology wasn't clear—was it the Giant or the Heroes or the leader?—and I was afraid of blaspheming.

"Will you get it back?" he asked. "After the Day of Change?"

"I don't know," I admitted, for once again I didn't have the right answer. I must ask Che; or Camba.

From Guevara's Journal

8/30/67: We moved along the lower edge of a thick junglelike area, then back towards the Rio Grande. Humid, yet we are far from water. Benigno found some small cane which we sucked on for moisture. But Pacho and Eusebio are falling to pieces and look on the verge of collapse.

8/31/67: Two of the *macheteros* fainted today. Eusebio, forgetting all that I had said, drank his own urine from his canteen cup, with the expected results of diarrhea and cramps. He didn't trust my word; or thought he couldn't be certain of a truth unless he tested it on his own body.

Benigno, our scout, brought contradictory reports about Joaquin's presence in the zone. Some of the local people say that guerrillas have been in the area, others deny it.

Monthly Summary: Until we rejoin with Joaquin our situation remains precarious. We cannot risk battle and further losses; but without battles there isn't even the possibility of new recruits. The myth continues to spread, taking unpredictable forms.

SEPTEMBER

9/1/67: Benigno went down into a canyon overgrown with thick bushes and vines and found a small stream.

9/2/67: A day scaling ridges between here and the river. We will wait in this area for Joaquin.

From My Journal

9/3/67: Che set up an ambush near the Rio Grande. I don't understand his thinking. We can't risk contact with the army if we are to remain in this area.

In the afternoon ten soldiers marched on the other side of the river as if they were about to cross. Che ordered us to wait until the column was all the way into the water, and then fire. But Marcos fired as soon as the point man came to the edge of the rocks. The other soldiers scattered.

Marcos is afraid of the army and wants to avoid a battle.

Che was furious with him, and called him a coward. Marcos bowed his head, and Che called him other names, like someone bringing a stick down across a mare's face, over and over.

From Coco's Journal

9/5/67: We camped an hour's march from the house of Honorato Ispaca, near the junction of the Masicuri and the Rio Grande. Che established an ambush with a good view of the hut, under El Chino.

A muleteer with a scarred face came down the dirt track near the river, and we took him prisoner. He was so surprised when I stepped out of the forest I thought the son of a bitch would shit!

I brought him back to camp for interrogation. He said that eight days ago, when he had stopped by Ispaca's house, Ispaca hadn't been home. Ispaca's wife said he was seeing a doctor in Vallegrande, about a tiger bite.

"So you had a nice visit with the wife, did you?" Ricardo asked. He and I laughed.

"You two are beginning to sound alike," Ponco said. He sounded sad.

"I saw a fire burning in the house," I said, certain that the man was lying to us.

"Maybe he's there now. I don't know anything about that. I told you what I heard. Maybe the army is using the house, sir." Ispaca's wife had said the army had beaten her husband up, killed all the pigs, and eaten all the food in the house.

Even as we talked to the peasant we heard shots coming from the ambush. A soldier had approached the house, leading a horse. El Chino saw a figure coming, but couldn't see it well, and shouted, "A soldier!" as if he were coming out of a reverie, surprised at what he beheld. The soldier shot into the ambush and ran away. Ponco killed the horse.

Che was furious with Chino. He said that Chino didn't have either the eyesight or the intelligence to be a guerrilla.

Now we had to withdraw immediately and move farther down the Rio Grande, to the northwest.

From Guevara's Journal

9/5/67: The reports from our scouts and the peasants add up to this: The Eighth Division is north-northeast. The Fourth Division is on the other bank of the Rio Grande, to the north.

From My Journal

9/6/67: The Bolivian announcer was jubilant with the news that ten guerrillas, led by a Cuban called Joaquin, real name Juan Vitalio Acuna Nunez, had been killed in the vicinity of Camiri, near the junction of the Masicuri River and the Rio Grande. Which is to say: where we were yesterday.

Che said immediately that the report was a lie. It had given no names other than Joaquin's, and no details. He said that if there were any truth to it there would have been more details. Joaquin was, he said . . . then he stopped. "Joaquin is," he said, "an experienced guerrilla. The whole group, led by an experienced man, could never have been killed all at once, unless they were attacked while they were sleeping."

Ricardo looked over at me at this last admission. Che had made it out of that boundless honesty of his, that honesty in which we all might freeze. I looked at Ricardo, but kept my face impassive. The radio glowed green on the forest floor, Benigno hunched above it.

There have been no recruits. If Joaquin's group is lost, we too are certainly lost.

Today there were fewer disputes in the group, the pointless constant haggling about jobs and food that has been our daily meal for the last month. We are twenty-four men. *We are all we have now, no life outside the revolution.*

From Coco's Journal

9/6/67: Che says it was a lie. The news was on the Voice of America, but none of the other stations. He said that they couldn't have been killed unless the army came upon them while they slept.

But what if the army came upon them while they slept?

From Camba's Journal

9/6/67: Che said it was a lie, but there was blood on his tongue when he said it.

From Guevara's Journal

9/7/67: Now the Voice of the United States reports that a guerrilla named Paco was the only survivor of the clash at the Masicuri. And they speak of one dead near Vado del Yeso, in a new clash where the other group was supposedly liquidated. These contradictions make the information about Joaquin seem like a farce.

On the other hand, they give all the evidence that El Medico Negro, the Peruvian doctor, has died at Palmarito.

From Coco's Journal

9/7/67: Che says that it was certainly a phony story about Joaquin's group. If there had been a clash we would have heard something about it. The ground, he said, couldn't have simply swallowed them up.

From Camba's Journal

9/8/67: I went with Inti and two others to the adobe houses with roofs of curved red tiles, near the Rio Grande, where we were to buy some of the merchandise that makes life more bearable.

Inti stopped a farm hand making holes in the field, to ask if there was anyone in the biggest of the houses.

"No," he said, not able to look at our faces—they were so terrifyingly bright —but staring up into the sun. "It's empty. There aren't any soldiers here, and the boss is away."

But when we entered the big house a group of forty soldiers sprang up in the field outside. Inti killed one of them, shooting him in the mouth, and the other soldiers took up positions in the empty field in front of the house. The man making holes was gone. He hadn't really been scared of us; he was a specter luring us to our death.

But Inti speaks for Che. He told us to make a loud noise and fire off our guns as quickly as we could. I aimed for the tender parts of the soldiers, where love also occurs, for Inti had shown that those parts, like their mouths, are sweet and unprotected. The noise of our shouting and firing turned the soldiers into rabbits, and they ran away. We escaped back to the river, taking a mule on the way.

From My Journal

9/8/67: Inti returned from his expedition with a mule. The peasants told him that they had seen guerrillas, a group that went to Perez's house before the carnival. But that was us.

That afternoon I felt Joaquin's presence lingering in the area, hiding among the leaves and bushes. He was the space between the leaves.

In the evening they played a tape on the radio, a scratchy thing that they considered a great prize, recorded, they said, on the day of the battle at Vado del Yeso. It sounded like Paco's voice.

"That was our chief," he said, "Joaquin. And the black man is what's left of Braulio. That one is Alejandro, a Cuban. That is Polo. That is Ernesto. That is Moises Guevara."

"You mean Che Guevara," a Bolivian voice said.

"No, Moises Guevara, the union leader." (The sound of firing: high, false, like the tinny sound of pebbles against a window.)

"And that was Freddy, our doctor."

Paco was identifying corpses.

9/9/67: Che sent eight men, under Ricardo, to establish an ambush in the forest between our camp and the river. It was possible, he said, that the army would see the footprints that Inti had left, if the cattle hadn't wiped them out. And Inti had spilled a lot of corn by the roadside.

At twelve midnight Che sent Benigno to tell Ricardo to suspend the ambush. Benigno moved down the trail into the darkness.

A few moments later we heard shots, and a burst of automatic fire. Benigno, all legs, came running back into camp. He had clashed with a patrol that was already bringing dogs down the path through the forest, towards our camp.

Che looked desperate. There were nine of our men on the other side of the patrol, and we didn't know exactly where they were.

The *macheteros* cut a new path to the river, and four men were sent ahead that way with some of our things. Che's plan was to transfer the knapsacks near the river, and keep contact, if we could, with the rear guard, until they could be reincorporated into the group.

At that moment Ricardo returned leading all his men, having cut a path of his own that went around the patrol.

I was very glad to see him.

Ricardo, that stupid asshole, had led his group off to find cattle without leaving a sentry on the path. When he heard the dogs barking, and the firing from Benigno's clash, he realized what had happened, that the army had set up an ambush ahead of him. So they cut a new way back through the woods.

Che was so relieved that he forgot to think of a suitable punishment for R.'s obvious gross criminal stupidity.

As we withdrew we heard the soldiers machine-gunning the place where we had camped.

Under a full moon, we marched all night to get away from the soldiers. The era of running away has begun. Che is certain that the army will think that we insist on the Masicuri region for supplies, or will wait for us farther south, towards the Nancahuazu.

On the radio, near morning, Jorge testified that Debray carried a gun. Debray said it was only because he sometimes went hunting.

"We will have to punish Jorge," Che said, "as an example."

Ricardo *laughed*.

9/10/67: Voice of America: The Bolivian Army today found the body of a woman guerrilla fighter called Tania, part of the band killed at a battle near the Rio Grande on August 31. Her real name was Haydee Tamara Bunkebider. Her body had apparently floated downstream and onto the shore, and was in an advanced state of putrefaction when it was finally discovered.

Her pocket diary, though, had been protected from the water by a leather pouch that she wore at her waist. According to the diary, the guerrillas had gotten lost and, unfamiliar with the Bolivian countryside, had been wandering aimlessly for months, hoping to stumble on the group led by the Argentine adventurer Che Guevara.

Tania was suffering from a fever, probably malaria, and complains in her diary that the other guerrillas refused to stop their ceaseless marching so she might rest. They held her responsible for their separation from Guevara. Tania writes of how they tormented her, waking her in the middle of the night, even threatening to rape her. She, in turn, said she would inform Guevara of the men's treatment of her so that they might be suitably punished, and each of their offenses is carefully noted in her diary.

The Bolivian Army has been patrolling the Rio Grande since the foreign guerrillas were first spotted in the area, more than eight months ago. According to the captain in command at Vado del Yeso, Tania had been trying to surrender when she was accidentally killed by one of the soldiers. Her yellow-striped blouse, the only piece of feminine clothing that she wore, made her an easily visible target, even from a distance. She was killed while standing in the river, and her body floated downstream to its resting place, not to be discovered for many days.

Documents found in the small leather bag attached to her belt, and information now in possession of the Bolivian Investigatory Agency, reveal a tale about Tania that the other guerrillas must never have suspected. She was a double, perhaps even a triple agent. A colonel of the East German secret police who defected to the West only this year revealed that he himself had originally recruited Tania into his spy force, to keep watch on the Argentine Guevara, who was then a high-ranking official in the Cuban government. The Russians, the colonel says, were often at odds with Guevara about his planned military adventures in Latin America.

It is possible, the Bolivian Minister of Information announced today, that it was Tania's mission here to betray Guevara, and to make sure that his expedition ended in defeat. This, the Minister said, would explain many otherwise very mysterious facts about Tania's conduct. In Camiri, Bolivia, where Tania based her undercover work, she often strutted about the town with two Bolivians, the Peredo brothers, announcing jokingly to shopkeepers that she and her companions were guerrillas. In those days no one even dreamed of guerrillas in Bolivia. Why would she so needlessly draw attention to herself? Of course the Bolivian Army began to watch them. Tania must have known, too, that the movement of jeeps on the road from Camiri to the farmhouse where the guerrillas were located had drawn the neighbors' attention, and that the police suspected them of being cocaine smugglers. Yet she conspicuously drove one of those jeeps about the town, and then simply abandoned it there.

The jeep was soon discovered by the Bolivian authorities, and a thorough search was made of its contents. The authorities found a number of incriminating documents, among them a list of the names and addresses of many of Tania's urban contacts, parts of her spy network and those of a Cuban guerrilla, an agent of Guevara's called "Ricardo."

This discovery led the army to investigate further, reconnoitering in the vicinity of the Nancahuazu River on March 13 of this year. Ten days later another patrol, of thirty-two men, marched towards the suspected location of the guerrilla camp. The guerrillas laid an ambush and killed seven of the unwary soldiers, leaving their unburied bodies for vultures to eat.

But this ambush alerted the Bolivian High Command to the magnitude of the danger. General Barrientos, the President of Bolivia and Commander in Chief of the Bolivian Armed Forces, said today that the war began long before the guerrillas were ready. All the guerrilla bases are now in army hands.

The final defeat of the foreign mercenaries, General Barrientos announced, will come in a matter of days.

Credit for this complete defeat of the foreign-led guerrilla movement, President Barrientos added, belongs not only to the Bolivian Army, which has battled so tirelessly and so courageously, but also to the Bolivian people, who have rallied to the cause of liberty and once again demonstrated their faith that social progress can be made without recourse to violence, through Bolivia's own democratic institutions.

From Coco's Journal

9/10/67: Che says that it is all crap about Tania. He had had a thorough investigation of her made, in Cuba, and we can be sure of her complete integrity. It may be that she was killed at the Rio Grande, but the rest of it is just crap.

I had never heard him say "crap" before.

I said that Inti and Tania and I did not "strut" around Camiri, but were always circumspect. I looked over at Inti who was seated cross-legged on the ground, staring at his own lap. Could he have done something I didn't know about?

No! Their propaganda corrodes even my faith in my own brother! I must not let it.

When we began to march again, Camba gestured at Che. "There's blood running down your leg," he said, trying to point at Che's tattered pants. But he couldn't keep his arm steady, and his finger moved up and down Che's body, from his feet to his neck, and then off to the trees and vines and sky. "She was a witch. There was blood running down her leg. That's why there's blood dripping from your prick. Her blood smelled. The army smelled it. That's how they got Joaquin. Now it will smell you, Che."

Before he could say any more my brother took him aside and slapped him. I would like to knock the bones of his nose back into his brain myself and shut him up for good.

From My Journal

9/11/67: General Barrientos himself honored us with a speech on the radio tonight. Tamara Bunke—who was called Tania by the guerrillas—will get a Christian burial despite her murderous past, for she was pregnant when she died.

I looked about and several men—Coco and Ricardo among them—were counting out the months on their fingers. We parted in April. Could it be true that she was pregnant? Could it have been . . . No. It couldn't. (We counted again.)

The enemy, Che said slowly, forming his words in pain, wants to turn the revolution into a romance called *Betrayed by a Woman*. A Hollywood movie instead of the miners' massacre; imperialism; and the class struggle.

From Guevara's Journal

9/11/67: How did Wolfe know we were in the country so long before the first battle? Certainly *someone* had spoken too loosely.

But most of this nonsense will work for us. The people protected us but we were betrayed by one of our own, perhaps killed by one of them—killed after death, like a bandit by the police.

[July 3rd: Killed after death! He imagined himself already dead! "This will work for us"—he means after we're dead. He already imagined our empty space filled by a story. He meant that the "nonsense" about Tania would be good for our story.

His story!

We could still have gotten away.

But it would have ruined his ending. He sacrificed us to his story, the one he thought he could write in the minds of the peasants, his new theology of Heroes and Giants.]

From My Journal

9/12/67: Each day we move farther from the river. The landscape has changed as we have moved north into the mountains. Reddish-colored hills, nearly bare, with small clumps of woods where we camp. Most of the trees are twisted and half withered from lack of nourishment. The dusty rock-filled soil kicks into clouds as we move.

Maybe he has come to his senses now that Joaquin's group is lost and is leading us towards Paraguay or Chile and away!

9/13/67: Today Che couldn't march and rode the pack mule. Everyone has the same thought, though no one has wanted to speak it, as·if saying it meant that one was responsible for what had happened.

Finally Moro spoke. "We are leaving the zone." He meant: This is admitting Joaquin's group has been killed. A simple sentence; a death sentence.

"Yes," Che said, from muleback. "We are slipping. But we are entering a new stage of intensified contact with the army. Our victories will bring new recruits."

So we are not going towards the border. We tasted the red dirt on our tongues, in our throats.

"Still," he said, as if talking to the mule itself, "they couldn't have wiped out the whole group. There will be survivors, and they will find us."

In hell, I thought.

From Guevara's Journal

9/13/67: A Budapest daily—Radio Moscow says—criticized Che Guevara as a pathetic and irresponsible figure. It hails the truly Marxist attitude of the Chilean Party, which assumes practical attitudes in the face of objective conditions. Guevara is a new Nechayev, who dreams of covering his continent in blood.

How I would like to take power, if only to unmask the cowards and lackeys of every kind, and rub their noses in their own dirty tricks!

9/14/67: A bad day. As we crossed one of the rivers not on any of our maps, my shoes fell from my hand and were carried away. I have bound up my feet as best I can with a bunch of rags and papers tied with pieces of string. This is not the sort of world yet where a man can take off his boots!

Isle of Pines, July 1968

JULY 4

Today I cannot bear to think of his life. Today I think there wasn't one moment of *pleasure* in it. If Che was a ladies' man, as they used to say in the mountains, then it was *without pleasure.* (Perhaps he—the hero—wanted them to say that he wasn't a sickly ugly little thing. Or perhaps he was never a ladies' man and it was all lies.) He couldn't hear music. And I don't think Che ever saw a color; if he did see a color he certainly did not see a *shade!* The only physical sensation I think he ever had intimately, fully, was his first attack as a child, giving himself without thought to the painful struggle to breathe. But after that moment I swear he couldn't hear, taste, see, feel—he was a doomed man, a dead man, already in the grave of his thoughts. He never loved anyone, any one person—certainly not me. He was always *talking* about love, *thinking* about love, trying to make it come out right, as if it were a problem not of the body, but of mathematics. "Altruism . . . anger . . . overcome by sharing the same condition, the fire of our continual suffering . . ."—all so much pigeon breath! Why couldn't he want simply to hit someone (or kiss someone)? Why couldn't he ever have been content with the way things look, smell, *are* in this imperfect perfect world? Why couldn't he have even been unhappy the way we—the rest of suffering humanity—are unhappy, simply unhappy, jealous, just desiring a woman who betrays us or makes us angry, without some theoretical escape, some escape into theory, a special exit into philosophy, a scampering off into a dream of absolute identity, instead of just eating the sublime muck we're served with *now.*

I *want* there to have been a romance between them. I *want* him really to have made Tania pregnant. He *was* the father. (Because *I* say so. Really, he wasn't. None of us had the energy for that. There wasn't any pregnancy. *But I will have it so.*)

When Tania told him she was pregnant his heart turned. Discovering this weakness that couldn't be called a weakness but a strength beyond willing, he didn't want to draw the lines more sharply. He wanted *simply* to embrace and protect her.

The first battle at the Nancahuazu River hadn't occurred yet. They made love. (What would he have thought making love to her? About the problem of tenderness . . . about a time when there was something beyond this sham tenderness which was only an inward-turned violence, about a new identity, One Body? No! *I say that he just liked the feel of her body.* And then he found it perhaps a little . . . disappointing.)

The first battle hadn't happened. Tania is pregnant. He doesn't draw the lines. It isn't too late for us to go out simply, the way we came in, running the film backward.

So we do.

Che and Tania don't go back to Cuba with the rest of us. They go on to Miami, for that is the place for luxury, for romance! "There all is but order and beauty / Luxury calm and sensual pleasure / My child, my sister, / Dream of the sweetness of going there to live together / To love at leisure and die / In the land that resembles you."

He becomes a doctor there, an allergist. She worked first as a secretary, until he was recertified to practice in the United States. Once they spoke of this, during the time when they were poor, how things would be handled differently in Cuba. *There* they needed more doctors. *Here* they protected their profits. Soon they were his profits, too, and they didn't talk of Cuba anymore.

They have a large ranch-style home. Two children. The first one was born while Ernesto was a student again, studying for his boards. They named him after Walter, Che's friend from the old days.

No. He would want to forget Walter. They gave the boy a British-sounding name: Alfred. Alfred Guevara.

The years go by like a soak in a warm bath. And now it's a spring night in Miami, a little humid but not too unpleasant, and Che and Tania have found a high-school student to watch the children so they can go to a movie at a theater near the Causeway, a highway that runs by the ocean. It's a big theater that looks like an office building or a mausoleum. Admission to the movies costs as much as a week's wages in Cuba. A month's wages in Bolivia. A year. A decade. *I want it to be luxurious,* I want to pile outrage on outrage, I want them to dive into a mountain of sugar until the white powder fills every crevice in their bodies!

It is a movie about a very rich man (richer than you can possibly imagine) and his problems when he falls in love with a shopgirl. His family disapproves. He forsakes her. She dies of a broken heart, and becomes his "good angel," guiding him through life, advising him who to marry. Giving him tips on the stock market.

That was the movie they meant to go to. But they couldn't get in, it is so popular, so they go to the one next to it, off the lobby of this entertainment complex. It's a mistake. It's a movie about Latin America.

During most of the film Ernesto keeps looking at his watch and thinking about other things. Recently he's worried that Tania had once been an East German agent, sent to attach herself to him and betray him for the Soviets. No! He worries about another sort of betrayal, about whether she's been having an affair. But with whom? There are too many candidates. Another doctor, a Cuban who works in the same medical building with him? He's been to the house sometimes and been very attentive to her, praising the watercolors she's taken to doing during their vacations. Or maybe it's the man from the office where she worked as a secretary? He thinks of her with that other man, a tall balding but boyish Anglo who calls everybody "pal." He thinks of Tania betraying him, making love to this red-faced fellow. It's painful but interesting to think about this man's cock inside her. He doesn't have a theory about why she's done it—if she has—or why he thinks about it lately. He just does, painfully, almost greedily. He strokes her hair, which she's pulled tight into braids. "The watery sun," he thinks, "in these misty skies / Has the same mysterious charm for me / Of your treacherous eyes / Shining through their tears." Funny, he rarely thinks of Baudelaire since coming here. What poem is it that just came into his mind?

Troubled by his jealousy he has hardly even looked at the movie, a European one as it turned out, and very arty. A card came on the screen saying LAST SCENE. He's glad. He wants it to be over. After all these years he's really unchanged, a restless man who finds it hard to sit still.

Medium long shot. An army patrol enters the scene and walks across a grassy field to a peasant's thatched hut. Sound of dogs barking.

Medium shot. Dogs running about and barking as the soldiers come up to the house. A peasant rushes out of his house, to keep the five soldiers from entering.

CAPTAIN VARGAS: We know you've given food to the guerrillas. We should kill you. Maybe we will.

ISPACA (the peasant): I couldn't help myself. They threatened to kill me if I didn't help. They killed all my pigs. There aren't any more pigs.

The captain shrugs as if to say, Why is the man talking about pigs?

He gives orders to a sergeant, who takes clothing out of his knapsack. He puts it on and is dressed as a peasant, in wide dirty pants, and a black jacket. The sergeant stays behind, and the patrol goes off. FADE-OUT.

Long shot. The guerrillas, led by a big man with a prominent Adam's apple, move horizontally across the field to Ispaca's hut. The camera follows them. Dogs are heard barking wildly again, and Ispaca rushes from his hut.

Interior of the hut. It is very dark and filled with dust and smoke. Close-up of a woman.

ISPACA'S WIFE: Someone is going to die.

Medium shot. The sergeant pulls a striped blanket over himself on the floor near the fire.

The rebels enter the hut.

JOAQUIN: Who's that? (His point of view: we see the sergeant, who looks worried.)

ISPACA: A neighbor. He is very hot. It's a witch who's done it to him.

JOAQUIN (to a woman who came in with him in a striped jersey. His p.o.v.: We see the woman. She is very beautiful, but her face is worn, as if she is feverish): They haven't learned anything. (To Ispaca:) We'll send a doctor for him.

The audience is mostly refugee Cubans and college students. The refugees are happy, confident that the guerrillas will be killed. They lean forward in their seats as if they can almost taste the happy moment.

But in this movie the guerrillas aren't all bad. Everyone in the film speaks German, and it was obviously made on a small budget, it has poor "production values." Ernesto wonders if perhaps he and Tania shouldn't have gone to Europe—not to East Germany certainly, but to the Federal Republic or to France. Politically they aren't so stupid. They have lost wars, and admit that they have lost them.

Like me, he thinks. Troubled by his asthma, he fishes in the breast pocket of his plaid sports jacket for his inhalator. For several years he's had unreasonable nagging worries that he might have to go without his medicine (he's even had dreams about it), so he keeps inhalators everywhere, in the jackets of his clothing, under seat cushions, by the bed, in the glove compartment of the Lincoln.

He goes up the aisle, feeling he's watched by the expectant faces of the audience, thinking he'll get some candy and go to the bathroom.

The bathroom light hurts his eyes, and the fixtures themselves look dazzlingly clean and white. "A veritable land of Cockaigne, I tell you, where all is rich, clean and shiny, like a clear conscience, like a magnificent set of cookware, like a gaudy set of jewelry." *Invitation to a Voyage,* that was its name. And surely *this* was the place he meant! What would his mother have thought of all this, he thinks, looking about at the empty urinals, the six polished mirrors, the chrome soap-dispensers. She would have understood, he thinks, the pleasures of living comfortably, the pleasure even of a bad conscience that had become as familiar as an old habit that will never give notice.

The huge lobby is almost empty. A few high-school kids. What are they doing out here? What are they doing anywhere? Their amusement seems to be in just lounging with each other. He stands before the candy counter, looking at the rows and rows of different candies, like a gaudy set of jewelry. It is all so overpriced. Monopoly capital. He thinks again that they must remember to bring their own food when they come to these places. Lukewarm orange drinks are no longer as delicious to him as they once were. Now he requires "a cooking poetic and rich and stimulating at once."

Medium shot. Joaquin and Ispaca stand outside Ispaca's thatched hut. Ispaca's p.o.v.: Joaquin towers over Ispaca. He is as tall as the roof of the hut.

JOAQUIN: We need your help. Tomorrow you must help us find a place to ford the river.

Ispaca nods, looking towards the mountains beyond.

Interior, Ispaca's hut. Daytime (which in the hut looks the same as nighttime). Medium shot. The soldier gets up from the floor and without a word goes running out of the hut.

Exterior. The field outside Ispaca's hut. The sergeant dressed as a peasant runs across the field (long shot) towards the river.

Exterior. Near the river, thick growth. Large rocks in the foreground. Close-up of the sergeant's face.

SERGEANT: They arrived. Ispaca will lead them to a ford tomorrow.

Captain Vargas smiles.

Exterior. Daytime. Near the river. Medium long shot. Vargas addressing his troops—thirty soldiers.

VARGAS: We must defend our country against the well-armed foreigners and killers. They may have defects and perhaps virtues, but they aren't invulnerable or invincible. (The camera pans across the frightened young faces of the men.)

Exterior. Nighttime. By the river. Shots of the soldiers taking up positions. Behind rocks. In the junglelike growth.

Exterior. Ispaca's hut. An army patrol crossing the field in medium long shot. Ispaca's family, sneaking out of their hut. They run into the patrol.

Medium shot of Ispaca and the army patrol. Ispaca has all the household things on his back. A soldier knocks Ispaca to the ground.

Close-up of Ispaca on the ground. Close-up of his farm tools and gourds rolling about in the field. Medium shot of the children gathering them up.

CAPTAIN VARGAS: You will return to your hut and wait for the guerrillas. Your wife will stay with us. Tomorrow you will lead the guerrillas to Vado del Yeso. The river narrows there but is sufficiently turbulent.

Ispaca's face in medium close-up.

ISPACA: Dear God please don't hurt me!

Vargas's face in medium close-up.

VARGAS: Your concern for your wife is touching. (Vargas laughs, an unpleasant breathy sound.)

Vargas and Ispaca in medium shot.

VARGAS: Of course we won't hurt you. You're our friend! You put on a white shirt, and it will be easy for us to recognize you.

Exterior. Night. Near the river. More scenes of the army patrols choosing positions in the high growth. High-angle shot so we can now see the layout of the forces around the river, in a horseshoe position.

Exterior. Night. Near the river. The army can't be seen. We hear the sound of mosquitoes, and can almost feel the heat.

We wait.

A card comes on the screen. Large black letters, filling the frame: THE END.

The audience stirs restlessly. Are they to be cheated of the *real* ending, the one they long for?

No. The movie goes on.

Exterior. Night. By the river. The captain's face in close-up. The captain's p.o.v. of the rest of the river, and the crossing.

Really, Ernesto thinks, it was all shot in the daytime. That's called shooting day for night. You put a filter over the lens until it looks dark enough on the film. Since coming to America he has learned how these things are done, learned words like "production values." It's the greatest American pleasure: being in the know, backstage. The whole country likes to think itself a theater. That reminds him of something Tamara once said, about intellectuals wanting to be in the know, and . . . And what? He can't remember.

Metaphysical speculations. That reminds him of Walter's play. Not physical. He smiles. But he doesn't want to think about Walter. Walter's play made his life then sound absurd. Was it absurd? Actually, he feels fine now. This particular place he's in, this movie theater that feels like being inside a cash register, *it's* absurd. Absurdity is a delightful privilege, like fancy French perfume or angst.

"Bolivians are funny people," he says to Tamara. It's absurd that they should be so poor and he so rich.

She takes his hand in hers, stroking it. "They *are* absurd," she says. Her Spanish still has a slight stiffness to it, a slight Germanic tinge. He is touched by how close together their thoughts are. Her stroking makes him feel restless. He looks at the beautiful strong lines of her face, her prominent bones, and feels how much he loves her and his sweet new life. *A veritable land of Cockaigne, where everything resembles you. Shall we ever live, shall we pass into this picture my mind has painted, this painting that resembles you? The beloved woman, the chosen sister.* He hands her the package of chocolate-covered raisins.

Exterior. Night. By the river. The captain's p.o.v.

We see a black knot of people moving alongside the bank of the river, the outline of the jungle in the back. The knot moves very slowly, stops, and waves a woman forward. She moves to the head of the group unsteadily, as if she has been pushed. She has a graceful figure, in blue pants and a striped jersey.

The camera pans to Braulio, a tall black man who is seen to be ahead even of the woman, by the bank of the river. Close-up of the black man. Head down, he studies the ground for footprints.

But the soldiers, Ernesto thinks, have erased their footprints with branches, the way their Yanqui advisers told them to. A clawing begins in his chest. Where is his inhalator? He feels furiously in his pockets till he finds it.

BRAULIO (speaking to Ispaca, who is a few paces behind him): What is that?
ISPACA (nervously): Those are my old footprints. I was out here not long ago.
    (Checking the spot.) Those are my footprints.

Sometimes Ernesto stays up all night, till daybreak, watching TV, nights when the temperature in the warm bath of his life seems to have gotten a little tepid. The stations here never go off the air, so there must be, Ernesto thinks, a lot of people who sometimes feel as he does. There are Spanish broadcasts late at night—but he doesn't care for those. He wants to learn about the United States of America. He is always learning, mostly from his children. Sometimes he feels that he and his children are the life forms of different geological epochs. They are the more evolved creatures, and he is a dinosaur. Everything gets reversed in the land of Cockaigne: the children know more about the U.S. than he does, about the essence of the place, how to dress and talk, and what to think about the popular music (it's easier for him than the complicated Latin tunes. 1, 2, 3, 4, like an army marching). A land of Cockaigne where the children teach the adults; the performer, the speaker, is the child; the audience are the adults. It makes leadership impossible.

Exterior. Night. Medium shot of the riverbank. The guerrillas and Ispaca embrace.

The captain's point of view. Medium long shot. Braulio walks into the river, a machete held in his right hand and an automatic weapon with a curved bullet clip in his left. His body is struck by the current and he staggers. Close-up of Braulio's face. The current was unexpected. Why had Ispaca led them to such a tricky crossing? But he walks on.

Medium shot. The water is up to his calves. He stops, puts machete and rifle in the same hand for a moment, bends over, and takes a drink. Close-up of his face as his hand brings the water to his mouth. The water is cool and delicious.

A card comes on the screen, filling the frame with big black letters: THE END.

Ernesto understands: the point of the movie is this: a man is about to die, and he tastes some water, and it is very cold and good. Why isn't the sensual world and the pleasures it offers us enough? My father, Ernesto thinks, would have liked that point. His father had thought that that would be the way to live, enjoying each moment—for just like this Braulio, we're always on the point of death, and we don't know when it's coming. That was his father's *theory*. His father had had the theory of enjoyment instead of enjoyment. That would have been his fate, too, if he hadn't found both Tamara (Tania, he thinks. But he only calls her that when they make love, and only in a whisper) and this country. *A veritable land of Cockaigne, where all is beautiful, rich, tranquil, honest; where luxury is pleased to mirror itself in order; where life is rich and sweet to breathe; where disorder, turmoil and the unforeseen are excluded; where happiness is married to silence; where the cooking itself is poetic, rich and stimulating at once; where all resembles you, my dear Angel.* He touches her braids, plays them between his fingers like the edges of a blanket, and she smiles, still looking at the screen.

Really it isn't the end. The movie goes on.

The river. Nighttime. The captain's p.o.v. Medium long shot. Braulio goes a little bit farther on, walking towards the center of the screen. The water is suddenly deep moving and extremely turbulent. Close-up of Braulio's face. He is very suspicious now. He looks around, but doesn't see anything.

Medium long shot. He walks forward.

The riverbank, behind some rocks. The captain and the lieutenant.
LIEUTENANT: They're close enough. Let's open fire.
CAPTAIN VARGAS (his face tense): No, I want to be sure of all the targets. Wait until the column is all the way in the water.

And his men, unlike some other men, somewhere, obey him.

The camera moves in a slow tracking shot towards Braulio as he walks forward, the water sloshing around him.

Braulio looks towards the camera, which is to say, towards the Captain's p.o.v. Cut to Braulio's p.o.v. He looks directly at the clump of rocks where the captain hides. We should feel for a moment that they look into each other's eyes. But the guerrilla doesn't see anything, for he continues to move forward, to the rocks and the shore.

Or does he? Perhaps he knows what he is moving towards, perhaps he has survived too many comrades and wants to die.

Tight close-up of Braulio's face and neck. We see his Adam's apple, prominent, bobbing up and down as he swallows.

Medium long shot. Braulio walks to the right of the captain's rocks. Braulio raises his machete as a signal for the others to come across.

Braulio's and the captain's p.o.v., which are virtually identical now. The guerrillas, spread out in a line as they enter the water. The woman carrying a knapsack, rolls her blue pants up to her knees. She is last. The camera pans across the line of guerrillas.

.   .   .

The guerrillas are all in the river, some close to the shore. The water is up to the woman's waist where she stands in the middle. The current pulls at her, and she loses her footing, putting her hands out into the water, as if it were solid. She regains her footing and stands.

A high-angle shot of the whole scene. The guerrillas halfway across the river. The soldiers hidden here and there in the foliage and rocks. They look like children playing hide-and-seek.

A wider higher angle still, and the people are little more than dots in the cartoon quilt of the landscape.

A wider higher angle still and you can't see the people at all, just mountains and deserts and rivers, the landscape of Bolivia, looking like a relief map.

A helicopter shot, Ernesto thinks, at first—in the know—laughing at himself for taking satisfaction, yet still taking satisfaction in knowing. But the highest angle of all, how did they get that?

A card comes on the screen, filling the frame with big black letters: THE END.

His father would have liked this part too, Ernesto thinks. Finding our place —our not-too-significant place—in the natural order. His father's emotions, his anxieties, his dissatisfactions with his life, they must have been terrible things, if he had to find such complicated ways to convince himself that they didn't matter.

High-angle shots were something you could do in the movies, but not in life. And Marxism? That was an impossible high-angle shot, too, on one's own petty concerns.

He squeezed Tania's hand.

"It *must* be near the end," she says, sighing reassuringly. "The *real* end."

For the movie has gone on.

Medium shot. From the bank of the river. The firing begins, a tremendous sound made up of a thousand little sounds. It should drown out the roar of the river. The guerrillas fire back towards the camera, but it is clear that they can't find any targets, they are firing in all directions, at the bank where they came from, at the far shore, even into the river or up at the sky.

Captain Vargas's point of view. Braulio is running towards the ambush. He comes face to face with the lieutenant. A close-up of Braulio's face, mad with rage and terror. A close-up of the lieutenant's, soft and scared. Braulio's machete blade starts at the upper-right corner of the frame and comes down in slow motion, splitting the boy's head. Blood gushes out.

The captain fires directly into Braulio's face.

Ernesto thinks about shooting a photo and shooting a man. Is the film-making a comment on that? Why is the word the same? But he finds he cannot think about it, he has to watch the screen, as if someone won't let him think, won't let him distract himself.

Close-up of the river water, a multitude of little red spots that turn into purple swirls.

THE END.

What does that close-up of the spotted water mean? Perhaps that even terrible events can release something beautiful if only we have eyes to see. He wants to make love to Tania/Tamara. He wants to feel her press her breasts into his hand. Could she have been so passionate with him lately if she were having an affair? Or does that mean that she *is* having an affair? He hopes that she'll be in the mood after all this carnage.

He remembers their first movies here, in this country. He had stood in front of the candy stand just staring, unable to believe the number of things offered, all beautifully packaged in bright colors. He had wanted to get the high-school kid behind the counter to describe each one to him. The people in line behind him had grown restless. Now he wondered if they had thought he was on drugs, for he has since then seen young people in a similar sort of stupor at the candy counter. Tamara had suggested that he try a new one each time, and he had found, to his disappointment, that most of the candies were variations on the same, a sugar and gelatin mixture, with coloring added. "A singular land," he thought, "superior to others as art is superior to nature, where nature is revised by dreams, where it is corrected, embellished, re-worked." Now he always got the chocolate-covered raisins—a pitifully small number of them, considering the price.

In those days he and Tamara had gone to the movies just to practice their English. They still usually went to American movies, trying to learn about their country, to keep up with their children. He hoped Tania enjoyed hearing the German tonight.

Medium shot. The captain's point of view. The woman waves a bit of white cloth torn from her blouse as a signal that the guerrillas want to surrender. The sounds of screaming now drown out the sounds of firing. The screams are so loud that they are painful to hear.

Medium close-up of Vargas's face. He is shaking his head no to his men. He isn't interested in surrender. The firing continues.

Medium long shot. Joaquin has gotten back to the bank they had started from. He runs along the edge, a fleeing shadow. The camera tracks him. He gets almost to the edge of the screen, as if he has outrun the camera, where he is shot and killed.

The river, from above. The dead, the wounded, the knapsacks are dragged along indifferently by the current. Medium long shot: the soldiers fire at everything that moves, killing the dead over and over.

We see that one of the smaller guerrillas, Paco, let himself be carried downstream, and another guerrilla, Freddy, swims over to join him. They get out and hide behind rocks, watching their dead comrades float by, swept past by the current.

The army p.o.v. Freddy's head is seen peering out from behind the rocks. Bullets begin to chip at the rocks. Screams. Close-up of Freddy as he is hit twice, once in the right forearm, and once below the shoulder, in the armpit.

Close-up of Paco, with his arm around Freddy.

FREDDY: Stop firing! Stop firing! We surrender! I am a doctor! For Christ's sake stop firing!

Medium shot. Three soldiers approach the rocks, shouting: "Come out with your hands up!"

Soldiers' p.o.v. Paco rises with his hands up. Then he bends down again, to hold Freddy up.

.   .   .

Medium shot. The soldiers enter the frame. They kick at the two guerrillas to separate them. They push them. The camera moves in to watch. They knock them down, and then order them to get up again.

When the soldiers stop, Paco tries to give Freddy first aid, ripping his own dirty shirt to get cloth to bind Freddy's wounds.

First soldier kicks at Paco.

SECOND SOLDIER: Leave him alone!

First soldier is from Paco's home town.

FIRST SOLDIER: You murdering son of a bitch!

He kicks at Paco's legs, trying to get him in the crotch.

Paco covers his genitals with his hands and tries to dance out of reach.

"Bolivians *are* funny," Ernesto says.

PACO (crying): Leave me alone.

FIRST SOLDIER: Sure. (He shoots Paco in the arm.)
THE END.

"It will never end," Tamara says with mock anger. "It goes on forever." She gives Ernesto's arm a squeeze.

It's impossible, he thinks. She couldn't be having an affair. He has never loved anyone so much, never perhaps loved anyone before. He hasn't tried to remain in touch with his former wives, children, lives. Better to make a clean break. But he couldn't stand to lose Tania. Sometimes when he comes home before her, he sees a pair of her shoes on the floor, little blue ones, like ballet slippers; they come from Hong Kong. How dear they look.

As the soldiers torment Paco we hear Vargas's voice off screen, shouting: "Bring the prisoners here!"

Medium shot. The two prisoners are half dragged over to where the other corpses have been laid out on the riverbank.

VARGAS: Tell us the names of the dead.

PACO: That was our chief, Joaquin. And the black man is what's left of Braulio. That one is Alejandro, a Cuban. That is Polo. That is Ernesto. That is Moises Guevara.

Vargas in close-up. It is clear that there is a certain name he is greedy for.

VARGAS: You mean Che Guevara?

FREDDY: No, a union leader from the mines, Moises Guevara. Che was not in our group.

Freddy collapses next to the dead bodies, as if he wanted to join them. Shot from above of Freddy writhing on the ground.

FREDDY: I'm being bitten! My arm is being bitten!

Medium shot. Paco tries to kneel down beside Freddy but is restrained. A corpsman bends over him.

CORPSMAN: Shut up!

FREDDY (shouting): I'm being clawed up! I'm being clawed up! For God's sake stop it! Stop it! Stop it!

The captain leans down and shoots Freddy in the chest and head with a burst of automatic fire.

PACO, in medium close-up: And that was Freddy, our doctor.

A card comes on and fills the frame with big black letters: THE END.

Then the whole thing starts again. The guerrillas come to the edge of the river. Braulio enters the cold water. But this time in the form of a drawing. Then it is as if someone were rubbing away at the drawing, blurring the outline to a dirty smudge. Then all the deaths—Braulio shot in the face, Joaquin falling by the riverbank, Paco shot in the chest—are clipped together. Hands reach up. A woman's body hits the water. Braulio's machete opens a man's head. A small boy, his head shaved for lice, lies arms akimbo in an open field. Braulio's head is blown off.

THE END.

A white light fills the screen. No end credits.

They weren't wearing coats, so there's nothing to gather up but their gray umbrella. They file down the aisle to the exit.

The night air is warm. They have parked by the Causeway, near the ocean. Ernesto puts his arm around Tamara, gathering her under the umbrella as a light rain starts to fall. *A veritable land of Cockaigne, where all is beautiful, rich, tranquil, honest; where luxury is pleased to mirror itself in order; where life is rich and sweet to breathe; where disorder, turmoil and the unforeseen are excluded; where happiness is married to silence; where the cooking itself is poetic, rich and stimulating at once; where all resembles you, my dear Angel.*

"What did you think of it, my dear Angel?"

She smiles at him, as if this were a new pet name, and she puts her hand out in front of her. Her hand wavers up and down. "So-so." For a moment she loses her footing as if water were pulling at her legs, but his hand around her shoulders steadies her.

They agree. It wasn't that good. It was mere rhetoric, not a real imagination of their dying.

"See on these canals," he says, "These ships sleeping / In vagabond spirit / It is to fulfill / Your last desire / That they come from the ends of the earth. / The setting suns clothe the fields, / The canals, the entire town / In hyacinth and gold / The world falls asleep / In a warm light."

JULY 6

It can't be done. By the end Ernesto was Che only, without possibility of change, without even the possibility of "descending." In one of his adolescent notes he wrote, "To be a revolutionary, finally: to create in one's own life the conditions so that there is no life outside the Revolution, so that if the Revolution does not win, you die." He cannot be translated; not there anyway, to the land of Cockaigne, to the life of luxury, of "petty" jealousy, of physical love—*of love!* "Our vanguard revolutionaries must idealize their love for the people, for the most hallowed causes, and make it one and indivisible. They cannot descend, with small doses of daily affection, to the terrain where ordinary men put their love into practice."

Descend. Or rise.

Anyway, he had his way. I cannot even imagine him doing it without it all—him, and the world he is woven with—becoming *absurd.*

Bolivia, September 1967

From My Journal

9/15/67: Pacho declared that he is tired of being bossed around by Cubans. He threw his knapsack into the dirt and pounded on Benigno's thin face with his fists—like a young girl having a tantrum—blackening our machine-gunner's eye. Inti and Coco separated them.

Sadly, it was not only hysterical, but unfair; Benigno is surely the mildest and least bossy of any of us.

9/16/67: The once fat Peruvian, Eusebio, says that the Bolivians are pigs. They eat up all the food. "They steal extra meals for themselves. They help each other out. They give each other extras."

We sat on the ground, cleaning our rifles, talking. "And you, Che," he said, "you let them get away with it."

9/17/67: Eusebio rushed into camp, in the small valley, to announce that soldiers were coming around the bare brown hill ahead of us.

We scrambled about collecting our knapsacks.

"How many?" Che asked.

Eusebio, struck suddenly dumb, held up a hand and showed five fingers. He kept his other hand up, too, showing a fist. Was that a zero? Eusebio's eyes looked suddenly blank and lifeless.

Che sent Benigno to look. The soldiers turned out to be ghosts, a hallucination.

"He's psychotic," Ricardo said to me, by way of showing off his clinical vocabulary.

Che took Eusebio aside as we prepared to march, packing the mule with the little firewood we'd been able to find. Eusebio swore that he wasn't worried, that he knew we'd get out all right. But he hadn't had any sleep because of the punishment Che had given him. (Eusebio had fallen asleep at his post, allowing the soldiers to attack us in camp a week ago. And he had denied it, so he'd been given six days' extra duty.)

9/18/67: Che talked with Pacho on the march. A little fellow, Pacho is worried by our lack of contact with the city, but remains, he says, firm in his commitment to country-or-death until the end.

Eusebio, skin hanging loosely on his neck, took me aside and begged me to speak to Che about taking him out of the vanguard. "I can't get along with Ricardo," he said. "The man is a monster."

I saw his point. I spoke to Che, but he refused to do it.

9/19/67: Ricardo, the monster, had another run-in with Eusebio; perhaps he'd gotten wind of Eusebio's complaints—Ricardo can smell that kind of thing. Ricardo says that Eusebio called him an asshole, so he gave him another six days' punishment of guard duty. Che respected Ricardo's decision, though no one thinks it is just. (After all, R. *is* an asshole.)

Eusebio accused Benigno of taking an extra meal. Benigno admitted that he had eaten some suet from hides.

9/20/67: Moro says that the men complain of him unfairly. He can't walk well because of malaria. And indeed Benigno screamed at Moro this morning that he was holding everything up, that his delay would kill us all.

The Bolivian radio reported that sixteen members of the underground network in La Paz have been arrested, among them Loyola Guzman, their leader. In her apartment they claim to have found a list of the guerrillas' city contacts—though I think she was a good intelligent person, and unlikely to keep a list lying around.

Still, the news had a demoralizing effect, like acid dissolving our bodies, lacerating into pieces the One Body of the guerrilla.

Pacho said that Marcos stole fifteen bullets from his magazine, because Marcos knows the army is about to attack and doesn't want Pacho to be able to defend himself. Pacho has sinister close-set eyes if you ask me, and speaks only to make trouble. He has run-ins with all the Cubans. Fortunately, the other Bolivians think he is as crazy as Camba and Eusebio and pay no attention to him.

9/21/67: Camba said that Benigno had allowed peasants to see him and had let the peasants leave the area. This seemed unlikely, but Che asked Benigno about it anyway.

Benigno admitted that it was true, and began to cry.

Che struck him across the face. Poor Benigno! "This is treason," Che wheezed.

Benigno continued to sob throughout the night.

9/22/67: Camba came up to me on the march today, as we clambered up one of the ravines that line the hillsides. He whispered in my ear, "She put his genitals right where his nose was. In the middle of his face. And then led him around by the nose."

"Whose?" I asked. "What?"

"No one's," Camba said. "Everyone's." He looked disappointed in me for not understanding and then walked away, to the side of us. Of course I had understood.

From Coco's Journal

9/23/67: Alto Seco. At five in the morning, when the early risers went about their business, they found us already occupying their town. I asked one of the peasants on the way to his fields where the phones were, and was directed to the magistrate's adobe house. (We took the peasant with us, since Che says no one is to leave the area.)

I walked in on the magistrate's breakfast, and cut the line.

The magistrate, a short man of about forty, smiled at us from his wooden table. "It hasn't worked for weeks."

A little later Che arrived with the center guard. He rode down the dirt track of the little village on our new pack mule. He can hardly walk anymore, and Marcos had to help him dismount.

Che had us set up sentry posts around the town. The place has about ten small adobe houses with red tile roofs. The peasants, most of them mestizos, looked out from the openings of their houses.

The center guard set up at the edge of town in a half-destroyed house—it had no roof—near the watering place.

The mayor, one of the peasants told us, had left last night, for Vallegrande, the army staging area, to inform on us. Inti and I went to the mayor's two-room house, which had a little wooden counter in the front room with cigarettes, candy, tins of mentholated vaseline, candles, etc. I stuffed all the merchandise into my knapsack as a reprisal for the mayor's treason.

His wife, Sara, cried when I loaded up the things. "In the name of God," she said, "you must pay for those things. That is how we earn our living. You can't take those things from us! Our children will starve!"

I told her that her husband was an informer, and that he and his whole damn family should rot in hell with all those who have betrayed Bolivia.

Inti, calmer than me as always, said, "Your husband is mayor. You are the town's richest family. Apparently your husband cares more for the government than for the people of his town. So let the government pay him."

"Let President Barrientos pay him," I said. "Let the Pope pay him," I said, nonsensical from anger.

The woman wailed, but we would not relent.

Elsewhere in town we had acquired some pork and a few eggs. These we paid for, of course. Ricardo tried to pay in U.S. dollars, but the shrewd townspeople weren't having any of this invaluable hard currency and insisted on our own worthless pesos. We took our booty back to the abandoned house and spent the rest of the morning cooking. We have moved really very high up into the mountains, though the Andes still tower above us on every side, covered with snow. Water, Ponco pointed out to me, boils very quickly.

From Guevara's Journal

9/23/67: After a fine breakfast we went back into the town. The peasants greeted us with a mixture of fear, awe, and their new curiosity, which seems strong enough to overcome their timidity. They go so far as to touch our arms, and want to examine our hands, perhaps for magic rings, perhaps for blood.

I talked with some of the townspeople, and a few children. There is a school here for the first- and second-graders of the area. One of the older boys, a bright-eyed lad of about fifteen, told me that the schoolmaster was a terrible fox, and not to be trusted. I said that I would keep an eye on him. The boy helps his family work their land on the mountainside, and sometimes joins the labor gangs that go into the valleys. His family's land is very rough—all stones he said—and they don't have enough to eat. I told him about socialism as we have made it in Cuba. There everyone shares tools so that the most advanced methods can be used. And the work, too, is shared by everyone, so no one does all the work for others, the way it is in Bolivia.

"Do the Heroes work?" he asked.

"I worked in the fields sometimes," I said.

He was disappointed, and looked away from me.

"But they thought I was better working with my head. We will make a world where everyone works at what he is really best at, no matter where he is born. Even in a little village like this. And where everyone takes what he needs to live, but no more than that. All will offer their work to the Giant each day, to the Nation, so that it might live and be strong and watch over all of us who live within it."

From My Journal

9/23/67: At eight-thirty, as the last light fled to the mountaintops for safety, we organized a meeting in the school, a two-room building, as usual collecting the townspeople by showing our guns, so that they wouldn't be implicated. But they seemed willing, even eager to come with us.

About forty peasants sat on the dirt floor, most of them wearing the long caps of the region, with ear flaps that make them look like cartoon characters to me. Some of the older peasants had come with loads on their backs in large white blankets that were tied around their foreheads; maybe they expected to do some trading after the meeting. These traders took off their rubber sandals when they entered the mud shack, though the floor must have been very cold.

Inti spoke first. "You must think we are mad to fight like this. The army says that we are bandits. But they are the bandits. We fight for you, the ones who work and earn little, while the soldiers who hunt us, who slaughter the miners, get high wages from their Yanqui masters. You work for them, and what have they ever done for you? Nothing.

"Today my brother cut the telephone lines to keep the soldiers away, and the magistrate said, 'It doesn't work anyway.'

"Here you don't have a doctor. You don't have a decent school. You don't have electric lights. You have been completely abandoned, like all Bolivians. That is why we fight. We ask you to join us, for we cannot succeed without your help. We ask you to join us to free our country, to fight with us for the final overthrow of Barrientos and the generals who work for the Yanquis."

Inti spoke in a slow sad unmodulated voice, hopeless for recruiting, but even he felt that the ending of a speech required some special rhetorical emphasis. So he lifted his rifle up over his head. This was greeted by a gasp from the audience, who may have thought that despite his reassuring words we intended to shoot some of them.

Then Che spoke. He, too, had interpreted their gasp. "We want you to come, to join yourself to the body of the Giant and live within his immortal life. But it must be of your own free will, not by force, or the Giant will not have you."

The teacher, a mestizo pleased with his own intelligence, smiled at Che. He kept his hands in the pockets of a worn black jacket without buttons and wore no hat. "But what if we are not ready to die for you, Professor?"

His challenge provoked a deeper gasp than Inti's rifle had. The others looked angrily at the young man, but I couldn't tell if it was fear that we might punish all of them for his outrage, or because he had frustrated their curiosity. How dare he interrupt this priceless lesson?

"You know," Che said, "that I am not asking you to die for me. I am asking you to find the courage to live as men, to fight for a world where the soldiers will not have the power of life and death over you. They can kill you any time, when you disobey them. And every one of you has heard of people to whom this has happened. I am saying that you can join us and become heroes, instead of slaves. If you join yourself to the life of the Giant you will share in his immortality and power. For now he slumbers—as the land sleeps in winter— but he always rises again, for he is immortal.

"The army says that it has killed our comrade Joaquin, and our comrade Tania, and many others in their ambushes.

"But it is a lie. They show corpses at the army laundry shed in Vallegrande. But those are just corpses that they have dug up from their own cemeteries, desecrating the graves, for nothing is sacred to them, not even their own dead. They haven't killed guerrillas. This I can assure you, because only a couple of days ago I was in communication with Joaquin."

This time *I* gasped. Such was my faith in Che and in the golden valor of his word that I believed him, and wondered at first why he hadn't told us before, and which of the peasants had brought him the message. But then I realized the truth. *Che had lied.*

"You do not die," the candid young teacher said, "because you have magic that protects you."

"Yes," Che said, and the world shook in front of me. "We have a power that comes from my vision of the people of Latin America. I see our people working the land together, free of the Imperialists, free of disease. Sometimes I and my men have failed because we have not been true to that vision. Sometimes we have been led by our own ambitions, and forgotten our vision, not keeping it constantly in mind. Then those whom we trusted, those who were close to us, have betrayed us. But the people have never betrayed us.

"If you want to share in my power, my power that is the power of the Giants of Latin America, of the Bolivian Nation, then you must share in my vision. And you will have the power I have, and that you have heard about.

"And it *is* a terrible and great power. Perhaps some of you know what it is like for me. Perhaps you saw me ride into your town this morning on a mule. You can see I have trouble standing, and you can hear that I have trouble speaking."

We had found three lanterns for this meeting and placed them about the room. Che, at the front, in his torn fatigues, with his wasted body, looked indeed like the shadow of a shadow.

"You can see that I am not a strong man. It is hard for me to breathe. Like the miners of Bolivia I have very weak lungs. Do you know how weak a hand is that cannot make a fist?"

Che held up his hand. His hand terrified the townspeople, for they shrank back.

He showed his long fingers struggling to come together. "That is how hard it is for me to squeeze the air in and out of my body. But you have all heard of me. I have come far in my life, and accomplished much."

He held up his hand again, open this time, and this was even worse for the audience. They could lean no farther back, so they shrank inside their bodies.

"I am a bloody man," Che said. "I have a bloody hand. And I will have revenge for all the wrongs that the people of Latin America have suffered. I see that some of you have come into my presence bearing a heavy load and barefoot. I know that you do this because you think I am a king. I am not. But I am a hero, part of the Giant, and so I am someone powerful and feared by the army. If you share in my vision then you too will be heroes. The weakest of you is as strong as I am. The weakest of you has the power to rebel against what is being done to you."

Afterward a few of the peasants gathered outside the school. It was a clear cold night with many stars. The peaks of the Andes were visible, as if they had some source of light of their own, as if they were beacons. Coco and Che and I spoke with two men about the best routes through the area, and what they had heard about the army's positions.

Near the schoolhouse door the young boy who had spoken with Che this afternoon approached Marcos, who was staring emptily up at the stars.

"Can I join you?" he said quietly. "I want to be a Hero. I want to fight for my nation."

Marcos shouted, "Don't be a fool!" He hit the boy on the shoulders with both his arms, and the boy simply bowed his head and accepted it. "Don't be crazy," Marcos said, and began to sob. "Can't you see that we've all had it? We don't even know how to get out of here! We're trapped! In a few days we'll be dead. Are you a fool? Do you *want* to die?"

Everyone up and down the little road could hear Marcos. The boy looked over at Che, then down at the ground. No one said anything. Coco had the townspeople sketch out a map for us.

When Che and Coco were done, the boy still waited for us. He came up to Che, made bold by his disappointment.

"So everything you said was a lie?"

"No," Che said. "All that I told you was true. But it is also true that we are in difficulties now. We have to run from the army even though our cause is just and my vision true and powerful, because I misinterpreted what a peasant told me. I have attacked at the wrong time. I was mistaken, though the people tried to warn me. But our cause is just and you will have another chance to fight for it. The Giant will awaken again."

On the march out of town that night a man approached me at the rear of the center guard. "We will sacrifice many of our guinea pigs for you," he whispered, "so you will be victorious."

I would have been shocked, I suppose, but Che's own speeches had exhausted my capacity for shock. I tried to think of what Che would do. "Thank you," I said. "The more the better."

9/24/67: I spoke to Che this morning. "But they misunderstood you," I said. "You must know that they misunderstand everything you say."

He walked beside the mule as we went up the mountainside, through some tall grass. "We must submit," he said.

"Submit?" It was an odd word, like "chaste," or "reign," or "forlorn."

But he had walked ahead of me and was half hidden by the grass.

It chilled me.

He is making shadows. He lets them understand as they wish. This is not like him. It can only mean one thing: *He is dying. We are dying.* He looks on from beyond the grave, having surrendered his will—and for Che that can mean only one thing: *he sees himself already dead.* I am terrified. But Che seems very calm, newly calm, strangely calm, having given his "life" to them.

And ours.

From Guevara's Journal

[No date. It must be from around 9/24/67, though I don't think it was one of his usual entries, but rather part of an essay on "The Hero." The fragment remaining comes after a ripped-out page.] . . . before his time, and so his gestures are absurd—or tragic. So they must be made more absurd so that he can be borne. The hero, at first, takes a comic or exaggerated form. A bloody man with a bloody hand. (Describe the mad fellow, the one with grease all over his chest who danced his mockery at the back of the church. Someone like him must be the hero's body for a time, someone who keeps his idea alive by mocking his heroism in mad speech, exaggerated stories, magical actions that make no sense, like thunderous farts. But it must be a mockery that mocks itself, and so points back to the hero's truth.)

As the people gain courage the hero returns in a form that speaks more directly, without mockery. A store dummy becomes a saint who talks to them in dreams and urges them to rebellion. He will speak the language of the people he appears among, here the purest Quechua. The hero is common property, the stuff of stories. Now they make him into a story in which they can see themselves, though only a small part of themselves at this stage, like in the saint's small mirror. But no matter how they tell the hero's story it keeps its meaning; it travels into the heart like the fatal blood-spotted kernel of the conjurer. *It is right to rebel. Even the weak can be terrible.*

When the rebellion begins, the hero's story becomes more real, closer to the tale, one might say, that he himself knew of his life as he lived it. (The staff Aaron threw down became a snake; and the people stood back from it in awe. That is the first stage. But now the snake becomes the image of a rifle, yet they are still afraid to pick up that rifle and join the hero.) The first hesitant actions are on the order of street demonstrations, where they chant the hero's name. A crowd moves towards the Government Palace, across the main square in La Paz, in Lima, in Buenos Aires, chanting a name, an empty name, a mirror that any might find himself in. A small boy carries a tall pole—a sign is extended from it on a piece of cloth—the other pole held by his father. They've forgotten to put holes in the cloth, so the wind billows it out like a sail, and makes the boy's hands ache. He shouts at the top of his voice, the name of the hero. The echo comes off the high stone wall of a church, the crowd's voice almost unrecognizable in its own ears, like the rushing of water, or the high buzzing of a saw. But the hero's power is only their own power deferred—that is what the echo tries to tell them—and in chanting his name they exalt him and mourn themselves, the death of their power, keeping it present to themselves in a kind of grief.

But when the rebellion continues, and the violence begins, then the hero's qualities are parceled out among them—before the hero flickers out. Of the fighters, one might say of another, His lungs are weak, like Che. He has a taste for chess, like Che. One man is a poet—as Che was. Or a doctor. Or has too much pride. Or a certain coldness. Or has to wrap his feet in rags as Che once did. But as the rebellion continues, the fighters become heroes themselves, their self-hatred and cowardice overcome, and the name that was their self-loathing magnified is forgotten. They will chant their own names, or descend upon the cities, like a curse, in silence.

From My Journal

9/25/67: Loma Larga. We arrived by climbing a ravine that runs up the side of the mountain, all the way to Alto Seco. The ravine was clogged with thick gray bushes, and ran a long distance, maybe as far as the Rio Grande. Loma Larga, when we emerged, was a small settlement of about ten huts, on a slant so steep that I thought the houses would tip over and start rolling down the bare mountainside. We came into the village at evening, and several men came out immediately to meet us—not to shoo us away, but for greeting. We talked about army emplacements, and food. Che looked particularly unsteady and weak in the afternoon, hardly able to stand.

But he revived a bit when they gave us some potatoes and plates of stew. I bit down on a soft bitter taste that still had skin on it. "Guinea pig?" I said to Ricardo.

"Who gives a fuck?"

I saw his point, and ate greedily.

After eating Che sent the vanguard on, and he and I went over to where a group of men sat on the ground by one of the huts, talking and chewing coca. These mountains are the place where the serious coca-chewing goes on. They stuffed great wads into their mouths, and spat to the side, spat above each other's head, spat indifferent to where the droplets might go. In black ponchos and brown caps, their shapes were rounded off, like stones. This group had been at its chewing for a long time when we came and stood behind them and listened to their stories.

If a hero is captured he is burned alive, or the dogs are set on him, the long sleek ones that rip their flesh. And once a hero's wife was captured and her breasts and arms were hacked off. Then they sent her back with a note, "All those who rebel must see that they will eventually have to submit to the knife."

But (another man said) *that makes the heroes fiercer and more determined, for they see that their opponents, our oppressors, are animals, not yet human beings. So when they move in a high gorge the guerrillas trap them, rolling boulders down so that the army can't move forward, and then the heroes roll more boulders down on top of the soldiers and crush them.*

An army general (one man said) *was taken captive by the heroes. They took him back to their kingdom near the Nancahuazu River, and the heroes made the general drink chicha, and tied him to a post.* (And at this a chicha bottle —a Coke bottle filled with the cloudy liquid—was passed around.) *Then the heroes made sport of him, throwing fruit at him, and they made the general shave off his beard, and cut his hair. The heroes changed him from a Spaniard and a general into a poor Indian, like us.*

But (another man said) *they weren't done with him. The heroes had all the general's bones taken from his body, leaving the skin intact. The heroes had made him into a drum! The shoulders formed one end of the drum* (the man touched his shoulders). *And the stomach was the other end.* (The Indian pounded on his own small belly, but it was muffled by his black poncho and made no sound.) *So when the general was stiff he was transformed into an instrument for their festivals.*

Their festivals! (another man said, and I felt I could hear the spark of inspiration in his voice, and that he was adding to the story as he went, saying things never heard before. Yet all he described was true for each of them, as soon as said, as if saying made it so. Can they, I wondered, make mistakes?) *At the festivals, when the llamas are sacrificed*

—*On the high white stone platform*

—*Yes, then all the dead guerrillas are brought out, each one preserved perfectly*

—*For they never let the army capture their dead, but take them back to the Nancahuazu*

—*Yes, and they look as they did when alive, their hair*

—*and even their eyelashes*

—*Yes, just as they were in life. They give food and drink to the dead, and the heroes drink a toast in chicha, swearing to kill all the soldiers who are here now, and all who will come.*

And nothing was said for a few moments, as the bottle was passed around in memory of the toasts the heroes drank.

And during the festival He looks into the entrails of the llama, and into the patterns of the clouds before the sun, and He knows from these when to attack.

—*Yes, and He marches before the heroes, chanting, Kill kill kill. And the heroes show their legs to the soldiers*

—*Yes, to display their contempt.*

—*Yes and He goes before the others, and holds up His hand,*

—*Yes, and it is filled with blood. Look, they say, He has a bloody hand, and the soldiers are terrified. He is a weak man, no stronger than we are*

—*Yes, so weak that the others must sometimes carry Him,*

—*Yes, yet He is terrible to the soldiers, when He holds up His bloody hand.*

—*A hand like Christ's, like Jesus.*

No one spoke, but they leaned back from the last man who had compared Che to Jesus, and a chorus of saliva pattered above his head, and onto the ground. He had made them angry. *He had made a mistake!* They weren't simply making it up any which way as they went, but were describing something that they all knew! But somehow they didn't know they knew it; so in a way they weren't describing it; they were discovering it by making it up.

—*Not like Christ, you idiot!* (one of them shouted, his voice filled with a very palpable hatred. To make a mistake here was a serious business. It required implacable opposition to erase it.) *Not like Christ! Nothing like Christ!*

—*Nothing like the stinking Christ.*

—Not like the sad little Jesus!

—Nothing like Jesus! They have sent many priests to him, to convert him and his followers. But he will not receive them.

—He has them killed.

—He has them killed, and he has their bodies made into drums for their festivals.

—And the heroes save all his hair, and all the bones of the food he has touched, so that they cannot fall into the hands of the priest to cast a spell on him.

—And there is a woman

—Tania

—His wife

—Who is also his sister, the beloved woman

—The woman who had his child, the chosen sister,

—And she takes the hairs from his clothes, and swallows them.

—And when he wants to spit she extends her hand and he

—for he is very powerful

—he spits into it.

—He is very powerful, for those who follow him are Heroes, and have the protection of the Giant

—But he is more than a Hero.

—He is more than a king.

Che stepped forward, standing above one of the men. The last light, a red glow, was all one could see by.

"I am your Che Guevara," he said.

I looked at their hero, their king, their . . . god . . . and he was a short skinny man, with a brown beard, and sorrowful eyes. A man almost without the spark of life in him; a revolutionary; a doomed man; a dead man; a specter's specter. His cheeks were hollow, his torn green pants held up by a piece of vine, his feet covered in rags caked with dirt and blood.

But the men didn't see what I saw, because they didn't look at him. They simply stopped talking, and passed the bottle around, and the bags of coca, and waited for him to turn away.

They had no more use for him.

So Che is first among the chiefs, first among the first (one said, as Che hobbled away into the dark). *And at festivals he wears the wings of the condor on his back.*

—Yes, that is how the Spanish got the idea for their angels

—And the other heroes wear small animals on their hands, as they do in battle, to frighten the soldiers

—And he wears the head of a puma, for he is descended from the puma.

—And so he killed his mother when he was born, for he ripped open her womb. The blood she spilled cost her her life.

—And he

And *he* called me, so I went back to the center guard, and the march away from here.

From Guevara's Journal

9/25/67: I say, You yourselves must rule. And they say, You must be our king. I say, You yourselves form the Giant, you shall see yourselves in the king. And they say, Show us the god!

Not of them, but utterly beyond them. Give us the god! Too early for an immanent deity. They say, Give us the Man Himself.

I must say now that I am that man? (As the Inca did. For the royal family knew that theirs was no lineage from the sun, nothing but a suit of shining armor that reflected light into their first followers' eyes. The Inca entered the top of the pyramid, the small foul-smelling room where Punchao the idol dwelled. Then he emerged to tell the Indians what *he* wished; and they obeyed.) Fidel would say, *I am that Man.*

The Bolivian radio announced that Loyola Guzman tried to commit suicide while being interrogated in the Ministry of the Interior. She jumped from a third-floor window (where once I had vomited on the minister himself), but her fall was broken by the cornice of the building and she was only slightly injured.

At the hospital, they say she told the press that she had wanted to kill herself because she had betrayed her comrades.

9/26/67: A kitchen in an apartment in La Paz, yellow wallpaper with milkmaids on it. The remnants of the city network meet, to talk over the day's events, the arrests. These are the very outer circle of our contacts, friends of friends, fellow travelers, men fascinated by the study of History, and its strange turns, by which out of the strong comes forth sweetness (or vice versa). "Yes, I knew one of the guerrillas," a bearded man says at a cafe. "But you mustn't tell anyone."

Now they sit at a round glass table with mugs scattered across it, and pieces of paper. One man points to a child asleep on the stone floor: "Is it all right to have him here?" The boy sleeps in his pajamas by his mother's seat.

"Of course," his mother says. "Let him dream his dreams. What harm can it do?"

Surely, someone says, there is something that can be done for the guerrillas? He stares into his coffee cup. Vile-tasting stuff. Does she draw the water directly from the tap, for her wretched instant coffee, without heating it?

The few dissidents from the Party suggest that maybe a group could be formed to reinforce the sectors we control.

Our remaining agent, or one who knew her, says that that is impractical. They had thought of it, in fact they had had seventy men ready to begin a month ago. But they hadn't begun, and now it is too late. There are too many soldiers in the area, with North American advisers. In fact, the guerrillas don't control any sectors anymore.

Another plan is suggested: a front could be opened in Cochabamba or Alto Beni, to relieve the pressure on us.

They analyze the proposal. Could it be done quickly enough? Who would lead? (Always a sticky point, worth squabbling over. The leader must have the right political tendencies.)

No, they decide, it is impossible now.

It is getting late, and it's dangerous (they pretend) to be together like this. They finish their coffee, turn their collars up before going out.

During the night one woman sits at the glass table, cutting articles from the newspaper. She keeps a scrapbook of the guerrilla campaign, of the History of the World in Its Many Disguises, her universal history of infamy. The guerrillas were fools, she had thought at first, adventurers, no better than bandits; they knew nothing of this country. But now that the last remnant is about to be snuffed out, die beyond help, become a fit subject only for discussion and mourning, not for action, she admires them, the purity of their hopeless action, the heroism of their leader, a man too good for this world.

It's unfortunate, the others think on their way home, walking quickly, head down. But it is too late. They have tried. But there is nothing to be done.

The radio also reports that the guerrillas are surrounded and will soon be wiped out.

9/27/67: Note for the revision of the essay: They will never chant their own name. Because they hate themselves they must have stories; and they will always hate themselves. The priest offers the sacrifice, separating himself from the masses. What if the revolutionary made himself the sacrifice, to shame them more? Then *they* have sacrificed *him*. (Not the god who rules, but the god who dies.) The hero must become the proper figure, the god they cannot forget, entering their flesh like a hook that they writhe about on, attracted by it, savaged by it, *until they act*.

From My Journal

9/28/67: Pichacho. Midmorning on a clear dry day. By the time the center guard arrived the men of the vanguard had already joined the festival. Our men were scattered about the sides of the large dirt square in front of the imposing church, Spanish-built, with carillons in towers on either side of the roof.

The Indians danced in the dirt to a three-man band—one man with a wooden harp, and two with flutes, a long wooden one, wound round with string, and another that looked like a dozen reed pipes banded together. The musicians were tranced; probably they had been drinking chicha and chewing coca since daybreak.

The dancers had their arms around each other's shoulders and bobbed up and down, bending their knees in time to the changing chords, a long line, a disorderly sort of procession, constantly losing its balance, then catching its footing and going on. The men wore embroidered shirts—festival clothes— and long caps that made them look like basset hounds. The women had on shawls of blue and red over their wide black skirts, a gay sort of mourning costume. And the thought of mourning made me tremble. I have been terrified every moment since my last talk with Che, when he said, *We must submit*.

Che sent the vanguard on to La Higuera, and stood with the old men on the edge of the square, watching over the big tin pots of chicha. The old men's mouths moved in time to the music, chewing their wads of coca, spitting in the dirt to punctuate the rhythm.

Only one of the old men spoke Spanish. He asked Che if our work for the Giant was going well. Was it true, he started to ask—and then thought better of it. Why let Che deny what they all knew, that we could turn ourselves into birds, that our farts were like thunder?

This man had a high womanly sort of voice and eyes clouded as if they were filled with broken pieces of translucent glass. Every so often he said something to the other men in the line with him, but even as he spoke with Che he stared straight ahead at the dance.

Che said that our work for the Giant was going splendidly. He held up his hand, and at that all the men turned towards him, and bowed their heads. "We cover them," Che said, "with blood."

Along one side of the dirt space there was a stone wall, its white paint flaking off to reveal the gray stone beneath. Coco and Inti sat on the wall, clapping to the music.

What did Che hear? I wondered. A few repetitive chords played over and over, endlessly, without variation, or something, now, more complicated?

I preferred the old days, when I was sure that he was simply tone-deaf.

The old man looked Che up and down, appraising his body as if it were a horse. He knew that Che had *submitted*, that this was a god who they might examine like a store dummy. He was theirs now. Che wore dirty clothes, his feet were wrapped in filthy rags and bits of paper but probably they saw light streaming from every opening, and the wings of a condor on his back. Che had the poverty of Christ, I thought, but a rifle in one of his bloody hands that made him as terrible as Jehovah. Maybe he is the god for our time, and our people, a pathetic little motherfucker clothed in the glory of his violence.

"The generals say you will be captured soon?" He made it a question, I thought, so as not to insult or provoke us.

"We have heard that many times before," Che said, "in many places. But we are here."

And I thought that that was true—in Cuba, the Congo, in Vietnam—and I took heart for a moment. We had escaped from scrapes as narrow as the defile between these mountains.

"You don't seek death?"

"No," Che said. "We want to live, to continue winning victories against the army and imperialists, until many men share our vision, and take their place in the body of the Giant. But the Bolivian people have not been worthy of the Giant, their nation. The Giant turns away, ashamed of this people."

And the old man looked away from the dancers, down at the ground, and scuffed the dust with his sandal like a child. He was ashamed to have disappointed the Giant! And I think that Che had intended to shame this old man.

"Is your father alive?" the man asked, still looking at the ground.

"Yes."

"Ah." He looked back at the dancers, his half-blind eyes filled with tears. I knew what that meant: it meant farewell. It meant that it was a sad thing for a son to die before his father.

Why had Che lied? Had he? I couldn't remember anymore if his father were alive.

The man said something that sounded to me like, He will have his own house, a grand one. For him and all his friends.

Che said nothing. But I knew what that meant, too: not a palace, but a grave. Che was—at least—king. He had to be buried like a pharaoh with all his line. I saw the palace, with the long steps in front. It filled me with more fear than my body could hold, my stomach turned in agony, wanting to spew out my terror.

The dancers, the white wall, my comrades shook. I wanted to tell someone how I felt, but if I tried to speak to Che or Ricardo I would stammer uncontrollably, I was that frightened. I hated the old man with his cloudy rheumy eyes. I hated all these people who set us apart.

The old man dipped the lip of an empty Coca-Cola bottle half under the chicha, and it made thick bubbles filling up. I tried a trick that has worked in the past, concentrating on one small thing: I tried to imagine myself inside one of the bubbles, but it broke, and spilled me out into the liquid where I was gasping for air, inside the bottle, drowning. He offered us the bottle with me inside it. But before Che could reach out, I took it and had a big swallow. It had a raw taste that set little fires in the desert of my throat. But it did nothing for my fear. I wanted to throw up.

When I handed the bottle back to the old man *he wiped the lip of the bottle on his shirt.* We were heroes. Kings. Gods. But we were lepers, too. He drank, and passed the bottle to Che.

The dancers bobbed up and down, their hands on each other's shoulders. A saint was brought from the church, and set in the center of the clearing. A plaster figure, a store dummy, like a parody human being. If it moved, I thought, it would be in spastic jerks, like Benjamin before he fell off the ledge; into the river. And if it talked it wouldn't be a sacred text, but a horrible dirty joke told by a man with a speech impediment, a stutterer who said the last line of the joke over and over, unable to complete it, until the words became unintelligible and terrifying. You would end up on your knees in fear before him.

The saint, a North American face, was dressed as an Indian, in a hat made of light-brown rushes with red ribbons on it. His pants were painted on him, and strings of dried fruit had been tied around his neck, with bits of bright red-and-gold cloth. He looked particularly stiff with all the swirling motion around him, sitting in a small light wooden chair, a child's chair, with long poles attached to the seat in front and back. The dancers picked him up and carried him aloft on their shoulders, passed him about, and moved around and under him, each person with his arm on another's shoulder, up and down. The band ran through its Che chords, the same ones over and over.

"Run the maze," Che said to me. "Coca music. Life will never change, life must never change. Not just a complaint, but a dream. They *want,* finally, not this life but a life that doesn't change."

I didn't know what he was talking about. I don't understand him anymore, and I knew, sadly, that my incomprehension would pain him. But how the fuck would he know what it sounded like? "It's a very complicated tune, actually," I said, lying, to annoy him. "It changes all the time."

Che ignored me. The crowd swirled around its center, the saint. Camba, our little crazy one with the eyebrows that met above his nose, came bobbing by, on the outside of the crowd, not far from where we stood. "Where's his rifle?" Che said—but not angrily, almost musingly.

No one had an arm about Camba. His big eyes looked sickly huge in his skull. He sang his own little song to himself in Spanish. "We must dance!" he shouted. He put his foot down hard in the litter of leather tatters that is all that is left of his boots. His ripped pants leg flapped in the wind as he went. "We must dance!" he shouted to us, by way, maybe, of offering Che further instruction. He lifted each foot very high, up to his waist, and then slammed it down to earth; I winced to watch. "We must *dance!*" he sang. "We *must* dance! *We* must dance! We must *dance!*"

I loved crazy Camba then, for I was fascinated by him in a way that distracted me from my terror. And it made me feel better to watch his high-stepping, as if his boots crushed the sharp-toothed weasel in my stomach. I wanted to give him a hug.

He looked at us looking at him.

"Why the long face?" he said to Che.

"What are you doing?" Che asked, stupidly.

Camba laughed—too fast, mechanically, more like someone imitating someone laughing, the way their saint would laugh, if he ever cared to. "We're dancing, Che. Can't you see? We *must* dance!" This time it sounded like an obligation, a curse even. Some of the other Indians smiled at him. "What did you think we were doing? You must join us!"

"No," Che said. He pointed to his feet wrapped in their rags and pages of Lenin's writings.

"Ah, Che," Camba said, "you know you lack a certain feeling. If you had your way there wouldn't be any dancing in the world to come."

One of Camba's lucid moments.

"Camba," Che said, "you're the giddy one. You do the dancing. Give them a new dance. The Camba."

From Guevara's Journal

9/28/67: . . . Further notes. His authors finish the hero's work, that he must leave undone. Only when he is not can they be. Are they taking his blood for their dreams, or offering him their blood, so that he might live?

A hundred shapes are given to the hero's life, by a multitude of authors.

An Indian imagines a store dummy, festooned with strings of dried fruit, speaking Quechua. But there will be psychoanalytic versions (the hero as case history). A movie—even a Hollywood movie! And other tellings, too, from northern climates.

But the best of my authors, beyond question, will be my one true friend, Walter Villamil Tulio, called Ponco

He didn't write that. I did. But he knew it was true. I see that now! He knew it long ago, on this island, where he trained me to imitate his style, so that I might change things, add things to his journals and manuscripts, as if in his own words, give the proper shape to his story, the one he would have wanted, the one it already has but no one knows it has until I say it.

NO! I AM LYING TO MYSELF! HE DIDN'T AUTHORIZE ME! HE DIDN'T CARE IF I WAS KILLED. HE LEFT ME, PART OF THE REAR GUARD, COVERING HIS RETREAT, CERTAIN TO DIE!

From Guevara's Journal

9/29/67: La Higuera. We arrived in the morning, yet there were no men in the town, and only a few women. A town populated by ten or twelve small children. Coco went to the mayor's house—which was empty—and to the telegraph office. He came back with a message: "Guerrillas in the zone. Wire news to Vallegrande."

We stood in the empty dirt street. La Higuera has fifteen crumbling mud houses, covered with flaking white paint.

Inti found the mayor's wife, hiding in the fireplace of her house. She said that the mayor hadn't told on us, he had gone to the next town, to Jaquey, for their fiesta. Inti asked why she hid from us. She wasn't hiding, she said, just sitting in the fireplace.

I sent the vanguard towards Jaquey at one o'clock and they left, followed by a group of small children. A woman ran after them, shouting.

A merchant arrived and was brought to me in the main square, by the well. He bought and sold coca, and had just come from Vallegrande, where he hadn't seen anything—not even any soldiers. This was nonsense, of course.

"What's wrong?" I asked. "Why are you so nervous?"

"The guns," he said, pointing to my rifle.

"We never use them against the people," Coco said.

"Though they have often betrayed us," I added, staring at him. "We fight for them. But we accept their betrayals."

At about one-thirty I led the center guard to the summit of a barren hill right outside the town so that we might have a better view of the field. As we neared the summit there were shots from all over the open field beyond, but some distance away. The soldiers weren't visible. They may be in the woods by the dirt road, or in the ravines beneath. It may be that they were firing on the vanguard group farther on.

I led the men back to the town and set up our defenses, planning to wait there for survivors and then take the road we came on back to the Rio Grande.

A few moments later Benigno arrived, wounded. Then Marcos and Ricardo. Marcos had his arm around Ricardo's shoulder, for Marcos had been shot in the foot. But Ricardo had been shot in the chest, and was dying. They reported that Miguel and Coco had been killed.

We went down the road, leading our two mules. Those in the rear were fired on at close range. The rear guard stopped to return fire and was delayed. Inti lost contact. I waited for him for half an hour in a small ambush we set up, at the edge of a ravine near the town.

But the hillside opened fire in our direction, so I decided to leave Inti behind and moved down the ravine. I sent the mules down another canyon to mislead the army. Our ravine had some bitter water in it. We slept.

From My Journal

9/30/67: I lay with Ricardo during the night. He is my oldest comrade. He was making a terrible racket, moaning, and I grew afraid that the army would hear him, and find us. I wanted him to shut up, even to die, and I held him more tightly.

"Did you ever do it with a man?" I asked him.

"Only with your father," he said, and tried to laugh. Blood came to his lips.

I kissed him on his lips to show him it was all right with me that he was queer like my poor dear uncle who raised me, and to keep him quiet. I even put my tongue in his mouth. His mouth was filled with blood, and soon after our kiss he died.

During the night, by a miracle, Inti found us, thank God. Marcos told him about Coco's death. Marcos had dragged him away from the army as best he could, by his legs. Coco didn't want to fall into their hands. They were getting very close. Marcos was still holding on to his legs when Coco shot himself. "I could feel them shiver."

Marcos had taken Coco's knapsack. He gave it to Inti, in case there were some personal things.

Inti wandered off for a while.

10/1/67: Inti didn't speak today; the gloom that has surrounded him as long as we have known him now has a name.

In the evening he distributed the contents of both Coco's knapsack and his own to the comrades. I took Coco's journal, for the time being, I said, for "safe keeping," until Inti wants it back. He smiled at me in that closed-lipped way he too has imitated from Che, and I felt like a son of a bitch.

But I wanted Coco's journal. When Inti was dividing up the things I put my hand on it, to keep it out of sight, and at the end I pushed it towards the dirt, as if it were a thing of no matter, and said I would take care of it. I didn't want to seem too avid, for it felt ghoulish to desire it so.

From Guevara's Journal

10/1/67: The area—hills with a few clumps of trees, and a series of ravines, thick with growth near the bottoms, bare near the tops of each side—is covered with soldiers. If we can escape detection we can perhaps move down ravines, as far as they go, and then cross to new ones, until we find a way back to the Rio Grande.

At dusk a peasant and a soldier climbed a hill opposite us, past the dirt track, and kicked a soccer ball back and forth.

Tonight I sent scouts to explore the area. Towards morning the scouts brought water in. The whole forested hill in front of us is marked by trails, and there are peasants riding on them.

10/2/67: Forty-six soldiers moved down the road at ten, with their knapsacks. There are twenty-two of us.

At twelve another group of soldiers appeared. Seventy-seven men in all. A shot was heard. Perhaps one of our scouts had been seen. The soldiers took positions on the road, and an officer said, "Go down into the ravine."

We thought he meant the one we hid in. Then voices were heard over the radio, a mixture of Spanish and English, and they started marching again. Our refuge has no defenses against attack from above.

. . . .

Later in the afternoon, a soldier who had fallen behind his buddies passed by with a tired brown dog. He pulled the dog's rope to make him walk, half choking him from the look of it. The peasant we had spotted farther up the hill returned after a while, going down the road towards La Higuera on a white mare.

The soldiers with their knapsacks may have been withdrawing from the area. This would give us a possibility for escape. There were no fires seen outside the town, and when night came, and the sun set, there were no shots heard. This adds to the evidence that the soldiers have withdrawn, for they usually fire off their rifles at sunset, just shooting up at the sky.

10/3/67: In the morning there were soldiers, Rangers, without knapsacks, traveling in both directions, like a bad dream, and other soldiers leading empty donkeys. The donkeys returned loaded with packs.

Inti, our scout, said the donkeys went down the trail into the farmland below us to the right and couldn't be seen anymore.

It is impossible to use the road, though that is the easiest and most direct route, for the soldiers may be in ambush along it, and there are dogs in the houses we would pass who would bark at us and give us away. Tomorrow I will send scouts to go out across the farmland and into the next ravines, to see if there is another way out of this area.

10/4/67: Inti and Willy returned with news that the Rio Grande is two kilometers straight down. We will have to move between ravines, but we can make camp in places that can't be seen from the side. We got some water, and at ten o'clock began a tiresome march to the end of this ravine. El Chino wandered off, delaying us. He is useless in the darkness.

10/5/67: No soldiers, but some little goats, led by a shepherd dog, passed by our position. No food or water today.

10/6/67: Benigno, today's scout, heard some peasants passing by on the road say, "Those are the ones we heard talking last night," and pointing towards our positions.

At three we began the march across the hill that leads to the ravine selected, which again has no water. Some of the brush by the sides is broken, indicating that the soldiers have already been here. I found a red-and-white cigarette package.

.　　.　　.

The radio gave news of where I will be tried when captured, though I told the men that this is nonsense, if I am captured I won't be tried.

The men are exhausted because of lack of water. Eusebio cried, saying he needed just one mouthful or he couldn't continue. But we haven't one mouthful. The march was very bad, with all the men complaining, so that we had to stop frequently, despite the danger.

Dogs barked. There is a high barren field at the edge of the ravine.

I cleared the pus from Marcos's wound, and I injected him with painkillers. When he is unconscious Marcos moans, troubling our sleep.

Eusebio woke with a white-ridged tongue, like the boy who lived across the street from us. How far I have come!

10/6/67: Our explorers found water in a ravine farther away. We went there and cooked all day long, under a big ledge.

On the radio they claim that Debray says he was not a guerrilla, but a reporter only, and never carried a rifle. He has called Che Guevara an adventurer, and not a true Marxist. A crowd in the background called for Debray's death.

Perhaps—if the story is true—Debray will have a good reason why it must be this way and no other. Or will this be the first time he recognizes the irrational power of brute force, its ability to make things happen that go counter to the march of history, that cannot be recouped by theory, that don't work to some good end? And if it could do that once, to him, couldn't it perhaps do it over and over, and triumph in that black senseless endless meaningless night that is one possible conclusion to history?

The day was spent bucolically, without complications, until an old woman herding her goats came into the canyon where we are camped, but farther down, to get water. Ponco and I followed her to her hut.

From My Journal

10/6/67: A child watched us from the corner of the shack. I say "a child," though she looked about twelve. Her eyes were dead. She was an idiot. She put dirt on her head, beat her fists together, and pushed her hands into her mouth. Her clothes were smeared with dirt and shit.

The old goatherd gave us a looking-over. "Welcome to our house," she said impassively. "You don't look well."

She was right.

"It's been very difficult," Che said. He poked his hand in at his waist, spreading his fingers. "We have not received enough to eat."

He's presenting us as charity cases, I thought. A new line!

"You are the guerrillas."

"Yes."

"What is your name?" This fat woman was too curious, I thought.

"Some people," Che said, "my parents especially, called me Ernesto. Most now call me Che."

I was surprised to hear how calmly he talked to the woman. I wanted to get food from here and run. I am terrified all the time now, and pray with every step I take that God may save me. We are all desperate and would scream at each other, but are afraid that the army would hear us. Che, though, grows calmer every day. He has no more bursts of temper; he has, as he promised, "modified." But I find his calm, as he sits at our center, horrifying.

The woman said that Che was very fortunate to have two names. People with two names, she had noticed, lived practically forever. It is difficult for death to find them. He's confused by the two names. He says, "I'm looking for someone named Ernesto." And all things say, "There's no Ernesto here, sir, only someone named Che."

"But," she sighed, sitting down behind her table in a little wooden chair, "you shouldn't have told me your secret name. Death has many creatures that work for him, and they may have overheard."

It's not enough of a trick, I thought at first, having two names, death being a clever fellow, after all, with North American advisers. He'll see through it after a while. Then I was angry with Che for giving away his secret name. Maybe it was bad luck.

Still, Che has a lot of names, some that only I know. Adolfo Mena, Ernesto Banana, Banana Guevara. *I* would never tell death (though maybe he has ways to compel me to speak the truth).

And there's one more name that even I couldn't tell death, the one his mother wanted to give him, before his father named him. So maybe, I thought, we were safe. (You see, I *believed* her for a moment, I was that far gone into my fear. It made sense to me. Death, after all, is what gave us our real names back.)

"But you are a Hero," she said, "you can only be killed by an ax in the head. One that has been kept a year in a dish with the first ear of corn, blessed by a priest on All Souls' Day, and over which twelve Masses have been spoken by twelve saints. The Giants protect you."

Again I had the feeling that she was making it up as she spoke, *and* that she believed it as thoroughly as if she were describing the color of a stone she held in her hand.

It was good news, I thought at the time. Where would they find twelve saints in Bolivia?

"Still," she added, "you'll be safe even from that if you follow the signs."

"We have followed the signs," Che said, "but though we lived for the people, they were weak-willed and afraid to help us."

Again, he wants to shame them.

"Well, why did you start all this fighting?" she said, suddenly angry with us. We stood in front of her table, and her tone made me feel like a child at school. Not that I've been to one, though. "Why have you gone around our country killing our soldiers? I've heard about that. You're a bloody man. You've killed thousands of Bolivians. You say you have a bloody hand."

Their crazy talk is driving me mad—Che and the Indians are in league together! Even the women's bowlers are part of their effort to be senseless!

"Yes," Che said, "and I will be avenged by the courageous ones who follow us."

Follow us? Did he mean the men? Or the ones who would come . . . later.

"I have fought for Bolivia," he said. "And we have killed only those Bolivians who are slaves to the North Americans, the ones who keep you countrypeople poor. We have fought so that children like yours will have enough to eat." He pointed to the girl on the floor, who was now putting dirt on her head. "If she had had enough meat or eggs to eat when she was younger she would be fine now. And after the Revolution there will be a place where she can be properly cared for."

The old woman smiled, changing the map of her wrinkles like a country suffering an earthquake. "She eats enough for three as it is! And she can stay here with me. We take care of the goats together." She was angry again, by the time she finished, thinking Che had accused her of negligence. "Anyway, you're foolish. You want to give her food when you don't have enough for yourself." She looked at her little saint, the kind taxi-drivers in my country which I pray to God I will see again used to keep on their dashboards. He stood in a little bowl that floated in a larger plastic bowl of water. White candles burned alongside it.

"But I can see you are a good man," she said, after consultation with her saint. "I want to give you something. You have difficulty breathing."

"Yes," he said, "I have asthma."

Even a weak man can be terrible, I thought to myself, or a fat woman—for this fat woman scared me. She could betray us to the army. Now we must take her with us.

The woman looked blank at the word "asthma." "If you have five bolivars," she said, not to be distracted from her business, "I can help you breathe. It will cure your as . . ."

"Asthma."

"Yes. That. The recipe came to me in a dream. I have had all the saints bless it."

"I don't believe in your saints," Che said. "Or in your Christ. He is not for us. We are for each other."

And for the Giant, I thought. And I hoped He, at least, was for us.

"Impossible!" she said to Che's blasphemy. "You are a good man!"

"And if I don't have five bolivars?"

"But of course you have them!"

"Why? Do I look like a rich man?"

No, I thought. You look like a dead man. My own thoughts made me chill. My body trembled. I hope to God I don't have malaria!

"You look richer than me," she said, matter-of-factly. Clearly she thought Che was trying to get her price down and wasn't having any of it. "You have so many things, you even carry some of them strapped to your back, like a turtle. And you have a rifle."

And so we could just take your fucking salve, lady, I thought. Why the hell were we spending so much time on this crap?

Che gave her a wad of bills, and she held out her hand to him. When she opened it to reveal the secret, there was a small tin in the center of her palm, about the size of a quarter.

It was mentholated vaseline, the kind sold in all the Indian markets.

Che laughed, a little wheeze that sounded to my ears lamentably like Ricardo's. I didn't see the humor in this bag of shit's cheating us, the dishonest crone.

But Che opened his shirt right there and spread the grease all over his chest. You could see his ribs poking through his skin, I thought, as they soon would. You could see mine, too, I suppose. Why are *his* more pathetic than mine? Why do I weep for *him* instead of myself? I fear for myself, I thought, but I mourn for him.

"It will take five or six days to work," she said. "You must use it every night. If it doesn't work bring it back to me."

"If it doesn't work," I said, "we'll be back to get our money." I wanted her to know that we would have our eyes on her.

She flinched from my voice, the bitch.

"Your money? No, I will give you special prayers that will make the salve work."

Che asked if she could sell us some coffee.

For another ten bolivars she offered us some grounds. Then she reconsidered. We could have them for nothing if we wouldn't judge Bolivians so harshly.

"You will judge yourselves," Che said, unrelenting. "And you will see that you have failed all those who wanted to help you. And if you have failed, then it is you who must make it right again, by helping yourselves, and completing their work."

So it all can begin again, I thought, as it was, as it will be forever, amen, everything in its proper place. *Except us.* Being under this stony ground was not the proper place for me, and it was where I was going.

"You must not tell the army we were here," I said, "or the Giant will spit you out. And we will be very angry."

She laughed, the nervy fat bitch! "Angry? My child and I aren't afraid of you. Look how thin you are," she said to me. "And you can hardly breathe properly," she said, pointing at my chief. "My child and I aren't afraid of anybody. But the army has never done anything for us. We won't be among those who have abandoned you."

That word again!

Che thanked her.

She took his hand across the table, and touched it to her wrinkles and furrows. She wouldn't touch my hand. She could feel how I hated and feared her.

"May the saints be with you," she said to Che, but tonelessly. Had she received some unfortunate augury from his flesh?

She handed him a pot made out of red clay but shaped exactly like a gourd with knubbly bumps. It had the coffee grounds in it. "You can have the grounds," she said, "but not the pot."

Che took what was left of a copy of *State and Revolution* from his knapsack —the last book he had taught us—ripped out another page, and wrapped up the grounds.

"You don't have to pay me for it," she said, looking down at the wood of the table. "But you could leave something for my saint."

"Your saint means nothing to us," Che said. I didn't want to hear another theological argument! "But we will leave something for you and your child." He put another huge wad of bills down by the little plastic bowl.

On the way back down the ravine, our hidey hole, I told him that we should have taken her with us. But he said no, that we could trust her.

From Guevara's Journal

10/7/67: We camped near the bottom of the Churo ravine. Willy unpacked the tin pot from his pack, and we scooped up some water from the clear stream that runs through the ravine. The water disappears during the hot day, and returns at night.

I took the well-used discolored grounds from Lenin. Willy filled the pot with cold water and brought it to a boil over our little brush fire. I dumped in the grounds, let them steep for a while over lower heat, tapped the container hard against a rock to settle the grounds.

Rolando tasted the coffee first. Not Rolando. He was dead. Eusebio. He needed the liquid.

We passed the coffee from hand to hand in a tin cup. Everyone took a few sips and passed it on. It tasted like heaven, bitter, but hot.

Isle of Pines, July 1968

JULY 22

A happy moment for him—sharing coffee with us, his comrades. So he did manage a moment of pleasure for himself—without the need of my imaginings, my land of Cockaigne—managed a swallow of pleasant bitter hot liquid on a cold night, warm beyond theory's ability to dream of. I remember now that he had told me of a time like that in Cuba, during the long difficult march, when he and Camillo's forces had split the island in two. He had, he said, "thrown himself upon the world, riding the tossed coin down. The world buoys you up." I would like to add: Well, sometimes it does. But that misses the point, for the issue isn't living or dying, but being altogether in love with the turning of the world, whether it's into darkness or light, in love with fate, beyond caring about the outcome. Not the gambler, on the ground, who waits to see the result of the toss, but the coin itself, spiraling downward, all eyes upon it.

I think that some men, like Che, feel their death inside them all the time, and to bear it they have to make it outside themselves somehow, stalking them, not themselves against themselves, but an enemy that they can see, something they can give a name to, like the Bolivian Army, like Imperialism. (Not that such things don't exist, mind you. They're what make the implacable ones so necessary.) And if the ones like Che succeed in putting their death somewhere else—on the whale's back—then they have a momentary respite, free for a while of the rat's teeth that otherwise gnaw constantly in their chests; they're released into the world—to enjoy a swallow of hot coffee.

Towards morning he let Camba go. I saw them get up while the men slept, and walk a little ways down the ravine, talking comfortably together, like old chums out on a stroll by the ocean. Che had attained that inhuman unforgivable calm of his last days, riding the tossed coin down. And not only because the army was near, was all around us. He had sheared himself from himself —if you can imagine such a thing—given up the burden of his personality to the Indians, for their stories. He had put himself in their keeping, in a way, as we were in his keeping. He didn't have to make himself known, declare himself, express himself, who he was, because he was (he had decided) whatever they said he was. He didn't speak himself anymore; they spoke him. No longer belonging to himself; already dead; given over; he had submitted. He had fulfilled his father's dream, as the old man lay on the floor of their living room, in corpse position: Che was *nonattached* to himself. It was as if he had two bodies, or as if one body (this one) were constantly leaving the other body (also somehow this one) at every moment. *He* was the story others made of him; and so he was always in the place "he" was meant to be, a figure being used by the impersonal cosmic drama.

Excuse me, please, if I do take it personally: *he let Camba go—to betray us—and he left me in the rear guard, to die.*

JULY 23

Che clambered down the long side of the ravine, holding on to the gray wiry vegetation to keep his balance. In the light of the red rising sun I saw that he was alone. When the men awoke Che didn't say anything about having released Camba; and no one suspected that he could have done such a thing.

Camba had left his knapsack behind, and later that morning, when the situation was already desperate, Che gave me Camba's journal, a black German-made diary, a few pages of which, here and there, were covered by Camba's small scribbling. Che didn't glance at the entries himself; no curiosity and no time; he didn't ask if I wanted the book; there was no ceremony when he gave it to me; he just shoved it into my eager hands, and I tucked it into my knapsack, with Coco's diary and my own. It was just another thing he couldn't carry. By that time the soldiers had already taken up their positions above us, on both sides of the lips of the ravine.

I think that Che knew that Camba would go to the army—or fall into their hands—and that he would give our position in Churo ravine away. Camba was not a likely man to stand up to the mildest physical persuasion, or even the threat of it. He was a milching little coward.

And I think that our death in those mountains was part of the story, an ending that Che wanted written. He chose Camba to betray us because he was crazy already—Camba, I mean—and so he would be able to bear the mental costs; or, anyway, he didn't have much to lose in that department.

So he let Camba go on his mission, and the rest of us—the rear guard especially—were left behind, to end in the ending he had written.

JULY 24

Start again.

Afraid, always afraid now, we marched the last night under a full moon. I made up superstitions—I was a tribe unto myself—about the clouds that sometimes cross the face of the moon. If a cloud went over the moon it meant we would get away. And if it didn't . . . I was terrified for a moment and then made up a new kind of omen. And if it did go across the moon, I was reassured . . . for a moment . . . and made up a new kind of omen. If my foot came down on a rock, it meant . . . If I heard the sound of a bird in the next ten seconds it meant . . . And all the time I prayed, prayed with each step, ceaselessly, over and over, *Dear God, please save our lives.*

At two that morning we stopped to rest. Everyone had been complaining on the march, in low whispers, about fatigue and lack of water. El Chino, who was courageous enough during the day, was a great problem on night marches, even with so much lovely dangerous moonlight. He could only see the most shadowy figures in the dark, and I had to lead him by the hand. He stumbled often, dragging me down, and shouted, terrified by some apparition, thinking it was a soldier.

"He's a regular old woman," Che said to me, mildly—though Che was showing a meaner streak sometimes, since R.'s death, it was without fury.

Chino overheard us, and laughed. He had a pleasant laugh. He wasn't a bad sort, Chino, though when he would stumble, making me fall into a net of sharp branches, or when he would cry out, terrifying me, and maybe giving away our position, I wanted to rip his tongue out and make him swallow it.

We made camp near a little creek at the bottom of a wide ravine—Churo ravine—so wide and deep it was almost a canyon. The creek was a clear thin rivulet that disappeared during daylight and returned at night, the stuff of parables once again, like the "flora and fauna" of the jungle. But once again none of us had the energy for parables. A fig tree a little taller than a man grew near the stream, and we camped by its base. We risked a small fire, and scooped a little water out of the creek to brew coffee.

And we shared it all around in a tin mug. I don't remember what it tasted like. But in the mountains at night it was very cold, my hands were numb, and I would have liked to have held the cup for a long time, forever, and never passed it on.

Before we slept, Che hung from the branches of the tree by his hands, and Camba beat him on the chest. Then Che lay on the ground—in corpse position —by the roots of the tree, and Camba—it was always Camba for the job, it was his new dance rhythm I guess, the Camba—beat on Che's chest some more, making him into a drum.

Then, while the others slept, Che led Camba away. I think.

When we awoke we saw troop movements, parts of the soldiers' arms and legs, rifle barrels, even some faces at the height of the ravine. There was thick scruff, and some trees all along the bottom of the canyon and halfway up the sides, but it thinned out as it went up—so we could see them, while they couldn't yet make us out. Camba was gone. I thought for a moment of Che's return alone, with the sun tinging him red. Had I dreamed it? Had Che finally found Camba as much of a burden as the rest of us did, and given him his release by killing him quietly, throttling him to death, as I had sometimes imagined doing? But then Inti thought he had seen him among the soldiers, waving at us—*the little prick!*—a crooked smile on his face. I was glad Che hadn't done what I imagined. And it was only later that I realized the far worse thing that he might have done.

Che said that we still had a good chance to get away, moving down the length of the ravine, to the Rio Grande. The wiry vegetation along the bottom and sides would provide cover. If we didn't exchange fire with the army until four o'clock we could hold out against them until dark, and make our escape.

He called for five volunteers to give covering fire to the rest of the group, as it moved down the ravine towards the river.

Everyone volunteered, each and every man.

But Che chose Dario, Inti, Urbano, Aniceto, and me. He gave each of us a hug. As I held him, half holding him up, I felt the continuous rattling tremor of his body, the tremor that *was* his body now. I was going to die to save this walking corpse!

But at the time I felt exalted. I had wanted him to choose me. I lived in them, in all of them, but most of all in Che, who had willed us there, and whose will supported us as the earth did, and kept us alive, like the flow of blood in our veins. His will seemed like the fruitful force of the earth itself. I wanted to do this thing, to sacrifice myself if necessary, as if that would weave me into the very molecules of my comrades' flesh. I would live forever in their bodies, and through them in the earth's vitality itself, in its recurrent transmutations; I would extend forever into the future if I gave myself up now. It was a way out of my fear.

I would live in the Giant!

Later, after we escaped, I didn't feel that way anymore.

Che gave us each a hug. I felt his beard against my cheek, and snuffed up his stink as if it were perfume—though his smell wasn't much different from my own.

If we were separated we were to meet again near Ispaca's house.

My group took up positions behind large reddish-gray rocks, and the others started off down the ravine, leaving us to die.

JULY 25

The rest I know mainly from newspapers:

THE DEATH OF CHE GUEVARA

Guerrilla leader killed in Bolivia

Shot in battle? Or executed by the army?

Was he betrayed by peasantry? Or one of his own?

Special from our correspondent

No. *He was my friend.* I owe him more than that, a more dignified and appropriate death, something less absurd—*even if he left me to die.*

No more today.

JULY 26

Dearest Che, please forgive me! How could I have been so blind to the obvious, to your kindness and love and mercy?

He gave me Camba's journal. He had said before that I was to be his archivist. Would he have given me the documents for his story if he were about to leave me to die? *He wanted me to live—me particularly.* In a precise serious voice, each word with its breathy halo of pain, he said that those who covered his retreat stood little chance of surviving, and he knew that if he said that we would all volunteer, for we all wanted to be heroes, worthy to live in the Giant that is our continent, and that is somehow Che's own body, the god he spoke for.

But really Che knew that what he said about the dangers was a lie, the complete opposite of the truth. For he knew that when he and the others went down the ravine they would certainly run into army patrols and be captured. And he knew, too, that when the army captured him they would go slack. They would have the red kerchief! The game would be over!

Then we in the rear guard would be able to make our way through the encirclement and escape.

But then why didn't he give me his journal? If it hadn't been for the Bolivian Foreign Minister—unable to live with his guilt, his offenses against the Bolivian people and nation, and the heroes who had tried to liberate it—we wouldn't have his pages. Che didn't care what happened to the journals. *His giving Camba's journal to me didn't mean anything!*

Wait a minute. Let's look at this calmly, rationally. Che couldn't simply hand me his notes while the others watched, for then they would have seen that we five had been chosen by Che to be the survivors, and they were walking towards their certain death. So he couldn't give me his journal; it would give the game away.

That must be true.

Time for dinner. Tonight I want—and will have—a spicy chicken dinner, a Ghanaian recipe, like a thick soup, with lots of red pepper and peanut butter; a "heavy soup," they call it. I must keep up my strength for the work he has left me.

JULY 27

The firing started at ten-thirty in the morning, and it came from all along the length of the ridge. Machine guns, as continual in their din as the roar of a saw, made a rapid staccato ringing that formed itself into one high-pitched tone that I thought would drive me mad. My group lipped the dirt or pressed ourselves like fossils into the rock. Mortars cratered the ground behind us and shook the bones of our heads to dust. The mortars splintered the reddish rocks into our faces. Things didn't want to stay together anymore. Most of the firing seemed to be coming from behind us, in the direction in which Che's group had retreated.

Towards noon the firing became less intense, as if a switch had been thrown. Isolated rounds clicked off, as if at particular targets. I couldn't tell for sure, but it seemed now as if all the firing was coming from above, and there was no return fire anymore from elsewhere in the ravine. The rest I know only from others.

They say that Che and Willy climbed up the side of the ravine, holding a screen of dry brown branches in front of them, a pathetic attempt at camouflage. Che had been wounded in the left leg, and had his arm clasped tightly around Willy's shoulders. Willy dragged the barrel of his sub-machine gun along the ground with one hand, and caught hold of the brambles with the other, pulling the two of them upward. *They say* that Che wheezed so loudly that the soldiers at the very top of the ravine could hear something coming— something that sounded like an old train engine—and knew that it was Che.

"Surrender!" the soldiers shouted. "Or we'll kill you!" They almost laughed with relief, the soldiers, for now the whole thing had become like a game for them, one without danger.

Che shouted upward at the faceless heaven of soldiers, up the long sloping rock and dirt wall that was the height of the ravine, "I am Che Guevara."

He didn't say, *"I surrender."* He didn't say, *"Don't shoot. I'm like you."*

Captain Prado, accompanied by two soldiers, clambered down the sides of the ravine, loosening rocks and dirt. The soldiers kept their rifles pointed at Willy and Che. Prado ordered the prisoners' hands and legs tied tightly with leather thongs.

One of these men, Prado thought, looked something like Che Guevara. But his cheeks were sunken, and his face emaciated—it gave a wolfish look to his jaw.

"You're so thin!" the captain said, his voice filled with a concern beyond his control.

He squatted beside Guevara, keeping his balance with difficulty, and took Che's hand, pushing back onto the wrist the thin leather thongs that bound it. Prado spit on the back of Che's hand, and rubbed at the dirt, so he might compare that hand to a picture from his wallet. Among the thick veins there was a scar running in welts from the wrist to the base of the third finger

the

mark of some angry young man's rugby cleats, the mark of Che's distance, and the fury it caused.

Reluctantly Prado let Che's hand go, giving it a little pat (as involuntary as his expression of concern).

I know what he received from the feel of Che's flesh. Holding his hand was like having your name already inscribed in the history books: it was like being on television, and seeing yourself through the audience's eyes. It was like looking down on the two of them from the mountaintop. Take this body away from beside him, this hand out of his, and he would lose that sense of things, that high-angle shot on his own life. He would be back at ground level, a man squatting in the dirt.

Che let Prado examine his hand, like a patient. "I would like to have a doctor for my comrade's arm," Che said—for Willy had a flesh wound in his right shoulder—"and for the bullet in my right leg."

"I have men," Prado said, in his overly precise way, "far more seriously wounded than you are." But he gestured to the soldiers to bandage Che's leg, to avoid hemorrhage. He wouldn't care to lose *this* prize!

". . . in my right leg." And then other accounts say his left. Which was it? And what does it matter? Yet I want to know. I want to hold the fact in my mouth and bite down on it. It matters to me. When he was alive, and here at this board, I wanted him to lie, to make it interesting. Now that he is dying I want to know exactly how it was—as if that might keep him alive!

The soldiers dragged Willy, then Che, up the ravine, and laid them down beside the corpses of Pacho and El Chino. A young soldier came up to Che, as he lay there. "You fuck, you stupid fuck!" he screamed down at Che. "You should die you little fuck, you should be shot you little motherfucking bastard bitch!" With his long boot he kicked Che in the chest.

Firing continued in brief bursts from the north of the ravine.

The corpses of soldiers and guerrillas, wrapped in striped blankets, were thrown across the mules. Che and Willy's legs were untied, so they could walk as best as they could manage. Che dragged *his right leg,* propped up by Willy from behind, and leaning on a soldier by his side.

Dead men on mules, soldiers, prisoners, made their way back to La Higuera along the narrow track of rocky gray soil. A field alongside the road sloped upward, dotted with patches of trees, to a ridge where the sun was setting.

Che *(they say)* pointed to one of the wounded soldiers. "If you don't apply a tourniquet that man will die. He is bleeding from the femoral artery."

I am suspicious of them now. Only the exact details, the truth, can keep him alive. They will lie in order to introduce impure elements, acids that will rot away the threads of the tapestry. But that last remark sounds true. He couldn't help himself; he had to teach everyone, to get things right, the right way to apply a tourniquet, the right way to run an economy, the right society for a man to live in, the right political line to bring that world about. At the end he detailed how to make coffee, so his followers in the world to come might drink his health, saying as they did, "That was how Che made coffee." God is in the details; his body would become the scattered details of what they did in his name.

I have left some of his instructions out of his journal: how to make a raft, how to bandage and tourniquet wounds, how to make a litter for the wounded from branches, how to remove a tooth, how to make a simple mortar.

"Didn't you receive training in first aid," Che asked, "in the counter-insurgency school in Panama?"

And this? Did he say it? Who is using him in this report? And why? There must be an account that isn't distorted by the use someone is making of him, a report called the truth. What God saw. Or is God just another point of view —the propaganda of heaven? the holy ideology? Or does He see the undistorted facts, for he is the One who doesn't distort, because he has no needs to serve —he has no use for us?

I want the truth. If there must be a God for that, to see impartially and judge, then there must be a God! I want to know exactly what he said, the words God heard. (The words my parents—the few times the sons of bitches were together —said to each other in bed; the secrets hidden since the beginning of time.) The truth.

"No," Prado said. "But the training was quite good otherwise." Prado, a tall thin man with a mustache clipped sharply into a precise rectangle, was called the English Gentleman by his men—because of his stiffness, his reserve, his way of speaking, his certainty about whatever he said.

"And you," *they say* Che said, to the wounded soldier, "what does your family think about what you're doing? Are they very rich, as your captain's family undoubtedly is?"

"There will be no more talking with the prisoners," Prado said.

The little parade moved along in silence. Sweat chills in the mountains when evening begins, a cold hand surrounding your body.

I can be sure of that!

Then Che asked for a cigarette.

Prado took a red-and-white package from his coat, a North American brand.

"No. Thank you anyway. But I don't smoke light tobacco."

"What would you prefer?"

"An Astoria, or some dark tobacco."

True to his taste, anyway, though it sounds like an advertisement for ciga-

rettes—The Brand Guerrilla Leaders Prefer. (I could have one of the soldiers say that.)

No!

Why do I want to make jokes?

Because I'm afraid. Writing this, I have pain swallowing. Does it remind me of the danger I was in then, how close I came to dying? No, I'm afraid that he is going to die, so I make jokes to distract myself, like watching the birds over the ocean outside this window—the way Che would follow his birds of theory off into the land of speculation.

And he is going to die.

One of the soldiers hesitated for a moment—calculating the effect on his career (who knows? maybe on his life itself, for this was Che Guevara, the chief of all demons, responsible for the ills of the world)—then reached into his long brown jacket for a package of Astorias.

At evening sweat (water) dries on the skin, becoming cool as it does. That is a fact of nature. Human beings calculate whether a kind gesture will have a bad effect on their careers—another fact of nature. So I can be certain that it's true.

Why do I keep interrupting their motion down the path?

Because I don't want them to get to the schoolhouse in La Higuera, where they will shoot Che.

Che took the package of cigarettes between his two hands—but they were tied together still. He could do nothing more with it.

The soldier took the package back, withdrew a cigarette from it; put the cylinder between Che's lips; and lit it for him.

"Look, Captain . . ." Che said, and paused, the smoke stinging his eyes.

This would have been a moment for the captain to have offered Che his last name. But he didn't; he didn't want Che to say his name

because death might find him? or history? because he knew that he would kill Che, and he didn't want a dying man's curse?

"Captain, don't you think it's unnecessary to keep me tied up? There's nothing I can do. It's all over."

"No!" Willy shouted, as if a fist had struck him in the belly.

Che was surrendering! Poor Willy, it was something more that he shouldn't have seen, shouldn't have heard!

The procession went down the little dirt track that runs through the town of La Higuera, past the brown mud shacks. Forty or fifty people stood by the side of the road. A woman pointed at Che, who leaned now on his friend the wounded soldier, and dragged his leg along. "Kill him!" she screamed. "Don't delay! He must die! Kill him now!" A few other voices *(they say)* joined her.

Whose voices? Who screamed? Probably it was the mayor's wife, the woman who hid in her fireplace. Or the goatherd. Was the woman fat? They don't say, afraid of how much I might deduce from that. It might have been her—she would want Che killed before the army could speak to him, find out that she had sold him things. I must find out the name of the bloodthirsty woman, record it for the history of infamy, the world in its many disguises, so that she might live as the very image of betrayal.

They put Che in the schoolhouse—that is certain, all the witnesses agree —a low-ceilinged mud shack with whitewash peeling from its walls. It had two rooms. They threw Che down on a wooden bench, against the back wall, and put Willy on the floor in the other room. The shack had two small square holes in the wall, with cross-pieces of wood that let the moonlight in—the moon just past full—in a lattice pattern.

Guevara sat in the dark, and puffed on his pipe.

Outside, Prado put a lantern on the edge of the town well, so that he might examine the contents of Guevara's worn green knapsack. He pulled out each item, and held it up to the light, like a jeweler doing an appraisal. The less valuable things he threw to his men, who traded them among themselves.

This, alas, sounds like someone else's story, the very tale that Che wanted to avoid. But Che is porous now, he who had, at first, held himself apart so that he might be a sign of intransigence, so that he might ring like a bell. Now— as he later wished—he takes the shape of older stories, the darkness that is already in our hands, his thin body filled out by shadows. His dream—not so very different from the first—was that there might be a core that would always show through the tellings, like the soul in all its transmigrations, still the same soul somehow, in a bug or a god, the soul that said, It is right to rebel.

Prado fished out a black velvet box, rimmed with golden thread, and immediately brought it in to the prisoner.

He placed the lantern down in front of him, and sat down on the bench next to Che, the open velvet box in the center of his palm.

"Are these yours?"

"Yes."

"I wouldn't have thought you would have much use for cuff links in the mountains. Did you have dinner parties?"

Once we did, yes, at Christmas, with nougat from Spain for dessert. —But Prado sounds too foolish. His taunts lack force. How can Che have the size he deserves if his tormentors aren't more skilled? Should I help them torment him, so that he might become even more clearly the hero?

"No. We ate badly. Like the peasants."

"Our peasants aren't unhappy with their fate."

"It isn't fate."

"It was a peasant," Prado said sharply, "who turned you in."

Was it? I thought it was Camba. Maybe Prado lied. Or maybe Inti hadn't seen Camba. Then what did happen to the little prick?

"If that is true then he was a weak greedy man who wanted the reward."

"No, just a man who hated you for disturbing his life. A man who wanted to be left in peace. Our peasants don't like people telling them what to do. This is not your country. They don't want to die for your plans."

"They prefer to die for yours," Che said, "and the North Americans." Che smiled.

His lips curled upward without parting and then clicked down shut. It's a bond between myself and Captain Prado—only he and I know what Che looked like at that moment.

"Please see that the cuff links are sent to my son."

Prado smiled,

"Don't be silly," Prado said—or should have said. "What do you really care about your children? You left them long ago."

Che slapped the captain across the face—infuriated by his smile, enraged that he was in someone's power.

Prado's head was knocked to the side, though the blow had been a weak one, from a sick, wounded man. The captain stood up, and stepped back a few paces. He unholstered his pistol, and shot Guevara in the right arm.

"See that he gets a doctor," Prado said to the sentry as he left. "And tie up his hands. He doesn't know what to do with them."

No. Too simple, crude, physical. Only someone who knew Che well, who Che loved deeply enough to share his thoughts, who loved Che deeply enough to understand him inwardly, only someone like that would be able to torment Che properly, so he might reach his true stature.

JULY 28

Prado materialized in the room, sitting beside Che on the bench. He had the lantern in his hand, a face with a body in shadows, a face lit from below, like one of those goblin heads that swing towards you in a funhouse—a not unattractive, though austere, face this time, thin, with well-chiseled features. Prado put the lantern on the floor between them, so half of their bodies were in light, half in shadow. Prado was a head taller than Che, so the top of his forehead reached into the darkness.

"It's a pleasure to meet you," Prado said. Usually Prado clipped his words, like someone cutting them from paper with a sharp scissors. The English Gentleman, they called him; he had a sense of efficiency in all his gestures, of polite decency in getting the job done, and of certainty about the rightness of his course. But when he spoke with Che his voice changed. His men wouldn't have recognized it. It wasn't a harsh ugly thing, like some people's voices, a tree's voice, no, it was smooth, fluent, almost musical.

"I have been waiting a long time for you," Prado said.

"A prize," Che said, "an asset to your career. It bodes well for your future."

"Yes. But more than that. Since I first heard of you I had the feeling that we would have a lot to say to each other. You understand?"

"No. We have nothing to say to each other."

"How sad for me, if true. I am as lonely among these people as an arctic explorer in a waste of snow. That's why I speak so curtly to the men, because I don't expect to be really understood. I cannot tell you how a man can long for some good conversation!"

Che said nothing.

"Well, in any case, I have so much to say to you. I've heard, you know, what you've been telling our villagers. I don't understand it all, of course. I don't pretend to be your equal. And I suppose in a way it wasn't meant for me to understand. I suppose you would have said something different—taken a new line—to win over the cities. Still, I think I can detect some problems with your thoughts."

Che puffed on his pipe.

"You're right about work, of course. All men must work. You know, though you may not see it my way, it's my opinion that even the very rich work now, in our world. They work at luxury. Court etiquette, you know—it's changed its forms, of course, but it's still absolute, imperious in the way it runs a person's life, as I know from my own. To be a king—or even a prince like myself—is like being a revolutionary—you must be already dead. The palace and the tomb, the same."

Che said: Hunger.

"Yes, hunger," Prado agreed. "I get your drift. But as I was saying, the rich work at their luxuries, all for the sake of the poor, who require it of them. The poor, you know, don't want everything shared equally. They wouldn't want to be denied the relief that the spectacles of the rich offer them. Not that they dream of having it for themselves, mind you, but they want to see it—the display, the variety, the luxury, the waste."

Che said: Cold.

"Yes, cold. Of course," Prado replied. "But you speak of suffering. Che, my friend, you cannot give a deeper meaning to suffering. Only God can give a meaning to suffering, not men."

Che said: Thirst.

"Yes," Prado replied. "Of course. Thirst. But I was speaking of God, wasn't I? And He must have priests, mustn't He? Priests who rule? who sanctify our suffering (or, like your party, justify it)? Then what difference between your way and ours?"

Che said: Sickness.

"Yes, yes, sickness. Of course," Prado said. "So you hate luxury, and you want to share suffering and poverty, because you—excuse me, I know this is a difficult time for me to bring it up, though I must say you are taking your situation very well, very calmly (though I think the reasons for your calm are quite ill-founded)—because you're a pathetic thing, Comandante Guevara. Even before this campaign and its hardships, you were a sickly creature, hardly fit to live in this world apart from your great sustaining willfulness. You hate luxury, perhaps, because you hate the body, the sensual pleasures? Or more: because you hate variety itself, don't you—all that you're cut off from? You can't hear tunes. Shades of color don't reach you. So you dream of an end to luxury, the elaboration of color and tone, you dream of shared work, shared poverty, shared suffering. One Body, all the same, a fire where everything is fused to one single color, utter blank whiteness."

Che said: Ignorance.

"Yes, ignorance. I see what you're getting at," Prado said. "But do you follow me? I think you need to study natural history, Comandante Guevara. Luxury means diversity, the elaboration of diversity and distinction for its own sake, and diversity is the very stuff of life. Display is what makes nature, and diversity is what allows a fortunate species to survive unpredictable changing conditions. The maximum diversity for the species, you see, many throws of the dice, so that one of them might be the lucky response to the next change, one of them might be the next, the necessary step. That's what happened to your friends the dinosaurs, don't you think? Not enough diversity in the gene pool, not enough waste (for, of course, most of the throws are wasted). Not enough luxury. You dream of uniformity, of one body, the Internationale, because you hate diversity, and so you hate life itself. You don't want order, as some of your critics say, or slavery—though I don't doubt that would end up being part of your new order, your faceless new man. What you want is death. A new man: faceless, without body: dead."

Che said: Suffering.

"Yes, yes, suffering," Prado replied. "But let me continue, please. You have misunderstood life, and you have misunderstood our peasants, Mr. Guevara.

They want luxury, you know, for their rulers, their gods, because they, too, want to see change, color, novelty, just as much as any Paris crowd. You looked at their weaving and you thought it is the pattern that they want to repeat, that it's repetition itself that they want. You thought the pattern had always been the same, and you must offer your new world of machinery as an endless repeating pattern. Nonsense! The pattern changes. Yes, our peasants, too, have their changes in fashion—only, of course, they change more slowly, because of their poverty. Bowlers aren't some archetypal costume for our Indian women, you know; they were brought here by the British. A recent development, only a hundred years old or so. They don't want repetition, they only suffer it for lack of funds and lack of imagination. You thought your story would be remembered here forever. Well, wrongheaded though your story was, it will be remembered here longer than most places—forgotten more slowly, let's say —after they've done with it, that is, made you over the way they want you, and that will have nothing to do with the themes you think, of violence and rebellion. Your story will last a bit longer here because poverty means a dearth of stories, too. Poverty has a bad effect on one's imaginative faculties. But you, too, will be sacrificed—and not to the victory of the Revolution where they all become heroes—but to the change of fashion. You'll be replaced by some new, equally foolish idea of the hero."

"Hunger," Che said.

"Yes," Prado replied. "Haven't you already said hunger? But let me add this: if the war had gone on—if you'd been the lucky one, and your fantasies about these people had been more than fantasies—then you would have let yourself been made into more than a leader, a hero. You would have let yourself be made into a god and obeyed as one. You wanted to feed these people. You wanted to offer them industry, but in the guise you thought acceptable to them, of the Inca, industry in the mass worship of your new-style selfless proletariat, joined to your ridiculous Giant by repeated acts of sacrifice and suffering, and listening to their leader with an empty face. But to have them build the industry they need to feed themselves would have required unquestioning obedience from these recalcitrant stones. And you—the god who would make the stones march to your will—would have required sacrifices and more sacrifices, hecatombs of death—to add to your terror, your luster, your distance—and their necessary obedience."

"Hunger requires food," Che said, stung into speech, almost crying, in a high rapid voice. "Thirst requires water. Cold requires shelter. Sickness requires medicine. Ignorance needs education. Our suffering requires stories. And this world," he said, "requires destruction!"

Prado clapped, slowly, his hands coming into the light for a moment, and *returning to the shadows. "Anyway," he said, "I forgot. I have something of yours." He took a small black velvet box with a thin gold thread embroidering its top, and held it towards Che, in the lantern light. "Gold," Prado said, "a piece of luxury that I see you kept with you."*

"Please see that the cuff links are sent to my son."

"Ah," Prado said mildly. "But what can you really care about your children? You cannot descend to that level where ordinary men put their love into practice. Descend?" Prado said musingly. "Or rise?"

Che cried out as if he'd been shot.

"Still," Prado said, "if you like, I'll see that they're sent to your son."

And those one-word answers of Che's, those monosyllabic grunts of man's needs, and (depending on your point of view) his apocalyptic hopes, or fears? I would have had Che remain silent, but that reminded me of Christ. And making him like Christ, if you ask me, is like translating him to the United States—it would make him and the world absurd. (The Indians understood this.) So what could I have him do? Babble? Speak the language of the future that we cannot yet understand—speaking in tongues, pentecostal. Have rainbows appear when he opened his mouth? Or fire? Have him change into a peasant, a prince, a seltzer bottle?

Che only knew one argument really, from the inside out, in all its endless permutations—his pain; pain itself; our need.

And the truth is, I don't know what he would have said to this Prado. I do know that he would have said something, something that would have made sense. He would have made a response, and if it were too early or too late for an action, then he would have elaborated a gesture. But I don't know what it would have been. I can't imagine the next, the necessary step.

That's why he's him, and I'm me.

JULY 29

OCTOBER NINTH

"A clean wound," the doctor said. He sounded as if he were praising Prado's efficient work, rather than reassuring the captain's victim. He dipped a cotton swab into a brown bottle of disinfectant by the prisoner's feet, and dabbed Guevara's arm.

"Colleague," Che said, "would you light my pipe? It's in my pocket."
The doctor did as he was asked.

With his pipe and boots a guerrilla is secure. He'd lost his boots. Shall I
provide the poem to his pipe that he never wrote?

> This was Che's pipe
> For the fag-end of butts
> It made his mouth smell
> Like an old whore's twat.
>
> Kneel down and suck it!

I'm going crazy. I want to pile obscenity on obscenity; I want to build a
wall with them. They shot him. That's it. The End.

No. Later that morning a muscular young peasant named Guzman, a
provisioner for the army, was let in to see the prisoner, a special favor for
services rendered.

"You're very courageous to come see me," Guevara said. He was slumped
against the wall, his legs almost straight out in front of him.

Guzman stared, his mouth open.

Which allowed for a lesson. "You have two rotting teeth in front. That
must be very painful. I would have taken care of them if we had met earlier.
We have always helped the people, in big ways and small, though few of them
had the courage to help us. You have to take care of your teeth, you know,
if you want good health."

"Go to hell!" Guzman shouted. "You can go to hell! Fuck you asshole, and
fuck your mother. Go to hell!"

Guzman ran from the room.

The High Command had left the manner of the prisoner's execution up
to Prado. He gathered his junior officers by the well, and had them draw straws
from his hand.

Meanwhile, while we await the winner, I go into the schoolroom to talk
with the prisoner. It's cold in the mountains near evening, so I turn my
sports-shirt collar up around my neck.

"Why did you leave me to die?" I ask. I want to hear from his own mouth that he hadn't. That really he had wanted to save me. That really I was to be his archivist, his author—authorized even to change things that would make the lines of his story clearer, that would fulfill his intentions.

"Give it up, Walter," Che says. He shivers on the bench. "This anger is a way of keeping me alive—alive and just for yourself, just as we were. You want to hear my voice arguing with you, unchanged. It's like your sudden love of facts."

Yes, I thought, the other authors want him to die, his name empty, severed from his intentions, his correcting voice, so they can use it however they wish. But I want him to be alive, just as he was. I want to hear him. Only I could be trusted with his story, trusted not to betray him. Why didn't he see that? Why wouldn't he say so?

He smiles, but his smile is the closed-lipped giving and withdrawing kind that I hate. After all, Walter—he should have said—you will always be first among my authors.

But *he* had authorized himself; he had known what History wanted to say, needed to say; and I—his truest follower, like him self-created or always responsive (which? both)—must do the same.

"After all, Walter," his voice says in the cold air of the schoolroom in La Higuera, in the warm air of our workroom by the ocean, "I taught you. You will always be first among my authors."

Anyway, I could only delay things so long. After I left, Sergeant Teran— the loser, the winner—a short fat skinny sweaty ugly handsome man, came a few steps into the room, holding a rifle with a curved clip.

The last face he would see. What in God's name did he look like, this hole, this bastard, this blackness!

Very well: it is up to me. He told me so himself, or wanted to, that last day in the ravine when he gave me Camba's journal. I can hear his voice (the man who has no voice of his own can conjure the voices of others from the air). "I taught you," he meant to say, as he handed me the journal. A short sentence that none of the others could understand—but I knew what he meant. He meant my word is his word is law.

So, Teran was a short man, Che's height, but well fed, with a paunchy belly, a sly smile, a broad flat nose, and a dark complexion like the blackness he came from. He looks exactly like my uncle.

As Teran entered, Guevara moved slowly to the end of the bench, and pushed himself off it, and upward against the wall. He half stood, and stared towards the man coming through the door.

Teran left the room.

Che heard Prado's sharp order, to return and finish the job he'd been given.

"Please sit down," Teran said, re-entering the room.

"It's easier for me to breathe like this," the prisoner said. The sound of his breathing was getting louder and louder. He gasped now with a loud metallic sort of racket. It frightened Teran. He feared for Che's life. Funny, Teran thought, that he should be concerned about this fellow's health! That's what it means to be famous, he decided. Everyone worries about your health. Well fuck him, Teran thought. No one worries about my health.

"People like you," the prisoner said, "have poisoned the air."

Fuck you and your nonsense! Teran thought. Fuck you fuck you fuck you!

"In any case," Guevara stammered between gasps of air, "you have only come To kill Me."

"No," Teran said soothingly, half believing his own lie for a moment, just as he half believed himself when he would promise to take care of my mother and me, to drink less, to get a job, to stay away from my friends. "I won't hurt you. Please. Look, I'll untie your hands." Why did he care, he wondered, what this dead man thought of him? He wasn't Teran's judge, after all. Why should he want Guevara to approve of him? He didn't, he thought furiously, he didn't care. Fuck him. Fuck him in the ass! Fuck him to hell! But why couldn't Che see his kind intention in undoing his bonds, why was his gesture refused? It made him angry. Teran was kind—kind, anyway, within the larger madness of their situation. He had to understand that, after all, he'd brought this on himself, that it wasn't Teran's fault.

Teran clumsily undid the thong, fumbling at the knot, freeing Che's hands. Dried blood and dirt flaked off as Teran received Che's thrilling touch.

"You are killing a man," Guevara said, barely able to get out the words.

"But you," Teran said, "have killed many men."

THE END

No. Teran walked a few feet towards the door, to the square of pale, criss-crossed light and shadow. There he turned and fired twice into the prisoner's chest, his poor stinking painful chest.

His asthma was the bullets already there, a spectral pain all his life long, now made real; the awful history of the continent already present in his lungs, moving towards this leaden realization.

No. That's nonsense. But his asthma brought him to this place. He wanted it to be a sign: as if the asthma had wanted the bullets, to give the grief of our continent a name, something outside him and inside him at once, always. Well, maybe it wasn't a sign, but a problem. It made him will himself into what he had become, the revolutionary will itself, his self-creation, which could only have this ending.

No. We might have won after all. Then what would he have done?

Oh shit, I'm trying to imitate him, trying to run off into metaphysics.

Che jumped and jiggled in the air and arced like a hooked fish, doing a dance so ugly that if you saw it you couldn't possibly take your eyes from it, it was that profound, and that right, the appropriate ending to his life, as if he had imagined the whole thing backward from this ridiculous jiggly motion that would transfix your gaze if only you had seen it, hypnotize you, until you, too, wanted to make those terrible motions. Che stuffed three fingers in his mouth, and bit down on them to keep himself from screaming. One finger he bit right through to the bone, filling his mouth with his own blood as he died, blood that soaked his hand

his bloody hand.

And as he died he saw himself. Not as a store dummy speaking Quechua, urging Indians to rebel; and not as the star of a Hollywood movie; not as a doctor who had discovered the cures for a dozen otherwise fatal diseases, a hero of medicine whose life was shown in serial episodes in the Cordoba movie theater, not as the Prince of Argentina, or a great violinist, or a child made of magical clay brought to life by the potter's love and longing; and not as an ascetic saint of nonviolence in a loincloth, marching to get some salt by the seashore; and not as a case history (the asthma of course, the central trauma), his body writhing then on a couch instead of a schoolhouse floor; and not as the main character, hardly even a hero, in the ambiguous story told by some North American, where he would turn and turn about as the winds of History turned and excited the author's angers and fears; not as any of those things, and not as a man with a robe of hummingbird feathers, or a man sacrificing a llama, wearing condor wings, or angel wings or a crown of thorns (certainly not that!) or with light streaming from every orifice; no, he didn't see himself as any of those things, he saw himself as whole, not only unwounded but well, always well, as he had never been well, not for one stinking moment of his wretched life; first he saw himself as a strong healthy infant, who watched his mother go into the sea, and waited patiently, without fear, unnervously, without ambition, for her return, and then as a young boy, about to go swimming, the sort of boy who was well liked, with many friends, a good team player; and then he saw himself as a healthy young man; and then at his own age—a perfectly formed man, naked now, and his chest was undeformed from the struggle to breathe, for this body didn't have to struggle, inside that chest there were some perfectly normal lungs; and this body was as transfixing as his had just been, doing its jiggly death camba, transfixing not because its movements were surpassingly sublimely ugly, but because they were so beautiful, though it was just an ordinary motion really, he was walking towards himself—but isn't the human body, when it is well formed and strong, and fed, and cared for, with firm muscles and tendons, isn't it beautiful? and this lovely body was his own age, was his, and so he stepped forward towards it, and became it, and so was supremely happy before he died.

"He's dead!" Teran shouted, but not at Prado—at the body he had just killed, and too loudly, as if he wanted to reach the dead man himself, wherever he was. "He's dead! I killed him! He's dead!"

Once again Willy had been in the unfortunate place, had heard what he didn't want to hear. From the other room he shouted, "We'll kill them Che! Someday we'll kill them all!"

Which wasn't what Teran wanted to hear. Those words, Teran thought, must be erased. I didn't hear them. No one heard them. They weren't spoken. He went into the other room, to the man who had cursed him, and, without waiting for further orders from Prado, he shot Willy.

THE END

Hardly. The captain came into Guevara's room, and fired a single bullet of his own, which pierced Che's heart and one of his lungs.

THE END

No. It doesn't matter how many times I write THE END; it's not over. The other officers begged Prado that they, too, might be allowed to shoot Guevara's body. "All right," Prado said, giddy, as if a weight had been taken off his chest, as if Che's life had made it harder for people like Prado to breathe. "But not above the waist."

The officers unholstered their pistols and shot Che in the legs and genitals, not laughing as they did it, one after another, as if they'd been ordered to take turns. This is as you wanted it, not a game, certainly, or accident, or play, we want to hurt you badly, do you damage, smash you down, pulverize your atoms, blow away the dust and erase your memory from the earth. Shoot him in the balls. That means he won't have any followers! You kept yourself apart, distant, judged us and what we did, you thought you could be our leader, our superior, better than us. This is your pride come home, you practiced making us keep our distance, compelled our admiration, and this is how we show it to you.

Che responded by jiggling a bit as the bullets struck him. When they were done he just lay there, of course, where he'd fallen, on the floor, in corpse position.

The doctor leaned over the corpse, putting his ear to its nose. "He's dead, gentlemen. I can't hear a thing. And a man you can't hear," the doctor said, smiling, "is a dead man."

He borrowed Prado's pistol and put a bullet in Guevara's neck. "A good hole for the formaldehyde," he told the officers, who stood over him, watching.

At five o'clock that day a helicopter flew from La Higuera to Vallegrande, with the corpse tied to a board across its runners.

As was the army's custom with the bodies of dead guerrillas, they put Guevara's corpse on display outside the hospital laundry, a shed with a red tile roof and no front wall, in the middle of a dusty field. The press might see the body and know Guevara was dead. Photographers were permitted to take pictures.

General Barrientos announced to the reporters that Che Guevara had been wounded in battle, and had died a few hours later, from his wounds.

The corpse was left outside the laundry, on a board across two sawhorses. At dusk the next day some peasants came from their fields and placed candles at his head and feet, kicking the sawhorses he lay on, and praying. And each evening the week thereafter they came, too, in increasing numbers.

This solemn attendance was not what the authorities wanted. They took the corpse away and loaded it on a small plane. It was thrown from the plane into a jungle region, a pointless place where no one ever went; or went and came out sane.

Before they discarded the corpse they cut off Che's hands at the wrist and stuck them in a jar.

JULY 31

THE DEATH OF
CHE GUEVARA

BY
Travis Tulio

—Because the first time is tragedy and the second time is farce. Because maybe he saved me, and maybe he left me to die.

The scene: November 1. Day of the Dead. Outside a laundry shed in Vallegrande. A corpse on a board laid across two sawhorses. A lime cross has been made on the ground nearby and around the corpse people had placed incense, a plastic bowl of water with a small saint floating in it, a plate of pork rinds, and some white candles.

Six peasants come down the mountain in the background. Or seven peasants. (They multiply like lice, as fast as the Lord can think up stupid names for them.) They have rented a truck for the occasion, for they couldn't afford a mourners' bus. FAITH IN GOD! ONWARDS has been painted on a board across the cab of the truck, in front. They have come because they know that where there is a corpse laid out there will be something to drink as well. But they have already started drinking. As they come down the painted mountain, a stream can be seen, like a rainbow in the last light of the setting sun, arcing over the back of the truck. It's their piss—several of them are pissing over the back, and the wind carries their urine away in this high lovely curve. They wear rags, and their faces are smeared with dirt.

On the front of the stage, near the corpse, they climb off the truck, looking about. One of them punches the air vigorously as he goes.

SHIT HEAD [*a professional mourner*]: Our father who art in heaven, hollow be thy name. Tower of David, forgive him!

SCUM MOUTH: Idiot! Shit head! [*He picks up a stick from the ground, and puts its end in the bonfire near the corpse. Then he swings the lighted torch at his friend's head.*]

BIG ASS: Give me that! [*He takes the stick, and burns his own arm to show how unhappy he is.*] The light has gone out of the world! Why should we be allowed to live when he is gone? But his spirit has come to me! His spirit has entered me! I'm not afraid of anything now! [*He looks about him to make sure there are no soldiers nearby. Reassured, he repeats:*] I'm not afraid of anything now! I am weak. I have a big ass, as he did. But I can be terrible!

SCUM MOUTH: The only terrible thing about you is the smell from your big ass. Pray Shit Head! That's why we pay you!

[*Stands have been set up by the board. Women with English accents, in bowler hats, sit behind them, selling mementos: Pictures of Guevara. Plastic inhalator models made from clay. Chicha.*]

SHIT HEAD: We have no respect for anyone. Here he is dead. He was a good person. He wanted to help us. And what do we do? We get drunk.

SCUM MOUTH: Help us? He wanted to help us get killed! Just like him!

SHIT HEAD: Shut up! He died a terrible death. He is set apart. And we have no shame! We act like drunks!

BIG ASS: Yes. Bolivians are shits, just as he always said. He was right. Bolivians are just pieces of shit.

SHIT HEAD *[walking around the corpse]:* Why don't they bury him?

SCUM MOUTH: They can't afford it. The army can't afford it. *[He takes down his dirty white pants and pisses on the ground.]* Let's take up a collection for the army.

BIG ASS: Let's piss and shit together in a pile. Then no one will steal from our collection!

[They do.]

SCUM MOUTH: They have no religion, these generals. They would even steal from our collection. They don't know what's right.

BIG ASS: Well, they knew enough to kill him. And now they're leaving his body out here to stink. That's why they haven't buried him. If he stinks, they think the stupid Indians won't go thinking he's a saint. But his friends came here at night, with a special syringe, and they put a magic fluid in him so he will never decay.

SCUM MOUTH: Think him a saint! This bandit! He was no saint! He could steal piss from your bladder if he wanted to! But, then, why would he want to? Who would want to steal piss? We're happy to give it away. *[He pisses, and once again his urine makes a magical arc that gleams like diamonds in the firelight.]* I'm tired, and out of booze. Let the women stay up with him. He *liked* women.

[The women enter, all in black, in layer after layer of black blouses and black shawls and black skirts. They look like giant lumps of coal.]

FIRST WOMAN: After he left us, my husband beat me. He was so ashamed of himself for not having gone with the heroes. He hit me on my face, made it all black and blue. That was the first time he ever hit me on the face. He does it all the time now.

SECOND WOMAN: The same thing happened to me.

THIRD WOMAN: And mine did it, too.

FIRST WOMAN: Did you bear a child for him?

SECOND WOMAN: For the dead one? Yes.

FIRST WOMAN: So did I!

SECOND WOMAN: Mmmm. He was good at that!

THIRD WOMAN *[hurriedly, not wanting to be left out]:* I did, too! I did, too!

FIRST WOMAN: My husband put me outside because I slept with him.

THIRD WOMAN: Mine did, too! Mine did, too!

SECOND WOMAN: I loved him. I would have done anything for him.

[SHIT HEAD, the professional mourner, falls across the corpse. The dead man

has flies around his eyes, eyes that bugged out when he died, from the asthma attack.]

FIRST FLY: Bzzzz! Delicious! Lots of nice morsels of blood and shit.

SECOND FLY: He really understood natural history! He took his proper place in the scheme of things!

[The men come back, staggering.]

SHIT HEAD *[from across the corpse]:* Look. They've cut off his hands. So he will be angry, and won't come back. Or if he does they think that he won't be able to fight!

DOG'S BREATH: But this is not his body. What they say he suffered, he did not suffer. What they do not say, that he suffered! He is still alive. He rules at his kingdom in Nancahuazu.

SCUM MOUTH: Idiot! It's him. He's dead.

BIG ASS: Still, you must admit, he died a hero's death.

SHIT HEAD: A king's!

SUCK BUTT: A god's!

DOG'S BREATH: You're right! He's dead. But this is not his body. The heroes have taken his body back to Cuba, and preserved it so it will last forever. They bring him forward on feast days, and offer him a meal. The heroes have his gun, called "Never Unsheathed in Vain."

BIG ASS: "Toledan quality, the soldier's dream."

SHIT HEAD: "For my lady and my king, this is my law."

SCUM MOUTH: What? What does that mean?

[The others shrug.]

SHIT HEAD: I don't know.

DOG'S BREATH: When he was captured they tormented him, for they knew how we loved him. They singed his eyelashes with a lighted candle.

BIG ASS: They urinated on him!

SHIT HEAD: In the battle, when he was captured, all his chiefs died the deaths of heroes, so they might be part of the Giant's body, and part of our immortal nation when it wakes again. His chief Joaquin hurled his weapons down on his attackers, in a frenzy of despair. His chief Marcos grabbed handfuls of earth, stuffed them into his mouth, and ripped his face with his nails. His chief Ricardo, the one who loved all men, covered his head with his cloak and leaped to his death from the top of the Nancahuazu fortress wall.

SUCK BUTT: When he died, many died with him.

DOG'S BREATH: More than ten!

SUCK BUTT: The number greater than more than ten!

BIG ASS: The number that is many many more than tens together!

DOG'S BREATH: Yes. I like that. I mean, that's true.

SCUM MOUTH [won over, his skepticism overcome]: He was a weak man. Yet he could stand it when they burned his eyelashes. He could stand great torture, for his will was strong.

SUCK BUTT: His will was strong because his love of the people was strong.

BIG ASS: His love was strong because his prick was big!

SUCK BUTT: Many many tens together in length!

SHIT HEAD: They tried to rape his sister, Tania, when they captured her. But she covered herself with shit, so that the generals would be nauseated.

DOG'S BREATH: So they killed her, and floated her down the river in a basket, so that Che's men would find her and be driven mad.

SCUM MOUTH: And they did find her, and they were mad! They attacked when they shouldn't have.

DOG'S BREATH: When the army caught a peasant who had helped the heroes —and we all wanted to help—they cut off her breasts or his hands.

BIG ASS: So we would be turned to stone, thinking all who help the heroes must suffer the knife!

SCUM MOUTH [now one of the most eager exponents of the life of the heroes]: But we suffered gladly. For we saw ourselves in him, as in a bright plate, polished, made of gold. We were turned to light.

DOG'S BREATH: The generals are stones, dead things. We can't see ourselves in them. They're not worth our spit!

SCUM MOUTH: More even than the army, the priests hated him. For he despised them as weaklings, who lied to us.

BIG ASS: It's the priests who led the army to destroy his well-ordered kingdom on this earth, in the Nancahuazu, where they sacrificed llamas, and told the future from the sun and the clouds.

SUCK BUTT: When he was captured, the priests called him an apostate, a liar, a homicide, a rebel, a tyrant.

SCUM MOUTH: And a worker.

SUCK BUTT: They said he was guilty of all the ills of mankind. But really, he has taught us, it is the Imperialists who are guilty of these things.

(I am like the peasant Guzman, who ran into the schoolroom, and couldn't stand Che's gaze. Fuck you! I scream.)

BIG ASS: Che was led by a chain of gold, and his comrade, Willy, by a chain of silver. The generals ordered the captives to bow when they passed the window where General Barrientos ate dinner with the Imperialists, the Kennedys.

SUCK BUTT: But he would not bow.

SCUM MOUTH: So they struck him across the eyes, like a mare, drawing blood.

SHIT HEAD: They say that he converted to Christ worship before he died.

SCUM MOUTH: But he didn't.

SHIT HEAD: They said they would shoot him if he converted, instead of hanging him like a common criminal.

SUCK BUTT: But he refused.

DOG'S BREATH: They said they would save him if he converted, and not shoot him.

SHIT HEAD: But he refused.

DOG'S BREATH: So they had a trial.

BIG ASS: They accused him of spreading disease, of laziness, of causing fighting between husband and wife, of poor crops.

DOG'S BREATH: Of all the things that have befallen Bolivians since Adam was tempted by the Imperialists, they accused him.

SUCK BUTT: And they condemned him.

BIG ASS: All the leaders of the world came to see his death. Barrientos, and the Kennedys, and Johnson, and Brezhnev, they came to watch Che die.

SCUM MOUTH: And the Pope, too.

SUCK BUTT: Who's that?

SHIT HEAD: The king of all the priests.

SUCK BUTT: So many Indians came to see the death of Che Guevara, their beloved leader, that there was no room on the ground.

BIG ASS: Indians covered the walls and roofs of the houses.

SUCK BUTT: The crowd was so thick in the streets that if a little boy had fainted the throng of people would have held him up.

SHIT HEAD: All the hills around were covered with a blanket of Indians, and when they lit fires at night as they waited it looked like the starry sky.

SUCK BUTT: The open spaces of the town were so crowded that if an orange had been thrown down from the roof it would not have reached the ground.

DOG'S BREATH: What's an orange?

SUCK BUTT: I don't know. But it wouldn't have reached the ground.

BIG ASS: They led Che Guevara, our beloved Lord, down out of the prison, and down a steep hill, to where they were to hang him.

SUCK BUTT: His hands were tied, and there was a rope already around his neck. He rode a small mule,

DOG'S BREATH: Called Rosinante.

SUCK BUTT: Yes, and it was covered in black velvet, and he himself was dressed in black.

DOG'S BREATH: And the Indians screamed, as if the sun were going down, and would never come up again.

SUCK BUTT: But when Che raised his right hand with the palm open—his great and bloody hand—to the right of his ear, and slowly lowered it to his right thigh, and said "Oiari Guaichic!," all grew silent.

BIG ASS: Though he had a weak voice! He was a weak man. He could hardly breathe!

SCUM MOUTH: But he was terrible!

SUCK BUTT: His voice was like a wisp of smoke from his mouth. But immediately all the lamentations stopped. For he was our Lord.

SCUM MOUTH: They wanted him to say, "Lords of all the four suyos, Be it known to you that I am a Christian!" They wanted him to say, "They have baptized me, not with chicha, but with water, and I wish to die under the law of their God. And I have to die, for I have stood against the all-powerful Imperialists." They wanted him to say, "All that I have told you up to now, about the Giant that is our Nation, and of the way to join yourself to that Giant, and live forever within that Giant by killing the soldiers, and driving the Imperialists from our land, all that is a lie. All that I have told you about becoming heroes, about the leader who will bear your own face, all that, too, is a lie, completely false. All that I said about my vision of a free people, working their land together, that vision which I said gave me power, that, too, was a lie. I did not speak for the Giant. The people did not speak through me. I alone spoke. For there is no Giant. There are no people. We are each separate, and must go down into the grave utterly alone. Each man should save his own soul." They wanted him to say those things.

DOG'S BREATH: But he would not!

SUCK BUTT: No! He would not. Our Lord Che held his hand up, and said, "I am a weak man. But a weak man can be terrible. I have a bloody hand. And you will avenge me. For no matter how you tell my story, Walter Ponco Travis Tulio, you son of a bitch, child of a drunkard mother, and raised by a faggot uncle you yourself killed, still you cannot hide the truth of it: I will be avenged. *For it is right to rebel!*

DOG'S BREATH: So they would not let our Lord Che speak anymore, and they shot him where he stood.

BIG ASS: But he has taught us to fight, and that we must fight, if we are to stop being clowns, and have names other than Dog's Breath, and Big Ass, and Suck Butt.

SHIT HEAD: And Shit Head.

SUCK BUTT: Yes, and Shit Head.

BIG ASS: And we will fight, when his son returns. For he fathered a son who lives among us now, in disguise, as an Indian.

DOG'S BREATH: For they buried an ax in Che's head after they shot him.

BIG ASS: And hanged him.

DOG'S BREATH: Yes, after they shot him and hanged him, they buried an ax in his head, and every time they abuse a peasant or cheat a worker, the ax will work itself free from his skull.

SHIT HEAD: By the breadth of a leaf of coca.

BIG ASS: And when it comes out, his son will declare himself. And when he announces himself we will follow him.

DOG'S BREATH: But until he does, we should drink chicha, so we will not see how disgusting we are.

SUCK BUTT: Yes, we must drink chicha and dance the Camba.

DOG'S BREATH: Though if our lord Che had had his way, there would be no dancing.

SCUM MOUTH: Yes, he lacked a certain feeling.

DOG'S BREATH: But we will drink and dance now before we fight.

[And so they all dance around the corpse on its two sawhorses, like the ones I write this scream on. And they make a big circle around him, passing the bottle filled with chicha from hand to hand, moving faster and faster, suddenly more graceful than you could have imagined, until you cannot see the corpse anymore within their rapid circling. Then they let the circle part. And the corpse is gone.]

AUGUST 1

Notes for revisions:

1. The boy with the freckles, the doll-faced one who sold Ernesto a game of catch for pieces of candy, is like the peasants who sold us information and food. They would help us, but they kept their faces blank, indifferent, to demonstrate to everyone that they had no part in our struggle, that we weren't friends—didn't have our cooties.

2. Running ahead of us in his floppy white shorts.

3. Drinking ink; killing soldiers—transgressing the natural order. Showing he is willing to risk more than others. Testing things on his own body first—

beginning the struggle. On his own body: military and political leader the same.

4. His father and he—their distance. Becoming the peasants' judge, inviting their guilt (and their anger).

5. A scene where Prado and the other soldiers put his head under the water in the well at La Higuera, bringing on an attack?

6. The soccer team of slum children. Show that I was already there, one of the children.

7. The board and the smoky light from the peasants' candles. The child's sickroom during an attack.

8. He would say perhaps, perhaps, perhaps, and then, as if he couldn't bear the world made cloudy by uncertainties, by different possibilities—he would act.

9. Jiggling with pain. He fell down at the foot of his parents' bed.

10. His mother returns from the ocean to gather him up.

Dates

<u>1967</u> Ernesto Che Guevara, captured in battle by the Bolivian Army, is executed at a schoolhouse in the mountain town of La Higuera, Bolivia. His voice is gone from these pages. Regis Debray, at his court-martial in Camiri, Bolivia, says, "It is not individuals who are placed face to face in these battles, but class interests and ideas; but those who fall in them, those who die, are persons, are men. We cannot avoid this contradiction, escape from this pain." He is sentenced to thirty years' imprisonment. "Bustos"—Ciro Roberto Bustos—is also sentenced to thirty years in prison. Fidel Castro declares a three-day period of national mourning for Guevara's death. There is a resurgence of difficulties between the Soviet Union and Cuba, on the issue of aid and of "moral incentives" for workers; Castro takes Guevara's position that socialism is built, that Socialist Man is formed, on the basis of a new morality, and not when work is done for material rewards. (Or perhaps the economy is such that there are no material rewards to offer.) The United Nations recommends sanctions against Portugal until she frees her African colonies—Angola, Mozambique, and Portuguese Guiana. Guerrilla movements in these countries continue their struggle against the Portuguese Army (including the indoctrination, the education, of the Portuguese soldiers that they capture). <u>1968</u> (Year of the Heroic Guerrilla) Fidel Castro introduces gasoline rationing for the Cuban people; he declares that the dignity of the revolution does not allow Cuba "to beg for Soviet supplies." Nine members of the Cuban Communist Party—members from before the revolution, members who were never part of the guerrilla struggle—are tried for divisive counterrevolutionary activities, for sectarianism that is harmful to the revolution; they are given sentences of three to fifteen years. The Cuban people—with less Soviet aid to rely on—are mobilized for voluntary work in agriculture, particularly sugar harvesting. Labor cards are introduced, to record acts that show "lack of discipline." Students and workers in France take to the streets against the bourgeois government of De Gaulle. The students are condemned by the French Communist Party as "Guevarist adventurers." (Are they his voice?) The demonstrations continue, gaining

support from workers who occupy their factories. The Communist Party, running to keep up with the class it is leading, calls for a general strike. Dubcek becomes first secretary of the Czechoslovakian Communist Party; he announces the Party's decision to build "socialism with a human face." The Soviet Union—Czechoslovakia's main "trading partner"—sends its tanks into Prague; Dubcek is stripped of his party position. The Vietnamese Communists launch the Tet offensive in Vietnam, against six cities in the South. (The country surrounds the city.) The U.S. embassy in Saigon is occupied for six hours by Viet Cong guerrillas. 11,000 people die in the offensive. President Johnson sends 10,000 more troops to Vietnam. Those who die are persons, are men. We cannot avoid   The United States begins Operation Complete Victory, involving 100,000 soldiers, and killing people here and there throughout the country. The United States ceases its bombardment of North Vietnam; the Paris Peace Talks begin. Liu Shao-chi is expelled by the Chinese Communist Party, for taking the capitalist road, for revisionist activities contrary to the people's interest, for stressing production of goods over Communist principles of production. Lin Piao, Minister of Defense, is named Mao's successor. Fidel Castro announces his approval of Soviet intervention in Czechoslovakia; the Cuban and East German governments issue a joint proclamation on the necessity of fighting against all forms of revisionism and opportunism. The President of Peru is deposed by a left-wing military coup; General Juan Velasco Alvarado decrees a radical agrarian reform. In Bolivia, the Minister of the Interior of General Barrientos's government admits that he sent a copy of Guevara's diary (seized by the army, never released to the public) to Cuba; Barrientos's Cabinet resigns. 200,000 students and others demonstrate against the Mexican government in Mexico City. The army occupies the university, jails, and then kills the leadership of the demonstration (and a good number of others). The Guatemalan guerrillas (the FAR) under Yon Sosa, break with the Communist Party; the Party sets up its own "FAR." Brazilian urban guerrillas kidnap the United Nations ambassador; he is exchanged for seventeen political prisoners. President Costa e Silva assumes emergency powers, and dissolves the legislature. <u>1969</u> (Year of the Decisive Harvest) The Cuban government introduces sugar rationing. The Revolution (in difficulty, or having come to its senses) declares its solidarity with the Soviet Union, and its admiration for the achievements of Stalin. Jan Palach, a student, burns himself to death in Prague, protesting Soviet control of the press. President Barrientos of Bolivia is killed in a helicopter crash; he is succeeded by Vice-President Salinas; Salinas is deposed by General Ovando (shuffling the deck a bit for the same game). Inti Peredo, still hiding, still fighting, in the Bolivian mountains, is killed by the army. In Panama, Brigadier General Omar Torrijos Herrera, a left-wing member of the National Guard, takes power. Brazilian urban guerrilla leader Carlos Marighela is killed. Dr. Mondlane, leader of Frelimo, the Mozambique liberation movement, is assassinated in Dar es Salaam. King Idris of Libya is overthrown by a left-wing military coup led by Colonel Qaddafi. (Pieces of a new interpretation:) The United States government, responding to the drain on its resources, the massive demonstrations against the war, its lack of success, begins a "phased withdrawal" of U.S. troops from Vietnam; the War in Vietnam continues. Neil Armstrong hits a golf ball across the moon's surface. The population of Latin America is 272 million.   **1970** China and the United States hold talks in Warsaw to discover their common interests. (A sadness. Or worse: big powers make deals; little countries squabble among themselves, hope for survival, vie for favors. Who needs heroes now? This play's turning into a farce! Good night, sweet prince!) Palestinian guerrillas blow up a Swiss aircraft in Germany as a step towards the liberation   The War in Biafra ends with the near total destruction of the Biafran people by the Nigerian Army; from battle and starvation more than 500,000 people die. The Portuguese government, seeing the light at the end of the tunnel, estimates that twelve thousand rebels have deserted Frelimo; the struggle in the colonies continues. Ethiopia declares a state of emergency in Eritrea; the Eritrean people continue their battle for independence. The Cambodian Army, with the aid of the United States, overthrows the government of Prince Sihanouk; the Khmer Republic is declared; Lon Nol makes himself military dictator of the Republic. The United States and the South Vietnamese attack Communist bases in Cambodia. Demonstrations against the War in Vietnam and the U.S. social system break out at Kent State and Jackson State; six people are killed by local police, and by national guardsmen (to freeze them in their tracks; to terrify them). A U.S. diplomat is kidnapped in Guatemala; the Japanese consul is held by guerrillas in Brazil; the West German ambassador to Guatemala is kidnapped; the West German ambassador to Brazil is exchanged for forty political prisoners; in Uruguay the urban guerrillas—Tupemaros—kill a U.S. adviser to the police. The Swiss ambassador is kidnapped in Brazil. (Our participation is not asked for; terror is spectacle. Sit still!) The Argentine military overthrows President Ongania. Worker unrest among both left- and right-wing Peronists—and urban guerrilla activities—continue throughout Argentina. General Torres, a left-wing member of the Bolivian Army, becomes head of the government in an urban putsch; Regis Debray is freed. Salvador Allende—despite the efforts of many corporations and the U.S. government —is elected the first Marxist-socialist President of Chile. The CIA and ITT begin operations for his overthrow. The World Bank cooperates in "destabilizing" the government by denying it loans.   **1971** The South Vietnamese Army invades Laos to destroy Communist bases and is badly bloodied by the opposition. The United States sends a Ping-Pong team to China (our enemy's enemy is perhaps our friend). Lin Piao, Mao's designated successor, is accused by the Chinese government of being an agent of Soviet imperialism; he has been "ultra-leftist" in the Cultural Revolution in order to hide his rightist deeds, to create disorder, chaos. The government reports that the traitor's plane has, on its way to Russia, crashed. Or not. In any case, he's dead. The British ambassador to Uruguay is kidnapped; 100 Tupemaro guerrillas escape from prison in Montevideo. (Pieces of a   ) In Bolivia, General Torres (not having armed the people) is deposed by a right-wing army coup under General Hugo Banzer Suarez (as if the name mattered). Middle-class demonstrations (a march of housewives, banging pots with spoons; a strike of truck owners and taxi-drivers) break out in Chile; a state of emergency is declared. The United States suspends hostilities in Vietnam, but continues to supply the South Vietnamese Army.   1972   The President of the United States, Richard Nixon, visits China; the United Nations admits China to its membership and expels Taiwan. 13 civilians are killed in demonstration in Londonderry; the IRA blows up the British embassy in Dublin. (is spectacle. Sit still!) The United States and the North Vietnamese sign a cease-fire agreement in Paris. The struggle in Vietnam continues. Eleven Israeli Olympic athletes are murdered by the PLO as piece of nw intri, for the librtni sit still! General Peron, invited by the army, returns to Argentina.   1973   The Revolutionary Workers' Party explodes bombs in Lisbon to protest the war in the colonies. Amilcar Cabral, leader of the liberation movement in Portuguese Guiana, is killed. Arab oil-producing states, in response to the outcome of the Yom Kippur War with Israel, cut oil production five percent. The oil companies find this convenient; they raise prices and tremendously increase their profit. (Terror of police; terror of conspiracies; terror of shortages. Our lives are in others' hands.) In Argentina General Peron becomes head of state; he amnesties political prisoners. Salvador Allende, attacked by the armed forces, without the means to arm the working people of Chile, is assassinated in the Presidential Palace (though many working-class groups in Chile do what they are able to protect him). General Pinochet takes power for the army, for the corporations. Serving different powers, Pinochet has the working-class leadership of Chile imprisoned, tortured, and then murdered.   1974   The Khmer Rouge, the guerrilla force in the Cambodian countryside, attacks Phnom Penh. Marshal Lon Nol declares a state of emergency. (The country surrounds the city. All fall down.) A left-wing army coup of officers who have spent long—and educational—periods in the colonies, fighting the guerrillas, comes to power in Portugal. Angola, Mozambique, Guinea-Bissau will be freed. Rebels aided by Cuban soldiers will battle rebels aided, at least monetarily, by the United States; the Communist guerrillas come to power. (The country. A children's nursery rhyme.) General Peron's Army Day address prompts fighting between left- and right-wing "Peronists." A matter of interpretation soon made clear: the army begins a drive against the People's Revolutionary Army. Peron dies; Mrs. Isabel Peron succeeds him. (The first time is tragedy; the second farce; and the third is I'm tired   I'm not sure how to make sense of   I'm not sure what to make sense of   ) Emperor Haile Selassie, Lion of Judea, is deposed by the Revolutionary Council, army officers called the Dirgue. They execute opposition elements within and without their ranks; they conclude treaties with the Soviet Union and pledge to build socialism. Hilda Gadea dies in Havana, of cancer. <u>1975</u> Khmer Rouge offensive begins around Phnom Penh. The United States reinforces the city with ships and supplies. The North Vietnamese and Viet Cong capture Phouc Binh; a tremendous number of frightened refugees clog the road moving south towards Saigon. Avoid this contradiction, escape from this pain. Now is the hour of the furnaces and only A state of emergency is declared by the Ethiopian government for the province of Eritrea. (The Cuban Army will assist the Ethiopian Army with its difficulties, a Communist government, an ally of the Soviet Union.) The North Vietnamese Army takes Da Nang. In Cambodia, Marshal Lon Nol flees. Lbrtoin The country surrounds   The North Vietnamese take Qui Nhon. The American evacuation of personnel in Cambodia (called Operation Eagle Pull) begins.   Tan Son Nhut air base in Saigon is shelled by the Vietnamese Communists. At 7:52 P.M., April 29, the United States leaves Vietnam, flying its embassy staff out by helicopter (refugees, clinging to the struts, have their hands beaten away by Marine guards).   The Communists advance in Laos, taking the southern area of the country. A general strike is declared in Argentina; the army moves against Isabel Peron. A more right-wing group of officers in Peru takes power. The Khmer Rouge take Phnom Penh. Now is the Lbrt imprls I can't read this story anymore   The Khmer Rouge guerrillas, many of them not more than fourteen years old, evacuate all people in Phnom Penh to the countryside. A forced march that empties the hospitals the I.V. tubes still in his arm, his bed being pushed by another patient. They're unlikely to make it, aren't they. Make it from where to where?I_m;

   p^{ri}al$_i$

      $_{be}$ra$_o$

         n

        His

voice would be useful to explain here. Pieces of a new intrp   It is gone from these pages   The old people too   All of them   The Khmer Rouge do not explain, they enforce   When the city is empty the soldiers who are left disdain the buildings, make cooking fires in the streets. The country surrounds the   All fall   A curse is on the city   An image is this the promised end or image of

       —No! *(I open myself to his friend's anger, his correction.)* This is no response! (he says). This is only an animal's howl of pain! You've misinterpreted the instruction you must take from the history you've been given. Your idealism (which no one asked for) sours into irony. But your irony corrodes only you, and not history. *Will you sit still?* Let his life interrogate yours; then improvise an answer—the next, the necessary step. Begin again! It all must be done over! <u>1976</u>   <u>1977</u>   <u>1978</u>   <u>1979</u>   <u>1980</u>   <u>1981</u>   <u>1982</u>   <u>1983</u>   <u>1984</u>

About the Author

Jay Cantor graduated from Harvard College in 1970 and now lives in Cambridge, Massachusetts. He is the author of a book of essays on literature and politics, *The Space Between*. This is his first novel.